Wendy Perriam was born in 1940 in an air-raid shelter, expelled from her convent boarding-school for heresy, and escaped to St Anne's College, Oxford, where she graduated in History Honours. She then worked as a barmaid, nanny, artist's model, carnation debudder, social worker, and researcher in the British Museum, before embarking on a successful career in advertising, which she combined with writing poetry and short stories. She now writes full time.

Her previous novels, which include *After Purple, Born of Woman, The Stillness The Dancing,* and *Sin City*, have been acclaimed for their explosive combination of sex and religion, humour and hang-up. She is at present working on her eighth novel and some new short stories.

By the same author

Absinthe for Elevenses
Cuckoo
After Purple
Born of Woman
The Stillness The Dancing
Sin City

WENDY PERRIAM

Devils, for a Change

PALADIN
GRAFTON BOOKS
A Division of the Collins Publishing Group

LONDON GLASGOW
TORONTO SYDNEY AUCKLAND

Paladin
Grafton Books
A Division of the Collins Publishing Group
8 Grafton Street, London W1X 3LA

Published in Paladin Books 1990

First published in Great Britain by
Grafton Books 1989

Copyright © Wendy Perriam 1989

ISBN 0–586–08937–3

Printed in Great Britain by
Collins, Glasgow

Set in Times

For Susan Watt,
with affection and admiration

He said not:

> Thou shalt not be tempested;
> Thou shalt not be travailed;
> Thou shalt not be disquieted.

But he said:

> Thou shalt not be overcome.

Julian of Norwich, 1317

Then came the words the cold wind brought our springs
And sprigs of blood: 'The past and present are as one –
Accordant and discordant, youth and age,
And death and birth. For out of one came all –
From all comes one.'

Edith Sitwell: 'The Wind of Early Spring'

Christmas

1

'What's happened? Why the hold-up?'

'Man on the line. He jumped.'

She didn't dare to look at them. Looked down. Looked down. They went on talking over her. Tall men who smelt of men, a smell she'd quite forgotten.

'Bad time of year for suicides.'

'Spring's worse. I wouldn't choose the Central Line, would you?'

'No. Pills for me. And a pint of Scotch in my own armchair.'

Their laugh boomed in her head. She shouldn't stand that close. Not to men. More men crowding on to the station, dark in suits and overcoats. A gang of youths in frayed and dirty jeans. Women big with shopping. Pushchair wheels nipping at her ankles; sharp-edged parcels jabbing in her side.

No light. No air. Someone lit a match, the tiny noise exploding in her face. She'd seen the headlines shouting from the papers: '*Bomb blast in Armagh.*' '*Earthquake latest: death toll now three hundred.*'

The platform heaved and trembled. She had just ten inches of it, the space her feet took up – her small, slim feet enormous in black wellingtons. Stolen boots, size eights. Other feet beside them – coloured feet, shades she'd never seen. Shoes were always brown before, but these were shiny purple, acid green.

'You're not allowed to smoke, you know, not since that frightful fire.'

'Oh, sod it! If they keep us waiting all this time, then . . . '

She looked up, watched the cigarette move from hand to mouth, spew a curl of smoke. She closed her eyes, heard angry hungry crackling flames charring the whole station into ash.

'Anyway, I thought you'd given up.'

'I had.'

'How long?'

'Four days. I put on half a stone.'

The girl was fat. Too fat. All these people, weighed and crushed together, would total tons and tons. Tons of flesh pressing into *her* flesh. Naked flesh. She had even lost her skin. Ripped off. Raw and bleeding.

O God, make haste to help me.
Lord, come to my aid.

The cigarette smelt strong. Everything smelt strong: women's faces; children's sweets. And people looked so strange. Some were wearing sports clothes, with running shoes or gym shoes, as if they'd just changed for PT. Why gym on Christmas Eve? And why those foreign letters on their clothes? She spelt them out: 'ADIDAS, NIKE'. Were they names of schools or colleges?

A dark-skinned lad had squeezed into the crowd. He wore a headband round his hair, attached to wires which trailed down to a small black box. His hands were clasped around it; his eyes were shut, lips moving. Was he praying? Why the wires? She'd noticed three other boys with wires, all four young and rough. Perhaps they were offenders, and this was some new punishment, to avoid sending them to overcrowded gaols: electric shocks jolted from those boxes right into their skulls. She tried to edge away, collided with another conversation.

'What's up? A strike or something?'

'No. A body on the line. They have to stop the trains until they've picked the pieces up.'

'Well, I wish they'd get a move on. My turkey's not defrosted, and I've got seven pounds of sprouts to clean.'

'They don't always find the pieces.' The girl removed her chewing gum, stuck it on the wall. 'I used to know this bloke who worked for London Transport, and he said they searched for hours, once, to find some woman's head. She jumped at South Ealing – you know, that open part where the line comes up from under ground, so her head must have spun off up the bank. They never found it, anyway.'

'God, Sue, you're disgusting! I don't want to hear these . . . '

A sudden roar. The earthquake. '*Two villages collapsed like children's toys; tiny babies screaming in the ruins.*' She shouldn't read the papers. Other people's papers. Shouldn't soak up other people's words.

'A train! Thank God. Now, *push*, Jen.'

Voices lost. Only crash and thunder, flare of sparks. Then sudden jolting stop. Voice from nowhere: 'Let them off first, please. Mind the gap.'

What gap? Doors opening. People pouring out, tangling with the people pouring in. She was squashed between, swept on. Impossible to move. More people jamming in, blocking up the doors. Lights frightening bright inside. Faces, faces, strained exhausted faces beneath their garish coloured masks; green eyelids, purple lips. One girl with tinsel in her hair, but frown-lines just below it, bitter twisted mouth. The faces in the posters didn't frown. Girls in swimsuits laughing on gold beaches. Real people wore heavy coats and scowls. She lost her balance, fell on someone's scowl. 'I'm sorry . . . '

No one heard. She'd lost her voice as well. The doors groaned and shuddered shut. Seething crowds still left behind, stranded on the station. She should have given up her place, let someone else get on, someone with a family, a turkey to defrost.

A Negro yelled 'Happy Christmas, man!' She hadn't seen a Negro, not for years and years. She tried to grab a rail. The train was moving, lurching from the station. Impossible to fall now. Too many people cushioned right against her, packed flesh on flesh on flesh. She kept feeling for her money, to check it was still there. 'Beware pickpockets!' she'd read, as she'd crept down to the tube. There wasn't much left anyway. She'd been amazed at what a rail fare cost. 'Single or return?' the ticket man had asked her, on the tiny Norfolk station with its two slow trains a day.

'Single.' Frightening word.

Someone leant across her – a sudden waft of scent and sweat – jammed the window open. A dirty wind blew in, tugging at her headscarf. She clutched it back. They mustn't see her hair. The scarf was far too skimpy, let in every sound; all her clothes too thin; musty tattered play-clothes from the ancient dressing-up trunk. She'd tried to choose the plainest: an old black skirt, though even that had braid on; a flimsy silver blouse; a tunic Herod wore, added not for warmth but to bulk her out, make her feel less frail. She'd put a coat on top – the gardener's anorak. It was far too big, yet light. She still weighed almost nothing, and without the boots she would simply fly away. She curled her toes, tried to feel the heavy rubber toe-caps; felt nothing, only space.

The train juddered to a stop. She couldn't see a station. Only black outside, a sudden hush inside. She felt the terror spreading, smelt the fear. Someone laughed, a scared laugh. A man peeled silver paper from a chocolate bar. The crowd inside was swelling, fear padding out each body. Soon they wouldn't fit. The crush would snap the train and they'd all fall into darkness. A tall man's knee was pressing on her thigh; a dark boy's curry breath reminding her of food. She hadn't eaten since six o'clock that morning. One dry slice of bread. She could feel the crumbs still scratching in her throat, couldn't get them down. Her mouth felt dry and gritty, her whole body light and saggy, as if she'd lost her bones.

The tall man kept on staring. He could probably see right inside her skin; see her cells, intestines. She shouldn't be with people, especially not with men. She was far too close to them, could glimpse the stubble pushing through their skin, the long hairs in their noses, coarse hairs in their ears. She tried to squeeze towards the doors. Impossible.

The silence seemed to gasp. She peered out through the window – nothing but dense black. Better to be a body on the line. Alone and quiet, at least. A child was wailing now, a skinny frightened child in a coat too big for it, screaming to escape. Supposing someone else should scream, start to fight or panic, lose control? One snapped or fraying nerve and the whole carriage would explode. She held her breath, watched the man eat chocolate, jumped as each square snapped. She could taste it on her tongue, sweet and melting chocolate, a shred of silver paper twingeing on one tooth. The child's screams went on. And on.

Oxford Circus. The one name she knew in London. She'd been to London only twice, and both times as a child. Shopping trips with Mother. She'd seen the letters singing on her tube map – OXFORD CIRCUS – looked forward to the lions and clowns, could almost smell the sawdust. They'd landed in a large and boring shop, bought gym-skirts and a blue felt hat. The 'Oxford' was misleading, too. Oxford wasn't London, but a place her father worshipped, twinned with Cambridge, hoped she'd go to one day, to make up for his own poor degree from Sheffield. Her father had taught geography, hadn't liked the subject or the boys, pinned all his hopes on her. Her father's brainy daughter who'd thrown it all away.

There were shops at Oxford Circus and she had to buy some shoes. The money wouldn't stretch to clothes. But she couldn't spend all Christmas in a pair of muddy wellingtons.

She stumbled up two escalators, found herself still underground in what looked like a cage. The low grey ceiling was roofed with bars, looped with tangled wires. She felt trapped, closed in, stifled by the fetid air. Two teenage boys were sprawling on the floor, slumped against a poster of a woman's naked leg. The fair one had his eyes closed, his skin transparent pale, empty bottles fencing him around. The darker one was staring into nothing, with an expression of such total desolation, she felt it was contagious, and he was giving off some virus of despair. She paused a moment, concern outlawing fear. They were both so young and thin, needed food more than she did shoes. She took a step towards them, fumbling for her money. The fair one opened his eyes, blinking at the light as if it stung; seemed not to see her, not to focus, even; started muttering ragged words, angry jumbled swearwords, directed not at her, but at the world.

She shrank back against the wall, watched the hordes of people fighting up the stairs. Those were skills she didn't have – pushing skills, shoving skills. Yet the shops would all be closing if she skulked there any longer. She wished she knew the time; had never owned a watch, never really needed one before.

She forced herself to brave the stairs, people charging past her, elbows used as weapons. A sudden lull, an inch or two of space, and she darted to the top, was swept towards the exit; stopped, bewildered, as stinging rain blasted in her face. She had walked into a phalanx of umbrellas, all jabbing at each other; a crush of people ten-deep on the pavement, swearing as their umbrella spokes entangled.

The sky was navy-dark now, not the sullen grey she'd glimpsed at Liverpool Street before bolting underground. Yet it was brighter than before – lights and colours flashing, more brilliant in the rain, reflected in the puddles; scarlet reindeer strung above the streets, Christmas stars twinkling and revolving. She stepped towards the kerb, dodged back again as a hot-red bus roared and panted past, spraying her with water. Traffic bearing down on her, policemen in the midst of it, shouting through tin trumpets as pedestrians disobeyed them, dashed out in front of cars.

She tried to shrink into herself, lose her limbs, her body; so she wouldn't have to touch people, wouldn't hold them up. She was jostled off the pavement, heard her feet crunch and squelch in something – rotting fruit fallen from a stall. More stalls selling garish Christmas paper, swathed in sheets of polythene to shield it from the rain.

'Ten sheets for 30p. All half-price now, ladies. Get your wrapping done tonight, half-price.'

The man looked ill. Black eyes sunken in a yellow face, dirty hands in fingerless red mittens. Rain beating on his head. No one bought. Too busy struggling home. Too much to carry anyway: parcels, bags, umbrellas. She was struggling now herself. It was hard to walk in boots. Huge and heavy garden boots dragging down her feet. Her legs felt cold, exposed. Her skirt was far too short, barely skimmed her knees; the anorak an inch or two above it.

She stopped a moment, stared in shock at the whirling drift of snowflakes. Could rain have changed to snow so soon? She glanced behind her; still the rain, and slackening off a little now. No – the snow was falling in the shop, inside the warm and lighted windows; falling on the mannequins who were dressed for summer parties, not for winter cold. They wore off-the-shoulder evening gowns, arms naked save for bracelets, heads bare except for tiny silver bows. They were lying in deep snowdrifts, in strange unnatural postures; frozen there for ever, their brilliant make-up perfect, their sandals flimsy gold. The snow looked cruel, not white and soft, but white and sharp, as if tiny splinters of broken glass had been trodden into it. Yet their blank unsmiling faces expressed neither cold nor pain. Their eyes were empty sockets, their mouths were scarlet holes. Like her, they dared not feel.

13

She walked on through the drizzle. Shoe shops everywhere. Racks and racks and racks of shoes, in every style and colour. She hardly ever wore them. Her feet had spread from going barefoot. They were probably even dirty and she hadn't any socks. She glanced in through a window at the thick-pile lilac carpet. She couldn't spoil that carpet with her muddy boots, or take them off and stand there with her calluses, the dirt engrained from walking on wooden floors.

Forget the shoes. If her feet were blistered, good. She ought to hurt, needed to do penance for the theft. She had to find a phone box, ring her aunt. Still difficult to walk with all the crowds. Umbrellas folding down now, but everyone with shopping; bags banging at her knees, a six-foot plastic Christmas tree butting her aside. The Three Kings shone in lights above the street, themselves weighed down with frankincense and myrrh. She stared up at their shoes – golden slippers, pointed at the ends – play clothes.

Three phone booths just ahead, a hunched shape inside each one, and a group of people queuing just outside. She stood behind a woman in an iridescent mac, her dyed two-colour hair escaping from its plastic clasp. She shouldn't look around, keep noticing such details. She'd been trained to keep her eyes down, block out all distraction; had never disobeyed until today. But now her eyes were aching, assaulted by the glare, the clash and jar of colours. She wasn't used to colours, kept jumping at the sounds: sudden blasts from horns, or wails from sirens; the steady roar of traffic, the steady roar of humans.

She checked her sodden pocket for her aunt's address and phone number – an aunt she hadn't seen in twenty years. Aunt Eva, next of kin. Her parents were both dead, had both died fairly young; her father in his fifties, her mother sixty-two. Life had been a trial for them, a purgatory on earth to be endured. Summers hot and airless, winter spoiled by Christmas, even spring uncertain. Prices rising, people getting ruder in the shops.

Aunt Eva was more cheerful. Her mother's younger sister who dressed in pinks instead of fawn, wore varnish on her toenails. She wrote once a year, at Christmas, never visited. She lived too far away, in a small market town in Gloucestershire – or had done till this year. Six months ago, she'd moved to London: Hurst Road, N14. Where was N14? Close to Oxford Circus? Or nearer Liverpool Street, where she'd first got on the tube? She ought to ask, but people looked so hostile – too busy to be questioned, too sullen to be stopped.

The phone-booth door was opening. A man came out, pulling at his coat. 'Damn thing's on the blink.' The queue muttered, stamped its feet. While she waited, she checked through all her coins. She couldn't remember money very well – vague memories of shillings, silver sixpences in Aunt Eva's Christmas puddings, chunky threepenny pieces, flimsy one-pound notes. This money she had never seen –foreign money for a foreign land. It seemed heavier and brighter, even somehow dangerous, perhaps because she'd stolen it. She'd give it back, she'd vowed to. Every penny. More.

By the time a booth was empty, her hands and feet were numb. She flexed her fingers, tried to make them work. Phones were black and bulky, with two buttons, 'A' and 'B'. This phone was slim and blue, and attached to a grey box. 'LIFT HANDSET,' said the instructions on the wall. 'INSERT CARD, GREEN SIDE UP.' What card? And why didn't phones take money any more? Was there a supply of cards somewhere in that grey box on the wall? She searched, found nothing but the slot for one.

She pushed the door, looked out. 'Not working?' someone asked. She didn't know; shook her head, then nodded. She could tell they thought her mad. She *was* mad. They had told her that already, back in Brignor.

She walked away, walked on; passed a strange shop open to the street, as if it had no doors; a throb and blare of music sucking in the customers. The lights were daylight bright; a dozen separate TV screens, suspended from the ceiling, showed long-haired men crooning to guitars, girls jigging in what looked like scarlet swimsuits. Records – hundreds, thousands – were racked up every wall, their lurid covers writhing with gyrating sequined bodies. A real man touched her arm. 'On your own?' he asked. She pulled away, dashed across the street, plunged into a side road, turned another corner. Now she was quite lost, in a different street, with different shops, different Christmas lights. The crowds were thinning, people going home. Her scarf kept slipping, couldn't hide her anyway. She ought to go back underground, somewhere dark and private, deeper than the tube.

> Lord, do not reprove me in Your anger.
> Punish me not in Your rage.

The Lord had heard her prayer. There was a phone box just in front of her, with someone coming out of it, a kind, good-mannered woman, who smiled and held the door for her. She almost wept in gratitude – the first smile she'd seen in London.

She picked up the receiver. It was a different sort of phone, with pictures of the coins it took stuck up on the wall; a phone box for a mental case, a child. She compared the drawings with the real coins in her pocket, found two or three which matched. Of course she wasn't mad. She'd always been described as capable and practical, clever with her hands. She pressed a coin in firmly, heard it cough and choke. Immediately, it rattled back again, appearing at the bottom in a small compartment marked 'returned coins'. She tried again, again, but every time it went straight through, its rattle like a jeer. Yet her 10p was identical to its double on the wall. Maybe phones knew stolen money, always spat it out.

'I borrowed it,' she whispered. 'I only borrowed it.'

She could see her blurred reflection in the glass. She looked dark and very old, though she was still only in her thirties, and remembered being fair, and even pretty. She tried to blank her face out, turned back to the phone; chose a different coin this time, the one they called a fifty, held her breath as she pushed it firmly in. It dropped, stayed put, and she heard the blessed dialling tone, checked her piece of paper for the number – that simple crucial number which meant a home for Christmas. She tried to rehearse her opening words as she listened to it ring; had gone over them already on the train. Her heart was pounding through her clothes, her freezing hands now sweaty. Her aunt might well be angry or incredulous; refuse to help, refuse to say a word. Was it fair to phone at all? Spoil her happy Christmas, turn up like a convict on her doorstep?

'Aunt Eva, it's . . . '

'I'm so sorry just to phone like this, after all these . . . '

'Look, I know this will upset you, but . . . '

No reply. No Eva. She clung on, hoping, praying. Her aunt might be out shopping like all these other people, could walk in any moment, scattering her parcels as she dashed to grab the phone.

Still the ringing tone – mocking empty ringing tone. Sadder now and slower. Her aunt must be away. Why should cheerful Eva spend Christmas on her own? She sagged against the wall, still holding the receiver. Just one more minute. Two . . . There was litter at her feet: a coil of withered orange peel, greasy papers, an empty battered can. She let her gaze creep higher, read the terse black messages scribbled on the wall: 'HELP ME,' 'FUCK ME,' 'A. LOVES E.'

E for Eva. Her last remaining relative. Her father was an only child, as she was; her mother one of two, and Eva hadn't married. She had never known her grandparents, not on either side. Not a long-lived family at all.

She jumped. Someone's fist was knocking on the glass, an angry face squashed up close against it. She dropped her coins in fright, scrabbled on the floor for them, collided with the couple trying to get in.

'Get a bloody move on! You've been hogging that damn phone for hours.'

'I'm sorry. Please excuse me. I didn't . . . '

Her words were lost and trampled. The couple had the door shut, arms around each other, their twinned backs like a barrier. Selfish of her, thoughtless; forgetting other people who had more pressing needs than she did – real relatives to ring, not names on scraps of paper.

What should she do now? Her thoughts stopped with Aunt Eva. She hadn't planned beyond her aunt, hadn't planned at all. Just found herself in play-clothes and the wellingtons, creeping through the garden, lurching over bare brown Norfolk fields; trembling in the village bus which took her to the station; a pant uphill, a change of trains, then main line on to London – a London closing down now.

All the shops were shutting, people bolting doors and pulling blinds. Gaps between the traffic, empty pavements with only litter left – shattered bottles weeping in the gutter, dirty streamers trampled underfoot. 'GRAND POST-CHRISTMAS SALE STARTS 27TH DECEMBER!' Bargain stickers already in the windows, huge posters declaring Christmas over before it had begun. Everything defunct now for two days. She hadn't any shelter, not a bite of food. A café was still open. She could see a few last stragglers warm inside. She daren't go in a café, brave those raucous strangers, eat those foreign foods. She tried to puzzle out the strange new words blazoned on the window. What were quarterpounders? Or double shakes and coke-floats? Franks, or fries, or Fanta?

She limped into a side street. The sky was darker there. No Three Kings, no Star. A couple slouched towards her, arm in arm. The girl had shaved her head, one scarlet crest sprouting from the centre, above the sandy stubble. She wore woolly tights, striped red and white to match; a skirt so short it was just a skimpy frill; her boyfriend in a ponytail and earrings.

She glanced down at the gold braid on her own skirt, the silver frills which drooped across her wrists. They were all in fancy dress. This must be a play, an unusual Christmas play, perhaps the dress rehearsal. She had always liked the plays, the fun they had rehearsing, the excitement on the day. She smiled at the young girl, couldn't place her features. She ran through all the names – none fitted – checked back on the face. There was nobody that young, no one with those piercing jolt-blue eyes. Was she new, perhaps, someone who'd just entered? No. They'd have told her that, rejoiced at someone new.

She smiled again. A welcome. Be gentle with the new ones, show them love, see Christ in them.

'Stop *staring*, you old fart.'

2

'Sister Mary Hilary?'

'Yes, Mother?'

'Would you like to be Mary in the play?'

She felt a rush of pleasure, even pride, tried to suppress them both. They had asked her because she was the youngest, that was all. Eighteen and three-quarters. The youngest and therefore the lowest. Servant to all. But Mary . . . Mother of the Saviour, Mother to the world. All nuns were mother to the world; contemplative nuns whose job was prayer, who renounced the world to save it.

She tried on the blue robe above her habit. She already wore a white veil, white for novices, already had bare feet. Her Order was a strict one; shoes only for the aged and infirm, apart from garden boots. She scrubbed her feet raw-clean for the dress rehearsal, tried to feel her part, imagine Mary pregnant. She placed her hands across her small flat stomach. She had never wanted babies. As a consecrated virgin, she could be mother to every soul on earth; nurture them and pray for them, implore her Bridegroom/Father to help and save them all. As Mary, she would be even closer to Him, carrying His child; the human vessel which would hold and shape His Godhead. 'Be it done unto me according to thy word.'

Was it pride to think like that? You had to be so careful. Pride was everywhere, she rank and riddled with it. She was nothing, nothing – a hole, a mess, a rubbish, Mother Mistress said. She stood on just one foot while they set up the props; a tiny penance to tame and quash that pride, rejoicing when her leg ached. She kept it up while St Joseph dressed: Sister Seraphina, tall and bulky in her thick brown robe – a Franciscan monk's old habit which they had somehow acquired and stored among the play-clothes. Amazing the things which people brought to convents – old vests, old rusty bedsteads, broken plaster statues, even chamber-pots. Once, a supermarket had sent two hundred chocolate yule-log cakes, all past their 'sell-by' date. Two hundred for their community of only twenty-three, which meant eight per nun and still some over. They hadn't got a freezer, had to share them with the hens. Sister Louis Marie was in charge of all the poultry, and also good at dialects, so she was playing the dozen rustic innkeepers who turned the Holy Family away. She wore a towelling turban above her flowing veil, and a multi-coloured dressing gown bulked out her stern black habit. They never took their habits off, or veils; were forbidden to wear trousers or moustaches. They were still nuns, not actresses; nuns celebrating Christmas, acting out the journey into Bethlehem.

'I'm sorry. We've no room.' A 'male' voice, deep but kindly, with a touch of Somerset.

'Can't take you. No, impossible.' Brusque now and more hostile, with flattened Midland vowels.

'You should have booked before.'

She felt Mary's pregnant tiredness, as she trudged on round the Community Room. Full up, no room, can't help. St Joseph steadied her. The third inn was the bookcase; Sister Louis Marie in a quick-change different turban. Still no joy, no bed.

This was the last rehearsal before the performance proper on Christmas afternoon, with Reverend Mother as audience and all those nuns who didn't have a part. Tomorrow – Christmas Eve – was a day of fasting and abstinence, and far too busy anyway for plays. She loved the day: the excitement and expectancy of the day before a miracle, the day before a birth; a birth in their own cloister. She even loved the extra penances, which made the Christmas feast more meaningful, more welcome. They stood, instead of sat, to eat their slice of plain dry bread, drink their tepid water. They never called it breakfast, just their 'drink'. The French Abbess who had founded the Order, back in 1556, had prescribed a mug of beer for each nun in the morning; nothing else, nothing solid. The beer had changed to water in the later 1890s, hot water in a teapot – without the tea.

On Christmas Eve morning, Sister Mary Hilary felt she had drunk beer herself; her brain light and almost fizzing, her stomach full of froth. She tried to think of ash, of coal, to keep her mind on penance, not excitement. It wasn't easy. The refectory was hung with stars and tinsel, and even with her eyes down, she could still smell the forced red roses – a present from a benefactor, arranged before the statue of St John. The crib was ready in the chapel. She had set it up herself, fetched clean straw from the chickens, shaped rocks from stiff brown paper; was helping Sister Sacristan with all her Christmas duties: pressing vestments, arranging flowers. They worked, as always, in silence. It was a day of total silence, their usual times for talking – one hour in the evening and thirty minutes midday – changed to silent meditation in the chapel.

Seven hours they spent in chapel, every day. Their other work was secondary, and still a form of prayer, performed in silence to keep their minds on God. On Christmas Eve, Compline was said earlier than usual, so that the older nuns could snatch an hour or so of sleep before rising at ten p.m. for solemn Matins, which lasted until Midnight Mass, with carols in between, then a whole night of Exposition on their knees. She could hear her stomach rumbling, a descant to the organ. Supper had been bread and jam. She had done without the jam, taken just the smallest piece of bread. She wanted to be one with Mary, cold and tired and hungry on her way to Bethlehem and birth.

> Mother most chaste,
> Mother inviolate . . .
> Virgin most prudent,
> Virgin most faithful . . .
> Health of the sick,
> Refuge of sinners . . .

The twenty voices rose as one. (Three nuns in the Infirmary, one half-paralysed, all too sick for Compline.) There was an art in unison. It took constant daily practice, attention to one's phrasing. No voice must be too loud, too strong, too slow. They must not be individuals, not in voices – not in any way. 'Emptied out for God,' was how the Novice Mistress put it. They called her Mother Mistress, and it was she who did the emptying; breaking down each novice, rooting out the self, all its petty likes and dislikes, its passions, failings, pride.

It had hardly started yet. Sister Mary Hilary had been a novice just two weeks, after twelve months as a postulant; was still awed by the Office, terrified of solos, scared by Mother Mistress with her blue-steel voice, her hundred eyes which took in every detail while always looking down. Yet she loved the Office – the ritual, the performance, the changing liturgy, circling with the seasons: Advent dark and pleading, spring and Easter rejoicing in new light; every day with its prayer, its saint, its purpose, lifting them to God.

'Into thy hands, O Lord, I commend my spirit.' Sister Michael, solo, with her pure and careful voice. All the nuns repeated it. 'Into thy hands, O Lord . . . '

Every night, safe within God's hands. Safe from nightmares, darkness, safe from Satan who loathed and taunted nuns. They bowed low for the Gloria, Sister Hilary lower than the rest, copying their Foundress who was said to offer her neck to an imaginary executioner at each and every Gloria, to show her complete surrender to God's will. They were reading her Life in the refectory. She still found it difficult to concentrate, remove fiddly little bones from fish, yet still take in devotions; digest syrup sponge along with miracles.

Sister Gerard switched the chapel lights out. Shadows from the candles fell across the wooden floor, duplicating vases, statues. The heady scent of freesias seemed stronger in the gloom. All the nuns turned towards the statue of Our Lady; blue robe again, bare feet, white veil, and eight feet tall. Their huge and powerful Mother, protecting them, listening while they sung the *Alma Redemptoris Mater*.

'*Succurre cadenti, surgere qui curat populo . . .*'

Sister Hilary struggled with the Latin. She had got an 'A' in her Latin A level, passed English and History, too, when only seventeen, but that was eighteen months ago, and her brain had dulled since then. Brains were part of pride, had to be subdued. She had done mainly manual work those first months as a postulant; scrubbing, sweeping, gardening, cleaning out the hens – work which kept the mind free, free for God. Now that she was a novice, she would learn Latin once again, but only the Latin of the Office, so she could understand the Lessons in the breviary, those lengthy expositions of Saints' and Virgins' lives.

'*Virgo prius ac posterius . . .*' She translated as she sang: 'You, a virgin, then and always, gave birth to your own sacred Creator, while nature watched in awe.' Only one more night before that birth, that miracle, the day of Christmas joy. The last notes of the anthem died away. She could feel the joy already, tried to burn it out of her, while she knelt praying for the joyless, the sick, the old, and dying, the homeless and the godless, the outcasts and the sinners. '*Peccatorum miserere.*'

The silence seemed to stretch to heaven. No page rustled, no nun coughed or fidgeted. The shadowed convent garden breathed softly, imperceptibly, outside the chapel windows, and beyond it watched the sombre Norfolk marshes, and above them both the waiting pregnant sky. It was so quiet you could almost hear the sand falling through Reverend Mother's hourglass, flowing silent as their prayers.

The Abbess rose, to bless her nuns, the last ritual before the night's Great Silence, sprinkling every nun with holy water, as she walked slowly down the chapel. Sister Hilary bowed her head as the cool drops spattered on her face. This was her second Mother – who had taken over from her own fussing, fretting mother-in-the-world – and who was Serenity and Strength; a woman over seventy, who, when she sat, never let her body touch the chair-back; kept her posture perfect, however long she knelt. Reverend Mother Benedict, who had been born 'the honourable', came from a wealthy, high-born family, with horses, servants, extensive lands in Shropshire; had renounced them all for God. Her final words of blessing seemed to lap them all in security, in peace. 'Vouchsafe, O God, to send thy holy angel from heaven, to guard, cherish, shelter and protect all that dwell in this house and grant them a quiet and peaceful night.'

'Goodnight' at home had been a cross shout up the stairs. 'You ought to have your light out, girl', or a tired grunt from her father. ''Night then, dear. You off?' Here, she was protected, blessed by both her Mothers, guarded by an angel, surrounded by her family. Reverend Mother's dog had wandered into the chapel. As old as Mother Benedict herself, but far less aristocratic and devout, he sat scratching his fat rump, the noise snicking through the silence. The only male allowed in the enclosure, and even he was neutered. Sister Hilary smiled. Could you pray for dogs, or for the greedy noisy Leghorns in the henhouse? She did. And also for the furled birds on the marshes, eider duck and grebe, cormorant and redshank, sheltering from the ruthless winter wind.

Sister Sacristan had extinguished all the candles. No light now, except the tiny scarlet flicker of the sanctuary lamp. She knelt silent in the darkness. She wouldn't go to bed. It was hardly worth it. In just two hours, they would be up again for Matins, then up all night. No room at the inn. There *was* room here, room in every cell, in every inch of corridor, every yard of refectory and chapel. Her Saviour would be born tonight in the crooked wooden manger she had set up on the straw, polished with brown shoe-wax, filled with fragrant hay.

She was thinking of herself again, risking pride again. She fell forward on her hands and knees, then lay prostrate on the floor, nose squashed against the wood, arms stretched out each side to form a cross, toes pressed down and hurting. She would lie there for the innkeepers who had turned away their God; lie there for her father who still had not forgiven her for entering; for her mother who could find no joy in Christmas, only worry, extra work.

Even through the pain, the sickly smell of floor-polish, the forbidden joy kept leaping up again as she thought forward to tomorrow and the play. She was Mary, virgin then and always, the holy pregnant Virgin, giving birth to her Creator, while nature watched in awe.

3

She mopped her burning forehead. Odd to be perspiring in midwinter in a cold unheated church. Stranger still to be alone on Christmas Eve, least of all in London. The church was empty, silent, seemed very much a haven. It was down a flight of steps, as if hidden in a basement, away from prying eyes: not bright and crowded like the tube, but solemn, shadowy, lit only by low lights and votive candles. She was back with her old friends, the statues of Our Lady, St Thérèse, St Patrick; a small wooden figure of St Genesius, standing on two masks of Comedy and Tragedy and with a notice underneath: 'Patron Saint of Actors'. She tried to still the questions as she knelt there in her play-clothes. Was her whole life just a sham? Had she been nothing but an actor, taking part in some ancient mystery play? Were her nun's clothes as spurious as her present fancy dress?

She sat back on the bench, to rest her legs. She had tramped for hours in those clumsy chafing wellingtons, trying to keep to darker streets where nobody could see her; had stumbled on this Catholic church, which stood beside a restaurant called the 'Greek Gods Taverna' and opposite a public house. The church sign was like the pub sign, both swinging up above. A strange place for God's house, its sooty brick hemmed in by worldly buildings such as betting shops and wine bars, a police van parked outside. The van had startled her, made her dart inside to the shelter of the church. Were they after her already, alerted by the Abbess?

She slumped back on the bench, too weak and sick to kneel. Crazy to trudge round all day, when she'd been told to rest, advised to stay in bed. She'd been taken ill that morning, fainted when she was laying out the vestments, and been rushed to the Infirmary. Could it really have been this morning, just thirteen hours ago? It seemed another age, a blurred and distant age; she a different person now from the quiet committed Sister slowly regaining consciousness in the convent's cold Infirmary.

'Don't stay,' she'd tried to whisper, as she struggled to sit up. 'I'm fine now, Sister, really. And I know how rushed you are.'

Sister Infirmarian had two invalids already, both crippled over-eighties; had just flurried from the kitchen, where she'd been helping out with all the Christmas cooking.

'But you've got a temperature. And you still look deathly pale.'

She'd murmured an apology, as she sank back on the bed, let Sister take her blood pressure. She'd no right to be ill, especially not today, when there was so much extra work. She was always needed, desperately, in such a small community, which had shrunk to only twelve; several of them elderly, two completely bed-ridden. She was able-bodied, strong, with skills – the sacristan, the vestment-maker, with a powerful singing voice. All the reasons why she couldn't leave; hadn't left for years and years, through all the doubts and struggles, when joy had changed to darkness, and superiors and priests kept urging 'Carry on. Accept it. Pray.' She'd prayed – prayed to darkness and to silence, prayed without an answer, without any consolation, yet continually assured by their chaplain, Father Martin, that this was just a proof of God's love. 'Those He loves He crucifies.'

She was still praying in the Infirmary when Sister Infirmarian at last went down to chapel, leaving her to rest. She didn't rest; staggered to her feet instead, removed the small white envelope from the pocket in her habit. A kindly local farmer had left a £20 donation, his annual Christmas offering to the convent. Twenty pounds in cash. The extern Sister had passed it through to her, to entrust to Reverend Mother. She was shaking as she crept up to the attic, the money in her hand. She couldn't steal, couldn't even think of it. If she rested for an hour or so, she would be strong enough to continue with her duties, be in choir for Compline. She rummaged through the play-clothes, heard rustlings in the attic – a mouse, a squirrel? – smelt mould and pigeon droppings. Of course she wasn't leaving; simply checking through the clothes in time for the next play. Except they never acted plays, not now. The community was far too small, too old for dressing up. No new recruits in five whole years. A struggle even to run the place, keep the huge house clean, weed and tend the garden. She was strong enough and young enough to hoe and dig and plant in her spare time.

She didn't feel at all young, but as if she'd lived for aeons, or had withered like some sickly plant kept too long in the dark. Yet she was still only thirty-eight, a child compared with all those nuns who had passed their Golden Jubilee, gone on to their Diamond. She didn't feel strong either, was often dizzy, nauseous, but those things you ignored. You could still dig with a headache, weed through pain or sickness. Impossible for someone strong to leave. She was feverish, that's all, hallucinating. Only dreaming that she went out in the freezing cold, couldn't find her boots, borrowed someone else's, snatched a dirty anorak from the spidery gardener's shed; then dashed across the orchard, past the chickens, though the gate. Still dreaming as she panted to the station, caught a train, arrived in teeming London, descended underground, then floated up again, walked and walked until she found this silent sanctuary.

'Maiden Lane', the street plaque said, and the church was Corpus Christi, Body of Christ. She struggled to her knees again, tried to feel His presence – failed – despite the seven sanctuary lamps flickering red above the altar. Christ present seven times, and she couldn't feel a fragment of Him. She must stay till Midnight Mass, remain there on her knees, however ill or faint she felt; beg God for the gift of faith, keep repeating with St Thomas, 'I believe.' She had doubted Him before, confessed to Reverend Mother, the new glacial Reverend Mother who had replaced saintly Mother Benedict. It was a sign of mental disturbance, she was told, to doubt one's Maker, Creator of the world. No one in their right mind doubted God.

She had redoubled all her penances, the fasts, the prayers, the vigils. 'God is kind in allowing you your Purgatory on earth,' the chaplain had explained. So her mother had been right about the Purgatory – her mother-in-the-world, who had died alone without a daughter's comfort. Selfish daughter shrivelling in the dark.

She clutched the bench in panic. Someone had come in. Slow uneven footsteps were closing in behind her. She shut her eyes, drops of perspiration snailing down her back, as a clumsy hand landed on her shoulder. She swung round, saw a nun – a modern nun, in a calf-length navy skirt and short blue veil. She must be still hallucinating, imagining a nun because her thoughts were on the convent.

'We're locking up now, dear.'

'I . . . beg your pardon?'

'We're locking up the church. I'm afraid you'll have to go.'

'But Midnight Mass?' Her voice was just a whisper, hoarse and rusted up.

'We're not having it this year. We've only got a tiny local congregation. Most of our regulars are office folk and so on, who come here after work, but live out of London. They'll have all gone off home by now. Public transport stops earlier than usual and British Rail packed up at nine o'clock. Try St Patrick's, Soho, or St Anselm's. They'll have Midnight Mass.'

She swayed slowly to her feet, still clinging to the pew. Their own Order hadn't modernised – no hair on show, or leg. This nun had thinning greyish hair, thick and swollen ankles. But she was still sacred in her habit, protected by her rosary, defended by her crucifix. The habit kept you safe: sound-proofed, world-proofed, endowing you with dignity and status. How could she have thrown hers off so lightly? The act seemed sacrilegious, almost unbelievable – stripping off the robes

25

she'd worn for over twenty years. Yet she had blanked it out completely. All she could remember was standing semi-naked in the attic, pulling on her play-clothes.

'You should be careful on your own, you know. There's a lot of funny types about, and it's even worse in Soho. A girl was knifed there just last week, *and* in broad daylight. I've got my car outside. I'll drive you to St Patrick's, if you like.'

She fought the tears back as she tried to mouth her thanks. Every kindness made her weep.

'That's it – mind the step. It's a bit gloomy down here, isn't it? I'm Sister Pauline, by the way. What's *your* name?'

'Sister Mary Hila . . . ' She stopped abruptly, gagging on the 'a'. That couldn't be her name – not now. Sister Mary Nothing. Twenty years ago, she had changed her name to Hilary. A man's name, a fifth-century Bishop's name: Hilary of Arles, an over-zealous prelate who had quarrelled with the Pope. She hadn't chosen it; had wanted to be Sister Anne, the mother of Our Lady who was mother to the world. She had never felt much sympathy with Hilary of Arles, an apparently high-handed man, from a rich and noble family in Northern Gaul, who had made a lot of enemies, was even excommunicated at one point in his career. He had been removed from the calendar in 1969, along with better-loved saints, such as Christopher and George. She kept his name and feast-day, but felt somehow disappointed in him; prayed to him only as a duty.

The nun drew both the bolts. 'I didn't catch, I'm sorry.' They were out in the cold again, cold and glare and fear again.

She didn't answer, couldn't. She was a nothing with no name. She'd been christened Gloria, because her father was a fan of Gloria Swanson, and had called his crumpled infant daughter, with her bald head and scarlet face, after an exotic *femme fatale*. The name had been a burden. Swanson was sophisticated, glamorous, every inch a star, with a voluptuous figure, wavy warm-brown hair, whereas she was flat – both sides – with hair so straight and heavy it wouldn't hold a curl, and a fairish wheaty colour. Swanson wore a different gown each day, all of them sensational, dripping fur and jewels; *she* wore boring blue school uniform five days a week, a bargain basement grey skirt most weekends. All they had in common was their height – or lack of it – both only five foot tall. At school, they'd laughed at Gloria, shortened it to Gee, but the *femme fatale* returned again when she entered as a postulant and became Sister Gloria. It sounded so pretentious, as well as inappropriate, but at least no one knew the Swanson connotation. *Gloria in Excelsis* rather than Gloria from Hollywood. And with names like

Seraphina and Agnellus all around her, she was really not conspicuous. Twelve months later, Gloria was dead; reborn as Sister Hilary.

Should she resurrect the Gloria, placate her father who had chosen it himself? She stared down at her clothes. How could she be Gloria in a dirty anorak, with an inch of hair, cropped ragged, and the boots?

'Er . . . Hilary,' she muttered. At least it didn't *sound* male. Hilary was either, male or female. She didn't feel a female, didn't have the parts required. Her breasts had grown at last, at the advanced age of sixteen, but two years later had been flattened by the stiff and swaddling bodice which went beneath her habit; her newly rounded hips lost in three serge underskirts. For twenty years, she'd been shapeless, breastless, spayed; a sexless neuter in service to her God.

'Well, happy Christmas, Hilary. My car's just round the corner.'

Hilary. The nun had christened her. Her new name in the world. It seemed too brief, too crude, without the 'Sister'; without the holy middle 'Mary' to uplift it.

She was nervous in the car. Only the two extern sisters drove – Sister Mark and Sister Bernadette, their link between the convent and the outside world, who ran the errands, answered phone and door bell, and so allowed the other nuns to avoid all contact with secular distractions which might interrupt their life of constant prayer. Only those two Sisters could venture out beyond the convent walls, contend with shops and traffic, handle money. The nuns in the enclosure never left it, save for hospital and dentist, flood or fire. One silent annual car trip to the dentist – an aged lady dentist who practised in a sleepy country town; one brief stay in hospital in her whole long twenty years.

This car was very different from Sister Mark's genteel aged Humber – smaller, more bad-tempered, as it jerked and whined through traffic lights, neon lights, Christmas lights, and flashing lights on hoardings. She kept her eyes cast down. It was Advent still, and her mind should be on the four Last Things: heaven, hell, death and judgement. She shivered – judgement – couldn't block the lights out. They were still flickering on her hands, tigering her clothes – lights from theatres, lights from dazzling windows. How did London nuns survive, drive in all that traffic, pray through all that din?

St Patrick's looked enormous. The nun had parked, walked her to the door. 'You're very early, dear. I'm afraid I've got to drive to Bath, otherwise I'd stay and keep you company. Don't trail around – it isn't safe. Just wait here till the Mass begins. At least it's nice and warm.'

Hilary faltered in the porch. This church was far too big, too grand; imposing vaulted ceiling arching over rows and rows of pews; pomp and pillars; gold and alabaster; huge statues frowning at her shabby clothes.

27

She glanced at the *Pietà*, Mary holding Christ's dead body, her marble face a mask of pain. She searched round for the crib – needed Mary joyful – found it in an alcove at the back. Not as nice as *their* crib. They had precious ancient figures brought from France a hundred years ago, carved in wood, dressed in silks and velvets, the Mary with real golden hair. These figures were just crudely painted plaster, which seemed cheap and out of place against their background of white marble.

She stared at the hollow in the yellow painted straw. No Christ in the manger, no God in His church. Mary still looked anguished. How could she not, when Bethlehem prefigured Calvary, birth leading on to death? The death of God. She fell onto her knees. No one in their right mind doubted the good God. *Good* God? Who let people jump from platforms, left broken bodies on the line, tiny babies screaming in the ruins?

She turned back to the altar: another dying God. A huge Crucifixion hung above the tabernacle, Christ's limbs starkly white against the rich gold of the frame.

'I *believe*.'

'Take this, all of you, and eat. This is my body.'

All heads in the church bowed low, as the priest recited the words of consecration; then held up the host – Christ's Body.

She couldn't eat it, couldn't receive Christ's Body, not in mortal sin. It was a mortal sin to leave one's convent, break one's solemn vows. The punishment was excommunication: exclusion from Communion and community, from the communion of believers in this world, and from the Communion of Saints in the next. It was an even graver sin to doubt God's goodness. If His world were less than perfect, then man's own free will had spoilt it. Free will in a baby who had perished in an earthquake? She tried to quash the thought, joined in with the prayers again, the eucharistic prayers. No unison in this church. Men's voices boomed, children's shrilled and wavered, everybody gabbling out of time. She had forgotten how distracting a congregation was – all those startling clothes and colours, coughs and fidgets, infants wailing, people dropping Mass-cards. Back in Brignor, the extern chapel was separate from their own, and set behind it; closed off with a grille. They rarely saw the villagers, and the few who came were always quiet and prayerful. Families and babies went to St Augustine's in the town. So many here were foreigners – black hair, dusky faces. Yet she herself felt more foreign than them all: someone who had strayed into an alien land and didn't know the rules or speak the language.

The priest was speaking now again, as he prepared to distribute the

Communion. 'Lord, I am not worthy to receive you, but only say the word and I shall be healed.'

God couldn't heal her, wouldn't say the word. She had sinned too gravely this time. She had never missed Communion before, had received it every day from the age of seventeen, and twice a week before that, since her First Communion at seven and a half. That had been traumatic. They had been strictly instructed not to touch the host. You didn't touch Christ's body unless you were a priest. And they were not to leave the altar rails until they'd swallowed it right down. The problem was she couldn't *get* it down. It seemed to block her throat, stick just above her windpipe. She'd coughed, panicked, stared blindly round at the throng of nuns and parents just behind. No one helped, or told her what to do. She was alone at the altar rails, which was also forbidden; the priest tutting at her, angry, motioning her to go. She touched the host with just one finger, managed to dislodge it.

Her cheeks were flaming as she slunk back to her pew. She had poked God's body with an unconsecrated finger, a finger used for dipping into sherbet or licking out the mixing bowl, a finger which had wiped her bottom earlier that morning. That was sin, grave sin. Which meant her First Communion was blighted, her frilled white dress and rose-wreath just a sham. She bowed her head as the nuns had taught her, hid it in her hands, felt hot and shameful tears splashing on the wood.

She wiped her eyes. The blue school nuns in their huge starched wimples, their elaborate fussy pie-frills, had changed into the sombre nuns of Brignor, kneeling in their dusty black for solemn Midnight Mass. She saw her choir stall empty, fought a sudden wave of shock. *She hadn't told them where she was.* They would be sick with worry, frantic, searching every niche for her, every inch of ground, even more alarmed for knowing she was ill and faint already. She must be gravely ill if she could forget a thing like that, wreck their peaceful Christmas through her thoughtlessness. Yet she hadn't meant to leave, had simply gone out for some air, sleepwalked in a fever. Sleepwalkers didn't plan, leave notes explaining where they were. She would have to phone immediately, tell them she was safe.

She struggled to the door, stood shivering just outside, looking out at neat black railings, bare but graceful trees. 'Soho Square', the plaque said. She recognised the name. That nun had mentioned Soho, warned her to beware of it. Yet the square looked safe enough, with its stylish buildings, quiet deserted streets.

She broke into a run. The nuns' Mass would be ending. They would be filing now, in silence, to the refectory, for tea and one plain biscuit, before returning to the Chapel. If she didn't catch them in that one short break, they'd be back in choir all night, till six a.m.

She dodged a crowd of party-goers in paper hats and evening dress, turned another corner. The hushed dark square had changed into a maze of narrow streets, throbbing with the lights from lurid bars. She crossed the road, skirted round a crate of mouldy cauliflowers, a box of black bananas rotting in their skins; turned right again, then left; was suddenly confronted by a blaze of spinning signs: 'PEEPSHOW', 'BED-SHOW', 'SAUNA', 'STRIPTEASE'. She stopped in shock. She could see two nuns – nuns in veils and wimples, but wearing black suspenders, seamed black fishnet stockings, and brandishing black whips. She backed away, disorientated, remembering stories of medieval saints who had seen such things, but only in their minds – peepshows staged by Satan, to wreck and taunt their faith. She glanced back at the window. Those nuns weren't in her mind. They were paper nuns, painted nuns, pouting in a frieze of flashing lights; crucifixes dangling between huge naked fleshy breasts.

She turned and fled, her heavy boots thrumming on the pavement, until she found a phone box, collapsed in it, still shaking. A row of small white cards were stuck up on the wall. 'Heaven or hell. Yasmin offers both. Phone 736 . . . ' 'Madame requires submissive subjects . . . ' 'Call Cherry, just eighteen, ripe, juicy and ready for picking.' She shut her eyes. She could see the stern black letters above her cell: 'Contempt For The World.' Each cell had its painted sign, its virtue – a custom brought from France, like so much in their Order. She had changed her cell so often, but, every time, she tried to live the virtue which came with it – Obedience, Holy Indifference, and these last two months, 'Contempt For The World' – as if God had picked the words to warn her and restrain her.

She lifted the receiver, suddenly swung round. She could hear a noise outside. A man was urinating, right against the phone box; a coarse-faced, drunken man, gnawing on a dirty piece of pizza, as he stood there with his legs splayed. She watched in horror as he dragged his trousers back, then lurched off down the street, colliding with another man who seemed to wrestle with him.

These were the souls she had prayed for in the chapel, these dirty vulgar drunks, their trousers tied with string and streaked with faeces; not souls, but bodies: dirty stinking bodies with gummy eyes, whisky breath. She had often seen them in her mind, as she knelt there in her choir stall, but seen them still as souls – poor perhaps, drunk perhaps, but clean poor and noble drunk. How stupidly naive she'd been, how sheltered. Christ had died to save these men, and she'd shrunk in sheer distaste at her first glimpse of a sinner.

'Christ is born,' she whispered; saw Him dying in the manger, a baby crowned with thorns.

The Mass was over, the last stragglers shuffling out. She crept back inside the church, tried to wrap herself in smells – candle wax and incense, damp coats, hot feet, ripe flowers. The congregation had left their smell behind – the good odour of good Catholics who believed in God, who had fed on Bread and Wine, not dirty pizza, urine. She was totally alone. The empty church seemed to echo all around her: heavy laboured breathing, whispered accusations, yet no one there except the ghostly watching statues. She had to pray. It didn't matter what she felt, believed. St Anthony had said that no man was really praying if he knew what God was, or what he was himself. The void, the mystery, was simply part of prayer. She looked back at the crib. The Christ was born now, a plump and solid bundle in a dirty plaster nappy.

She limped towards the figures, swaying, almost falling, as a sudden wave of dizziness seemed to make the church dissolve. All the flashing lights and flickering signs had come in from the street and were whirling in her head. Slowly, she bent over, picked up the plaster baby, held Him very awkwardly, His pudgy feet jabbing in her side. She wasn't used to babies, had vowed her womb to God. 'Rejoice, thou barren, that bearest not, for many are the children of the desolate, more than of her that hath a husband.' 'Rejoice,' she repeated silently, tears sliding down her cheeks, splashing on the infant's face, so that He was weeping, too. She ought to rest, sit down. The hammering in her head had merged now with the throbbing in her feet; the double pain dulling thought and will. The baby felt too heavy, His naked body dragging down her arms. She wasn't a good mother, was letting Him get cold – burning hot herself, but her baby stiff and chilly like a corpse. She returned Him to His coffin, sank back on her knees. Must pray – not rest – pray for souls. She was Mother to all souls.

The noises in her head had changed, sounded now like footsteps, heavy booming footsteps tramping closer, closer. She mustn't listen, must block out all distractions, keep her mind on God; pray in sickness, darkness, as Father Martin urged. She closed her eyes, bowed low.

'I'm sorry to disturb you in your prayers, my dear, but it's getting on for two o'clock, so I'll have to lock the church.'

She glanced up at the shifting blur of black. A larger, kinder priest than Father Martin, but without a clear-cut outline; maybe two of him, or three.

'It's time you got back home now. You have a home, do you?'

She tried to think through the fog and swirl of images, the stab of

31

hurting lights. Oxford Circus. N14. 'My aunt,' she said. 'Aunt Eva.'

'You live with her?'

She shook her head. Words seemed very difficult.

'She's meeting you from Mass?'

'Yes,' she said, uncertainly; could hear Aunt Eva's pounding feet rushing down the platform, as time hurtled back to childhood and she met her from the train; saw the clashing swirl of colours as Eva's emerald raincoat embraced her blue school mac.

'Well, if you could wait outside . . . All right? If there's any problem and she doesn't show up, I'll get Father John to sort it out. Okay?'

Priests didn't say 'okay'. He was someone in the play. The one with the deep voice. St Joseph, or an innkeeper. 'No room at the inn. I'm sorry, we're full up.'

'Sure you'll be all right, dear?'

The innkeepers were surly, didn't call you 'dear'. He must have got his lines wrong. She was forgetting hers, as well. Yet she'd been given the main part – Mary, God's own Mother, trudging into Bethlehem. Would she ever get there, when she felt so weak and faint, or simply fall, lie useless in the road? Mary hadn't fainted. Mary always smiled and struggled on.

'You're not ill or something, are you? I mean, if you need a doctor, I can always . . . '

She shook her head, made one last desperate effort, gripped the bench in front of her, used its strength to haul her to her feet; then smiled at him, as Mary would, as she staggered to the door.

4

Hilary lay, still half-asleep, groping for the shreds of psalms which kept drifting through her head; fumbling for the blankets – those thin grey scratchy blankets which must have fallen off the bed. The bed itself felt hard, so hard it made her ache. She was stiff all over, could hardly move her legs, which seemed encased in plaster casts. It must be time for chapel, time for Morning Prayer. She forced her eyes to open, blinking in the harsh and jolting light. Light? She always woke in darkness; Morning Prayer was said before the dawn.

She glanced around her, startled. Her tiny cell with its plain white walls, its window too high up to give a view, was swelling into a tangled maze of buildings, lampposts, windows, rooftops, sky. The jumble settled, steadied, though not her sense of shock. She was lying in the open, in an anorak and wellingtons, in an exposed and public street. Her bed was just a dirty piece of cardboard, laid out on the pavement against the warm flank of a building. *Warm* in late December? She felt her hands, her head – both sweaty hot. She remembered being very ill, must still have a temperature, but it wasn't simply that. Some sultry breath was blowing on her body. Slowly, she sat up, turned round to find a metal grille set into the wall, hot air panting out of it from a basement boiler-room, a grotesque and filthy dungeon, housing hugely swollen pipes. It must belong to some hotel, be pumping out the heat for baths and breakfasts.

She heard a cough, swung round. Just beyond her lay a huddled shape, also sprawled on cardboard and wrapped in three old coats. What was it? Male or female? Human, certainly. She could hear its laboured breathing, see one hand flung out, a large hand in an old brown glove, with holes in all the fingers. The face was turned away from her, a fringe of greasy hair flattened beneath a black and broken hat.

Her first instinct was to run. That body might be dangerous, or even verminous. She struggled to her feet, about to dart away, then glanced back at the heap of tangled coats, the battered shoes tied round with dirty newspapers. That 'thing' could be her rescuer, could have brought her here, shared its cardboard couch with her, laid on central heating. She had prayed so often for the outcasts and the homeless. Had one of them repaid her prayers, shown her how to manage when the pavement was her mattress and her alarm clock a police siren? Or had she just collapsed here? That could be a proof of God – a good God – that He should have saved her from exposure, hypothermia; made sure she fell where there was heat and help at hand. She could remember nothing, except a frightening snarl of noises in her head, looming faces, then falling into black. If she had stayed in the Infirmary, she would be restored to health by now. The contaminating world had made her worse, kicked her in the gutter with the lowest of the low – which was what she was – lower than the lowest.

The piled coats jerked and shuddered in a second rasping cough. She glimpsed a bony foot, the ankle bare, engrained with filth, the shoe gaping at the sides without its fastening. There was still no face – no ear to hear her thanks, no mouth to answer if she asked what had happened in the night. Perhaps better not to know. 'Thank you,' she said silently, as she crept away, limped off down the street, then turned into a dark and narrow alley. She still felt the need to hide – from God, from tramps, from further punishment. She smoothed her crumpled clothes, re-tied her scarf. Important to be neat. Nuns could look shabby – patched habits, veils with darns in – but never messy or unkempt. She glanced down at the baggy skirt, the oil stains on the anorak. Today she should be in her best, for Christ, Christ's birthday. Was it really Christmas Day – this grey and silent morning with overflowing dustbin-bags the only decorations in the street?

Twenty-two long years ago, she had woken on a different Christmas morning, a radiant one, with a new-born sun spilling its gold tinsel on her curtains. She'd flung them back, stood exultant at the window, greeting God in sun, in sky, in the glinting furrows of frosted winter fields. She was going to be a Sister of Notre Dame de Bourges! She hugged the secret to herself, knelt down to say her thanks. God had revealed His will to her last night at Midnight Mass – not the perfunctory gabbled Mass at St Augustine's, where the priest was old and irritable and her mother's sniffs and shufflings made it hard to concentrate, but the exquisite chant and singing of the nuns of Notre Dame. It was the first time she had seen them. The convent was remote; not far in terms of miles, but buried in the Norfolk wilds, deliberately removed from human noise or commerce, even from a bus route or main road. But her best friend Katy's parents had a cousin there, who'd entered seven years ago, invited Katy's family to come for Midnight Mass, meet the Sisters afterwards for coffee and mince pies.

'Like to come along as well?' Katy had asked casually, the last afternoon of term. 'They're nothing like our school nuns. All they do is pray all day. Imagine!'

She warmed to Katy's family; her funny scatty father who was always making jokes, her calm and kindly mother, her two kid brothers who bulged at hip and cheek with pocketsful of marbles, huge half-sucked gobstoppers. The six of them had knelt in the tiny extern chapel, peering through the grille at the rows of black-robed nuns, who seemed to move and chant as one. She was utterly transported; had never heard such pure and perfect singing. She was musical herself, on grade seven for piano at sixteen and a half. She shivered with an almost hurting pleasure at the high soprano solo from a young and ardent novice, her white veil standing out from the black ones all around it. Everything was perfect – the plain white chapel walls, uncluttered by the plaques and pomps which carbuncled St Augustine's; the ancient figures in the Christmas crib, the soaring Latin anthems. But it was the nuns themselves who drew her. They seemed so other-worldly with their bare feet, straight black backs; their complete absorption in the Mass, as if nothing else existed – no villagers behind them, no fidgety kid brothers; nothing but their God.

She had thought, already, of a future as a nun, hoped for it and dreaded it alternately; though feared to say a word back home, where the only talk was A levels and Oxbridge. She'd even braved her own headmistress, to discuss the issue with her. Mother Gabriel suggested that she wait till after university, then, if she was still certain God was calling her, she could enter their own mother-house in Ely.

That Christmas night, as she went up for Communion, received the host through an opening in the grille, she knew suddenly, indubitably, that it was *this* house she must enter; this strict and silent convent where 'all they do is pray all day. Imagine!'

'Wake up, Gee! You haven't said a word for hours.' Katy had nudged her in the car, as they motored home through dark and winding lanes. 'Tired from all those prayers,' quipped Mr Brent, passing back the mints. 'Have a Polo, Gloria – hole-y sweets, for after Mass.' She didn't take one, didn't even laugh. God's Body was still blazing on her tongue.

She licked her lips, tasting neither host nor mint, only the sour taste of her illness in her mouth; smelt mould and urine as she leant against the crumbling alley walls. She eased her rubber boots off, wincing at the pain. Her feet were sore and swollen, the skin rubbed raw in patches. Too bad. She rammed them back. She had to walk, walk for souls, as St Thérèse had walked for missionaries in the last months of her life when she was dying of consumption, hobbling up and down her sick-room, offering her exhaustion to lift or lessen theirs. *She* would walk for drunks, for huddled shapes on cardboard, for Katy Brent – now Dawes – who had left her husband, run off with an artist.

She trudged on down the alley, crossed a wide main road. A car flashed past, three balloons streaming from its bonnet – on its way to celebrate, or perhaps speeding home for Christmas. She hadn't got a home.

> My dwelling is plucked and removed from me
> like a shepherd's tent;
> like a weaver I have rolled up my life;
> He cuts me off from the loom . . .

She struggled down an incline, crossed another road, found herself facing a wide river, a sad and sluggish river, the colour of stained concrete. Everything was still – dead tugs, sleeping barges, huge hibernating bridges slumped heavy over heavy brooding water. She would walk beside that water, seek to find her God.

> When you pass through the waters, I shall be with you.
> And through the rivers, they shalt not overwhelm you.

She set off along the bank, watching the reflections: wharves trembling on the water, huge warehouses dissolving into ripples. The road beside her was lined with naked plane trees; grey clouds streaked with purple barely breathing overhead. Everything seemed muzzled – birds silent, branches drooping – as if somebody had drugged both earth and sky. Her own legs felt dead and lumpen as she forced them to trudge on, her skirt clinging damply round her thighs. Strange to have no wide black sleeves to hide and warm her hands in; no long and heavy habit to protect her from the wind. She was even walking differently without the habit to restrain her, walking like a secular, lurching like a drunk.

She stopped to rest a moment, grateful for the hard iron bench which looked out across the river. It was probably only hunger, this dizzy nauseous feeling, this sense of constant weakness. She felt no hunger, but she hadn't eaten since her 'drink' the day before, a whole day and night ago. No – more. It must be well past noon now. She sat straighter on the bench, smoothed her skirt, as if to spread her starched white linen napkin on her lap. She was sitting in the refectory at Brignor, her eleven Sisters smiling round the table, about to start their Christmas dinner – never turkey – fried fish and Christmas pudding. Meat was forbidden, even on Christ's birthday, as was speaking in the refectory; both invariably prohibited, regardless of the feast. The silence, though, was joyful, broken by the snap of Christmas crackers – plastic rings comic on old fingers, paper crowns set rakish on black veils – even the stern-faced statue of St John softened by his second tinsel halo. The food itself was something of a trial – fish too flat and greasy for their rounded wooden bowls, pudding damply heavy after all the weeks of fasting.

Christmas dinner changed to Christmas breakfast, her favourite meal of all, and eaten in the Community Room, which meant that they could talk. They even called it breakfast, since it was much more than a drink – real tea with tea leaves in, fresh white rolls with butter, which they never saw all year; sometimes even porridge, made with milk. She could see the bare wood table festive with its cloth, flowers and holly glowing in the centre, paper napkins twisted into swans; hear the happy music, as they processed in, two by two, Sisters Luke and Anna on recorders, Sister Gerard entrusted with the drum. Everybody bubbled – gnarled old nuns like children, opening gifts, and giggly. The gifts were tiny, often useful items which were needed in their work: a packet of red cabbage seeds for the nuns who did the garden; needles or a thimble for her, as vestment-maker; new dusters, wooden spoons. The extern Sisters bought them, with a few precious pounds squeezed from the donations which benefactors sent in through the year. Or someone's friend or parent might contribute a few chocolate bars, or a box of home-made fudge, which went straight to Reverend Mother, were stored and saved for Christmas, then shared around the nuns. They couldn't give each other presents, only holy pictures, but those, too, were loving offerings, prayers and greetings written on the back.

And then there was the excitement of the cards – Reverend Mother as Santa Claus again, handing out the Christmas post which had piled up during Advent, when letters weren't allowed. Her letter from Aunt Eva, the large untidy writing, the row of slanting kisses at the bottom of the page.

She ached to see those kisses, to be back there with her 'family', sipping that rare tea, exchanging squares of Milky Bar. She could almost hear Sister Clare slurping down her porridge, Sister Joseph's phlegmy snuffling wheeze – all the petty maddening things which had strained her screaming nerves for years, tested her compassion. Now she missed them.

She eased up from the bench. She would never find her Lord and God, if she didn't keep on calling Him, didn't keep on walking, offering Him her pain. She shivered, as she plodded on. The tide was ebbing, the listless water silting into sludge; two glossy magpies squabbling over a carcass on the bank. Two for joy. How long this Christmas Day seemed, how sluggish, like the river. At Brignor, it would race – every hour accounted for, every minute sanctified, Christ and the community sharing it together.

She paused to watch a surge of gulls, wheeling swooping past her, their soaring white breaking up the stillness and the grey. She envied them their wings, felt some tenuous link with them. Had they flown from Norfolk, from the bleak and lonely coast beyond the convent?

> Have mercy on me, God, have mercy . . .
> In the shadow of your wings I take refuge
> till the storms of destruction pass away.

She followed where they led, turning up a narrow lane into a labyrinth of streets, dark confining ancient streets, which seemed to turn her footsteps into empty echoing sighs. Each time she turned a corner, she prayed to see another human face, even a blurred form through a window, or a driver in a car. There *were* no faces – save painted ones on pub signs, peeling ones on posters.

She stopped, disorientated. Windows windows windows all around her and beyond her – hundreds of them, thousands, reflecting nothing but themselves. The streets had opened out, and she was standing in a square, gazing up at a massive soaring tower block, its dizzying glass and concrete rearing up so high, she was forced to tilt her head right back to see its topmost storeys. Another monster faced it, a third beyond, blocking off the sky. The three giants stepped towards her, closed her in, whittled her to nothing, as they had squeezed the ancient churches trapped and pinched between them. Those churches must have once been free to soar, spires thrusting up to a huge uncluttered heaven. Now, they, too, were dwarfed.

She backed away, still dizzy, read the sign blazoned on the square: 'City of London'. She had heard about the City, the seething hub of London, with its banks and finance houses, its million people packed into one square mile. Where were they, all those million? Did not one single one of them still live here after work, or return to walk these streets, buy a Christmas drink? Every pub she'd seen was locked and shuttered, every restaurant closed, and those tower blocks seemed like vast abandoned monuments, left behind by a vanished master race, who had built higher and more daringly than any tribe before them, then been swept away themselves.

At least nobody could see her in this City of the Dead; criticise her crumpled skirt, shrink from her old clothes. She had made herself a rag-bag and a solitary, when, once, she'd taken such great pride in belonging to an Order renowned for its ideals – one of the strictest left in Europe – who got up every midnight for the Office, and were back in choir again by six a.m.; still observed silence for the best part of the day, went always barefoot, even in the winter, refused to shorten their devotions or their skirts. Other nuns had modernised, relaxed the rules, relaxed the fast, docked their floor-length robes. The Second Vatican Council had ended in December 1965, just a year before she entered; had urged all nuns to embrace the twentieth century, update ancient practices which wasted time or money. Vacuum cleaners instead of besom brooms; habits which would wash, and took fewer yards of fabric; wimples with less width and starch, so that nuns could drive and still see out both sides; less starch altogether, both real and metaphorical.

Some Orders rushed to change, took things far too far – shouted in the corridors, escaped to cinemas, gossiped over wine. A few firebrands in America went further still: started using contraceptives, wearing dungarees. Other Orders compromised – hair cut short instead of cropped, sober calf-length dresses, months of agonised debate before deciding to use Christian names. But the Sisters of Notre Dame de Bourges remained faithful to the spirit of their Foundress. They hadn't ignored the Council; had bought their Hoover, removed the most medieval of their undergarments, trimmed their habits from eleven yards of serge to only seven. But those were merely details. Should their Foundress have returned, glided from her coffin to inspect her modern heirs, she would have found no major deviation from her own sixteenth-century practices and Rule.

Her old headmistress, Mother Gabriel (now 'Nancy' in a skirt and blouse, and well into her eighties), had warned her, long ago, of the rigours of the enclosed contemplative life, counselled her to wait, to reconsider. 'With your gifts, my dear, your good exam results, you could probably serve God better in an active teaching role. I know you're keen to enter right away, but if you wait until your eighteenth birthday, you can do your novice year at Ely, then go on to our scholasticate at Cambridge University, study as a nun, Gloria.'

'I'm sorry, Mother, but I know that isn't right for me.' God had given her the words, the courage. Contemplatives were special – only six thousand out of a million total nuns. And their lives could touch and succour the whole world, not just one trifling school. 'Separated from all and united to all,' Evagrius had said. She had discovered him in the library: a fourteenth-century monk and mystic who believed that man must mortify himself until he became spirit more than matter, and could then experience union with God. She had thrilled to his ideas, longed to be pure spirit like an angel; didn't like her body with its newly rounded breasts, its messy monthly curse, its down of pubic hair. God was Pure Light, Evagrius declared. That, too, she understood. She had often stood, transfixed, at Blakeney Point, watching the sun alchemise the sea; exulting in God's presence as the sun went down in a blaze of painted sky.

She was reading other books, not just for her A levels, but preparing for a future far removed from History, English Literature. One Trappistine had written that the life of a contemplative 'prefigured heaven' because when all other jobs had vanished – nursing, teaching, running schools – the work of contemplation would go on for all eternity. She loved that word – eternity.

'Bloody waste,' her father said. 'Waste of education, throwing your whole life away, your chances.'

In one sense he was right. Another book she'd borrowed described contemplation as 'wasting time with God', like Mary Magdalen's precious ointment 'wasted' on Christ's feet.

She had always been obsessed with God, playing saints or hermits when other girls played dolls. Aged just ten, she had found her desert cave in an abandoned worked-out quarry; fasted forty nights in it – or would have done, if her mother hadn't dragged her back to liver-sausage salad and rice pudding. Later, she played martyrs – stakes thrust in her heart, lions slavering round her bound and naked body. She begged God to give her the stigmata, kept examining her hands and feet, waiting for the bleeding wounds which would prove she was a saint. She pretended she could levitate, or spend entire nights praying on a sixty-foot-high pillar like St Simeon Stylites, who lived for nearly half a century without a wink of sleep. They weren't just foolish games. She wanted to be special, vow herself to God.

'GOD IS LOVE', she'd seen written on a poster, when she was only eight or nine; stored the words like treasure. She knew love was important – all the grown-ups said so, and the songs. She didn't think her parents loved each other. They shouted such a lot. God never shouted, banged His fist on tables, or complained about burnt toast. She yearned to run away from it – the rows at meals, the nagging, the brown skin on the rice, the dingy khaki kitchen which seemed to have soaked up all the rows. Heaven would be gold, she knew – and quiet.

By seventeen, she was less naive, though still in love with God; realised now that martyrdom could mean something rather different from stakes or ravening lions. The contemplative life was itself a form of death – the equivalent of being stripped and stifled, gagged, imprisoned, bound. There was an intoxication in renouncing everything, breaking self to powder, keeping nothing back at all. Outwardly, she still laughed and joked and studied, went picnicking or swimming, shopping with her friends. She was always popular, had her crowd of cronies. She and Katy dared miniskirts and eye gloss, giggled over desperate readers' letters in the women's magazines. But she also had a secret life, where she tried to skimp on meals, bath in icy water, put pebbles in her shoes, sleep without a pillow, or

40

blankets on her bed – anything that would break or hurt the body. She also refused to apply to university. Degrees were pointless, if your true work was praising God. Her parents were outraged.

'I never had your chances. If you'd had to work through college, do it all the hard way, then you wouldn't take this line. It's completely irresponsible.'

'And what about my grandchildren? I'd always hoped you'd marry, settle down close by and . . .'

She heard a clock strike one, braying through her mother's wail, returning her to London; one chime for twenty years. It was echoed by a deeper chime, a sudden peal of bells. Churches everywhere. She couldn't get away from them. Convent bells calling her to dinner. First, she had to find it. She must eat something to get her through the day, allow her to keep walking. She should have plucked a few bananas from those bulging crates in Soho, grabbed a mouldy cauliflower. These litter bins seemed far more mean and meagre: old papers in their stomachs, dirty crumpled cartons. She stopped to check a pile of cardboard boxes, a great load and spill of rubbish heaped outside an office door – empty bottles, dribbling cans, Christmas wrappings stained with wine – a drunken office party with no food.

The bells were ringing still – the second call for dinner. Almost automatically, she joined her hands, said grace. 'We hope in you, O Lord, and you give us food in due season.' She bowed for the 'Our Father', which always followed grace, then rummaged in the next few bins, repeating just one line: 'Give us this day our daily bread . . .'

Her hands closed round half a loaf – best white bread, fine and clean, the sort they had for Christmas, not coarse brown Advent fare. It was stale and hard, but clean. She broke a tiny piece off, ate it very slowly, as she offered up her thanks. It was difficult to swallow. Her throat felt parched, constricted. There was a puddle in the gutter, a swirl of muddy water above a blocked-up drain. She dipped the dry crust in it, sucked the moisture out. A few grey bedraggled pigeons flurried round her feet. She threw them half the bread; must share her Christmas dinner, extend her prayer of thanks.

'Your mercy, O God, is boundless, and your gifts without end.'

Two hours later, she brought the dinner up, vomiting and spitting, as spasms shook her body, racked her throat. Could one small half half-loaf take so long to void? She retched again, again, as if she were sicking up her past, her twenty years as a nun, the endless months of struggle when she'd been told by Father Martin that she *should* feel crushed, annihilated, totally destroyed; that only then would her humility be deep enough for her Saviour to return.

She spewed up a last drool of smelly fluid, clinging to a ledge to keep her balance. Her whole body craved to rest, but where? She couldn't lie on pavements, and if she fainted in the street again, there would be no obliging tramp, this time, to share his precious cardboard. Was it only yesterday she had been lying on a Dunlopillo mattress? The beds in the Infirmary were kinder than the hard ones in their cells. They even had sheets, which were normally forbidden, a luxury for invalids alone. Cool white sheets against her burning head, an iced drink on a tray . . .

She inched on down the street, stopping every pace or two, to try to calm the queasiness which still churned and griped her stomach. She crossed the road in front of her. 'NO ENTRY,' said the sign which barred her way. That sign was right. She had no business to be out at all, when she'd made solemn vows to leave the world, shun streets and shops and cities, stay till death within the convent walls. She turned the other way, towards the shelter of a building. 'KEEP OUT. NO ADMITTANCE.'

She stood paralysed between both signs, both forbidding her approach. There was nowhere she could go – not back to the enclosure, nor forward anywhere. How could she go forward when she had doubted God, abused Him?

Slowly, painfully, she knelt down where she was – her damp skirt flecked with vomit, her rough boots splashed with mud – begged her loving Saviour to return.

Winter

5

'I just don't understand how you could have behaved so irresponsibly –
someone with your background, under vows . . . '

Father Anstey was pacing up and down the kitchen of his Earlsfield
presbytery, his tight black suit straining at its buttons, plump hands
sawing the air. 'Your Abbess has been absolutely frantic. She's been on
to the police, had half the village scouring fields and woods, every nun
praying for your safety . . . '

Hilary said nothing. Her own selfishness and thoughtlessness had
shocked her into silence. She was stunned by what she'd done – even
without this priest's reproaches – to have dared to leave at all, tell no one
where she was; to have taken money which had been donated to the
convent, which belonged to Reverend Mother and therefore ultimately
to God.

'Couldn't you have phoned yourself, far earlier than this – not
wrecked their Christmas Day?'

'I did, Father, honestly. Well, I tried, but . . . ' She was adding lies to
theft now. She hadn't tried, not really, had found another phone box,
but stood there paralysed, unable to explain, or even dial the number,
when there *was* no explanation, no excuse. She'd wrecked Father
Anstey's Christmas Day as well as the community's. He should be at his
sister's, sitting down to Christmas supper – cold turkey and mince pies –
and, instead, he was on duty, making soup for vagrant nuns. She forced
the oxtail down, though it was still almost cold, with lumps, and she'd
already had two other soups in just the last two hours. She'd been found
that afternoon in the graveyard of a London church – found by the
police. They had made her Cup-A-Soup, asked her a few questions,
which she'd answered with evasions, terrified to say too much, in case
they locked her up, or sent her back to Brignor. 'I . . . I'm fine,' she'd
said. 'No, really. I was just looking for a priest.'

After half a dozen phone calls, and a few jokes about priests vanishing
once they'd said their Christmas Masses, while coppers had to sweat it
out all day, they found her one – miraculously – a kindly priest, with
sparse white hair, whose name she never heard. He served her home-
made turkey soup, bones and skin and all, then went straight to phone
his colleague, Father Anstey; returned, smiling, to his guest.

'The good Lord must have sent you, dear. You say you need a job,

45

and Father Anstey's got one. He phoned me just two hours ago, desperate for some help. One of his parishioners is really in a spot. She had a stroke a while ago, but still needs live-in help. Her usual nurse is away on Christmas leave, visiting relations in New Zealand, so she won't be back for weeks. They fixed her up a substitute, but the poor dear soul collapsed this very morning, and was rushed to casualty. What timing! You'd think an appendix might do the decent thing, and not perforate – bang! – on Christmas Day. Poor Father's in a spin himself, hasn't had much Christmas yet at all. But if I drive you down to Earlsfield right away, you can meet the invalid, then maybe . . . '

Hilary drained her oxtail soup, followed Father Anstey from cramped kitchen to plush parlour. *Had* the good Lord sent her, arranged this whole affair, offered her a job which included a Catholic roof above her head? She'd hardly heard a word about the job, yet. The priest was too annoyed to find his instant help had turned into just another problem, and that he had to make more phone calls, assuage a frantic Abbess.

'I told your Reverend Mother you'd send the money back. She wanted *you* back – straight away – but I said there were no trains, either today or Boxing Day, and I'd no intention of driving up to Norfolk, just to pander to . . . Anyway, now you're here, you might as well help out, at least for just a week or two, until I've made some other arrangements. Miss Pullen hasn't a relation in the world, which doesn't make it easy. She's lost her power of speech, as well, but that doesn't mean you have to shout. She hears everything you say. Now, about your duties . . . '

Hilary felt more and more uneasy as the priest ran through the list, casually referring to cooking, shopping, washing, managing the house. All were mysteries to her. She hadn't braved a shop since the age of seventeen; had all her own meals cooked for her, as if she were a child, all her laundry done. Cookers, boilers, washing machines, were hostile dangerous strangers, which might try to play her up. She had never run a house, never even spared a thought for what it might entail. How could she compare with Miss Pullen's usual nurse, who was not only fully trained, but sounded a true paragon – a shrewd resourceful woman, who could turn her hand to anything; a skilled cook, a careful driver, even a devout and pious Catholic?

The priest plumped into an easy chair, arranged his small feet on a stool. His shoes were highly polished calf, his socks a bishop's purple. 'I'm afraid the wages aren't a fortune, but you'll be getting room and board, and for someone with no training . . . '

'*Wages*, Father . . . ?' Hilary's voice faltered to a stop. It seemed extraordinary that somebody should pay her, provide not only food and roof, but actually give her money, when she deserved only reprimand.

She had seen the job as penance, done willingly, for nothing, as atonement for her sin.

'You'll find this first week pretty painless, anyway. Miss O'Connor stocked up before she went, and did all the heavy washing – sheets and towels and so on. And she left very detailed lists for Mrs Clarke. Which reminds me – I ought to ring the hospital, find out how that wretched woman is. She should never have taken on the job, not if she had pains. I *asked* her how her health was, and she told me excellent, yet the doctor on the ward said . . . ' The priest broke off, seemed too impatient or exhausted to finish all his sentences. 'After that, I'll drive you to Miss Pullen's, show you round the house, and then maybe I can get back to my sister's – some time before midnight.' His laugh was unconvincing, his face still cold and closed. He dragged up to his feet again, looked her up and down. 'I'm not sure about those clothes. Miss O'Connor wears a uniform. Have you nothing else to . . . ? No? Well, I suppose there might be something in the jumble box, at least something a bit longer. That skirt's not decent, is it, and you'll need some proper shoes.'

Hilary sorted through the box of musty garments, wincing at the brilliant reds and greens, the garish flower-prints, jaunty stripes and squiggles. Was there nothing unobtrusive, nothing plain? At last, she found a prim grey dress which reached almost to her ankles, had long tight sleeves, a high and modest neck. She felt better with it on, though wished it were less flimsy, did more to bulk her out; wished it didn't smell so, of cheap scent and nicotine.

She limped back to the parlour in her gaping slip-on shoes, found it empty, Father Anstey already in the hall, impatient fingers tapping on the table. 'You took your time, didn't you? Miss Pullen goes to bed at nine, and she's been left far too long alone. She's just not used to that. Miss O'Connor always . . . '

The drive was just five minutes, through drab South London streets. They drew up outside a narrow house, squeezed between its neighbours, with dark and frowning gables, drawn down like heavy brows; dank walls of yellow brick. She followed Father Anstey up the gloomy, ill-lit staircase. He stopped outside Miss Pullen's door, eyes and nose screwed up. She wrinkled her own nose, drew back a step or two. They could both smell something stronger than the vague whiff of damp and cat which had met them in the hall.

The priest knocked, strode in, let out a little throttled cry, as he flapped back to the door. Miss Pullen had her eyes shut, was slumped on her commode, pink bloomers round her feet – bloomers, stockings, floor and feet, caked with excrement. She had tried – and failed – to wipe herself, transferred the stuff to face and hands, daubed it on three towels. It was crusted on her bottom, clinging to her clothes. Father Anstey plunged straight back downstairs. She hoped he'd gone to find a bucket, fetch some disinfectant. She herself got to work immediately, running water in the basin, removing the soiled clothes. Miss Pullen's eyes were open now, the cold blue stare swivelling round to face her. Her right arm and leg looked stiff, seemed joined on to her body at slightly the wrong angle. Her face was thin and sallow, drooping to one side; the skin flabby and unhealthy, as if it had been left in a cellar with neither light nor air. Her hair was dry, discoloured – permed and dyed so often it had faded to a dingy yellow-grey, the wispy strands straggling down her neck.

Hilary forced her mouth to smile. 'I'm your new . . . ' She faltered, couldn't truly call herself nurse, or cook, or housekeeper. 'Helper,' she said softly, as she soaped the flannel, made a timid start on cleaning up that bleak and bitter face.

Miss Pullen swatted at her, with a frightened whimpering sound, as if to pull the flannel from her hand. Hilary tried to reassure her, smoothed her hair, stroked her arm, then reapplied the flannel, keeping her touch as gentle as she could. She had never had the job of Infirmarian, but she knew the principle – care for every invalid as if she were Jesus Christ Himself.

She kept running more clean water, wringing out the flannel. The stench was overwhelming still. She needed Dettol and detergent, more rags, a few clean towels; couldn't understand why the priest had not located them, not reappeared at all. She crouched down on the floor, sponged Miss Pullen's lower parts, trying to ignore the sudden raps and bangings, as her patient used her good (left) hand to ram the wood of the commode. She was obviously frustrated, and probably embarrassed to be found in such a state, treated like a baby, cleaned up by a stranger. Hilary understood; could imagine the sheer terror of being trapped, without the power of speech, in an old and useless body. She tried to make some recompense, put mercy in her hands, keep her voice as soft and kind as possible.

'There, that's better, isn't it? Though you do need some clean clothes. I can't seem to see them in any of these drawers. Perhaps you'd show me where they are. Just point or . . . '

Miss Pullen sat immobile, though she must have heard quite clearly.

'Well, I'd better go and ask, then. Will you be all right alone for just a moment?'

Miss Pullen's strangled cry seemed to pursue her down the stairs. But she had to find the priest, find out where things were, ask him if Miss Pullen could be moved. She could hardly spend all night on a commode.

48

She checked the kitchen – empty – knocked shyly on the closed door of the sitting room.

'Yes. Come in, come in.'

Her hand froze on the handle. Father Anstey was reclining on the sofa, his pipe smoking in the ashtray, a tumblerful of whisky cradled in both hands.

Hilary eased up from the lino, where she had been lying prostrate with her arms out in a cross. She heard the clock downstairs strike two. Night Office would be finishing at Brignor, the nuns returning to their cells to sleep. She still always said the Office, prayed for the depressed, the indecisive, the terrified, the sleepless. She could rarely sleep herself, these days, felt frightened in her room, claustrophobic somehow – though it was far larger than her Brignor cell, and had a window with a view, a grey-rinsed panorama of streets, shops, buildings, roofs. And yet she felt closed in, particularly at night, as if the bedroom were her coffin and she were wrapped in a black shroud. Miss Pullen's house seemed far too small, despite its three bedrooms, its square of concrete garden. She had become so used to the space and breadth of Brignor, its old grey stone softened with wisteria, its high ceilings, lofty rooms. Though everything was convent-plain – no carpets on the wooden floors, nor curtains at the windows – it was still a mansion, however much they kept it bare and poor; a mansion with extensive grounds, rolling fields beyond. Miss Pullen had her pot plants, her floral curtains, her rugs across the lino, yet the house seemed bare and grudging, didn't welcome strangers.

She still felt a total stranger, though she'd been there ten long days now; should feel more at home. Had she *ever* felt at home, even in her parents' house? Brignor was her 'home' – at least legally, officially – but it had become a place of suffering, her land of bitter exile.

She sat down on the bed, uncomfortably aware of the picture of Our Lady, whose sad eyes seemed to watch her from the wall. She ought to feel relieved to have such a sheltered job, in a safely Catholic house, where she could still keep her silence, still live as a nun, instead of being plunged into a bustling shop or office. She'd hardly had to venture out at all, yet, save twice to Mass, and once to the small corner shop, which was mercifully self-service, so there was no need to speak a word. She'd tamed the ancient boiler; washed everything by hand, so she didn't have to grapple with the moods of the machine, and Miss Pullen ate so little, her cooking was confined to making porridge or mixing mugs of Complan. No one ever bothered her, no one knocked or visited, except Father Anstey on his brief twice-weekly calls, which he spent mainly with Miss Pullen, only speaking to her afterwards in the bare and draughty hallway. 'Do you understand the cooker?' 'Are you managing all right?'

She said 'yes' to everything, tried to make as little fuss as possible, yet the terror was still there – that overwhelming feeling of being the only one in charge. Supposing something should go wrong, a gas leak or break-in, or Miss Pullen have another stroke, or heart attack? She'd been so totally protected in the convent. Reverend Mother, however strict and cold, had been a genuine mother, in the sense she took control, made all the decisions, coped with any crisis. Each nun had her job, her own 'obedience', as they called it, but only as part of some larger system, which, carefully controlled, shielded them from all the myriad concerns, all the other jobs and worries, she realised now were part of normal living.

There was also God – Father God – who, like any decent father, took responsibility for His family, allowed them all to lean on Him. God would provide – and did. She remembered times when there had been bills they couldn't pay. Sister Procuratrix had taken the bills to Him, literally stuffing them in the pocket of her habit, then hastening to the chapel, kneeling by the statue of the Sacred Heart, begging instant succour from that Heart. The next day, a cheque would come, an anonymous donation, the exact amount they needed; or someone leave them money in a will. If a nun were ill, she had God as specialist as well as just the local Brignor doctor. God could deal with strokes and heart attacks, gas leaks, break-ins; everything. He was always there, taking on their worries, acting as their bulwark and their bank.

So why was he not *here*, in Rosemont Road? God was omnipresent, didn't confine Himself to Norfolk. And yet she couldn't find Him, couldn't make Him hear. She had never felt so totally alone. She was living now in London, a city of nearly seven million people, if you counted all its suburbs; hemmed in by close-packed houses, a thousand other dwellings massed outside her window, and yet it felt as if no one else existed in the world. At Brignor, there were just twelve nuns, twelve nuns in a wilderness – no other house within twenty miles or more – and it had seemed like a metropolis, an empire.

She had still failed to reach her aunt, though she had phoned her three more times. Phoning wasn't easy. She had to ask the priest's permission to use Miss Pullen's phone, and he seemed always disapproving, as if he imagined she were wasting time and money on idle chats with friends. Friends! She hadn't any. She'd had to give up friendship when she took her vows. But she longed to hear Aunt Eva's voice, her mother's sister, next of kin; family, real family.

No reply. Even when she hung on fifteen minutes. Was her aunt away, in hospital? Or dead? Please, God, not dead. She had hoped so much to reach her before New Year's Eve, so at least they could exchange greetings, maybe even see each other. She had never spent a New Year's Eve alone. At Brignor, they didn't break their silence, said the Midnight Office the same as every other night, but it was special, nonetheless. They added extra bidding prayers, thanking God for all the joys and sorrows of the old year, begging Him for peace throughout the new: peace at Brignor, peace to all the world. The next day was a holiday – Exposition in the morning, pink ice cream for pudding, a beetle drive or puppet play to enliven their free afternoon, even extra talking.

This New Year's Eve, she had spent up in her room. Miss Pullen seemed especially irritable, had fussed and squirmed and fretted, until she subsided into exhausted sleep at nine. She should have slept herself, but the night seemed too important. A new year was struggling to be born, a year she feared and dreaded more than any other in her life; a year which couldn't bring her peace, however much she prayed for it; a year beginning without the blessing of her aunt, without even the comfort of her voice.

Well, at least she had survived that night, survived almost a whole fortnight without any major crisis, which was something to thank God for. She offered up a prayer of thanks, then settled down in bed. She had to sleep tonight, or she would be ill again and no help to Miss Pullen. She reached to switch the light off, was plunged instantly in fear. The dark was solid, like black and smothering earth being heaped on her live body. She tried to slap it off, but her hands seemed paralysed, sucked into that blackness as if they had no more weight or substance than her frantic choking prayers. God couldn't help her, couldn't even hear. Nobody could hear. She was totally alone, buried underground, where the earth itself acted as a muzzle, deadening every sound, pressing on her eyelids, filling up her mouth.

She sat bolt upright, ramming on the light switch, grinned in sheer relief as she saw the pale blue nylon sheets, the old-fashioned satin eiderdown, not a winding sheet or shroud. She was still dressed in her old brown frock, not swaddled in her grave-clothes. She hadn't worn a nightie since the age of seventeen. Most Orders wore a high-necked, long-sleeved nightgown, but the Brignor Sisters preferred to be 'in uniform' every minute of their lives, never off-duty, even in their beds. They slept in a night-habit, which was identical to the one they wore all day, except older and more shabby; the one they also used for gardening or rough chores. They changed at nine p.m., so that when they rose at midnight for the Office, they were already girded for God's service; had

51

only to remove the shorter softer night-veil, replace it with the choir-veil.

She had become so used to sleeping in a habit, it felt strange and quite immodest to slip into a nightie. She had found two among the jumble, silky sheer creations with lace panels and pink frills. She had tried them on, even tried to sleep in them – felt exposed and almost naked, as well as freezing cold. She had rifled through the jumble box again, found another dress: a good plain boring brown, and safely long and thick. That was now her night-habit.

The habit was your bridal dress, so that if your Bridegroom called you in the night, you were ready to accompany Him to heaven. Every evening's Compline was an immediate preparation for that death. After Compline, the lights were all extinguished, and the Great Silence of the night began, unbroken till the morning. She had never feared the dark before. Nuns developed a sixth sense, found their way like cats, along corridors, round corners, and upstairs to their cells. Nor had she feared death before. Death was welcomed by a nun as her reunion with God, the completion of her goal. The corpse was crowned with a wreath of pure white roses, buried in their flower-filled private cemetery. There was chocolate cake for tea, and extra recreation – a day of joy, not dread. But now death meant damnation, a going down to some black and fearful region, where she would be dead and yet still conscious; dead and yet still screaming in the dark.

Shivering, she clambered out of bed, ransacking the psalms again, as she knelt to pray this time. 'Deliver me, O Lord, from everlasting death . . . from the pains of hell, the deep pit. Deliver me from the mouth of the lion, that hell may not swallow me up . . . ' She tried to keep her eyes closed, but lurid images still surged beneath the lids. She could see funerals, damned corpses – not roses round their heads, but black and stinking weeds. She jerked out to the bathroom, found Miss Pullen's sleeping pills, old ones in a bottle with a faded smudgy label. It seemed wrong to help herself, like another form of stealing. They had to ask for everything at Brignor. 'I humbly beg, Mother, for a sheet of writing paper.' The same formula for toothpaste, or for soap, even for their sanitary towels, or more than two clean handkerchiefs a week.

She unscrewed the bottle, shook out just one pill, sat on her bed with the tablet on her tongue, too scared to swallow it. It might be even worse to sleep, than not to. Suppose she never woke again, wandered for eternity in that black pit beyond God's mercy, caged in the dark jaws of the lion?

She spat the pill out, hid it in a Kleenex. Must keep awake, keep conscious. She was alive, alive, still loved by God. She drifted to the window, pulled the curtain back. It wasn't even dark. Traffic lights and car lights were flashing through the night, shops and houses still lit up. London didn't sleep much, burnt the midnight oil. And yet she couldn't feel a bond with any of those other sleepless souls: all those people working, reading, driving; maybe even weeping in their cold and lonely rooms. It was as if she were shut off from them by a rigid wall of glass, far thicker than the window pane she stood at; a wall which closed her off from everyone. She could see them, hear them, but she couldn't touch, reach out.

She returned to bed, smoothed the tangled sheets. How could she be frightened, with everything so solid – the high and creaky bedstead with its wooden head and footboards, the thirties wardrobe which was too big for the room, the battered chest of drawers? She was behaving quite hysterically, like an indulged and stupid child. And she'd no right to keep the light on, as she'd done the last five nights. It wasted the electricity and Miss Pullen paid the bills.

She had barely clicked it off again, when her frantic hand was back, fumbling for that light switch, groping through the darkness, to turn the terror off. Fear and dark were one now. She could hear the chaplain's voice: 'Perfect love casteth out fear.' That was it: she didn't love enough. She felt pity for Miss Pullen, but no real Christian love; had even banged her cup down when her charge had spilt the tea. Miss Pullen spilt things purposely, kept dropping spoons and books, but that was no real reason to stop treating her as Christ. She had to keep her mind on Christ, keep searching for Him, even in the dark. *His* was perfect love. Hadn't Father Martin told her that the cruellest desolations were proofs of that great love, since He was allowing her to suffer here on earth, and not in hell? So why did she fear hell still?

Exhausted, she sat up again, abandoned bed for chair. She'd better read, distract herself, give up thoughts of sleeping. The only books she'd found, so far, were a shelf of lurid paperbacks and a seven-volume set of *The History of the English-Speaking Peoples*. She picked up Volume One, blenched to see the letter she'd been using as a bookmark – her letter from the Abbess, whose cruel and wounding phrases were now incised into her skull. 'By leaving in this fashion, you have shown blatant disregard for your vow of Holy Obedience, scandalised your Sisters, made your life a mockery . . . ' She couldn't blame the Abbess, who bore a grave responsibility, had to account for each nun's soul on Judgement Day; pledging each Eternal Life, on the day of their Profession, if they were faithful to their vows. She had not only cast aside those vows, but laid guilt on her superior as well. Mother's letter demanded a reply. Sister Mary Hilary had either to return forthwith, or write requesting formal leave of absence.

Sister Mary Hilary refolded the blue paper, closed the heavy book. Both steps were impossible. There was no way she could return, yet to obtain a leave of absence meant writing to the Bishop, setting out her reasons for needing time away. He might well dismiss her reasons as mere neurotic weakness, refuse to grant the leave. She replaced the history on the shelf, took down a lightweight crime novel. She'd never had much interest in criminals or crime until now she felt condemned herself, alone and shunned and guilty in the dock.

She stood rigid, rooted to the floor, staring at the orange blob, the only patch of colour in the darkness. What was it? *Where* was it? Who had brought her here? She tried to remember names for things: the thing she stood on, thing above her, those small hot heavy white things which seemed attached to her. The names had disappeared; everything had vanished except the darkness and that one bright blob. She couldn't move. Who *was* she? Terror surged and spiralled as she realised she didn't know the answer, didn't know her name. She searched back in the reaches of her mind. No clue, no pictures, no memories at all. Time passed. She was aware of that, at least; time slowly moiling on, while she stood, stranded, a mind without a name.

Supposing the name eluded her for ever? This could be eternity, trapped and banished on her own, not knowing who she was. She was aware of endless passages, dark and low and maze-like; corridors of dense black fear, stretching on for ever. No doors or windows anywhere. No way out. No way in to who she was, or where.

She could feel her heart pounding through her chest – which meant she was alive still. Yet the state felt more like death. She tried to move towards the orange, touch it with the white things. It felt hard and cold, with two protuberances. The word was coming back. A word she knew, everybody knew, except it was still not on her tongue. She made one last effort, stormed and dragged her mind, struggling through the tangled coils of what seemed like black barbed wire.

Kettle! Yes, a kettle. The thing she made the tea with. Tea – another word she knew now. All the words were flooding back, even in the darkness. Floor – the thing she stood on; ceiling up above her; hands – the things attached to her. And *her*? Sister Mary Hilary.

She groped towards the light switch, blinked in the bright neon at the fawn Formica table, the scuffed and chequered lino, the shiny orange kettle on the range. She was in Miss Pullen's kitchen, must have sleepwalked there from her bedroom one floor up. She shuddered. That flight of stairs was steep, the hallway full of hazards – sharp edges, jutting furniture. She crept back to the stove. She ought to make some tea, strong sweet tea to calm her down, stop her hands from shaking. No. Tea was not allowed, only lukewarm water, and it was forbidden to make snacks, to eat or drink at all, except at mealtimes, unless a nun were ill. She wasn't ill. This was sheer indulgence. She had sleepwalked several times before, and the Abbess had dismissed it as hysteria, a bid for attention, a proof that her emotions were still not disciplined, her self too strong, trying to take over, even in her sleep.

She clung on to the kettle, as if its cheerful orange could warm her like a fire; was surprised to find it cold. It seemed too bright and modern for Miss Pullen's dingy house, where so much else was old, or barren brown. It felt important, somehow – the beacon in her nightmare, the first word to return.

She cleared her throat, just to hear the noise. She was used to silence, but this silence seemed more total than at Brignor, where an hour or so of talking was permitted every day. Those stiff-necked recreations when they sat round in a circle, darning socks or sewing, had seemed sometimes an ordeal. You could be lonely in a community, as well as on your own, especially when all close ties were forbidden, and conversations must be always safely general and polite. No confidential chats, no personal disclosures. A young American retreat priest had told them, just two years ago, that a good contemplative would make a good prostitute, because she had to give herself to everyone, regardless of her feelings, couldn't pick and choose her favourites. The older nuns had been distinctly shocked, but she had understood him. You loved and 'serviced' everyone, even those Sisters who annoyed you most. Sister Anna, for example, with her high-pitched girlish giggle, had been a constant trial. She had often sat there, wincing at that giggle, cringing at the jokes, yet outwardly serene, only screaming silently from the months of doubt and darkness which she couldn't, mustn't share.

Now she realised she hadn't been as friendless as she had allowed herself to feel. Some nuns had antennae, understood, without the need for words. Sister Luke was sensitive, had often smiled at her, even touched her hand a second, though that was quite forbidden; a fleeting, caring touch which said, 'I feel your pain. Take courage.' And at least she'd not been physically alone: other nuns beside her in the refectory; other Sisters' voices lapping hers in choir, a dozen people always in the house.

Here, the silence stretched in all directions. Only Father Anstey's brief remarks, Miss Pullen's angry grunts. And once her charge had gone to sleep, the stillness seemed to freeze and stiffen round her, especially in the death-hush of her bedroom. Her convent cell was one in a long row, and although you never spoke there, and would be most severely punished if you dared invite another nun in, at least you had the comfort of noises through the wall: the friendly splash of water from a ewer, the creak of a loose board. Miss Pullen's room was at the back. The walls were thick, conducted not the faintest human sound.

She fumbled for a chair, still feeling half-disorientated, as if she wasn't quite awake yet, perhaps not even quite alive. She wondered what the time was, wondered what the date was, tried to work it out. The Feast of the Epiphany had been four days ago, the feast on which God 'manifested' Himself – though He hadn't done to her – a solemn feast at Brignor, with tall candles on the altar, symbolising the bright star over Bethlehem, which led the Three Kings to their greater infant King. That was January 6. Which meant today must be the tenth. Her birthday! The one she'd dreaded for so long, tried to keep dismissing, blank out of her mind. Nuns didn't keep their birthdays, only the anniversaries of their Clothing and Profession, and the feast-days of their name-saint. Age shouldn't matter in a convent. One's age in religion was the only thing which counted, and that was reckoned from the year a nun first entered, so that a fifty-year-old Sister would be younger than a twenty-year-old, if she had joined the Order after her. Yet, for months she'd been aware that she would be thirty-nine in January. Why was it so crucial? Because there was only one year left till forty, the real start of middle age? No. Something more important.

She rose slowly from her chair, seemed to be drawn towards the range again, its cheerless black enlivened by that kettle. She ran her hands across its pregnant orange belly, then down to her flat stomach. You could have a child at thirty-nine, but you were old already, had lost your really fertile years, couldn't waste more precious months, agonising, hoping. It was that American retreat priest who'd first sown those dangerous longings – something else he'd said: 'A contemplative praying for the world is like a mother feeding a baby. Both get up at night to give nurture to the weak and helpless.' As he spoke, a disconcerting image had flashed into her mind. She was a mother with a baby, a real and solid baby pulling at her nipple, nuzzling at her breast – breasts hot and tight with milk. The image kept returning, was especially vivid now, as she still clutched that stupid kettle, feeling not its hard cold metal, but the soft flesh of a child. She darted to the sink, let the blast of the cold tap dispel her vacuous motherhood. A kettle was for making tea, not for playing babies. The first grey light was filtering through the curtains, the clotted dark dispersing. It was far later than she'd thought – not night at all, but morning – time to wake her charge up, make her early tea, wash and dress and feed her. There wasn't room for self-indulgent fantasies. She had a child already: Miss Ethel Margaret Pullen.

Could you hate a pair of boots, really loathe them? It was wrong to hate at all, but Miss Pullen's stiff black boots seemed somehow evil; battered leather ankle-boots with slimy knotted laces, dirty yellow insoles which showed the impression of misshapen feet. Hilary crouched to lace them up, remove the woolly bed socks. Miss Pullen never went out, but she wore her coat all day, a thick tweed skirt, lisle stockings, and the boots. The house was always cold. Miss Pullen wasn't poor, could have afforded central heating, gas fires in all the rooms, but she preferred to keep her money in the bank. In her will, she had left it to the church, to Father Anstey in particular.

Hilary stood up, shook out the crumpled coat, a once-expensive raincoat, now stained with food and grease. It was never washed or cleaned, since Miss Pullen wouldn't part with it for longer than a night, and even then, she wanted it beside her, draped across her chair. First thing in the morning, it went back on again.

Hilary could sympathise, would have liked to wear a coat herself, not only for its warmth, but to use it as a tortoise did its shell. She fastened all the buttons, then went to fetch the porridge, which already had a scum on top and had started to congeal. She ought to reheat it, but it would only go cold again, while Miss Pullen pushed the bowl away, or refused to open her mouth.

'N . . . N . . . N . . . ' she stuttered, as she jerked her head right back. That was 'no', could go on for minutes, as she fought to get the word out, growing more and more frustrated. She had refused to have speech therapy, or any other therapy; refused all help at all, save Miss O'Connor's. So how did Miss O'Connor manage? She was probably a much better cook, made porridge with no lumps; served all the little delicacies she'd mentioned in her notes. 'Try egg custard and blancmanges, soufflés, creamy soups. And don't forget a cake or two. You can nearly always tempt her with a light Victoria sponge.'

Hilary refilled the spoon, watched the porridge drool down chin and coat. She had never made a cake, not even as a child. Her mother always bought cakes from the grocer, discouraged her from messing up the kitchen. And in all her years at Brignor, she had never cooked at all. They couldn't spare her for domestic chores, when she was so handy with her needle, and could actually earn money by the labour of her hands. Of course, she never saw the money, or thought in terms of wages. Her work was prayer, obedience. But her skill as vestment-maker had spread far beyond the county or the local village priests.

She'd been designing vestments recently for bishops, Father Generals; elaborate brocade chasubles for Golden Jubilees; matching stoles with appliquéd silver chalices, shining jewel-grapes, ears of silken wheat. She had also made the cloaks for the Knights and Dames of the Holy Sepulchre – white cloaks with scarlet crosses for the Knights, black velvet for the Dames. Yet her skills now seemed so narrow, and quite pointless in the world. Who wanted satin-stitch on hand-embroidered orphreys, or elaborate cope-hoods sewn with flowers and gems? Ordinary women had to cook as well as sew, nurse and launder, drive and shop – all the normal routine things she'd never done.

Miss Pullen made a grunting sound, tried to grab her *Daily Express*. Her sight was bad and she refused to wear her glasses, so she liked it read aloud – especially the disasters – wars and armed rebellions, earthquakes, bomb attacks. Hilary unfolded it with her usual twinge of guilt. Papers were forbidden in the convent. The Abbess took *The Times*, but pre-censored it severely, consigning humour, arts and gossip to the waste bin, along with business news and sport. A few remaining articles were carefully cut out, pinned up on the noticeboard for the other nuns to read: crises which demanded prayers: peace talks, or elections, or international incidents, but only those with no hint of sin or scandal.

She glanced briefly at the headlines – 'Heroin shock. "Dirty Dick" confesses.' 'Yard man on call-girl charge' – searched the sea of print for something more salubrious, something Reverend Mother would permit. She read the main news story on violence in Armagh – Ireland always needed prayers – continued with a report on the social life of dolphins. Miss Pullen seemed restive and was pulling at her coat. She searched for a disaster, found an air crash and a flood, read out the fatalities, her voice dwindling to a whisper, as she tried to deny those pointless savage deaths. She craved to believe in a good God's ordered world, not this hell of twisted wreckage, dismembered bloated bodies. She knew now why the Abbess banned the papers. It wasn't just the scandals, but the danger to their faith. If the world was rotten, then how could its Creator escape all blame? 'Free will,' she kept insisting to herself. But who had made that will . . . ?

She continued reading till Miss Pullen nodded off, then laid the paper gently on her lap; cleared away the breakfast things, pausing at the larder door as she put the milk away. Wasn't this her chance to do some cooking – make that cake, perhaps – a light Victoria sponge to tempt Miss Pullen, a cake of recompense? She started searching through the cookbooks, looking for a recipe. Sponges all took eggs, and she hadn't any eggs, had never thought to buy them. She remembered in the War, her mother had made cakes from things like swedes and carrots – or so she'd always claimed. Her mother enjoyed complaining about the War: the way bananas simply vanished, the indignity of ration books, the cheek of Mrs Grant next door who wangled extra sugar. She murmured a brief prayer for the safety of her mother's soul – only hoped Eternity would please her – then went to check the larder; found several shrivelled carrots, even a fat swede. She had always hated swedes. They figured at the convent three or four times weekly, a cheap and staple vegetable the Sisters grew themselves. In twenty years, she must have eaten over a thousand pounds of swede, plain unbuttered swede, sometimes woody, or only semi-cooked. (Sister Cook wasn't always skilled.) But maybe in a cake, you wouldn't taste them, especially if she added some strong flavouring.

'Cream 6 oz butter with the same amount of sugar, and beat till light and fluffy . . . ' At least she had butter, and a good two pounds of sugar, though the butter was rock-hard and seemed hostile to the sugar, patently unwilling to merge or mix at all. She beat until her arm ached, but the butter stuck in small hard lumps to the bottom of the bowl, while the gritty stubborn sugar sprayed across the work-top. She'd better add some water. She ran a little in the bowl, watched with pleasure as the sugar soaked it up. The butter was less tractable. She used her hands, tried to knead and pummel it, as Sister Gerard did, when she made the convent bread. The butter only oozed between her fingers, still refused to cream. Perhaps it needed eggs, some slimy gum to bind it to the sugar. She'd substitute her vegetables, grate them first, to make them light and moist. The only problem was she couldn't find a grater. She searched all the drawers and cupboards, turfed out a floral chamber pot, some stuff for killing ants, an ancient tin of cat-food, but still no grater. Well, she'd simply have to chop them, chop them very fine, an exercise in patience.

She sat down at the table, listening for Miss Pullen's bell, ready to respond the instant that it rang. That was second nature. You obeyed the convent bells without the slightest pause, without crossing your 't', if you were writing; or pulling through your needle, if you'd just stuck it in the fabric; without finishing your sentence, if you were speaking to a Sister. The bells were honoured as the voice of God, calling you to chapel seven times a day. Obedience to a Lover, not a tyrant. She missed the bells, tolling for the Angelus, or choir, pealing out at the beginning of each hour, to remind the nuns to devote that hour to God.

She mixed in her vegetables, followed by the flour, and the teaspoon of vanilla essence suggested in the recipe. A teaspoon seemed so little, especially if it were fighting with the flavour of the swedes, so she shook in the whole bottle, then transferred the sticky mixture to a tin. She felt a sense of real achievement as she shut the oven door; had to stop herself from running, as she returned upstairs to spread the news: 'I've made a cake – the first one in my life!' Miss Pullen was asleep still, couldn't share her triumph. She walked on down the passage, too elated to sit down, stopped a guilty moment outside Miss O'Connor's door. There was a mirror in that room, the only full-length mirror in the house. She had been avoiding mirrors for the last two weeks, yet utterly obsessed with them, seeing them in every shiny surface, every pane of glass – a sudden jolting shock as the reflection's eyes met hers, or a face she didn't recognise mimicked her own startled flinch of panic. She'd look away, look down; immediately immerse herself in some job or safe distraction. There had been no mirrors in the convent. Most Orders allowed a small one in each cell, so that nuns could check their veils were straight, or snip off a stray whisker. But the Notre Dame Sisters had refused to introduce them. However small the mirror, it could still encourage vanity, or lead to self-absorption.

This house was no convent, yet seemed strangely short of mirrors; both her room and Miss Pullen's totally devoid of them. The old one in the bathroom showed nothing but your head, and was stained and spotted, anyway, with its backing peeling off. She had still not seen herself – not *all* her self, not clearly – in a cold and honest light.

Impulsively, she slipped in through the door, turned the key behind her. She was grateful for that key, which seemed to lock the Abbess out, or any charge of vanity. This didn't feel like vanity at all. She took a quick breath in, turned to face the mirror, stared in shock at the startled girl reflected there. A girl? At thirty-nine? Impossible. She kept on staring. That mirror must be wrong. She still looked young and slim, even quite presentable, not the freak, the bundle, she'd felt in her old clothes. She had struggled for so many years with depression, darkness, near despair, she had imagined all the conflict would be stamped across her face, larded round her body like an ugly layer of fat.

She must be standing too far back, so that the mirror flattered her, prevented her from seeing all her flaws. She took a few steps forward, peered more closely at her face. Her eyes looked bright, alive, not dull and somehow dead, as she'd imagined. Her cheeks were pale, admittedly, but the skin was well plumped out; no wrinkles round the eyes or frown-lines on her forehead. She had assumed she had the same lines as the Sisters all around her; lines from nose to mouth and mouth to chin, criss-cross lines etched above her lip. Those ageing nuns had seemed patterns for herself, as she grew stout and shrivelled with them – or so it always felt – grey in mind and spirit, not just greying hair. She untied her old blue headscarf, which she kept on day and night, so Miss Pullen needn't see her convict's hair. It was longer than she'd realised, growing well already; raggedy, uneven – yes – but still its wheaten colour. When she'd cropped it in the convent, the clippings always looked a dullish grey. Was that just depression, turning everything to ash?

She ran her hand through the short and stubbly growth, took in her whole form again. Was that really her, that slim and fair-haired stranger in lay clothes? The mirror in her mind had told her she was ugly; a sapless burnt-out creature, not woman, even – neuter. She had felt so sterile sometimes, that it seemed as if parts of her were missing; that some ruthless surgeon had yanked her womb out, sliced off both her breasts. Occasionally, as she knelt there in the silence, wrestling with the absence of her God, she imagined that her mouth had gone, as well, and that she would never form another word again. Other times, in the darkness of her cell, she had touched her eyes, to make sure they were not missing, not just empty sockets.

She was startled now to see herself so whole: face no longer cut off at the brows; eyes somehow larger than they'd ever been before, burning through her face; even the outline of two breasts beneath the dress. She seemed to be three people all at once: the nun in veil and habit whom she had left behind at Brignor; the ugly freak washed up at Rosemont Road; and this figure in the mirror – female and an interloper.

She didn't like its clothes, the droopy dress which flopped around its calves, the shapeless navy cardigan. Why should any Order want to modernise? The habit gave you dignity, both physical and spiritual, had weight in every sense. It still seemed strange to walk without that swirl of heavy fabric, the anchor of the veil. She missed the veil the most. A bare head was so vulnerable, so cold. The nun's veil symbolised fidelity, virginity. 'Receive this veil,' the priest had said, 'the token of purity and modesty . . . that thou mayest, at last, with the wise Virgins, be ready to enter into the joyful marriage of the Lamb.'

She snatched her scarf up, secured it round her head again. Her vows were made for ever. All the words they used stressed that. Final Profession, perpetual Profession, unbreakable union, lifelong service. She had sworn obedience and fidelity till death.

'Are you resolved to serve Christ and His kingdom for the whole of your life in solitude and silence, in unceasing prayer, in lowly work and willing penance, persevering unto the end?'

'I am so resolved.'

It *was* a sort of death. She had lain prostrate on the chapel floor, covered with a thick black pall, to symbolise her death to the world, while the other nuns had sung the *Dies Irae*, as if it were a funeral. For almost half an hour, she had lain buried beneath the musty stifling darkness of that pall, embracing death, rejoicing in it, while her Sisters begged their Saviour to help her die to earthly love.

She had even made her will. That, too, was symbolical, since after her Profession a nun could own absolutely nothing; must have legally disposed of her possessions, however small or trifling. No photographs, no letters, no trinkets, keepsakes, mementoes of her parents. She had no parents now, belonged to God alone.

She wore His ring to prove it. The priest had placed it on her wedding finger at that same Profession ceremony. 'Receive this ring, that you may be called the Bride of God, and be conscious of the faithfulness of the Eternal King, who has bound you to Himself.'

A silver ring – not gold – to symbolise her poverty; a ring shaped as a crucifix to remind her she must suffer for her Bridegroom. Yet 'Joy' was written on it, joy in suffering. She had exchanged her crown of roses for a crown of thorns – not mere symbolic thorns – but long and spiky hurting ones which pressed down on her head. Hers was a crucified Lover. She must feel not just the thorns, but the nails and spear as well, sweat blood with Him in the garden of Gethsemane.

She tugged at the ring, which refused to budge past the obstruction of her knuckle. She had been trying to remove it for the last two weeks, but that finger must have swollen. It seemed proof of her betrayal – the professed nun's ring worn with an unveiled head and worldly clothes; Christ dying on her finger. All she'd managed was to twist the slim band round, so that the figure was concealed on the inside of her hand, and the word 'Joy', once inconspicuous, now clear for all to read. The letters seemed to haunt her, as she recalled the real and brimming joy she had felt at her Profession, as she repeated St Paul's words: 'I am nailed with Christ to the Cross. I am dead that I may live for God alone.'

She sat staring at the cake. No – that heavy gluey hotchpotch bore no faint resemblance to any cake she'd seen. It had failed to rise at all, was burnt around the edges, sticking to the tin, yet soggy in the centre, orange lumps congealing in a curdled greyish pap. Miss Pullen's cat was dead, alas, or she'd have saved the hash as cat food. Though even a mere tomcat would probably take one sniff and run. She suddenly burst out laughing, the first time she'd laughed in months. This was her great triumph, her culinary achievement, the news she'd longed to holler from the rooftops. Well, that would cure her pride.

She strode towards the waste-bucket, tipped the whole mess in, stood rigid for a moment, her foot still on the pedal. How could she be laughing? She had wasted fuel, wasted good ingredients, and waste was always sin. She had been taught that as a postulant; been rebuked for wasting food her very first day in the convent, as a foolish raw recruit of seventeen. Sister Cook had burnt the fish, each portion black and charred, impossible to cut. She had tried to stick her knife in it, but the rock-hard plaice had skidded to the floor. '*There is no health of soul, nor hope of eternal life, but in the Cross. Take up, therefore, your cross with Christ, and . . .* ' The spiritual reading, which accompanied each meal, went calmly, quietly on. No mouth had twitched, no eye looked up, save hers. Once again, she had made waste worse by laughing – just one stifled nervous giggle, which had swiftly changed to horror when she was ordered to retrieve the fish and eat it – grimy now, as well as burnt – and eat it on her knees, with her chair-seat as her table, since she'd disturbed the others' silence, insulted Sister Cook. She had struggled with her pride, struggled with a sudden wave of homesickness. Her mother's cooking was plain and unpretentious, but it didn't break your teeth.

She had soon learnt better, begun to grasp the principle that no crumb of Christ's creation should ever be spurned or squandered – had even warmed to the idea, which seemed entirely different from her mother's dreary economies, stressing shortages and worry. Their vow of poverty promised, rather, joy and freedom; freedom from possessions and attachments, the joy of travelling light.

Light. The word seemed mocking. 'You can nearly always tempt her with a light Victoria sponge.' She fell to her knees beside the bin, started spooning out the cake mixture, trying to rescue every morsel, ungluing it from newspaper, scraping it off tins. She packed it back firmly in its own tin, smoothed the surface, returned it to the table; sat staring at her failure, as she slumped down in a chair. Had she ever understood the vow of poverty? It wasn't just a matter of giving up possessions, or even skills and talents like her music (the highest use of anything was its sacrifice to God); but of being emptied of one's feelings and emotions, of memories or fantasies, prejudices, pride; even being stripped of one's opinions, since those, too, smacked of self. After two whole decades, she'd still nowhere near succeeded, and these last few days she'd been especially lax – vain in seeking mirrors, pleased with her appearance, obsessed with both her body and her birthday. She had indulged in childish terrors every night, criticised a priest, allowed herself to loathe a pair of boots. Even in the convent, her emotions had been far too strong, not emptied out at all. She had given way to fear, to depression and self-pity, allowed herself to want – want a child, want peace.

She reached out for the cake, heard the mixture glug and squelch as she heaped a generous serving on a plate. It was getting on for lunchtime, and she couldn't waste more food; help herself to bread or soup, when lunch was ready-made. She forced down the first spoonful, trying not to gag on a slimy piece of swede, sweetish and half-raw still. There was no taste of cake at all, just a strangely bitter flavour she didn't recognise. The texture was still worse – sudden gritty mouthfuls, followed by damp and glutinous lumps. And the cake was oddly speckled now, mixed with dirt and tea leaves, potato peelings, porridge – extras from the waste-bin. She must rejoice in that, welcome any chance of extra penance. She had promised daily penance when she made her solemn vows – had broken all her other vows, so that one she could keep.

She swallowed a large dollop as slowly as she could, to spin the penance out, make it really meaningful – a mouthful for each sin. She worked through waste, and pride, and vanity; looked up a moment – chewing – caught the brilliant orange eye of the kettle on the range. 'Thirty-nine,' it whispered. 'Your birthday, your last chance.' She tried to fight temptation, as the image of the baby surged back into her mind – so vivid, she could see its mouth closing round her nipple, smell its sweetish milky smell. Frantically, she searched her plate for the largest piece of swede, jammed it in her mouth, to quash and void that image, cancel out the date. This was not her birthday cake, but penance cake.

6

Hilary clung on to the rail, jolting with the bus, almost overbalancing on to a buxom woman's lap. The woman glared and muttered. 'I'm sorry,' Hilary whispered. She had apologised seven times already; for treading on an old man's foot; for being in the way, for holding up the bus queue, not understanding that you paid the driver when you first got on, instead of waiting for the conductor to take your fare. Conductors seemed to have vanished in the later 1980s, as had also any joy. People seemed so miserable and rude; not the chatty jolly passengers she remembered from her childhood, or the conductors who were friends, gave you fruit-gums, tweaked your blue school hat.

She couldn't blame these Londoners. Half of them looked ill, many were overweight or elderly. The woman who had glared at her was loaded down with shopping, one bag splitting open, a wailing infant struggling in her arms. A gnarled old man was strap-hanging, though he looked too frail to stand, legs unsteady, scrawny hands clutching at the rail. Her own feet burned and pinched. She still wasn't used to shoes. The battered gaping slip-ons had finally slipped off, been thrown out with the rubbish. She had changed to bedroom slippers, an unobtrusive brown pair she'd rescued from the jumble box – but you couldn't wear slippers on a bus. The only other shoes she'd found were black patent with high heels, a scuffed and smelly pair which needed soling. She had forced her feet to fit them, but the pain was still severe, and she hadn't learnt to balance yet on what felt like wobbly stilts.

Frightening to be out at all – at least to venture further than the tiny Earlsfield corner shop. Even unenclosed Orders preferred nuns to be in pairs, not go out unaccompanied. On her one and only visit to the hospital, Sister Mark had driven her, made all the arrangements, done the talking for her, acted as her chaperone and nanny. These people had no chaperones, no warm and waiting cars to whisk them home. She felt a rush of shame as she glanced around their strained and stoic faces. It had seemed their natural right as nuns to be protected – from crowds, or buses, or coping on their own.

She kept peering through the window, watching for her stop. 'Look out for the Goat in Boots,' Father Anstey had told her. 'It's a big pub on the corner, opposite a garage.' It was he who'd forced her out, at last. Miss Pullen wore a surgical belt which was old and wearing thin, had to be replaced. The local chemists didn't stock them, only Wright's, in Wandsworth.

'I'll jot down the address, draw you a rough map. And while you're there, perhaps you'd go to Tesco's for me, and buy half a pound of Roquefort. That branch is really good for cheese. Oh, and get some decent coffee for Miss O'Connor. She likes the fresh-ground beans.'

Miss O'Connor. Expected back in just three days, to resume her duties, oust her substitute. She would lose her job, her refuge. The priest was trying to help, find someone else who needed her, could offer her a room in return for nursing, charring – anything. She trembled at the thought of moving on, having to face a normal household, eat her meals in public, become a relaxed and chatty person who could crack a joke, conduct a conversation. She had considered doing office cleaning, so she could work at night – alone – but she'd have nowhere then to live. A residential job meant other people, fitting in with them. How could she fit in, when everything about her shrieked 'alien', 'outsider'? Yet worse if no one wanted her. She would be on the streets again, homeless, penniless.

She had written to her aunt, enclosed a stamped addressed envelope, but hadn't had it back. If a reply arrived eventually, who would send it on to her – and where? That letter had been difficult, taken two whole days. 'Praised be Jesus Christ!' she'd written first – which was how a nun began a letter, dedicating all its words to God. But this was a letter explaining she was *not* a nun; that she had left her convent and was living in the world. She tried again, remembering to put just the date, and not 'the feast of St Benet Biscop'. Lay people thought in terms of simple days and months; knew little of the hierarchy of feasts, as the Church's year circled round from one Advent to the next, matching its liturgy to the colour of the vestments, to each martyr, pastor, virgin, saint, each period of penitence or joy. Half the saints she knew and loved would be empty names to these people on the bus.

She'd kept crossing out, re-starting, as if aware of Reverend Mother reading every line. All their letters in and out were read. She found herself writing not to dear Aunt Eva, but a stilted, halting letter to the Abbess, trying to defend herself, explain. In the end, she scored that out as well, penned just a few brief lines, explaining nothing, just begging Eva to get in touch immediately. 'A corpse can't get in touch,' mocked a cruel voice in her head. She had tried to quash that voice, dropped the letter in the postbox with a desperate whispered prayer.

The bus was now less crowded. She took the one free seat, felt guilty as she sank down into plush, though no one else was standing. The boy next to her was eating a jam doughnut, its brown bag stained with grease. She could hear her stomach rumbling, as he chewed the last small mouthful; licked imaginary sugar off her lips. She'd been hungry now for days. She had finished up the penance-cake, then eaten a few vegetables she'd found rotting in the rack, boiled them first, to kill off any germs. The larder was still full of tins, but she hadn't liked to touch them. It seemed wrong to help herself, still wrong to make a cup of tea, or switch the one-bar fire on. The only tin she'd opened was the ancient can of cat food, which had made another penance, with its putrid fishy smell, its slimy jellied globules slithering down her throat. She couldn't stop her penances. And yet today should be a joyous day – the feast of St Antony of Egypt, who was regarded as the founder of monasticism, though he'd lived mainly as a hermit in the desert. He was a fitting saint for her, with his rigorous austerities, his desperate daily struggles with temptation, his diet of dry bread. She could see him suddenly, a fourth-century recluse in goatskins and a beard, riding on this twentieth-century bus with her, more startled even than she was by the traffic and the din.

'Goat in Boots!' St Antony plunged back to his desert cave as he saw the lewd and leering grimace of the goat, swinging on its sign. She stepped down off the bus, was immediately engulfed in noise and bustle; traffic roaring past, a man with a pneumatic drill blasting concrete and her ears. She turned the other way towards Albert Road and Wright's, following her sketch-map. London was a maze to her, far too vast, inhuman.

She jumped at every sound: a car backfiring, a sudden squeal of brakes. Her nerve ends felt exposed, as if she had been prised out of her shell. No one else seemed bothered by the noise. They slouched along, faces closed, impassive, struggling with their children, dogs or shopping. Few people seemed alone – all anchored to a pram, a lead, a toddler's hand, a husband's arm. She longed for her own anchor: the weighty silver cross she'd always worn around her neck, the heavy rosary dangling at her side; both left behind at Brignor. For twenty years, she'd dressed not just in the habit, but in the prayers she'd said as she put each garment on – a prayer for guimpe and cincture, a prayer for habit and veil. 'Clothe my soul, O Lord, with the nuptial robe of chastity . . . Place on my head, O God, the helmet of salvation . . . '

Once robed, she'd felt protected. God Himself had dressed her, buckled on her breastplate and her shield. But now she stood in silence, as she dragged on her grey dress each day, pulled up the blue school knickers she had found among the jumble. She had dared, at last, to remove her convent underclothes – the tight and swaddling bodice, the scratchy knee-length drawers. But she couldn't bring herself to change them for the flimsy scraps of nothing which seemed the secular equivalent – pants which weighed an ounce or less, wisps of cobweb lace. All lay clothes seemed strangely insubstantial, especially here, where you needed heavy armour to protect you from the dangers: angry drivers honking at each other, swarthy men in crash helmets tearing down a building. She stopped a moment to watch the burly foreman, who was bellowing out instructions as he balanced on a half-dismantled wall; the greedy yellow maw of a machine eating into solid brick and stone. She herself felt bulldozed, her whole foundations wrenched up and smashed to powder, but with no prospect of rebuilding, no future plan at all.

She dodged a piece of flying brick, walked on to the chemist, stood behind a woman in a sari, who was buying cough sweets for her five small black-eyed children. They all had colds, their noses sore and running, their anoraks too thin to keep them warm. Again, she felt ashamed. She had always worn warm clothes, made from thick expensive fabric, despite her vow of poverty; had always eaten wholesome home-grown food. That Indian woman's shopping bag was full of paper food – everything in packets – custards, curries, soups. She was still astonished by all the coloured people, especially here in Wandsworth. No coloured nun had ever joined their Order; no Indian or African been seen within their walls. Had they been hiding from reality in all-white, all-English Brignor? She'd sometimes read an article (one salvaged in the censorship) about immigrants or race riots, but it had seemed to have no relevance to peaceful cloistered Norfolk.

At last, she got Miss Pullen's belt, felt much the same distaste for it as she felt for her black boots: though she wished there were a spiritual equivalent – a truss or corset for the soul, which would support her faith, keep it firm, strengthen it against doubt and desolation.

She checked her map again, wasted five whole minutes trying to cross a road, then found herself face to face with an ugly foursquare building, which seemed to be constructed not of the grey concrete rearing all around it, but of the huge multicoloured posters plastered on its windows, the breathless urgent promises emblazoned underneath. 'Chicken prices slashed!' 'Super freezer savers!' 'Biggest value ever on . . .'

So that was a supermarket. She had never seen one in her life. Her mother had shopped at the local village store, a tiny cosy place where you were greeted by your name, looked after individually. Its owner, Mrs Baxter, even helped you choose. 'That Cheddar's good and strong, dear. It's just come in this morning. Or how about a piece of ham?' No buxom Mrs Baxter here; just anonymous people gliding through a dozen sets of automatic doors – doors opening, shutting, opening, as they swallowed up the shoppers, spat them out again. She followed, stepped inside, blinking in the neon glare at the huge blown-up, close-up pictures of every type of food. She was dwarfed by a colossal wedge of cheese – not Mrs Baxter's Cheddar, but some foreign brand with holes like yawning craters; a grape or two beside it, black and big as bombs; a bush-sized parsley sprig. Beyond it, was a cake with icing whipped in peaks, as dazzling-white and towering as the Alps, and then a slice of German sausage, its individual fat-globules glistening like great puddles.

Her eyes tracked lower to the real food on the shelves – a spate and swarm and flood of food, stretching on all sides; its blurring colours and looming shapes settling only slowly into tins and jars and cartons, meats and milks and fruits. More food than she had ever seen gathered in one place: at least a thousand jars of jam, several thousand cereals; whole sacks of polished carrots, oranges in mounds – pulsing, jostling, dazzling foods, which seemed to assault her eyes and brain.

She crept along the furthest aisle, keeping to one side, trying not to tangle with the bold aggressive women bearing down towards her, with their children, loaded trolleys. She stopped at the biscuits, gasped at the array – cream biscuits, chocolate biscuits, wafers wrapped in gold and silver foil, every flavoured filling from peppermint to cheese. Crazy names she remembered only vaguely from her childhood; some she'd never heard of: Toffeepops and Wagon Wheels, Jammie Dodgers, Yo Yos. How ever did you choose? She felt dizzy just looking at the wrappings; the shouting slogans, sickly coloured pictures – all different, all the same. It was still worse with the breads. Brignor bread was home-baked, plain and brown. But here were fifteen shelves of loaves – pitta bread and currant bread, Farmhouse Brown, Supa-White, low-calorie, high-protein; bread for diabetics, slimmers; unleavened bread and gluten-free, malt loaves, Extra-Bran. She reached her hand out, let it drop again. Did she even need bread? They were playing music – maddening bouncy music, which seemed trapped inside her head, spinning round and round it, so she couldn't think at all. Why music in a food shop? Was this some special day, some Tesco's gala, when you shopped to jolly tunes, like their feastdays in the convent, which they celebrated with joyous extra hymns?

A woman rattled past her, reached out for two loaves. She looked only twenty-five or so, yet she moved with such brash confidence, manoeuvring her trolley round corners, other shoppers; snatching what she wanted without the slightest hesitation. Hilary followed, mesmerised. Who told her what to buy, how much to spend? And however did she concentrate, with that baby in her trolley, poking at the shopping, those other two small children tagging on behind, knocking all the packets off the shelves? The girl stopped at the pet foods, grabbed two tins of Whiskas. So she had a cat, as well. The convent cats ate scraps, had never tried these gourmet tins of Super-Fish With Salmon, or Chicken Breast Supreme. You could spend a whole week's wages on a cat – cat vitamins, cat chew-bars, even cats' Christmas stockings, now marked down to half-price.

She watched the woman tie her small son's shoelace, distract the baby with a rusk. She had more than just two hands – hands for pushing, reaching, choosing, feeding, soothing. She knew her way around as if this were her own home, swinging right and right again to the aisle marked 'Baby Care' – a whole aisle just for babies. How could that tiny infant in the toddler-seat need all those racks of complicated things; all those oils and creams and cleansers, all those tins and jars of food, those juices, syrups, dishes, rattles, toys?

She slowed her pace as the woman strode away, vanished round a corner. How spoiled she'd been these twenty years: food appearing as if by magic on the table, no decisions as to what she'd eat or buy; clean clothes neatly folded on her bed each week, no family or pets to feed. Her world had been so small. They had kept it simple by cutting down their needs. She had seen that as a penance, but now she realised it was more a blessing and protection, a haven of a world made safe by rules, by lack of choice. She glanced up at the mirrors, glimpsed herself tiny and distorted; a feeble useless figure, cowering in a corner, while other women ran a dozen lives. She could see them all around her – women who could cope, women who had children. Babies everywhere: in prams parked in the street, in shopping trolleys, baby-slings; wriggling on the nappy packets, smiling from these tins of baby food.

She hadn't found a trolley yet. Did you simply take one, or pay a fee to hire it? Those trolleys seemed so public – your shopping on display, everybody knowing what you ate or could afford. Yet the store itself was totally anonymous: no one chatting, or even exchanging brief 'hallos'; the long queues at the checkout full of silent, separate people, every face turned inwards, on itself.

She forced herself to move. She was wasting time – God's time and Miss Pullen's. She was here to buy Father Anstey's Roquefort, Miss O'Connor's Mountain Blend; yet she hadn't even seen a cheese – save that gigantic painted one – or caught a glimpse of coffee beans. She'd never get another job. Nobody would want such a stupid country bumpkin, who was dazed by all this choice, scared of these exotic things she hadn't known existed: Pour-a-Quiche filling in a carton (ham or

70

mushroom flavoured), spaghetti tongs, blue ice-cubes, gadgets for making radish flowers, or tins for heart-shaped pizzas.

'Excuse me, please, could you tell me where the cheese is?' She tried to stop the tall man in an overall who was striding down the aisle – the first assistant that she'd seen, but obviously too busy to be questioned. 'Over there,' he called across his shoulder, pointing to the left, where a thousand different products jostled for attention, though no sign of any cheese. She walked in that direction, past rows and rows of cold white chests, marked 'Freezer Foods', 'Convenience Foods' – complicated dishes from a dozen different countries, ready on the table in the time it took their Sister Cook just to assemble her ingredients. The Brignor nuns were still living in the fifties – or perhaps the 1550s – still preparing simple fare from whatever was in season, spending patient hours peeling, chopping, simmering. She felt a sudden longing to smell those homely smells – onions, nutmeg, home-baked bread. She missed *all* the convent smells: incense and wax polish, hot candles, altar wine. Nothing smelt at all here. A million different foods, but all deodorised.

She passed the fresh fish counter: scaly fins, staring eyes, a long black claw, still writhing and alive. Her hunger had abated – vanished altogether when she saw the joints of meat: raw and bleeding slabs of cow, feathered necks on turkeys, innards, gizzards, black and slimy ox liver. She turned her back, found herself facing shelves of cleaning products. Those she did need – stain-remover, dishcloths, a whitener for Miss Pullen's ancient vests.

Miss Pullen. In just a few days' time, it would be Miss O'Connor wringing out those vests, Miss O'Connor making porridge; she herself homeless, unemployed. She had failed in her first job – been too proud, too critical, secretly resented scrubbing smelly underclothes. '*Each Sister should go deep into the knowledge of her nothingness, and considering herself least of all, should receive with joy the most humble or degrading charges, as well as the contempt and humiliations permitted by Divine Providence.*' She knew the Constitutions off by heart, yet had flouted them continually; had never worked with joy, only with a steely sense of duty. She had forgotten how to feel joy, forgotten what it was. Three letters on her finger, with a dead and bleeding God the other side. Yet Hilary meant 'cheerful', her new name in the world; the same root as hilarious. It still sounded wrong if anybody used it, wrong without the 'Sister' – yet 'Sister' was a lie.

She slumped against the shelf. She was tired of names, confused by all the brand names, all these different products. How could anybody want so many, or use them in one lifetime – Heavy Duty Cleanser, Stain and Soil Remover, Deodorising Cleanser, Oil and Grease Dissolver, Car

Upholstery Foam? She was stained herself, indelibly, but nobody could make her clean – carpets, toilets, car seats, yes, but no whitener for the soul. Blackness surged and loomed again, as she reached out for the Glo-White. Every month at Brignor, they held a day of preparation for their death, a day of total silence, extra prayer and penance. Many of the prayers they said had been written by their Foundress, who urged them to imagine that they were already dead and damned. Only that, she'd counselled, could make them see the gravity of sin. 'Depart from me, ye cursed, into everlasting fire, prepared for the devil and his angels. Depart from me, ye faithless spouse, I am no longer thy Bridegroom or thy Father; depart for all eternity.'

She clung on to the shelf, could hear the flames behind her, hear that hideous 'Depart', all the voices shouting it – Father Anstey's, Miss O'Connor's, God's own voice repeating it. Even Aunt Eva, shocked and disappointed, was telling her to go, tearing up her letter, refusing to reply. They didn't want her near them. She couldn't run a home, couldn't find a trolley.

But *where* to go? She was useless in this fast and frightening world; had been dragged out of a silent womb into the harsh slap and glare of an operating theatre. Yes, she could feel the fierce lights panting on her skin, see surgeons in white coats, slicing into raw flesh just behind her. Trembling, she turned back again, tried to choose a cleaner; reached instead for a packet of black dustbin bags. She was rubbish, rubbish, those Constitutions said, a rotting hulk of flesh. The bags were huge and shiny. She couldn't seem to hold them. They were slipping from her hand; so black, so black, so heavy – blackness, darkness, pressing down, stifling hot; lion's mouth closing in a shining trap of teeth. 'Depart from me, ye cursed, into . . . '

'Hey! Watch out. Are you okay?'

Someone steady. Someone with kind hands. Picking up the dustbin bags, reaching out to steady her. She edged away. A sin to touch a hand.

'Here, lean against the shelf. That's it. You're boiling hot, you know. I'll find an assistant, see if you can lie down. They've probably got a first-aid room or something.'

'N . . . N . . . ' That was 'no', Miss Pullen's no. She couldn't get the word out, couldn't speak at all.

'Can you hear me? Look, I'd better get a doctor. Sit down where you are.'

'N . . . N . . . '

'What's your name?'

Hilary meant cheerful, and she was sad, like Ruth.

'I'm sorry. I didn't hear. That music's so damned loud.'

'H . . . Hilary,' she whispered. Perhaps she *was* a Hilary, someone proud and stubborn, who'd defied authority, been demoted, excommunicated.

'I'm Liz. Liz Kingsley. Christ! You gave me quite a scare! I thought you'd copped it for a moment. Your face went sort of greenish. It looks a little better now – thank God. All the same, I don't think you ought to charge around. I've got my car outside. I'll run you home, if it's any help.'

Home. Home was Norfolk. A quiet place, green and brown, with huge, silent, empty skies. Why was it so difficult to speak? She ought to thank this person, this kind unselfish person, who took Christ's name in vain, but had still cared enough to stop, to offer her a lift. Her mouth felt dry and hollow, empty of all words. Had she lost her voice, as she feared she'd lost her body once – her legs, her breasts, her gender? Or was she growing like Miss Pullen, the nurse catching symptoms from the patient?

'Where d'you live?'

That was a question, had to have an answer. She dragged three words out, wished they had more power. 'R . . . Rosemont Road, Earlsfield.' Father Anstey's housekeeper was sitting with Miss Pullen – a tall and frightening spinster called Miss Baines. She'd be there till late this evening, as they'd given her the day off. She didn't want it off, but Miss Baines had insisted that she enjoy a change of scene, sign up for an evening class, buy herself a meal. If she returned too soon, they'd think she was ungrateful, or had disobeyed her orders. And if she turned up with a stranger, Miss Baines would tell the priest – tell him 'Sister' had been ill again, hadn't bought his cheese. She let Liz take her arm, lead her to the exit. It felt strange and almost frightening to walk so close to someone, to be joined and part of them.

The car was brilliant orange, like a toy, looked far too small and vulnerable beside the real and dangerous cars which kept revving, roaring past it. Liz chattered as she drove, asked questions, frightening questions.

'What d'you do, Hilary? For your job, I mean?'

'Sounds pretty grim to me. How long have you been there?'

'Oh, I see – a new job. So what did you do before?'

She jammed the brakes on suddenly, drew up in a street of tall Victorian houses, built in warm red brick, with stone steps leading up to them, small and neat front gardens. 'This is where I live. You don't mind if I stop off for a moment, do you? I've got a crowd for supper, and I ought to get the oven on before I run you home. Come on in and I'll make a cup of tea.'

* * *

73

Hilary tried to keep her eyes fixed on the vivid blush-pink tablecloth. Tea had stretched to supper and she was still in Liz's house. She'd kept saying she must leave, but she didn't, couldn't leave. She was trapped in warmth and colour. She'd forgotten one could feel so warm – warm all over, even hands and feet. The kitchen seemed to pant heat: heat from oven, boiler, radiator; heat from all the people; heat even from the tablecloth, echoed by the deep rose of the walls. She had never seen kitchen walls that colour, or pictures in a kitchen, proper ones in frames. It was hard to keep her eyes down, when so many objects were shouting for attention – shiny coloured pencils in a ceramic mustard pot, a shelf of wooden ducks, a vase of paper poppies beside the tea and coffee jars. The Brignor kitchen was plain and functional, contained only the essentials. Its walls were bare, its floors were stone, the sink an old white china one which had been there fifty years. There were two sinks in this kitchen, both shining stainless steel, both piled with coloured crockery, every plate and soup bowl with its dazzling golden sunburst.

Twelve people round the table – the same as in the convent – yet it seemed triple that, at least; all those close-up faces zooming into hers, all those eager voices rising; people interrupting, shouting down each other's conversation; one small boy making noises like an aeroplane, another kicking at his chair; the constant clunk and clatter of knives and forks and plates. At Brignor, they used wooden bowls, to cut down on the noise. And meals there were a ritual – the procession in and out with its solemn Latin chanting, the grace before and after, the bowing to the crucifix every time you passed it, the curtsey to the Abbess before you sat down at your place. Here, everyone had scrambled to the table, jostled elbows, squeaked back chairs, argued about who'd sit next to whom, plucked lids from dishes to see or sniff the contents, even poked their fingers in, to taste. The only grace had been Liz's casual mumble: 'Okay, you lot, dig in.'

She was still confused by half these strangers, the relationships she hadn't yet worked out – who belonged to whom, who had children, husbands; who lived here, or was visiting. The only ones she'd really grasped were Liz and her two daughters, because she'd met them first, before the crush. Liz had introduced her to all these other people, but she'd been too shy to take them in, seen just a blur of faces. The men had scared her most. There were only three in all, yet they seemed to take up half the table, fill more than half the space. Men still seemed so strange to her – a foreign race. The one called Robert was especially overwhelming, with his loud excited voice, his laugh which shook the room, his sudden savage flare-ups.

'No, I damn well didn't, Sue! What d'you take me for – a total bloody fool?'

'Okay, cool it, Robert. I only meant . . . '

'Well, you shouldn't start accusing, when you don't know all the facts.'

'Look, cut it out, you two. We had all this last week, and it was pretty boring then.'

'Hey, did anyone see that fantastic exhibition at the Imperial War Museum – the one on Second World War art?'

'No, I won't go there on principle. If you believe in peace, then . . . '

'Come off it, Anne. That's stupid. Half the artists were probably pacifists.'

'Angus went last week and wasn't that impressed. Apparently, they got the . . . '

The voices went so fast, she couldn't follow, couldn't even fit them to their owners. She made herself look up, so she could sort out a few faces, get those straight, at least – that plump and rather breathless girl, who was eating with her fingers and had yellow wooden earrings shaped like two bananas – was she Juliet, or Anne? She was talking to a tall man, with floppy sandy hair, neatly dressed in a formal charcoal suit. Were they man and wife, or was he married to that darker girl who was recovering from a cold, and kept dabbing at her nose with torn-off lengths of toilet roll?

The third man looked more singular, with his thick dark springy beard, and wearing not a suit, but a sort of purple jerkin, over black and baggy pants. She liked his face, a kind face, with a gentle voice to match. He seemed gentle altogether, almost fatherly, though he was only in his thirties, as far as she could judge. Was that his son beside him – that bouncy, boisterous, dark-eyed child, who still thought he was an aeroplane? They'd been larking around together, mock-wrestling, swapping jokes.

The second little boy was Luke, the smaller, quieter, fairer one, who was sitting almost opposite. *His* name she remembered. She had always loved St Luke, the poetic-penned evangelist who was the patron saint of artists, doctors, surgeons. It was also Sister Luke's name, and Sister Luke was special – not her friend – friends were not allowed, but the nearest thing she'd had to one at Brignor. Luke seemed strangely silent, hunched at the table as if he didn't quite belong; the only guest – bar her – who wasn't chattering and laughing. His long untidy hair needed washing and a trim. He'd used both his hands as jotters, so they were scrawled with smudged blue biro. His grey eyes matched her own. She caught those eyes a moment, looked down as fast as he did; both of them embarrassed, both with untouched plates.

She had eaten almost nothing. It was so difficult to talk and eat at once, a skill she'd quite forgotten. If she forked in a small mouthful, somebody would ask her something, and she'd sit there paralysed, trying not to choke. It seemed so easy for the others, just a natural habit they didn't have to think about. She'd never learnt that habit, ate all her meals in silence; slow and solemn meals where no one grabbed or guzzled; where everything they did, even boning fish, or chewing a tough cabbage stalk, must be dignified, unhurried, and above all, prayerful. The rules here were quite different. You were meant to look at people, not stare down at your plate; take an interest in them, not keep your mind on God; above all, answer when they spoke.

'Did you train as a nurse, then, before you took this job?'

'Er, no, I . . . '

'I'd loathe a job like that – looking after half-wits.'

'Oh, she's not a . . . '

'She sounds like one to me.'

Hilary gripped the table. She shouldn't talk about Miss Pullen. It was uncharitable, disloyal, but everyone kept pelting her with questions, especially Della, Liz's younger daughter, a fair and very tall girl, with spiky hair which seemed to stand up on its own. She was wearing a green sweater, with rows and rows of frogs on, frogs with bulgy eyes. Her own eyes were icy-blue, nothing like her mother's. Liz was dark, more like her elder daughter, Di; the same warm brown eyes and bronzy hair, which didn't look quite natural. Di's hair was swept on top, a glamorous, rather frightening sort of woman, who jangled with gold bracelets, wore rings on every finger. She ran her own boutique, a stylish place in Wimbledon, which attracted wealthy customers from the whole of south west London – or so Liz had told her earlier. She was only in her twenties, but seemed far older somehow, a sophisticated worldly type, who made her feel a child. She, too, had endless questions.

'So you come from Norfolk, Hilary. Where in Norfolk? I know it pretty well.'

Hilary paused, took a sip of water. If she said Brignor, Di would guess. There was nothing much at Brignor, except the convent itself and a few ruined tenant cottages. She could give the village she was born in, but Di might know that too, know she hadn't been there for more than twenty years. She fumbled for her napkin, to cover her embarrassment – the huge starched white linen napkin she kept forgetting wasn't there. There were at least a dozen separate rules about its use, which made it seem more central than the food – sixteenth-century rules, which had been laid down by their Foundress. At breakfast, it remained folded on the table, like a mini tablecloth beneath your bowl; at lunchtime, you kept half beneath your bowl and the other half fanned out on your lap; at collation, the whole thing was spread out, covered half your habit, like a towel. Overnight, the napkin became a cover, a receptacle – the cloth you swathed your mug in, wrapped around your cutlery – again following an ancient rule in the exact way you had to fold it, turn the corners in. It was ludicrous the way she missed that napkin, almost ached for it, as the starched and formal symbol of all that she had lost.

She'd still not answered Di, though the question had now foundered in a general noisy argument about some movie they'd all seen.

'It's absolutely riveting – the best film he's made in years.'

'Riveting? It's crap – pretentious arty nonsense, but packaged as . . . '

'That's not fair, Di. He's trying to make some really serious points about society – how the whole thing's built on lies and fake, yet if you try to champion so-called truth, then . . . '

'You just stole that from the *Sunday Times*. Those critics read things into films which simply aren't there. If there was any theme at all, it was personal obsession – the way jealousy can . . . '

Hilary lurched from voice to voice. How did they all know so much, or form these fierce opinions? It wasn't simply films – they had views on everything: fashion, theatre, war and peace, exhibitions, art.

'The photography was stunning – all those moody shots of dawn breaking on that sordid highway with its crappy little diners and godforsaken gas stations. I mean, you feel he's saying that only nature's unpolluted.'

'*Now* who's being pretentious? Real "Pseuds' Corner" stuff, Phil. Dawn's a cliché, anyway. I'd like to see a movie which banned all dawns – and sunsets.'

'Have *you* seen it, Hilary?' It was Robert who had asked, leaning down from the far end of the table, where he'd been placed between the two prettiest of the girls. It was the first time he'd addressed her, and she felt instantly self-conscious; could hear the silence gaping as the others turned to look at her, waited for her answer.

'Er . . . no,' she said. 'I haven't.'

'How about his other films? You must have seen *Last Call*?'

She cleared her throat, tried to play for time. The last film she'd seen was *The Sound of Music*, at the age of seventeen.

Ivan saved her – changed the subject, swept them on from films to the rights of unborn foetuses; all the voices rising with the passions. Ivan was the bearded man, whose name she'd grasped, at last, and who was something called an Alexander teacher, though she'd no idea what that was. She'd assumed he was Di's husband, until she discovered that he lived down in the basement – which Liz called the garden flat – a lodger, not a husband. No one had a husband, as far as she could tell. Yet Di did have a child. The taller boy was hers, the noisy one called Stephen, who kept jumping up and down. That had startled her – Liz a grandma, when she didn't look much older than herself?

There was a sudden shout of laughter at a joke she hadn't caught. They'd somehow moved from foetuses to cats; the plump girl speaking now, through a mouthful of potato.

'At least cats don't have abortions. We've just had Rosa spayed. It's changed her whole character. She's a matron now, instead of just a slut. She couldn't say "no" before, not even to an alley cat.'

Hilary glanced across at Luke, astonished they should discuss such things with two small children present, use words like abortion –though neither child was paying much attention. Luke's whole concentration was focused on his fork, which he was using not for eating, but to jab into his palm. Stephen seemed more interested in *her*. For the last few minutes, his unflinching gaze had never left her face.

'Why have you taken off your tights?' he blurted out, at last, his piercing voice alerting the whole room.

Everyone stopped talking, as all eyes switched to her. She could feel herself blushing; a stupid, childish, endless blush, which seemed to be spreading from her cheeks and chest, right down to her guilty naked legs. Stephen must have seen those legs when he was crawling under the table to retrieve his paper napkin.

'I . . . er . . . haven't, Stephen. I don't wear tights.'

'Aren't you cold, then? Mummy only has bare legs in the summer.'

She gulped her water far too fast, to hide and cool her face, gain a few brief moments to find a better answer. She could hardly tell him that there were no tights in the jumble box, that she'd always had bare legs beneath her habit, and that, without a habit, yes, you *did* get very cold, especially in mid-January, but that made a useful penance, helped the holy souls in Purgatory. He was staring at her hair now, would probably ask her next ask why it looked so short and raggedy and was sticking up in tufts – or why she'd gone so red. The blush was getting fiercer, her whole body burning hot. She longed to run away, bolt out of the room, or at least retrieve the headscarf she'd been wearing when she came, swathe it like a yashmak, so it covered her whole face.

'Stephen, don't be rude.' Di fumbled for her lighter, lit a cigarette, as if she, too, felt the tension.

'I'm not.'

'And don't keep dropping food. You're a great big boy of six, not a baby in your highchair. Go and get a cloth and wipe that mess up.'

Stephen jerked out of his seat, caught his glass of water with his arm. It crashed on to the tiles, the noise echoing round the room. Hilary slumped back in her own chair, guilt fighting sheer relief. At least the spotlight was off *her* now – with people jumping up, mopping water, clearing shards of glass. Yet the poor child would be punished, sent upstairs, or slapped – which was hardly fair when it was partly her own fault. If you broke anything at Brignor, you had to kiss the floor in penance for disturbing others' silence; carry the smashed pieces around with you all day, abase yourself in public, since you had broken your vow of poverty, as well as just a glass. She watched, amazed, as Stephen just plumped down again, his glass replaced, refilled; no punishment at all, beyond a mild rebuke from Di.

She took one last sip of water, then forced a piece of meat down. It still seemed wrong to eat meat, an almost dangerous luxury she had done nothing to deserve. The casserole was rich, buttery, with garlic; all the vegetables also cooked in butter; the table strewn with extras – sauces, pickles, ketchups, three different sorts of mustards. At Brignor, they ate their food unseasoned – even salt and pepper both forbidden; everything served plain, so that appetite would be restrained, not stimulated. If they did enjoy a dish, found themselves deriving any pleasure from it, then they must immediately deny that pleasure, pour a little water on the food, or imagine they were eating coal or mud. Here, it wasn't easy. Her taste buds were continually delighted, startled sometimes, tantalised, but when she tried to think of mud or coal, someone asked another question, or distracted her again. Every sense was being titillated – sight, smell, taste; even the feel of an upholstered seat beneath her, instead of a rigid wooden bench; her ears syruped with soft love songs, crooning from a radio.

'More wine for you, Hilary?'

She started. Robert was standing just behind her, a bottle in each hand.

'She can't have "more",' Della said, sarcastically. 'She hasn't had a drop yet.'

'Well, white or red?' Robert proffered both. 'I recommend the claret. It's certainly an improvement on that poisonous South Thames water.'

She mumbled a refusal, prayed that he would move, not hover by her chair like that, still trying to change her mind. His sheer male bulk seemed to threaten and disturb her. His amused and teasing voice made her own sound prim and feeble.

'What do they say – a meal without wine is like a brother-in-law's kiss?' He splashed the red into her glass. 'I wouldn't know – I've never had a brother-in-law.'

'You've never had a meal without wine, you mean.'

'Hey, come off it, Liz. That's snide.'

'Just my little joke, Bob.'

'Not a very funny one. And I'm Robert, please, not Bob.'

'You were Bob when I first met you.'

'Maybe. I'm different now.'

'Oh, really? You surprise me.'

Hilary heard the sudden sharpness in both voices, saw the mutual hostile glances, before Robert moved away, changed places with the tall thin man called Philip.

'Come on, Phil, give another chap a chance. You've been monopolising Sue the whole damned evening, and she's dying for a change of face – aren't you, Susie darling?'

Sue giggled as he edged his chair in closer, put an arm around her shoulders, started fondling her bare neck. Hilary glanced at them, confused. They'd been fighting earlier on, and now they were embracing. She couldn't understand it. And Sue didn't pull away, didn't seem to mind being stroked and touched in public. She herself felt embarrassed and exposed, as if the hand were on her own neck –that hot and heavy male hand with its tangle of fair hairs. She forced her eyes away. She'd no right to be watching; had been trained at Brignor never to look up. Even if someone fainted in the refectory or chapel, it was the Infirmarian's job to pick the body up, and no other nun so much as raised her eyes. Far harder at this table, though, with all the banter and distractions, the four-way conversations, the arguments, and sudden strange hostilities.

Even the radio was adding to the din, though no one else seemed aware that it was on. How could they ignore it – all those urgent breathless voices peddling dandruff cures or motor oil, yet sounding as ecstatic as if they'd just seen the living God – and all mixed up with weather forecasts, news flashes, shrill and raucous songs? She'd been amazed to hear advertisements on radio; startled by the casual way the announcers joked and chatted – everyone a pal – even accidents or hold-ups a subject for their wisecracks. Yet she envied them, in one way. They were so at ease, so friendly, wouldn't cower at this table without a word to say, but would galvanise the group with their superlatives – every guest the greatest, every dish 'super, fab, fantastic'.

She suppressed a sudden smile as she imagined Sister Gerard putting on a voice like that for the *Life of John Bosco* or *Journey of a Soul*. The readings in the refectory were always slow and solemn. You had to practise first, enunciate each word, give each page the reverence it deserved. She almost missed the readings – the way they helped to sanctify the meal, kept your mind on God. The week she'd left, they'd been working through Thomas à Kempis's *Imitation of Christ*, a book well-suited to the refectory, since the fifteenth-century monk believed that if only men could be weaned away from their need for food and drink, they would then be free to praise God without pause or interruption. '*If you desire to be God's spouse, then drink only the chalice of suffering, eat only the dry bread of mortification.*'

She jumped as a pea flicked in her face. Stephen was using peas as bullets, now, and had selected her as target. 'Bang, bang, you're dead!' Liz removed his plate, leaned across the table.

'Are you all right, Hilary? You've eaten almost nothing. If you don't like the casserole, I can do you something else. How about an omelette?'

'No, really. It's . . . ' She struggled for the word. At Brignor, you must never mention food, never comment on it. *Did* she like the casserole? She wasn't even sure. She'd spent so many years trying to eradicate her personal likes and dislikes; punishing all failures by forcing down a double portion of any dish she loathed, she was now thoroughly confused about her natural preferences. Except for swedes, of course. Those she knew she hated, always would. But there were no swedes here, only delicate courgettes, tiny tender peas, creamy mashed potato. So why was it so difficult to swallow?

She realised to her shame she was the only one still eating. She was holding them all up. They had taken more than she had, talked far more than she had, yet all their plates were cleared, even second helpings – well, all except for Luke's. He had pushed his plate away, was slumped back in his chair, yawning, half-asleep. His tiredness seemed to creep across the table, infect her limbs, as well. She laid her own fork down, could hardly hold its weight. It was late for little boys to eat, late for nuns to eat. It also felt quite wicked to be talking after nine o'clock at night. The Great Silence started then – or always did at Brignor – lasted till the morning, was totally inviolable; not one word to be spoken, except in real emergencies. No problem in observing it when she was safe at Rosemont Road. Miss Pullen went to bed at nine, and she herself followed not long after – her evening ending as most people's in the world began. They would scoff if she explained to them that the evening was God's time, when you kept your mind and thoughts on Him, undistracted by the duties of the day; spent part of every night as preparation for the next morning's Holy Communion.

She glanced across at Luke again, wondered when he went to bed, who and where his parents were. There was no one he called mother here, no one he seemed close to. They were still the two outsiders, the two awkward, silent, tired ones.

Liz was on her feet now, collecting up the plates. 'Don't force yourself

81

to finish, love, just to be polite. I know you've been unwell, and there's nothing worse than . . . '

'Love.' Liz had called her love. She didn't even know her, and yet she'd called her love. She was a freak in old grey castoffs, with bare legs and stupid shoes, and this woman loved her, in the sense she understood, treating her like Christ, offering help and food. She mustn't cry. She mustn't. She clasped her hands together on her lap, gripped them till they hurt, digging in her nails. Pain always ousted tears. She'd learnt that as a postulant.

'I'm sorry, I didn't catch . . . ' Someone was addressing her and she hadn't even heard; was still savouring that 'love'.

'That's okay. I only asked if you'd been to Alexander lessons. You sit so straight, you see.'

'Er . . . no.' What was Alexander? Should she ask, or was she meant to know? The girl who'd spoken was one of Ivan's pupils, the brunette with the snuffly nose, who seemed to be wearing her pyjamas.

'She's been to bloody prison, not to Alexander, that's what I'm beginning to think.'

'Della!'

'You can see her head's been shaved. And she's nervous as all hell. It's her first week out, I bet, after a whole long stretch inside.'

'For God's sake, Della. If you can't be civil, shut up, or go upstairs.'

'It's my house, isn't it? I'm sick of Mum's lame ducks.'

Hilary stood trembling in the bathroom. Liz had come to fetch her, twice, but she'd said she was all right, would be out in just a moment. Prison! So they thought she was a convict, someone who had stolen or . . . She checked her face, staring in the mirror, as if her crime were branded right into her skin. She *had* stolen. She'd returned the twenty pounds, in fact – sent it from her wages the minute she'd received them – but it was still a theft, and she'd still broken every rule and run away. She could see the high stone walls which confined them night and day, rearing up around her once again. A girl like Della might see it as a prison – the shaven heads, the uniform, the lack of privacy and loss of all personal possessions, the bare white cells, the endless rules and punishments. She'd even had a number stitched or stamped on to everything she used. She was a number, an offender, someone people shrank from – normal girls like Della – *all* of them, most likely, except they weren't as frank as Della, probably kept their horror to themselves.

She'd have to leave, immediately, without waiting for dessert. They wouldn't want her back there – not one of Liz's lame ducks, resented by her daughters. It was getting late, in any case. Miss Baines would be expecting her. She'd slip out, catch a bus, leave a note of thanks for Liz, even leave some money for the meal. Except her bag was in the kitchen, and, more important, Miss Pullen's surgical belt. How was she to fetch it, face all those jeering eyes, those stares of accusation? She should have stayed inside her prison. At least she fitted there. Even when her hair grew and she'd dared to buy some clothes, she knew she'd still be different, someone who was stigmatised, could never learn the casual ways of relaxed and normal people.

She sank down on the bathroom stool, too tired to move or think. The supper had seemed endless – an ordeal, and one she'd failed. Yet she wanted to belong, wanted Liz to call her 'love' again, be offered luxuries like wine and OK sauce.

She froze as someone knocked, not Liz's gentle tapping, more a thump. She unlocked the door. Luke was standing there, his jeans already half-unzipped. 'I'm busting for a pee. There's spiders in the one upstairs.'

He dashed in, started urinating, right there in front of her. She tried not to look, or hear, as she crept towards the door. His high voice called her back. 'Have you really been in prison?'

She shook her head. He couldn't see the gesture, was still standing at the toilet, legs apart. 'I won't tell if you have.'

'No, I haven't. Really.'

'Cross your heart?'

She smiled, despite herself. She liked this child. They even looked alike – not only the same colour eyes, but the same straight, thick, fairish hair – though his was longer, fell across his forehead. He left the toilet unflushed, went to close the door, stood in front of it, as if he were acting as her jailer, preventing her escape. 'My Dad's been in prison.'

She received the news in silence. It felt like a secret, something he was offering her, an overture, a confidence, a bond between the two of them. She owed him something in return. Would it really matter if she told him? She'd have to tell someone, apart from priests and housekeepers, so why not a six-year-old she'd never meet again? If he fetched the bag and belt for her, she need never see the rest of them again, just grab her stuff and run.

She pulled nervously at her hair. It felt long to her, not cropped, certainly much longer than it had been for twenty years. 'I've never been in prison, Luke, but I . . . I used to be a nun.'

'What's a nun?'

She didn't answer. It seemed extraordinary, incredible, that he didn't know, had never heard the word. It was as if he had negated her with just that one short question; made her realise, suddenly, how marginal nuns were – not the prayer-powerhouse of the world, as they had seen themselves, but an almost extinct and peripheral species, which the younger generation had never even heard of.

He was still waiting for an answer, eyes huge and fixed on hers. He was expecting something exciting, or even excitingly horrendous; something worse than his father's spell in jail. Her first words petered out. She didn't want to let him down, bore him with accounts of prayers and penances; repeat the standard answers about nuns devoting their whole lives and selves to God. How could he understand that? She suddenly craved to give him something – this pale, tired, grubby, crumpled child – even if only a white lie or two, to make nuns sound more enthralling.

'Well,' she said, still groping for the words. 'They're perhaps a bit like soldiers. But they don't fight in wars – they fight for God, in secret.'

7

Hilary trudged up to the entrance of the lowering concrete building, its rash of signs daubed with paint, spattered with graffiti. 'Department of Social Security', 'Department of Employment', 'Unemployment Office'. She shook the sleet off her shoulders as she stepped into the bleak and dirty hallway, which smelt of disinfectant. She refused to cower any longer in that biting wind outside, too frightened to go in. It was time she made some effort, did something for herself, stopped depending on a priest for food and work. Miss Baines had told her much the same – a sarcastic and irate Miss Baines, still smarting from the night before, when she'd kept her from her bed. She'd been so upset about running out on Liz, escaping from the supper and from Wandsworth, that she'd caught a bus going the wrong way, landed up in Shepherd's Bush; finally limped in to Miss Pullen's as the clock was striking twelve.

'It's high time you learnt some sense, Hilary. It's your own fault, you know. You'll never find your way about if you always stay indoors and hide away. You've got to make some effort, learn to cope with things like shops and buses. Miss O'Connor's back in just two days, *then* what are you going to do?'

'I . . . I don't know.'

'Well, you could always try the dole. If half the country's on it, why not you, as well? At least it would let poor Father off the hook. He's got enough on his plate already, without trying to find employment for nuns who run away.'

She had winced at that remark, resisted the idea of taking money from the State; joining all those desperate souls she'd read about – or prayed for – single parents struggling with sick children; the handicapped, the destitute, people with no help or hope at all. She was able-bodied, healthy, and still officially a nun; had no real right to handouts.

'I . . . I'd rather find a job,' she'd said, as she helped Miss Baines into her coat, saw her to the door.

'Well, that's not easy, is it? Father's tried, for heaven's sake, done his level best. But if you go up to the dole office, at least they'll give you some advice. I'm not sure how the system works, but maybe they have jobs as well, or someone there who knows about employment. It's worth asking, isn't it?'

Hilary paused in the vast hallway, with its bare and shiny walls, its rows of dull green doors, its shabby people shuffling down the corridors or toiling up the flights of steep stone steps. She was confused by all the signs. The benefits on offer appeared to stretch from birth to death; cover all contingencies from illness to retirement. What had Father Anstey said? That if you haven't paid your stamps, you couldn't get unemployment benefit, but went on supplementary. Yes, there it was – 'Supplementary Benefit, 2nd Floor, Door C.' It all sounded very complicated, and she'd never heard of paying stamps, but she must show the priest she wasn't quite the ninny he assumed.

She hurried up the steps, trying to ignore the scum of litter silted on each landing, the obscene remarks scribbled on the walls. Door C was right in front of her. She knocked softly. No reply. She opened the door a nervous inch or two, stood staring at the crush of huddled bodies, packed thigh to thigh on rows of metal benches. Her first instinct was to run. She couldn't go in there, join those frightening blue-jeaned youths slouched against the wall, those sad old men and women staring into space, that ox of a young man with three days' stubble grizzling his huge jaw, greasy hair hanging to his shoulders. An aura of sheer hopelessness seemed to be rising from them all, drifting into the air with the grey haze of cigarette smoke, the sour smell of damp clothes. Despite the fact they were jammed so close together, each person seemed imprisoned in his own cocoon of private misery; torpid bodies slumped, faces closed and hostile. The room itself looked desolate – its scuffed grey floor engrained with dirt, its walls tiled in dingy white, like a public lavatory; no curtains at the windows, only bars. Even the sleet was falling very listlessly, as if too tired to make its way from sky to earth.

'Mind your feet!'

Hilary jumped back, as a woman with a pushchair and three young children clinging to her coat struggled through the door, her long wet hair dripping down her neck. Hilary paused a second, still fighting the desire to run, then tagged behind the woman, like her fifth and youngest child. At least she could hide behind this family, escape notice on her own account as she followed in their wake. The woman seemed to know what she was doing, moved purposefully towards the last bench at the back, finding room for all her children as she parked her pushchair, removed their sodden coats. Hilary squeezed between the smallest and a tall unshaven youth with tattoos of naked women on the backs of both his hands, whose bare flesh seemed to ripple as he lit a cigarette. No one spoke, no one even glanced at her. Only the three children showed any sign of life, crawling on the floor now, picking up cigarette ends, then fighting with each other as to who should 'smoke' the longest ones. Their mother took no notice, just sprawled back on the bench, her mouth a shiny purple gash clamped round a cigarette, her gymshoes torn and dirty. Another child was screaming, a baby in the row in front, whose mother looked a child herself – except that she was pregnant – a pale and very nervous girl, obviously embarrassed by her infant's wail of fury. How long had she been waiting? Since opening time at nine? There seemed no sense of urgency, no efficient busy hum, just a general torpor which had infected the whole room. The three partitioned cubicles at the far end of the room were all occupied by claimants, but the clerks kept disappearing into the labyrinth behind them, returning with more forms – or still more questions – as if totally oblivious of the sullen crowd still waiting.

Hilary jumped, as a sudden yowl of fury drowned the baby's cries, answered by an angry shouted barrage. A row had broken out between a client and a clerk. She couldn't hear the details, but could feel the tension screwing tighter, tighter, in the room. All heads were looking up now, all eyes focused on the middle cubicle, where the huge stubbly youth was screaming out expletives – words she'd never heard and shouldn't know. She tried to block her ears, terrified that threats would turn to blows. Violence must be common here, judging by the notice which threatened imprisonment or heavy fines for anyone attacking staff, and the thick glass barriers which divided clerks from claimants. It was as if the clients were wild beasts who must be caged up in their zoo, or quarantined like lepers. She shuddered as she realised she was one with them; one with the infected and the animals. If her parents were to see her now, they would shrink in disbelief; her mother with her horror of what she called 'scroungers'; her father with his high ambitions for her.

The door slammed with a final shouted curse. The man had gone, but left his mood behind. People started muttering and fidgeting; the three children on the floor were no longer squabbling mildly, but grabbing at each others' eyes and throats. She tried to calm her own unease by reading all the notices jumbled on the board; suddenly realised to her horror that she should have taken a numbered ticket as soon as she arrived. The whole system worked on numbers, which came up, turn by turn, on the indicator-panel set above the cubicles. They didn't make it easy. The panel was so small, she hadn't even seen it; the ticket dispenser half-concealed at the far end of the room; the notice itself defaced and vandalised. She'd wasted half an hour now, lost her turn to all those milling people who'd come in after her, experienced folk who knew their way round, didn't need a guidebook to all the different systems in the world – rules for supermarkets, rules for dinner parties, rules for finding jobs or claiming money.

She slunk up to the front to get her ticket, aware of countless eyes boring into her, noting her bare legs, the high-heeled patent shoes which must look so incongruous with a shabby gardener's anorak. Her ticket was number sixty and the indicator-panel said only seventeen. She squeezed back to her seat, found she'd lost it to an old woman in an army coat who was talking to herself, patches of pink scalp showing through her scurf of greyish hair. She felt conspicuous, self-conscious, as she went to join the people slumped against the wall – mostly tough young men, whose nervous hands seemed never still, jangling coins in pockets, rolling cigarettes.

She edged towards the radiator, which felt just faintly tepid, as if even the heating system had been affected by the general air of sluggishness. The whole room was dank and chilly; paint peeling off the window frames, one cracked pane stuck with grimy tape. Was it really necessary for this place to be so desolate, with no single softening touch: no plant or picture, no easy chairs – or chairs at all – no magazines to read, not even a calendar to brighten the bare walls? It was as if poverty were a crime and must be punished by the most miserable surroundings. At Brignor, things were plain, but beautiful, the place kept always spotless, in and out. If man were God's creation, then he had dignity and value, and his surroundings should reflect it. How could these people feel any sense of worth, when they were trapped in rooms like this, which no one seemed to clean, or heat, or paint?

She rubbed her eyes which were smarting from the smoke, tried to block out the endless whining questions of the small child just in front of her, a boy of six or seven, who was sucking half a Mars Bar, chocolate dribble leaking down his clothes. How did these mothers cope all day, providing answers, stopping tears and fights? She was exhausted after just an hour, and she only had to watch, not take responsibility, feed and clothe a family, deal with all their problems. She was mother to the world, mother to all souls, but souls didn't wrestle on a grubby germy floor, or wet their pants in public, or get chocolate in their hair. And was enclosure such a hardship, when it meant you stayed in, warm and dry, instead of battling with the elements in cheap and flimsy clothes?

How sheltered she had been, totally protected from the horrors on the noticeboard – posters about AIDS or heroin addiction, advice for single parents or those with partners in jail. Nuns were spared such crises, and if they got old or sick or feeble, they would be nursed with love for the remainder of their days; food and care provided, no need to queue for handouts, or trail a troupe of children from one bench to another.

'Help them, Lord,' she whispered, ashamed that she had sat so long without a word of prayer. Had she ever prayed with any real discernment, ever grasped what 'poor' meant, when she'd used the word so easily at Brignor? She would say the rosary – all fifteen Mysteries – which would take her a good hour or so; offer up its hundred and fifty 'Hail Marys' for all the hopeless people in this room. And she would start with the Joyful Mysteries, to remind herself there *was* still joy – and hope.

She said the first 'Our Father', then began on the 'Hail Marys', eyes half-closed, fingers fumbling for her non-existent beads. 'Holy Mary, Mother of God, pray for us sinners, now and at the . . . '

She broke off in the middle of her ninety-eighth 'Hail Mary', as her own number clicked up on the panel; weaved her way past children, bodies, pushchairs, to the now empty middle cubicle. The clerk was male – and smoking – sounded hoarse and croaky, as if he were suffering from a cold. She had hoped to see a woman, would have felt less shy and stupid as she stammered out that she'd never made a claim before, didn't know the system, wasn't sure if . . .

'Well, you're in the wrong department, then, for starters.'

She stared in disbelief. 'But . . . '

'You need the Unemployment Benefit Office. First floor, door E.'

She tried to calm her voice, remember what the priest had said. 'But I haven't paid my stamps.'

He shrugged. 'It doesn't matter. Even if you don't qualify for unemployment benefit, you still have to register, make yourself available for work, sign on as unemployed.'

'Can't I do that here, though?'

'No way. We're two completely different sections. You need a B1 form, which they can only give you there. When you've filled it in, you send it back, and the DHSS decide what you're entitled to. Just one flight down. Door E.'

He gestured with his cigarette, dismissed her with another casual shrug. She still hovered, fighting panic. How could she wait a second time, in a second dreary room, wait all those hours and hours? Miss Baines was kindly sitting with Miss Pullen, but had offered only grudgingly, couldn't stay all day.

'You stupid bloody cunt! Don't think you'll . . . '

Hilary swung round. The huge long-haired youth was back, striding from the door towards her cubicle. He elbowed her aside, swept into the booth, clenched fists raised, tears streaming down his dirty stubbled face. 'You'll pay for this, you see. I'll smash your fucking face in!'

* * *

The second clerk was also male, though he was wearing a gold chain above his scruffy V-neck sweater, a matching bracelet engraved with 'Mike'. He shook his head impatiently as he peered down at her form, still left mostly blank.

'I need your National Insurance number. You should have put it on here.'

'I'm afraid I don't know it. I don't think I've even got one.'

'Haven't you ever worked before?'

'Er . . . no.'

'You're living with someone, are you, who supports you?'

Another mumbled no. The questions hammered on; all answered in the negative, or with awkward gaping silences. How could she explain those blanks, unless she told the truth? She glanced around her nervously. Could that other woman hear her – the one in the next booth? She lowered her voice to an embarrassed halting whisper, stared down at the desk. 'I . . . I've been a nun, you see.'

Silence. She couldn't see his face. Had he even heard her, or was he trying not to laugh, or jeer; or about to repeat Luke's question – ask her what a nun was? She added quickly, 'You know – in a convent. For the last twenty years or so. That's why I haven't worked.'

'You've been a *nun*?' His own voice rose in sheer surprise. He made it sound extraordinary, like being in a circus or a zoo.

She nodded, face now crimson. Both the clerk and claimant next to her had heard; four more eyes swivelling round to stare, their own consultation halted, so they could listen in on hers.

'For twenty years?'

'Twenty-one.'

Her own clerk seemed incredulous, his sharp eyes tracking up and down her body, as if to check she was quite human, had all the normal parts. He wrote 'WAS NUN', in capitals, right across her form. She felt nervous of that 'was'. She was still a nun, bound by vows of steel. And if her whole role and life and calling were cancelled by one word, then what was left of her? He handed her another form, a much larger and more daunting-looking one, with a vivid purple border round each page – purple for penitence, for mourning. 'This is your B1.'

'Oh, I see. I thought I'd filled that in.'

'No, that was your UB461. The B1's much longer – about a hundred and forty questions, as far as I remember. It's best to take your time and fill it in at home.'

Home. She hadn't got one. She was here to try to find one, ask about employment. 'I really came to get a job, was told you could advise me.'

He shook his head. 'Not here. Your best plan is to go down to the Job

90

Centre. They'll be able to help. The only problem is it's quite a hike. Hold on, I'll get a map.'

He was trying to be kind now, returned with piles of leaflets, as well as just the map. She thanked him, backed away, saw him whisper to two fellow clerks behind him, caught their stare of fascinated prurience – the nun, the curiosity, the one you gawped and sniggered at. She rushed out of the room, escaped to the toilet, which was mercifully empty, spread out the B1. There were eight large pages in a dozen separate sections – endless detailed questions about her husband, children, property and savings, employer, landlord, home and job. Those clerks were right. She *was* a curiosity – some creature from another age, who had no job, no partner, no dependants; who paid no rent nor rates nor mortgage, no heating costs, insurance; who'd never saved or borrowed money in her life; who fitted nowhere, had no real past at all. And how could she take money from the State, when so many people were in more desperate need than she was – people not just unemployed or homeless, but also fighting disease and disability, all the chronic illnesses spelled out on this form, all the different handicaps she hardly knew existed?

She tore her form up, dropped it in the bin. She'd had nearly forty years of security and shelter, two good meals a day, a safe and solid roof above her head. She had to find some work, not take funds from people who were truly poor – poor in health and prospects, poor in hope, poor even in their pasts. She threw out all the leaflets on rent rebates and housing, kept only those on jobs, put them in her pocket with the map which showed the Job Centre, then walked swiftly out to find it.

'Can I help at all?'

A friendly grey-haired woman was smiling from her desk, gesturing to the empty chair in front of it. Hilary sat down. The chair was sunny orange, with a comfy cushioned seat, the whole place bright and cheerful – plants in the window, carpet on the floor – yet her spirits didn't match. She had already read the job-cards plastered round the walls, realised all the skills she didn't have. There was not one slot she fitted – not Building, Engineering, Catering or Chefs, Secretarial, Motor Trade, Young People. Prayer was her profession. One priest had called contemplatives the Brigade of Guards of Prayer, God's crack troops. There were jobs in hundreds, rows and rows and rows of them, but no vacancies for pray-ers. Pastrycooks were wanted, bricklayers, cost accountants, plumbers; things she'd never heard of like VDU ops or software engineers. Even the humblest sorts of jobs demanded people with experience, and she'd had none at all, except as sacristan and vestment-maker. What use were hand-embroidered chasubles or highly polished chalices to a 'busy friendly office' or 'expanding modern company'? Even her personality was wrong. 'Must be ambitious and self-motivated.' 'Bright bubbly extrovert required.'

She forced her mouth to smile, tried to sound extrovert, ambitious, despite her string of 'noes'.

'Are you married?'

'Children?'

'Have you trained for anything?'

'Ever worked abroad?'

'Do you type?'

'Or drive?'

'Any special skills at all?'

'Er . . . dressmaking,' she mumbled. Six 'noes' were enough – though talent with a needle would hardly land her a residential job. Those seemed non-existent, except for nurses, nannies, or other fully trained professionals who could also drive and cook. She tried to fight the slow despair seeping through her body, made herself sit straighter. 'How about a job in a hotel? A receptionist, or . . . '

The interviewer shook her head, still searching through her job-sheets. 'Receptionists have to work a switchboard and they usually do all the accounts as well, so if you've no experience with either, there's no chance, I'm afraid. You might get a bar job, but most hotels prefer a married couple.'

She shuddered. An ex-nun pouring drinks, having to ward off the advances of raucous tipsy men. She should be searching for a useful job, some service to the poor or sick. 'I could look after invalids, or work in an old people's home.'

'Well, again you'd need some training, and we don't get many jobs like that, not here. You could try the social services, but I doubt if it would lead to much, and they'll be shutting now, in any case.' The interviewer checked her watch, gave a final clinching smile. 'So are we, in fact.'

Hilary got up, walked slowly to the door, the lush green plants and cheerful orange décor seeming now to mock her. She was ashamed of her despair. It was an insult to God to worry about the future, since everything was in His careful hands. Sister Clare had said once that even if she landed in a concentration camp, she would accept it as God's will. Auschwitz in Norfolk was, to say the least, unlikely, but all the same, she could do with Sister Clare's strong faith, her fighting spirit.

She stopped to check the Temporary Jobs, the only board she hadn't scanned. Her whole life was so temporary, maybe better to accept that, try to find some stopgap job, just to tide her over. If live-in posts were difficult, took time and effort to arrange, perhaps she'd be allowed to stay at Rosemont Road for just another month or two, while she sorted something out; tried the social services, tried anywhere and everywhere. She read the cards as quickly as she could, since it was three minutes to closing time, staff locking drawers and files now, collecting up their bags. She mustn't be too fussy, be willing to take anything, however hard or humble. 'Kitchen porter urgently required. Large hotel needs strong and willing man or woman, for cleaning, washing up, and heavy physical work. Hours: 6 a.m. to 3 p.m.' She copied out the details. She was very willing, fairly strong, not scared of heavy work, and used to clocking on at six a.m. She jotted down the phone number, heart sinking as she read the bottom line. 'Two references essential.'

References for kitchen porter work? It seemed absurd – though perhaps they'd be working with valuable equipment, must be trusted not to steal or spoil it. Who ever could she ask for references? Miss Baines? Father Anstey? Both disapproved of her, and there was no one else she knew in all of London. Except Aunt Eva. She could see her aunt, suddenly, dressed in a plaid skirt, exotic red-tipped fingers passing her the cake plate when she was only nine or ten – not her mother's heavy rock cakes with burnt currants, uncooked middles, but ethereal creations from a local French *pâtisserie*. 'Go on, love, take two.'

She hardly knew how she got down to the tube – or even found a tube – let alone the confidence to make the trip to Eva's London home, especially in the rush hour. She had planned the journey several times, even bought an *A–Z*, marked Hurst Road in biro, but had never plucked up courage yet for feet to follow fingers. It was crazy to go now, with Miss Baines already angry that she'd spent so much time away, but she'd phoned Miss Pullen's, nonetheless, begged another hour or two, said there was one last possibility she just had to follow up.

'It may have slipped your mind, dear, that you've rung three times already, and asked me the same thing. I've been sitting here since nine o'clock this morning, and now you're demanding the evening off, as well. I have a job to do myself, you know, and Father wants his dinner.'

Wretched, she'd apologised, said she'd catch a bus immediately, be back in fifteen minutes.

'No – don't do that – not if you're just on to something. I'd rather stay here half the night again, than have you trail back in with no money and no job. But this is your last chance, d'you hear? It's no good crawling to me tomorrow and expecting . . . '

The sarcastic tone hadn't hurt as much as usual. She'd felt a sudden burst of hope that she was going to see her aunt, at last. She could hardly understand it, but it was as if God Himself were telling her to trust in Him; that an unanswered phone needn't mean disaster, as she'd feared so often previously. Eva might have changed her number, or the phone be out of order, or she herself copied down a digit incorrectly.

'Lord,' she prayed, as she squeezed into the crowded train. 'I trust in Your great mercy.' There were no free seats, so she clung on to the rail, stood studying the tube map – Eva's station smiling like a beacon at the far end of the line. In just an hour or less, she could be standing face to face with her astonished radiant aunt.

Two hours later, she was travelling back again. At least she had a seat this time, and could read her *A–Z*. The two long journeys had given her the chance to learn her way around, work out all the postal districts, the railways and the tubes. If she got out at Vauxhall, she could change on to the mainline and take a train to Earlsfield – though she dreaded going back, facing Miss Baines's fury, felt almost desperate as she ran through her long day. Was there nothing she could salvage from it? What about that kitchen porter's job? Should she rush there now, apply without the references, explain she'd been a nun? She could almost hear the titters, or the scoffing disbelief. No. Why add one more failure to her list? It had been bad enough last night, when she'd returned from Liz's, crept in late and guilty like a . . . .

Liz! Liz Kingsley! She'd quite forgotten Liz. Liz would write a reference. Liz was kind and generous, had called her 'love', as Eva used to do. Did she dare to go there, seek her out again? She might even get both references, if Di wrote one, or Ivan – and perhaps some other work as well, babysitting, ironing. Liz was part of a whole circle, with endless friends and contacts. Some of them might need her, if only for an hour or so. They'd know by now she hadn't been in prison. Luke would have told them she'd been a nun and not a convict, and at least most nuns could be trusted not to steal from hotel kitchens.

She went racing through her *A–Z*, found two Wandsworth stations – Wandsworth Town and Wandsworth Common. Which was nearest Liz, and would she find the street at all, remember which the house was? A small stern voice was whispering that the idea was quite impractical. She'd simply waste another hour, keep Miss Baines still later. And supposing they were out? She closed her eyes a moment, saw Eva's house again – that cramped and dingy terraced house with neither tree nor garden, which seemed so wrong for Eva, who loved nature, colour, space. She had stood shivering on the step, listening to the doorbell pealing through the hall – pealing twice, three times. The house stayed deaf and dark, the heavy curtains all drawn close, as if to shut her out. She'd walked slowly down the street again, sleet stinging in her eyes, then turned round, indecisive. She couldn't simply leave, trail back to

94

the station without making some enquiries. Her aunt might be a wall away, sitting with a neighbour. She braved five different neighbours – a suspicious dusky woman who spoke no word of English, an angry man who shouted, a child in its pyjamas who said its mother wasn't back yet, and one good-natured couple who said they'd like to help, but had only just moved in themselves and didn't know a soul yet.

She closed her *A–Z*. The tube was slowing as it drew into a station, shuddered to a stop. Vauxhall. She must go straight back to Miss Pullen's, not risk a second empty house, a second disappointment. She crossed from tube to mainline, found the ticket office. 'A single, please, to Earlsfield.'

'Hey! Don't forget your change, Mrs.'

She turned back to the counter. The man was grinning, friendly, asking if she'd meant to leave a tip, or was she just a millionairess who couldn't be bothered with loose coins. She felt a sudden desperate longing to stay there the whole night, clinging to that counter because there was a kindly voice behind it. Liz's house was like that – full of jokes and banter, human noise and contact, which had frightened her before, but now seemed infinitely preferable to Miss Baines's cold contempt. She was cold enough already – her feet and fingers numb, her mind frozen in despair. She could almost feel the warmth of Liz's kitchen, thawing her, reviving. She'd hardly realised till this moment how utterly alone she was. The man had called her 'Mrs', must have seen her ring, but her husband-God had left her, and there was no one else at all. She could hear Miss Baines's cutting voice deploring her ineptitude. ('So you've spent thirteen hours of your time – not to mention mine – getting absolutely nowhere'); see her fawn and frowning face as she stepped into the hall.

She left her tenpence pieces where they were, cleared her throat, to get the ticket man's attention. 'I'm sorry. I've just changed my mind. Does it cost any more to Wandsworth?'

Ivan let her in. She stood nervous in the hall; could hear not friendly voices, but angry bitter ranting ones, booming from upstairs. The woman's voice was Liz's, but not a Liz she knew – a Liz close to tears and shouting. The man's voice she didn't recognise, but his rage was unmistakable.

She edged towards the door again. 'Look, I'd better go, really. It's obviously not convenient.'

Ivan shrugged. 'Take no notice. Whenever Ken turns up, they have a row.'

'Ken?'

'Liz's first ex-husband. They fought when they were married and they still fight, cat and dog. Don't worry. He'll slam out in a moment and I'll let Liz know you're here. You look frozen stiff. Like a cup of tea?'

She didn't answer. She was still dazed by that casual 'first ex-husband'. So Liz had been divorced, and more than once. She felt a rush of pity for her, yet also deep unease. In Reverend Mother's eyes, divorce was a sin, divorcées hard and brazen. She was also shy of Ivan, shy even of his clothes. He was dressed in the same black baggy trousers he'd worn yesterday, at supper, but this time with a green embroidered smock, which looked almost like a vestment, the way it hung loosely from his shoulders. His long untidy hair was falling in his eyes. The eyes themselves were kind – the sort of soft brown melting eyes that cocker spaniels had. Yet it felt almost dangerous to be sitting with a man alone; a man not a priest or monk.

Somehow he had swept her into the kitchen, sat her down, closed the door behind them. She hardly dared look up, just stared into her cup, hands slowly thawing from the warmth of tea and boiler. He had made a pot of herb tea which she had never tried before – Lemon Balm with honey, which smelt sharp and sweet and spicy all at once. Should she explain about the references, or wait till Liz appeared? Suddenly, the door burst open and Di strode in, her pale cheeks flushed, her hair spilling from its chignon.

'That bloody man, I'll kill him! Okay, so he's my father, but . . . ' She stopped dead, stared at Hilary with a mixture of suspicion and bewilderment, seemed hardly to remember who she was.

Hilary stood up. 'I'm sorry. I'm intruding. I'm the nun, ex-nun – you know, the one who turned up yesterday.'

'*Nun?*'

'Didn't Luke tell you?'

'Tell me what?'

She wished she hadn't spoken, though Di seemed not that interested, her whole attention focused on what was going on outside, angry taunts and yellings still echoing from the stairs. Ivan offered tea, but she poured herself a stronger drink, turned to Hilary with the gin bottle uncapped. 'Care for one yourself?'

'N . . . No, thank you.'

'I'm sorry if I snapped. I've had a real bitch of a day. It gets harder and harder to run that blasted shop. The girl who helps me has gone off sick with flu, my new stock's been delayed, this lousy bloody weather keeps the customers away, and on top of that, I find my father here . . . Cheers, anyway!' She downed her gin and grinned. 'With that lot off my chest, I feel a whole lot better. So how are things with you, Hilary?'

So Di *did* know who she was, had even remembered her name. She felt touched by the 'Hilary', but still awkward, ill at ease. Not only had she barged into a private family row, but Di would wonder why she'd come at all, suspect she was a scrounger, begging a free meal again. She got straight on to the references, asked if they could help.

'What's the job you're after?' Di refilled her glass, lit a cigarette.

'A kitchen porter.'

'*What?*'

Liz walked into the silence which followed Di's 'You're joking!' Her eyes were sore and swollen, arms hunched across her chest, as if holding in bruised or broken pieces. Di jumped up, steered her to the table, poured a drink for her.

'Hilary's just told us she's a nun, but she'd rather be a kitchen porter, and would we write a reference for her.'

They all laughed, even Liz, which broke the tension. Hilary let Di explain. She felt too tired herself, too scared by all the wild emotions raging in this house. Nuns were trained to hide what they were feeling, be it joy or anger, exhaustion or resentment.

'Good God!' said Liz, letting out another bray of laughter, while still dabbing her red eyes. 'You must be kidding, surely? You don't look like a nun – and even less like a kitchen porter. Though I must confess I've never met either in my life.' She gulped her gin, lounged back in her chair. 'Can't you get a teaching job, instead? Nuns all teach, don't they?'

Hilary took a sip of tea. 'Well, no. Not contemplatives.' Would they even know the word, or understand that some nuns spent their entire life in prayer; that prayer was the Church's official work, and that other jobs like pottery or printing, making hosts or vestments, were merely secondary, just a way to keep themselves, as an alternative to begging? She remembered the words written in the Community Book, justifying their role. 'To pray for those who have no time for prayer; to believe for those who can no longer believe; to give praise for those who are lost in pain; to accept death, that they may live.' If she recited that, they'd laugh again, or worse still, be embarrassed. Yet, they were still all looking at her, waiting for some further explanation. 'I did mostly sewing,' she added lamely. At least vestment-making would be easier to explain than singing the Divine Office seven times a day, succouring the world.

'Sewing?' Di was on her feet. 'Why ever didn't you say so? I'm desperate for someone who can sew. My alterations lady is really almost past it. She'd got arthritis in her fingers, and must be pushing eighty, though she swears she's sixty-five. I've had three complaints already, just this week, and a pile of work mounting up. If you need work, my love, I've got it – loads of it – and you can do most of it at home, without having to trek out to some bloody great hotel where they'll probably only treat you like a skivvy.'

Hilary flushed. It would sound just too pathetic to say, 'I haven't got a home.' She thanked Di instead, told her she'd love to have the work and could fit it in in her spare time, evenings and weekends.

Di frowned. 'No, the shop's shut then, and I'll need you there occasionally – you know, for fitting customers. Anthea and I do the simple things like pinning up hems, but if someone wants a garment more or less remade, then we need an expert on the premises. Even fitting can be tricky, as I'm sure you know, judging where to make a tuck, or when to take a seam in.'

'Yes, of course.' She hesitated. 'But I'm afraid I need a live-in job as well, something residential. I could try to do them both, but . . . '

'Are kitchen porters residential? Surely not?'

'Well, no . . . ' Hilary pushed her cup away. There was so much to explain. Miss Pullen, the Job Centre, her lack of any training or experience, her need to rent a room. She tried to compress her whole dismal endless day into just a few brief words. Di cut through them.

'Don't worry. You can have my old room here. I hardly ever use it any more. It's full of junk and stuff, but we can soon shift that. I'm sure Mum can find you some work as well – you know, instead of rent, maybe. And what I pay you for the alterations will be cash in hand. Okay, it won't be a fortune, but at least you needn't declare it, or pay tax or anything.'

Hilary sat silent. She knew nothing about tax, felt highly nervous of moving to this household, meeting fussy wealthy customers in a fashionable boutique. And why had Liz said nothing? She probably didn't want her there at all – was annoyed with Di for putting up the scheme – if she'd even heard it. She wasn't listening any more, had moved to the far end of the kitchen where she was standing by the cooker, *tête à tête* with Ivan. She was obviously upset, still reeling from the quarrel, and probably hoping for a private word with Di. They'd all heard the front door slam, the shell-burst of an engine as Di's father drove away, the car horn like a final jeering taunt. She ought to leave herself, still felt in the way, someone who had walked into an explosive situation and was now preventing it from being sorted out. She leaned towards Di, kept her voice as low as possible. 'But how about your mother? She may not want me here. I mean, even now, I feel I'm . . . '

'You'll be doing Mum a favour.' Di crunched an ice cube, wincing as the cold shocked through her teeth. 'She's got far too much to cope with. She helps out at the shop at least three days a week, takes Stephen to and fro to school, has him half the evening, if I'm working late, and a good chunk of the holidays, as well. Then there's all the housework and the cooking. I mean, you could help with that, to start with. Do you drive, by the way?'

'No, I'm afraid I . . . '

'You can cook, though, I presume?'

Hilary flinched at all the questions starting up again. Why were contemplatives so useless? 'No, I've never really . . . '

'Well, at least you can sew, and frankly I'm quite desperate. Some of my customers drive me almost mad – want something taken up, then immediately let down again, or keep fiddle-faddling about every tiny detail. If you've been making clothes for twenty years, your God must have sent you here on purpose.' Di laughed, flicked her worm of ash into a saucer.

Hilary sat silent. *Had* God sent her here? Was this her new mission, to help this family, pray for it, try to reduce the strain on Liz? She wouldn't mind the housework, it was the shop which frightened her. When she'd made vestments, she'd never met her customers, just worked from measurements, and she'd always viewed her handiwork as something quite impersonal she created for the Church, not individual garments for individual vanities.

'Good God!' said Di, glancing at her watch. 'Is that the time? I promised Madge I'd pick Stephen up by nine and it's already quarter past.'

'Quarter past *nine*?' Hilary sprang up. In twenty-two years, she'd never once been late, or not without a really good excuse. Yet, in just the last two days, she'd twice kept Miss Baines waiting – and waiting hours and hours – with no real reason save self-absorption, thoughtlessness. She'd also broken the Great Silence once again.

Di was dragging on her coat, searching for her car keys. 'Are you late yourself? Well, don't look quite so frantic. I'll just fetch my poor kid, who must be longing for his bed, then run you back, right to your front door. And on the way, we'll talk about that job.'

8

'Is that all your luggage?' Liz picked up the two carrier bags, strode out to the car.

Hilary followed, nodding. It seemed a lot to her. Father Anstey had brought her round another jumble box, let her take her pick: his farewell present to her. She now had two good skirts, half a dozen jerseys, some matted, some quite reasonable; even a green mac which came right down to her ankles.

'Right, in you get. Chuck that clutter in the back and you'll have a bit more legroom. Sure there's nothing else to bring?'

Hilary wished there were, fought a sudden craving to rush back to the house, barricade the door and stay behind it. However much she'd hated Rosemont Road, it had been somewhere safe and sheltered, where she'd been free to hide away, avoid a lot of problems, including other people. The car swept round the corner and onto the main road, turned left for Wandsworth High Street. Was she a fool to stay at Liz's, with all those raucous voices, all those complications? Did they even want her there, or was Liz simply being kind, or giving way to Di's continued pressure? Whatever else, Di required her sewing skills, and had overridden all the other factors, including her own fears. She'd called round twice, once with Stephen, adding lures and bribes. She could have her own television, she needn't work weekends, except in real emergencies. Hilary felt embarrassed, over-cosseted. Were people who could sew so truly rare? Couldn't Di find someone else, someone much more suitable, who could cook and drive as well, and had somewhere of her own to live? Apparently not.

I should never have agreed, she thought, as they drew up outside the tall brick house, which looked bigger now, and somehow even threatening. She hadn't had much choice. She had phoned about the kitchen porter job, but it had gone already, taken by a male – and one who had two references, presumably. Father Anstey had found a worthy Catholic lady who'd agreed to take her in, but couldn't offer work. She'd be a charity case, eating someone's food, but giving nothing in return; still tied to a priest who saw her as a renegade. Yet she ought to live with Catholics, stay in touch with priests. Reverend Mother had just written to her again, a less stinging angry letter than the first, but pointing out that if she wished to take formal leave of absence, then she must be very

100

careful how and where she spent it. It should be a time of prayer, reflection; her most important task to discover what God planned for her, and she must therefore shun all company which might mislead her as to the value of her faith. She must also remain faithful to her vows. She was allowed to work, to keep herself, pay her bills, but must still observe the spirit of the vow of poverty, not deviate at all from her vow of chastity, and observe her vow of obedience in informing her superior of any changes in her lifestyle or her plans.

But did she really want just a leave of absence? She was almost sure already that she would never return to Brignor; couldn't face that life of ceaseless prayer again, when she had lost her sense of God; been tempted by such doubt and desolation, that every hour in chapel seemed a mockery, every act of faith a blatant lie. So why live as a nun still – least of all a hybrid nun, who had left the cloister, didn't wear a habit, but was still bound by ties of steel?

She must obviously go further still, ask for dispensation from her vows. No! Impossible. It was just too terrifying, painful – above all, far too final. Supposing she didn't make it in the world? She hadn't done too well yet, and things could get still worse. Di might find her hopeless with the customers, or Liz resent her presence in the house. She might fall ill again, or even have a breakdown; be out of work or starving, forced to change her mind, crawl back to Brignor on her knees, and beg for readmittance. Even well and working, she couldn't seem to break the tie with Mother – who'd been not just mother, but God's deputy, His whip; the superior you knelt before, to confess your faults and failings, the mistress you obeyed, instantly, invariably. She longed now to kneel in front of her, be forgiven, back in favour, an obedient child again. Yes, too much a child. She seemed to need approval for everything she did, still dreaded Mother's anger, knew she'd disapprove of this move to Cranleigh Gardens, were she aware of all the facts.

She felt worse as she walked in, met Della in the hall, her hair a different colour from a week ago, but the eyes as cold and piercing as before. Even here, she was still a charity case, whatever Liz pretended, still one of her lame ducks, at least in Della's eyes.

'So you're our fun new lodger?'

Wrong on both accounts. She'd forgotten what fun was, and lodgers all paid rent – a lot of rent in London, so Father Anstey said. Liz hadn't mentioned rent, and Di had simply shrugged it off, said they'd talk about it later. She followed Liz upstairs, noise and voices fading, as they reached the top floor of the house.

'This is your room, love. I'm afraid I haven't cleared it out yet. I've been up to my eyes this week, but at least the bed's made up, and I've turned the heating on. It's really nice and warm now.'

Hilary stood, marvelling, at the door. A large untidy room, with real carpet on the floor, and wallpaper, not paint, the sort of formal stripey wallpaper you only got in sitting-rooms. And two lamps with frilly shades, and mirrors, mirrors, reflecting three or four of her. She tried to dodge their stare. This couldn't be her room. Even as a child, bedrooms had been plain – plain and simple, plain and cold. This room was tropical.

'Di'll be round tomorrow and she can sort out all this clobber. I don't know why she leaves it here, when she's got her own big flat. Mind you, that's chock-a-block as well. She always was a hoarder.'

Liz was opening all the drawers, trying to find one empty, squashing up the dresses in the wardrobe, to make an inch of space. Hilary followed, dazed. She'd never seen so many clothes – clothes of every sort and style, from boiler-suits to evening gowns, fur coats to bikinis. It felt wrong to hang her sludge-green mac beside a lurex cocktail dress, to put her blue school knickers in a drawer with satin briefs.

Liz was handing her some towels, huge coloured towels with ships on; fetching soap and toothpaste. 'If there's anything else you need, just shout. Okay?'

'Okay.' The word was difficult, not one she'd used before. But she'd have to change, to modernise, if she was going to live in this house.

'*Ciao*, then. Come down when you're ready and I'll show you round the house.'

The house-tour hadn't started until midnight. Too much else had happened in between: a constant stream of visitors, including Della's father; two meals, one cooked by Liz, one an Indian takeaway; and a crisis at the shop, when someone rang to say the burglar alarm was wailing and had there been a break-in? It was now after one a.m. and Hilary was exhausted. Even talking was an effort, the constant need to think up things to say, or find answers to their questions – though there hadn't been as many as she'd feared. Liz had probably warned them all to keep off dangerous subjects, not mention nuns at all. Was she a joke to them, a weirdie, someone even threatening, a sort of witch or killjoy? It was so hard to un-become a nun. She'd spent years and years becoming one, going through the training, studying the Rule. Now she had to undo it all, but without the help she'd had before, without a Mother Mistress to provide the guidelines, correct her every lapse. She had also learnt to smash her personality, erase every thought or fancy which might distract her mind from God. The process had been arduous, demanded total concentration and commitment. But now she *needed* thoughts and viewpoints; required a personality, a 'self'; was expected to contribute to every conversation, have ideas on every subject. The reversal was confusing, left her floundering and dazed.

She'd gone pretty wrong already, not known who people were – pop singers and sports stars, whom everybody else knew, everyone save nuns. It was also odd, apparently, to have never tasted Indian food before the age of thirty-nine, to think poppadoms were flowers. The day had seemed so long, so totally unstructured. She'd kept fighting down the urge to creep away, obey the bells she still heard in her head, follow her own timetable, as she had done at Miss Pullen's, even say each Office. Today was January 21, the feast of St Agnes, Virgin and Martyr, a young girl of only twelve or so, who'd been stabbed in the throat for standing up to Roman persecution, refusing to yield the treasure of her maidenhead. She had acted out her life when she was a child of twelve herself – had loved that strange word 'maidenhead' –played all the parts in turn: the cool and saintly Agnes, the mocking Roman soldier with the knife, the shocked and weeping parents. They hadn't mentioned parents in her Children's Book of Saints, but she'd invented them herself, making them quite different from her own; the mother noble-born, the father quiet and gentle, both idolising, devoted.

Today's Office of Readings praised Agnes's steadfast chastity, the courageous way she spurned mere earthly suitors. 'He who chose me first shall possess me. Why do you delay, executioner? Let this body perish which could be loved by eyes I do not desire.'

She missed her breviary. She could remember many of the psalms, but not all the prayers and readings for specific days and feasts. She had hardly had a chance to say any of the Office today; felt deprived, excluded from the Church's public prayer. She had always loved the thought of being part of that great work of prayer – priests and religious in every country of the world, stopping at the same set hours to recite the same words of praise or supplication.

They are happy, whose God is the Lord,
the people He has chosen as His own.

She switched off the main lights, kept just the bedside lamps on – though it was more the mirrors she needed to turn off. She kept seeing her own body, walking into it, wanting not to see it, yet somehow fascinated. Whatever else, she had to see her bra – Della's bra, a lacy one with a tiny pink rosette where the cups joined in the front. She took her dress off, stood staring at her chest. It had felt odd at Miss Pullen's to be without her swaddlings; odder now to feel her breasts supported. She could no longer fear they'd disappeared, or been hacked off by a surgeon, when they were cradled and defined in stiff white cups. Della had asked her why she didn't wear a bra. Had she burnt it, or was she still living in the sixties? She hadn't understood, just been horribly embarrassed. Stephen was listening, a boy of six, a male, and they were talking about brassières. Liz had rescued her, as usual, changed the subject, come up later to her room with one of Della's bras.

'This may fit. What size are you?'

She'd no idea. She hadn't seen a bra in twenty years, couldn't remember sizes from the scant eleven months she'd worn one as a schoolgirl. She fumbled for the hooks. She'd lost that knack of reaching up behind, fastening or undoing it without being able to see, which must seem second nature to most women. At last, she got it off, glanced at her bare breasts, which seemed blatant, far too large. Nuns were always warned not to look at their own bodies, almost to disown them. It still felt very wrong to be examining herself, noting the pink circle round each nipple, the way the skin was slightly puckered there, as if someone had sewn it up too tightly, then ripped the stitches out, leaving faintish marks. Her nipples were a deeper pink, standing up like tiny snouts.

Her eyes went lower, gazed with fascination at her legs – tanned and sheeny in the sheer nylon tights which Liz had given her. The tights felt strange, confining, like clingfilm on her legs, and were also quite tricky to put on. She'd succeeded with the left leg, rolled it to the thigh, but the other one had twisted and she'd had to start again. It seemed easier to take them off, though she was terrified of snagging them. None of her clothing had ever been that delicate. Convent clothes were always thick and practical, even underwear. She removed the blue school knickers, stole a brief and guilty glance at her quiff of pubic hair. It looked fairer than her head hair, seemed alive – standing up and springy, glinting in the light. Yet she was blushing as she glanced at it, ashamed of this new interest in her body, aware still of the Abbess, as if Reverend Mother were watching through the ceiling, her face a mask of horror and distaste.

She pulled on the pyjamas, to hide and clothe her nakedness. They felt strange, as well. She had never worn pyjamas, not even as a child. These were, in fact, a child's pair – Della's once again. Della had outgrown them at thirteen and a half; was now seventeen and five foot ten. Hilary stood up straighter, wished she had that height. The pyjamas were bright scarlet with a Snoopy on the front – another word she'd learnt today, along with dreadlocks and chapattis. Yet, despite the Snoopy, she was a woman, not a child; her thighs defined by the tightly clinging fabric, her breasts pushing out the dog's droopy comic ears. The colour seemed quite startling after twenty years of black. Black for mourning, death; death to the world, death to womanhood. Red was Della's colour, red for anger, danger. She was scared of Della's sharpness, tried to understand it. Perhaps the girl felt neglected, with her father gone, her mother always busy. Did she resent the way Liz spread her love and time beyond the family, treated Ivan's pupils as her daughters, or Luke as a spare grandson?

Luke was sleeping next to her in the small room at the back. She'd been to say goodnight to him, several hours ago.

'I didn't tell them, honest.'

'Tell them what?' she'd asked.

'That you was a . . . a nun.'

'I know you didn't, Luke.' She'd had to smile. He made it sound like something criminal, on a par with his own father's spell in prison. She had wondered about that, wondered why Luke stayed here, instead of at his own home. Liz had told her, briefly, that he was the last of seven children, years younger than the rest of them and obviously a 'mistake', born when his mother was almost forty-four – the age that Liz was now – and Liz had already been a grandma for six years.

'I married at just seventeen, you see, had Di two days before my eighteenth birthday. Then Di married at nineteen herself, and was already pregnant on her wedding day, with Stephen.'

Liz had told her that so casually, as if she were merely describing the bridesmaids or the dress. Disasters and disgrace were shrugged off in this house as just bad luck, just life.

'I suspect that's why her husband left. He never really wanted kids at all.'

'Oh,' she'd asked, embarrassed. 'Di's divorced, as well?'

'Well, only separated. Bill may come back, perhaps when Stephen's older. He's a freelance photographer, so he's always travelling anyway. He's in the Cameroons at present, doing some big thing on wildlife. *He* bought Di her shop. Bill was never mean, whatever else.' Liz sounded almost fond of him, certainly not bitter. 'It's a shame for poor old Stephen, though. Maybe that's why he and Luke are pals – Steve's Dad seven thousand miles away, and Luke's disappearing half the time. Luke's in Stephen's class, though he's almost a year older, should be in the form above. He got a bit behind, poor lad. His mother's always ill, and the old man's a queer fish – runs a scrapyard, among other things. They're Catholics – well, *she* is, anyway, which explains her seven pregnancies. Your Holy Roman Church has got a lot to answer for.'

Hilary had let that pass, feeling guilty, yet disloyal for saying nothing.

So Luke was a Catholic and had no idea what nuns were. Perhaps his poor, sick, worn-out mother had given up the struggle to instruct him in his faith. His school certainly wasn't Catholic, since she'd been told already that both he and Stephen attended the ordinary local primary school.

She knelt to say her prayers, to pray particularly for Luke, but she couldn't seem to concentrate, felt God was no more here than He'd been at Rosemont Road. Sleep was also just as difficult. Even with the lights off, she was aware of all the colours, all the objects, clutter, clothes, not just in this bedroom, but in each and every room. Liz's house was pretty but untidy; elegant but crowded, and all those busy objects seemed to have squeezed into her head. She couldn't shut them out, or block out all the people who still circled in her brain – Luke and his sick mother, or Bill, festooned with cameras, tracking tigers in the Cameroons; Liz's second husband, a tall fair man in jeans, who had popped in for an hour or so, showered Della with gifts. It seemed strange that he and Liz had once been married, intimate, in love. Liz treated him so casually, almost like another child or lodger. And yet he seemed at ease there, not so much an 'ex' as someone who belonged still. What happened if he met the first ex-husband? And why did either of them visit still? She had always thought divorcés kept apart, communicated only through lawyers or the courts.

She discarded two of the three pillows, usually slept without one, as a tiny nightly penance. The duvet was too pampering, far too snug and sensuous, pressing close against her, moving when she moved. All this luxury was wrong. Perhaps Reverend Mother was punishing her by preventing her from sleeping. No, that was quite absurd. She should be grateful that the Abbess was concerned with her at all. Ten years ago, another nun had left. There had been no farewells, no explanations, just an empty choir-stall, a spare place in the refectory at supper time. The next morning, in the Chapter Room, Mother had announced: 'The Lord giveth and the Lord taketh away. Sister Mary Damian went home last night and will not be returning. Now the order of work today is . . . '

Sister Damian had been professed for thirteen years; erased in just three seconds. The other nuns had been forbidden to discuss the matter, nor even mention Sister Damian's name, except in private prayers. Hilary had struggled to obey, tried to blot out the whole incident. Only now had it come surging back with renewed and poignant horror. She felt erased herself; nothing left of her save some brittle outward husk. That's why she couldn't sleep. She was trapped, not in a coffin, but in the cage of her own nothingness. Every time she closed her eyes, she seemed to tip into darkness, into void; lost any sense of self or even substance, as if she had dissolved like smoke, like vapour. She had to keep awake, in order to cling on to something else – something bigger, stronger. How did other people cope? Liz and her family had no religious faith, no God to give them hope or strength, yet seemed confident and cheerful nonetheless. Could a child make you stronger, or a boyfriend? Was that why Della was so tough, because three different boys were all in love with her; or Liz, because she had two daughters and a grandson?

She turned the other way in bed, removed the last remaining pillow. Liz had borne a child at seventeen, the same age that she herself had entered Brignor. How stubborn she had been then, seeing herself with what she called humility, as God's base instrument, required to do the work He wanted, ignore all other needs or obligations. In obeying God, she had disobeyed her parents – worse than that, had hurt them. And now it was too late – too late to make amends, tell them she was sorry, admit that they'd been right, that she'd made a huge mistake, wasted her whole life.

She remembered their first visit to the convent. They hadn't seen her for a whole six months, yet were allowed to stay for only half an hour, and couldn't take their tea with her; were ushered to a separate chilly parlour. Nuns must never eat with seculars, not even their own parents. Her father had been shocked by that, more shocked by the grille; said it reminded him of monkeys at the zoo – no, worse than monkeys – he was obviously a wild and dangerous animal, if he couldn't see his only child except through wooden bars. She had tried to laugh it off, told him it had been far stricter in the old days, when they'd had double grilles, two sets of bars, as well as a thick curtain, dividing nuns from visitors. It had been hard to say too much at all, with Sister Edwin sitting just behind her, acting as her chaperone. Chaperones had lasted well into the seventies, by which time her father was dead, and her mother's few brief visits were sadly silent anyway.

She sat up, put the light on, startled by the scarlet arm reaching for the switch. Did Della mind her wearing her pyjamas? She was still too preoccupied with Della, who seemed like the model for another sort of life – a life in the world, with lovers, clothes, possessions, a career. Della was training to be a beautician, hoped one day to open her own salon, rival her sister in running her own business, attracting wealthy clients. She'll succeed, thought Hilary, with a sudden stab of envy. She was old enough to be Della's mother, yet felt little more than seventeen herself – a shy and awkward teenager wrestling with the adult world. She'd never had a boyfriend, never tasted gin, knew nothing about make-up, fashion, business; had almost no experience of life. She had tried a drink

107

this evening – not gin, but sherry; found it bitter and unpleasant, was relieved to change to Stephen's Seven-Up. She must have drunk too much of that, felt a sudden urgent need to find the bathroom. She got up very quietly, scared of waking anyone, though only she and Luke slept on this top floor; Liz and Della just below, Ivan in the basement.

She was surprised to see a light on in the bathroom; stopped outside, uncertain what to do.

'Who's that?' a scared voice called – Luke's voice.

'It's only me. Can I come in?'

He didn't answer, so she pushed the door, saw him standing in the middle of the room in his stripey blue pyjamas, as if he'd been frozen there, rigid, for some time. 'Are you all right?' she asked.

'There's something in my room.'

'What? Spiders?' She remembered now he didn't like them.

'No. Something big.'

She hoped he hadn't found a rat. Surely not, in such a well-kept house. 'Shall I come and look?'

He nodded, followed her. The room looked much the same as it had done earlier – toys piled on the floor, posters on the walls, Luke's bed rumpled, Stephen's neat, unslept in. Stephen had gone back with his mother to their Putney flat; spent many evenings here, but rarely stayed the night.

'Where is it, Luke, this thing?'

'There,' he said, pointing to an empty patch of floor.

'I can't see anything.'

'No, you never see it, but it's there.'

Both of them were whispering. It felt sinful, almost wicked, to be talking in the early hours. She had grown so used to the Great Silence, that all this evening, after nine, she'd been fighting guilt and habit; kept wishing she could slip up to her room, escape the noise of television, radio, laughing chatting people. Silence seemed more natural – or had done back in Norfolk, where everything was hushed and calm at nightfall; birds no longer singing, fields and marshes muzzled by the darkness. But London was so different, lights blazing everywhere, traffic hooting through the night, six million television sets blaring out till closedown. She had envied Luke when he went off up to bed. Now she wondered if he'd slept at all. To be insomniac at thirty-nine was one thing, but at only six years old . . . No, he must be seven. Liz had said he was nearly a year older than Stephen. Yet he was smaller by a head. She wondered if he minded. She'd hated being small herself, called 'Titch' and 'Shrimp' at school, envying friends like Katy who could reach apples on the tree, ride a grown-up bike.

She glanced at him again. He looked so crushed and weary, the dark circles under his eyes like bruises on the pale and fragile skin, a Band-Aid on one thumb, the hands themselves half-lost in drooping sleeves. She longed to comfort him, find the magic words, those powerful mother's words which could banish spectres, horrors. Yet all she could recall were a few stern and stoic lines from the Office of St Agnes. 'She chose to love the Author of life alone; in the full flower of her youth she died and found life.' Agnes was always pictured with a lamb, the emblem of purity, virginity. '*Agnus Dei*,' she said suddenly, out loud.

'What?' said Luke.

'It's Latin.'

'What's Latin?'

'It's a language. They used to speak it long ago, in Rome. *Agnus Dei* means lamb of God. It's the beginning of a prayer for peace and mercy.' Would he know what mercy was – or even Rome? '*Agnus Dei*,' she repeated to herself. '*Qui tollis peccata mundi . . .* ' How could she translate that? A lamb who took away the sins of the world would sound peculiar to a child, unlikely to a lot of people. '*Miserere nobis.*' She realised only at this moment that she must have repeated that 'Have mercy' several times a day for twenty years. Had no one heard? Have mercy on this child, she begged again, in silence.

Luke was staring at her. 'Do nuns speak Latin all the time?'

'Oh, no,' she laughed. 'It's what they call a dead language.'

'Dead?' He looked alarmed.

'Not really dead.' She reassured him, reassured herself. She had hated it when they had swept away the Latin, changed to the vernacular – though unlike most other Orders, they still sang Vespers in Latin, still retained it for several of the anthems and the hymns, still had a Latin Mass each month. She had come to love the language; its economy, tradition, the sense of dignity and drama some words seemed to carry, which were only thin and flimsy in the English. Even *nobis* had a certain weight.

'*Nobis* means "us",' she explained to Luke, hardly knowing why, except she longed to share the language with him.

'How d'you mean, "us"?'

'Well, you and me.'

'We're "*nobis*"?'

'Yes.' That wasn't quite correct. She should tell him about cases – genitive and dative – but would he understand? He'd probably never learn Latin in his life. If not dead, then the language must be dying; almost no one left who would value it as she did: a doomed species, like most nuns.

109

She started to explain about declensions, heard herself sounding stilted, even boring, no use to him at all. This child was frightened, needed love and comfort, not some lecture on stuffy Latin grammar. He was still standing very stiffly, casting nervous glances round the room. Had he always had these fears? Did he miss his mother, worry that she'd die, or not return? Perhaps he'd had a nightmare and was still half-trapped in its clutches.

'Did you have a nasty dream, Luke?'

He shook his head, started pulling at the Band-Aid, gnawing his sore thumb. The silence seemed unkind. Liz would hug him, cuddle him against her. She herself stood rooted where she was, realised with horror that she had forgotten how to touch, couldn't even hold a frightened child. Another complex skill she didn't have. Her arms felt stiff and heavy, as if she were made of wood, not flesh. Could she actually be scared of a small boy? She was aware of the glass wall again, rearing up between her and other people, preventing any contact, even with a child. Her own fear was infecting him, as they both stood tense and silent. Now she, too, could feel that 'something big', that something black and dreadful, which you couldn't see, but was somehow always there. Everything looked menacing. The toy monkey on the bed seemed to be screwing up its face in pain; the lorry on the floor had crashed, lay bleeding on its side. She jerked to the window, drew the curtains close, eclipsing the thin moon, the slice of angry sky. She must pull herself together, try to act the mother. Liz might be annoyed if she encouraged Luke to stay awake or give way to his fears.

'You're shivering, Luke. Why not hop back into bed?'

He didn't answer, didn't move.

She sat down on the child's chair, a child herself in terms of her experience. Should she take a stricter line with him, or resort to bribes and blandishments, or soothe him with a story? Red Riding Hood? Hansel and Gretel? Wolves and witches weren't exactly soothing. How about the story of St Agnes? No. A martyr's death at twelve was even more unsuitable, would hardly help him sleep. She glanced around the room at the jumbled tide of toys, glimpsed a snakes and ladders board, trapped beneath a pile of other games. She had played that with her father when she was little more than Luke's age. Her father liked to win, took the snakes too seriously, as he'd taken everything too seriously in his short and serious life.

'Shall we play snakes and ladders, Luke?'

'What, *now*, you mean?'

She nodded. He rushed to fetch the board, collect up dice and counters, find the shaker. 'You're red, I'm blue, okay? Same as our pyjamas.'

'Okay.'

She threw a six almost first time off, went skimming up a ladder. Luke kept throwing ones.

'It's not fair.'

'Yes, it is.' Another six, another soaring ladder.

'You're cheating.'

'No, I'm not. I'm lucky.'

Luke kissed the dice, whispered something private to it, then threw a two, grimaced. 'Damn!' he shouted, ramming down the shaker.

'No, not "damn",' she told him. 'You're lucky now, as well. Two for joy.'

'What d'you mean?'

'It's just something people say. It comes from an old rhyme – about magpies, actually.'

'What's magpies?'

'They're birds,' she said, surprised he didn't know. 'Very handsome birds – black and white, with long and glossy tails.'

'And what's the rhyme?'

She collected up the dice, stowed it safely in the shaker. They appeared to have moved from snakes to birds, at least temporarily.

'"One for sorrow, two for joy,
Three for a wedding, four for a boy."'

'A boy?' he interrupted.

'Yes.'

'What d'you mean, a boy?'

'Well, a boy like you. If someone sees four magpies, all together, it means a boy baby will be born.'

'Did my Mum see one, then?'

She laughed. 'You'll have to ask her. What's her first name, by the way?'

'Rita. Why?'

'I thought it might be Margaret. That's what country people call the magpies.'

'What, Margarets? You're kidding.'

'No, I'm not. It got shortened into maggot-pie – then magpie.'

'I ate maggot-pie, once. We had it at our school. The meat had all gone wormy.'

She grinned, felt easy with this child, more relaxed than she had done all day long. 'It's not that sort of pie, Luke. Pie means pied.'

'What's "pied"?'

'Two colours – black and white.'

'You do know funny words.'

'So do you.'

'I don't.'

'Yes, you do.'

'What sort of funny words?'

'Well, trainers. What are trainers?'

He shrugged. 'Just shoes.'

'*Shoes?*'

'Yeah.'

'And what's a leotard?'

'Oh, girls wear those, not boys. For P.E. and stuff like that. Della's got one. It's a bit like a swimsuit.'

'And what's a Filofax?'

He shook his head. 'Dunno. Will you go on with that rhyme – the one about the maggot-pies?'

'I'm not sure I can remember it all. Where did I get up to?'

'Four for a boy.'

'Let's see. "Five for a christening. Six for a death."'

'A death? You mean, if you see six magpies, someone's going to die?'

'No,' she said quickly. Luke seemed too concerned with death. She tried to change the subject. 'They're dreadful thieves, magpies are. They love all bright and shiny things. In fact, they'd steal these counters if they ever caught a glimpse of them. Shall we get on with our game?' She shook the dice out, threw a two. 'Look, two for joy again.'

He watched her move her counter, scale another ladder. 'Your ring's got "Joy" on, hasn't it?'

She nodded. So he'd noticed that as well.

'Can I try it on?'

'I'm afraid it won't come off. It's stuck.'

'Let me see.' He tugged it, seemed impressed. 'Do they have rings with "Sorrow" on?'

'No,' she lied. 'They don't.'

She threw a four, shot up a long ladder, which took her almost to the last square on the board. She tried to suppress a surge of childish glee. She was winning, for a change. But it wasn't only that. It was really rather fun to be sitting with a seven-year-old, in the middle of the night, playing a simple but most satisfying game – a definite improvement on lying in the dark, fighting guilts and terrors on her own.

Luke threw a six, at last, went careering up a ladder, and then a second one, did a triumphant little war dance before passing her the dice. 'I'm really catching up now. You haven't got a hope.'

'Oh, yes I have! The game's over, more or less. This one's going to take me to the top.'

112

They both watched, breathless, as she threw a five, landed on a snake, a treacherous, scaly, slit-tongued snake, the longest on the board, which wound round and down, round and down, almost to the bottom.

Luke crowed with raucous laughter. 'I'm winning now. I'm winning! You're right back where you started.'

No, she thought, I'm not. The Thing had gone away, and both of them were very nearly happy.

9

At five a.m., Hilary crept out of Luke's room. They had played eleven separate games of snakes and ladders. She'd won five, he six. He'd been asleep since half past three, but she'd sat there with him, on the child's chair by his bed. He had begged her not to leave, asked her for more rhymes, then wanted rhymes in Latin; had finally closed his eyes to the *Salve Regina*.

It was now time for the Office, and later, Mass. Today was Sunday, so she couldn't miss it. She had already missed Mass on far too many weekdays, knew Father Anstey noticed. Mass should be the centre of the day. A priest had once described it as the precious jewel shining in the setting of the Divine Office, which reflected and enhanced it. And on the one and only occasion when their Brignor Mass had been cancelled, because the chaplain was unwell and his substitute cut off by ten-foot snowdrifts, Sister Clare had said, poetically, that it was as if the soul had departed from the day and left it with a dead body of mere hours.

Yet she herself felt increasingly distressed at Mass, an alien who didn't quite belong, who still couldn't take Communion. Father Anstey had noticed that, as well. It was a relief to be away from him, though she'd have to find another priest, have to go to confession. Every time she went to church, the confessionals obsessed her. She had knelt outside them, many times, but not yet found the courage to go in. She was terrified of questions which perhaps she couldn't answer. Was she truly sorry for having broken solemn vows? Was she planning to return? Was she doubting God still? Surely no priest could absolve her while she continued in her doubts.

Today she would be kneeling in a new and different church – St Agatha's – the nearest one to Liz's, which had a Sunday Mass at seven. At least that was a boon. She could be back by eight, ready to help with breakfast, be some use to Liz.

There were only fifteen people at the Mass, most on their own, and elderly. Hilary knelt, unnoticed, at the back, felt a strange relief in the gabbled hasty service; no sermon and no singing; the air of anonymity as people hurried out, set off home with no greetings or farewells. The priest himself had vanished, after his final 'Go in peace'. She'd hardly had a chance to see his face, try to judge how stern he was, how strict.

She was back in Cranleigh Gardens before the clock struck eight,

114

found the house still deathly quiet; the kitchen empty, stacked with last night's dishes, greasy and unwashed. She ran some soapy water, spent half an hour working through the pile, then laid the breakfast, put the kettle on. She was longing for a cup of tea, but there was still no sound from anyone and she didn't like to make it for herself. Liz had urged her to treat the place as home, help herself to anything she fancied, but that wasn't very easy after years of never eating outside formal meal times, never making snacks. Even at Miss Pullen's, it had seemed strange and somehow greedy to eat all on her own. A meal was always shared – with God as well as Sisters – always an occasion, however meagre the fare. And the price of food appalled her. She had never even thought of it before, never had to worry about best buys or value for money. Food was God's free gift to them, graciously accepted. But in the Kingsleys' home, it was the fruit of Liz's labour in the kitchen, Di's slaving in the shop.

She ran half a glass of water from the tap, sipped it very slowly, then went back to her room, passing all the other rooms with their closed doors, silent occupants. On Sundays, they slept late at Brignor – got up at six instead of half past five – spent Saturday preparing for the Lord's Day – cleaning the whole convent, baking bread, re-doing altar flowers. 'This is the day the Lord has made, let us rejoice and exult in it.'

By eleven-thirty, it was harder to rejoice. She felt weak and faint with hunger, yet no one had got up yet. She crept into the kitchen once again. The cereals looked wrong, lined up on the table when it was nearly time for lunch. She shook out a tablespoon of cornflakes, ate them dry, yet still felt guilty, as if she'd stolen them. She almost choked on the scratchy flakes, as the phone shrilled out, alarming her, as usual. She could never quite get used to that imperious ringing sound, kept expecting Reverend Mother, her cold contemptuous tones. She'd have to pick it up herself, since there was no one else around.

'Hallo,' she said, uncertainly. The voice was male – a confident and friendly voice, and one she recognised. 'No, this isn't Liz. She's still asleep. Yes, I met you just last week. Yes, Hilary.'

Ridiculous to feel so scared and threatened. It wasn't Father Anstey, or the Brignor chaplain demanding her return. Just that impetuous man she'd met at Liz's supper party – the one called Robert, who remembered her, surprisingly; seemed actually quite pleased to hear her voice.

'I'd love to chat, Hilary, but my damn car's broken down, so I'm phoning from a call box. Perhaps I'll see you later? Liz is expecting me for lunch, though I'm not sure if I'll make it now. I'm still forty miles from London, stuck in some God-forsaken village. Look, could you be an angel and go and shout for Liz, and could you make it speedy, because I'm running out of coins?'

She ran – forbidden – knocked on Liz's door. No answer. Knocked again.

'Who the hell is it? I was hoping for a lie-in. Okay, okay, come in.'

Liz was sprawled diagonally across her kingsize bed, half the covers off it, three cups and a wine bottle empty on the floor, clothes piled on two armchairs.

'Oh, it's *you*. I'm sorry. I'm so used to being jumped on by stray guests or nomad kids. If you've come to get me up for Mass, no thanks! Any religion mad enough to make claims on a woman's one free day won't get *me* as a convert.'

Hilary explained about the call, already fearing that Robert had been cut off. Liz sat up and groaned. 'Wretched Bob! I'd forgotten he was coming. I asked him weeks ago, and was really hoping he'd forget, as well.' She reached out for the phone extension. 'Bob, how rotten for you. Have you phoned for the AA? Yeah, I know they keep you waiting hours, but don't worry on my account. Make it supper, if you like. It doesn't matter, honestly. We haven't had our breakfast yet. Just relax and enjoy the view, until they come and bail you out. See you when you get here. 'Bye.'

She put the phone down, stretched and yawned. Hilary hovered at the door, uneasy at the thought of another rowdy supper, another encounter with a man who made her nervous, yet intrigued by Liz's room. That mixture of luxury and squalor was completely new to her: the smart white bedside television, the padded velvet chair, the pile of glossy magazines, the plants; yet everything messy and untidy – dirty clothes strewn across the floor, make-up jars without their lids, jumbled on the dressing table.

Liz switched on the television, shouted over it. 'Are you all right – found yourself some breakfast?'

'Er . . . yes.'

'If there's a cup of tea left in the pot, could you be an angel and bring it up? I'm useless in the mornings, and my tongue's just hanging out.'

'Yes, of course.'

Hilary made the tray as pretty as she could, used coloured paper napkins as a tray-cloth, cut the toast in quarters, chose a pink-flowered egg cup; flushed at Liz's pleasure as she laid it on her knees.

'Breakfast in bed? Fantastic! I haven't had that since Neville left. And you've remembered every tiny thing. Poor Neville always got it wrong. No salt for the egg, or a teapot full of water with no tea bags in. No, don't slink off like that. Have a cup of tea and stay and chat. There's a spare

116

cup on the floor.' She scrabbled for it, scoured it with a Kleenex. 'Shut the door, can you, there's a draught.'

Hilary shut it, feeling guilty as she did so. As nuns, they'd been forbidden to sit in twosomes with the door closed. Twos were always dangerous. 'The devil makes a third,' her old Mother Mistress always said. Walks in twos were equally forbidden, or even sitting next to the same Sister at recreation twice running. Occasionally, she'd seen two nuns get close, despite the prohibitions, but they were always punished, separated.

Liz lounged back on the pillows, smoothed a stretch of counterpane beside her. 'Come and sit here on the bed. I'll have to shout if you skulk there by the door.'

Hilary tried to keep her eyes down, as she perched stiffly on the bed. Liz's ample breasts were spilling from her nightdress; the soft hair beneath her underarms also on display, as she reached back to plump the pillows. The only naked flesh she ever saw at Brignor was hands and feet, and faces – and even faces were always half-concealed. She felt her gaze drawn back. Now she'd seen her own body, she somehow needed to look at someone else's – compare the two – make sure she hadn't lost some vital organ or appendage which other women had. Liz's body was fuller altogether, the breasts heavy, unsupported, in the skimpy black lace nightie; the bare arms chubbier.

Liz poured tea for both of them, handed her the cleaner cup. 'You look a bit washed out, love. Did you sleep all right?'

Hilary suppressed a smile, remembering Luke's great whoop of triumph as he won the final game. 'Yes, thank you,' she replied. She had learnt already that social lies were kinder than the truth, even half-expected in the world.

'Good. I was worried you'd be feeling rather low. It must be bloody painful leaving a convent after twenty years.'

Hilary nodded, tried to edge away. She still found those 'bloodys' worrying, and was far too close to Liz; could see the outline of her nipples beneath the flimsy fabric, smell hot body and stale scent. Liz seemed strangely different without her clothes and make-up – more vulnerable, yet larger, as if she'd spread and sagged. Her face looked paler, slacker, a private face, off duty.

Liz rapped her egg, unpeeled the shreds of broken shell. 'I suppose it's a bit like a divorce – something breaking up when you thought it was for life, and losing your routine, or even your reason for living. When Neville left, I really went to pieces, couldn't sleep, couldn't eat.'

'I'm sorry.' Hilary sipped her tea, longed to sound less distant, longed for Liz's gift of being instantly warm, immediately sympathetic. She was touched that Liz should talk to her, confide. She had never really thought about divorce, except as a general evil which needed constant prayer. Yet Liz, like her, would have broken solemn vows, vows made for life, sanctioned at a ceremony.

'When did Neville leave?' she asked, though the question sounded gossipy, intrusive, when she'd been trained so long not to indulge in personal conversation. But she'd never make a friend if she didn't open up and take some risks.

'Six years ago – though it seems more than double that. I kept delaying the divorce – just couldn't bear the thought of having two bust marriages. It felt like total failure.'

Hilary put her cup down. If Liz was a failure, what did that make her? Liz could drive and cook, ran this whole big household, coped with all the crises and the bills, had brought up two daughters largely on her own. Gloria Swanson had been married and divorced five times. As a prig of seventeen, she had been shocked by that, disgusted. Now she began to see the pain in it.

Liz dipped her toast in egg yolk, sucked it like a child. 'Once the divorce was final, I went back to my maiden name. I suspect it was a fear thing, really – wanting to be a little girl again. The problem is, Kingsley doesn't feel like me – not any more. I outgrew my parents long ago, all their petty values, all they stood for. But then I couldn't be Buchanan, either. That was Neville's name and Neville had pissed off. I've had too many names, I suppose. I was Mrs Carr to start with. Yet Mrs Carr's been dead and gone for years. Then Mrs Buchanan died, as well. Now I'm Mrs Kingsley, which is crazy – Daddy's wife, instead of Daddy's little girl.'

She licked butter off her fingers, took a swill of tea. 'Perhaps we ought to choose our own names, when we come of age. I had this girlfriend once, called Heather, and she joined some Eastern sect or other – started signing letters with what looked like gibberish, but meant "free and running antelope".' Liz made a face, grimaced. 'She was thirteen stone at least, couldn't run a step to save her life, but she said the name expressed her new self, her new way of looking at the world. The trouble is, when *do* we come of age? They say it's twenty-one, but I was still a booby then, and not much better now, at forty-three. We probably only grow up on our deathbeds, and by then it's far too late. Unless you believe in the afterlife, which I presume you do, Hilary. Nice to choose a name for heaven and keep it for eternity. I'd choose something classy, or maybe something pious, so I'd get good treatment from the saints.' She laughed, spooned out a last white curl of egg. 'Della changed her name, you know. We christened her Jane – my choice, actually – but she didn't like it once she got into her teens. Plain Jane, she thought, and no way was little Madam going to be plain. She was mad about make-up, even then, spent all her pocket money on eyeliner and lip gloss. She chose Della after Della Montefiore – you know, the singer.'

'Er . . . no.'

'She was all the rage two years ago. Then she was killed in an air crash, which was ghastly for poor Della – though she kept the name. The only problem is, she'll probably loathe it later. It's a sort of trendy name which is bound to date and won't fit her when she's older. I chose Jane specially, because I thought it was a classic.'

Hilary shifted on the bed, felt a sudden bond with Della, a new secret sympathy. Gloria and Jane.

'Want this piece of toast, Hilary? Before I pig the lot? No? I'll have to force it down myself then.' Liz larded it with marmalade, talked through her final mouthful. 'What was *your* name as a nun?'

'Hilary.'

'Oh, I see, you kept it. Do you still feel like a nun, then?'

I am a nun, she almost said, bit it back in time. What else could she call herself, when she was neither wife nor mother, not a beautician or a dress-shop owner, not an Alexander teacher? 'Spinster' was the only word which fitted, and that sounded cold and prudish. Or perhaps an alterations hand, except she hadn't started yet. Liz was still waiting for an answer. 'It . . . It takes a while to throw it off,' she said.

'I bet it does.' Liz wiped her mouth, flicked toast crumbs off the sheet. 'I think you ought to work out who you are. Oh, I don't mean your identity, or heavy stuff like that, but just your style, your image – what clothes you want to wear, how you do your hair – all that sort of thing. One advantage of today is that we're free to choose, as women, far more so than in the past, when fashion was more or less dictated. We can be ourselves nowadays, but first we have to choose which self we want, how we want to look.'

Hilary sat silent. Liz made it sound as if there were a variety of selves, each waiting to be fleshed and clothed, whereas she herself could hardly scrape up one.

Liz hitched up her nightie. 'I had to do the same myself.'

'You?'

'Oh, yeah. I started to go grey when I was only twenty-nine, so I had to decide whether I'd just shrug and let it happen, wind up old and faded, or get busy with the hair dye. It's not just a question of how much it costs in time and cash – though that's a factor, obviously, but of how one sees oneself. Am I still an attractive woman, in the running, so to speak, available to men – all that sort of thing. And even if the answer's "yes",

119

you've still got to decide what *sort* of attractive woman – glamorous, or girlish, or maybe just maternal. It's damn hard work deciding to be glamorous. Look at Di. She has to watch her weight every second of the time, keep her eye on fashion, so she's always way ahead of it; never be seen without her make-up, or wearing last year's style. It's not so bad at her age, but once you're over forty, it's a constant running battle against nature. Though even at Di's age, I had to fight nature. I had that awful frizzy hair, the sort that's like wire wool, and I wore glasses at thirteen.'

Hilary looked up in surprise. Liz's hair was only slightly wavy and she'd never seen her in glasses, not even for reading. 'But . . . '

'Hair-straighteners, my love, and contact lenses. The trouble is, it all becomes a sort of trap. No one's seen me in thick specs or with a mop of frizz on top, so I've got to keep up the illusion, so to speak, or they may not like the real me, or even recognise it. I sometimes long to revert to nature – grey wire wool, granny specs, the lot.'

Hilary glanced again at Liz's hair – semi-straight, glossy brown. That fight against nature was not so very different from the training to become a nun – the same remaking of the self, the same constant battle with one's faulty raw materials, the same striving for perfection, transformation. Would she have to do the same herself, take a second training to fit her for the world? But what image could she choose? Glamour was beyond her, and 'maternal' quite impossible when she'd never mothered anyone.

Liz poured the last dregs from the teapot. 'Mind you, even really famous people like film stars, or top models, seem to battle just as hard. They say Marilyn Monroe was constructed piece by piece, rather like a car or plastic dummy. Her hair was dyed, her name invented, her jaw rebuilt, her voice desqueaked, and she was pumped with anti-ageing hormones as early as her thirties. By the way, how old are you? You don't mind me asking, do you, Hilary?'

'No, of course not. I'm thirty-nine – just.'

'You can't be! You look years younger than that. It's not fair. Nuns seemed to lead charmed lives. I read somewhere that they live longer than the average woman, have less cancer, fewer heart attacks, and far less mental breakdown. It must be all that peace – unless it's anti-ageing wonder-pills like Marilyn's!'

Hilary laughed, said nothing. Sister Louis Marie had died of cancer; so had Sister Edwin. Several of the nuns had heart conditions, took pills in handfuls with their meals, not to stop them ageing, but to stop them dropping dead. She herself had felt perilously close to breakdown, as she'd knelt in what might seem like perfect peace to Liz.

Liz was leaning out of bed, trying to glimpse her face in the dressing table mirror, smoothing out the lines which ran from nose to mouth, as if she could erase them. 'I'd go on hormones myself, if it wasn't for the side effects. Every treatment seems to have its risks. Hair dyes give you cancer, sun beds ruin the skin . . . That's what really bugs me about the beauty business. Half the things they push are either bad for you, or completely bloody useless. A dermatologist told me once that all the fancy claims they make for facials, or cosmetics, or those wonder slimming treatments, are just a load of gobbledegook. And yet my own daughter's in the business – selling women things which waste their hard-earned money, or actually do harm.'

Hilary glanced up at her own face, still obsessed by mirrors. She knew nothing of the beauty business, yet she had noticed already how hard it was in other fields to tell truth from lies and sham. People in the world seemed to have a special knack of reading things in advertisements or newspapers, and sorting wheat from chaff; shrugging off the mirages and make-believe, the glitter and the guile. She herself found it much more difficult – the obedient nun, who swallowed everything, who'd been trained in faith, not scepticism; taught to accept unquestioningly what people said, be they Pope or priest, abbess or superior – and now politician, advertiser, beautician. She looked down again, aware of Liz's eyes. Liz was studying her, frowning, trying to appraise her face and figure.

'You know, if I were you, Hilary, I'd go for Laura Ashley.'

Hilary fiddled with the fringed end of the bedspread. Another name she didn't know. A friend of Di's, perhaps?

'She'd even suit your background – innocent and wholesome, all that sort of stuff. It's amazing how that shop's caught on – sham again, I suppose. We're all crying for that cosy world where Nanny always tucked us into bed, and girls were sweet and virginal, and we still made hay with scythes, instead of combine-harvesters. They had a window display this summer, with yokels in smocks leaning on their pitchforks, and frilly girls picnicking with hampers among the buttercups. All the city secretaries who work in high-rise office blocks, with plastic wipe-clean plants, were snapping up the flower-prints. We'll go there, if you like, pick out something pretty. Or perhaps you ought to speak to Della first. She's got a gift for finding people's styles. She's already said how she'd love to do your hair, cut it sort of urchin, put some highlights in.'

'Highlights?'

'Blonde streaks. She's right. Your hair's a lovely colour, but the highlights would make more of it, really bring the fairness out.'

'But I thought you said hair dyes give you cancer.'

Liz laughed. 'Streaks are only little bits, so I shouldn't think they

121

count. Anyway, it's worth it. Women take worse risks than that, in order to look good. I mean, think of plastic surgery, or even high-heeled shoes, which sound innocent enough compared with surgeons' knives, but which cause all sorts of ghastly foot deformities. You're very lucky, actually. You look pretty good already without hair dyes or high heels. Your skin's fantastic, and you haven't got a single grey hair, or not one that I can see.'

Hilary turned back to the mirror, as if to check on Liz's words; realised she was smiling, a happy startled smile. She'd just received a compliment – her first in years and years. And even Della didn't see her as simply someone with a prison-cut.

'I envy you, Hilary, being able to start again, and with a sort of clean slate behind you. My life seems such a mess. Fights and rows and one-night stands with guys I hardly knew or . . . ' She broke off, made a little clatter with her cup and saucer, to cover her embarrassment. 'I'm sorry, love, forgive me. I'm so used to talking frankly with my mates, I keep forgetting I ought to watch my language. I suppose I'm just not used to nuns.'

Hilary mumbled some inanity, tried to analyse her feelings – a mixture of pleasure and annoyance: pleasure that Liz should speak so freely, trust her with these confidences; annoyance that she'd stopped halfway, obviously regarding nuns as sissies, who must be protected from reality. Yet didn't nuns bring that on themselves, hiding away in their prim and narrow cloister; referring to 'the world', which made it sound like some alien place they had transcended and condemned; praying for 'sinners', as if they were plaster saints themselves? If they were one with all the world, then they, too, were responsible for every sin committed, even the grossest, most revolting ones. So why had she shrunk at that coarse term, 'one-night stands', guessing what it meant from Liz's own reaction, feeling just a shudder of revulsion?

Liz shifted on her pillows. 'It's strange to think our lives have been so different. I mean, what makes a girl give up everything for God? I simply can't imagine it – or what it's like once you're locked inside with just a gang of women.'

Hilary said nothing. How could she explain that there were no bolted doors, no keys; that a nun entered willingly, with joy, a sense of honour that God had chosen her; that the grilles were only there to protect her from distraction, so that her whole mind and heart and purpose could be fixed on God alone; that you lived with God – and for Him – not with 'just a gang of women'. Liz wouldn't understand. Once you talked of God, you sounded preachy, sanctimonious. And there simply weren't the words. Supernatural concepts slipped through and past the language, like trying to package smoke in brown paper and string.

'Perhaps you'll tell me a bit about it sometime. I must admit I'm curious. I've always thought of nuns as sort of . . . ' Liz paused, seemed to be censoring a host of different words.

'Freaks?'

'*You* said it.' Liz laughed. 'Or maybe paragons.' Liz was fidgeting herself now, pulling at her shoulder straps, playing with her teaspoon. 'I know I shouldn't ask you, Hilary, but don't you often think about – you know, men and sex and stuff, wonder what it's like, what you're missing?'

Hilary held tight on to the fringe. 'No,' she said, almost to herself. Liz would think she was lying. Was she lying? She hardly even knew. The subject was too dangerous, and she had thought so long in nun's terms, followed the official line, there seemed no personal feelings left, no opinions of her own. She could tell Liz what the books said, the Rule, the Constitutions; that chastity was a glory, not a deprivation; that celibacy was part of poverty, and since nuns didn't own their bodies, they had no right to any pleasure from them. Their hearts and bodies belonged to God alone, and love of God was far higher than carnal or conjugal love. Yet terms like that would seem as strange to Liz as words like punk or Walkman seemed to her. And wouldn't it sound priggish and superior to repeat what they'd been taught: that marriage was of brass, virginity of gold?

She glanced down at her tights, still felt a shock of pride and sheer surprise that those blatant sheeny brown-gold legs could actually be hers; legs on show, and worldly. She had read spiritual books on temptations of the flesh, but her own trials at Brignor had centred on the mind: temptations against faith and hope, not stirrings of the body. She had managed to subdue the flesh, disown her body, or view it like a punch-bag; something dead which needed pummelling, attacking. Even now, if she tried to think of sex, her mind went almost blank, as if the years and years of censorship had become strictly automatic. One priest had advised them that if they ever had problems with what he called concupiscence, they were to think of men as merely a mass of bone and muscle, a collection of red and white corpuscles, a sack of coiled intestines. It had always proved effective.

A younger priest had taken a more jokey line, suggested that they view their sexuality as something like a spare tank on a car, which, as sworn non-drivers, they never had to use; simply carry but ignore. She thought back to her convent years. Had people disobeyed that priest, siphoned off their tanks? She doubted it profoundly. Liz probably saw the convent in very different terms from the cool and brisk reality. She had read accounts of nuns in Miss Pullen's daily papers, realised people viewed them as objects of desire; or suspected secret wild liaisons between nun and nun, or nun and priest; their outward primness masking raging passions. It simply wasn't like that. Most of the nuns at Brignor were now elderly, dried up; Father Martin seventy next birthday. Yet, even in their younger days, sex was something they'd deliberately and happily renounced, and not just as a penance, but a privilege.

She smoothed her skirt, clasped her hands, unclasped them. The silence seemed uneasy. Liz was waiting for an answer, some confession, revelation, more than just that muttered 'no'. Yet she couldn't give it, felt loyal still to her Order, was aware she'd gone far too far already, at least in Reverend Mother's eyes. Her embarrassment was catching. Liz, too, was looking down, making some pretence of tidying the breakfast things.

'Well,' she said, at last. 'I wouldn't mind another hour in bed, but I promised Tim and Jenny I'd meet them in the pub. Why don't you come along?'

'Oh, no. No thank you.' More names – Tim and Jenny. More strange faces, questions, more risk of breaking confidences, offending Reverend Mother. It would be bad enough tonight, with that boisterous Robert there – and probably several others – all drinking, laughing, arguing; plunging head-first into deep and turbulent subjects, while she stood shivering on the edge.

'Why not? You don't always have to hide away, you know.'

Hilary tensed. Miss Baines's phrase. She had left Miss Baines, Miss Pullen – two other joyless spinsters who saw Sundays as a day for only prayer and naps, piety and Complan.

'And have a drink for once, a proper drink with a bit of kick behind it. It'll help you to relax. Okay?'

'Okay.' Hilary nodded, collected up the tray, smiling to herself as Liz still yawned and groaned, unable or unwilling to pluck herself from bed. They'd been told as postulants to spring up in the morning at the first sound of the bell, as if their bedding were on fire and they were leaping from the flames. She had done it ever since. But poor Sister Mary Liz would have charred to a cinder seven hours ago.

'What? Speak up, Hilary. I can't hear a single word.'

Hilary tried to shout above the music, the roar of other voices, the sudden brays of laughter, yelled orders from the barman. Her throat felt hoarse already from the smoke. She barked her brief remark again, was

124

relieved when Tim looked satisfied, smiled and nodded at her. She forced a smile herself. Could this be pleasure? It must be. Everyone else was chatting and relaxing, downing drinks, tapping feet or fingers to the rhythm of the band. They were privileged, apparently, to be enjoying what was called a live group – five frightening-looking youths dressed in black leather jackets and blue jeans, who played a type of music she'd never heard before – wild insistent music, which seemed angry and alive, booming and slamming into every niche and corner of the pub, invading even her body, so that frantic drums were pounding in her stomach, hysterical guitars trapped and twanging right inside her skull.

She tried another sip of gin. It was worse than sherry, far worse – had an evil oily taste which lingered in her mouth, even when she'd swallowed it. Reverend Mother should buy some gin for Brignor, as a new and most effective penance. She giggled suddenly, startled by the sound. She must be careful or she'd land up drunk. They had bought her what was called a double; Liz insisting on 'the hard stuff', saying she mustn't be a party-pooper. More words for her collection. She was doing rather well with words. 'Okay' was easy now. She'd managed 'Hi!' to Tim and Jenny, and even 'great'. In just a day, she'd learnt the difference between a tee shirt and a sweatshirt, a tracksuit and a catsuit, and discovered Malibu, Cinzano and even Bloody Marys, though that name seemed so blasphemous she couldn't get it out.

She'd even learnt to look around, forget her usual 'custody of the eyes', which meant looking down, looking inward, keeping her attention on God and only God. If she were going to pluck up courage to ask for dispensation from her vows, then she'd better make some effort to learn to break the minor rules, at least. She'd seen an unsteady singing Scotsman spill two beers in turn, a woman feeding steak and kidney pie to her obese bull-terrier, and a passionate young couple kissing very publicly, their arms entwined, joined at mouth and groin. That she knew she shouldn't watch, yet her eyes kept flicking back to them, noting how his lips crushed into hers.

Sex kept cropping up today, and her strict internal censorship was crumbling. She realised she was wondering what it felt like – to be kissed like that, so roughly and intensely. She didn't think she'd like it. Men still seemed alien creatures – not Tim perhaps, or Ivan – but all the rest of them; all those raucous guzzling strangers at the bar, with their loud guffaws, their bellowed orders, the way they gulped their beer or shovelled in peanuts, spraying salt and foam, as they ate and drank and talked and laughed at once; used their hands to thump or grab or grope. She was fascinated, frightened, kept fearing they'd turn violent, like those scenes she'd watched on television, where men in bars suddenly smashed glasses – or each other – whipped out loaded guns.

She fumbled for her glass again, tossed back a generous gulp of gin with what she hoped was nonchalance, if not exactly relish. If this was Sunday in the world, well, she wasn't doing badly – though it did seem a waste of time. At Brignor, they'd have celebrated Mass, said a good half of the Office, spent two hours at Exposition, and another hour, at least, in spiritual reading; eaten dinner, washed it up, and she herself would be preparing the chapel now for Benediction. Tim and Jenny had only just got up, they said, never ate breakfast, and couldn't face lunch today, after something called a 'thrash' last night. They'd been Neville's friends from long ago, still stayed loyal to Liz – an easy-going, friendly pair, who had laughed quite loudly when she tried to make a joke, a feeble joke, which had sounded forced to her. She wished Sister Luke could see her – sitting in a real live pub, with a glass of gin in front of her and a man on either side. Yes, Ivan had come over, joined them at their table, told the others she had the straightest spine he'd ever seen and she ought to train as an Alexander teacher, set up as a rival.

'What *is* Alexander?' Hilary asked, at last. Gin made questions easier and she didn't have to shout now. The band were taking a break.

Ivan grinned. 'If you've got three hours to spare, I'll tell you – well, just an introduction. First of all, it was a who and not a what. Frederick Matthias Alexander, born in Tasmania, 1869, died in London, 1955 – praised by Aldous Huxley, Bernard Shaw, Colin Davis, Sir Adrian Boult, Lord . . . '

Liz groaned. 'Ivan, *no*! I've got to get back home and think about a meal. It's all to do with posture, Hilary – how you sit and stand and walk and breathe and everything. They're obsessed with backs and necks. I tried a few lessons myself and got so confused, I couldn't do the simplest thing like sitting on a chair, without feeling my head was in the wrong position, or my legs too bent, or straight, or . . . '

'You're telling it all wrong, Liz.' Ivan turned back to Hilary, drew his chair up closer. 'It's really all to do with how we use ourselves – you know, like using tools or instruments. You have to do it skilfully, learn the right techniques. If we rely just on our feelings, we can go completely wrong, because feelings spring from habit, and habits may be bad ones, which cause stress and even pain. Alexander started on himself. He was an actor, actually, a Shakespearian orator who kept losing his voice when he tried to go on stage.'

Liz split a bag of crisps open, passed them round. 'You can't explain in theory. It's far too complicated. It's a body thing, Hilary. The teacher uses his hands on you, to put your posture right, correct any part that's

126

stiff or out of line. Hey, Ivan, why not give Hilary a lesson, sometime when you're free? It'll make a lot more sense then.'

Ivan shrugged, seemed hurt. Hilary would have liked him to continue. She was intrigued by the thought of learning to use oneself; surprised to hear him say that one mustn't rely on feelings. At Brignor, too, feelings had been suspect, had always to be discounted. Yet this was 'a body thing', not soul.

Jenny brushed crisp crumbs from her skirt. 'I had a lesson once myself, but the teacher chap was really very formal – all dressed up in pinstripes and a watch chain, as if he'd come from Harley Street, or some swanky City bank. Forgive me being personal, Ivan, but why do your crowd look so weird?'

Ivan grinned, gestured to his own strange combination of loose multicoloured waistcoat over purple tracksuit bottoms. 'We believe in being comfortable, that's all. You can't do body-work in pinstripes – though the old school do, of course, and dear F.M. himself always wore a suit, and even spats.'

'I wouldn't say you're typical, though, would you, Ivan?' Liz shook out the crisp bag, retrieved a few last broken shreds.

'What's typical?'

'Well, take Keith Thompson. He's an Alexander teacher, but much less way-out than you.'

'And what's way-out? A very relative concept, and often a judgemental one.'

'Oh, Ivan! You're impossible.'

'No, I'm not. And anyway, it's really very simple. As far as I'm concerned, clothes reflect the spirit, and vice versa, so if you're imprisoned in tight belts and stiffened collars, you can't feel free or open. The way most people dress is only sheer convention. They're mostly far too scared to break the rules or differ from the herd. Yet people just don't realise how simple it is to dress the way they want, rather than be dictated to by fashion – which is only another name for tyranny and money-making.'

'Strong talk, Ivan! You should have brought your soapbox.' Liz drained her glass, stood up. 'You layabouts can stay here. I've got work to do – a meal to cook and about five full loads of washing. I don't know why I do my daughters' washing, when one's left school and the other's married.'

Tim lolled back in his chair. 'People wash too much these days. Labour-saving machines actually make more work. Jenny keeps bunging in my shirts to justify the expense of our new Zanussi Super. Then someone has to iron them.'

'Someone?' Jenny asked. 'I wonder who.'

'That's not the point. It's extra work, whoever does it. If I were female – which God forbid – I'd rather have dirty sheets, but more time to sleep on them.'

Hilary was tempted to agree, once she saw the pile of washing – almost spotless sheets and shirts, things worn twice, at most, yet all bundled into the dirty linen basket. She wouldn't dare confess to Liz that their Brignor habits were washed just once a year, and blankets every three years. (Sheets they didn't use at all, except in the Infirmary, and even those were rarely laundered, unless a nun had something contagious like mumps or shingles.) They had lived like sixteenth-century peasants who had to wash their clothes in ponds and streams. She was beginning to feel more and more extraordinary, a throwback to medieval times, who had been pitched into the present with all the wrong conditioning and customs.

'If you bring your washing down, Hilary, I'll bung it in as well.'

She stood rigid, unresponsive. She hadn't any washing, had been there just one day, couldn't bear anyone to see her underclothes; private things like knickers which might be stained or even smell. People were so open in the world – everything offered freely for inspection: feelings, sex-lives, underclothes. She had been private for so long; no one entering her cell, or mind; her whole life and body covered, under wraps.

'Look, let me help,' she offered, as Liz sorted clothes into piles of whites and coloureds. This was Sunday, so all work was forbidden, but Liz had called it woman's one free day, so why should she work, either?

'No, you sit down. You'll have enough to do tomorrow, once Di throws all those hems at you. Why not read the papers? We get three or four delivered every Sunday and they're chucked away unopened half the time.'

Hilary obeyed, although the papers seemed more a chore than washing, especially the fat Sunday ones with all their different sections, which made her feel so ignorant. She had tried to learn from them, but even that was tricky, since they assumed you knew so much already, were aware of the whole background to a story or an issue, and didn't need a child's-type introduction. There were such a lot of complicated crises – faction fighting faction for no reason she could grasp, and in esoteric places she'd never even heard of, or countries which had changed their names since she'd learnt them in the sixth form. Names, in general, were an endless shaming problem – so many people she ought to know, and didn't – not just heads of state and politicians, but chat show hosts, or leading lights in what were called 'the soaps', whom other people seemed to know as friends.

Their world at Brignor again had been medieval, restricted to their village and a few scraps of news from the bigger town beyond. She had prayed for places like the Middle East and Ireland, but they always seemed remote, not dragged into the chapel bombed and bruised and bleeding. Did people really need all that information, detail; all those gruesome close-up pictures of casualties or kidnaps? She'd found, even in her own case, that she was already becoming blasé, less shocked by atrocities, less outraged by injustice. When you saw so much of it, it seemed impossible to respond, each time, with quite the same pity and compassion. You could weep for one man's fate – your neighbour's, or your relative's, or your fellow villager's, but the bleeding millions left you still dry-eyed. And those blandly smiling newsreaders, who reported daily carnage without ever breaking down or displaying any emotion of their own, somehow made disaster more acceptable. A global village, they called it now, but a medieval village was simpler; heaven above, hell below, and a few simple Catholic peasants in between.

She refolded the *Observer*, picked up its colour supplement. Everyone inside it seemed confident and glossy, loaded down with things she'd never needed – cameras, cars, computers – complicated things again, which she knew she'd never master. Yet Della, at seventeen, could drive; owned a fancy camera, was learning word-processing on her boyfriend's Apple Macintosh – another strange new word she'd stored away. She flicked on through the pages – a cooking feature by a star she'd never heard of, who drove a hundred miles each week to get goat's cheese and fresh chervil; a fashion spread which forecast that women would have to change their shapes again, as curves went out and the Belsen Look came in. What had Ivan said? That fashion was tyranny and money-making. And yet Liz had claimed the opposite: that fashion left you free to choose – except then she'd talked in terms of 'fighting nature', complained of 'sham' and 'traps'; none of which sounded much like freedom. It was all most bewildering, and easier for Ivan, anyway, since he worked from home, didn't have to meet the sharp-eyed scrutiny of all those stylish customers, as Liz and Di did – she, too, in just a day or so.

She tried to drown her wave of apprehension by skimming through the bookshelves; soon overwhelmed again by the scores of things she didn't know – books on psychology and physics, politics and history, antiques and art and sculpture; books on aircraft, war, and stamp collecting; travel books and cookbooks. In their tiny Brignor library, almost every author was a devout and narrow Catholic, if not a priest or monk. Every tome led back to God, blinkered the community from knowledge of the world. Was that a good thing, or a bad – good because they avoided a tidal wave of information, much of which was peripheral, or petty, and which might well swamp them anyway, leave them still ignorant and helpless, distract them from their work of praising God; or bad because they remained too insular and narrow, cut off from the rest of humankind? She hardly knew – knew less and less, in one way, each day she spent outside the convent walls, despite the mass of so-called knowledge cascading into her ears.

She crossed the room, stood by the piano, an old Broadwood upright which no one ever played. She stroked the polished rosewood, saw herself reflected in its shine; not a middle-aged woman who had forgotten how to play, but a young girl in her teens, working through the Mozart sonatas, practising for hours, bringing the same obsession and perfectionism to her music as she'd brought to her religion. The two were linked. Music led to God. She'd assumed as a child that people always sang in heaven, rather than merely spoke; that if you asked for manna or a halo, you must set your request to music, make it soar; that God Himself spoke, not in words, but music, in chords and cadences, a whole orchestra booming through His voice.

Her fingers itched to play again, yet she didn't even lift the lid. Her skill in music had been rendered back to God at the age of seventeen, and she'd no right to reclaim it. It had been hard, at first, extremely hard, and she'd always hoped secretly that she would be allowed the job of organist. When she'd entered as a postulant, a nun called Sister Dimpna had held that envied post. Wrong to criticise; brazen and conceited to assume she was more skilful on the keyboard than a nun of sixty-five, but all the same she'd longed to make the music breathe and kindle, provide the feeling Sister Dimpna lacked. After seven years or so, her longings faded. Sister Francis Xavier was now the organist – competent, no more – but Sister Mary Hilary had more pressing problems than how to shape a phrase or pace a cadence.

She turned her back on the piano, as if renouncing it again, sat by the window watching the slight movement in the bare branches of the sycamore. Doing nothing was an art, and one she hadn't mastered. For twenty years and more, every minute of every day had been rigidly accounted for, so no nun would ever idle, doze or daydream. She looped the curtains back, missing the wide sweep of Norfolk skies.

'Are you all right, my love? You look the picture of misery, perched on that hard chair and staring into space.' Liz had sauntered in, carrying a tray with a bottle and two glasses. 'Liquid lunch today. We'll have the

130

beef this evening, once Bob's here – or Robert, I should say. He was Bob for years, you know. No wonder I get muddled. Names again.' She shrugged. 'I sometimes wonder, if I'd stayed Elizabeth, my whole life would have been different. Or maybe Beth. Beths are always demure, marry the right men, get looked after and protected, then finally expire sweetly and courageously, with a throng of grief-choked mourners round their bed.' She poured two glasses of something pale and yellowish, set them on the coffee table.

'Have this chair. It's really nice and comfortable. That's it, put your feet up. Relax and drink your wine.'

'But can't I help, or . . . ?'

'No, really. I know I should be cooking, or at least peeling spuds, or something, but the meal can wait a while. It's so rare to have the house to ourselves, we ought to make the most of it. Della's out with friends, and Di's taken Luke and Stephen to some Fun-Day thing at Battersea. Rather her than me. Cheers! Here's to peace and quiet, good French wine, and Sunday afternoon.'

Liz sprawled back in her chair, cupped her wine glass in both hands. Hilary tried to copy her, though she was highly nervous of drinking any more. She'd moved from a lifetime of non-drinking to a double gin and half a pint of wine in just one day. It was also hard to sprawl. She'd spent months as a novice learning just the opposite, not to run, stretch, wriggle, fidget, slouch. Both the long skirts and the Rule had helped to slow her down, restricting all her movements, limiting her freedom, both physical and mental. She hadn't sat on a sofa or armchair for at least two decades. There was no single chair at Brignor that wasn't hard and wooden, and at Miss Pullen's she'd avoided all upholstered seats, partly out of habit and partly as a penance.

Liz passed her some pistachios, took a handful herself. 'It's odd that Robert hasn't rung again. I suppose he must be stranded in his car still, waiting for the AA. Poor sod! He'll have all that time to ponder on life's miseries. He's usually a very positive sort of chap, but this last month, he just hasn't been himself. God knows what's the matter – he'll never say, just arse about in company and pretend he's on top form, but I always seem to pick it up when he's going through a bad patch. It's like I've got antennae.' She reached out for a cushion, made herself more comfortable. 'Mind you, I really got annoyed with him last week. He was drinking far too much, and then pinching Sue from under Philip's nose like that, when he's well aware how jealous poor Phil is. It's stupid, really. He gives quite the wrong impression, when underneath he's a very serious decent guy who cares passionately about things. I mean, I bet you didn't like him?'

131

Hilary flushed, swallowed her pistachios too fast. 'Oh, yes, I did.' Another social lie. 'What does he do?' she added quickly, to make the conversation more impersonal. 'For his job, I mean.'

'Well, he trained as an architect, and was doing bloody well, in fact, once he'd got a partnership, but then after a few years he suddenly jacked the whole thing in, said he hadn't any scope to follow his ideals, and all the other partners in the firm were just soaking up Arab cash by churning out these monstrous swanky palaces in the Middle East – you know, for diamond-studded oil sheiks. Well, that was true, of course. Lots of firms were doing the same thing – cashing in on the oil boom and making a quick killing in places like Bahrain.' Liz removed her cushion, pummelled it a moment, then put it back behind her. 'I must admit, I admire him, in a way. I mean, people called him a total bloody fool, but it must have taken guts to start again from nothing, after all those years of training and when he was earning a good screw. I know this sounds crazy, love, but there's a part of Bob which reminds me of *you*. I can't put it into words, exactly, but it's something about ideals, I suppose, or maybe . . . Oh, I don't know.'

She shrugged, as if embarrassed, seemed to change the subject. 'Funnily enough, his first big commission, way back in the seventies, was to build a Catholic church. Christ! He sweated blood and tears to get it right, must have worked through a dozen different schemes. He wanted the whole building to be a sort of . . . meditation – I think that was the word he used. The church was called St Bridget's and he mugged up her whole life, tried to express her spirit in his structure.'

'Is he a Catholic then himself?'

Liz laughed. 'God, no! An atheist, I think, now. He dips into religions like other people try new beers. He's been through his Buddhist phase, flirted with the Quakers, once, got hooked on T.S. Eliot for a while – you know – why and how he became an Anglican and the effect of the religion on the poetry. Last time we discussed it, he was full of some fantastic book he'd read, on how Hindu harvest rituals affected Coptic art. No, that can't be right, can it? Never mind, he'll have changed his mind anyway, by the time I've got it straight.'

Hilary forced a smile. The man still sounded frightening, would trap her with more questions, confound her with his learning, and whatever Liz might claim, she couldn't see the slightest similarity between an unruly six-foot atheist ex-architect, who gobbled art and poetry when he wasn't chasing girls, and a five-foot-nothing nun, whose intellect and love-life had both been amputated. Could she escape the meal tonight, plead a headache, say she wasn't hungry?

She was starving, actually; drank her wine too quickly, as if it could fill the hole, relishing its sharpish, almost fruity tang – the first alcohol she'd liked so far. She let her neck and back relax, aware that she'd been holding them too tightly. Liz was right. She needed to let go, allow herself one day off, at least. She glanced around the room, its mixture of untidiness and stylishness, which seemed the hallmark of the Kingsleys. She'd been untidy as a child, but nagged and chivvied out of it, and once a nun, neatness was the rule; a rule applied to everything, be it bed or cell or habit, or each and every convent room. There was something rather appealing about the clutter on the sideboard, the books disordered on the shelves, one of Stephen's games still set up behind the sofa; yet the furnishings themselves so tasteful and sophisticated: the use of creams and oatmeals with a sudden splash of orange, picked up in the amber of the huge dried flower arrangement which stood in the old fireplace.

Liz was kicking off her shoes, curling one foot underneath her, a plump black-stockinged foot. 'I haven't answered your question yet: what does Robert do? To be truthful, love, I'm not exactly sure these days. He's done so many things, you see – building, teaching, dabbling in antiques, writing articles for journals, and buying and selling everything from wine to railway stations. He even ran a diving school in Crete, once, and took English tourists on trips to Turkestan. He's been all around the world, even camped in swamps and jungles, or so he always claims. It's a bit like the religions – nothing fixed or permanent. Though he's much more settled now, in fact. He's been living down in Sussex for the last eighteen months or so, running some weird commune; shares this huge old house with a bunch of artists and musicians, and a few oddballs and dropouts, to make the numbers up.' She grinned. 'Rather him than me. Though I suppose even that's quite brave, shows spirit, don't you think?'

Hilary nodded, tried to think up some reply, or perhaps another question. She had learned already it was important to keep talking. Silence in the world was considered rude, not holy. But the drink had made her sleepy, lulled and numbed her mind. She closed her eyes a moment, savouring the two new tastes – pistachios and wine; relishing that novel sense of dizziness which made everything seem just nicely slightly blurred. The new words on the bottle were jumbling in her head; words they'd never taught her in her French lessons at school: *Vouvray, Clos du Bourg, Appellation Contrôlée*. She started at a new and deeper voice – Ivan's voice – Ivan's head poking round the door.

'Can I come in? Or is it strictly girls together?'

''Course not.' Liz got up. 'Want a glass of vino?'

'No, thanks. I really came to ask if you'd like a lesson, Hilary?'

'A . . . . lesson?'

'You know, Alexander.'

'Oh, no. No, really.'

'Why not?' Liz put the bottle down, finished her own wine. 'I suggested that myself. You'll learn more in just one lesson than any amount of yakking in the pub. Anyway, it can be quite relaxing – if Ivan doesn't make you practise sitting down and standing up a mere two hundred times.'

Ivan laughed. 'I promise. Look, give me half an hour, okay? I just want to pop out. See you down in my flat about ten to four or so.'

'No, honestly, I . . . '

No one heard her. Liz was collecting up the glasses, chattering herself. 'Why not go and have a bath? It'll prepare you for the lesson, make you more relaxed, warm your muscles. The water's nice and hot. Use my bathroom, not that tiddly one upstairs. I'll run it for you, shall I?'

Hilary lay back in the foam. This was the nearest she had ever come to playing Gloria Swanson – lying in a queen-sized bath with Mozart on the radio and her wineglass still in reach. She daren't drink any more, though; already felt light-headed, yet heavy in her limbs, as if she were sinking down and down. The water was deep blue and smelt of freesias. Baths were few at Brignor, always rationed. The nuns washed every day, but in a small bowl of cold water which they collected in a ewer the night before. In the winter months, when it had stood all night in a damp unheated cell, it felt like melted ice. All toiletries were totally forbidden, save plain carbolic soap which doubled as shampoo. Once, when Sister Gerard was suffering from psoriasis, she'd been allowed a grudging tablespoon of cooking oil, which had been sent up from the kitchen in an empty mustard pot. She appeared in chapel glistening, and with a faint smell of salad-dressing wafting from her choir stall. Hilary smiled as she remembered, reached out for the flower-soap, soaped her breasts. Liz had left her matching talc and scent, shampoo and conditioner, both perfumed and expensive, and something called Body Spray, which came in a black aerosol with a picture of a voluptuous naked woman. She'd use them all in turn. This was Sunday – not the Lord's Day – but the day of colour supplements, where everyone was worldly, rich and glamorous.

Liz had said, 'Enjoy your bath.' She was trained in obedience, so she'd better do her best. She held the soap heavy in her hands, sniffed its musky scent of summer roses. She was so warm, it felt like summer; a kind and caring season which lapped her in its fragrance, contradicted the steel grey sky outside. Summer flowers were blooming on the walls,

134

so real she could have picked them. She enjoyed those, too; the contrast with the shiny paint at Brignor, which seemed to sweat in winter, crack in summer.

The Mozart was so beautiful she shivered in the fug. She had played that piece herself, as a girl of seventeen, played it for the final time the night before she entered as a postulant. She might never play again herself, but she had a new exquisite pleasure – listening. One huge advantage of the world – and especially of this house, where she'd been given her own radio – was that she could hear music when she wanted, just flick a switch to have it pouring out; that vital, powerful music, which had once been so important in her life – Bach and Handel, Beethoven and Mozart. She let herself respond to the impetuous eager scherzo, which sounded almost skittish; used one naked foot to conduct the piece a moment, feel its rhythm pulsing through her body. The foot plopped back in the water. Conducting was too strenuous for this indulgent Day of Rest. She stroked her arms instead, admired her new smooth skin, silky from the foam. She was becoming quite a sensualist, now she'd got the hang of it and kept pushing down the guilt. The wine had helped, of course. She took another gulp, held the glass cool against her chest. Both legs were lost in bubbles now. She'd seen a picture in her father's book of thirties Hollywood – some sultry star or other, lazing in a bubble bath with nothing but her pout above the water.

She shut her eyes, submerged her body right up to the chin, revelling in the water's warm embrace. She had progressed light years in a single day, from medieval peasant village to swinging Hollywood.

'Sister Mary Swanson,' she said suddenly, out loud, heard her giggle skid across the Mozart.

10

'Come in.'

Hilary stepped into Ivan's basement living room, surprised to find it almost bare of furniture, but enlivened with unlikely things like a Victorian rocking horse with a real hair mane and tail, and an ancient cast-iron sewing machine dismantled on the floor. The window was high up, and the already fading light seemed greyish and half-hearted, which increased her nervousness.

'Sit down,' urged Ivan, pointing to a cushion. He sat himself, cross-legged. She hadn't crossed her legs since the age of seventeen, let alone squatted on the floor. Liz had lent her an old tracksuit, which at least was less revealing than a skirt, yet it still felt wrong to sit so casually beside him, legs splayed out in front. Although they covered more, the trousers seemed immodest – emphasised her legs, her woman's hips. And if it were wrong to sit alone with Liz, then how much worse to be shut up on her own with a stranger and a man. Though was it really fair to class Ivan as a stranger, when he was part of Liz's family – or so she'd claimed this morning – who had lodged there seven years, watched Della change from a gawky ten-year-old to a glamorous seventeen? She glanced down at his feet: bare feet, with dark hairs on the toes. The hairs disturbed her, seemed so male, so animal.

'Right, Hilary, I suggest we plunge straight in. Liz says we're eating early, so we haven't got much time.'

Not much time? Two hours, or even three? She'd thought in terms of half an hour, at most. She glanced behind her at the door, then up at the small window. Basements were like dungeons: you felt trapped.

'Are you comfortable like that? Don't worry, I don't intend to bore you with a load of dreary theory, just the barest outlines.' He clasped one foot in each hand, his knees so supple they touched the floor each side. 'Remember what I told you in the pub, how we have to change bad habits?'

She nodded, tried to make her back as straight as his.

'You see, habits are so crucial, they affect not just our posture or our health, but our feelings and emotions, even our relationships. Okay? So we have to change the bad ones, replace habits with more conscious control, try to develop an awareness of what we're doing with our body, and especially the relationship of the head and neck and back. Once we've got it right, we can just leave ourselves alone, let our body be. It knows how to function, if we don't keep hindering it.'

He suddenly got up, opened a cupboard door, on the back of which was hanging a full-length skeleton. She jumped in shock, tried to edge away as the grisly yellowed skull moved towards her, grinning. A skull was the emblem of the hermit, emphasising the vanity of earthly things, which would all end as ash and bone. The empty sockets seemed to stare into her own eyes, reminding her of death again, damnation.

'Meet Rose,' he said. 'Yes, she's female and quite friendly. Why don't you shake hands?' He held the hand-bones out to her, the jointed fingers dangling. 'It's a miracle, that hand. Eight bones in the wrist, five more in the palm, and fourteen hinged ones, which form the thumbs and fingers. She's got about two hundred and fifty bones in all, counting all the tiny ones and give or take a few. So have you.'

She glanced down at her own hand. There was no resemblance to the gruesome bony object Ivan was insisting she admire.

'Now, see her head?' Ivan dropped the fingers, stroked the blank-eyed skull. 'It's heavy, very heavy. Most heads weigh a good nine pounds.' Ivan rummaged in the cupboard, brought out a canvas bag tied round with string. 'Hold that,' he said.

She was startled by its weight, her arm dragged down and hurting.

'That's nine pounds of sand. I measured it out specially, to try to show my pupils what their spines have to carry every day.'

She was relieved to put it down, less happy when she felt his hand move from Rose's skull to hers, stroke along its outline. No one ever touched her, least of all a man.

'Relax,' he said. 'You're very stiff. The first rule in Alexander is to free the neck, so the head goes forward and up, instead of back and down.'

The hand was moving on her neck, as if rearranging it, steadying her head, her spine; finding knobs, protuberances, she didn't know she had. 'That's it, drop the nose. Now try to let your shoulders go. You're tensing up against me. I won't hurt you, Hilary, I promise. I want you to trust me. Just let me lead you while we walk around the room.'

Walking seemed impossible. How could she manoeuvre all those different bones, make sure they worked together? She was aware that she was stiffening even more, as Ivan led up her and down, using both his hands now, guiding her, gently repositioning her head and neck and back.

'Drop the nose, drop the nose! No, not the eyes as well. Look up again.'

'I can't. It doesn't work. If my nose goes down, my eyes do, too.'

137

'No, they don't. Like this, see? That's better. Now free the neck.'

'I'm sorry, Ivan, but I don't know what you mean by free the neck. I thought it *was* free. It all feels so confusing, as if I've never walked before.'

'Don't worry. It's okay to be confused. Just stay with the confusion. Don't fight it, Hilary. You've dropped your eyes again. Keep them looking up and out. Don't try so hard. Just *be*, forget yourself. Try smiling, if you like. It'll help you to relax. That's not a proper smile. Make it more convincing. Better! Now smile with your back. Smile with your buttocks. Smile with the soles of your feet.'

She was laughing now, not smiling. It sounded so absurd – and laughter helped to cover her embarrassment when he used words like buttocks, a word no Brignor nun would have in her vocabulary.

'No, I'm serious. A smile is a great release. Now smile with your whole body – let it go still more. Good! That's good. We'll do it one more time, okay?'

He led her up and down again, up and down, round and round, at the same slow but rhythmic pace which seemed gradually to calm her, mesh in with her breathing. She felt a sudden joy in the simple fact of her bones and body working; in her slow breath going in and out, her face and body smiling, the touch of Ivan's hands. She passed the rocking horse, a piebald with a scarlet bridle, flaring scarlet nostrils. She was a horse herself, stepping out, going through its paces, guided by its trainer. Nice to be an animal, with no restraining conscience, something wild and free.

'Right, now I want you to lie down – just stretch out on the floor here.'

Lie down? She couldn't, wouldn't. When he'd said a lesson, she'd thought in terms of theory, the principles on paper, rather like her novice year at Brignor, when they'd sat at desks in rows – good obedient children in a classroom, studying the Scriptures and the Fathers, the Rule and Constitutions. But to stretch her body out, let some man stand over it . . . Impossible. He had turned his back to her, was fashioning a mattress out of cushions and a rug.

'I'd like your head at this end, and both your legs bent up.'

'No, Ivan, really. I . . . '

'What's the matter? Does your back hurt?'

'No, it doesn't, but . . . '

'What's wrong, then? You're so tense now, we're undoing all the good we've done. Just sag like a rag doll and allow me to position you just the way I want, okay? You don't own your body now. It's mine, like Rose's is. No, let me move that leg – not you. Just feel its weight sinking into my hand and then into the floor. Don't look so worried, Hilary. Forget yourself – relax, release.'

138

Reluctantly, she lay back on the floor, tried to release not just her limbs, but her inhibitions, terrors. It felt extremely strange and dangerous to be touched – a man's hands actually moving down her body, coaxing it to lie the way he chose. Yet the hands were very gentle, seemed to treat her body as if it were something rare and precious, not the mass of sinful flesh it had always been before. It was almost a relief not to own that mass of flesh, to let someone else dispose of it, take charge. She hadn't realised how profoundly tired she was; exhausted from her night awake, sleepy from the wine; had no more energy to argue or resist. She closed her eyes, sank down, suddenly heard music, strange Eastern-sounding music, slow and sinuous.

'Now, I want you to try to concentrate on just that line of music, follow where it goes, stay out of your head.'

It was so different from the Mozart – mysterious, unstructured – yet she tried to enter it, be part of it, feel herself a sitar or a gong, softly beaten, gently played upon. Her eyes jerked open as she heard a match strike. Ivan was lighting candles, two stubby scented candles, set in saucers, as if he were preparing for some ritual. This was his religion, he solemn as a priest. She shut her eyes again. It was easier to relax if she saw him as a priest – not a man at all, just a minister, a celebrant. Priests must be obeyed. Again, she tried to fix her mind on the undulating spiral of the music, do as he had told her, let her fears and worries melt away. She hardly stiffened as she felt his hands return to her again, massaging her shoulders.

'What you've got to realise is that you're made like Rose, with bones, and be aware of all those bones. I'm going to point them out to you, tell you all their names and what they're for.'

His voice was like a mantra, very soft and soothing. She felt him trace each vertebra in her neck – seven tiny separate discs – then gently press her collarbone, her shoulder blades. She marvelled as he said each name, as if he were presenting her with new and priceless gifts. She had always felt strangely insubstantial, as if she didn't have a body, let alone these complex clever bones. Bones endured for centuries, while vegetation rotted, flesh putrefied and fell apart. She had just been made immortal – not her soul – her solid, iron-hard skeleton, a rare and precious fossil, dug up by Ivan after millennia had passed, discovered whole and perfect in some lonely Norfolk ditch.

'Feel your ribs,' said Ivan. 'A dozen pairs of them. They're connected to the spine at the back and the breastbone at the front.' He took her hand, laid it on her ribcage, made her touch each rib in turn. Her heart was beating far too fast, thudding through her body. Would Ivan notice, wonder what was wrong? She hardly knew herself, except that it was an extraordinary sensation to have a man's hand on her chest, just below her breasts; aroused a frightening mixture of excitement, panic, guilt. Yet Ivan himself seemed totally relaxed – just the teacher with his pupil, nothing more alarming. She must see herself as pupil, or as child or baby, even. The lesson *did* stir memories of babyhood; dim recollections of her lying on a rug as a tiny helpless infant, some dark and shadowed figure cosseting her body, talking to it gently. Yes – 'it', not her. 'It' was safer.

'Now, just lie still a moment, and concentrate on all those bones I've mentioned – try to own them with your mind, make them a reality.'

That wasn't difficult. Never before had she felt so grounded in her self, so conscious of her body's power and structure. They were *her*, those bones, as much her as her conscience, or her will; more solid and more central than her faith. Yet, for thirty-nine years she'd been completely unaware of them, lived as if without them, put all her concentration on her soul.

Ivan's hands were creeping lower now. She tensed in sudden fear again, heard her stomach rumble; flushed at the loud noise it made, as if it were expressing her unease. She was so open to him, vulnerable. Although fully clothed, she felt naked and exposed, her whole body in his power, like a specimen on a dissection table; its skin split open, its rumblings magnified.

'Don't worry about the gurgles,' Ivan smiled. 'That often happens when you're learning to relax. Let it rumble all it likes. We're so embarrassed by our bodies, so terrified they'll belch, or fart, or otherwise disgrace us. But none of those things matter. A fart's no worse or better than a cough.'

Her face was crimson now. No one said such things, used such words in polite society. A nun would no more fart or belch than run naked through the chapel. Yet she was intrigued by Ivan's view. Okay to be confused, he'd said; okay to do the things which others labelled vulgar or disgusting. She had spent so many years condemning everything she did as wrong, or at least as less than perfect, it was a relief to feel she was all right as she was; all right gurgling, nervous, muddled.

Ivan was still talking, working through her bones. She felt humbled yet inspired by his attention, the way he seemed to make her so important, as if her bones, her body, were the only things which mattered in the world – the first time she'd ever felt that in her life.

'Feel the wide wings of the pelvis, the big hollow space inside. I want you to rock your pelvis gently to and fro, so you can feel it working, be more aware of it.'

She didn't move. Her other bones were fine, but not her pelvis. She

140

knew little of anatomy, but morality alone put the pelvis out of bounds. She felt so flustered and self-conscious now, she had missed what he was saying, tried to pick it up. His voice was slow and serious, a teacher's voice, lecturing to his pupil.

'The pelvic girdle is rather like the shoulder girdle, in some ways, anyway. They diverged in evolution, but they're patterned on the same basic plan. Or you can see the pelvis as another sort of head – two very heavy weights, one at each end of the spine. In fact, that's quite a good analogy, because the skull protects the brain, while the pelvis surrounds all those vital bits and pieces, like the bladder and intestines – and the ovaries, of course, in Rose's case, and yours.'

She tried to concentrate. Did she really have to worry, if the pelvis were just another head, another heavy weight, not private or embarrassing at all; just a bone, an amazing bone which supported the spine, provided attachments to the legs? Yet still she hesitated. Rocking seemed so blatant, and completely inappropriate for someone who'd been taught so long to live like a statue, rigid and restrained.

'What's the matter, Hilary? Have you nodded off or something?'

The teacher – sounding sharp now. She dared not disobey him. She screwed her eyes up tight, as if disowning her own body, tried to escape into her head, keep her real self separate and apart. Then, nervously, reluctantly, she started rocking; not daring to let go, at first, just moving very stiffly, as if her joints had rusted up. Yet the rocking itself began to calm her and relax her; became gradually more confident, built into a rhythm, a lulling gentle rhythm, fusing mind with body, breaking down the boundaries she'd erected in her mind.

'That's fantastic, Hilary! You're doing really well.'

His praise was like a blanket, warm and cosseting – the first praise she'd ever had – and for something so ridiculously simple. Now she'd got the knack of it, she couldn't stop her rocking. It felt soothing, strangely comforting, as if her body were in tune with some larger, cosmic rhythm, expressed also by the music, which seemed to spiral on and on, never came to rest in a climax or a cadence, but worked through endless new and lilting harmonies. The square of window had darkened into black, no daylight left, no dull and cold grey clouds; only the bright flames of the candles sending nervous shadows flickering up the walls, the smell of wax and musk. She was excited by the fact she owned a pelvis, a moving working pelvis of her own. She rocked harder, faster, feeling her whole spine press against the floor, vertebra by vertebra. The movement seemed quite natural now, helped express her triumph that she had bones – not just that awesome pelvis, but two hundred and fifty other bones – all hers, all indestructible.

Ivan was still praising her. 'You're so much more relaxed now. You've really opened up. It's important to be open. Think of all the "open" words – open-handed, open-minded, open house – all good words, aren't they? To be open means you're vulnerable, okay, but that's better than being closed through fear. People waste so much time on fear: fear about the future, or a constant nagging dread that the things which happened in their past will poison them for ever, or recur again to trip them up. You've got to let that go, trust life to be good.'

She stared at him. If only it were possible . . . She felt she had stumbled on some new religion, with Ivan as its priest – a priest in purple tracksuit bottoms and a tee shirt with the logo 'Bulmers Devon Cider'. She had been so self-absorbed, so nervous, she'd hardly noticed that he'd changed his clothes, at least his top and shoes. He was wearing soft suede boots now, fringed around the calves. She glanced up at his body – the strong but narrow shoulders, mobile hands, flat stomach – let her eyes go lower, quickly looked away again. She had seen the bulge between his legs, outlined by the clingy purple fabric. He was man, as well as priest, and the fact frightened and disturbed her. How could she have rocked like that, so blatantly, so eagerly; lain down on the ground, with that . . . that bulge so close to her, maybe almost touching her as he reached down to guide her movements? She had tried to kid herself that she was just a tiny baby, but the truth was far more shameful. She was a mature and adult woman, who had allowed a man to stir up dangerous feelings. She scrambled to her feet, appalled. She had totally forgotten that she was still bound by her vows – a vow of chastity, which included not just deeds, but thoughts; which enjoined her to avoid even occasions of impurity.

'Don't get up so quickly or you may feel dizzy. What's the matter, anyway? We haven't finished yet.'

'No, really, Ivan, that's enough. It's so . . . new for me, all this.' She forced a nervous laugh. 'I need to take it slowly, like the gin.'

'Well, I hope you enjoyed it. It's meant to be a pleasure, not a penance.'

'Oh, I did.' She tried to sound more gracious. There were sins against charity, as well as against continence. It would be wrong to bolt away, let Ivan think she had derived nothing from the lesson, when he had given up his time. 'I mean, just to realise that I've got a body . . . It's funny, really, we use the word so often, yet as far as I'm concerned, bodies never have much weight or substance. I mean, "Body and blood of Christ" – you know, in Communion. I'm always saying that, but I must confess I've never realised all its implications. It was a kind of . . . spiritual formula, something miraculous and precious, but still rather

142

formal and remote. But when you think just what it means. Real blood, real body.' She broke off, startled, could suddenly see Christ Himself with bones, a rocking pelvis; struggled to suppress the image, which must be blasphemy.

'Well, blood's as much a miracle as bones, of course. Have you ever seen blood under a microscope? No? Hold on a sec, don't go.'

He disappeared himself, returned in just two minutes with a stout mahogany box, which opened up to reveal an antique microscope, its dark-grain wood and shining brass cradled in a handsome case.

She touched the highly polished grain. 'It's beautiful.'

'Yes, isn't it? It was a present from my father when I was studying Biology.'

She felt almost surprised to hear he had a father. He seemed so self-sufficient; living on his own, working from this basement flat, without colleagues or an office, that she couldn't quite imagine him with parents or a family, with fixed or formal ties.

'Are you scared of blood, Hilary?'

'Oh, no.'

'Would you like to see your own? It means I'll have to prick your finger, but I'll only need a drop. And since you've got a good nine pints . . . '

She tried to picture nine pints, like bottles on a doorstep. It seemed excessive, though she'd never really thought about amounts. Blood was simply there – like bones, like pelvises.

'We'd better go into the kitchen, so I can sterilise the needle.'

She blinked in the strong light. Her eyes had got so used to the soft flicker of the candles that the kitchen seemed as harshly lit as an operating theatre, though far smaller and more cluttered. A bust of a Greek god sat between the toaster and the kettle, its nose chipped off, a dog's lead round its neck. A poster of French cheeses had been tacked up on the wall, beside one of human muscles. At least fifty different herbs and spices were lined up on the shelves, including things she'd never heard of, like cassia and fenugreek. She also noticed baby food, several different cereals with chubby naked infants smiling from the packets. Ivan with a baby seemed even more unlikely than Ivan with a father.

He was clearing the table, setting up the microscope. He had also put the kettle on. 'Cup of tea?' he asked. 'They always give you tea when you've donated blood.'

She didn't laugh, suddenly felt scared again. It was too intimate, this ritual. She remembered her and Katy both pricking their fingers when they were just thirteen, mingling their bloods, to make themselves officially best friends. Later, she had confessed it in Confession, felt disloyal to Katy. Yet if she hadn't done, she would have felt disloyal to God.

As Ivan stood above her with the needle, she kept recalling fairy tales – sleeping for a hundred years, waking up to princes, or bad fairies. Her blood looked far too red, a vibrant pulsing shameless red, which seemed to spurt too willingly. He placed one drop on the slide, adjusted lens and eyepiece, then motioned her to look.

At first, she could see nothing, only greyish blur. She tried another angle, suddenly saw a cosmos on the slide, a whole new world of what looked like tiny planets: hundreds, thousands of them, packed close against each other, yet gently floating in some mysterious aether. She watched, astonished, as they slowly drifted, some somersaulting, spiralling, others motionless. It was as if she had stumbled on a secret universe, closed to her before; awe-inspiring, infinitely complex. She looked up, dazzled. 'That can't be just one drop of blood.' She grinned. 'You've tricked me, Ivan, haven't you, put something else on the slide?'

'Oh, no. That's your blood all right – a few odd million cells of it. The body always seems so reckless in its numbers. We're all made up of at least a thousand billion cells apiece, with some twenty thousand genes in just one chromosome, two hundred thousand hairs on the average head, and about two hundred and fifty million red cells in one small drop of blood.'

'Red cells? But these ones are all white.' She stared down at the slide again, where her brilliant scarlet blood looked colourless, transparent – what she might call bloodless, if the word weren't so inappropriate.

'No, they're not. The magnification just dilutes the colour. There are probably only a few thousand white cells on that slide, and all the rest are red. It's amazing, really, that something quite so tiny should be so vitally important. I mean, those red cells must be five or ten times smaller than a pinprick, yet if they ever stop whizzing round the body, you're dead. And the whole system's so elaborate. You could spend fifty separate lifetimes studying just the blood cells, and still not know it all.'

She continued peering down. If just one drop of her blood was so astonishing, so complex, then she was a miracle *in toto*. Nine more pints of blood were flowing through her veins – universe on universe. She ran her fingers through her hair, no longer short and butchered, but a dense and tangled forest with two hundred thousand separate trees springing from her skull. She had always seen her body as a puny paltry thing; sought to punish it, downgrade it. But now Ivan had transformed it, made it huge and powerful.

She took her tea almost in a daze, burnt her mouth drinking it too fast. She didn't want to talk, only reflect on how incredible she was. She had blood, a body, bones; a dozen pairs of ribs, two dozen vertebrae; a hundred thousand genes. She refused a second cup of tea, said she'd better leave now, help Liz with the meal, though it was hard to have to plummet down to roast beef and Yorkshire pudding, when she'd soared to such great heights. They walked back through the living room. The candles had burnt out, left only their sweet scent. She stopped by the rocking horse, stroked its coarse black mane.

'Have a ride, go on.'

'Oh, no, Ivan, I can't. It's a child's horse and I'll break it.'

'No, you won't. It's really strong, that thing, built to last. It's already survived a hundred years, and with all sorts of people riding it, far heftier than you. You look pretty light to me.'

She *was* light – buoyant with elation, light-headed from the wine again, which seemed to have returned in its effects, made her feel floaty, as if she might take off and fly away. She climbed into the saddle, with its real stirrups, leather straps, gathered up the reins. She began to rock, cautiously at first, as if nervous of the horse, fearing it might bolt or rear, then gradually relaxing, as it responded to her movements, obeyed her as its mistress. Never before had she been so exaltedly aware of her body moving, working – all the bones which Ivan had created just by naming them, were now gloriously in action, proving their existence. The humerus, connected to the radius and ulna at the elbow by a hinge-joint, flexing as she pulled the reins; the femur, longest bone in all the body, pressed against the smooth flank of the horse; the fibula and tibia hanging free; the tiny tailbone coccyx snug against the saddle.

She galloped faster, faster, back across the centuries, until she was a mighty brontosaurus, a powerful creature with no brain, no soul, nor will, nor conscience, to keep plaguing her, oppressing her; just a huge impressive body, with bones the size of columns; a proudly crested tail, and some forty billion blood cells coursing through her veins.

Spring

11

Hilary ran along the path, skirt swirling out around her, face up to the sun. It was still a strange – and glorious – sensation to feel the sun fingering her bare arms, a brisk west wind blowing through her hair. Liz had warned her not to wear short sleeves, said it was too cold, still March, still really winter. She glanced up at the sky, the offcuts of deep blue between the clouds. It didn't feel like winter, and anyway, Liz didn't understand that she was trying to make up for twenty years of being swaddled in a veil and long-sleeved robe. She kept going out without her coat, even in the rain, to feel the wind and weather on her skin; to revel in that heady sense of lightness – no longer insubstantial-light without the shield and anchor of her habit, but a new and soaring freedom.

She stopped to admire a blaze of daffodils, gawky long-stemmed trumpets, some bent and trampled down. She picked one of the casualties, secured it in the V-neck of her dress, let her hand linger there a moment, touching the bare skin. No secular could ever know the sense of almost wicked liberation in a V-neck – to have one's throat on show, display all that naked flesh, even draw attention to it by wearing a gold chain. She had bought the chain herself, bought her yellow slip-ons, the first shoes she'd purchased since the age of seventeen. Yellow shoes! Crazy and extravagant, yet somehow right for spring. There was so much yellow in this tiny children's park – crocuses the colour of an egg yolk, riotous forsythia sunshining the fence, at least three different yellows in the frilly daffodils, even a yellow metal slide. She had found the place a week ago, much preferred it to the waste of Wandsworth Common, with its constant roar of traffic, its sweaty pounding joggers, its fierce and threatening dogs. The park was quiet and fenced; dogs on leads, children with their mothers; lovers holding hands.

She didn't feel alone. Ivan was beside, around, within her, stopping when she stopped, admiring birds and flowers with her, seeing through her eyes. He was always with her – always – even when he was working in his flat, or had gone to see his mother in East Grinstead, or was lying fast asleep at night, three floors down from her. His physical presence wasn't really necessary. He had seeped into her mind now, transformed her whole perception, so that she saw the world quite differently, as less menacing, less dark. Liz had noticed how she'd changed, attributed it to the lessons, which she now had twice a week. Yes, of course those helped – had made her more relaxed, taught her how to own and use her body, but it was the Alexander teacher, not the Alexander method, which had made the crucial difference.

She glanced at a young couple who passed her on the path, envied them their closeness, shoulder touching shoulder, fingers linked through fingers. Ivan kept his distance – not literally, of course, since he had to touch her in the lessons, keep showing her body how it should stand or sit or lie, but he had never yet suggested that they take a walk together, or go out for a meal, although she had known him two whole months now. She suspected he was shy – like her – which increased her liking for him. Sometimes she felt jealous of all his other pupils, most of whom were female, several young and glamorous. She hoped, secretly, that he was shy with them, as well; found it quite intolerable to imagine him entangled with that sultry brunette she'd seen chatting in the garden with him, or the tall and stately redhead she had met once at his door.

She dismissed brunette and redhead, broke into a run again. It was exhilarating to feel her body moving, using all those joints and muscles which Ivan had reawakened after a hundred years of sleep; hear the sound of silly shoes skittering on the path, feel as free as those young children rolling down the slope. Today was her day off. Liz had said she was not to sew a stitch, and Di had excused her from attendance at the shop. She was glad of that. The customers still daunted her, imperious wealthy women who talked over her and through her, while she knelt to pin their hems, ignoring her completely, as if she wasn't there. Yet they were delighted with her work – or so Di kept reporting – asking for her name, where she'd learnt her skills, learnt to sew so beautifully. She only did what she'd always done, made every stitch an act of love, a prayer; worked silently and swiftly with total concentration.

She had even made herself a dress – the one she had on now – feeling wickedly indulgent as she shirred the floral fabric with its vibrant blues and golds, hemmed the full and flouncy skirt. Nuns never made their own clothes. You could sew another Sister's habit, take pains to make it neat and strong, but it was wrong to lavish time or care on something for yourself. Sister Anna had made her habit for her, and Sister Anna couldn't sew. The seams were bulky, the cobbled hem uneven. She had rejoiced in that, in fact, used it as another way to conquer vanity. Now vanity seemed less heinous, even quite defensible. Ivan liked the dress, and it was a virtue to please Ivan, not a vice.

She checked her watch, a scarlet Mickey Mouse watch, which Stephen had rejected as too babyish. She felt important with a watch – someone with appointments, responsibilities, who belonged now in the world, which measured time by clocks, and not by bells. It was time to do her shopping, buy Liz's fish and double cream, her own shampoo and tights. Liz was cooking bouillabaisse, which she had never even heard of, though it was Ivan's favourite dish, which he'd chosen for this evening's birthday dinner. He was thirty-three today. He looked much younger, though in some ways seemed as ancient as Methuselah, as wise. She had bought him a present, a Victorian puppet she'd found in an antique shop. Another first – the first time she'd bought a gift for anyone at all, since her mother's fortieth birthday. In her postulant and novice years, she had longed to have money, not for herself, but to buy some little keepsake for her idol, Mother Benedict, or for an ill or aged Sister cooped in the Infirmary. It had been hard to learn she couldn't, that a holy picture must suffice, or a small posy from the garden – perhaps in winter nothing more substantial than a crumbling fir cone or shivering skeleton leaf. She had money now – a fortune – could buy everyone a present, light everyone a candle. Yes, she'd do that first – slip into the church and light candles for the Kingsleys, for Luke and Di and Stephen, for Di's assistants in the shop, and the biggest one for Ivan, since it was he who'd brought her God back.

She could hardly believe the difference that had made – to have her faith again, not as a mere formal word or concept, but imbuing her whole life, suffusing it with peace, bringing that same sense of joy and purpose she had felt in her late teens. No, not the same – not quite. Her new God was subtly different, no longer deaf, reproachful; but permitting her more freedom, more worldly pleasures, even. That, too, was due to Ivan, though she couldn't quite explain it. They hadn't discussed religion, not explicitly, but his own kindness and serenity had leavened her, inspired her, so that she had begun to see Christ in him, and then Christ in and for Himself. She had been reading Isaiah, surprised to find such comfort there, where before she'd seen stricture and admonishment. 'I will console you then like a mother comforting her child.' 'It is I, the Lord thy God, who hold thee by the hand and whisper to thee, "Do not be afraid, I am here to help thee."' God even seemed to speak with Ivan's voice.

She left the park, Ivan still beside her, strolled up Atwood Avenue and into Bulmer Gardens; the red brick of St Agatha's rising high above the skewbald plane trees. She had come to love the church, which no longer seemed anonymous, but a friendly welcoming place. She now knew both its priests – balding Father Hollings and boyish Father Frobisher – had been introduced to them by a girl called Susan Wallis, who had approached her after Sunday Mass, a good four weeks ago, was now a friend herself. Friends were still a rarity, and Liz the first and best;

151

someone very special who had done much more for her than anyone, indulged her like a daughter, offered her a home. But Susan was important, too, as her only Catholic friend, and one she felt a bond with, since they were both convent girls and country girls, both serious, both single, and both roughly the same age.

She walked into the airy church, its wooden floor chequered with bright sunlight, stripy red-streaked tulips glowing on Our Lady's altar, amidst a froth of white narcissi. She'd been astonished to see flowers in a Catholic church in Lent. At Brignor, they were totally forbidden from Ash Wednesday till Easter Sunday morning, and Lent meant daily fasting for the nuns, extra daily penances, bread and water only, twice a week. This church was more relaxed, more in tune with the new God she'd discovered, who stressed joy as well as penitence, who allowed a gleam of Easter into Lent, allowed a birthday dinner, with wine and friends and gifts.

She lit Ivan's birthday candle, all the other candles, included one for Eva. She had been back to N14; this time found a neighbour who at least knew who Eva was; said he thought she'd moved away again, though he'd no idea where, or even why. She'd been enormously relieved to know Eva wasn't dead, but still baffled by the problem of how to track her down. She had contacted the Post Office, who couldn't help at all; even phoned the police. They had shrugged her call off, refused to share her worry. People often disappeared, they said, and in the absence of a body, there was nothing they could do. She had stopped worrying herself now; knew she had to trust instead – and pray. God would keep her aunt safe, give her news eventually, in His own good time.

She rummaged in her purse to find some coins for all the candles. That Woolworth's plastic purse had been a crucial acquisition –another badge and symbol of her entry into the world, and important-looking, anyway, with all its different pockets for credit cards and season tickets, banknotes, stamps and photograph. She also had a bank account at a Trustee Savings bank, a cheque book and a savings book, both printed with her name. She would never forget her ridiculous excitement as she signed the first cheque of her life; felt the entire shop was watching her, mannequins included. That was at Laura Ashley's, with Liz as chaperone. But two weeks later, she'd braved a different shop, gone all on her own; worked out what the sizes meant – ten, twelve, fourteen; even dared a communal changing room, with half-naked girls undressing all around her.

The purse was special for another reason – as a frame for Ivan's photo. The tiny plastic-covered square had stayed empty for a month. She had no photographs of anyone, least of all of Ivan, though she longed to have his striking face smiling from her purse. She knew she couldn't ask him, nor mention it to Liz, but just last week she had come across a brochure for an Alexander course, found Ivan, one inch small, tucked between two female teachers at the bottom of the page. The photo didn't flatter him, was blurred and out of focus, but she'd snipped around it carefully, pasted it on cardboard to give it weight and strength, and now it accompanied her everywhere like a talisman, a life-support.

She stowed it in her bag again, knelt before the candle-stand, the flame from Ivan's candle leaping higher than the rest. She clasped her hands, gave thanks to God for Ivan, for all her new and marvellous gifts; gazed up at the icon, gilt-framed on the wall – a picture of Christ before His Passion. The beard was dark and springy, the eyes a gentle brown, the whole expression on his face compassionate and sensitive. The two images were fusing – the icon on the wall, the photo in her purse – as the eyes returned her scrutiny, keen yet loving eyes, which seemed to bore into her soul. Ivan was thirty-three today, the age that Christ had died – died that she might live.

She could smell the garlic as she stepped into the hall. Liz had started early, preparing vegetables and fish stock, as they both had hair appointments later on. Hilary burst into the kitchen, loaded down with a huge bouquet of flowers – all different dazzling yellows.

'Good God!' said Liz, looking up from her pile of glistening onion rings. 'You look like Callas at La Scala, on her final curtain call. Who sent those?'

'No one. They're for you. Just a little present.'

'Little!' Liz rushed across to hug her, flowers and all. Hilary made an effort not to pull away. Hugging was still difficult, kissing even worse. Stalks were sticking in her stomach, blooms crushed against her chest.

'And here's your fish.' At last, she put the flowers down, extracted a damp package from her bag; the smell of fish competing now with the almost rancid sweetness of narcissi, the cloying scent of freesias. At Brignor, it had been forbidden to smell flowers, since all sensuous experiences were wrong, and anyway, the scent belonged to God, but in the exotic Wandsworth florist's she had breathed the blaze of different scents right down to her diaphragm.

'Yuk!' said Luke, from his dugout under the table. 'I hate fish. They've got eyes.'

'So have you.'

'Not fish eyes. Or a tail. Or all those nasty little bones.'

Hilary tended to agree with him. She had always thought of fish as penitential. She glanced down at the bodies which Liz was now unwrapping; not their greyish Brignor coley, but more outlandish breeds: long and slimy eel things, spiny monsters complete with tasselled beards, pretty rose-pink flat fish, a huge crab, barely dead.

'Hey, guess who's just phoned up?' Liz was groping for a tea towel, mopping onion tears.

'Who?' Hilary immediately felt nervous. Even now, she still thought in terms of Reverend Mother, insisting she return, or Father Martin phoning to rebuke her, his thin voice cold, accusing. She was still absent without leave, shrugging off her vows, yet too cowardly to beg release from them; answering Reverend Mother's letters with lame excuses, or scribbled hasty notes begging for more time.

'Robert!'

'Robert?'

'You know, Bob. Bob Harrington.'

'But I thought he was abroad.'

'He was. He got back yesterday – invited himself to dinner.'

'But you said you'd never have him here again.' Hilary broke off, realised Liz had flushed, probably had no wish to recall that painful Sunday, way back in January, when Robert's car had broken down, the whole evening broken down. The row had terrified her, though she'd only heard one side of it – Liz's, on the phone – at half past ten. They had waited dinner all that time, and still Robert hadn't rung. They even feared he'd had a crash, perhaps had tried to drive his faulty car and landed in the ditch. She remembered Liz's growing agitation, her almost tearful fury when she spoke to Bob, at last; found him full not of remorse, but of some fantastic place he'd stumbled on, while waiting for the AA to come back with his fan belt; how he'd spent two hours exploring it, planned to make a bid for it, renovate it, sell it, or maybe move in there himself and . . .

'Congratulations, Bob! It sounds amazing. Though it may have slipped your mind you were expected here for dinner – well, actually for lunch, but let that pass. I've ruined my digestion, as well as an expensive roast, worrying about your safety and whether we'd meet next in a mortuary, rather than round my kitchen table.'

They hadn't seen Bob since, and Liz had barely mentioned him, save one brief remark about him going to Kuwait as a consultant on some project.

'It's time we made it up.' Liz decapitated a fish, ripped out its slimy innards. 'It's crazy for two adults to keep up a sort of feud like this. And it was my fault as much as his. I mean, I know I over-reacted, and then he took offence, and the whole thing just went sour. To tell the truth, I've missed him, so I'm glad he's got in touch, and, anyway, if I'm cooking for eleven, why not a round dozen?'

154

Hilary could think of several reasons. She didn't want the evening spoilt, more arguments or upsets; Robert hogging all the limelight when it was Ivan's birthday dinner, or maybe arriving late again and ruining the meal. She went to fetch some vases for the flowers, started arranging them in silence, as she used to for the altar, reverently, devotionally, and using all her skills. If today was Ivan's birthday, then that must be the equivalent of a first class feast with octave, so she had to make them look especially beautiful.

'Gosh! You really are artistic.' Liz paused in gutting fish, admired the marshalled tulips, layered with fern and freesias, which formed a horseshoe shape. 'If it was left to me, I'd bung 'em in just anyhow.'

Hilary tweaked a wayward tulip into line, tried to hide her pleasure at the compliment. In the past few weeks, she'd received more praise than in all her life to date, and for things she'd done at Brignor without a single word of acknowledgement. Why be scared of Robert, when she'd made so much real progress since she'd met him that first evening? She was a different person now; had learnt to talk at meals, learnt to eat with relish, to answer to her name, even just to 'Hil'; learnt to look at people instead of staring at her plate; to drink a glass or two of wine without giggling like a booby. She had other skills, as well. She could walk in heels, make a decent omelette, stay in bed as late as seven without suffering pangs of guilt, knew where Nicaragua was, had even learnt to slouch and sprawl, though Ivan disapproved of that.

Ivan! She owed so much to Ivan, so much of her progress and her happiness; planned to look her best for him tonight. It was only in his honour she was going to the hairdresser; had been reluctant up to now, despite Della's constant urging to let her do the highlights. But when he'd mentioned, last weekend, how much he liked fair hair, and what a pretty colour hers was, she'd changed her mind immediately, fixed a time with Della, who had a Saturday job in a salon up the road. If Ivan liked fair hair, then she must make hers fairer still, get it cut and shaped, at last, be worthy of his compliment. Though she was a little apprehensive now that perhaps he'd disapprove, accuse her of submitting to the tyranny of fashion. She'd tried to make a joke about it on the special card she'd chosen for him, which she was saving for this evening, together with his puppet.

She checked her watch. Eight hours till dinner still. She was like a stupid child these days, counting hours, dreaming dreams. She removed a pouting iris, which was too tall for the vase, snipped it down to size. Robert couldn't spoil the birthday dinner – she simply wouldn't let him.

* * *

Hilary gazed at her reflection in the ranks of salon mirrors. That couldn't be her, surely – that sophisticated woman with her dazzling two-tone hair, still short, but now designer-short, not simply hacked and cropped, and cut in layers to give it bulk and body? Her hair had been dead before, raggedy and dry from twenty years of harsh carbolic soap. Now it was alive – sheeny, glinting, polished; reflecting all the salon lights in its bold and brilliant blonde streaks. The resurrection had taken several hours, and Della hadn't finished yet, was using heated tongs now, to give what she called a 'lift' to the curved sweep of the sides.

She'd felt increasingly uneasy as the salon clock ticked on. To spend that much time on primping, on herself . . . Her old nun's conscience had returned, as she had offered up the pain – yes, pain. She had always assumed that hairdressers meant pleasure, the sort of sensual experience forbidden to all nuns. Now she realised it was penance – the confining rubber cap, the tugging at her hair roots as Della yanked the strands of hair through tiny holes; the stinging in her eyes as she brushed on the thick bleach; the long wait in public with her hair swathed in towels and plastic, when she felt everybody's curious eyes turned in her direction. A second wait, when they'd hosed away the bleach, applied conditioner, left it for what seemed like half a day; then hauled the rubber cap off and washed the hair again, slapped on something else which smelt of peardrops. Still a third delay, while Della worked on Liz, and a young girl brought her coffee, which she didn't dare to drink, since she'd no idea if hairdressers had toilets.

At last, Della had slouched over to do what she called a blow-dry, which pulled again and burnt her ears. She hadn't realised, when she'd leafed through Liz's magazines, trying to choose a style, admired a model's curly-cut or blonde streaks, how much sheer time and suffering were involved. And it had been impossible to read or think, or pray – not with that loud music booming from the amplifiers. She had become more used to music now, the fact that it was quite normal in restaurants, pubs and shops; that people seemed to need it as a comfort or a background, perhaps to fill the void because they didn't have a God – or have an Ivan. The nonstop chatter of the girls had proved still more distracting; gossip about their boyfriends, their diets, spots or flaking nails; the discos they had been to, the clothes they planned to buy. At least four or five assistants had been working on her hair – not just Della, who was officially the manicurist, and only allowed to help out with the hairdressing because she had an obvious flair, and was friendly with the manager. All five seemed so confident, so worldly-wise, so *au fait* with the jargon – that riot of new words: neutraliser, scrunch-dried, balsam, body-wave.

'Is that full enough, do you think?' Della stepped back, frowning, to assess her handiwork, brush and tongs still poised.

'Oh, yes. It's fine.' Hilary's voice competed with the singer's, an ardent breathless girl, repeating and repeating the pains of earthly love. There had been so many questions since she'd stepped into the salon. Would she like a half-fringe or a full fringe; full on top, or flat? Which shampoo did she prefer? And how about a protein treatment first? Her own private questions were every bit as difficult. Was this the self she wanted, the self Liz had said to think about, to choose with care, discernment, make sure that it was right? And would Ivan think it right, or despise her for going through such agony in such a trivial cause?

Liz herself seemed sure, had already praised the colour and the style, came over now, to admire it once again. They were all surrounding her: the shampoo girl, the other young assistants, the manager, two clients who had just come in, Liz herself, and Della. 'Fantastic!' was the verdict. Universal.

'It's *fantastic*!' Robert said, moving closer, so he could touch one curving wing. 'You look totally transformed, Hilary. I mean, don't get me wrong, you were pretty before, but this is something else. I just can't . . .'

Hilary cursed herself for blushing. These last few weeks, she'd hardly blushed at all, assumed she'd overcome the habit, yet Robert's praise, his presence, had reduced her to a bashful tongue-tied schoolgirl once again. It had been something of a shock to find him on the doorstep when they returned from the hairdresser's at only four o'clock. Liz had simply laughed.

'Trust you, Bob! Last time we invited you, you don't show up at all, and this time, you come for tea, instead of dinner. I know I said we're eating early, but I didn't mean *that* early! Okay, come in, but don't expect my full attention. I've got a hell of a lot to do still. And I'll need Hilary to help.'

Robert shrugged his coat off, presented Liz with wine and handmade chocolates. 'You both look far too glamorous to be slaving in the kitchen.'

'You don't look bad yourself, Bob. I like the Kuwaiti tan.'

Hilary dared to raise her eyes. She had hardly glanced at Robert yet, simply been aware of him as too tall, too male, too close. He, too, looked very different, and it wasn't just a matter of the sun-bleached hair, the tan. She had met him only the once, dismissed him as a man she didn't like, and that dislike had somehow influenced the picture in her mind. She was thrown now by the reality, and especially by his face, which she had remembered as much slacker, a weak man's face, a drinker's. In fact, it had great strength – a complicated face, in one way

157

conventionally handsome, with its thick fair hair, its slatey-coloured eyes, which seemed to mix steel-blue and sombre grey, the generous full-lipped mouth. But the eyes were wary, troubled, dark-shadowed underneath, as if he hadn't slept; seemed to contradict the easy grin, the eager voice, the boyish thatch of hair. And the lines around his mouth weren't just simple laugh-lines, but suggested discontent, and even bitterness.

He was wearing a black shirt beneath a light-olive corduroy suit; the expensive and distinguished clothes counterbalanced by his casual open shirt-neck, the lack of any tie, the coarse fair hairs tangling at the throat. More hairs on his hands, bronzed intrusive hands, one stretched across the scrubbed pine kitchen table, as if reaching for her own. She edged away a little, picked up a second peeler. Liz was paring apples for a pudding, Robert sitting opposite, broad back to the window, so that the waves of weak spring sunlight broke across his shoulders, as if he were giving off light and heat himself. He licked his finger, dipped it in a spill of sugar, slowly sucked it clean. 'I love your dress, Hilary. It's a really happy blue.'

How could blue be happy? Was he mocking her? Or was it a real compliment? Compliments appalled her. She always felt unworthy of them, had no idea what to do or say. It was easier with Ivan. When he'd told her she was pretty, it had sounded genuine, unforced, whereas Robert's tone was always slightly stagy, as if he were sending himself up. How different the two men were – Ivan, dark and lean, a controlled and serious person with his soothing voice, skilled hands; Robert, fair and brawny, with some impetuous boisterous quality, like those huge unruly dogs she'd seen on Wandsworth Common, straining at their leashes, or leaping on a ball.

'Damn!' said Liz, sniffing a sliced apple. 'I've used the garlic knife. Now we'll have apple garlic flan instead of *tarte aux pommes*. The meal's awash in garlic, as it is. That bouillabaisse alone took fifteen cloves.'

'Good God!' Robert rocked his chair back, convulsing sun and shadow. 'What's Ivan trying to do – lose us all our friends? If it was *my* birthday, which it isn't, I'd stick to something safe, like fillet steak.'

'Ivan's more romantic.' Liz rummaged for the lemon squeezer, the astringent tang of lemon suddenly covering all the other smells – fish stock, garlic, freesias. 'This cookbook I'm using says Venus invented bouillabaisse. Isn't that nice? There's even a poem written in its honour, sixteen verses long. I'd read it out at dinner, if it wasn't all in French.'

'More romantic.' Hilary smiled to herself, wound a loop of apple peel round and round her finger, like a ring. She kept listening for the sound of the front gate. Ivan had gone out all day, but was expected back at

158

teatime. 'Teatime' could mean anything – four, five, or even six. She always felt a sense of sweet relief when he was back indoors, safely in his room, as if a missing part had been restored, her own semi-self completed. She was aware of Robert watching her, as she peeled her final apple, feared another compliment, racked her brain for something to say first, something not a cliché. Liz couldn't help her out, was hunting for a flan tin, head inside a cupboard, hadn't even noticed there was silence.

'Er . . . how's your car?' she asked, at last, and desperately. 'Did they ever manage to repair it?'

'No, I'm afraid we had to part. A case of major incompatibility. I've got a new one now, more obedient altogether. Perhaps you'd like to try it sometime. Hey! Why not now – this minute? I know I'm in the way here, but if Liz could spare you for an hour or two, we could go out for a drive, maybe have some tea together.'

Hilary gripped the table edge, as if to clamp herself to something fixed, immobile. A drive was quite impossible. To be imprisoned in a car with a man she hardly knew, driven miles away from Liz and Cranleigh Gardens, all she felt was safety; to spend two whole hours with him, have to keep on talking, answering his questions, fobbing off his compliments. She grabbed the peeler, removed a second layer of skin from her already naked apple, as if to prove she was still needed; glanced at Liz imploringly, tried to frown and shake her head, without Robert noticing.

'No, I'm sorry, Bob. Hilary's my *sous chef* and the only help I've got. Di's at the shop, you see, and Della never finishes till six o'clock, at least. And we seem to have got terribly behindhand, which I'm sure is partly your fault. We can't concentrate on anything with your gorgeous hulk distracting us. Look, tell you what, could you be an angel and nip out to the supermarket and get me half a pint of cream?'

Hilary said nothing. She had bought the cream this morning, two whole pints of it. The supermarket was crowded on a Saturday; long queues at all the checkouts, no parking space for miles. By the time he'd struggled back, there would be no chance whatsoever of their fitting in a drive. She smiled into her mangled pile of apple flesh.

'That was cruel,' grinned Liz, once they'd heard his car accelerate away. 'He looked really hurt, poor lad. You realise he's quite smitten.'

'What d'you mean?'

'Look, I know Bob pretty well, love, almost like a brother, and it's obvious that he's hooked. Actually, he was pretty damn intrigued the first time he set eyes on you. Oh, I didn't tell you then. He made me promise not to. But he rang up the next morning and asked me all about you – who you were, where you lived, and why on earth you'd scarpered in the middle of the meal.'

'Scarpered?'

'Bolted, run away.'

Hilary was crimson. To be reminded of that shaming meal, when she'd cowered like a convict with bare legs and butchered hair. Liz must be inventing things. No man could be intrigued by such a dumb and gormless ninny. 'But I hardly said a word, Liz, just . . . '

'That's exactly what intrigued him – the fact you *were* so shy, so unlike those other pushy girls. "Untouched", was how he put it. Funny that, he'd no idea you were a nun – nor had any of us – yet he somehow put his finger on it.'

Hilary collected up the peelings, swept them in the waste-bin. 'And he doesn't know now, I hope.'

It was Liz's turn to look embarrassed. 'Well, I did just mention it. Don't go mad – he was bound to find out anyway. I mean, Della would have said, or even Luke. And what's the point of hiding it? It's not a crime. If it was *me* who'd been a nun, I'd shout it from the rooftops, be bloody proud I was Reverend Mother Liz.'

Hilary laughed, tried to imagine Liz as Mother Abbess, with her newly coiffed and coloured hair, her emerald linen trouser-suit, her cheerful casual 'bloodys'. Why allow Robert to destroy her peace of mind? Liz was bound to be exaggerating his apparent interest in her, and even if she weren't, she was too concerned with Ivan to have any heart or mind left for any other man. She swept up the pool of sugar on the table, which Robert had been shaping into letters, dispersed his white and ghostly 'H'. 'Shall I lay the table now?' she asked. Best to use her energies preparing for the birthday – preparing the room, the meal, herself.

'No, it's far too early. Luke and Stephen have got to have their tea first, and Stephen won't be in for at least another hour. I do hope Luke's okay. He's been stuck up in his room all afternoon, and was really stroppy, earlier, when his father brought him round. I don't know what's got in to him – unless it's another row at home.' Liz was whipping cream with brandy, flecks spraying on her blouse. 'You know, I worry sometimes that I'm only making things more complicated by offering him a bed here. I mean, originally I tried to help, but the kid must feel uprooted, spending some days here and some days there, and never really knowing which and when. Look, could you be a darling and go and check on him? Try one of your magpie stories. They always go down well.'

Hilary walked slowly up the stairs. She had been worried about Luke herself. He was waking in the night still, often sullen and bad-tempered after school; then he'd vanish for a week or more, return to his own home, until a phone call from his mother begged Liz to help her out again. If she ever tried to question him, he'd stall; seemed to resent her curiosity about his unconventional home, which Liz had now described in much more detail – the handicapped sister who shared his mother with him, a thirty-one-year-old baby weighing nearly thirteen stone; the tide of elder children who had now all left the nest, but who returned frequently and raucously with their own spouses, kids and problems; the constant rows, the mess. His father ran a breaker's yard in Wandsworth, a country lad by origin, who also kept rabbits, ferrets, hens. As far as she could gather, the livestock shared the house, and no one seemed to bother much about trivial things like cleaning. The mother seemed most shadowy of all, though Luke had once passionately defended her, when Della made some critical remark – the only time she'd heard him raise his voice.

She knocked softly on his door. 'Can I come in?'

'No.'

'Oh, go on, let me in. Don't you want to see my hair?' She pushed the door, put just her head round, struck a comic pose. 'There. What d'you think? Do you like it?'

Silence.

'It's so bright, you'll need your sunglasses.'

He didn't smile. He was lying on the floor, face down, scrunched-up sheets of drawing paper littered all around him, one picture half-completed. She edged in a cautious yard or two, peered down at the drawing. He usually drew cars: cars in pieces, smashed cars, cars piled in heaps like junk. That was understandable, when his back garden was a scrap yard, but now he'd drawn a human wreck – a burly, vicious-looking man, with his purple face punched in, his whole body bent and twisted. His father? She'd never met Joe Craddock – had missed him when he called this morning – but from all accounts, he was not an easy man.

'That's a funny picture, Luke. Who's it meant to be?'

He didn't answer, used both his hands to hide the drawing. The red crayon on his fingers looked like blood. There was real blood on his knee, congealing round a graze. His hair was now so long it fell across his face. He had blocked her out entirely – with his hair, his hands, his silence.

'Do you want a magpie story – Son of Droopy-Wing?'

He snapped a crayon in half.

'Don't do that, you'll spoil them. Here, let me have some paper. I used to do a lot of drawing once.'

161

He raised his head, the faintest stir of interest dislodging his dark scowl. 'What, when you was a nun?'

'Yes. It was called illumination.'

'Is that Latin?'

'No. Well, yes, I suppose it is. *Illuminatio*. We had to decorate these manuscripts.'

'What's manuscripts?'

'Sort of books. We drew little coloured pictures on the pages.'

'I did that once and the teacher slapped my wrists. She used a metal ruler.' He crumpled up his drawing, passed her a clean sheet. 'Do nuns get slapped?'

'Well, not with metal rulers.' She paused, could hardly explain self-flagellation, or spiritual abnegation, the slapping down of lust and pride and self. Though she was tempted sometimes to tell this child not magpie tales and fables, but true stories about her life at Brignor, which he treated with more gravity than Liz or Della did. His own religious faith seemed tenuous. His father was aggressively non-Catholic – resented his sick wife's sick religion, to use Liz's damning phrase. Yet religion might have helped the boy, as it had helped her as a child; holding out a whole new world of ritual, colour, drama, which could transcend the dreary nag and squall of home. She herself had feasted on the liturgy, long before she was old enough to understand it rationally; had got drunk on solemn music, drugged on clouds of incense.

'What's that?' asked Luke, squinting at her paper.

'It's meant to be a magpie, but it looks more like a peacock. I've overdone the tail. Hey, have you seen their nest today? It's huge! The male's still bringing twigs and things – well, hardly twigs. Some of them are two foot long and he can barely stagger back with them. Perhaps we'll leave him out some bits of silver paper, so . . . ' She swung round at the knock. Liz and Della never knocked. 'Come in,' she called, half-rising from the rug.

'So what's happened to the *sous chef*?'

She was blushing instantly, registered the veiled rebuke behind Robert's jokey tone. He always made her nervous, but now she knew he was what Liz described as 'smitten' she felt even more self-conscious. He was meant to be at Tesco's, a good mile or two away, not sneaking up to find her on the top floor of the house. He swooped into the room, hair dishevelled, jacket half shrugged off.

'I rushed back with the cream, bought it at another shop, just along the road, almost broke a leg hotfooting it back here, and what do I find? Both the hard-pressed cooks have disappeared.' He grinned, plumped down on the bed. 'Or is this an official tea break, as laid down in your union rules? If so, I'll stay to tea.' He made a flamboyant gesture of drinking from a cup. Luke giggled, copied him.

'What's this, then?' He picked up the peacock-magpie, traced its sweeping tail. 'That's good, Luke, bloody good! You've really got a flair.'

'It's not mine, it's Hilary's.'

In the tiny pause which followed, she could feel his own embarrassment; tried to fill the gap by describing the pair of magpies in the larch tree up the road, their huge domed nest right up at the top, which swayed with every gust, yet . . . She could hear her voice sounding breathy, almost false. Why did Robert affect her in this way? All the progress she had made seemed to be unravelling in an instant, as she stumbled over toys and words in her effort to avoid him. He was too big for this child's room, seemed to threaten and invade it, blocking out the light from the one small window, breathing all its air. She faltered by the door. She couldn't just walk out. It would look too rude, too obvious.

Luke seemed less concerned. He was peering over Robert's shoulder, pointing at the bird. 'It's meant to be a magpie – probably Droopy-Wing. Or maybe Mrs Swagger-Tail. She's the female. They're a family, you see. They used to live in this funny place called Brignor, but they weren't allowed to go outside the walls, so they flew all the way down here and . . . '

Hilary recognised her own words, prayed that Luke would stop. It was rare for him to talk so much, least of all to strangers. Though Robert seemed so thoroughly relaxed with him, he could have been his father – except the two looked quite mismatched; Luke's face pale and peaky beside Robert's bracing tan; his bird-bones dwarfed by Robert's bulk.

Robert suddenly slipped down off the bed, grabbed some crayons, a sheet of paper, and began to draw with total concentration, squatting on the rug like a child himself, brows drawn down and frowning, tongue trapped between his teeth. Hilary took a step towards him, leaning over to see what he was drawing; far less apprehensive now his eyes were on the paper, rather than on her. She watched, astonished, as a magpie hatched in minutes from his hand – strutting, preening, feather by black feather – beak gleaming, eye alert. The female took more time. He spent longer on her tail, using blue and purple to tip and gloss the feathers, then shading them with green. The fledgling sprang between them next – an eager, gangling, clumsy bird, with a squat and almost comic tail, a wide-gape beak which seemed to shriek for worms. He finally drew a worm, a flaccid writhe of flesh, which seemed impossible to coax from any crayon.

There was silence when he finished. She and Luke had both moved closer to him on the rug, as if magnetised, drawn in; both crouching down to watch; Luke staring at the paper with a mixture of awe and fascination; she herself trying out adjectives, dismissing all as lame. Robert sat back on his heels, eased his aching neck, then suddenly reached out both his arms, put one round each of them. Luke escaped immediately, ducked down and dodged away. She herself went rigid like a block of stone, every muscle tensing, as she sat crushed beneath the arm. It felt highly, wildly dangerous to be joined to him like that, to the rough graze of his jacket, the ripe smell of his skin – a smell she couldn't quite define – not obvious things like sweat or aftershave, but the subtle smell of maleness.

She dared not pull away, could see he meant the gesture as just a casual friendly one, part of his expansiveness, his general bonhomie. When she'd seen that couple in the park, joined at hip and shoulder, she had envied them their closeness, but only because she'd imagined Ivan close. She tried to turn Robert into Ivan, became still more confused, shrinking from them both now, from any touch at all, wanting only to escape into her room. She glanced across at Luke, as if begging him to save her, but he was standing by the window with the drawing in his hands, talking to himself as he gave the birds their names – names she herself had invented for her stories: Droopy-Wing, Swagger-Tail, Son of Droopy-Wing. He suddenly looked up, must have felt her scrutiny; his own eyes shifting slowly from Robert back to her.

'Did you both have your hair dyed in that shop?'

Robert's spurt of laughter gave her the chance to make a move, scramble to her feet, pretend she was only getting up to check her hair in Stephen's mirror.

'Why?' said Robert, grinning still. 'D'you think mine looks as glamorous as Hilary's?'

Luke shrugged. 'They're both the same.'

'Ssh! Don't say that. She'll kill me! Hers cost pounds and pounds, while mine came free, courtesy of the sun.'

Luke didn't understand, licked his finger, smeared the greasy plumage of the birds. 'Nuns don't have any hair. They have to shave it off. Hilary couldn't go out 'cause she was bald.'

The tiny gasping silence seemed to choke the room. Hilary tried to laugh, to break the tension; hoped Robert wouldn't laugh himself – a hoot of sheer derision. She had never been so pleased before to see Della at the door, plunged across to greet her, started swamping her with words, to cover her embarrassment, thanking her for all her time and trouble in the salon.

Della flicked her red-tipped nails. 'You've said all that alre₂dy.

Anyway, it *wasn't* any trouble. I like to get experience. In fact, will you be my guinea pig again? I want to do your make-up. We've been learning at college how to do a total look – you know, face as well as hair, tie them in together, plan them as a whole.'

'I . . . I don't wear make-up, Della.'

'It's time you started, then. In fact, tonight's our perfect chance, with all those captive guests. You'll get all the compliments and I can get some feedback.'

'No, honestly, I can't, Della. I've got to help your mother. She said we're eating early and . . . '

'She doesn't want any help. I just offered her a hand myself and she said everything was under control and she'd rather finish on her own. Anyway, it won't take long, I promise. You can help her afterwards.'

Robert had got up, joined them at the door. 'Can a mere male come and watch?'

'I want to watch, as well,' said Luke, who seemed a fan of Robert's now, and was tagging on behind him.

'No,' said Della, coldly. 'We don't want any men.'

Hilary followed her downstairs. No men, she echoed silently, with a shiver of relief, as Della slammed her bedroom door, barring all intruders. Well – no men except for Ivan, who could never be shut out, and whom she'd glimpsed just coming up the path – smiling, special, safe.

12

'No, not so bright, Della. Please. I just won't dare to face them. I've never worn make-up in my life.' That wasn't strictly true. She and Katy had bought greasy Woolworth's lipsticks in their teens, even rubbed them on their cheeks as rouge; borrowed Katy's mother's powder, puffed it everywhere. But they had never had this range of different products – things she'd never heard of – highlighters and blushers, gloss-sticks, shaders, fixers; nor these unlikely garish colours: purples, puces, mustards. Her eyelids had changed colour several times, from jade to aqua, from mulberry to rose.

'Wait! I haven't finished. I'm just experimenting. You're my guinea pig, okay, and guinea pigs can't speak. We can rub it off, anyway. It's not indelible.'

Hilary sat silent. She was still scared of Della's tongue. And how could Della ever understand how extraordinary it felt to sit staring at a face she couldn't recognise, which seemed to mark the final break with Brignor? That hussy in the glass could never have been a nun, with her glossy wet-look lips, her stiffened curling lashes. She gripped the stool, fighting sudden panic. Who *was* she? That mirror-face was merely Della's model, nothing more; a canvas or a collage which could be wiped clean, painted over. She had lost her convent self, but she hadn't got a new one – only greasepaint and peroxide. She gave a sudden nervous laugh.

'What's the joke?'

'I was just thinking of our Abbess. I sometimes worry that she'll storm down here to find me, but I don't think she'd even know me now, just pass me by and start searching somewhere else.'

Della paused a moment, her eye-brush dripping green. 'What's it like being a nun?'

Hilary was immediately on her guard. Della's public questions were insensitive enough, but at least she'd managed all these weeks to avoid being alone with her, avoid an inquisition. It hadn't been too difficult. The girl was out all day at college, out most evenings with her friends, and often disappeared for whole weekends. But now she was her captive, trapped in a chair with a towel pinned round her neck, tied to Della's eye-brush and her whims. She struggled for an answer, one neither priggish nor disloyal. 'Well, it was easier at the beginning,' she admitted. 'I went in at just your age and then it seemed . . . ' She

166

faltered. Glorious? Or simply safe? A consummation, or a cowardly escape?

'I'd rather *die*! All those ghastly dreary clothes and endless prayers, and everyone so gloomy all the time.'

'Nuns aren't gloomy. We all laughed quite a lot.' Hilary surprised herself by saying it, yet realised it was true, despite her painful memories. Even in the later years, when she'd felt broken into pieces, tried and tested by what seemed God's insatiable demands, she had still been able to laugh at recreations; spontaneous and childlike laughs over tiny stupid things, such as their tame mouse in the chapel, or the time they built a snowman and dressed it in a wimple. She racked her brains for something more substantial to recount, to prove that nuns were human.

'Funny things do happen. I mean, Sister Mark went out one day, to do a bit of shopping in the town. She's what we call an extern sister, who does our errands for us. She saw several people staring at her, but didn't take much notice until she got back to the convent and realised why. It was her Golden Jubilee, you see, and Jubilarians always wear a wreath of golden flowers – faded ancient silk ones, on top of their black veils. It's a very old tradition, dates back years and years. They're meant to keep them on all week, as a sort of celebration, but only in the convent. Poor Sister Mark forgot to take hers off.'

Della didn't laugh. 'It sounds pretty weird to me. Like kids in fancy dress.' She refilled the eye-brush, continued with her daubing. 'What makes people enter in the first place? I mean, you're not bad-looking, Hilary, and you said you did your A levels and everything, so why in God's name did you shut yourself away?'

Hilary fiddled with a lipstick case. It *was* in God's name, but how could she explain that; explain that daunting sense of being chosen; that sense of God, which she had experienced so early, as a mere child of four or five. She had been helping her mother put a huge white tablecloth on their dark old kitchen table, which seemed very high in those days, so she couldn't see its top. She had closed her eyes, had a sort of revelation that God was like the cloth, shining white and endless, out of reach, yet one end in her hands. Another time, when just thirteen, she had knelt at Benediction on an August evening, with the ardent sun forcing an entry through the darkly rich stained glass, throwing blue and scarlet on the chaste and chilly stone. The priest had held the monstrance up – gold spikes kindled by gold sun – and she had felt as if a flash of light had fallen on her soul, suffused her with that sense of God, which flooded through her veins like an injection. How pretentious it all seemed now, even suspect. Psychiatrists might say she was an over-impressionable child, seeking the poetry and passion she couldn't find at home – or, worse – in search of status. Every Catholic girl knew that nuns were superior to laywomen or married women, came before them in the hierarchy; that the brightest girls at convent schools were always skimmed off as 'the cream', groomed to be Christ's brides.

She cast around for a simpler explanation, something Della might respond to. 'Well, I suppose a vocation's a bit like toothache. It just won't go away. Whatever else you're doing, it keeps nagging on and on, until you're forced to take some action.'

Della screwed her face up, as if rejecting the idea. 'But didn't you have a boyfriend? I mean, someone who'd have stopped you; married you or something, so you wouldn't have to go?'

Hilary shifted on the stool. Once they were on to boyfriends, the talk would turn to sex, as it had already done with Liz. She realised with a sudden sickening dread that everyone she met, who found out she'd been a nun, would probably show the same curiosity, ask the same distasteful questions.

'Er . . . no,' she said. 'I didn't.'

'What, never? You mean, you haven't had a bloke in all your life?'

She was grateful for the make-up now, that tactful rouge and blusher which masked her own deep flush. 'Well, there was just one. Peter Clark – or was it Clarkson? I can't even remember. He was eighteen-and-a-half and what I thought was terribly good-looking.' She tried to laugh, hoped Della wouldn't ask her any more; discover Peter Clark had lasted just three days, that his first kiss had appalled her, a wet and frightening kiss in which his tongue had seemed to thrust right down her throat, choking her, invading her. She knew that it was wrong, wrong for her especially. She yearned to be immaculate, like Mary, betrothed to God, who didn't have a tongue, or clammy hands, or a spiky metal tie-clip which had poked into her chest, even through her blazer, left faint red marks. She had never mentioned Peter, never brought him home. Her mother hated sex. She was well aware of that, though the subject was taboo. She sometimes wondered if her parents had ever consummated their marriage, or whether she, like Mary, had been conceived without the sexual act – conceived long-distance, as it were, by some mere word or sign.

'Did you – you know – do it?' Della frowned in concentration as she shaded green with ochre.

'I . . . I beg your pardon?'

'This guy, Peter Whatsit, did you have it off with him?'

Hilary kept tight hold of the lipstick case. No good pretending that she didn't understand the phrase. She had been long enough in Liz's house

168

to have heard it several times. She recalled Liz's own probing, that first Sunday in her bedroom. She had managed then to avoid giving any answers, but Della was less merciful.

'Well, did you?'

'No.'

'So you've never done it?'

'No.'

'That's wrong. It must be. I mean, it's going against nature. And if you believe in God, then it was Him who made us horny in the first place. Why give us all those urges, or make men with all those dangly bits and pieces, if they're not allowed to use them?'

'But that's for married people, Della, not for nuns.'

'You weren't a nun when you were going out with Peter – or now, come to that.'

'I'm not married either, though.'

'Nor am I. But it doesn't stop me having sex. Don't get me wrong, Hilary, I wouldn't sleep around. It's far too dangerous nowadays, apart from being cheap. But if I meet a bloke I like enough – and trust – then I'll go to bed with him. It's part of being human, part of living.' Della tissued eye-gloss off her fingers, crumpled up the Kleenex. 'All my crowd feel much the same. I know people say we're too young and everything, but the average age for having your first sex today is actually fifteen years and three hundred-and-something days. I read it in *Cosmo*, just last month. That's officially underage, which seems to show it's just a basic urge, and whatever laws they pass, or ghastly warnings they keep giving about AIDS and stuff, people will still do it. D'you want to see the survey? The whole thing was on sex – who does it and how often, and when and where and how. I've got it here somewhere, if you're interested.'

No, she tried to say. She had no business to be interested, should be telling Della that a nun's life was deliberately 'unnatural', that the whole point and glory of it was that they were striving for the supernatural. One book she'd read had compared contemplatives to consecrated objects like chalices or patens, reserved exclusively for use in worship. If she repeated that to Della, she'd laugh her out of court, and even to her own ears terms like 'consecrated objects' or 'consecrated virgins' sounded rather strange now, which only showed how worldly she'd become.

'There you are. It's right at the beginning, after all the ads.' Della had been rifling through a pile of magazines, now tossed one in her lap.

Again, she tried to shake her head, push the thing away, yet part of her burned with curiosity. She had read so many books on chastity,

169

virginity; none at all on sex. And if she refused to read the survey, Della would regard her as the sort of old-fashioned narrow prude who gave convents a bad name. She picked up the glossy monthly with its young girl on the cover, dressed in black net tights and leopard top, although she looked not much more than twelve. Women's magazines still startled her – the idea that life was fun, that woman's role was to look good, smell good, catch a man, but do as little as she could for him; to be liberated, free, yet a slave to every diet, every fashion, every latest fitness fad or make-up range. And all those intimate subjects, medical and personal, discussed so openly; the private shameful details poured out on the page. And blatant pictures of women with their legs apart, or hugging their own breasts, or posing in just bra and pants – or less.

'Can't you find it? Here, let me. That's it – "Sexational". Actually, a lot of it's quite boring. I hate all those statistics – don't trust them anyway. I mean, they're claiming there that the average number of times people have it off each week is 3.9, and that's all ages, up to seventy-five. Well, I just don't believe it. I bet people lie, or boast.'

Hilary sat staring at the print. She had found the statistic for herself now: almost four times every week. That made two hundred times a year, two thousand times a decade, ten thousand times a lifetime – no, more, if you still had sexual intercourse up to the age of seventy-five, which seemed incredible to her. She had never done it ever; never even wanted to. Yet children only ten years old had already lost their virginity – it said so in bold print – girls of just sixteen enjoying several different partners. She couldn't stop her eyes from reading on. Eighty-five per cent of women of all ages masturbated regularly. She sat aghast, trying to take it in. She hardly knew the word, except as sin, found it embarrassing and shameful, yet the average age they started was fifteen and a half. At that same age, her overriding aim had been to deny and disown her body, not touch it or indulge it. Was something very wrong with her, that she'd never had what Della called 'basic natural urges', that she fitted nowhere in that eight-page survey, was just a freak, or frigid?

Yet now she was experiencing a curious sensation, a mixture of excitement, shock and envy, which seemed to have affected her body, as well as just her mind, left her flushed and sweaty, as if the words she'd read were hot and somehow charged. Other words were churning through her head – those graffiti in the phone box, her first day in the world, which she thought she had forgotten, but had suddenly returned. 'Cherry, just eighteen, ripe, juicy and ready for picking . . . ' 'Yasmin, young and beautiful . . . ' Women selling sex; women built the same as she was, yet so different they were like another species. Or were they?

170

maybe she had started off the same, with the same desires, same urges, but had denied them so vehemently, with – ironically – such passion, that she hadn't even recognised them.

Della was still talking, and she hadn't heard a word. She tried to laugh it off, sound casual, unconcerned. 'I'm sorry, Della, I was miles away.'

'I was just on about my Auntie Vi. You haven't met her, have you? She's my Dad's eldest sister and the perfect case of what you call the dried-up loveless spinster – hates men, hates sex, hates bodies – even hates dogs because they crap. There's plenty like her, though you wouldn't think so, judging by that survey. And *why* are they dried up? Because they've never had it, which makes them mean and miserable, and often narrow-minded, so they disapprove of anyone who does.'

Hilary knew that she should argue, put the case for chastity, but she was seeing Father Martin in her mind, Miss Pullen and Miss Baines, Father Anstey: all those strait-laced celibates who were, indeed, intolerant and miserable. Liz was far more warm and loving, far more truly Christian, in the real sense of the word, yet she had indulged in 'one-night stands', which they (and she herself, indeed) viewed as sinful and disgusting.

Della had moved from eyes to cheeks again, began toning down the blusher on Hilary's flaming cheeks. 'Some nuns do have sex. I read it in the *Sun*. I mean, they're not just breaking the rules. They actually believe in it – say you can love God through your body, as well as just your soul, and if you don't have close relationships, you stay immature and childish.'

Hilary said nothing. She had heard of nuns like that, mostly small free-thinking Orders in America; had condemned them automatically. Now she was less sure. Many of the Brignor nuns were immature and childish, and Della probably thought the same of her. And wouldn't Ivan side with Della in believing that the body should be used? She could suddenly see her pelvis rocking on the floor in Ivan's room. Could that have been what Della called an 'urge'? Had she kidded herself all this time that those Alexander lessons were strictly therapeutic, a way of improving her posture, breaking habits which might result in aches and pains? She had enjoyed the rocking, hadn't she, enjoyed it every week, liked the feel of Ivan's hands, the closeness of his body, the stir of his warm breath. He was rocking too, now, in her fantasy, her mind. Their rocking synchronised, and they were no longer on the floor, but lying in his bed, that double bed she'd glimpsed just once, when she went to use the bathroom.

'Immaculate heart of Mary,' she repeated desperately. They had been taught at Brignor to say that instantly, if an immodest thought should take them unawares. She was still under vows, still bound to God, not free to indulge in fantasies of such a blatant kind. She had continually reassured herself that her thoughts of Ivan were completely innocent, that she admired him and respected him, valued all his help; loved and sought his company, but only as a friend and teacher, not as man *qua* man. She slammed the magazine shut. She couldn't end her relationship with Ivan, yet how could she defend it? She needed him, revered him, yes – but there were also far more dangerous thoughts breeding in her mind.

She dropped the magazine back on the pile. She must never read such things again; must start monitoring her every thought and word, refuse to indulge in such loose and idle talk. She ought to change the subject right away, steer the conversation back to Della, ask about her college, her plans for Easter – anything.

'Easter? Don't remind me! Me and Dave are hoping to go to Paris, but we haven't booked the flight yet, and it's a mere two weeks away. I'm really looking forward to it. Dave's great! He's the new one, works as a DJ on Capital. That's his photo there.' Della pointed to a board, pinned up on the wall, a sort of memento of her life to date, crowded with photographs and cuttings, theatre programmes, menus – all the things she'd done and men she'd met; her own picture in the centre, surrounded by a group of laughing friends.

Hilary tried to quash a sudden stab of envy – to be that experienced, that popular, at the age of seventeen; to have slept with men, enjoyed it, felt no pangs of guilt, or fears that she was frigid, no constant churning worries about her soul, her sins, her vows; to be so confident, so casual, so at ease with people; to own a room with such a sense of style, such a profusion of possessions: the stereo, the records, the daring clothes discarded on the floor, the blue suede boots, the tee shirt with a tiger on the back. And all those fancy beauty aids – most of them electric and expensive – heated rollers, heated tongs, styling brushes, sun lamps, even a battery-powered manicure set and massager. She could suddenly see her own room back in Norfolk, a schoolgirl's room with textbooks on the shelves, neat and boring essays on the desk, her school coat in the cupboard, and no one on the walls except the Blessed Virgin Mary; nothing electric save the light. She kept gazing at the board, trying to imagine that it was her, instead of Della, dressed up in that ski suit, or waving from that sports car, sipping that champagne, or lolling on a palm-fringed beach with that handsome doting father. 'Oh, look! There's Ivan.'

'Yeah. Mum took that a year or so ago. It's a good one, isn't it? He's even smiling. Though actually, he was still in quite a state then.'

'Oh, really? Why?'

'Well, he hadn't recovered from Barry's death. I guess he never will, not completely.'

'Barry?'

'His lover. They used to live together – here – shared the flat downstairs. But then Barry smashed his car up, was dead before the ambulance arrived.'

Hilary sat absolutely motionless. Barry was a man's name.

Della licked her eye-pencil, tried it on her wrist. 'We never talk about it. It seems more tactful, really. I mean, Ivan went quite batty for six months or so, cancelled all his pupils, removed everything of Barry's, wouldn't even eat – well, nothing except baby food. I shouldn't laugh, but that was quite a hoot. Mum meant to buy him Complan, because she was worried about how much weight he'd lost, but she picked up the wrong packet, came back with infant groats –you know, that ghastly mushy stuff they give to tiny tots. Well, Ivan got quite hooked on it, ate nothing else for months. I suppose it was a comfort thing – all hot and sweet and soothing.' She laughed again, then shook her head. 'Poor Ivan! Di got fed up with him, said he was overreacting, but he and Barry really loved each other, and they were married, more or less.'

'M . . . Married?'

'Well, poofters can be married in a sense. They were faithful, anyway. And Ivan's never looked at anyone else, not even recently.'

Hilary reached out for a Kleenex, scrunched it into nothing. Poofter. A word she hadn't learnt and didn't know – didn't want to know.

'I'm surprised Mum didn't tell you. Perhaps she didn't want to shock you, though, or put you off agreeing to the lessons. There was quite a lot of hassle about those lessons.'

'How d'you mean?' Hilary kept her eyes down, fixed them on a grease spot on the carpet; tried to keep control.

'Oh, forget it. I shouldn't have even mentioned it. Mum made me promise not to. It's nothing anyway – just that Mum pays for your lessons. I don't see why you shouldn't know, do you? I mean, all the argy-bargy's over now.'

'Argy-bargy?' She must be sounding witless, repeating Della's words in that strangled shaky voice.

'Well, Ivan refused to take a penny first of all – said Mum did enough for him already, and a few free lessons were neither here nor there. But she wouldn't hear of that, and anyway, she wanted you to have a proper course – you know, to help you loosen up and get more confidence and stuff. So he finally agreed, but said he'd give you extra time.'

Hilary pushed the brush away, pushed off Della's hand. Her own hands felt cold and clumsy, yet her head was burning hot. She couldn't sort her thoughts out: a shocked confusing tangle of shame, distaste and horror – horror at her self – her own vanity and folly in assuming that those lessons were a proof of Ivan's affection; that he'd taught her for nothing just because he liked her, gave her extra time because he enjoyed her company, even returned her interest. Liz had probably paid not just for the lessons, but for the compliments, as well. 'Tell her she's attractive, Ivan. She needs a bit of boosting. Say her hair's a pretty colour.' So Ivan liked fair hair. Fair hair on men, on Barry. How fortunate his puppet was a male – that Victorian puppet she'd bought him for his birthday – a simpering boy with pretty golden curls, everything he wanted. Except she wouldn't give it to him; would never set foot in his flat again, or have another lesson.

What an adolescent fool she'd been, touring all those shops to find him something special, spending all her money on him, treasuring his photograph, mooning around like a pathetic lovesick schoolgirl. Worse than that – actually desiring him, lying on the floor with him, allowing him to touch and stroke her body, even touch her pelvis. Those lessons seemed so different now – not freeing, not releasing, but dangerous and shameful. She had never met a homosexual, but she knew the Church condemned them, refused them the sacraments if they practised what it called their vice; referred to it as 'serious depravity', 'intrinsically disordered'. It was her duty to avoid him now, have nothing more to do with him.

'Is that Christian charity?' another voice demanded. She had loved Ivan till this moment, loved him for qualities which had nothing to do with his sexual preferences. He was still lovable, still gentle, still the same basic kindly person. And yet . . .

'What's the matter, Hilary? I haven't shocked you, have I?' Della was sharpening her eyebrow pencil, flicking the fine shavings in the bin. 'I told Mum she was way off beam if she thought you'd never hear of things like poofs. I mean, with all this AIDS hysteria, they're headline news most days.'

'Y . . . Yes, of course.' She had read those headlines often, but they'd had nothing to do with Ivan – or with her – just sick and tragic people who needed help and prayers. Poofs. She shuddered. The words were so unpleasant. Even 'gays' seemed ironic, when they were so often sad or bitter. She stared down at her finger. It was like her ring again. 'Joy' – which meant suffering, disillusion. Ivan himself must have suffered horribly – to have lost the person closest to him in such a tragic death; mourned him all those months, unable to teach or eat or sleep. She ought to feel compassion for him – *did* feel pity, overwhelming pity,

174

longed to comfort him and help him, make up to him in some way. But he wouldn't want that, would he, wouldn't want a woman close to him, concerned for him? He wanted only Barry – only men.

Della scrutinised her eyebrow pencil, gave it a last twist in the sharpener. 'Some people say Jesus was a poofter. There's this big new book about it, with what they call new conclusive evidence.'

Hilary jerked up from her chair. Della was just shocking her on purpose; must have realised she was fond of Ivan and had set out deliberately to hurt her; probably resented the fact that her mother spent her money on expensive lessons for some naive mixed-up nun, instead of on her daughter. She had always been unfriendly, unpredictable.

'Hey, Hilary, sit down! I haven't finished yet.'

'No, really, that's enough.' She unpinned the towel, forced her voice to sound less brusque, as she added a lame thank you. Why take it out on Della? That was only further proof of how unpleasant she'd become – vindictive and unfair, blaming other people for her own wounded self-esteem, her pathetic ignorance. Was Jesus *really* homosexual? Did people in the world accept that now, as they appeared to accept so many other things, which would have seemed unthinkable at Brignor, truly scandalous? She fought against a sudden tide of images: Christ in Ivan's baggy pants and green embroidered smock; Christ and Ivan living in the flat together, lying in that double bed; Christ and Ivan rocking . . .

She stumbled out of Della's room. This was sin, grave sin. She had never had such thoughts before, entertained such blasphemies. It had been wrong enough to have muddled God with Ivan, allowed herself to reinterpret her religion in a softer, more indulgent way, just to suit herself; relaxed the rules, believed she had found man's love, then confused it with God's.

God was angry with her, as He had been for years and years – more angry now, in that she had given Him short change, cut her church attendance to Sunday morning Mass and nothing more, avoided the whole issue of confession. Confession . . . She halted on the landing, leant against the wall. How could she tell those two priests at St Agatha's that she had allowed herself immodest thoughts towards a homosexual; indulged in sensual pleasures with him? She had told them nothing yet, had hushed up all her problems and her past, acted out the part instead of devout but cheerful spinster. She couldn't change roles now, admit she'd been a nun; was still a nun in one sense, in that she hadn't been exclaustrated, hadn't even returned to see her Abbess; a negligent and weak-willed nun who had become emotionally involved with a gay, a poof, a poofter. If she did confess it, then she would never dare to face those priests again, would have to stop going to that church. And that would mean losing Susan Wallis, her new important Catholic friend.

She struggled up the stairs, relieved to find that Luke had disappeared. She had to be alone, to think. She must get in touch with Susan right away – not to tell her about Ivan – she could never tell a soul, but to say she'd changed her mind about the conference. Susan had suggested that they both attend a Charismatic Conference to be held in Sussex during Easter week. She'd declined before, disliked the little that she'd heard about the Charismatic movement; feared the thought of travelling to a new and alien place, being surrounded by strange faces. And, anyway, she'd especially wanted to stay at Cranleigh Gardens over Easter. Di, Liz and Della would all be going away, leaving only her and Ivan in the house. She'd made no plans, just allowed herself to hope.

Now it was essential that she, too, went away, and the conference would be a perfect chance to renew her spirituality, perhaps find a new confessor who would be a total stranger, one she'd never need to see again, once he had absolved her. She needed absolution; had needed it since Christmas, and more than ever now. And before she went to Sussex, she'd travel the other way – to Norfolk – sort out her position with the Abbess, make her apologies in person, before begging a formal dispensation from her vows. She felt sick with dread to think of it, but like confession, she'd put it off too long.

She grimaced as she saw her face reflected in the mirrors. All that paint and powder seemed to symbolise the petty trivial person she'd become. Her eyelashes felt sticky, stiff; her face camouflaged, as if she wore a mask. It was like another sort of habit, confining and uncomfortable, hiding the real her. It was all false, all sham, all proof of her vanity. She kicked off her new shoes: high heels ruining her feet, as the bleach would harm her hair. How could she have allowed herself to get caught in the beauty trap, spend money on such trivia, when no one had released her from her vow of poverty? 'Thou hast made us for thyself, O God, and our hearts are restless until they rest in Thee.' St Augustine's words, which she had totally ignored, seeking empty happiness in paltry worldly things – and all this during Lent, a penitential season when she should be fasting every day, her thoughts fixed on the Cross, not on hairdos, make-up, clothes.

She grabbed a tissue, tried to scrub the lipstick off, the blusher. The Kleenex was soon scarlet, but her lips looked no less pale. She used some spit this time, scoured her lips, her eyelids, but only smeared and smudged the colour, without removing it. 'It's not indelible,' she remembered Della saying, yet she couldn't get it off. She needed soap and water, crept into the bathroom, flinched at still more mirrors.

First, she used the lavatory, stared in horror at the piece of toilet paper stained crimson like the Kleenex. Her period had begun, the first one she'd had since June last year. She hadn't worried overmuch. Periods were a nuisance, so she was glad to be without them; aware that they could stop because of stress. She'd been under stress for years, wrought-up about her faith, her future as a nun; often sleepless, or suffering blinding headaches. She'd deliberately avoided the jolly Brignor doctor, who hadn't any pills for doubts and desolation; could only give her hormones to restart her menstrual cycle. She didn't want those pointless monthly cramps again, those regular reminders that she could still conceive, still bear a child.

She didn't need reminders. Even without periods, the thought was always nudging her, especially recently. She had allowed herself to indulge in secret sinful fantasies of her and Ivan conceiving their own child. Each time they had tea together, those pink and chubby faces on the baby foods had smiled down from his shelves, refuelling her desires. She flushed the toilet, as if flushing Ivan away, aborting their frail child; remained standing by the cistern, wondering what to do. She had no sanitary towels, hadn't used them for nine months. Nine months without a period usually meant pregnancy. Hers was a phantom one, the phantom child of Ivan's phantom love. She mustn't think of Ivan any more, must ban him from her mind, concentrate instead on practicalities: how did she get towels? It was half past six already. The nearest chemist would be shut, and it was hardly fair on Liz to go traipsing round the shops to find one open, when the birthday dinner was just about to start. She'd forgotten Liz completely; should be in the kitchen with her, tossing salads, shining glasses, twisting paper napkins into swans. If she rushed down straight away, she could ask Liz to lend her towels, then make up for her negligence by doing all the washing-up, at midnight.

She lined her knickers with several sheets of toilet paper, limped downstairs, fearing they might slip; was horrified to find the kitchen crowded. Half the guests had arrived already, drifted in from the sitting room, so they could chat to Liz while she made the last adjustments to the bouillabaisse. She stopped rigid at the door. Mouths were opening, shutting; hands reaching out towards her, exclamations, compliments.

'Wow! I like the hair.'

'You look marvellous, love, fantastic!'

'I wouldn't have recognised you, Hilary. It's absolutely stunning.'

She suddenly glimpsed Ivan, who looked completely different, no longer wise and gentle, but mocking, threatening, stupidly effeminate. He, too, was praising her, his false face wreathed in smiles, easy empty flatteries dripping from his lips. Liz had paid for all those compliments, paid too highly. She edged away, shrinking from his voice; shrinking from the heat, the glare, the reek of fish and garlic, which made her stomach heave. A plate of discarded fish bones was lying on the side: Ivan's bones – her own – which he had shown her, celebrated.

'Hilary! You look sensational.'

Robert's voice above the rest, Robert striding now towards her, his eyes and voice admiring. Had Liz paid them all to praise her? She couldn't look 'sensational' when she'd smudged her make-up, hadn't changed her dress. She might even smell of menstrual blood, as Sister Dunstan did each month at Brignor: a sickly sweetish smell, which had made a welcome penance for the other nuns, but would be quite repellent here, in this deodorised and glamorised society. She backed away, out into the hall, stood clinging to the coat stand.

'What's the matter, Hilary? You're not usually so shy these days, and you've met this lot before – or most of them. They all think you look great.' Liz had come out after her, took her arm, tried to steer her back.

Hilary flinched at the contact, wondered why certain words were so difficult to utter, never sounded comfortable or casual. She had hated asking for sanitary towels, even at the convent, where they were never given as a right, but must be begged as a favour every month. 'I humbly beg, Mother . . . ' Not quite the formula for Liz. She mumbled an alternative, followed her upstairs.

'You're in luck! I bought a super-pack last week. There's a good three dozen there.' Liz passed a box to Hilary, still wrapped in its Boots' bag. A super-pack? Three dozen? It felt light, looked very small.

'Are you okay? Or do you want some Feminax, as well?'

'What's that?'

'You know, a kind of aspirin, but made especially for period pains.'

'Oh no – no thank you.'

Period pains were there to be endured, like labour pains; reminded women they were Eve's descendants, responsible for her sin, the fall of man. Modern nuns scoffed at such ideas, took aspirin, paracetamol, probably even Feminax. But the Brignor Sisters refused all palliatives on principle, except in serious illness or emergency. Anyway, she had no pain. This period had surprised her unawares, crept up on her with no warning signs at all, no pre-menstrual backache or bloated tender breasts.

She locked herself in the bathroom, removed the package from its bag, felt an instant surge of guilt, dismay, as she found not towels, but Tampax. Tampons had always been forbidden in her life, not only at the convent, but also at her convent school. If you inserted a tampon, then you had to touch yourself, and that was wrong; might stir up forbidden

178

feelings, result in sexual pleasure. She had accepted the ban unquestioningly, relieved to be allowed real towels at all, since during her first Brignor year, they'd had nothing more than torn-up rags – old vests, old flannel petticoats, formed roughly into pads which were not disposable, had to be washed each month, reused. They had felt bulky and uncomfortable and were often stained and stiff from cold water and cheap soap. In her novice year, when the rags had disappeared, replaced by soft white Kotex, used only once, then conveniently flushed away, she had felt reprieved, elated, as if she had been given some expensive gift. It would have been churlish and ungrateful to expect to go one better, start demanding Tampax.

Nor would she have wanted them, she realised, once she'd read the instruction leaflet, which looked alarmingly involved, had unpleasant diagrams of a woman's naked body, a sort of see-through body which showed the womb and bladder. There were also frightening warnings – what to do if you couldn't remove a tampon, or 'lost' the removal cord inside you; how you must always call a doctor if you developed a disease called toxic shock syndrome, which could be caused by wearing tampons. Tampons sounded dangerous altogether, yet what was the alternative? To bother Liz again, go down to that busy crowded kitchen, begging now for Kotex? She was sure Liz wouldn't have them, and anyway she'd cautioned her to hurry, said they'd be sitting down to dinner any moment.

She retrieved the leaflet, studied all the diagrams, surprised to find that she was meant to have two holes between her legs – one they called 'vaginal', and one 'urinary'. She had assumed they were the same; blushed at her own ignorance, almost longing to be back in the safety of the convent, where there was no need to know these details, no need to touch herself. She spread the folds of skin apart, as the diagram instructed, fearing yet expecting some forbidden stab of pleasure. The only stab she felt was from the cardboard applicator, as she pushed and twisted it, obeying the instructions on the sheet. She winced at the discomfort, which was fast becoming pain. There seemed to be a barrier inside her, some blockage which resisted her, however hard she rammed. She removed the applicator, now smeared and stained with blood, tried to insert its crimson tip at a slightly different angle. It still felt hard, unkind. Perhaps she was trying from the wrong position. The leaflet suggested three alternatives, one of which was sitting on the toilet, which she had selected as the simplest.

Now she tried squatting, crouched down on the floor like an animal, a primitive, yet still no more successful. She was beginning to tense up so much, she could hardly feel an opening, let alone one several inches long

179

– as long as that rigid cardboard tube. Yet how could she relax, when she was so conscious of the minutes ticking by, the impatient hungry guests, awaiting only her? Supposing Liz asked Robert to go upstairs and fetch her, warn her they had started? Worse still if Ivan came, played his usual role of loving friend, unaware that everything had changed. She could almost hear his footsteps on the stairs, cried aloud as a fierce pain seemed to tear at her insides. The sharp cardboard applicator refused to move another inch inside her, yet it was nowhere near inserted. What a fool she was, a bungler, who couldn't do the simplest things. Girls of twelve used Tampax, yet here she was, a woman almost forty, squatting on the floor, half paralysed and leaking, hands wet with fear and blood. She hated all that blood, which reminded her of Ivan once again. On his microscope, her blood had seemed miraculous, but congealing on her fingers, pooling on the lino, it looked squalid and repulsive.

She struggled to her feet, the cardboard tube protruding still. Could she leave it sticking out like that, cover it with pants and tights? No. She couldn't walk, or only with her legs apart, and her whole insides were aching, as if objecting to that foreign body, which felt huge and hard and stiff now, as if it had spread and swelled inside her.

She removed it gingerly, flushed it down the toilet, tried not to see her watch; that stupid Mickey Mouse mocking her concern with his maddening 'don't care' grin, the minute hand creeping past the seven. They would have started their first course by now, or worse still, *not* have started it; all sitting round the table with just one empty place. She glanced in desperation round the bathroom, grabbed the cleaning rag which was folded on the Vim, refolded it to form a pad. It felt rough, looked stained and grubby. Too bad. The older nuns at Brignor had used rags for thirty years, had never had the luxury of Kotex, the boon of Feminax.

She longed for Feminax herself, as a dull but throbbing pain seemed to spread from her vagina right round to her back. Eve's pain. It was right she should be reminded of Eve, who had been vain and disobedient, committed the first sin, deserved punishment and penance. She pulled her knickers up around the pad, washed her hands – refused to check her make-up or her hair – then walked slowly down to Ivan's birthday dinner.

13

'My friends and God's friends, this is the happiest day of your life. There should not be one sad face in this room, because the Lord has chosen every single one of you to be here this afternoon, sent you here to spread His word, to praise Him.'

'Praise the Lord! Praise the Lord!'

A thousand voices shouting, two thousand hands clapping, men and women springing up, dancing in the aisles. Even the speaker gyrating on the stage now, arms outstretched, hips jerking; three of his disciples dancing with him – wild immodest dancing more suited to a party, or one of Della's discos. It *was* a disco – a religious disco, organised for Christ: hot-blooded headstrong music, a large live band with guitarists in Hawaiian shirts, a huge black-bearded drummer with hair right down his back; amplifiers, TV cameras, the whole hall throbbing with 'Hosannas!', 'Alleluias!', stomping feet, applause.

Hilary sat rigid in the last row at the back. This was Lent – Maundy Thursday, Passion Week – a time for silence, reverence, not this giddy celebration. The girl beside her had jumped right up on her chair-seat and was shouting 'Jesus, Jesus, Jesus!', arms aloft. The whole row in front was swaying to the music, two people leaping up to join the jigging revellers; a young girl with her eyes shut, huge breasts wobbling in a 'Jesus Loves Me' tee shirt, and a balding man in glasses hopping on one leg.

Applause and music died away, as the speaker raised his arms again, moved to the centre of the velvet-curtained stage, lit only by multi-coloured spotlights. 'The key word, my friends, this whole four days, is Resurrection.' He paused a moment, repeated it, half-singing. 'Res-urr-ect-ion! The Resurrection is a happy whoopy thing, because it means we're saved from sin, and saved from death. And the Charismatic movement is a kind of Resurrection in itself – God's springtime in the Church. Brothers and sisters, just look out of those windows. See the sky, smell the flowers! It's spring out there, as well, God's annual jamboree, with Resurrection running riot everywhere – bulbs and blossom, new growth, re-creation. This week we're going to grow and blossom too, grow in our faith, blossom in our prayer.'

Hilary glanced towards the windows, which were double-barred with blinds and heavy curtains. Impossible to see the sky or flowers. Spring had been shut out, to give more dramatic light effects on stage. She peered down at her programme in the green and purple gloom. The speaker was a Mr Duck – Jim Duck – not Father, not Reverend, not even a Catholic. Had Susan Wallis *known* this conference wasn't Catholic? Oh, there were Catholics present, certainly. She'd met quite a few already, seen the names of Catholic priests printed in the programme, but they were far outnumbered by the rest – the throng of Pentecostals, evangelicals, Charismatics from a score of different churches and traditions, all joined by their insistence on spiritual renewal through the gifts, or charisms, of the Holy Spirit poured down on the faithful.

She herself felt empty of all gifts, nervous, out of place. Her own Abbess had never really approved of the ecumenical movement, claimed it weakened and diluted the primacy of Catholicism in its rightly Roman form, threatened the authority of the Pope. And Charismatics had earned only Mother's contempt – even Catholic Charismatics, whom she regarded as emotionally unstable. No mature or professional pray-er, she insisted, should need all that commotion and hysteria, all those dangerous and divisive goings-on.

Hilary now secretly agreed with her, appalled that some plump and coarse-faced layman, in a crew cut and a blazer, with a slight South London accent and a frankly comic name, should be trumpeting the Resurrection four full days too early, ignoring the Crucifixion altogether. She grimaced at his plastic shoes, his polyester slacks in powder blue; rebuked herself for snobbery, a lack of Christian love. She should be trying to reap some value from this talk, not criticising the speaker's clothes and person, as Di or Della might. The Kingsleys had influenced her far more than they should, yet it wasn't only that. When you were used to a Father Martin in a long black cassock or traditional sacred vestments; a *Reverend* Father Martin with his sternly solemn voice, his six years of training, seven years in Rome, it was hard to hear this tyro rant and vaunt.

'The Resurrection means that Jesus loves me. Yes, me! If I was the only person on this earth, He'd still die for me, just me. And you! He'd die for you. He'd go through all that agony, just for each of you alone. But you've got to get to know Him, get to know Him personally.' Jim Duck moved downstage, the spotlights following, one lone guitar sobbing with emotion. 'D'you realise, friends, that Jesus Christ is the greatest guy you've ever met? He's not a wimp, not a prig. He wasn't even religious. You read your Bible and you'll see He had a pretty short fuse with those scribes and Pharisees. He was just an ordinary sort of bloke, like you and me. And that's how you've got to talk to Him. Not fancy formal prayers. Just "Hi, Lord! How are you?" when you wake up each morning, or "Gee, Lord, you're the greatest!" through the day. And listen to Him, friends, because He's probably answering you. He's probably saying "You're not so bad yourself, Jim." That's what he says to me.'

Laughter rippled through the hall. Hilary stayed stony-faced, unable to join in. She had never heard the Son of God discussed in such a way – this crude colloquial language, this slangy matiness, as if man and God were just two pals, not creature and Creator.

'My God's a jolly God, with a broad grin on His face, not a stern and angry judge. I often roar with laughter when I pray. He always has a joke with me Himself, or shares a pint. Jesus wasn't scared of having fun. He often went to parties, let His hair down. He wants us to enjoy ourselves, not sit with long sad faces in a pew. But in return, we've got to go out to the world and declare to all the hordes of hell that Jesus is our friend and He's the tops.'

Hilary was wincing still. Could any Christian see God in those terms? Even an aloof and angry Judge was preferable to this jokey jolly Jesus, with His belly laughs, His chummy camaraderie. She knew instinctively that a God like that couldn't possibly exist, that He was an invention of Jim Duck, of all this throng of people who wanted fun rather than faith, jokes instead of sermons. She tried to find her own God, a dignified and grave God, whom you respected and deferred to, a God of might and majesty, with a sword and sceptre in His hand, not a frothing beer glass.

She glanced back at Jim Duck, realised with a sudden shock that he would no more believe in *her* God than she in his; would claim she had invented Him because she had a psychological need for an Avenger and Chastiser, or was an intellectual snob, who required a God Who spoke in Latin and preferred plainsong to guitars, cathedrals to saloon bars. But if people just made up the gods they wanted, modelled them on their own individual needs and temperaments, then what about truth or revelation?

She gazed up at the banners which framed the stage – elaborate silken banners, like those she'd made herself in the Brignor Vestment Room; their huge embroidered letters proclaiming 'PEACE', 'PRAISE', 'JOY'. Joy. Those three letters seemed to haunt her, and always when she felt no joy at all. She was confused enough already. Her visit to the Abbess had been more painful and upsetting than her worst imaginings. She had returned tired and shocked from Brignor to an empty house. Liz, Di and Della had all departed for their Easter break, leaving her a scribbled note and a Snoopy Easter Egg. She had packed her case, travelled down to Sussex on her own. Susan had arranged to meet her at the conference, since she was staying with her mother on the coast and would come on straight from there. Impossible to find her in the swarm and tide of people converging on the campus, drawing up in cars, shouting to each other, exchanging hugs and greetings. She had queued at the reception desk in another crush of bodies, asked timidly where she might find Susan Wallis.

'Are you Miss Reed?'

'Er . . . yes, I am.' The name seemed unfamiliar – far more so than Hilary. No one used her surname, either at Liz's or the shop.

'Miss Wallis left a message for you. She's terribly sorry, but she'll have to miss the conference. Her mother fell and broke her wrist. It happened just this morning. She says she tried to phone you straight away, in London, but there was no reply, so . . . '

She hardly heard the rest. She was fighting terror, panic. How could she face the conference on her own, without a friend to cling to? Susan should have warned her how large the numbers were, how completely overwhelming; prepared her for the shock. But had she known herself? She'd seemed vague about the conference, vague about the Charismatics generally, had simply warmed to the idea of a religious movement which stressed joy and spontaneity, and which allowed laymen a less passive powerless role.

'That's right – you laugh!'

Hilary jumped. Everyone around her was in fact guffawing, the noise swelling, roaring through the hall, she the only one who hadn't heard the joke.

'Yeah, I want you all to laugh today – laugh the whole weekend. If you love the Lord, you've got something real to laugh about, something to tell the rest of the weeping world. God's laughing too, I can guarantee you that.'

Wild applause took over from the laughter. Jim waited till it died away, his grinning face now grave. 'There's just one thing He's not too pleased about. Jesus wants to know where the hell are all the guys. We've got seven hundred and sixty ladies booked on this conference and only one hundred and ninety men. My sisters, I congratulate you; my brothers, I beg you to go out and bring in more recruits. Storm into the pubs and bars and offices and tell your fellow men that their Lord is waiting for them – waiting for them here.'

Hilary glanced up and down the rows. Jim Duck was right. Almost every head was female, many of them young – attractive lively-looking girls, whom she'd never have expected to find at such a conference – except they'd probably come more for the whoopee than for any deep spiritual experience. The whole audience had now broken into song.

She ought to say 'hymn' and 'congregation', but both those terms seemed wildly inappropriate.

> Let us praise His name with dancing
> Let us shake the tambourine.

Half the hall instantly obeyed, tambourines appearing as if by magic, their shrill and jangling sound competing with the band. Men, women, teenagers, started pouring on to the stage, to join the dance with Jim.

'Dance, dance, dance before the King!' the impassioned choir beseeched. The dancing grew wilder, as if in answer; people flinging up their arms, shimmying their hips, using their whole bodies to express their prayer and praise. This was a religion of bodies, not souls; a religion of rapt faces, throaty cries. Hilary felt a jolt of startled recognition. She had seen that ecstatic expression somewhere else: in the Soho sex-shops, her first day in the world. She couldn't kick Soho from her mind – those flagrant posters, photographs, girls with half-closed eyes, grimacing mouths. Here they were again, in these fervent Christian worshippers, breasts thrusting, bellies shaking, as they danced to please the King.

> Let us celebrate with dancing,
> Sound the trumpet, beat the drum . . .

Drums and trumpets answered, the hall booming and vibrating, not just from the band, but from a thousand open throats. Only she was mute, didn't know the words, knew no hymns at all which fitted with this frenzied jungle music. She felt totally excluded, a foreigner, an alien, someone who belonged to a completely different tribe with different rituals.

At last, the hall subsided, people returning to their seats, as Jim claimed solo stage again. 'Not bad for a warm-up! And now we're all relaxed, my friends, I want us to introduce ourselves. Will you all please say hallo to the person sitting next to you – both sides, not just one. And don't forget the folks in front of you, and those behind, as well. You can shake hands, if you like, or if you prefer a hug, that's fine. Just let the Spirit move you. Say your name, exchange a word or two – why you're here, what you're hoping for. And if the Lord has touched you, or you've been born again or baptised in the Spirit, share that too. Share it with a stranger. Go out and touch that person – touch him literally.'

Hilary sat motionless. All around her people were embracing – kissing, clasping, squeezing hands. A babble had begun, was slowly rising like a tide, as greetings were exchanged, confidences swapped. Arms were reaching out to her, as well, the girl beside her closing in, the men in front turning round to claim her. Faces seemed to loom and swell, hands huge and hot clamping on to hers, sweaters prickling, whispered words drilling through her skull.

She kicked her chair back, made a dash for the huge closed double doors, prised one open, heard it slam behind her as she fled.

She sat trembling in her room. She would have to leave the conference, could never stand four days of such emotional and physical unbuttoning. But where could she spend Easter? Liz's was impossible, with Ivan there, alone. And who else did she know? Susan, who was nursing a sick mother; a few odd customers who would never take her in, and elusive silent Eva. The only other person was Robert Harrington, who lived in Sussex, just a brief drive from the campus. Liz had actually suggested she try to call on him, or at least phone to say hallo, but the last thing she wanted was to re-excite his interest, allow him to assume she was available. Anyway, didn't he live in some terrifying commune, with what Liz had called oddballs? No. He'd moved since then – had told them at the dinner – though, as far as she remembered, it was to somewhere else just as weird and whimsical, and she craved for peace, normality. She could go to a hotel, perhaps, but hotels were expensive, and she had paid enough already for the conference – four full days of bed and board, which had taken all her earnings. Anyway, a lonely and impersonal hotel seemed almost as daunting as a campus full of Charismatics.

She walked slowly to the window, stared out at the glaze of new green leaf, the splash of purple crocuses. Jim Duck was right: spring was running riot just outside. It had seemed winter still at Brignor, only yesterday, a cruel wind from the coast sawing at bare boughs; the only leaves a dead mulch underfoot. It was still hard to believe that the Abbess had forbidden her to set foot in the enclosure, had received her in the extern parlour, with a grille between the two of them. Brignor was her home, her home of twenty years, yet she was now forbidden entry, except as a secular, a stranger. She had assumed she'd be allowed to see the whole community, say her goodbyes in person, thank Sister Luke especially, for her kindness in the past. Instead, she'd been treated like a leper, kept away, for fear she might infect her fellow Sisters.

No, not her fellow Sisters. She had no sisters now, not even any Mother. The Abbess had been steely, perhaps shocked by her appearance. She had worn no make-up, gone back to her jumble clothes, tried her best to look dowdy and unworldly, but she couldn't disguise the highlights in her hair, and had totally forgotten to remove the rose-pink nail varnish which Della had applied two days before. She had also annoyed the Abbess by her dithering.

'It's time you pulled yourself together, child, and worked out what you want. Your position is already most irregular. If you are refusing to return, then the only other course is to request formal dispensation from your vows. You've had a full three months to make your mind up.'

Three years was hardly long enough to make such a cruel decision. Release from vows was an extremely grave affair, worse than a divorce, since you were divorcing God, not man. She would be obliged to write to Rome, with a statement from the Abbess sanctioning her letter, and the council in the community would have also to agree. If they were uncertain, or divided, there could be delays, re-votings, agonisings. Any nun who left was a threat to the stability of those still under vows, a challenge to her superior's authority. She dreaded causing all that aggravation, all that extra strain, when they were already so hard-pressed to run the convent, so short of new recruits. They needed her, and – worse – she needed them. Back at Cranleigh Gardens, it had seemed increasingly impossible that she ever could or would return, but once sitting in the convent, she'd felt a violent longing to be part of it again; craved purpose and security, rituals and order, even rules. She hadn't forgotten the years of desolation, her ever-growing doubts and darkness, yet even they seemed bearable, compared with the alternative of being barred from her own home, cut off from her past.

She had heard a bell tolling through the cloister, the urgent throaty midday bell, summoning her to choir. Instinctively, she had risen to her feet, then realised with an aching sense of loss that the chapel, too, was out of bounds, that she would never see it in her life again, unless she knelt behind the grille in the separate extern chapel, with the villagers, outsiders – or unless she changed her mind.

She faltered to the door of her fifth-floor Sussex room. She could leave for Brignor now, be there for the evening Mass, the Maundy Thursday ceremony of the washing of the feet. Maundy Thursday was a day of total silence – a silence which began on Wednesday night and lasted until Easter Sunday morning, unbroken by a single word, save those sung or said in prayer – yet a serene and happy day, since it commemorated the Eucharist, Christ's giving of Himself in bread and wine. The Abbess herself washed all the community's feet, as Christ had washed those of His disciples, to symbolise the fact that a superior is lowly, one who serves, as well as rules. Every year, she had marvelled at the sight of Reverend Mother, enveloped in a huge white apron, with her sleeves rolled up, working through a row of calloused feet.

She stood, undecided, half in the room, half out. How could she return, interrupt the silence, spoil the ceremonies, cause even more disturbance? If she wished to be a nun again, she had better practise here, not waste time and money trying to run away, but seek to gain some value from this conference, attend some service or event which would reroute her thoughts to Christ. No need to go to Brignor for a Maundy Thursday Mass – there was one on offer here, to be said in chapel by a Father Simon Tovey, and billed as an alternative to the main meeting in the hall. It was bound to be much quieter than the session she'd just left – only Catholics present, not a crowd a thousand strong. She checked her programme – yes – it was scheduled for six o'clock. Still three hours to go. Well, if she couldn't face Jim Duck again, she should at least pray alone in chapel. She hadn't found the chapel yet – another proof that the Abbess had been right: Sister Mary Hilary was becoming worldly, self-absorbed and neglectful of her religious obligations.

'Excuse me, please. I wondered if you could direct me to the chapel?'

'Yes, of course, but there's nothing going on there. It's tea time now, and such a lovely day, we're having ours outside. Why not come and join us? My name's Sally, by the way, Sally Burns.'

Hilary gave her own name, wished she'd worn a skirt and not a dress. Sally looked quite dowdy, and most of the other conference members were dressed very casually; women with no make-up, men in open-necks. She realised once again how Liz and co had put their stamp on her. In Di's high-fashion shop, she was expected to look stylish; here, she looked frankly overdressed. She followed Sally through a door into the garden, bore left along a path between two lawns.

'Oh, look! There's Heather. I expect you know her, don't you? No? Heather Tait. She's what we call a charismaniac. Don't look so worried – that was meant to be a joke! I'll introduce you, shall I? She's really big in the Charismatic movement.'

Not just one name, eight. Heather was surrounded by seven eager acolytes. Hilary tried to keep on smiling, as she shook hands, answered questions. She could see the chapel now, a stark white modern building, at the far end of the path, but how could she retreat there, when she was trapped in faces, voices?

'I never thought I'd get here,' a breathless girl was saying. 'I was driving on my worn spare tyre and I didn't find a garage for a good thirty miles or so. They told me there the tyre was just about to burst, and I could have had a really nasty accident, if I'd gone on any further. I reckon it was God who saved me. He wanted me to be here, made sure I found that garage with a mechanic free to deal with it.'

Hilary fought a wave of anger. People had no right to drive on faulty tyres. Would Jesus really bail them out if they took such risks, endangered others' lives? *Her* Jesus wouldn't, certainly, but then she had never been on such familiar terms with Him as these women were with theirs. The Abbess had just told her that if God seemed distant still, she was to accept that as inevitable. Fallen humanity were like blind and deaf children, who lived with a Father they could neither see nor hear. Yet this group of women appeared to claim a Father, who, far from being deaf, popped in for coffee every morning, or phoned them for a chat, and had nothing else to do but grant them favours, especially on their journey down to Sussex. He'd filled one woman's tank, when she was running out of petrol, saved another the last ham and tomato sandwich in a café on the motorway.

'I'm allergic to dairy products, you see, and all the other sandwiches were cheese. I thanked the Lord, rather than the waitress. He must have known I was stopping at that café. It was even margarine, instead of butter.'

'Talking of cafés, we'd better get our tea. We're having it outside, Joan.'

'Oh, goody! I always love a picnic. Come to that, Jesus did as well.'

Hilary tagged after them, stared in shock at the crowded stalls being set up on the lawn, like a garden fête or jumble sale, except all the wares were Christian – beer mugs with 'The Lord Refreshes' engraved into the glass; tea towels printed with the Lord's Prayer; 'I'm hooked on Jesus' sweatshirts; dolls called Faith, Hope and Charity, which, according to their cartons, prayed out loud if you pressed a secret button in their navels; their pious hands clasped cleverly with Velcro.

'Aren't you coming, Hilary?' Sally had slowed down for her, was waiting by the hedge. 'We can do our shopping later, after tea.'

'You go on. I'll catch you up.' She pretended to be examining a pink plush bear called Grace, which sang *All Things Bright And Beautiful*, then, as soon as Sally's back was turned, she fled the other way, towards the chapel. She craved its peace, its silence; had to find her own God, a God not of trash and trinkets, but of Truth.

Three hours later, the chapel was transformed. The rows of empty pews had disappeared, nearly fifty people now sitting in a circle with bare feet. Hilary stroked one foot with the other. It felt really strange to be without her shoes again, as if three short months had wiped out twenty years. Father Tovey was washing all their feet. She could hardly take her eyes off him. Jim Duck in a blazer was one thing – Jim Duck was a layman. But this man was a priest – a priest in jeans and sweat-shirt, with a towel tied round his waist, and wearing bright blue flip-flops. Flip-flops! Those cheap and nasty plastic things which children wore on beaches and which cost less than a pound. The sweat-shirt seemed too big for him, had 'NIKE SPORTS' printed on it. He didn't look a sportsman – a youngish man, admittedly, but pale and slender-boned, his narrow shoulders lost in baggy folds.

He was kneeling by his bowl of water, filthy water now, covered with a scum of grease and soap. Reverend Mother's washing had been more of a symbolic gesture – just a token finger dipped into the bowl – just the right foot dabbed with it. And the nuns had washed their own feet first, in the privacy of their cells, making them as spotless as they could, before the Abbess touched them. Father Tovey was tackling really dirty feet, some grass-stained, even smelly, using soap and elbow grease to scrub and scour them clean. She was touched by his humility, his total dedication, as he lingered over old or bunioned joints, treating them with reverence, as if they were rare and precious objects; even kissing every pair of feet before moving to the next. At Brignor, they had sung the words from St John's Gospel, as a background to the ceremony: 'A new commandment I give unto you, that you love one another, as I have loved you.' The whole Maundy Thursday washing centred on that love, that giving of oneself in service, selflessness. Yet, never before had she seen it acted out with such devotion, actually experienced that love, dripping from the fingers of a humane and humble priest. Even the saintly Abbess Benedict had not abased herself like Father Simon Tovey, who was crawling on his knees around the floor, his clothes splashed with dirty water, his small hands chapped and reddened.

Her turn now. She tensed as he approached her, felt she had no right to sit, while he grovelled at her feet; then remembered Peter in the Gospels. He, too, had objected on the grounds of false humility. And Christ had replied that only if He washed his feet would Peter be His friend, and made clean like the rest. Made clean. She knew suddenly, instinctively, that this was the priest she must go to in Confession. He could make her clean. She also knew he would understand, treat her with compassion, even love.

A young red-headed man was carrying in a bowl of fresh warm water, set it down at Father Tovey's feet, removed the dirty one. 'You're in luck,' the priest said, smiling as he wrung out his two sponges. Was it simply luck? They were bound to change the water halfway through, but to do so at that moment seemed to her a symbol, a promise of new hope. Clean water, a new start.

She felt awed to have a consecrated priest kneeling at her feet, Christ's delegate on earth, acting as her servant – awed, yet also nervous. He was so close to her bare legs, his wet hands gliding down them; each separate sensation shocking through her body – the slippery soap slicking round her ankles, the smoothly probing sponge, the rough and nubbly towel between each toe – and finally, his soft lips on her skin. With any other man, she might have felt threatened, or immodest, but he was Christ for her, girded in his apron-towel, as Christ Himself had been that night of Passover.

When every pair of feet was washed – and kissed – Father Tovey vanished for a moment, reappeared in the same damp and shabby clothes, but with a white stole round his neck, a drab and dingy thing, with no embroidery or trimming. Father Martin wore ceremonial vestments in elaborate white brocade for the Maundy Thursday Mass; a gold-fringed stole she had made herself, ornate with grapes and wheat sheaves. Yet Father Tovey's solemn voice belied his casual clothes. He seemed to be thinking out each word as he pronounced it, coining it anew, so that every phrase of every prayer sounded fresh and newly minted – the word 'love', especially, spoken with a fervour, almost hunger. He was an insignificant man, as far as looks and stature were concerned, with pale and fragile skin, mousy hair flopping limply to his collar, and only five-foot-six or so in height. Yet there was beauty in his bearing, beauty in his manner, which was dignified and gentle, full of the love he kept referring to in words.

'Christ's love has gathered us together into one. All mankind is one – one in ancestry; one with the plants and animals, the planets and the stars; one in our common life and purpose.'

Hilary listened, fascinated, marvelling at his almost cosmic vision, which drew all history, all creation, into one. She was still nervous of these strangers all around her, a group of mainly women, whose ages ranged from seventeen to seventyish, yet she was beginning to feel a bond with them, simply through the power of this priest's words. She was aware of them relaxing, too, exchanging friendly smiles, thawing in the warmth of Father Tovey's presence. He was so different from Jim Duck. There was no hysteria, no matiness, yet he could still stress love and friendship; humble himself, without descending into bathos.

He was now begging pardon for his sins – in public, and specific sins, not just the general Confiteor which they had already said at the beginning of the Mass. He was accusing himself of greed in food and drink, of worrying about his work, instead of relying on God's goodness, of speaking unkindly of a fellow priest. She heard him out, incredulous. Never before had she known a priest confess his sins to laymen, rather than vice versa. Unthinkable with Father Martin, Father Anstey – almost any priest she'd met. Yet it showed such deep humility, a sense of being equal, equal with his flock, not a self-important leader, set apart. Could he really be greedy, when he looked so lean and slight, or have spoken unkindly of anyone at all, when he seemed imbued with such deep charity? Or was he simply over-scrupulous, so genuinely humble, that he saw himself as a sinner, when to others he was saintly? She warmed to that, warmed to the thought that he was a worrier, like her; listened in amazement as he implored not just God's forgiveness, but their own.

All through the Mass, he had inserted his own words, departing from the standard formula. It made the service longer, yet he spoke with such sincerity, intensity, she hardly noticed the chapel windows darkening, the grey-blue dusk muting all the colours. They had now reached the Communion, the most sacred moment of the Mass, and he invited all his 'guests' to join him on the floor. People got up from their chairs, sat cross-legged on the parquet, displaying half their underclothes, or sprawled full-length, as if they were attending Sally's picnic, not a solemn sacrifice. She watched, astonished, as the red-haired man spread a scarlet gingham tablecloth between them, then carried in a long French loaf, a litre bottle of red wine, and a tray of plastic glasses. Bread and wine meant hosts and chalices – or always had at Brignor – tiny fine white wafers, heavy golden chalice, with rubies and white sapphires round the rim.

Two girls were breaking up the loaves, tearing off rough uneven chunks, using just their hands, and grubby hands, in one case. Another girl was pouring wine, a generous splash in each cheap glass. Hilary tried to hide her sense of shock, as shreds of bread-crust flaked on to the cloth, dribs of wine soaked into it. She, as sacristan, had been trained to handle hosts and wine with the utmost care and reverence, since they were to become Christ's Body and Blood. Was she simply out of touch with modern customs, used to sixteenth-century rituals which had become fossilised at Brignor? No. Even at St Agatha's, the Communion was formal – each host merely moistened with the wine, then placed directly on the tongue by a priest in proper vestments. Yet maybe that was wrong, and Father Tovey right. He was pointing out to them that this was a true meal, that too much pomp and ceremony could make people forget that Christ Himself sat down to simple fare with friends. And those humble fisher friends would not have drunk from precious gold or silver, nor expected fancy hosts in fine-milled flour. They had eaten real rough bread, drunk full-bodied wine; sat, not knelt, talked amongst themselves.

'I invite you all to come together in this sacrament of love – whose chief purpose is to fill us with more love – love for God, love for one another, love for the whole world.'

He was now about to consecrate the bread and wine, but still he didn't stand, simply sat back on his heels, blue flip-flops half kicked off; spread his arms above the fifty chunks of bread, the fifty plastic glasses.

'This is my Body. This is my Blood.'

She had heard the words so often, yet never spoken with such reverence, such conviction. She longed to kneel, prostrate herself, express her own devotion, but all the rest were sitting – most of them inelegantly, legs spread-eagled, or knees hunched up to chests. Then, suddenly, there was a stir and tide of movement as the priest handed out the bread and wine. 'I share with you this bread of life, this food of love, this cup of peace . . . '

A glass of wine was pushed into her hand, a piece of bread offered with a smile. Her own smile faded from her lips, as she sat paralysed with horror. Until this actual moment, she had totally forgotten the problem of Communion – that she was still in sin and unabsolved, and therefore couldn't take it. She had expected a traditional Mass, where the congregation would surge up to the altar rails and she would stay behind, kneeling in her pew, as she always did at Wandsworth, hoping nobody would notice in the general crush and bustle. Here, she was a member of a circle, unable to conceal herself, expected to partake like all the rest. True, some seemed a little awkward, chewing on their morsels of dry bread, or wincing at the roughness of the wine. Father Tovey was young enough himself to have overlooked the fact that French bread was a problem for those with false or faulty teeth. One woman was obviously embarrassed, sucking at her crust to soften it, eyes screwed up in pain and concentration. Others were trying to disguise the amount of chewing necessary to get the stale bread down. Yet all were eating – all except for her – hers the only bread untouched, the only glass undrained.

How could she eat Christ's Body or drink His precious Blood? For all the other hundreds at the conference – Anglicans, Evangelicals, Baptists, Presbyterians – there wouldn't be a problem. For them, the Body and Blood of Christ were present only figuratively, symbolically, not in actuality, as the Roman Church believed. But for Catholics, here, and everywhere, 'This is my Body' meant just what it said: Christ's real and literal presence in the sacrament. Which is why it would be sacrilege to swallow it, in her state of mortal sin, yet also sacrilege to leave it or reject it. Every morsel of consecrated bread, every drop of consecrated wine, had to be consumed by the communicant. You couldn't drop it, hide it, conceal it on your person, or leave even a small crumb, since that was Christ's own Body you were slighting. If there were any hosts left over at a conventional Mass, the priest either returned them to the ciborium and placed them in the tabernacle, or he swallowed them himself; finished up the last dregs of the wine.

She could return her bread and wine to Father Tovey, for him to eat and drink, but it would be so public, so humiliating. Several people had already started looking at her with a mixture of concern and curiosity. 'Are you all right?' one whispered. Hilary nodded, palms sweaty, as she moved the scrap of bread towards her mouth. She was being forced to sin through sheer embarrassment; more eyes on her now, as she sat tense and rigid, the bread just a hair's-breadth from her lips. All she had to do was open her mouth and swallow it, yet if she did so, she would be defying God deliberately, sinning mortally again. She glanced around the circle, the ring of pious faces, the tray of empty glasses. These were her friends, her fellow Catholics, all one with her, united, yet she felt more alone, more alien, than even with Jim Duck.

The inch or two of bread seemed to be swelling in her hand until it was a whole French loaf; the drop of wine a vatful. Yet the larger they became, the more her stomach shrank, her throat constricted. It was like her First Communion, when the host had stuck and she had touched it with a finger. That had been a sin, one which had haunted her for years, cast a blight across her childhood. Yet, ironically, they'd changed the rules since then. Now you were allowed to touch the host, even in a formal church, receive Communion in the hand, instead of on the tongue. If that had changed, then why not other things? Would it really be so wrong for her to take Communion in this one emergency, to save embarrassing the priest, upsetting all these kindly friendly people?

The bread was right against her lips now. She opened them, swallowed only terror, as she seemed to hear Christ's words spoken at that Maundy Thursday supper: 'One of you shall betray me. Better for that man that he should never have been born.' Not man, but woman; not Judas, but herself. She jerked up to her feet, rammed glass and bread into Father Tovey's hands and blundered to the door.

14

Hilary checked her watch. She could hardly see the figures. The bedside lamp was tiny, with the lowest wattage bulb, threw dim and frightening shadows on the wall. She held the watch-face nearer to its light. Nearly two a.m. She ought to get some sleep, or she would never cope with the rigorous Good Friday programme, planned for the next day. At least her stomach had calmed down. She had explained to Father Tovey that she had suddenly been seized with the most violent cramping pains, which was why she'd left the chapel so precipitately. It had, in fact, been true. She had fled straight from church to toilet, sat there half an hour voiding lunch and breakfast, probably through sheer nerves. The priest had been extremely understanding, and several of the group had come up to her room with medicines and sympathy. She had felt a total fraud, yet was touched by their concern, especially by the girl who slept next door, a fellow Catholic – Bridget – who'd gone out specially to buy her milk and sandwiches, since she'd missed the canteen meal.

She took a sip of milk, wished she had some sleeping pills, something to block out the confusion of emotions still raging in her head. She felt newly orphaned away from Cranleigh Gardens, which had become her home, her refuge. Without the Kingsleys, all her earlier fears and vulnerability had come flooding back again. She was even missing Ivan, though still shocked by what he was, and especially missing Luke – the bond she felt when he stayed the night at Liz's, the sense of his small but friendly presence through the wall. She wondered if he, too, were lying sleepless. He had gone back to his family for Easter, after a row with his father, which had involved Liz and Di as well, had left the Kingsleys and the Craddocks shouting at each other down the phone. She pulled the blankets round her, shivering suddenly, as her own father's features replaced those of Mr Craddock. He had died eleven years ago, almost to the day, died in Passion Week – although Easter had been late that year, late April, almost May: a brilliant blowy day, with the last almond blossom drifting like warm snow. She had missed the funeral – home visits were not allowed in Lent – had been forbidden even to grieve.

'You gave him up already, when you entered, Sister Hilary.'

'Yes, but my mother . . . '

'You gave her up as well, child.'

Hilary reached out for her milk again, choking as she gulped it far too fast. Anger was forbidden, just as much as grief. Father Martin had told them to reflect on the story of Job, if they were ever tempted to resentment – Job, who trusted God, yet was stripped of wife, children, friends, health, possessions, and still begged pardon for daring to complain. Or St Paul, in his letter to the Philippians, who wrote from prison – confined in chains, eating rancid food, breathing fetid air, yet never whining, indeed repeating the word 'joy' eleven times.

Joy. She tugged guiltily at her ring for the umpteenth time since coming back from Brignor. Mother Abbess had insisted she return it. She had slipped into a jeweller's, before catching her train back, but the tiny Norfolk shop didn't have the proper tool for sawing off stuck rings. They had tried their best with pliers, only hurt her finger, marked the silver. She had almost missed her train, had to thank them, rush away. 'If you're going to London, lady, try a jeweller's there. They'll do it for you easy.'

Easy, no.

She slipped out of bed, switched on the main light. Now she could see the posters on the walls: pop stars, ponies, sunset over Malibu; the warm orange of the chair. Stupid to feel wretched in such a bright and cheerful room. She pulled back the curtains, gazed out at the shadowed campus buildings, the rolling downs beyond. She had been looking forward to four days in the country, back with fields and trees again, and not far from the sea. She missed the sea. Although she never saw it in the convent, she had always been aware of it, consciously, subconsciously; a huge and boundless presence just ten miles away, tugging at her mind, as it threshed in and out, in and out, following the moon. So why did she ache for London streets again, feel so vulnerable and lost, like a tiny child torn forcibly from Mother Liz and dumped in a strange house? She was thirty-nine years old, should have outgrown the need for mothers, Reverend or profane.

She let the curtain fall, forced herself to kneel. It was already Good Friday. She should be reflecting on Christ's death, begging pardon for the sins which had nailed Him to the Cross; her own most recent sin in even contemplating sacrilege at the Maundy Thursday Mass. She prayed first for her father, begged his forgiveness, also; implored God to give him the happiness he had never found on earth.

Her eyes flicked open. She could hear a noise – someone gasping, wheezing, as if they couldn't breathe. The girl next door. She sounded in distress, in pain. Hilary got up from her knees, stood nervous by the bed. She ought to go and help, as Bridget had helped her, yet it still seemed wrong to enter someone's room, or intrude herself where perhaps she wasn't wanted. She could hear voices now – a man's voice, very low, with Bridget's cries above it. Perhaps they'd fetched the warden, or a doctor. No. The man was laughing, an excited throaty laugh, followed by a bout of urgent whispering. Then Bridget started whispering herself; no longer sounded ill at all; was even laughing now, as well, instead of whimpering. She felt embarrassed to be eavesdropping, but the walls were cardboard-thin, conducted every sound. A louder giggly '*No*, Ian!' was followed by a warning 'Sssh.' Hilary knelt down again, tried to block her ears. She had better stop her private prayers, change to something with a formula, which would help her concentrate. She had already said the Office – what she could recall of it. Now she started on the stations of the Cross, in keeping with Good Friday, trying to call up the first station in her mind, repeat the prayers they said each week at Brignor.

'Hail, Jesus, who, though guiltless, didst will to suffer the sentence of death, even the death of the Cross, grant that . . . '

There was silence now next door, but a strangely threatening silence, which made her somehow nervous, distracted her from praying. Had he gone, the man? She hadn't heard footsteps, or the creaking of a door. She had no right to be listening, nor even curious. She put her hands across her ears, forced her attention back to Christ condemned.

'Grant that, out of love for thee, I may not . . . '

She flinched. There *was* a creaking now – but not the door, the bed. And the voices had returned again – different voices – strangulated, jerky. She abandoned the first station, leapfrogged to the second, words slipping from her grasp, as they jumbled with the frenzied sounds next door.

'Hail, Jesus, who didst patiently accept the death of Crucifixion, may the wood of thy Cross be as a soft bed to me, and may I die for . . . '

Soft bed. Those two were in bed – Bridget and that man – in bed together, a creaking rocking bed, its iron legs skidding wildly on the floor. And yet Bridget was single and a Catholic, a devout and pious Catholic, or so she had implied, when they'd had their chat this evening. She mustn't think about it. It was wrong to judge or criticise, and she was muddling all the stations, skipping some, forgetting some, her flustered prayers skewing out of sequence.

'Jesus, who before thy Crucifixion was stripped naked, strip me of the things of this world, so that naked I may . . . '

Naked. Why were all the words obscene, even in the stations of the Cross? She could see Bridget naked on her bed – plump pale thighs apart, large breasts falling sideways, as she lay back on the pillows. The man was much more shadowy, just a silhouette, like the man in the advertisement for Camel cigarettes. She had started noticing advertisements, especially those with men in, started looking at their bodies. She jerked her head violently, trying to jolt the pictures out of it. It was sacrilege and blasphemy to confuse Christ's death and Passion with these vile disgusting images. Half her mind was praying still, as she hurtled on towards the Crucifixion – Christ naked now, as well – naked on the Cross, just a flimsy drapery bunched around his loins. She gripped the bed, appalled and half-incredulous at the contents of her mind. There had been naked Christs throughout the convent, cruci-fixes everywhere, so why had they never troubled her before? She had never even thought of them as naked. They were sacred icons, a focus for her prayer, for her contrition. Now she could see only Christ's bare flesh – bare chest, bare thighs, bare . . . This must be the devil. Mother had warned her that Satan would be using every wile to wean her from the faith, would take advantage of her lawless state, to try to win her soul.

'Lord, help me, save me!' She couldn't find the words, kept repeating 'Help me!', as she tried, in vain, to block out what was going on next door. The rocking had intensified, much faster now, more violent; the gasps turned into cries, terrifying cries, a sudden muffled scream, then silence. She gave up all pretence of praying, sank back on the bed. The room was dankly cold and she was sweating, her whole body burning hot, throbbing with some restless agitation. She seized her dressing gown, slipped out to the bathroom, splashed her face with water – freezing water – soaked a flannel in it, pushed it down between her legs, as they had been taught to do at Brignor, if they were ever tempted by what Mother called stirrings of the flesh.

Gradually, her heart stopped pounding, the sweating changed to shivering, but there was still no way she could go back to her room. That man might stay all night with Bridget, the noises start again . . . She would never sleep now anyway. Best to try to calm herself, make a cup of tea in the students' kitchen, two floors down, stay there till the morning. She buttoned up her dressing gown, so that it concealed her damp pyjamas, crept along the hushed and dim-lit passage, tiptoed down two dark flights of stairs.

'Who's that?'

She froze. Someone else awake. A light on in the kitchen, a girl's voice calling out to her. She pushed the door, almost bolted back upstairs. The room was full of women – women in their nightwear, women lounging, smoking, sprawling, drinking coffee. Not a soul she recognised – not Sally, Heather, Joan, and no one from the Mass.

'Can't sleep?'

'Er . . . no.'

'Come in.'

She stared confused at all the faces, bodies; hand still on the door knob. 'No, really, I . . . '

'Come on, come and join us. But shut the door – it's draughty. There's a spare seat over here.'

'Cup of coffee?'

'Th . . . Thank you, but I . . . '

'White or black?'

'White, please.' Simpler to give in.

'What's your name?'

'Hilary.'

A babble of 'hallos' from all the rest, names flung at her too fast for her to catch – except Elaine, the one who'd spoken first, a crop-haired girl, wearing blue pyjamas, with a creased and grubby anorak on top.

'I hope you're a rebel, because we're the ginger group.'

Laughter.

'We're just discussing the iniquities of churches, especially the Holy Roman one. You're a Catholic, aren't you?'

She nodded. They must have seen her at the Mass. How else could they know?

Elaine grinned. 'An ex-nun, too, I bet! Don't look so startled, Hilary. I used to run an ex-nuns' group and I developed a sort of eye for them. Even in mufti, there are always telltale signs – no bright colours or dangly jewellery, back too straight, voice too low, whole manner too polite.'

Hilary crossed the room, feeling every eye upon her, her own eyes cold, as she sat stiffly on the one spare chair. Politeness had its value. It was extremely rude to label her like that, divulge her secret to this crowd of unknown women, make her feel stupid and exposed. And could it really be so obvious? She'd assumed she looked nothing like a nun now, had lost all her old habits of timidity, submissiveness. Even her dressing gown, although not exactly bright, was still a daring shade of salmon; something she would never have bought without Di and Liz's prompting.

'Don't worry, I used to be a nun myself – Anglican, not Catholic. They're just as bad, though – worse, in some respects. I was in for fourteen years, escaped in a gymslip with 10p in my pocket.'

Hilary almost jumped out of her chair. A fellow criminal, someone else who had dared to run away, risked excommunication; must have gone through the same agonising fears, the same battle with her abbess. Yet Elaine seemed nothing like a nun: a forceful, almost vulgar sort of woman with a shrill laugh, raucous voice, now slumped back in her chair with her legs crossed at the thigh, and puffing on what looked like a cigar.

'I'd run away before, but in my habit that time. I lasted just three hours. We wore those huge white stiffened wimples, which stuck out miles each side. I felt like a dinosaur, something far too big and clumsy, which ought to be extinct. I seemed to take up too much room, be blocking people's way, yet inside I felt tiny, like an ant – a nobody, a nothing.'

Hilary's annoyance all but seeped away. This girl understood, understood completely. She longed to talk to her in private, find out when she'd left, how long had it taken her to adapt, adjust, stop agonising. But other girls were talking.

'They're ridiculous, those habits. I mean, a lot of nuns still wear them, yet they cost a bomb, far more than normal clothes.'

'It's not just that. It's psychologically wrong for women to have only one outfit, which they have to wear for everything from a major feast like Christmas to mucking out the henhouse.'

'No, but the money thing's important. I mean, what about dowries? All those convents raking in the cash, investing it and living on the interest, then daring to talk about vows of poverty. I read about a convent just last year, which had only nine nuns left, rattling around in a fifty-five-room mansion with grounds to match. When at last they pulled it down, they built housing for four hundred. Yet the Reverend Mother defended it for years, kept out the developers, said her Sisters needed peace and space to preserve their interior life. I ask you! What about the interior life of Bangladeshi families living in one room?'

Hilary flushed, still felt a sense of loyalty to her own eleven sisters in their spacious Georgian mansion. Yet she herself had criticised their easy sheltered life.

'Well, that's true of the Church in general,' someone else chipped in. 'The Vatican's sitting on a gold mine, while peasants starve in Ecuador. And the C of E's as bad. Those fat-cat Church Commissioners own so much land and property, they can hardly . . .'

'Oh, don't start that again, Pat. We've been talking politics since ten o'clock. We're meant to be discussing the Charismatic movement.'

'It's still relevant, isn't it? I mean, what do Charismatics do to help the starving world, or even help the hungry here in England? For lots of them, it's just an ego trip – people getting high on their emotions, then calling it the Spirit. And even for the saner ones, it's still all prayer and praise and meetings – letting off spiritual steam, hanging loose with God. But what difference has it made to our society? And it's even worse in the States. There's this Charismatic pastor in Dallas who's a multimillionaire and says God made diamonds for His own flock to enjoy, not for Satan's crowd. He even believes in segregated churches. I suppose he fears his faithful congregation might feel a bit uncomfortable with poor blacks and shabby Spaniards envying all those sparklers.'

Hilary glanced up at the speaker, a tall and angry-sounding girl, who was snapping used matches into splinters. Why had she come to a Charismatic conference when she seemed so disenchanted with the movement? She longed to slip away herself, felt more and more uneasy in this cramped and ugly room, with its overflowing ashtrays, its scuffed and speckled lino. The girls themselves looked shabby and unkempt, one in just her raincoat, with bare legs underneath. She tried not to notice the dirty toenails, cheap blue vinyl sandals. She was becoming far too critical, expecting elegance, good taste, in her surroundings, other people, just because the Kingsleys all stressed style. A different girl was speaking now, a small and rather sallow one, with ragged cropped brown hair.

'Another thing – take the role of women. D'you realise, not one single speaker at this conference is a female? Oh, I know they've got women running workshops, but all the "stars" are men, and yet it's meant to be a democratic movement which gives power to the layman. Layman, true, but what about us laywomen?'

'That's not fair, Jane. I can think of lots of women who've made it in the . . . '

'Name just one.'

'Heather Tait.'

'Okay, her. Who else, though?'

'Mary Clarke. Mary Holdsworth.'

'Interesting they're Marys, when it's Mary who's to blame – the BVM, I mean.' Elaine again, stubbing out her cigar in a puddle of spilt coffee. 'In the Catholic Church, anyway,' she added. 'What a model for us women! A virgin who produced her child without a man, and apparently no pain; was hauled straight up into heaven, rather than plain died, and was always passive, docile, silent and submissive. No wonder most Catholic girls feel guilty, or end up in a mess. And look at Southern Ireland. Divorce and contraception and abortion are all still mortal sins there, not to mention masturbation. Bloody hell! If we read that Soviet Russia had forbidden wanking, or refused to allow the sale of contraceptives, we'd call it tyranny and all be signing petitions to allow them greater freedom.'

Hilary sat aghast. Elaine's language was more outspoken even than Della's. And the way she talked of Mary, God's own Mother . . . Could she have really been a nun, undone those years and years of training so completely?

'I couldn't be a Catholic,' said a young and skinny girl, munching

201

biscuits in the corner. 'No way! Just that whole Virgin Birth thing is enough to put me off. I mean, you're either a virgin or a mother. You can't be both at once.'

'Oh, yes, you can.' Elaine was grinning now. '*I* was, for fourteen years. Mother Immaculata. What a name! The first thing I did, once I'd returned to plain Elaine, was to get rid of my virginity, as well – just to prove I could, I suppose. When you've been called "Immaculate" for fourteen years, and you're not the Virgin Mary with a Holy Ghost on tap, it's not that easy.'

Some of the girls were looking quite uncomfortable, others laughing outright. Hilary kept glancing at ex-Mother Immaculata, hardly able to believe what she had heard. Elaine wasn't even pretty – downright plain, in fact; with a lumpy figure, coarse-pored greasy skin. Yet she'd found a lover, been to bed with him.

'They say it's the most pleasurable experience known to human beings, so I didn't want to miss it. Better late than never!' Elaine let out a loud and vulgar laugh.

Hilary heard the noises from the next door room again – gaspings, moanings, sudden whimpering cries. It hadn't sounded pleasurable, rather animal and painful. If only she knew more. She was so ignorant, so sheltered. Had *all* these women had sex, all except for her – even single Catholic girls like Bridget, ex-nuns like Elaine?

'I was lucky, really,' Elaine went on, lighting up a fresh cigar. 'A lot of women in my group were still living as half-nuns, even years after they'd left. I remember one poor soul. She fled straight back home and stayed there, a little girl of fifty-three, doing what her parents said.' Elaine guffawed suddenly. 'Her convent name was even worse than mine – Sister Mary of the Seven Dolours. I ask you! No wonder she was suffering from depression. Even when she changed it back to Brenda, she wasn't exactly a ball of fun. And she knew absolutely nothing about sex. She came to me once in private, after the meeting, terribly concerned because her Ma had mentioned something about her father having a bulge in his left side, and Brenda thought that must be his . . . you know – whatsitsname. In fact, the poor chap had a hernia, but she was so completely unclued-up about male anatomy, she assumed that men kept their vital bits and pieces on the side.'

'I don't believe you.' Pat reached out for the biscuits, passed them round.

'It's true, I swear. You just don't know what goes on in these convents – the mixture of plain ignorance and sort of creepy fascination with anything remotely sexual. I mean, even the way they called us "Brides of Christ", and had these quite explicit prayers about "panting for our

spouse" and "fruitful seeds" and things. What was it we used to say?'
Elaine took two biscuits, shuddered. '"Let Him kiss me with the kisses
of His divine mouth". Just the stuff for virgins.'

Hilary put her cup down. She had said it, too, had never even thought
of it as sexual. She had loved the bridal imagery sung at her Profession.
'Come, my chosen one, the King has greatly desired your beauty'; had
felt cherished to be chosen by the King of Heaven. And when they'd
placed the veil upon her head, she had repeated twice, three times:
'Christ has put a mark upon my face, that I should admit no other lover
but Him.'

'That "Brides of Christ" thing really gets me,' Pat said with a grimace.
'I mean, what does it make monks – homosexuals?'

Everyone was laughing now, everyone save Hilary, who sat shocked,
incredulous. She had always considered it the greatest of all privileges to
be the Bride of Christ, a soul He wanted entirely for Himself. Man's love
could cool or slacken off, whereas God's love was eternal.

'It wouldn't appeal to me,' the skinny girl was saying. 'He's married to
too many. I'd choose someone more available.'

An aggressive-looking woman in glasses and a bun jerked forward in
her chair. 'Look, let's be serious, can't we? Whether we're Brides of
Christ, or brides of plain John Smith, we're still mere appendages to
men, and that's the whole damn . . .'

'I *am* serious,' Elaine interrupted. 'In fact, I'm bloody furious,
wasting half my life like that. What do *you* think, Hilary? You haven't
said a word yet, but you can't support the system if you left it.'

Hilary fiddled with her teaspoon. All the faces had turned to her
expectantly. She longed to hide, sink down through the floor, melt away
to nothing like the wisp of steam still drifting from her cup. 'Well, I only
. . . I mean, there were other sorts of problems, private ones, and . . .'
Her voice tailed off. Was it any wonder Elaine had guessed she'd been a
nun? She had none of these girls' confidence, or spirit, no opinions of her
own, no voice above a whisper, and she was looking down again. She
forced her eyes up, found herself lassoed in a ring of curious stares.
Elaine broke the sudden silence.

'I just can't understand why you're not bloody raving mad. I mean,
the way we were treated like small children, with no freedom or
responsibility. *Worse* than children. Kids aren't made to recite a sixth-
century Rule, written for male masochists, off by heart and on their
knees. Or forbidden to have friends. I mean, all that crazy stuff about
the danger of "particular friendships". All friendships are particular,
otherwise the term's quite meaningless. Anyway, Christ Himself had
friends, though not a bunch my abbess would have liked – adulterers and

tarts and such, but definitely "particular". Mind you, there weren't a lot in our community I was that keen to be pals with – a load of crooks, crocks, cranks and creeps, I'd say. But then what can you expect, when you break nuns' spirit, muzzle them, load them down with sin and guilt, but still keep on insisting God is Love?'

Hilary felt scared, not angry – scared of Elaine's own anger, her depth of bitterness. She hated being lumped with her: two ex-nuns, fanatics. And yet hadn't she felt something of the same resentment – far more furtive, maybe, and never actually expressed, but still present, nonetheless?

'I'm a thorough-going feminist now. Okay, it may be just reaction, but no wonder, after all those years and years of having the traditional female virtues like meekness and submissiveness dinned in to us by Holy Mother Church. God! That's a fraud, if ever there was one. The Church is Patriarchy pure and simple. Male cardinals elect a male Pope who consecrates male bishops who ordain male priests who worship a male God in a male-orientated language.'

'You ought to stand for politics, Elaine. You're wasted on us here.' An older, grey-haired woman grinned around the circle, then turned to Hilary. 'Were you one of those enclosed nuns – you know, who never go out at all?'

'Y . . . Yes, I was.'

'That's another way men keep women powerless – shut us up, in all senses.' Elaine was on her feet now, like an orator. 'D'you realise there are far fewer enclosed Orders for men – in fact, far less monks than nuns. A lot of men wouldn't take what we did. I mean, I got a First in Maths, from Bristol, and as soon as I'd graduated, they stuck me in the kitchen to humble what they called my pride, wouldn't let me teach for five whole years, and then RI instead of Maths. And as a bit of extra penance, I had to swab the refectory floor – all ninety feet of it – with a tiddly little dish-mop, made for washing cups. It took me three whole hours. I could have done it in twenty minutes if they'd let me use a floor-mop. But a nun obeys blindly, doesn't she? And even when I was teaching, all the footling rules continued. I couldn't borrow someone's pencil, or throw away a scrap of paper, without permission from a superior.'

'Please, Reverend Mother, may I have permission to go to bed?' The small girl on her knees, hands clasped, face demure. Everybody laughed.

'Yeah, I'm shagged myself. And there's no hope of a lie-in. What time's breakfast? Eight o'clock?'

'Seven-thirty.'

Groans all round. The girls started stretching, getting up; collecting lighters, kicked-off slippers, shuffling to the door.

'Coming?' Elaine asked, as she paused by Hilary's chair.

'Er, not just for the moment. I think I'll have another cup of coffee.' She prayed Elaine wouldn't stay and join her, try to strike up a friendship on the flimsy grounds of what they had in common. What they didn't have in common seemed far more fundamental.

'See you at breakfast then, okay?'

'Okay.' Hilary watched Elaine slouch across the room, then stop a moment, heave up her pyjamas, scratch crossly at her bottom. This girl astounded her. Her language was so violent and fanatical, yet she must be brilliant to have got a First in Maths. And what about the other girls, who all seemed so critical and bitter? What had made them come at all, if they were so contemptuous of the Church, so obviously unspiritual?

She sank back in her chair. At least they had convictions, whilst she herself was totally confused, still a child, an innocent, living as a half-nun, to use Elaine's own words. She picked up the cigarette packet, which Elaine had left behind, one long thin brown cigar thing crumpled at the bottom. She hesitated a moment, glancing round the room, as if to make sure she was alone, then found a match, tried to copy Elaine in the way she lit the thing, held it in her mouth, sucked in very deeply. She choked immediately, swallowed smoke and air, gagging at the rough taste of tobacco. She tried again, refusing to be daunted. If one ex-nun could do it – smoke and swear and sleep with men – then why not her, as well? She inhaled more slowly this time, managed not to cough, but now her eyes were streaming, tears running down her cheeks. She mopped them with her sleeve, stubbed out the cigar. She was just a baby, a crying clueless baby, who should never have ventured from her sheltered Brignor nursery.

15

Hilary sat in the far corner of the canteen, hoping no one else would join her. At least two hundred other people were queueing, jostling, eating, most in jolly parties, exchanging chat and laughs. She was astonished at such hubbub on Good Friday. Even in her childhood, the day had been a gloomy one, her mother tense from fasting, her father irritable because he was expected to survive on pilchard salad and a pot of tea. Here, nobody was fasting. The counter groaned with food – eggs boiled, poached, scrambled, fried; bacon, sausages, baked beans and tomatoes; a whole row of different cereals, fruit juice, porridge, prunes.

She shook a douse of salt on her small helping of dry All-Bran, helped it down with black unsugared tea. However much she'd relaxed her fasts this Lent, Good Friday was still sacrosanct, still meant rigorous penance, though she'd no wish to draw attention to herself, which was why she'd chosen a table on her own. It was also quieter in the corner, further removed from the swarm and scrum of bodies, the rowdy kitchen staff bumping trolleys, clattering knives and forks. She put her cup down, wiped her mouth. Someone was approaching – a nun in a black habit, the old-fashioned full-length habit, very like the one she'd worn herself. She stared at it in shock. She had never realised before how conspicuous it looked, how much it marked you out from other people, how cumbersome, impractical, it seemed. She could feel herself shrinking from that drab funereal black. Had her parents felt the same, seeing their own daughter as a depressing, even menacing figure, who had stepped out of another, sadder century? She'd always imagined herself as gracious in the habit, dignified – set apart in the best sense of the word. And, even now, she missed it; felt not just distaste, but a confused irrational envy for the portly Sister standing by her table. At least the habit gave you status, denoted your role as a professed religious, made you part of something so much bigger than yourself – the Church with its history and its hierarchy, an Order with authority and purpose.

'Mind if I join you?' The nun put down her tray, introduced herself as Sister Mary Lucian. She envied that as well – the title, the tradition – was tempted to reply with 'Sister Mary Hilary'. But someone else had joined them, a balding burly-shouldered man, who seemed to know Sister Lucian well, exchanged greetings, even banter, as he pulled his chair out, installed himself beside her. Sister Lucian flashed them both a smile.

'Do you know Brian – Brian Pagley? I'm sorry, I didn't catch your name.'

'Hilary.'

Brian murmured a few pleasantries, then turned back to Sister Lucian, started discussing a past conference, where the two of them had met. She and Brian were probably roughly the same age, though the nun looked much the younger. That was another advantage of the habit. If your hair was grey or scanty, nobody could see it; veiny legs were hidden, thickening waists disguised. Sister Lucian seemed totally at ease, laughing, almost flirting with the man, insisting that he move his tray, to make more room for hers. Hilary tried to hide her sense of shock as the nun unloaded Sugar Puffs and fruit juice, bacon, eggs and beans, three pieces of toast. The Brignor nuns would be standing now, in silence, as they drank their lukewarm water, ate their one dry piece of bread; would stand again for dinner – just swedes and boiled potatoes – nothing else all day. Good Friday was the strictest day of the year, a day of penance, total silence. Yet Sister Lucian was sprinkling extra sugar on her Sugar Puffs, drowning them in milk, talking through a mouthful. She and Brian were now discussing the recent reforms in convents and why some nuns wore mufti – as if they'd read her thoughts.

'I prefer the habit, and I'm sure it stops me sinning. If I didn't have it on, I might be tempted to pop into a pub and have a pint – or two!'

Her laugh was genuine, unforced. She used her hands to gesture with, used her eyes expressively. Hilary felt more and more dejected. She had prided herself on making so much progress, yet now she realised just how stiff she was, how stilted, how still so over-scrupulous. Here was a room full of Christians, Catholics, whose God had been crucified this day, yet all around her mouths were munching, chattering; greedy hands grabbing for more food. Even Sister Lucian was larding mustard on her bacon. Mustard was a stimulus, a relish which inflamed the taste buds, and bacon was forbidden on this day of abstinence. She reproved herself for criticising, longed to be as casual – less a judge, a goody-goody. She herself had swallowed just two salty spoons of bran, yet still felt guilty, gluttonous.

She could suddenly see Miss Pullen in her mind, one half of her face twisted and distorted, the other half quite normal. That was how she felt – half a normal woman in the matter of her dress and hair, her changing views and outlook; yet still half a nun, warped in some way, freakish, permanently retarded. Would she ever catch up, feel at home in the world, or remain a permanent outsider – some extraterrestrial, whose inner core and yearning dragged her always God-wards? How strange that Sister Lucian had no inkling of her past, nor of what they had in common, but saw her as a secular, maybe even married. She touched her 'wedding' ring, made sure the Christ was hidden. The nun's own ring was silver, engraved with a small dove: the Paraclete, the comforter.

'Brian, can I steal some marmalade? These pots are so darn tiny, they don't go anywhere.' The nun pushed her plate away, started on her toast. She had left an egg, a whole poached egg, untouched, flecked with mustard. Hilary couldn't keep her eyes from it, could taste mustard in her own throat, hot and stinging like Reverend Mother's voice. 'Waste is a sin, Sister Louis Marie, and a breach of our holy vow of poverty.' She was back in the convent, still a nervous postulant, watching Sister Louis Marie beg her soup at dinner, as a penance for leaving half a crust at lunch. The heavy-eyed French Sister prostrated herself humbly before each nun in turn, holding out her empty bowl to cajole a tepid spoonful from each one – Sister Louis Marie, who came from a wealthy family in Lyons; would have been used to eating the finest food at home, served on the finest china by a maid in uniform. The other nuns had already started eating, so their spoons were dirty, the soup maybe even germy, yet she thanked each for the favour with another deep prostration. Her main course was taken from the scrap-dish, one small cold boiled potato, pock-marked with black eyes, a few skins and bones of fish. Sister Mary Gloria shouldn't have been watching, should have kept her eyes down, been listening to the reading, but it was only her fourth week in the convent, and she hadn't yet outlawed curiosity – or horror.

'Where you from, Hilary?'

She jumped, realised Brian was speaking to her; almost answered 'Brignor', changed it into 'Wandsworth'.

'I don't know it, I'm afraid. I'm a stranger in the South. Sister Lucian and I first met in murky Manchester. Hey, Sister, do you remember that young monk who said he kept a rattlesnake . . . ?'

The two were laughing now again. Hilary edged her chair away, glanced around the huge canteen, which was echoing and booming like a public swimming baths, bursts of laughter exploding from the tables, a sudden crash as someone dropped a pile of dirty plates. She still missed the Brignor refectory, despite the penances, the strictness. Meals, however simple, had been almost sacramental, the serving nuns processing in, with cabbage soup, or swedes; eyes cast down, steps exactly matched, as they bowed low before each Sister, offering her the food. Even clearing the table became a solemn ceremonial with its own set rules; nothing rushed or casual, the whole elaborate ritual like a prayer. And if a Sister wanted something, she would never ask or grab.

There were special signs to indicate her needs: a circled thumb and forefinger for water, two fingers raised for bread – even signs for illness so you could excuse yourself, in silence, with just one finger touched against your pulse. She longed to make that sign herself, creep back to her room, avoid the need to socialise, to talk.

'Which workshop are you going to?' Sister Lucian was trying to include her, not make her feel left out.

'I hadn't thought. Do we have to choose?'

'Oh, yes. We all break into groups this morning. Haven't you read your programme? *I'm* going to Bodywork. There's this Reverend Mother running it. I've never met her, but they say she's very good. Why don't you come along? Brian's coming, aren't you, Brian?'

He swallowed a last white frill of egg, nodded, wiped his mouth. 'I'm not sure which is most unfit – my body or my soul. But we get so much soul-stuff anyway, I've decided it's my body's turn this morning.'

'What is Bodywork, exactly?' Hilary asked, to gain some time, though she had decided already to avoid it at all costs – to avoid anything and everything run by a Reverend Mother.

'I'm not quite sure.' Sister Lucian had cut her toast in soldiers, like a child, her chubby fingers glazed with marmalade. 'A bit of everything, I think – dancing, exercise, encounter groups – sort of acknowledging your body and relating to it.'

Hilary's 'no' boomed louder in her mind, though she merely smiled politely. She'd choose something more cerebral, more spiritual, in keeping with Good Friday. But what? The names of the other workshops were slowly coming back: Painting and Praying, Sing Joyfully to God, Renewal through Yoga, Jesus Rock. Nothing suitable at all. She drained her tea, mumbled some excuse about going to her room first, moved towards the door, almost collided with a woman striding in – a woman in man's dungarees with a red shirt underneath – Elaine, from last night's ginger group.

'Hi, Hilary! I'm knackered – and missed breakfast by the looks of it. They're just clearing all the food away. Bloody hell!' Elaine reached out for a sausage left on someone's plate, crammed it in her mouth. 'By the way, I hope you're coming to the painting workshop. It's great! I went last year and we all did finger-painting and squirted huge great aerosols around.'

'No,' she said, suddenly decisive. 'I'm sorry, Elaine, but I've just promised to go to Bodywork with Brian and Sister Lucian.'

'Right, I'd like everyone sitting on the floor – crosslegged, if you can manage it. I want us all to ground ourselves, to actually feel the ground through and with our bodies.'

People started getting up, mostly nervously, reluctantly. The plump and well-dressed leader smiled encouragement.

'Don't skulk against the walls like that. We're here to share our bodies with each other. Can we make a circle? That's better. Now, is everyone quite comfy? No? Well, take a few deep breaths.'

Hilary inhaled, let her breath out slowly. She was surprised how shy this group seemed, far smaller and more inhibited than Jim Duck's ecstatic mob. Each event seemed different – different in its atmosphere, different in its members. Apart from Brian and Sister Lucian, and a woman called Thérèse who'd been in the kitchen with Elaine last night, but hadn't said a word, there was no one else she knew, or even recognised; certainly no wild unbridled revellers. Perhaps Bodywork attracted all the misfits, self-conscious shrinking people, who were unhappy with their bodies, unable to let go.

'Now let's introduce ourselves. Each one say their name and add a few brief words to tell each other who they are – what they do, how they feel. I'll start, shall I, break the ice? Right, I'm Molly.'

'But I thought they said . . . I mean, I understood this was run by a religious.' The speaker sounded angry, cheated in some way, a thin and sallow woman in her sixties, who was having obvious difficulty in sitting on the floor. Several other people mumbled in support, as if they'd been thinking the same thing, but were too scared to voice objections.

'We're all religious,' Molly smiled. 'That's why we're here. Yes, I am a nun, in fact, and I do run a convent, but the title "Reverend Mother" has always seemed rather inappropriate, since I'm neither reverend nor a mother. I prefer plain Molly. I was christened Amanda Margaret Mary by my parents, but it's a wee bit of a mouthful, don't you think? Still, if you'd rather call me Amanda, please do go ahead. Call me anything you like, I shan't mind, I promise.'

Hilary simply stared. She was used to nuns in mufti – or at least to the idea – the sober skirts in grey or navy blue, the loose and shapeless blouses, low-heeled lace-up shoes. But Molly wore a tartan pleated skirt, a scarlet shirt with ruffles down the front, matching scarlet slingbacks which Della would have envied, with high stiletto heels. Yet Reverend Mother Molly was still bound by vows of poverty, of chastity. It was one thing for Elaine to wear dungarees and gym shoes. Elaine had left her convent and the clothes were old and shabby. But Molly's clothes looked new, the sort of stylish snobby outfits they sold at Di's boutique. Who paid for them, she wondered – guessed others in the group were wondering too, especially Sister Lucian, whose habit now seemed quite archaic, compared with Molly's glad rags.

They had all assumed this worldly made-up woman was a substitute, a stand-in; that the Reverend Mother detailed on the programme had been delayed or taken ill. Hilary had been secretly relieved. Now she was confounded. She tried to imagine her own Abbess dressed in a kilt and three-inch heels, sitting cross-legged on the floor, saying 'Call me what you like. I am neither reverend nor a mother.' She could feel a laugh threatening, a laugh of sheer shocked disbelief, tried to turn it into a smile. Molly smiled back warmly, obviously glad to see a face which wasn't simply hostile or incredulous.

'I'm here today to try and teach you how to use your bodies, to love and own the body God has given you, whatever its age or shape. Bodies are the only thing we have to express our love of God, so we mustn't ignore them or neglect them. My body's feeling extra good this morning, so I hope to share that with you.'

The silence was embarrassing. Everyone was staring at Molly's auburn hair, which seemed to owe less to God's own bounty than to the skills of a good salon; the glossy scarlet lipstick which exactly matched her blouse, the flash of white lace petticoat beneath the tartan flounces.

'Well, is no one going to speak? Come on, don't be shy. We're all in the same boat, you know. I'm shy as well, very shy. In fact, when I first became a superior, I really had to fight that.'

Hilary wondered if she'd heard right. *Shy?* This relaxed and chatty extrovert, who'd chosen brilliant colours, clothes which drew attention to herself? She glanced again at Molly, who was wiggling her toes, knees splayed out, expensive shoes kicked off now. Wiggling her toes! The gesture seemed obscene. The Brignor Abbess kept all movement to a minimum, could kneel for hours in chapel, as if she were a statue; appeared to glide on castors. Hilary had sometimes even wondered if her heart beat, or if that, too, had been stilled, in the interests of total reverent silence.

Molly flexed her shoulders, clasped an ankle in each hand. 'Let's go round the circle anti-clockwise, and let's start with a man, since we're lucky enough to have one – two men, in fact. Wonderful! Right, you with the nice beard, what's your name, my dear?'

Hilary hardly heard the names. She was too concerned with what she'd say herself. Should she admit she'd been a nun? Thérèse already knew, might somehow let it out. Then Brian and Sister Lucian would think she was a fraud, for concealing it at breakfast. Was it wrong to try to hide it, deny her whole adult past to date, pretend her life began three months ago? She glanced at Sister Lucian, felt the same confusing mixture of envy and aversion; became more and more uneasy as it got closer to her turn. Just two to go. Just one. Just . . .

211

'I'm Hilary,' she managed. 'I live in London and do mainly sewing work.'

'And how are you feeling, Hilary?'

'Terrible.'

Everybody laughed. At least it broke the tension. Molly smiled at her, squeezed her hand encouragingly. Hilary froze. Her own Abbess would never touch a fellow nun, except at her Profession and the Renewal of her Vows, when she would clasp the Sister's hand in hers, receive her promise to observe her vows till death. Till death . . .

Molly had moved on to the next name – Marie-Clare – a French girl, who admitted stumblingly that her whole life was a mess. Molly slipped into the circle, put her arm around her. Hilary watched, envious of the girl who didn't pull away, or freeze, but seemed to relish the experience, even laid her head against Molly's shoulder, as if she were her child. Whatever she said, Molly *was* a mother, a mother with a lap and arms, large and obvious breasts. Hilary could suddenly see her own mother, lying in the nursing home, her scraggy chest covered with a dressing. She had never been able to breast-feed, had produced abscesses, not milk – or so Aunt Eva told her twelve years later. Why had both her Mothers been so grudging? Mother Amanda Margaret Mary would have gold-top in her breasts, the full cream milk of human kindness. She envied her, as well. To be able to show such warmth, be so relaxed and easy-going. She herself was still too inhibited to put her arm round Luke, let alone an adult and a stranger.

Molly hugged the French girl, assured her they'd talk later, then retrieved her shoes, stood up. 'Right, now we're going to do an exercise, just to get us going. I want you to imagine that you've all been stuffed in the bottom of a large brown paper bag, and the bag's been tied securely at the top. First, see what it feels like, what your reactions are, then use every effort possible to try to escape, get out of that confining bag. All right?'

No one stirred at first. There were a few nervous titters, coughs, then suddenly Sister Lucian got up to her feet and started wrestling with an imaginary paper sack, pushing at the sides, wrenching at the top, even kicking out with one black-stockinged foot. Hilary watched, astonished. Was the nun obeying simply out of duty, or enjoying the experience? Despite her age and girth, and the restrictions of the habit, she seemed supple, energetic, using her whole body as she bent and reached and stretched, flinging up her arms, butting with her head. Other people were now slowly getting up, emboldened by her courage. An obese and dumpy woman wobbled onto the floor, punched the air with fat and feeble arms. A younger girl began threshing furiously, as if fighting off

212

an army. Both men now joined in, and then an older woman, whose white hair and bandaged ankle didn't stop her running round in tiny frantic circles, trying to break out of her bag. At least three-quarters of the group were now in bags and fighting to escape: shadow-boxing, grappling with brown paper, lunging at thin air.

Molly skipped around them like a referee, laughing her approval. 'That's good! That's very good. Now make sounds, as well. You don't have to be silent. Match your movements to your grunts and groans and yells.'

Again, Sister Lucian was the first one to obey, letting out a strangled shout, surprising in its force. Hilary longed to scream herself, scream her sheer frustration at being unable to break out, express herself, let go. *She* was the one who had left her Order, thrown off her long robes, yet she was still too scared, too hidebound, to behave like Sister Lucian. The nun was like a model, one she couldn't follow, only envy and resent. She felt even more a failure, as howls and moans and whimperings began to pour from every throat, swelling in a babel. She retreated to a corner, watched burly Brian crawling on the floor, petite Thérèse charging, tussling, punching; everyone save her trying to break or tear or burst their paper bags.

'Having trouble, Hilary?' Molly had come over, crouched beside her on the floor. 'Don't worry. Just take your time, do it in your own way. Have you got into your bag yet?'

'Er, no.'

'Well, try that first, and just see how it feels.'

Self-consciously, she climbed into a bag, a non-existent bag, felt the brown walls close around her, the string fasten at the top. So how did it feel? She wasn't sure, at first, was aware only of embarrassment, of Molly watching her. She closed her eyes, tried to block out everything, to sink down in her bag. That was better – peaceful. She had shut the others out now, was in her own quiet space. She slumped even further down, relishing her privacy. She felt safe, protected, back with walls again and boundaries; a confined and sheltered space where nobody could touch her. She liked the bag, surprisingly. Why should she escape from it, waste all that fruitless energy trying to get out? She was tired already, sluggish from her night awake, exhausted from the confusion in her mind. Each new group she met seemed to throw up more conflicts, contradictions. Did Molly's loving warmth give her leave to break her vow of poverty, or Elaine's bitterness justify her anger? Were Sister Lucian's easy-going ways a virtue or a danger? She didn't know the answers, didn't like the questions; didn't even want a mind at all; a mind which kept criticising, questioning, contradicting everything by turn.

And she didn't want a body – a body which had periods, or strange and shameful urges, set off by those noises through the wall – a body too like Bridget's, which might betray her sometime, even make those same wild threatening noises.

She curled up very small, hid her eyes in the dark carpet, put her hands across her ears, so she could shut out all the grunts and yowls and scufflings. Why settle for a flimsy paper bag, when she could pack herself away in corrugated cardboard, layers of strong brown paper? She started imagining the wrappings, feeling safer with each one, as she retreated to the centre of her parcel, shielded by stiff cardboard, armoured in brown paper. No one could get in, nobody could touch her. Every other person was trying to escape, yelling as they struggled up and out. She alone sat absolutely still, picturing the firm string knotted round her, the final daub of sealing wax to secure and seal the knots, so no one would be tempted to undo her.

16

'Come in.'

Hilary opened the door, stepped back again, confused, when she saw Father Tovey lying on his bed, the curtains drawn, the room dark and musty-smelling.

'Oh, I'm sorry, Father, I didn't realise . . .'

'No, do come in. I had a splitting headache, but it's gone now.' He swung his legs off the bed, pulled the curtains back, started hunting for his shoes – running-shoes this time, not bright blue plastic flip-flops. He seemed fond of sports clothes; was wearing a grey tracksuit top, with a tiny motif of two crossed tennis rackets. She couldn't imagine him playing tennis, even less running marathons. He looked too pale and delicate, as if he spent all his time indoors. He removed his coat from the one small upright chair, a pile of books and journals from the stained and mottled carpet.

'Can I get you a cup of coffee? One of the perks of being a priest is that we have kettles in our rooms.'

She refused the coffee, glanced around his room, which looked much the same as hers, save more untidy. His desk was heaped with papers, and a large and showy Easter egg in a gold and scarlet box seemed to be serving as a paperweight. The posters on his walls were very different from her own guitars and Shetland ponies. He had women on his walls – three blown-up women in different clothes and poses, but all blonde, curvaceous, pouting.

He saw her looking, smiled. 'Yes, I'm sorry about the pictures. I'm surprised the students aren't made to take them down, but I suppose term restarts in just a week or two and it's hardly worth their while. I've got tea, if you prefer it. Or Ribena.'

'No, nothing, thank you, Father.'

'Well, sit down, anyway, and please do call me Simon.'

She tensed. 'Simon' would only make it harder. Confession was a sacrament, not an encounter group or bodywork. She realised suddenly that Molly and this priest had certain things in common – the same warmth and informality, the same refusal to pull rank. Perhaps they'd worked together, or been to the same trainings. She mustn't get sidetracked onto unimportant issues, or even friendly chat. It was imperative to tell him why she'd come, blurt it out, if necessary, before she lost her courage, fled.

'I was actually wondering, Father, if you could . . . hear my confession.'

He paused at the window, stood looking out across the grounds. 'I don't hear confessions any more – not private ones.'

She stared at him, astonished. Surely *all* priests heard confessions. She was beginning to feel more and more out of touch, even with her own Church. Had things changed so much without her even knowing?

'But if you'd like to talk to me, or if I can help in any way . . . '

She got up stiffly from her chair, sick with disappointment. Talking was no good. She must have absolution. She had spent the last two hours preparing for confession, had missed lunch deliberately, so that she would have more time for examining her conscience, reflecting on the Passion, on her sins.

'No, I must go to confession. Is there another Catholic priest here, or a local Catholic church that's not too far away?'

'What's wrong, Hilary? You're sounding quite upset.' He sat down on the bed, motioned her to sit beside him. She remained standing and distraught, listening to the noises from outside. A group of people were playing ball, running in wild circles on the lawn, their shouts and whoops of laughter intruding on her gloomy thoughts. She shrunk back against the wall, so that none of them could see her, lowered her own voice. 'I'm in mortal sin, Father.'

'I doubt it.'

'I . . . I beg your pardon?'

He clasped his hands, pale eyes almost lost as he stared down at his fingers. 'One of the reasons I no longer hear confessions is that they result in too much guilt and introspection, on the one hand, and too much sheer arithmetic, on the other. You know the sort of thing – how many times; when, where, how, how much? It's *why* that's more important – our inner motivation. A mortal sin is a deliberate desire to deny, flout or injure God, cold-bloodedly and consciously, whereas most lesser sin, the common everyday sort, results from muddle and confusion, or fear, or conflict, or just simple human weakness.'

'You don't understand, Father. This isn't just a common everyday sin. I'm a nun . . . I mean, I *was*. I left my convent.'

'So have several thousand others, and it may be a good thing. Too many girls entered the religious life for all the wrong reasons. A true vocation is a wonderful thing, a precious gift from God, but it's all too easy to confuse it with a longing for security, or a fear of men or marriage, or terror of the world.'

She winced as the ball shot past their window, two men in pursuit, young boys in jeans and sweatshirts. 'But I ran away, Father. I didn't ask

216

permission or discuss it with my Abbess. I just walked out and . . . '

'Poor girl. That must have been quite terrifying. Which Order were you in?'

Hilary stumbled out her answer, subsided in her chair. Had he really said 'Poor girl', shrugged off what she'd said, called it a good thing? Perhaps even now he hadn't understood, didn't know she'd made – and broken – solemn Final Vows.

'I was in for twenty years, Father – twenty-one. I wasn't just a novice or . . . '

'It took courage, then, to leave, enormous courage. How long have you been out?'

'Just over three months.' She thought back to Christmas Eve, the frantic limping criminal in play-clothes. That three months seemed a lifetime.

He frowned. 'Not long. Have you had counselling? There are people who can help, you know, talk things over with you, try to find you work and a decent place to live.'

'I've got work, thank you, Father, and a room. I'm very lucky.'

'No.' He shook his head. 'It's an enormous upheaval leaving the religious life, and it can affect you very deeply, both physically and mentally. I've known ex-nuns get really ill, or land up in a psychiatric ward. You're doing very well, Hilary, believe me. The last thing you need is a load of guilt, on top of all the other problems you must have had to face.'

He was being kind, too kind. She must make him realise how bad she felt, how much she needed confession, absolution. 'But I *feel* in sin, Father, as if I'm damned already. I even have nightmares about hell.'

'There is no hell, I'm pretty sure of that. Look at it this way. I couldn't be happy in heaven, if I knew there was even one poor soul in hell. And I'm only human, with a limited compassion. So how could an all-merciful God damn His own creation?'

She was touched by his remark, his obvious human warmth; less happy with his theology. 'Yes, but it says in the Bible . . . '

'It says a lot of things in the Bible. We aren't meant to accept them all as literal truth, but interpret them symbolically, use our imagination as well as just our reason. I mean, I've often wondered if the idea of the flames of hell first arose from things like fiery lava or volcanoes – physical phenomena which people didn't understand, couldn't explain in terms of natural causes. Or maybe methane gas, which seeps up to the surface of the Middle Eastern oilfields and catches fire, if there's any breath of wind around, burns along the sand. I saw a picture of that, once. It looked really rather strange, with these fierce and crackling flames, but nothing actually burning – no wood, or fuel, or anything, just a mysterious fire, which seemed to be coming up from underground. Easy enough to imagine that hellfire was underneath, instead of natural gas.' He flicked his hair back, shifted on the bed. 'True hell resides in our own minds, in our misery, our weakness. You may be in hell, in that sense, but not in the sense of being damned.'

Hilary looked up, hope and doubt struggling in her mind. Was she truly not in sin, or was he just too liberal? Father Martin had mentioned priests like that, priests who made things easy, to suit their own lax standards. But Father Tovey was so obviously devout – unconventional, yes – but basically a holy person. She could tell that from his whole demeanour, the prayerful way he spoke, even when dismissing hell. How could two priests be so different? It was Father Martin who had made her fear damnation in the first place, fear the devil.

'But what about Satan?' she asked, falteringly.

'He's just another name for the evil in the world and in ourselves. I'm not denying evil – alas, it's all too obvious – but the Church has stressed it far too much, especially *our* Church, I'm afraid. D'you realise, Hilary, there are far more Catholic convicts, Catholic alcoholics, Catholic prostitutes and drug addicts than their actual numbers in the population warrant? Maybe that's because Catholics are made to feel guilty right from the word go, told they're bad so often, they become bad in the end. And half the time, it's we priests who are to blame, threatening little kids with hell, or insisting they keep rooting for their sins. We need to stress God's love, rather than His fury. People are good because God made them, precious because He died for them, and holy because they're made in His own image. Yet mostly they feel wicked, undeserving and unworthy. It's even worse for women. When I think of the early Fathers debating whether women had souls at all, or Thomas Aquinas concluding they were simply defective men, who . . . '

Hilary hooked her feet around her chair-rung. She was beginning to feel nervous. Was he a feminist, as well, like those rebels in the kitchen, a rebel altogether? His radical views and casual shabby clothes seemed to link him with their circle. He was wearing the same old denim jeans, which looked even more incongruous with his sporty tracksuit top, and both were badly creased where he'd been lying on the bed. So what? She could hardly criticise Reverend Mother Molly for her glamour, then slam Father Tovey for his lack of it. Yet it was somehow so much easier if people wore their uniforms – superiors in habits, priests in long black cassocks. Once they changed to mufti, it was so hard not to judge them; put them into categories like glamorous or scruffy, top-drawer or

Bohemian. And that, in turn, seemed to remove them from their office, dilute their authority, make them semi-seculars.

'Christ Himself loved women, mixed with them quite freely, yet His Church has taken quite a different line – feared and even hated them, tried to suppress their sexuality, which has only led to more guilt – an attempt to deny the body, a harping on celibacy, virginity, which brings us back to nuns. It's hardest of all for nuns, Hilary. I've known many paralysed with guilt, because they've infringed some minor rule, yet they're living a life that's unnatural, near impossible.'

Hilary's legs were hurting, twisted on the chair-rung. She must be very careful, or he might only confuse her more; add self-pity to her already muddled feelings of resentment, self-disgust. Yet he seemed entirely different from Elaine's shrill and vulgar ginger group. Even when he was criticising, he spoke very quietly, gently; less in anger than a sort of quiet regret. He had turned towards her now, his whole face solicitous. 'Tell me, Hilary, what made you leave the convent after all those years?'

Hilary glanced out of the window. She could no longer see the players, but could hear the ball thudding on the grass, the skid and swoop of feet. 'Your turn!' yelled a shrill-voiced girl. 'Quick, Avril, over here!' She stared down at the carpet, tried to blank the voices out, creep into her silent Brignor cell. 'I . . . I lost my sense of God,' she said. 'I know that's fairly common, and for years I just accepted it. I felt so sterile sometimes, spiritually, it was as if I'd died inside, but our chaplain told me that I wasn't dead at all: God had just anaesthetised me, so He could carry out life-saving surgery. He said I might have to accept living in that sort of dark and frightening coma for the whole rest of my life, but that a lifetime was nothing compared with Eternity. He advised me to "let go", to embrace the darkness, allow it to become darker still, if necessary.'

The uncertain April sunshine was trembling on the carpet, casting shadows, patterns. Hilary moved her chair back, as if escaping from its light. 'Often, I felt close to real despair, especially in the winter. Winters were the worst. Each one seemed colder, bleaker, longer than the last. I felt frozen over, like the ground, and barren, Father, useless. And I kept on getting ill. Oh, only minor things like colds and flu, or styes or stomach pains, and I always tried to shrug them off or blame them on the weather. But even when the spring arrived, nothing really changed – well, the season did, of course, but I stayed sick and shrivelled, even after Easter. Easter always seemed a sham – the greatest feast of the Church's year, yet I couldn't feel the joy of it, couldn't seem to believe in Resurrection, only Crucifixion.' She broke off suddenly, realised with embarrassment that it was the longest speech she had made in twenty years, perhaps the longest in her life. 'I'm sorry, Father. I'm talking far too much.'

'Not at all. You're here to talk, and I understand your pain. I've been through a lot of it myself.'

Hilary shifted on her chair again. The sun was fingering her shoes, creeping up her legs. 'Well, our chaplain didn't understand. He said despair was just a form of vanity, and that my real fault was wounded pride, in that I couldn't accept my misery and nothingness, as a sinful creature's natural state. He told me the devil works overtime on cultivating vanity, tempts people to despair, then drags them down to hell.' She smiled shyly at the priest. '*He* believed in hell, Father – very much so, I'm afraid. That was half the trouble. I could never work out what I really felt, or what was Satan tempting me. I began to feel split in half, like two separate hostile people, who kept quarrelling and shouting at each other, though always in dead silence – one doubting, questioning; the other instantly reproving, or even scandalised. Then that wretched doubting Person One started to rebel against tiny petty things, like the way you have to fold your habit in exactly the same way, day after day, year after year, or ask permission to use an extra hankie or drink a glass of water between meals. But Person Two would say: "None of that is petty. Just pour an infinity of love into every infinitesimal thing; make each second of each day a prayer, an act of service."

'I tried, Father, believe me. I warmed to that ideal, longed to really live it. It wasn't easy, though, and I probably went too far; made every detail of my life a kind of test-case; had to do every single thing better, harder, longer, than anybody else, which I suppose is just another form of pride – though I didn't see it then. You see, I was determined to murder Person One, whom I'd come to see as Satan, Satan right inside me, speaking through my mouth, as Father Martin said.' She stopped again, ashamed of her own outburst. How could she be pouring out these private shameful things, and to someone who was still basically a stranger; things she had barely admitted even to herself, and which must sound self-pitying, neurotic? It was disloyal, as well as feeble; disloyal to Father Martin, to her Order.

Father Tovey got up from the bed, stood in front of her. 'You've had a tough time, haven't you, a really wretched lonely struggle. Far be it from me to criticise another priest, but my personal belief is that if God is good, then He wants us to enjoy our lives, live in light and peace and happiness, not shrivel in the dark, or burn in hell with Satan.'

'But *is* He good?' The cry escaped her before she could suppress it. 'I'm sorry, Father, you can see now I'm a sinner. I've had doubts about

God's goodness for years and years, and they've become much worse since leaving, seeing all the horrors in the world.'

He walked slowly to the window, kept his back to her, spoke so softly she had to strain to hear. 'I know exactly how you feel. I've wrestled with those doubts myself, almost left the Church, at one point. It's much the thorniest problem of them all. There *is* no answer, I'm afraid. I've read the books, worked through the old arguments about free will and the Fall and original sin, and all the rest of it, but I found none of it convincing when I was lying awake at night struggling with the problem of how God allows the murder of six million Jews, or even the suffering of just one old woman who dies of hypothermia, or one mixed-up kid who takes an overdose. And when you think of . . . ' The door suddenly swung open and a fresh-faced girl bounced in, a fat and glossy pigtail swinging down her back.

'Simon . . . Oh, you're busy. Sorry! I'll come back later, shall I? And don't forget you promised me a drink – a double. I'm keeping you to that.'

The priest seemed thrown, confused. He had moved towards the girl, but she was already prancing out again, her pert 'Ta-ta' vibrating through the room. Hilary winced as the door slammed. Couldn't she have closed it, knocked before she entered, and was it really fair to wheedle drinks from priests? She was annoyed that Father Tovey had been stopped in his account, and just when he was admitting his own doubts. It amazed her he should do so. Father Martin had always made her feel that doubts were a sign of weakness, a proof of her inadequacy; had even hinted, like the Abbess, that she was mentally disturbed. Was Father Simon Tovey equally disturbed, then? He had used the very words she might have used herself – *had* used, indeed, in the frantic anguished silence of her mind. She glanced at him again, his young face almost haggard, his smoke-blue eyes dark-shadowed with fatigue. Did he still lie sleepless, wrestling with those doubts? She must return him to the subject. 'But how did you resolve it all?' she dared to ask, half-rising from her chair.

He walked back to the window, stood leaning on the sill. 'I don't think I ever did, you know, not completely, anyway. I've come to see that the price of faith is doubt.' He paused a moment, sombre, weighed down by that doubt. 'People argue that without free will we'd be lesser human beings, that as co-creators with God, we must have power and responsibility, and power includes at least the possibility of evil. But I'm not so sure. I mean, if God could create the Blessed Virgin Mary sinless, yet still possessing free will, then why not a billion billion Marys?' He let out a brief laugh, but his eyes remained troubled still, as if he were searching for an answer.

221

Hilary had no answer. She had put almost the same question to a visiting retreat priest, seven years ago, though she hadn't used the term 'co-creator'. She liked the word, relished it a moment – the power to create life, to have a baby, form another human being, a complex personality – the nearest thing to playing God on earth.

The priest was fiddling with the curtain, scrunching up the cretonne in one hand. 'In the end, I stopped expecting foolproof rational answers. And two things helped a lot. One was the Agony in the Garden, which is relevant today, of course, Good Friday. Christ suffered so desperately Himself then – not just the physical horror of sweating blood, which I believe is physiologically impossible, but the utter loneliness of being let down by His closest friends, and apparently abandoned by His Father. He begged God to take away the anguish, but God didn't choose to hear, so He had to say "Thy will be done, not mine", and I suppose in the end, that's all that *we* can do. Do you know the El Greco painting, by the way?'

She shook her head, knew little about paintings, except those which hung at Brignor, mostly nineteenth-century watercolours of pious praying saints with lilies in their hands.

'In my poor view, it's the only painting of the Agony which really puts across the intensity of the suffering. The others may be moving, like the Giovanni Bellini, or majestic, like the Rembrandt, but they don't give you that sense of total racking anguish. It's not so much the figure of the Christ itself – the whole composition seems tormented. The rocks are very cruel and sharp, painted in these strange and lowering shapes, and the trees are bare and dead, and the sky looks really menacing, with a ghastly lurid light and a sense of things cracking up all round. And there's this little band of men approaching on the right, already come to get their man, with their spears and torches reflecting back the moonlight, and the shadows on Christ's robe look like gaping wounds themselves and . . . '

The priest's plain face seemed transfigured by his fervour. Hilary could almost see the painting in her mind, could feel Christ's suffering far more tangibly than she had managed yet, all day. Father Tovey seemed to have lived Christ's Passion with Him, shared His last few days, interpreting them in his own new and vivid way – the Last Supper, the washing of the feet, and now the Agony. She looked up at him again, surprised to see a pouting blonde behind him on the wall, and not Christ sweating blood.

'Careful, John, you idiot! You've just battered down a good two dozen tulips. Let's push off to the sports field. It's too dangerous here. We'll break a window next.'

222

Hilary waited till the voices died away, ball bouncing still, footsteps slowly fading. 'You said two things helped you, Father. What about the second?'

'Oh, that's much less dramatic – just the ordinary decent people I've met along the way. If I'm still a priest, and still worshipping a good God, that's partly due to His creation, to the courage and compassion of parishioners and friends, and even total strangers. A good few of those people have suffered pretty terribly themselves, yet their desolation gives them greater sympathy with others. Because of suffering, they can somehow channel love – love of God, love of neighbour.'

Hilary glanced up at his hands, saw them in her mind, still wet and chapped from the washing of the feet. How could he be a fraud? His favourite word was 'love' and it was obvious that he lived the word himself. Perhaps he looked so tired and drawn because he'd been up all night helping a sick person, or counselling a potential suicide. She slumped back in her chair. 'That's another reason, Father, why I feel in sin. I just can't love enough. I seem to be so critical, and wary, and sort of muddled up inside. I mean, I've just been to a workshop where everyone else could hug and touch and share – everyone save me, that is. I feel as if there's this thick glass wall in front of me which prevents anyone from coming close, or me from reaching them.'

He crouched in front of her, as if pleading with her, forcing her to see his point of view. 'That's completely understandable. Your Order was extremely rigorous, if not downright punitive. I knew a girl who was going to enter Brignor, even spent a week there, but she just couldn't take the training. Even now, it's hardly modernised at all, and twenty years ago it must have been archaic. You've been through a system which suppresses all your feelings, tries to break your spirit and your self, crush you, strip you, divide you from your body. Is it any wonder that you can't respond? You will, I know you will. You need more time, that's all.'

She shrugged impatiently. She'd had so much time already, done so little with it. 'It can't be just the convent, Father. I've just met another nun – a Sister Mary Lucian, and she quite put me to shame. She's so free and uninhibited and . . . '

'Hold on a second, Hilary. I know Sister Lucian. Her Order's different altogether, far more up to date. And it's a teaching Order, anyway, so her pupils keep her on her toes, and then she meets parents all the time, and goes out and about to educational meetings and conferences and so on. Of course she's more relaxed. You were a contemplative, totally enclosed, and in one of the strictest Orders left in Britain – left anywhere, for that matter. You must believe me, Hilary, you're doing very well.'

'I'm not, Father, honestly. I'm totally confused. I don't know what I think, or even if I'm still a nun or not. I mean, if I *am*, or want to be, then why am I so negligent? I've stopped attending Mass, except on Sundays, I haven't been to Confession since the first week in December and . . . '

'All those are healthy signs. It's probably good for you to start letting up a bit, after twenty years of strain and grind. You said yourself you were becoming over-scrupulous, and it's as wrong to be obsessional as it is to get too lax. You should be gentle with yourself, you know, love yourself a little more. If you don't love yourself, how can you love God, or anybody else?'

Love – that word again – and one which kept leading back to Ivan. If this were confession, which in a sense it was, however casual and informal, then she ought to mention Ivan. She longed for the privacy of the confessional box, where the priest couldn't see her face, where the darkness would hide her blushes, as she struggled to explain what had happened in the Alexander lessons, what had happened to her body, to her mind. There was silence now outside, only the faint snort of a chain saw droning from the far side of the campus. She longed for the intrusive thud of feet again, to mask her voice, make it sound less tremulous. She feared Father Tovey's own voice might sharpen in rebuke, but it stayed gentle, unperturbed.

'God made our bodies, Hilary, as well as just our souls. There's nothing wrong with experiencing certain feelings, or even doing certain things, so long as we're not harming anyone else.'

'But he was . . . homosexual, Father.' The word seemed so embarrassing, almost worse than Della's 'poofters'.

'I know. I understood. That's sad for both of you, but hardly sinful, surely. You did nothing wrong, as far as I can see, and as regards your friend, well, many doctors nowadays believe that homosexuality is a matter of biology, or chemistry. If God made gays that way, then we must love them as they are, try to help them.'

He reached forward, took her hand. 'But first we must help *you*. God doesn't want you crushed, Hilary, or racked with guilt, or broken. If He called you once, then He called you as an individual person, and that unique and special person is still very precious to Him, very dearly loved. You must have confidence, that's all. You're attractive and well-dressed, and obviously a caring decent person, and intelligent and . . . '

She hardly heard the rest. She was aware only of his hand on hers, the intense and vital pressure of its grip. If it had happened any earlier, she would have been shocked and disconcerted, but she could accept it now as an act of Christian love. He was trying to show her that she mattered, to him as well as to God; trying to give her that confidence he had already said she needed. He moved a little closer, put his arm around her. She tensed at first, almost automatically, had to fight the urge not to shrink away, remembering Robert's arm, that sense of being crushed and threatened, in danger from a man. But this was something different – just a simple loving gesture from a holy man of God. Reverend Mother Molly had done the same with the two men in the group, both young attractive men. There was no flirtation in it, only spontaneous human warmth, a warmth she lacked herself, yet deeply craved. It was all part of the healing, the need to fuse soul and body, which would make man whole and holy, and had been divided for too long.

She let herself relax, realised with a slowly mounting pleasure that the arm felt good, that she was actually in contact with another human being, and in contact not just physically, but mentally. There was a sense of real release in the fact she'd shared so much with him, had managed to communicate. The word startled her a moment. Communicate. Not bread and wine this time, but something nurturing and precious just the same. The pressure of his arm felt strange, the closeness of his body. Miraculously strange. He found her attractive, thought she was well-dressed. She had received compliments before, from Ivan, Robert, Liz, but never from a priest – God's representative. It was because he *was* a priest that she could allow herself to break the years and years of rigid separateness, which had forbidden any touch at all, any reaching out of either mind or body. She must be less relentless with herself, do what he advised, stress God's love, instead of her own sin. Already she could feel God's grace restored to her, His warmth across her shoulders. Yet she still craved absolution, formal forgiveness from His minister on earth.

'I wondered, Father, if you could give me absolution? I know this isn't quite confession, but . . . '

There was a sudden thumping on the door. She sprang away, darted to the window, feeling instant though irrational guilt. She heard the door creak open, two male voices talking; kept her back turned, as if she wasn't there.

'Okay, I won't be long, Paul. Just two minutes, right?'

'Yeah, fine.'

The door clicked shut again. The priest approached her, touched her shoulder. 'I'm afraid I have to go now. Don't worry, we'll talk again – we need to. It's wrong to rush these things and the Healing Service starts in just ten minutes. In fact, I'm late already. They've been wondering where I am.'

'Oh, I'm sorry, Father, really. I should have . . . '

He smiled. 'No more guilt, remember. Try to stamp out all those "shoulds" and "sorrys" – and all those "Fathers", too. If you call me

Simon, like everybody else does, then we can talk more freely, as two equal human beings.'

'I'm sorry,' she began again, bit her words back, had the grace to laugh.

He grinned himself. 'That's better. You've got a lovely smile – just use it more, all right? And by the way, why don't you attend that Healing Service? It's for healing of the soul, as well as just of sickness, and a marvellous way of making your new start.'

'Yes, I will,' she said, and added shyly, 'Simon.'

17

Hilary sat drowned and trapped in Babel, nine hundred mouths around her emitting weird unearthly noises, which were swelling to a tidal wave of sound. She could recognise no words. Sudden plangent yodellings rose above soft and crooning wails; strings of babbled syllables with no meaning and no end echoed and resounded through the hall. She couldn't run away this time – she was trapped right in the middle of a close-packed middle row, beads of sweat sliding down her back. She was frightened of the sound, frightened of its power, its sheer hurting whooping volume; her sense of being the one and only mute amongst a hall of trumpet-tongues. It was as if she had blundered into a foreign country where the natives spoke a completely alien language and spoke it in a roar. The noise kept rising, falling, fading to a whisper, then reverberating out again. Each time it dwindled, she dared to hope. It would stop now, spare her, restore the hall to silence, but no – some individual voice would suddenly take up the cry again, rise to a crescendo, as a squall of other voices swooped around it. There was a strange harmony about the sound, an insistent soaring rhythm, as if some invisible conductor were keeping everyone in time.

'Stop!' she whispered soundlessly. 'Please, God, let them stop.' The noise had reached an even higher pitch now, a new intensity, as voices wailed and keened against a descant of low and rhythmic moans. Then suddenly it did stop – dramatically, abruptly, as if a switch had been turned off – no tardy voice left lingering, or finishing a cadence, just instant shut-off, silence.

'What was that?' Hilary spoke in a dazed whisper, inquiring of the plump young girl beside her, who had already held her hand, introduced herself as Karen, Born Again.

'You mean you don't *know*?' Karen looked incredulous, almost pitying. 'You've never heard singing in tongues before?'

Singing in tongues. Of course! How could she have not realised? She'd heard so much about it, read exuberant accounts of it in all the Catholic papers, knew it was one of the most important gifts claimed by Charismatics from the Spirit. And yet she had expected something different, something far more spiritual, not that jungle noise which bordered on hysteria.

Karen nudged her suddenly. 'Look! There's Danny Greaves. He's really famous. He's raised people from the dead.'

'Which one?' she whispered back. There were eight men on the stage now, one in cowboy boots and lanyard, none at all in priestly garb, though according to the programme six of them were ministers, including Pastor Danny Greaves.

'Ssh! He's speaking now.'

A tall lean man in glasses, dressed totally in cream, from his expensive three-piece suit to his shirt, tie, socks and shoes, walked down to the footlights, raised his arms. 'Let every eye now close and every hand be raised, as we welcome the Holy Spirit down into this room. Alleluia!'

'Alleluia! Alleluia!' The entire congregation took up the cry, as a forestful of arms shot up, Karen's almost first. Hilary didn't shut her eyes; there was still too much to see – not just the seven healers, who were standing in a semicircle behind the Reverend Danny Greaves, lips moving as they prayed; but also the scarlet-shirted band, dressed identically and showily in black trousers, red bow ties. It was a different band from yesterday's, more a full-scale orchestra, which included piano, cellos, violins, already playing soft romantic music. Both band and healers were hemmed in by banks of flowers – plastic flowers in plastic pots with shrill-green plastic leaves: blue tulips, purple roses, stiff and waxy lilies, too tall for their pots. And beyond them, as a backdrop to the stage, was a huge white screen with blown-up coloured pictures flashing on and off, mostly of Christ's miracles: Christ healing Jairus's daughter, Christ driving devils out, Christ raising Lazarus from the dead. Christ was fair, with ringlets and blue eyes, and appeared to be wearing lipstick.

Hilary glanced nervously around her. She'd been looking out for Simon since the service started an hour or more ago, but there was still no sign of him. Every other eye was closed, every face devoutly rapt. She shut her own eyes, guiltily, tried to concentrate on what Pastor Greaves was saying.

'The Spirit is now with us. He will heal our pain and sickness, heal our doubt and fear. Brothers and sisters, I have experienced His power in my own life. Just last year, my eldest son, Nigel, fell off a rock ledge when he was mountaineering in Wales. He was black and blue, with severe concussion and several badly fractured bones. The doctors said they doubted he would live. We prayed all night, laid hands on him, and when Nigel woke next morning, there was not one single mark on his whole body, not a scratch, not a bruise. He sat up and asked for Shreddies – that's his favourite cereal – Shreddies and fried eggs. And where is he now, this very moment? Climbing that same mountain ridge in Wales!'

The applause was deafening, drowned the violins, which had been gently throbbing as he told his story. Hilary tried to clap with more conviction. Cries of 'Praise the Lord!' were exploding all around her, people whispering to each other in excitement, admiration.

'God didn't want my boy to die. He died Himself, this very afternoon, to take away our suffering. Brothers and sisters, He died to heal our slipped discs, our arthritis, our duodenal ulcers, our angina. He died to heal our broken marriages, our broken nights, our lonely vigils with the whisky or the Valium. He is with us now – look at Him! – walking up and down the rows, laying on His hands. When He touches you, respond. God has given us emotions, so let Him see them, show Him how you feel.'

Hilary shifted in her seat, nervously aware of how far back the exits were. She had deliberately decided to sit up near the front, to prove her commitment, her desire for healing, wholeness; but also to be close to Simon, whom she assumed would be participating. He must be in the crèche, instead, where they were carrying out individual healing sessions, which were offered as an alternative for those with private problems, or who needed personal counselling. He would be marvellous as a counsellor, supportive, sympathetic. She should have gone herself, except he'd urged her to attend the public service. Perhaps he hadn't realised quite how stagy it would be, how histrionic, rowdy.

She looked back at the healer, who seemed to catch her eye, be talking just to her, one finger pointing straight in her direction. 'If He lifts your depression, sing with joy to thank Him. If He restores your faith, let the whole hall know. Right, all close your eyes again and I'm going to ask the Lord to start His miracles.'

The pastor's voice had changed, now deeper, more dramatic, as he sank down on one knee. 'Yes, the Spirit of God is moving, moving in this room. There's a woman in the thirteenth row who was involved in a car crash seven years ago and has suffered serious back pain ever since. That pain is going from her back – it's going now – it's gone! She's just felt that pain leave her back and shoulders. You know who you are. Can you get up from your seat, please? That's it. Has the pain gone?'

An ecstatic cry of 'Yes!', as an elderly woman in fawn slacks and a green home-knitted cardigan clumped up to the stage.

'What's your name? Alice? Alice, thank the Lord for healing you. Show Him you can move. Bend and twist and dance for Him.'

The woman started moving, gingerly at first, just a few shy shrugs and shakings of her arms, then she touched her toes, started skipping round the stage, to a hail of 'Alleluias!' from the hall.

'Someone else in the back part of the room has been deaf since childhood, deaf in her left ear. That ear has just popped open, praise the Lord! Can you hear me in both ears now?'

Two women shouted 'Yes!' at once. The healer barely paused this time, didn't ask for names; seemed possessed by his own power, as he spoke faster and more urgently. 'There's a man who's had a migraine since he first arrived, but it's lifting, it's lifting as I speak, and he'll never have a migraine in his life again. Another man has cancer of the liver. In the name of Jesus, I command that tumour to shrivel up completely. Yes, it's disappearing. The Lord is just breaking down that tumour. If you feel a cool breeze round your liver, Sir, that's the Spirit.'

Hilary sat rigid and incredulous. Were these people truly healed, and from conditions as serious as cancer? What real proof was there? Doubting Thomas had asked for proof and been rebuked by Christ Himself. Yet even Christ had never worked miracles in such profusion and so quickly, one following the other with barely a pause for breath between.

'There's a man there on the left, who's just been healed from asthma. Breathe freely in and out, Sir. Praise the Lord with every breath. And a woman further back is now free of all her allergies. You can eat cheese now, and chocolate, drink all the milk you want. Alleluia! The Spirit of God is moving in this hall. I can feel power flowing through my hands like an electric current of half a million volts. Many of you have been healed without me saying. If God has touched you, slip out of your seats and come up to the front, so that everyone can see our Saviour's power.'

People began surging from their seats, crowding the aisles as they struggled to the front, shouting out, 'Hosanna! Praise the Lord!'

'Those with fears, come up now, as well. People scared of heights or lifts, or moths or mice or spiders, come up and be healed.'

Another tide of people started fighting their way out, squeezing past those still in their seats, tangling in the aisles with those already healed; the weeping and the fearful pushing past the brave and joyful. All eight healers began laying on their hands, their voices overlapping as they touched foreheads, shoulders, hands.

'Lord, I command this fear to go.'

'*Vaia, vaia, vaia!* Out, out, out! I drive every fear away in the mighty name of Jesus.'

'Your fear of spiders has completely disappeared. When you leave this hall, you'll be able to pick one up in your bare hands, have it run across your arm.'

Hilary shuddered, frightened not of spiders but of the whole disturbing uproar. Cries of terror mixed with cries of joy. Sudden chilling screams petered out in a storm of alleluias. Pictures of Christ's miracles were still flashing on the screen, each greeted by a drum-roll. Violins and cellos were swamped in wild applause, as many of those

230

healed were presented with a microphone and began testifying publicly.

'I could feel this heat moving to my knees, and then a sudden click. The pain's completely gone now.'

'I can move my neck! I can even look behind me. Yet it's been stiff and locked for years.'

'I'm no longer scared of dying. I've been terrified since my mother died of cancer, but now I . . . '

There was a sudden disturbance in the rear part of the hall, as a grey-haired woman started running with a wheelchair, jostling people in her way, bumping and shaking the large and dumpy invalid who sat inside, clinging to the sides. As they neared the stage, several people helped heave the wheelchair up, pushed it right towards the Reverend Danny Greaves. The hubbub in the hall gradually subsided, as all eyes turned towards the pastor, who was conversing with the older woman, nodding vigorously. Suddenly, he seized the microphone, addressed the whole hushed audience.

'Brothers and sisters, this is Ada in the wheelchair. She's been in it thirty years. And this is Marjorie, who looks after her poor daughter when she's not in hospital. Ada has multiple sclerosis. That's a serious disease. But our God is a God of miracles. If He worked them two thousand years ago, why not now, as well? I ask you to join your prayers with mine, as we beg for healing for our sister.' He stretched out both his hands, laid them on Ada's shoulders. 'Sickness, I bring the very power of Christ against you. I command you to go now.

'*Now!*' he repeated, louder and more vehemently.

The silence was electrifying, not a murmur from the audience, not a ripple from the band.

'Brothers and sisters, Satan is present here, as well. I can feel him in this hall, trying to fight this healing, trying to keep this woman locked in her paralysis and pain. Pray, my friends, storm heaven.'

Hilary couldn't pray, felt paralysed herself. Simon had cast doubt on Satan. Would he approve of this at all, or see it as hysteria? Ada was still passive in her chair, her mother looking haggard, close to tears. All eight healers were joining in the prayers out loud, all standing round the wheelchair, their hands stretched up to heaven, imploring and beseeching.

'Lord, hear us . . . '

'Mighty God . . . '

'God of Signs and Wonders . . . '

Pastor Greaves let out a shout of triumph. 'Yes, yes, yes! He hears us! Satan has been cowed. The Lord is working here. I can feel his healing flowing through my hands. Ada, I say to you, in Jesus's name, "Get up from your chair and walk."'

Slowly, as if sleepwalking, Ada rose, took a few steps forward, unsupported. The entire hall boomed with triumph. Everyone was springing to their feet, as if copying Ada's movement; laughing, crowing, exchanging hugs of jubilation. Hilary felt her hand seized, met Karen's shining eyes. 'A miracle! A miracle!' She tried to babble back, doubt and wonder fighting in her mind. Was Ada truly healed, or was the whole thing just a hoax? Had she been paralysed at all, or able to walk anyway, at least a few short steps? She searched the stage for proof. If Ada were still walking, instead of slumped back in her wheelchair, then . . .

Impossible to tell. At least two hundred people were fighting to get close; to touch her, touch the pastor, have some part in the miracle. All she could see were tangled arms and legs, backs pushing, shoving, flowerpots overturned, nervous instrumentalists trying to protect their music stands.

Karen dragged her by the hand. 'Come *on*,' she urged. 'Come up.'

Hilary let herself be led, joined the euphoric throng of believers in the aisles. Other hands kept grabbing at her, as people touched, embraced; everyone united by their rapturous sense of wonder. She lost Karen in the crush, found herself face to chest with a six foot man whose shirt was drenched with sweat. She pulled away, stood thunderstruck a moment as she caught a sudden glimpse of Ada, still walking unsupported on the stage, her face transfused with joy. She broke into a run – not towards Ada – the other way, towards the door, the exit. She must find Simon, find the crèche, seek individual healing. If even a true miracle could leave her doubting and uneasy, then she was in desperate need of help.

'I must see Father Tovey. He said he . . . '

'I've told you, he's not here. Can't I help instead? We're all trained counsellors.'

'Yes, I know, but . . . '

'Okay, I understand. You need a priest. I'll try to find him for you, but it might take a few minutes. You'd better sit in here.'

The tall woman in tweeds opened the door of what looked like a child's classroom, with tiny desks, tiny chairs, children's drawings on the walls. Hilary sank down on a yellow chair which had been constructed for a four-year-old. This building seemed more a full-blown nursery school than just a simple crèche. She'd passed several rooms already, some with pictures on the doors, cut-out cats and rabbits. She'd heard noises through the doors – weeping, shouting, singing. One group was singing still, women's voices mainly, piercing the thin wall.

232

> Thank you, Lord, for this fine day,
> This fine day, this fine day . . .

Hilary glanced out of the window. The fine weather had broken. It was raining now, a heavy stinging rain, lashing the bare and bony branches of a beech. Penitential weather, fitting for Good Friday.

> Thank you, Lord, for loving me,
> Loving me, loving me . . .

A branch had broken off the beech, splintered at the end. The grass was bruised beneath it, slimy green. A cruel east wind was pouncing on the last dead leaves, left over from November. Hilary shifted on her chair. 'Simon,' she said, suddenly, out loud. 'Please come. Please help me.'

The door opened. Two faces wreathed in smiles, four arms reaching out to her; a short man in his thirties, already balding, in neat grey flannels and a blazer with a badge on; an older woman with glasses and a bun. Hilary stood up. 'I . . . er . . . wanted Father Tovey.'

'He's not well, I'm afraid. He's lying down. We've come to help instead. I'm Olive. This is Ted.' More smiles, a lingering squeeze from clammy hands. 'We're your prayer-team. There should be three of us, but Hannah's just dropped out. She's having problems. Don't worry. Numbers make no difference. It's faith that counts with Jesus. I've brought you this, dear.' Olive held out a man's handkerchief, a crumpled dingy white one, with a blue border round the edge. 'It's one of Danny's prayer-cloths. He can't heal everybody in person, so he prays over these cloths – sometimes hundreds at a time – and his power goes into them. If you put it on your head, your sickness will depart. Praise the Lord!'

'But I'm not sick. I only . . . '

'It works just as well for sickness of the soul. Praise the Lord! Just try it. Trust in Jesus.' Olive levered Hilary back into her seat, then spread the prayer-cloth on her head. One end was drooping in her eye, so she could no longer see Olive and her smile. She longed to snatch it off, make a quick dash for the door, but Ted was standing just in front of her, with his hands stretched up and out. He was praying ostensibly, lips moving, eyes raised up, but he'd probably also read her mind and was positioned there to prevent her from escaping.

Olive rearranged the handkerchief, started rummaging in her bag, brought out a tiny tin. 'Now we're going to anoint you with this holy oil. Danny's blessed that, too.' Olive eased the top off with her thumbnail,

233

dipped it in some greyish stuff which looked like rancid lard, dabbed a blob on Hilary's hands and forehead.

'Don't look so worried, dear. I was healed myself, you know. Jesus gave me the Kiss of Life. I was living in a dark cave and He took my hand and led me to the light. All I said was "God, I hurt. Help me" – and He did. I was born again at Swindon, at a conference, baptised in the Spirit. I saw Jerusalem outside my window, all its spires and churches shining in the sun. Yet it was January in England in the snow. I'm so happy now, I feel I'm walking on water half the time. Jesus told me it was okay to be me, you see. And it's okay to be *you*, Hilary. Even if you're a sinner – and we're all sinners, I'm afraid – you can still be a happy sinner. Have you given yourself a hug today?'

'No, I . . .'

'That's all right as well. Even if you're down, that's okay with Jesus. He meets us where we're at, accepts us as we are. But you have to let Him in first. If you let Him in big enough, He'll change your whole life.'

'Look, really, I'm all right. I'm not sad or sick or anything. I just wanted a brief word with Father Tovey.'

'We're priests as well, you know, spreaders of God's love. Ted here joined the Ministry just three months ago. He lost his way last year. His youngest daughter died when she was only three. He couldn't take it, was heading for a breakdown, but then Danny made him see that his daughter wasn't dead, that she'd only gone to God. God wanted her, you see, wanted her so much, He couldn't wait till she was sixty-five or seventy.'

'Oh, I'm sorry. How awful. I . . .'

'Don't be sorry. Ted's not, are you, Ted? He was proud to give his little girl to Jesus. Instead of a funeral, they had a Mass of celebration and afterwards . . .' She broke off, listened through the wall. 'It's a shame about that noise next door. Are you finding it distracting?'

'No, I'm not, but . . .' Hilary tried to struggle up, find some excuse to leave. She'd been so unnerved by Olive, she'd hardly been aware that the voices were still shrilling on, the pelting rain now thrumming out a descant to the hymn.

> Thank you, Lord, for setting us free,
> Setting us free, setting us free . . .

She subsided on her chair again. Olive's hands were hurting.

'They'll probably stop quite soon. I don't know what they're up to. Hymns don't mix with private healings, not in my experience. I prefer to sing in tongues, and Jesus likes it, too. It's His favourite form of praise, no question about that. I do it all the time now – in my car, in the supermarket, walking my two corgis. Right, my dear, if you close your eyes and bow your head, we're both going to pray over you, okay? Ready, Ted?'

Ted moved in closer, seemed in awe of Olive, hadn't said a word yet. He was a mousy shambling man, with a slight stoop to his shoulders, as if he were recoiling from a blow, but he had kindly doe-brown eyes, a mild and gentle face. Perhaps she could appeal to him, beg him to release her. She touched his arm nervously, kept her eyes on his blazer badge, which showed an owl above a shield. 'Ted, I . . . '

Her voice was lost completely as Olive's strong contralto bombarded both of them, singing strings of syllables with no sense to them, only shrilling sound. 'Eu-wawa-vanni-loga-dani-eo-nada-ahahahah.' Olive nudged Ted in the ribs, to urge him to join in. He broke into a thin and piping wail, but soon ran out of breath and sounds, petered out uncertainly. He cleared his throat, began again, but his reedy tenor voice was cowed by Olive's, and lagging way behind. At least Olive's sounds had some power and mystery to them, and were always different, changing, as if some outside force were dictating what she sang, perhaps even inspiring her. But Ted was faltering, now desperately repeating the same word on and on: 'Dora, Dora, Dora.' Was that his wife, or the daughter who had died, or some coded evocation of the Spirit? Hilary tried to shut her mind off, force herself to pray. It was wrong to be so critical when this pair were trying to help her, had given up their time. Why did she keep finding fault with people, people far more charitable than she was? 'Lord, take away my pride,' she whispered silently. 'My mocking way of . . . '

A sudden terrifying scream cut across her prayer. She jumped out of her chair, clutching at the prayer-cloth, which had almost fallen off.

'Don't worry, dear. It's just the girl next door. She's demonised.'

'She's *what*?'

'Possessed by devils, maybe ten or twelve of them. They'll drive them out, you'll see. Jesus always wins. How are you feeling now yourself? Any better?'

'Y . . . Yes, much better, thank you.' Hilary held on to the wall, tried to edge away. 'In fact, I think I ought to . . . '

Olive's smile closed in on her, forced her to sit down again. 'We praise you, Lord, for healing our lost sister. Thank you, Jesus, for dying for her today. Do you realise, dear, if you were the only person in the world, Christ would still have died for you alone? He loves you – so much you'd never grasp it in a billion billion years. His love for you's so high, so deep, so great, so wide . . . ' Olive groped for adjectives, spread her arms apart, to indicate infinity. 'And He'll never leave you, ever. He holds your hand. He walks beside you, night and day.'

'Yes, I know. Yes, thank you. But I've really got to go now. I . . . '

They couldn't hear. Ted was muttering in a low and throaty monotone – 'Praise Him, praise Him, praise Him' – as Olive's words poured on.

'He's prepared a pure white robe for you. I want you to put it on, as a sign of your rebirth. Slip it on right now. No, don't get up, don't move. It's just symbolical. What's wrong, my dear? You're very tense. If you feel still lost or sad, hold God's hand, hold it very tight.' Olive proffered her own hand, now damp with heat and sweat.

'Jesus, Jesus, Jesus,' Ted continued, the reiterated s's sounding like the hissing of a serpent. Hilary suddenly felt scared. She was hot herself, sweating, with a strange throbbing in her head, a queasy feeling spreading through her body. Was she ill, about to faint, or just weak from lack of food? She had eaten nothing since her two small spoons of All-Bran, seven hours ago, and had missed both lunch and supper yesterday. She kept her eyes fixed on the wall, tried to calm herself, breathe deeply. She was staring at a lurid Crucifixion, a young child's handiwork; the matchstick Christ lopsided, His mouth a crayoned blue line, vermilion blood pouring from His side.

'Christ is dead,' she whispered.

'What, dear?'

'I don't believe. I don't believe in anything. Perhaps I never did.'

'Can you speak a little louder. With all that noise next door, it's . . . '

Hilary hardly heard the screams resounding through the wall. She was deaf to everything save the screaming in her mind.

'Ted, go and ask them if they can be a little quieter. It simply isn't fair. They're not the only pebbles on the beach.'

Pebbles on the beach. She could see the beach at Weybourne, the miles and miles of shingle, shining in the rain. She was just a random pebble, just a grain of sand. A nothing, with no Maker, something to be tossed away, worn thin by the tide. She heard Simon's voice, booming like the sea. 'I've come to see the price of faith is doubt.' This wasn't doubt, but cold and fierce conviction, as forceful, overwhelming, as her call to be a nun that Christmas Eve in 1965. *There was no God*. If anyone had called her, it was her own pride, or fear, or fantasy. Simon had been right in that respect: she had become a nun for all the wrong reasons – for security, for status, to replace her own bad-tempered father with a superior Heavenly one. But Simon was wrong in still believing. His kindly left-wing God was as much a myth as Jim Duck's jolly pal, or Danny Greaves's God of miracles, or Molly's God of Bodies. They were dead, all dead; had died today, this afternoon, Good Friday, and there would be no Resurrection, no joyful empty tomb.

Empty – that was it. Man's emptiness had created all these gods; his need for love and power, his longing for certainty, for comfort, a hand to hold, a beacon in the dark. All the Popes and priests and pastors had been totally deluded; all the thousand members of this conference seeking the same thing: answers to questions which hadn't any answers; love from a Lover who would never let you down, and whose love was higher, deeper, wider, than any mortal man's; Eternity to save you from your coffin, reunite you with your daughters snatched away at three; your past forgiven, your future life assured. She had been fooled herself, fooled from early childhood, fooled from her late teens; had tried to clothe her puniness in long black robes; add rings and crosses, rosaries, to give her power, make her less a nothing.

Olive was still praying. 'Hilary needs you, Jesus. Please help her. Hold her in your arms. Help our sister, Hilary.'

Sister Hilary. Sister Mary Hilary. All a lie, a lie. She sprang up from her chair. 'I'm *not* Hilary. That's not my name, so please stop using it.'

'I'm so sorry, dear. They told me it was Hilary. I asked specifically. We always use first names, you see. It's more friendly, isn't it? Perhaps I heard it wrong, though. My hearing's not so good these days. What *is* your name? We'll start again.'

'No, please. No, don't. I'm sorry . . . I'm not feeling well at all.'

'But that's why you need the healing. That's exactly what we're here for. We'll sort you out, don't worry. Ted! Where's Ted? I told him to go and ask for quiet, not disappear completely.'

The door swung open suddenly, and a screaming weeping woman flung herself face downwards on the floor. Then a group of men burst in, tried to seize the woman, as she writhed and struggled, spitting in their faces, punching with her fists. Her screams were so deafening they seemed to terrorise the room, every blockish piece of furniture petrified with horror, the walls themselves shrinking back in fear. Hilary knew they were her own screams, could feel them graze and bruise her throat, as she stood shivering in silence; screams for her lost childhood, her lost twenties, thirties; her frightening loss of purpose, her lost reason for existence, above all, her lost God. She clung on to the wall. Olive grabbed her, prevented her from falling, held her close against her bosom, as if to shield her from the terrifying howls.

'Don't worry, dear. It's just the demons leaving her. They always put up quite a fight. We'll go on with our own prayers. If you come into this corner, we'll make our own quiet space.'

'No, please. I've got to leave.'

'I know it's frightening, but at least it shows how powerful Satan is, how much we need God's mercy.'

Satan – gone as well. The bogeyman who made little kids behave; little kids like the ageing nuns at Brignor, little kids like her. She was sitting at her child's desk, as powerless as she'd been for twenty years, Nanny Olive standing over her.

'Right, now let's have your real name, dear.'

Real name. What was real? Bread and wine? Croziers and mitres? Her Rule and Constitutions? Advertisements, commercials? Fashion, beauty? Hell?

The woman on the floor was barking like a dog now, frothing at the mouth, four strong men all trying to hold her down, the others praying publicly; Ted amongst them, with his serpent's hiss of 'Jesus, Jesus, Jesus'. The rain had changed to sleet, sleet lashing on bare branches, weeping down the panes. Hilary peered out through the window, saw flowers and blossom guillotined, winter murdering spring. Yet she had to go out there, cool her burning head, escape the noise, the prayers. She pushed past Olive, dodged the group of healers, the foaming choking body on the floor; slammed the door on Olive's cry: 'Jesus *loves* you, Hilary. Don't run away from the best friend you'll ever have.'

238

18

Hilary dashed across the lawn, sleet stinging on her face, feet slipping on the soaked and slimy grass. A sudden strobe of lightning zigzagged laser-blue across the sky. She ran on, stumbling, blinded, frightened by the gloom. It was only four o'clock, yet an eerie greenish light was spreading from the west, all natural daylight gone. Two thousand years ago, the whole sky had darkened, as Jesus died in anguish on the Cross. Was this some sign, some warning to her? Could she hear God's anger in the cannonade of thunder now echoing and booming through the buildings, blasting the whole campus? She'd have to shelter somewhere, swung left towards the lake. There was a Grecian temple just behind it, a modern man-made ruin, where nobody would find her. She zigzagged down the path, dodging puddles, broken twigs, past a row of creaking larch trees swaying in the wind. The whole lake seemed alive, as sleet churned and threshed its surface, water slamming water in a sullen foaming swirl.

She sped towards the temple, slipped inside, shoes sodden wet and squelching, hair plastered to her face. Rain was drumming on the roof, bouncing back from the slabs of broken masonry littered round the ivy-strangled columns.

'Out of the depths I have cried to thee, O Lord. Lord, hear my voice.' Why did she keep praying, psalms from the Office, prayers for the dead? He wouldn't hear – He wasn't there. She had to grasp that, grasp it finally, realise exactly what it meant. No more prayers, no Office, no Holy Mass, no confession, absolution, no feasts and fasts, no resurrection of the dead. She would never see her parents, rush straight to them in heaven, as she had always hoped, expected, so she could make her peace with them. They would be simply bones by now, rotting in their coffins.

A last faint roll of thunder grumbled through the sky: not God's Wrath, not Jove's thunderbolts, just a meteorological phenomenon with scientific causes. She'd better learn some science, recite formulae, equations, instead of rosaries. The rain was easing now. She walked slowly to the lakeside, stood staring at the wreckage: reeds maimed and mangled, water muddied, debris from the bottom floating scum-like on the surface. She looked up at the sky, still bruised and swollen; grey and festering clouds lying lumpen on the soaring chapel roof.

The Lord is in His holy temple.
The Lord whose throne is in heaven.

No Lord, no heaven; His holy temple ruined like the Greek one. How long would it take her to remember not to pray; how long to see the sky as just cumulus or nimbus, and not the realm of Angels? 'Have mercy,' she begged no one. '*Miserere nobis.*'

'Hilary!'

She jumped. They'd come to get her, come to lock her up for not believing, the gravest sin of all. She turned and ran, away from temple, chapel, trimmed and nannied lawns, towards the wilder grounds beyond.

'Hilary, stop! Wait! What's wrong?'

Simon's voice, not Olive's, or the Abbess's. She slowed her pace, heard his footsteps drumming into hers, slumped against him, as he caught her in his arms. He, too, was drenched, without a coat, his light hair darkened by the rain, his khaki sweat-shirt clinging to his back.

'I saw you from my window. You looked utterly distraught. What's happened? What's the matter?'

'My . . . My father's dead,' she stuttered, startled at her words.

'Oh, my God! When? How? What happened? An accident? Who told you?'

She shook her head, half-smiled. 'He died years and years ago, but it's only now I've realised.'

He was staring at her, aghast, uncomprehending, perhaps fearing she was mad. 'Look, come inside. You need to take those clothes off, lie down for a while.' He led her back across the lawn, paused a moment as they walked into the corridor. 'We'd better go to my room. I've had the fire on quite some while, so at least it should be warm.'

She didn't argue, felt too tired and dazed. He sat her by the gas fire, put the kettle on, fetched two of his old sweaters and a duffle coat. 'I'm going to find some brandy. I think you need it. While I'm gone, dry yourself really well and change into these clothes.'

'But you're wringing wet yourself,' she said, cold droplets from her hair trickling down her neck.

He smiled. 'I'll survive.'

She felt nervous undressing, even with him gone. This was a priest's room and it seemed wrong to take her clothes off, wrong to wear a priest's clothes, even casual ones like sweaters. She was aware of eyes upon her, invisible but hostile eyes, as she slipped out of her blouse. Her brassière was soaking wet beneath it. Should she take that off, as well? She unhooked it very quickly, tried to hide her breasts while pulling the two sweaters on, one above the other, to disguise any hint of curves. The wool felt rough against her skin, smelt of peppermints and woodsmoke, strangely mixed. Both the jerseys were very large and shapeless, came down to mid-thigh. Simon's clothes all seemed far too big for him. Did he get them from the jumble-box, as she herself had done, or were they passed on by some larger sporty friend? She approved his lack of vanity, his lack of worldliness. Even Father Martin had fussed about his albs – their fit, the way they fell.

She tugged the sweaters down as far as they would go. Her skirt and tights were drenched, but she could hardly take them off and sit there naked-legged. She towelled her hair, stuffed Kleenex in her shoes, wished she had a comb, or Della's hair dryer.

'Yes, come in.' Simon was knocking, entered rather cautiously, with a bottle in his hands and a whole clutch of other things, including his wet clothes. He had changed into dry ones – smarter altogether: well-cut trousers, an expensive-looking sweater, with a jaunty matching scarf.

'Colin's a marvel! Who else would come to a Charismatic conference with brandy, aspirin, Lemsip, and a whole cupboardful of clothes? I'm afraid I brought just those two spare sweaters.' He glanced down at her sodden skirt and tights. 'You've still got those wet things on. You'd better slip them off and wear my coat. That'll keep you warm and decent both at once. I'll wait outside. Call me when you're ready.'

Hilary watched him close the door, touched by his thoughtfulness, his tact. He was so concerned about her, yet sensitively aware that she wouldn't want him there while she struggled out of a tight and dripping skirt. She eased her tights off next, fastened the last toggle on the coat, which only reached her knees. *Did* she look decent with those pale and naked legs? She wrapped the towel around them like another dampish skirt, before calling softly, 'Simon!' It still felt odd to be using a priest's Christian name, odder still to be sipping brandy with him. He poured her half a tumblerful, started making a hot drink, set the steaming mug beside the glass.

'Both strictly medicinal,' he assured her with a smile.

'So why aren't you having some as well?'

'I'm not ill.'

'They said you were.'

'Who said?'

'Well, Ted and Olive. They . . . ' She broke off, had no wish to think of them, relive that whole experience. It was better just to sit, let the warmth of fire and brandy thaw and comfort her. 'I wish you'd have a drink, Simon. I feel sort of . . . wicked drinking on my own.'

He shook his head, mock-angry. 'You're still so full of guilts. Of course I'll drink, if it makes you happier.' He went to fetch the bottle, sat beside her on the floor. There was not much room on the skimpy little rug, and his knee was touching hers. She was somehow too aware of it, tried to edge away.

He leaned forward, put his glass down. 'What was that you said about your father, about not realising he was dead?'

'Oh, nothing. It was stupid.'

'It wasn't stupid, Hilary. I realise how upset you are. Can't you try and talk about it?'

She gulped her brandy, needing instant courage to spell out her loss of faith. 'I've just realised that I don't believe in God,' she said, speaking very slowly, and almost shrinking from the words, as if they had the power and force to damn her. 'He's gone, completely gone. I mean, I know as certainly as I've ever known anything in my entire existence, that there's no Creator, no First Cause, no Heavenly F . . . Father.' She heard her voice break on the Father, and suddenly Simon had both his arms around her. She clung to him, felt his lambswool sweater soft against her eyes, his arms very strong and safe across her back. No one had held her since she was a tiny baby, and she couldn't remember that. She tried to imagine her own father's arms around her, to turn Simon into him. The arms immediately felt wrong – colder, more reluctant, with a hint of real impatience. She pulled away.

'What's wrong?'

She didn't answer, just hugged her knees up to her chest, then linked her arms around them; shoulders hunched, head down, blocking off everything and everyone.

'Don't shut me out, Hilary. I can feel your pain, so let me try to share it with you. You're very low today, need someone else's strength. I've got that strength, so just accept it. Please.'

'Yes, but . . . '

'What?'

'You're a . . . priest.'

'Of course I am.' He smiled. 'That's all the more reason why I should try to help. You mustn't be so scared, scared of contact, simple human warmth. There's nothing wrong with an arm around your shoulders.'

Reverend Mother Molly's words. She yearned to be like Molly, to be able to give and receive affection without always feeling guilty or alarmed. Molly had deplored the fact that so many people were frightened of their bodies, especially priests and nuns; had tried to make them see that 'body and soul' was a phrase with real significance; that bodies must be used to express love of God, love of fellow creatures. She uncrossed her legs, uncrossed her arms, let Simon take her hand in his,

242

allowed herself to sink back against his chest. She shut her eyes. His navy V-neck sweater was changing into Molly's scarlet blouse, a blouse open at the front. She was a tiny baby, with Molly as her mother, Molly's nipple in her mouth, Molly's gold-top flowing through her body, transforming her from a cold and puny starveling to a warm and loving woman. Molly held her firmly. She couldn't fall, seemed to fit into her arms, as if the two of them had been sculpted from one piece. She felt very warm, very still and peaceful; the faint hum of the gas fire fusing with the rhythm of the rain.

'You'd better take that coat off. It's getting really hot in here.'

She jumped at Simon's voice, had been hearing Molly's softer one whispering against her face, as she suckled her full breasts. She sat up, half-confused, started tugging at the coat.

'It won't come off if you don't undo the toggles.' He was laughing at her now, helped her with the fastenings, his hand brushing her bare legs. Quickly, she rearranged the towel, feeling vulnerable, exposed, with the heavy tent-like coat gone.

'You haven't had your drink.'

'Nor have you.'

'I meant your hot one. Don't let it get cold.'

She sipped it while he refilled her brandy glass. She had never drunk brandy in her life before, wasn't sure she liked it. He took a long draught from his own glass, then put it down, touched her forehead, frowning. 'You're still very hot, you know. I wouldn't be surprised if you've got a temperature. Why don't you lie down – just stretch out on this rug and try to doze a bit?'

'No, really, Simon. I'm quite all right, honestly. I feel much better now.'

He seemed not to hear her, stretched out on the rug himself, drew her down beside him. 'You're obviously dead tired. Your body needs to rest. Why deny what it tries to tell you, Hilary? You're always doing that.'

Rebuked, she lay in silence, aware the towel had shifted, one leg bare almost to the thigh. He placed his hand across it, as if to fill the gap, smiled again. 'Mustn't let you get too cold.'

She tensed. No fear of that. The hand felt burning hot. Heat everywhere – in her throat and stomach where the warm drink and the brandy had scalded their way down; in the prickle of his sweaters on her skin; in the panting of the gas fire, the strange disturbing tingle on her thigh. His hand was stroking slowly up and down it. Was this simply comfort, or something much more intimate? She didn't know, couldn't tell. Her brain was fazed by brandy, fugged by too much warmth. The

243

hand moved upwards to her breasts, strayed above the left one, stroking the rough wool.

'N . . . No,' she said, uncertainly.

He appeared not to have heard, slipped his hand beneath both the baggy sweaters, found her breast again, cupped his hand around it, naked hand on naked breast.

She jerked up suddenly, almost threw him off. 'You don't believe, do you – in God, I mean? You've lost your faith as well. Is that the reason you no longer hear confessions – because you're in sin yourself? It *is* a sin for a priest to touch a woman – touch her there and . . . ' She blushed, draped the coat around her, so it covered everything. 'And it's worse to call it simple human contact, try to put me off my guard by pretending it's just therapy or something; say you want to share my pain when all you're really after is . . . ' She took a gulp of brandy, coughed and choked it down. 'I confessed to you I'd lost my faith and you didn't say a thing. You didn't try to show me I was wrong, or find me some new arguments, or pray with me or . . . *That*'s what priests should do, not . . . not . . . ' She forced her voice to right itself, went on. 'I'm sure you don't believe, and I want you to, I *want* you to. I know it sounds irrational, if I don't believe myself, but I can't bear it if you said that Mass, and washed those people's feet, and it was all a sham or . . . '

His own voice was very steady, his face calm, expressionless. 'I *do* believe, Hilary. My faith is very strong, in fact – strong enough to know what Christ wants of His disciples. I love my God and I try to serve Him in the way that I think best. But some things I've rejected, maybe *can't* believe in – so you're right in that respect. Though, even now, it's not easy to acknowledge it. It took me many years of soul-searching, many sleepless nights, before I could admit it, even to myself. I could have left the Church, or at least have left the priesthood. Some would say I should have done, or that I'll be turfed out anyway, once my superiors get wind of what I think. Maybe. I hope and pray not.'

Hilary clutched her glass so tightly she was frightened it would break. Her cheeks were flaming as she realised what she'd done: shouted at a priest, accused a priest of sinning. She felt so ashamed, so horrified, she could hardly bear to look at him. 'I'm sorry,' she whispered, voice barely audible.

He smiled. 'No sorrys. Didn't we agree that? Except it's me who should apologise. I'm sorry, too, Hilary. I didn't mean to hurt you or upset you. I genuinely felt that you needed human warmth. You've been very hurt and damaged, and only love can heal that.'

Love. She trapped the word, examined it. Did he mean he loved her, that there was some real bond between them? Certainly, they had a lot

244

in common – the same faith and values once, the same doubts and struggles now; the same long and rigorous training to wean them from the world. How could she have repulsed him quite so violently? 'Forgive me, I was rude,' she said, still not daring to look up.

'You weren't rude, not at all. You're never rude, Hilary. You're a very gentle loving person, which is why I care about you.'

So he did care. She could hear it in his voice, feel it in the pressure of his fingers, as he laid them on her arm. A priest who loved her, longed to make her whole. She shrugged the coat off, pushed it to one side. Why shouldn't she be healed, made adult and humane, instead of turning into one of Della's loveless spinsters, or remaining a semi-nun for ever, like the ones Elaine had mentioned, terrified of any human contact? If her God had gone, there was nobody to stop her. In fact, she should feel better, with no judgement and damnation, no constant daily sin and guilt re-crucifying Christ, no Rule, no vow of chastity. But what about *his* chastity? She tried to put that question to him, struggling with embarrassment, stumbling on the words, washing down the hardest ones with brandy.

He leant back against the wall, eased and stretched his legs. Colin's smart blue trousers were much too long for him, and had been rolled up at the ends. He still had his wet shoes on, the pale suede black with rain. 'No, Hilary, I don't believe in celibacy, not now. I did, of course – right through my twenties and up to just three years ago. Well, I struggled with it, actually, and believe me, it was a struggle. But in the end, I came to see I was wasting too much energy on fighting something natural and perhaps not that important. It seemed all wrong. It was making me bad-tempered and far too self-absorbed, turned in on my petty sins and weaknesses, when there was so much major misery screaming out for help.' He reached out for his glass, cupped it in both hands. 'Perhaps you don't realise, but parish priests are often very isolated, living on their own, or with just an ageing housekeeper, and if they let themselves get lonely or embittered, what use are they as caring human beings? I know in my own case that once I was less frustrated, less hung-up about what I'd come to see as basic human needs, I had so much more to give – more energy, more love, more sheer humanity.'

He took a sip of brandy, frowned into his glass. 'But it wasn't simply personal, of course not. You can make quite a case against celibacy on theological grounds. The first priests weren't celibate and there's no scriptural justification for it anywhere. It came in very slowly, especially here in England, where it wasn't fully recognised until as late as the twelfth century. And it's bound to change again. The Church *has* to change, or die, Hilary. Do you know what Cardinal Newman said? "To live is to change, and to be perfect is to have changed often."'

Hilary shifted on the rug, struggling with a sense of shock. She'd read a lot about the case for married clergy, but affairs for single priests were another thing entirely. Even more extraordinary was the fact he seemed to be admitting that he'd had affairs himself; seemed not ashamed, not worried that he might give scandal to her, or other people, be found out, removed from office. And even while he was talking about basic sexual urges, he did it with a sort of spiritual fervour; eyes blazing with conviction, voice solemn and intense. She found herself excited, excited by that fervour, excited by her very sense of shock. She glanced at him again – his pale hands locked together, the fall of hair hiding half his face; tried her best to concentrate; hear him as a priest, not fear him as a man.

'I also feel it's wrong that celibates with no experience of life or love or sex should make the rules for married people. That seems to me plain arrogant, as well as psychologically wrong. And anyway, it doesn't work in practice. I mean, the present system's crazy. At least eighty per cent of Catholics in America are using contraceptives, despite the Church's ban, and in Ireland there's enormous opposition to official Catholic teaching on divorce and sex and so on. That all results in a lot of guilt and conflict, a lot more wasted energy, and resentment on both sides. And the Church is losing clergy. Thousands every year are leaving to get married, or because they simply can't accept these . . . '

Hilary clung on to her glass. She'd missed his last few words, had been seeing him with women – naked women, Catholic women, women she both envied and abhorred. She ought to argue with him, challenge his loose statements, his too permissive views, but she could hardly think at all. What he was really saying, beneath the arguments, the rhetoric, was that he was free to touch her, free to go to bed with her. She swallowed brandy, tasted only fear. Her head was throbbing, her heart pounding in her chest. Was she ill, as he'd suggested, or simply terrified? She could feel the tension building in the room, the choking shouting silence closing in on her. Why had he stopped speaking? Was he expecting some reply – or worse – some move from her, some encouragement, caress?

'Your . . . Your shoes are wet,' she stuttered.

His burst of laughter startled her. 'That'll teach me not to lecture. I try to expound my deepest and most heartfelt views, and you fuss about my footwear! Though you're absolutely right. My shoes *are* soaking wet. In fact, I'd better take them off.' He started tugging at the laces. 'I think you'll have to help me. You've got longer nails to deal with all these knots.'

As she struggled with the tangled laces, he reached forward, stroked her hair, kept stroking as she eased the muddy trainers off.

246

'Your socks are wet, as well.'

He grinned. 'So what are you going to do about it?'

She shrank back from the damp and matted wool. It seemed wrong to take his socks off, far too intimate. She glanced up for a moment, saw the three blondes on the wall mocking her rigidity, her inexperience. She turned her back on them, tugged his socks off almost angrily. She'd seen his feet already, at the Maundy Thursday Mass, but then they had looked holy, a humble servant's feet. Now they looked obscene – small and white and plump, with dark hairs on the toes. He looked different altogether in Colin's stylish clothes, the knife-crease in his trousers, the blue scarf at his neck. She had felt more at ease with shabby Father Tovey.

His hands were still stroking down her hair. He moved her closer, began taking off her sweaters. She didn't help him, stayed rigid, unco-operative, as he tried to coax her stiff arms through the armholes. He had turned her round, so she could see the blondes again, all three posing, pouting, begging to be touched. Suddenly, she pushed his hands away, dragged the sweaters off herself, flung them in a corner. What was stopping her, for God's sake, when those stupid blondes had done it, and all the women in her mind, women from his parish – perhaps devout and Catholic women, like devout and Catholic Bridget creaking on the next-door bed; and when Elaine herself had done it, even coarse and shrill Elaine, and Della, seventeen, and all those women in the survey, and those ripe young girls in Soho. Why should she be the only one left out, the only one bodiless and loveless?

She tried to strike a pose like the most blatant of the blondes; one hand on her hip, naked breasts stuck up and out, the other hand across her open lips – felt utterly ridiculous – absurd and shameless both at once; subsided instantly, used her hands instead to try to hide her breasts. Simon was on his knees in front of her, as if worshipping her body. Gently, he prised her hands away, replaced them with his own, started using just his thumbs to rub across her nipples, up and down, up and down. She tried to like it, tried to get out of her head, stop worrying and fretting that someone might disturb them, which had happened twice already, when she'd been with him after lunch. That pigtailed girl had just barged in, said she'd come back later. Supposing she came now, found her naked on the rug? Had Simon locked the door? Did he even have a key? *Her* room didn't have one. And even if it were locked, someone could still knock, or call out through the door; somebody in trouble who was seeking help or guidance, or another priest or pastor come to fetch him for a service. What time was it? What session were they missing?

He had edged closer to her now, and had one nipple in his mouth, tonguing it and sucking it. She had never heard of that, felt sure it was all wrong. Babies suckled breasts, not grown-up men. From what she'd seen on television, he should have kissed her first, then taken off his clothes. He'd done neither yet, was still fully dressed, apart from socks and shoes, and still sucking at her nipple, so hard it almost hurt. His eyes were shut, his face screwed up like a pale and greedy baby. He'd confessed to greed in public at that Mass. He wouldn't get much nourishment from her. She could see her breasts dribbling out a trickle of the tepid water they sipped at Brignor for their morning drink, brownish water with a bitter brackish taste. Her long stint as a nun had made her mean and grudging, dried her up, as Della said. And yet Reverend Mother Molly had stressed giving, not just taking, offering one's body as a means of love, support.

Ashamed, she drew him closer, let him lie across her lap. He'd been giving to her since the moment they'd first met; washing her feet, comforting and counselling, boosting her, supporting her. But what about his own needs? She knew nothing of his background, yet suspected he had suffered, since he spoke so much of suffering; had mentioned doubts and struggles, sleepless nights, loneliness.

She tried to make her arms more welcoming, smooth his fine fair hair, only wished she felt less awkward. Her back was aching, with nothing to support it; one foot scorching from the fire, the other jammed against the skirting. In the few sex scenes she'd watched guiltily on television, the couples seemed to melt and float together, whereas Simon's bony shoulder was pressing into hers, his legs cramped and probably hurting. And those TV settings were always very gracious, either large and stylish hotel suites, or lush and sheltered gardens; romantic music playing, even in the shrubberies. This room was small and basic, with a smell of damp and steaming clothes, no music save the rain. And shouldn't she be feeling something more, some pleasure or excitement, as he nuzzled at her breasts, instead of wrestling with inadequacies and worries?

At last, he pulled away, and she was shocked and disconcerted to see the same expression on his face as at the consecration at the Maundy Thursday Mass – a look of solemn bliss, which she'd regarded then as holy. She watched him tug his jersey off, astonished by the coarse hair on his chest, much darker than his mousy-coloured scalp-hair. Never in her life had she seen a naked male, just assumed unconsciously they would all more or less resemble the stripped and dying Christ – be passive, pale and hairless.

Simon was yanking at his belt now, anything but passive. She felt a sudden terror, as if Christ Himself were tearing off His draperies. She struggled to her feet, tried to back away from him. 'Sh . . . Shall we draw the curtains, shut the rain out?'

'I think it's stopped now, actually.' He drew them, all the same, roughly and impatiently, then took her hand, steered her to the bed. 'That floor's a bit uncomfortable.'

She mumbled some reply, stared down at the bedspread while he removed his vest and jeans, turned her back abruptly as he bent to take his pants off. If she had imagined nuns with wombs and breasts cut out or simply missing, then priests, too, were always doctored, had nothing but air between their legs. She didn't want it otherwise, didn't want a priest to be a man; a completely naked man now, reaching out towards her, trying to slip her own pants down. She snatched them off herself, dived between the covers on the bed.

'On, not in – otherwise I can't admire your body.' Gently, he uncovered her, hands straying down her breasts. She kept her eyes tight shut, as if that way he couldn't see her; lay heavy like a corpse. Their Brignor Rule had urged them to yield themselves to their superiors, as if they were dead bodies with no needs nor minds nor wishes of their own. She barely stirred as he kissed her neck and shoulders. 'Let Him kiss me with the kisses of His Divine mouth.'

'You're beautiful,' he whispered, his mouth going lower to her breasts. He had said that twice already, as they also said it twice at her Profession. 'Come, my chosen one, the King hath greatly desired your beauty.' 'Forget your people and your Father's house, for the King has greatly desired your beauty.'

'Happy?' Simon smiled.

She nodded, could think of nothing except that any moment she would be no longer a virgin, would have broken lifelong vows. Vows don't matter, she kept repeating to herself, as he used his teeth very gently to graze across her belly. Unless I'm wrong, she thought, half-sitting up in horror; unless there *is* a God.

'What's wrong? I didn't hurt you, did I?'

She shook her head, hardly heard him; was more concerned with her other former Lover. 'Christ hath put a mark upon my head that I should admit no other Lover but Him.' Why not test her Spouse? If He really did exist, then He could punish her immediately, show His anger in some way, maybe send the storm back – thunder, lightning, pelting sleet again.

Simon was kneeling now above her, one leg on either side. Slowly, very carefully, he lowered himself down, until his hair was dangling in her face, tickling on her skin. She heard the bed creak, froze in embarrassment as she remembered Bridget and the man next door. Was someone listening on the other side to *her* – perhaps people on both sides – pious Catholics, maybe, who knew Simon was a priest and were now registering every incriminating sound, every slightest whimper of the bed springs? She prayed he wouldn't move, lay motionless herself, until a sudden stabbing pain made her almost cry aloud. He was hurting, probing, hurting, as he tried to slide inside her. She tensed everything against him, sick with fear as she heard Bridget's cries resounding in her head; cries of pain, not pleasure, as he seemed to meet some barrier, some block. If she couldn't fit a tampon, then how could she expect to fit a man? A tampon! She'd quite forgotten periods, the whole business of fertility; started counting in her head, counting frantically, as Simon still inched in, hurting with each thrust, however slow and gentle. Her period must have started about twelve or thirteen days ago, which meant she could conceive; her most fertile time, in fact – a time any Catholic woman would most definitely avoid, if she didn't want a baby.

'I'm hurting, aren't I, Hilary? Shall we wait a while, cuddle a bit longer?'

'No, don't stop, please don't!' She heard her voice frantic, almost desperate. She craved to have a child – his child – a consecrated priest's child, whose father was God's representative; ached to be a co-creator with him. She could bear the pain, however bad, could view it as a penance. She shut her eyes again, tried to make herself relax, as Simon lowered himself once more. There must be something wrong with her that it should hurt so much, yet still seem not to fit, as if she were made differently, or smaller, than most normal women were. She tried to think of babies, distract herself with good things, but she could only see the Christ-child in the crib, a wooden child, a dead child. Simon felt like wood himself – hard and rigid, stabbing, far too big. Both their bodies seemed feverishly hot, Simon's sweating into hers, sticking to it almost. *Was* it sweat, that slimy, tacky film? She could see Christ's body in her mind again, not the infant Christ-child, but Christ dead and crucified: nail-holes in His hands and feet, blood trickling down His side. She could feel that blood coating her own body, see Christ's contorted face in Simon's – eyes shut, mouth hanging open, lines of anguish etched along his brow. 'Your sins have nailed Him to the Cross, your lusts have . . .'

'Get *out*,' she cried. 'Get off!'

'Hilary, I'm sorry. I didn't mean to hurt you. But you're very tense and tight, you see, so it's hard to . . .'

'I said get out, didn't I? Please leave me. Go away.'

'All right, relax. Don't worry. I'll fetch your brandy glass.'

'I don't want brandy. I don't want anything. Just leave me on my own.' She slumped back against the pillows, watched him fumbling for his clothes, straighten out his underpants. How could it have hurt so much, that small and rather stupid-looking thing, barely showing now between his legs? She'd been too scared even to look at it, that bobble of pale flesh, which seemed now so insubstantial, unimportant. Yet so much fear and sin and guilt, so much ecstasy and passion, had been built around male genitals. 'The greatest pleasure known to human beings.' She shuddered, hid her eyes.

'Hilary . . .' He was dressed now, looked quite different, more dignified, less puny, as he came towards her, smiling and solicitous. She could see the whole ghastly thing restarting – the straying hands, the sympathy, the fervent explanations and excuses. He sat down on the bed, held her tumbler out to her. She didn't want his brandy, which he'd only used to knock her off her guard, soften her up, seduce her. She flung the covers off, heard the glass smash against the radiator, as she pushed him off, struggled from his bed.

19

Hilary slunk along the corridor, keeping to the sides, terrified she'd meet someone before she reached the safety of her room. Her shoes were muddy, wet still; her skirt had shrunk, clung damply to her legs – cold and naked legs. She'd left her tights behind, left her pants and bra behind, just snatched up the first clothes she could find. Thank God the place seemed empty. All the conference members must be at some event. She ran up the last flight of stairs, relief replacing panic, as she darted down the passage, escaped into her room.

'Hilary!'

'Elaine!'

Their voices overlapped, collided; one staring at the other, both startled, off their guard. Hilary sprang forward, almost lunging at Elaine. 'What are you doing in my room? Get out, get *out*!' She heard her voice sounding ugly, uncontrolled; heard the fury in her words – the same words she'd used to Simon . . .

'Don't blow your top, old girl. I'm not reading your diary or pilfering your diamonds. I only came to see if you'd like to drop in at a sort of workshop thing we're running. I couldn't find you, so I thought I'd leave a note.' Elaine thrust a scrappy piece of paper under Hilary's nose. 'Ten o'clock tonight. The subject's church reform. Okay? Happy now? No, you're not too happy, are you? What's happened, for God's sake? You look as if you've been dragged through a hedge backwards or ducked in the village pond.'

'Nothing. I just got . . . wet.'

'And changed clothes with Father Tovey?'

'What d'you mean?'

'Well, not many Catholic priests strut around with "NIKE SPORTS" on their chests, especially when the only sports they practise are strictly indoor ones. Christ! I should have warned you, Hilary. He did the same to Pat last year – or tried to, anyway. How far did he get with you?'

Hilary sank onto the bed, stared down at her khaki chest and arms. How could she be wearing Simon's sweatshirt, instead of her own floral patterned blouse? 'Go away,' she whispered – to Simon, to Elaine. She couldn't bear her vile insinuations.

'The problem with poor Tovey is he's so hung-up on virgins, he just can't keep his creepy hands off them. Oh, he tries to justify it. I expect you got the spiel about love and bodies, didn't you? Pat did, anyway. It makes me mad. Celibacy for priests like him doesn't mean resisting sex, but just avoiding all commitment.' Elaine plonked down on the chair, crumpled up her note. 'Pat got quite fond of him, in fact, but he didn't want to know. He always wriggles out of any real attachments. He's married to God, you see, which is a pretty useful let-out for taking any responsibility for anybody else – well, after just the first few thrills, of course. He'll do anything for those, especially if he's stalking an ex-nun. They seem to turn him on, though God knows why. Mind you, he didn't get the thrills from Pat, but from what I gather he's often more successful. It beats me really how he gets away with it, except he's so devout in public, I suppose that fools a lot of people. All that "holy radical" bit, and the fact he's done a course in psycho-whatsit. The tutor was a "Miss", so I expect he chatted *her* up.'

'Elaine, would you leave, please. I . . . don't feel well.'

'Oh, don't you, love? I'm sorry. I'm ranting on, as usual, and you've probably caught your death. Which reminds me – you still haven't told me how your clothes got so messed up, or why you're wearing Tovey's little number. Was it a straight swap? I mean, should we expect to see him at supper in your daisy-patterned blouse, with a gold chain round his neck? Okay, okay, I'm going. Can I get you something, though, before I disappear – tea, aspirin, some nice thick woolly socks? No? Right, see you tonight, then, if you're feeling up to it. We're meeting in my room, starting sharp at ten. Church reform, okay? But don't bring Tovey.'

The door slammed on her raucous burst of laughter. Hilary sat shivering, her whole body shaking, trembling, as if she'd lost control of it, or already caught a chill. So Simon courted nuns, had tried to sleep with Pat, wanted only thrills – and virgins. She'd imagined that he loved her, thought of her as special, when she was really nothing more than just another name on a whole list of sordid conquests. How long was that list? He'd certainly seemed experienced, at ease; not at all the nervous shy beginner. Had he slept with Elaine herself, then dropped her or rejected her, which might explain her bitterness; or with Reverend Mother Molly or . . . ?

She tried to fight the pictures in her mind – Simon tangled with a score of women and still not satisfied; Simon in his parish, wooing all the single females; Simon with that pigtailed girl, plying her with alcohol, so she'd submit to him more easily. Greedy? Yes, he was. She could see his face again as he pulled back from her nipples, slavering yet solemn. And she could see that Easter egg, half-eaten on his desk, a huge milk chocolate one with caramels inside – or their empty wrappings, rather. It hadn't really registered before, but now all her hurt and anger seemed to centre on that egg. How could he have sat guzzling in his room, pretending to a headache, while the other priests shouldered all the services – and on Good Friday of all days? That egg was far too big for him, in its gold and scarlet box, gaudy with a ribbon and a bow; showy and specious like all the showy chalices and patens back at Brignor, the heavy jewelled monstrances adding weight and mystery to a religion which was hollow like an egg.

How could she have swallowed all that cant about him caring, when he hadn't cared at all about the fact she might get pregnant; hadn't even broached the subject, except to say how many in America disobeyed their priests on contraception. No wonder! What were priests except frauds in fancy dress; sweating, panting, unconsecrated frauds. She stared out at the lawns, the riot of spring flowers; trees and shrubs in bud, burgeoning into life. She had actually desired his child, believed it would be sacred – a bastard child, with a liar for one parent, a cretin for the other.

The sky had cleared, a shaft of late bright sunlight knifing through the window, carving up the floor. Sun, not storm. So God hadn't sent a sign, wasn't angry, wasn't there at all. And if there wasn't any God, could she really be so angry with a priest? After all, it was her fault as much as his. She could have refused him, simply left the room. And whatever else, Simon had been gentle, hadn't forced himself upon her, either physically or mentally. It was she who'd been the violent one, breaking a glass, actually kicking out and wrestling when he'd tried to stop her leaving; she who'd given in, let him touch her, take her to his bed. And why believe Elaine at all, when she was anti-priest on principle, an evil-minded gossip who thrived on lies and slander? She was probably slandering *her* now, telling all her cronies that a woman still a nun had just been coupling with a hypocrite who called himself a priest. Except it wasn't slander, was it? That's exactly what they'd done.

Slowly, she got up, removed her skirt, Simon's clammy sweat-shirt, examined her body in the mirror. It looked completely different now – bloated and disgusting. She ought to take a shower – a hot shower to wash his smell off, a freezing one as penance – but she dared not leave her room. She might bump into someone *en route* to the bathroom, and she couldn't face more questions or more lies. She soaked Kleenex in cologne – a recent gift from Di – scoured her breasts and body, stared in shock at the ooze of blood dribbling down her thighs. She was bleeding, bleeding from inside; not menstrual blood, but a brilliant crimson trail, like the clotted plaster gobbets which trickled down the Brignor crucifix. She dabbed between her legs, kept dabbing with the Kleenex, until she was surrounded by a scum of bloodstained tissues. The cologne stung against her . . . her . . . She still had no word for that shameful private place which she had ignored throughout her life, but which seemed now to be screaming out in pain, as if it were bruised and raw, exposed. Had Simon injured her in some way, done some lasting damage? Too bad. She'd have to live with it, could never admit to anyone what had happened, and who with. Even the smell of the cologne seemed a reproach – the clean fresh scent of lilies of the valley, flowers which symbolised virginity and innocence.

She went to fetch clean pants, clean clothes; her drabbest skirt, her plainest high-necked blouse. The skirt was steely-grey with a matching leather belt, another gift from Di. Almost without thinking, she removed the belt, stood naked in the centre of the room, whipped the belt hard across her shoulders. The metal buckle stung. She made no sound, just hit herself again, again, lashing harder with each stroke. You could ask for extra penance, if you felt that it were warranted, or your sin were grave enough. They were usually such small things; petty misdemeanours, minor breaches of the Rule.

'I confess to you, dear Mother, and to you, dear Sisters, that I have failed in obedience by opening a window without first asking permission; I have failed in silence by letting a door slam; I have sinned against my vow of poverty by spilling half a cup of tea, then made it worse by failing to report it.'

She was back at Brignor, lying on the floor, face down, the hard and musty wooden floor of the tomb-cold Chapter Room, which had no heating even in December, her arms stretched out like a cross. 'I humbly beg God to forgive me for all the faults and negligences I have committed, for the bad example I have given to you, my Sisters, and for any pain I have caused you, dear Mother.'

The Abbess rose slowly to her feet, her thin face pale and closed. She would now mete out the penances, public penances, such as kissing every Sister's feet, or missing a meal, lying prostrate – and hungry – on the refectory floor, while the other Sisters stepped over your slumped body on their way to table; private penances which Sister Mary Hilary practised anyway – wearing the armlets all day long, instead of just three hours, their sharp raised metal points piercing and pricking with any slightest movement; or adding a wooden cross strapped around her waist or thighs, and studded with blunt nails which pressed into her naked flesh.

She could feel them now – the points, the nails – tearing, jabbing at the skin, but still not sharp or fierce enough for the sins she had committed; flagrant sins she hadn't even mentioned yet, hadn't dared to mention. If you hid a sin, suppressed some fault or negligence which others had observed, then another nun was permitted to accuse you, though only for your good, and in charity, humility. She could see Sister Gerard rising now, kneeling on one knee, eyes down, hands clasped, bony hands twisted with arthritis.

'Sister Mary Hilary stripped naked with a priest. Sister Mary Hilary had congress with that priest. Sister Mary Hilary has lost her faith in God. Sister Mary Hilary doubts His goodness, doubts His whole existence.'

Even in the silence, she could feel their sense of outrage, though no one moved, no one said a word, not even Reverend Mother meting out a penance. How could any penance be heinous enough? She already used the discipline twice a week, or more; a whip of thin waxed cord with nine separate knotted tails. If you were tempted to indulgence, or some sudden longing sprang up to distract you – a craving for a slice of beef, or an unbroken night in bed, or to hear a piece of music, or simply curl up with a book and be alone, you must lash and beat it out of you with ten sharp strokes of the whip; must scourge yourself for laziness, for greed, for disobedience; above all, for concupiscence, since the body must be punished for the body's lusts. She had been too lax recently, must use the whip more often, use it every day now, use it longer, harder; use it till she bled.

She slipped back to her cell, unclipped the soft black cover which she had sewn herself, embroidered with her number, removed the discipline. She stood hunched in the corner while she whipped her thighs, her shoulders; building up a rhythm. She thrashed harder – this was nothing. St Rose of Lima had carried a heavy wooden cross for hours and hours on shoulders already raw and bleeding from the discipline. And St Margaret Mary had carved 'JESUS' on her bare breast with a knife, then burned the letters in with a lighted candle. Those were straight historical facts, not pious fabrications. And both those saints were nuns – devout and faithful nuns, who had never sinned as she had, yet still felt the need for penance.

Again, she raised the belt, brought it down across her breasts, as she heard the Abbess's voice: 'You must scourge and wound your flesh, as your Holy Saviour's body was also scourged and wounded.' She knew the ruling, didn't she? Each Sister in good health was obliged to use the discipline in the privacy of her cell, at least once or twice a week; offering the pain in reparation for her own sins and the world's. Those who had been longest in religious life were expected to inflict more and harder strokes. She had never shied away from it; had indeed regarded flagellation as a means of crushing not so much her body, as her rebellious doubting mind. Why stop now, then, when both mind and body had so flagrantly rebelled?

The heavy silver buckle was tearing at her skin, marks and weals rising on her body, blood flowing to its surface like the tide of scarlet anger surging in her mind: anger with Simon, with Elaine; fury with God for not existing, fury with the Abbess for pretending that He did; contempt for herself for being so passive and accepting, for wasting half her life. Things might have been so different if she hadn't been a Catholic, hadn't been a nun. She could have married and had children, lived a normal happy life, clocked up some small achievements, instead of twenty years of penance, deprivation. She was whipping not herself now, but all those who had crippled her – Mother Mistress, Mother Abbess, her father, Father Martin, even God the Father – thrashing really wildly, tears of pain and anger streaming down her face.

Suddenly, she stopped, stood paralysed a moment, her right arm raised above her head, frozen in mid-air. Someone was outside. She'd heard a sudden knock, and now the door was opening, opening very slowly. It must be Simon – Simon come to get her. She rushed to shut him out, force and wrest the door shut. He mustn't find her naked, see her bleeding body.

'No, Simon, *no*. Please, no.'

'*Simon*?' said a voice. 'Who's Simon?' Then, 'Oh, my God! What's happened?'

Everything was blurring – words, walls, the man himself – a tall and startled-looking man she wasn't sure she knew. She took a step towards him, to tell him he must go. It was Passion Week, Good Friday, a day of total silence. They couldn't speak till Sunday, joyous Easter Sunday, when Christ their Saviour would have risen from the dead.

'No,' she sobbed, as two arms closed around her, seemed to drag her down into Christ's dark and endless tomb. 'That's all a lie. There *is* no Saviour, *is* no Resurrection.'

20

No curtains. Light nudging at her eyelids through small and naked windows, throwing patterns on the bare stone walls. Where was she? It must be Brignor. There were never any curtains in the convent. You didn't need them when you lived so far from any other house, with four high walls to screen you, and when you got up every morning in the dark; winter, summer, winter. Except it wasn't dark, wasn't winter, but bright full-bodied morning, with eager sunlight flickering on the counterpane. Hilary tried to sit up – worried, yet still dazed. She'd overslept, missed the bells, missed Office. She could hear the other Sisters chanting in the chapel, somewhere far below. 'This is the day the Lord has made. Let us rejoice and be glad.'

That was from the Easter Sunday Mass, the most important joyous Sunday of the entire Church year. She should be down in choir. Why had no one woken her, or come to fetch her when they realised she was missing from her stall? And why were her cell walls that roughcast sallow stone, instead of smooth and whitewashed plaster? Round walls, very thick walls, with bars across the windows. She must be in a prison cell, not her Brignor one. She'd done something very wrong, though she couldn't remember what, couldn't remember very much at all. It felt rather peaceful really, not to have a mind, to be just heaviness and warmth, as she slumped back on the pillows, turned her head a fraction so she could see the Easter flowers – not simple Brignor daffodils, but majestic trumpet lilies.

'The Lord has brought us to a land which flows with milk and honey. Alleluia!' Male voices now, mingling with the shriller female ones, a loud full-throated organ booming out behind. Could that be the prison choir, singing so professionally? She made herself sit up again, struggled out of bed, hobbled to the window. It was difficult to walk, as if her legs were someone else's, someone very old, who'd just recovered from an illness. She peered out through the pane, astonished when she realised how high up she was, as if she could reach out and touch the sky. There was only sky and downs – hills in folds, clouds in furrows, a brilliant sun enamelling greens and golds. It was as remote and quiet as Brignor. No roof, no house, no curl of smoke or sign of human habitation. Was she all alone, alone in some high tower? Had they left her here as punishment, and she'd merely dreamt the music? It had stopped now, anyway. But she could hear another noise – heavy male footsteps on a staircase made of iron. This must be her gaoler. She'd find out what she'd done now, why they'd locked her up.

'Hilary, are you awake? You're *up*, for heaven's sake! How are you? How you feeling?'

'I'm fine.' Suddenly she was. This was somebody she knew, not a prison guard, or stranger, but someone kind and solid connected with the Kingsleys. He was smiling, knew her name, though his was still eluding her.

'Thank God you've woken up. I was getting rather worried that I'd overdone the sedatives. You've slept for hours and hours, you know, missed lunch and dinner yesterday. You must be ravenous.'

She tried to think of food, recall what hunger felt like. No, she wasn't hungry, but full and fat and satisfied, as if she'd been stuffed with soft white feathers.

'Well, how about a cup of tea?'

She nodded. Tea would be quite perfect – real tea with tea leaves in, not just tepid water; tea to slake the dryness in her mouth.

'Strong or weak? Milk or sugar? Both?'

How strange he didn't know. She felt she'd known him years, remembered he'd been with her in a dark and endless dream, where she'd been trying to climb to safety on the frail and slippery deck of some black ship. He'd been captain of the ship; saved it, saved them both.

'Strong, please, with milk and two large sugars.' It was Easter Day, so she was allowed to be indulgent; the long fast over, the penance and the vigils at an end.

'Shouldn't you get back to bed? You still look pretty groggy and the doctor said to rest.'

Doctor? Yes. A large one with cold hands. He'd been in the dream, as well, had found her naked at the bottom of the sea, examined all her bruises, wrapped her in a winding sheet.

'Hilary, are you sure you feel all right? You look so sort of dazed. You do know who I am?'

'Oh, yes,' she said. 'The captain.'

He laughed. 'I like that! We need a ship or two here, not to mention a stretch of real live ocean. Look, let me help you back to bed and I'll go and make the tea.'

He was there again before he'd gone, sitting on the bed now, holding out a cup. 'I brought some croissants, too, just in case you've found your appetite. Happy Easter, by the way. I hope you like your flowers. Those are genuine Easter lilies.'

'Mine?'

'Yes, to cheer your sickroom. And I've got some grapes downstairs. Hey, why not come downstairs? It's a right mess, I'm afraid, but much less claustrophobic than up here. I only brought you this far up, because it's the one and only room that's really finished, and also furthest away from the smell of paint and plaster. I started at the top and I'm working my way down, turning a lighthouse into home.'

'A lighthouse?'

He nodded, grinning at her startled face. 'You probably didn't realise since there isn't any sea. It's more a folly, really. Some nutcase built it in 1810, perfect in all details and with a proper flame-holder on the top, for guiding ships around the rocks. The only problem is there *are* no rocks, and the nearest ship must be fifteen miles away. Still, I like it, and it's ripe for a conversion. I mean, if I don't live here myself, I can always sell it and move on. There must be quite a lot of weirdos in the world, who can't wait to buy an inland lighthouse looking out across the downs. Tell you what, you rest here and drink your tea, and I'll go and tidy things a bit, make your bed up on the sofa. Thank God I've got a sofa! A lot of things I haven't got, including a cooker and a fridge. Never mind, we'll manage. Don't move till I come back.'

She didn't want to move. It felt wonderful to be drinking tea in bed, with a shaft of sun pawing at the honey, turning it to amber. She spread amber on her croissant. She'd never had a croissant, relished its rich taste, its unusual melting texture, which combined crisp and flabby both at once. He'd spoilt her, brought her breakfast up, brought her flowers, expensive flowers, worthy of an altar. She turned again to look at them, the exotic ice-white trumpets, with their gaping golden throats, their veined and speckled petals; the velvet-pollened stamens sticking out their tongues. No one had ever bought her flowers, least of all such glamorous ones, so why should Robert Harrington; crass and noisy Robert, whom she'd thought she hadn't liked?

It was all slowly coming back now – images and memories flashing through her mind: not just Robert pestering her at Wandsworth, his arm across her shoulder on Luke's floor, his constant teasing compliments at Ivan's birthday dinner; but Robert in her Sussex room – a completely different Robert, calming her, dressing her, packing up her things; Robert grim-faced in his car, driving fast through Sussex lanes while she sat silently beside him, some other stranger-woman weeping through her eyes; then stopping at the doctor's, where that woman kept on crying – a terrifying sound, which seemed to claw and rack her body; a needle in her arm, then blackness and the nightmares. She'd woken once and found him there, Captain Robert Harrington, very strong and sure. They'd talked a while, together on the deck, and then she'd plunged down down again, surfaced once or twice, always found him watching at the wheel.

She pulled up her pyjama top, shuddered at the red and angry marks. What in God's name had she told him, how explained those marks? Strange they didn't throb or hurt, when they'd been so sore before. Nothing seemed to hurt, except the questions in her mind. Who had put on her pyjamas, brought her up these stairs? What had really happened in the night? Had he touched her, tried to share her pain – and body – as Simon Tovey had? Her suitcase was unpacked; slippers by the bed, sponge bag on the windowsill, dressing gown hanging on a hook. Someone had looked after her, found the things she needed.

She limped out to the staircase, stronger now, with food and drink inside her, started creeping down it, clinging to the rail. The steps were steep and dangerous. She stopped several times to get her breath, or peer out through the tiny stone-framed windows, marvelling at the view. It *was* a sea out there; the hills themselves rolling in like breakers, capped by white-foam clouds; a strong sea-wind roaring round the tower. There were even sea gulls circling, as if they'd been fooled by the lighthouse and were searching for a shoal. All the smells were wrong, though – not the salty tang of seaweed, but turpentine and paint, new-sawn wood, fresh plaster, now wafting up to meet her, as the stairs curved round towards an open door.

She paused on the last step, exclaiming at the bright and airy room, a perfect circle, with light pouring in from deep-embrasured windows. The room was bare of furniture, save a trestle table piled with paint and tools, and the sofa Robert had mentioned, which looked completely out of place with its curving wooden arms in the shape of dragons' heads, its luxurious crimson velvet. It seemed to form a small oasis amidst the clutter all around it – cardboard boxes pressing in, packing-cases spilling half their contents; more tools and paint-pots on the floor. One crate had been upturned and placed beside the sofa to form a makeshift table; two dirty mugs on top of it, half a staling sandwich, and a small transistor radio tuned to Radio 3. So that had been her Brignor Mass, a recording from the BBC. She smiled, walked over to the window. The view looked very different from lower down the tower. She was no longer poised beneath the sky, but enfolded in the hills, every detail sharper now in the dappled patchwork morning. She swung round as Robert entered, carrying a pile of rugs and cushions and whistling to himself.

'Hilary! You shouldn't be down here yet. I wanted to make it nice for you.'

'It *is* nice. It's wonderful. I've never seen a room like this before.'

'Well, there's a long way to go yet – months and months of work.

Though I suppose I'm lucky to have got this far so quickly. It all happened so damned fast – stumbling on the place at all, then finding it was actually for sale – and cheap at that, then moving in last month and going at it fourteen hours a day. Hell! I never even meant to move. I was living in this commune and . . . I'm sorry, I'm boring you. I've told you all this before.'

'Before?'

'You know – at Ivan's dinner. Liz says I drove her crazy, raving on about the place, but I suppose I'm just in love with it.'

Hilary tried to think back to Ivan's birthday dinner. She did remember Robert talking – talking long and loudly about a whole storm and shoal of things, including his precious acquisition. Though she hadn't even grasped it was a lighthouse, only recalled that strange word 'folly', which she'd applied immediately to herself. *She* was a folly, a naive and stupid laughing stock, who'd fallen for a man who loved only his own sex. She'd been so concerned with Ivan, so embarrassed in his presence, so conscious of her period – blood soaking through the cleaning rag, maybe staining Liz's chair – she'd had little time or interest left for Robert's latest passion. She'd hardly even listened, just tried to tune him out. Now, she felt ashamed.

'It's fantastic, Robert, honestly – like something in a dream, or film, or . . . '

'You wait! This is nothing. I've got some really dazzling schemes – not just inside, outside. See those stinging nettles – a good ten ton of them, and those huge great ugly boulders? Well, imagine Kew Gardens crossed with Hampton Court, and that's what I intend.' He laughed. 'Right, your throne is ready, Ma'am.' He gestured to the sofa, where he had plumped pillows and spread rugs. 'And if I just clear away this debris, you might feel more at home.' He started lunging round the room, stacking boxes, making space.

'Leave it, Robert, honestly. There's no need to do all this for me.'

'There's every need. I want to make you comfortable.'

She watched him from the sofa as he strode in and out, banishing coffee mugs and paint pots, bringing her more things: a carafe of orange juice, a bunch of purple grapes, a twig of blackthorn blossom in a United Dairies milk bottle. 'Sorry about the vase. Half my things are still in packing-cases. You like grapes, do you, Hilary? I tried to get you strawberries, but the damn shop didn't have them. Mind you, I was lucky to get anything so late on Easter Saturday. *And* delivered to my door. I had to phone the shop and really woo the girl. Girl! She's nearer fifty-five, but never mind, she came up with the goods – even found those lilies. I'd have preferred to choose the stuff myself, but I didn't like to leave you, not the way you looked.'

Hilary said nothing, stared down at the grapes, plump expensive grapes with an iridescent bloom; the spray of blackthorn blossom pastel-frail against its gnarled black twig. Why should he do all this for her, look after her two days and nights, stay in all Easter Saturday, so she wouldn't be alone? She ought to thank him, but she couldn't find the words, felt utterly confused. This was the Robert she'd always endeavoured to avoid, yet now she'd been alone with him since Friday – alone in some strange dream, where he had been her anchor and her rock. Things still seemed rather dream-like, her brain unplugged, her body like wet sawdust, as she lay back against the cushions, suddenly dead tired again.

'What time is it?' she asked him. Her watch had disappeared and she had lost all sense of time, all routine, all boundaries.

'Ten past twelve.'

'*Twelve?* You mean midday?'

He grinned. 'Well, certainly not midnight.'

'But I've never slept as late as this, never in my life.' Not even as a teenager had she been allowed to laze in bed, or have lie-ins at weekends.

'Well, I must confess you had me worried, especially when you sleepwalked. That's really why I moved you to the bedroom at the top. It's the only one with bars across the windows, and tiny windows anyway. I was terrified you might fall out if I left you where you were, or might try to break the glass or something. As it was, I had to bar the stairs.'

She took a sip of fruit juice, so she wouldn't have to speak. What did he mean by 'If I left you where you were'? Where *had* she been, and just what else had happened in the night? It was bad enough that he'd seen her sleepwalking – seen her dishevelled and unconscious, a puppet and a prisoner, completely in his power. 'I . . . er . . . never seem to hurt myself,' she muttered hesitantly, still not looking up. 'Well, I never have before. It's as if I keep away from windows almost from some seventh sense.'

'You mean you sleepwalk quite a lot?'

'I used to, a few years ago. But our Abbess said it was really just attention-seeking and I ought to try to . . . '

'For God's *sake*, Hilary! Was the woman mad or something?'

She flushed at his sharp tone, felt a duty even now to defend her Reverend Mother. 'Well, you *can* control a lot of things which people tend to think of as just "happening" – I mean, things like tears or illnesses. The Abbess said they were often self-indulgence.'

'Hilary, it's crazy, that sort of iron control. Don't you see, that's

263

probably just the reason why you sleepwalk in the first place? If you keep yourself so rigid all damned day, then something has to snap at night. Your mind and body are simply shouting out for freedom and a chance of self-expression. You were beside yourself last night, literally shouting in your sleep – and sobbing, really sobbing, tears pouring down your face. You must remember, don't you? I had to wake you in the end.'

She put her glass down, locked her hands together, her whole body tense with shame. 'I . . . I'm sorry.'

'Don't say sorry. Please. I'm the one who owes you an apology. I should have said it sooner, but to tell the truth, I felt a bit, well . . . ' He broke off, veered away from her, started pacing up and down. 'Christ Almighty, Hilary, I've been dead worried all this time, not just about the fact you seemed so ill, but as to what you'd feel when you woke and found me there.'

Ill. He meant mad, unbalanced. Hilary's cheeks were flaming as she recalled the scene again: the sudden knocking at her door, as she held the belt suspended in the air. Had he known what she was doing? How else could he – or she – explain the marks?

He suddenly plunged back to her, sat down on her feet. 'Look, I've barged into your private life, and that's embarrassing for both of us, but if I *hadn't* found you, Hilary . . . ' He paused again, reached out for a grape, as if to stop his mouth with it.

She listened to the crunching of the pips. Of course he'd known, though he wouldn't understand. She hardly understood herself what had made her go so far. She had broken rules again, rigid rules, laid down deliberately so that Sisters wouldn't harm themselves. It was as wrong to overdo the discipline as to avoid it altogether. You were not allowed to mark the skin, forbidden to draw blood. She ought to tell him that; owed it to her convent, to its name and reputation. She tried out words and phrases in her mind, rejected all of them. Why were words so treacherous, always too simplistic or too literal; never seemed to fit the things you tried to say with them? She plucked a grape herself, held it on her palm. The blackthorn blossom was already falling, pink and white confetti on the crate.

Robert had shifted to the far end of the sofa, chin cupped in his hands. 'You're not angry with me, are you – I mean, that I brought you here at all? It must seem a damn cheek, but what else could I do, with Liz and Di and Della all away? It was Liz, in fact, who suggested that I call on you, before she left for France. She phoned to say you'd be staying just ten miles away, so why didn't I pop over in the car? I did phone first, I promise. But the guy who answered said they didn't take messages for ordinary conference members, only for the staff. So I thought I'd take a chance and just drop in. I'm sorry, Hilary, honestly I am.'

She watched another blossom tremble from the twig, fall between the grapes and disappear. He'd apologised – three times. For saving her, for nursing her, for buying grapes and lilies.

'Don't cry,' he said, springing up awkwardly to try to find some Kleenex; passing her his handkerchief instead.

'I'm not.' She touched her face, surprised to find it wet. She had forgotten how to cry – crying was forbidden. But how often had she cried at night, unknowingly? For months, or even years, perhaps? And that woman in the car, that sobbing, screaming stranger, who'd lost all control, all dignity, could that really have been her?

'If you're upset about the doctor, he's a pal of mine and absolutely trustworthy. I had to find a doctor – you do see that, don't you, Hilary? I was frightened you'd been raped, for heaven's sake. Okay, you told me about Simon, so we can forget all that bit now. I just wanted you to know I didn't . . .'

She stared at him in shock. Told him about Simon? That was quite impossible. She'd resolved to hush the whole thing up, never say a word to anyone. And they hadn't talked at all, not that she remembered, or only in a dream. Yet he'd hardly mention Simon's name, unless she'd let it out herself. How many people was she – an hysteric and a sleepwalker, a gossip and a telltale? And why had it all vanished from her mind, as if those dangerous alter egos had taken over in the night, said things she'd never say herself, shamed her and betrayed her – betrayed Simon, too, most likely.

'It wasn't Simon's fault,' she faltered, concerned now that she'd slandered him, portrayed him as a bully or a brute. 'I . . . let him. I mean, it didn't seem to matter if there wasn't any God.'

'No God?'

Suddenly she was blurting out the whole grotesque Good Friday – Jim Duck and Elaine, Reverend Mother Molly, the so-called 'healing' session, when she'd lost her faith, her God.

'But you *are* healed, don't you see – or at least well on the way.' Robert seized her hand, almost knocking over the milk bottle in his eagerness to speak. 'You say you've lost your faith, but actually you've gained something, and something really vital – the freedom to be yourself. Your faith was acting like a straitjacket, keeping you confined in a narrow set of rules. For the first time in your life, you can be free from all those rules, free from guilt and punishment, free to grow. You're a passionate person, Hilary. I realised that the first moment I laid eyes on you. Oh, I'm not talking about sex. I mean feelings and emotions, the capacity to respond to things, enjoy things. All that's been forbidden up to now. You've been taught to seek perfection through constant self-denial. But perfection isn't possible, not for human beings. We all goof, or make a hash of things. It's simply part of life – like pain and mess and mystery are. If you try to avoid them, you'll always end up miserable and frustrated with yourself. I know – my wife was a perfectionist.'

'Your wife?' She'd no idea he had a wife, felt a sudden rush of guilt; glanced behind her, startled, as if expecting Mrs Harrington to walk in through the door, find her in her nightclothes, dishevelled and . . .

'Well, *ex*-wife I should say, though it's funny how the "ex"-bit hurts, even after all these years. And talking of messes, I made a mess of that – not just the marriage, but the divorce as well. I never see my son now. He lives right up in the wilds of Scotland and calls someone else "Dad".'

'I'm sorry.' Hilary eased her hand from his, embarrassed by its stickiness; nervous at this talk of his relationships, his past. She had seen him as a bachelor, free and unencumbered, roaming round the world, changing jobs and houses, in the way Liz had described. Had his wife and son tagged after him on all those exotic trips, or had he divorced them long before? She felt somehow disconcerted to know he had been married – almost angry with him, as if he'd deliberately misled her.

'Don't be sorry. I wasn't cadging sympathy, just trying to show you that my own life hasn't exactly been plain sailing all the way. In fact, I messed up my career, as well, stopped working as an architect because I didn't want to compromise. And actually' – he laughed – 'I lost my own religion, so I do know what a wrench it is. I was brought up C of E, but not the merely social sort who specialise in garden fêtes. I took it very seriously, spent a whole ten years trying to replace it with some other faith. Any one would do, I felt – Eastern, Western, mongrel, even political or secular – so long as I had certainties and dogma, something to make sense of things, explain them. Then, one night, I was reading Thomas Carlyle – well, I was devouring books at that time, reading anything and everything from Marx and Confucius to Nietzsche, Jung and Zen – but there was just one sentence which stuck in my mind. Carlyle said: "I don't pretend to understand the universe. It's a great deal bigger than I am." Okay, I admit that's so damn obvious, it's just a cliché really, but it seemed to shake me up, made me realise I was trying to make the universe much *smaller* than it was, a nice safe cosy world, where everything was neat and orderly, instead of huge and wild and random. *All* religions do that, limit truth, instead of widening it; hand out answers, rigid ready-made ones, which only blinker you.'

He paused a moment, fished an ice cube from the jug of orange juice, sucked it like a gobstopper, went on talking with it still stowed in his mouth. 'I began to see most faiths as merely props and crutches, or maybe cosmic sunglasses which screen out all the glare. But perhaps we need that glare, need to be almost blinded by the sheer maze and swarm of things. Okay, we lose our safety, lose our "Man-From-The-Pru"-God, with his life assurance policies and his comprehensive cover, but once we accept uncertainty, plunge headlong into doubt and risk, we're somehow far less shackled.'

Hilary glanced up at his eager face. She was still shocked by his losses – loss of wife and child, career and God – yet amazed that he could shrug them off so lightly. 'But isn't it rather frightening, not to have the answers? I mean, not to know why we're here, or even who we are?'

'Frankly, yes it is, but it's also quite exhilarating. It depends on how you look at it. I got a bit depressed at first, like you – saw myself as just an ant, one of five billion people on a minor planet in the solar system, which is itself a minor system in an unremarkable galaxy in a whole vast collection of several billion galaxies . . . ' He removed the piece of ice, let it melt between his fingers, hardly seemed to notice it was dripping on his clothes.

'Then I started reading scientific journals and they can really cut you down to size. I mean, half the boffins writing in them, ten years or so ago, believed that human life is just an accident and probably an irrelevance, and the whole damn universe is just a huge great random bubble, which popped into existence out of absolutely nothing, and will ultimately pop back into nothing. Yet the latest theories are much more optimistic, put man back in the centre. They seem to be saying that this universe couldn't be there without us, that human life is the inevitable and almost pre-determined goal of evolution – I think that's the phrase they use. In other words, we rational thinking beings are an essential part of the process, who keep the whole thing going, so to speak – so that it's consciousness, in essence, which gives meaning to the universe.' He paused, to take his jacket off, as if his ideas had made him hot. His face was flushed, eyes burning.

'Oh, a lot of other experts disagree, and disagree quite violently; prefer the random view. In fact, I've heard it said that, far from being inevitable, the odds against man being here are something like one in ten to the six hundredth power – if you can grasp that, which I can't. It's all *I* can do to grasp the basic outlines of the arguments. But whoever's right or wrong, here we actually are – a talking, thinking, writing, building animal, reflecting on itself. Amazing, isn't it, all that sophisticated brainpower evolving out of nix, and even more so when Darwin's crowd keep telling us there's only a one per cent difference between ourselves

267

and chimpanzees. Well, that one per cent is all the more astonishing when it has to account for the whole of civilisation – for art and literature, even science itself. That's the line I take now: a sense of mainly wonder, mixed with a dash of residual fear, plus a strong dose of comedy at the absurdity of it all – the fact that no one really knows the answers anyway. Hell! We may not even know the *questions*, or be asking the wrong ones.'

Hilary was twisting his handkerchief round and through her fingers. For her, the fear far outweighed the wonder. 'But I hate the absurdity and I especially hate the random bit. I mean, take today. What's the point of Easter if you don't believe in Resurrection? It's just a day, isn't it, the same as any other?'

'Of course it's not! You don't need Christianity to put triumph into Easter. It's a pagan feast, anyway, from the Teutonic goddess Eastre. And you've only got to look out there to see things resurrecting – trees in leaf, birds nesting, light and warmth returning.'

'But that's just nature, Robert. I'm not talking about . . . '

'What d'you mean "just nature"? It's desperately important. Why d'you think we're all so terrified of nuclear winter? Because there *won't* be any spring then; no green, no life, no hope. But for centuries and centuries spring must have seemed a miracle – a sudden end to dark and cold, dead trees springing back to leaf, bare ground seeding crops again. Death and resurrection myths are two a penny, once you study ancient cults, but you don't need any myths at all to rejoice in spring itself. Spring's *there*, a simple fact you can't refute.' He pointed to the blossom in the bottle, the sun and birds and green beyond the window. 'In fact, I've always thought the year should begin now – in spring, instead of winter. In most of medieval Europe they did just that, used to start their year in March – March 25th, to be precise – but April's even better, don't you think? I mean, look at the two names: March called after the god of war, and with French and Saxon names meaning "rough month", "windy month", which bracket it to winter; but April sacred to Aphrodite, goddess of love, and also meaning "opening month", when everything is opening and unfolding. Hey, what's the date today? April 5. Perfect! Let's make it New Year's Day today, as well as Easter Sunday.'

She stared at him, intrigued. To begin again, blank out the pain and loneliness of that New Year's Eve cooped up with Miss Pullen; to celebrate a pagan spring and Easter. She glanced up at the blossom, saw the grapes instead, the curling sandwich crusts. Bread and wine. How could she exist in a world devoid of sacraments, where bread was Mother's Pride, wine just Liz's burgundy? She recalled Easter in the convent: all the leaping Alleluias in the Office; the solemn younger Sisters acting out the Resurrection, with an old tin bath as the empty tomb; the paschal candle lit at midnight on the Vigil. 'This is the night on which heaven was wedded to earth. On this night, Christ broke the bonds of death. The night shall be as light as day.' She had often sung those words with no sense of that light; the chapelful of candles mocking her own darkness, yet at least she'd had a structure built on hope; a belief – however desperate – in life and light beyond; rituals and symbols to cling on to. She tried to explain their aching loss to Robert.

'You keep talking about losses, girl, but what about the gains? You've got a host of new religions to explore now, a score of different ways of relating to the world – new ways of even praying, if you like. I'm not trying to throw out soul. Far from it. We all try to be too rational and logical, and ignore the other side – the intuitive, the spiritual. It's just that the Roman Catholic Church doesn't have a monopoly in souls. Nor does any church. What *I'm* against is any kind of "ism" which tries to close our minds, tries to categorise or structure, so as to clear away loose ends, instead of leaving them open and mysterious.'

Open. Ivan's word. Open-minded, open-ended. Hilary picked a grape pip from the fuzzy tartan rug. A mere two weeks ago, she had regarded the two men as completely different, different both in outlook and in temperament. Now she realised they had vital things in common.

Robert was pacing up and down again, as if the energy in his words had poured out to his limbs and he had to work it off. 'I mean, even in science there are no fixed and certain truths. The world may stay the same, but we keep modifying the way we see it and make sense of it, according to our knowledge or the culture that we live in. And whatever our advances – which is a dodgy word itself – we're probably never really there. How can we be, for God's sake, when we're locked in space and time, yet trying to understand things outside them or beyond them? Sometimes I suspect that the laws of physics are like a never-ending set of Chinese boxes – each new box we open reveals yet another box, with even more complexities, and there's never any "last" box. It may sound trite, but I've come to realise that life's a mystery to be lived, rather than a problem to be solved.'

She didn't answer, felt too confused, too dazed. The whole universe was suddenly wide wide open, instead of closed off with a God, buttressed by theology, explained by laws and absolutes.

'Hell, I'm sorry, Hilary. You look quite washed out, and you're meant to be resting, not listening to me rant. It's just that this is something I care so passionately about, I feel I want to share it with you, let you see how strange and rich the world is. But I'll shut up now, I promise, leave you here in peace.'

'No, please don't go,' she said, jerking up and deranging all the rugs. She was worried he might disappear, the nightmares start again.

'Okay, I'll get on with my shelves then. That way, I can keep an eye on you, stop you galloping round the place, or trying to break your neck. I'm building shelves in here, to go all round the room. It's quite a challenge, really. The curved walls make extra work and waste a lot of wood. Though I was lucky with my wood. I found this superb oak panelling in an old Victorian house they were pulling down to build a block of flats. I bought it for a song, plus a lot of other bits and pieces I salvaged from the wreckage. I need shelves badly, so I can unpack all this clutter.' He gestured to the crates. 'I'm a bit of a collector – not the sort who hoards, because I sell a lot of stuff I buy, or get rid of it again, but all the same, it seems to overflow or just pile up.'

'What do you collect?'

'Oh, anything and everything – nineteenth-century gardening books, English sporting pictures, wood-carvings from Fiji, medals from the First World War, even dragons.' He grinned. 'I used to own a good five hundred dragons – painted ones and carved ones, dragon bookends, dragon plates and vases, heraldic dragons on coats of arms, dragon everything.'

'What happened to them all?'

'I'd like to say I slew them, so you'd toast me as St George, but I'm afraid the truth's more boring. I was very pushed for cash about seven years ago, and lucky enough to meet up with a fellow dracontophile – d'you think that's the word, or did I just invent it? Anyway, Mr Elmer Waldo Wallace – American, of course – was really into dragons, bought the lot, lock, stock and barrel.'

'Except for these,' said Hilary, stroking one of the wooden sofa arms.

'Well, Wallace wanted those, in fact, but that sofa's rather special. It was the first thing I ever bought, when I was still wet behind the ears, and it's something I cling on to now, even when the rest goes. I suppose it's become a sort of security blanket.'

She touched the rich red velvet – at least five foot of it. 'Rather a big one.'

'That's the trouble. We've had a few sad separations, when I've been gadding round the world. I especially used to miss it when I was living in the bush, squatting on a chair made out of fuel cans. Mind you, I was still collecting even there – not exactly dragons, but not far off. I had a sort of zoo – rounded up rare animals threatened with extinction. I even owned a scimitar-horned oryx, if you know what that is. Not many people do.'

Hilary smiled and shook her head. There was so much she didn't know, not just about the oryx, but its owner – this new complex Robert

Harrington, who had such exotic tastes, yet still mourned a wife and son, still needed a security blanket; so different from the simpler Robert she'd met – misjudged – at Wandsworth. Even Liz seemed to have told his story wrong, left out the important bits. Her hand strayed back to the dragon, traced its bulbous tongue, its carved and fretted wings. 'You ought to start a zoo here, or at least buy a dog or something. It must be rather lonely, so far from any neighbours – especially after living in a commune. Don't you miss the company?'

He shrugged. 'Yes and no.'

'Liz said you'd been there quite a while.'

'Nearly eighteen months. But I wasn't all that sorry to have an excuse to up and leave. It didn't really work that well. Too many rampant egos all fighting for supremacy.' He stripped a few grapes from the bunch, offered her a cluster. 'What else did dear Liz tell you – all my secrets?'

She flushed. 'Well, no, she only . . . '

'I should have phoned you, talked to you myself. I kept wanting to and meaning to, but I always felt too shy.'

'*Shy?*'

''Fraid so. I know I don't exactly look the modest shrinking violet type, but underneath I *am* shy, and used to be far worse. I learnt to disguise it pretty well through putting on an act – life-and-soul-of-the-party sort of thing – talking too much, hogging the limelight, sitting up on my hind legs and begging for the titbits. It worked so well, I think I've even fooled myself now.'

'Well, you certainly fooled me. I can't think of anyone less shy.' She remembered Reverend Mother Molly, dancing like a dervish in the exercise called 'Loosening', then still insisting she was shy. The word was too elastic.

Robert returned to the sofa, crouched down at her feet. 'D'you realise, Hilary, I've never really had the chance to talk to you before – I mean real talk, one to one, not just social chitchat? Even the last time we met, on Ivan's birthday, I seemed to louse things up. I was furious with myself. I wanted to be serious, impress you, or at least make you notice I was there, and all I did was play the fool, impress you in the worst sense. I could see you disapproving, but I couldn't seem to stop.'

Hilary removed her hand from the dragon's trap of teeth. How could she tell Robert that she'd hardly been aware of him, that her whole mind had been on Ivan?

'The trouble was I knew about your background, knew you'd been a nun. It was the first time I'd seen you since Liz told me, and it seemed to make a difference, screw me up still more. I just felt so in awe of you – your courage and . . . '

'Courage?' Hilary stared. 'What courage? What d'you mean? I'm the biggest coward going.'

'Oh, no, you're not! It's heroic, what you did, leaving that convent after all those years and years. A coward would have stayed there, not just for the safety, but because it takes a special strength to admit you've been wrong, that your original ideals have come unstuck. It happened with me when I gave up architecture – far less dramatically, of course, but it was still an awful wrench. I mean, I lost my whole status and profession, my colleagues, my ideals, or at least the chance to put them into practice. Well, there *wasn't* much chance, actually – that's the reason why I left. I started off wanting to change the world, play God, if you like, rethink our whole society, reorganise our cities and our living-space. But I was forced to drop all that, start cutting corners and licking boots, or keep talking sordid money, instead of space and scale and light. Then, once my partners began wooing those damn Arabs, architecture just went out of the window. Oh, it solved our money problem, but – Christ! – at what a cost. We had to hitch twentieth-century modernism to ancient Islamic tradition.' He grinned. 'Imagine Corbusier smothered with mosaics. No – don't! It's quite grotesque. Don't get me wrong, Hilary. I've nothing against the Arabs. They're just not my favourite clients.'

He paused a moment, swallowed two grapes whole. 'Still, I don't regret my training. I wouldn't be tackling this conversion quite so confidently if I hadn't been through all that slog. I'm sure that's the secret, actually, to value what you had, see the good in it, then try to take it with you, use it in your new life. I know when I was trying to run my potty little Noah's Ark in the outback of Australia, I still needed courage and ideals. Robert, *stop*!' He rapped his own wrists, knelt back on his heels. 'I'm jawing on and on, and I promised half an hour ago that I wouldn't say another word.'

'I like you talking.'

'Do you?'

She wished she hadn't spoken, when it seemed to stop him dead. He *was* shy; he was right. She was suddenly aware of it as he caught her eye, looked down; pretended to be fiddling with the corner of a rug. He needed help. She gave it. 'What about your shelves?'

'You're right! My shelves. This stuff will still be sitting in its crates on Christmas Day 2000, if I don't get a move on. Are you sure you'll be all right, though, just lying there while I leap around a bit? Actually, I don't think I'll disturb you. I've finished all the sawing and the sanding down, so the noisy bits are done. I've got two last shelves to finish off, then I'm going to polish the whole lot, just a gentle rub with beeswax. No noise, no smell, as they say in the commercials. All the same, if you'd rather escape into another room, or go back upstairs to read, or . . . '

'Oh, no, I'm fine. This is really rather new for me, just lying doing nothing.'

'Yes, and vitally important, woman. You've got to practise every day. And also practise *enjoying* life a bit. In fact, let's shift the sofa, so you're closer to the window and can feel the sun and start basking in the spring. And how about some music? There's a Schubert concert starting any minute. And food – you must have food. I've got some duck terrine. It's only in a tin, but the picture looks quite fancy. I'll bring it in. Don't say no. That word's on the Index from now on. Pope's orders. Pope Robert. Was there ever a Pope Robert?'

She was laughing now, enjoying, doing what he said. It wasn't even difficult. Both sun and Schubert were deliciously relaxing; warmth seeping through her skin, horns and strings beginning an antiphony, the melody repeated by a pleading oboe. Music was still a real indulgence. Stephen had walked off with her radio, at least six weeks ago, never brought it back, and the other Kingsley sets were rarely tuned to concerts. She had been starved of music in the convent; this rich and urgent music with its fierce rhythms, startling contrasts; had been rationed to an organ, or unaccompanied chant. She felt her spirits soar with the soaring woodwind, her heart twist over on the downward glide of the cellos. Robert had called her passionate, able to respond to things. He had also called her 'woman'. That could have sounded rude, but it hadn't, and she'd relished it. *Woman*. She'd been scared of him at Liz's because he seemed so male; male and threatening, male and coarse. He was still male, very much so, but it intrigued her now, rather than alarmed her.

She watched him planing wood, his total concentration on the plane; his body thrusting back and forwards with it, both hands tensed and braced. He had rolled his shirt-sleeves up, and she could see the startling contrast between his tanned and roughened hands – workman's hands, with broken nails, stained fingers – and the pale skin of his forearms, which looked delicate, almost womanish, despite the long fair hairs. His brows were fairer still, but heavy, well-defined; his strong and squarish jaw suggesting tenacity – or stubbornness. The word 'strong' kept returning. Strong voice, strong hands, strong principles – strong appetites, as well. He had poured himself a pint of beer, and swilled it every now and then, in noisy eager gulps. Or he'd reach out for the long French loaf, which he'd brought in with the terrine, rip a rough hunk off, almost seem to throw it down his throat. She hid a smile as she tried to imagine him in the Brignor refectory, eating with that passion,

273

declaiming through the silence, dropping forks or food, as he tried to make his points. He stopped his planing suddenly, as the music reached a climax, started conducting with his French-bread baton, arms sweeping up and out.

'I love this bit, don't you? But they're taking it so slowly. I've got six different recordings of it and none of them's quite right. Perhaps I should have been a conductor, instead of a mere architect.' He gestured to his orchestra, beckoned in the strings; suddenly stopped dead in the middle of a phrase. 'Hey! Is this your sort of music? I didn't think to ask, don't even know if you like music at all.'

'I *love* it!' She flushed. She had replied with too much vehemence, surprised herself – and him – by almost flinging out the words, half-rising from the sofa, as if scared he'd turn it off. 'It's terribly important – I mean, it was, once, still is, but . . . ' How could she explain – that aching sense of loss again, music sacrificed so young, flogged out of her at seventeen, labelled 'dangerous', 'indulgent'? She sank back on the sofa, tried to blank out all regrets, feast herself on the exuberant violins, which were exploring the main theme, embroidering it, enlivening it.

Robert chewed a bit of baton, watched her anxiously. 'Are you all right, Hilary? You don't feel ill again?'

'No, I'm fine.'

'Sure?'

'Yes.'

'Good.' He broke her off a piece of bread, spread it with terrine, put it in her hands with a sudden explosive laugh.

'What's funny?' She was amused already by the way he kept on talking, interrupting the music he claimed to find so riveting.

'They thought I was your brother.'

'Who did?'

'The people at the conference. Well, I mean, I told them so. I thought it would be simplest. I just said you weren't too well, so I was driving you back home. The problem was I'd already given them my name and they picked me up on it – some awful bossy girl, with a "Jesus Loves Me" badge, who said how come you were Miss Reed – and she really stressed the "Miss" – if I was Mr Harrington? I told her you were "Ms", married and divorced.'

'Oh, you *didn't*, Robert.'

'Yes, I did. Serves her right for being such a nosy parker. Hell! I'm yakking again, aren't I? Sorry, Schubert; sorry, little sister.' He picked up a piece of sandpaper, gave the wood a final rub; started humming the last phrases of the scherzo, as if it were impossible for him to be completely quiet.

Little sister. She smiled down at her plate. She'd always wanted a big brother, someone she could turn to when her parents quarrelled, someone who'd be proud of her. And brothers were quite safe, safer than priests. She did feel safe with him. He hadn't tried to touch her, save once, to take her hand, and that, too, had been more brotherly than lustful. She was certain now he had done nothing in the night, except look after her. She still marvelled at his kindness. She must have disturbed his sleep for two consecutive nights, if she'd been sobbing, shouting, threshing in and out of nightmares, yet he hadn't once complained. In fact, those things, however shameful, had somehow bonded them; made them closer, in a way, than if they'd shared their bodies, or a bed. How odd to think this almost-stranger, whom she'd met only three times in her life, knew more about her now than anyone in the world, including Liz. He knew about Simon and her loss of faith, about the whipping and the sleepwalking; had seen her cry, heard her rant; and still he hadn't shrunk from her, just acknowledged all of it, and then gone on to compliment her.

She glanced at him again, admiring his mixture of energy and patience, the eager careful way he worked. She liked to think of him building shelves for books, for treasures gathered round the world, a world he saw as rich and strange. She'd seen so little of that world, knew nothing of its riches. But she could learn, use him as her teacher. Teacher-brother.

The plate felt very heavy in her hands, the inch or two of bread too daunting for her mouth. She was still so tired – often was at Easter, after all the fasts and strain of Passion Week. It had been impossible at Brignor to snatch an extra hour in bed. Easter Sunday was the greatest of all feasts, but still vigorously timetabled, with extra time in choir, extra recreation. Recreation meant sitting on a hard wood chair, sharing safe and cheerful subjects with your Sisters, not creeping up to bed to snatch a nap. By the time they'd reached their tipsy trifle in the evening, she had often felt too tired to lift her spoon. But now she was allowed to sleep, sleep all afternoon, if that was what she wanted, do exactly what she liked.

It still felt almost wicked, yet she lay back, closed her eyes. They had reached the slow movement in the symphony, and even the music seemed to be telling her to rest, to ease up, just let go. The music of the plane was also slower now, and had somehow joined the orchestra, with Robert as conductor. She looked down at her score, saw it was marked 'rest', the remaining pages blank. How wonderful, how kind. This particular Easter, all the other nuns could sing, while she slept through till summer.

21

'It's like summer,' Robert said. 'The first week of April and too hot for a jacket.' He took his off, used it as a pillow as he lay back on the grass.

Hilary removed a tiny crawling insect from her dish, parked it on a leaf. 'I thought you said it was our New Year.'

'It is. And quite right, too! One should always start a new year with some hope, not in dark and cold and snow. All we need is flowers. Another month, and there'll be harebells and blue scabious in their hundreds here. It's all blue in May, isn't it – forget-me-nots and speedwells, borage, bugloss, bluebells – blue like you.' He reached out to touch her dress, a meld of several different blues. 'How d'you like your tipsy trifle, by the way?'

She spooned neat brandy from the bottom of her bowl, nodded her approval. 'There's more tipsy than trifle. That beetle thing was reeling. And Sister Gerard would have gone into terminal shock. She used just half a spoon of cooking sherry, and thought *that* was pretty daring. Even so, some nuns got giggly on it. It was the only sniff of alcohol we got all year, so I suppose it went straight to our heads, or maybe just the thought of it. It was really children's trifle – you know, custard and red jelly, with glacé cherries on the top and wet sponge at the bottom.'

'I've made it all wrong, then?'

'Yes, wonderfully wrong.' She scooped up a fresh strawberry, layered between ratafias and double Jersey cream; held it in her mouth, let its winey flavour jolt and tease her taste-buds. She was still practising enjoyment, learning to be a hedonist, a pagan. All their meals had been improvised so far, since Robert had no cooker, but this was the first real picnic, with the springy turf as tablecloth, the curve of downs surrounding them, like the plush and padded back of some gigantic sofa. They could see the lighthouse far above them now, dwarfed into a pepperpot, a toy. They had walked down the hill to find shelter from the wind, but the terrain still felt high and breezy, with other hills below them, a humped quilt of graded greens. It was Easter Monday, Bank Holiday, yet the crowds were somewhere else. This whole wide sweep of downland seemed like Robert's private sanctuary, which he had bought to please her, as he'd also bought the strawberries and the wine; found delicacies in tins, like olives and smoked oysters. He was gobbling olives now, spitting out the stones, arranging them in patterns.

'I envy you, in one sense – the way everything's so new for you – books, ideas, philosophies, even wine and food. So often, by your age, people have become blasé, with jaded palates, jaded minds – seen it all, done it all. But you're just starting, coming fresh to everything.'

'But you're not jaded, Robert. In fact, you're the least blasé person I can think of. You sort of crackle with enthusiasm.'

He laughed. 'All the same, I can't eat a mere smoked oyster the way you did just now, with that mixture of surprise, delight and terror.'

'Well, it sort of looked . . . alive, and anyway, it did taste strange, coming after – what were they? – black truffles?'

'*Truffes à la Périgourdine*. I've been saving that small tin for years, waiting for someone worthy of them.'

She was touched by all his trouble, the way he'd picked out books for her, marked passages, suggested other authors; ransacked his cupboards for exotic foods and fruits; had even made the tipsy trifle, not just because the name had charmed him, but also so she wouldn't miss it, wouldn't break tradition. She had been telling him about traditions in the convent, reluctantly, at first, since it still seemed like betrayal; then more enthusiastically, as he seemed to understand, and, finally, the little things – the posies at each place for Easter Sunday, the way even meals had to match the liturgy: boiled turnips for the fast days, jelly for the feasts.

'Right, it's jelly for a year then. You deserve it.'

She let the last fat strawberry slip slowly, richly, down, then sucked the word 'deserve'. Such a new and unfamiliar word, which brought an immediate rush of pleasure, followed by a feeling of complete unworthiness, and a small sour voice saying: 'All you deserve is penance for a year.' She had to quash that voice. Robert, like Ivan, had urged her to leave the past behind, concentrate on 'now', the precious present moment. It wasn't easy, when she had spent so long with her sights set on eternity. And she would have to unlearn all that anxious looking inwards, all that concentration on soul and sin and conscience; look outward for a change. In just two days, the world seemed so much larger. Robert had expanded it, not only with his trips abroad, his constant references to philosophers or writers she had never even heard of; but also through his interest in things like science and cosmology, so she was aware now of other galaxies, other forms of being, worlds on worlds.

She gazed up at the clouds, their strange and various shapes – lozenges and anvils, swags and plumes and streamers, a squat truncated gargoyle – clouds changing as she looked at them, merging, breathing, bits breaking off in ragged wispy trails. She had called them white, but that was far too simple. They were every shade of pearl and milk and oyster, with a touch of pink magnolia, a hint of amethyst; some streaked and fretted grey. As a child, she had loved the natural world – walking on a winter beach beneath a sky as churned and angry as the sea; or seeking lugworm casts on the glassy tide-washed sand, where her feet glugged in and out and the wind whipped her streaming hair. Sometimes, she had stretched out on the dunes and gulped down great strong draughts of sky, or imagined the waves breaking right across her body, instead of further down the strand, as if she were the sand itself, pounded and sucked down.

All that had been forbidden in the convent. Brignor stood just ten miles from the coast, yet she never saw the ocean in her life again. They had lived in unspoilt country, beneath vast dramatic skies, yet had to keep their eyes down, not feast them on raw nature. She had missed so much, she realised now; had never looked before with such intensity, seen all the different greens, all the different grasses: tall and bearded ones with coarse and wiry stalks, shorter mossy growths, frail yellowed stems which trembled in the wind; had never fully noticed the way the shadows fidgeted on folds and falls of hills, or the exact shape of the gorse buds, the mixture of dead wood and new bright leaf. She picked up a grass, examined it, felt its whiskery softness on her cheek. 'I had another dream last night. That ship again.'

Robert reached out for the cheese, cut himself a hunk. 'It must be the lighthouse. It's hungry for a ship or two, so it sails them through your dreams.'

'No, this was a ghost-ship, but with lots of high frail rigging. I was climbing it this time. It's funny, really, I haven't dreamed in years, yet now the dreams are coming thick and fast.'

'You must have dreamed, Hilary. We all do every night, or so those sleep researchers say. Hey! Perhaps I'll be a sleep researcher, instead of an Otto Klemperer. It must be really strange staying up all night with rows of snoring bodies twitching all around you.'

'Well, at least I've given you some practice.'

He grinned. 'You didn't snore – not once – and if all the subjects are as fascinating as you are, I'll apply for the job this instant.'

She forced some light reply, still found it very difficult to accept his compliments; was never really sure what was joke, what not. 'Fascinating': that was a term which applied to Cleopatra, or Helen of Troy, or to the glamorous Ms Swanson, not to her mere namesake.

Robert swigged his wine, refilled both their glasses. 'Tell me about the dream.'

'There's not much to tell, except the climbing, which seemed absolutely terrifying. Oh – and yes – the end. That was ghastly, too. There were all these small white bodies like cocoons. There were babies inside, baby pupae with their eyes still open – not dead at all, yet I was flinging them overboard, really hurling them in the water with an awful sort of glee. I didn't seem to care a fig, just watched them drown and struggle, then went back for more. It felt so violent, not like me at all.'

'Are you sure of that, Hilary?'

She flushed. 'What d'you mean?'

'Well, sometimes I suspect you're quite a violent person. I mean, isn't a nun's life pretty violent in itself?'

'Violent? That's the last word I'd use.'

'Think about it, though – those things you told me just today: the whole concept of putting yourself to death, breaking down your personality – what's that but a kind of violence and destructiveness? And I suspect some nuns become addicted to it. There's excitement in extremes, and even pride; seeing how far you can go, how much pain and humiliation you can take without cracking. I've told you before, you've got very strong emotions, so if you're stuck in a system which won't allow them out in normal ways, is it any wonder that you crack? Look, Hilary, my sweet, I realise we're both avoiding the subject, have been avoiding it two days, in fact, but I'm also well aware that those marks are hurting you. Oh, I know you haven't said. You wouldn't, would you? That's all part of the package – suffering in silence, avoiding human comfort, but I can't bear to think you want to spoil and scar your body. You ought to cherish it, look after it, not flog it into pulp.'

She winced, fought a jumble of emotions: embarrassment, resentment, shock at that 'my sweet'; surprise at his own mixture of tenderness and anger. The marks *were* hurting, especially when she moved, and the rough fabric of her dress chafed the open skin. Whatever had sedated her had also been a painkiller, and now both effects had faded, leaving her whole body sore and throbbing. Yet she resented him for mentioning it, shadowing their day, smirching its soft colours with darker threatening tones. She caught his eye, looked down.

'I'm sorry, Hilary, that must have sounded cruel, and the last thing I want is to upset you any more. But someone's got to make you realise what you're doing to yourself. Don't you see, it's very bad for you not to allow yourself to dream, or cry, or even lose your temper?' He was fiddling with his olive stones, disrupting their neat patterns. 'D'you know what I suspect?'

She shook her head, didn't trust herself to speak.

'That you entered the convent to escape your own strong feelings, and that what you saw as the dark night of the soul was plain and simple depression. Because you'd suppressed all your vitality, you see, your whole sensitive and creative personality, tried to become someone else completely, a sort of saintly robot, serene and even-keeled and totally controlled.'

She still said nothing, thought back to her child-self, lying on the sand dunes, those wild imaginary waves crashing over her body, foaming through her hair. She'd been only twelve or so, yet she'd felt so old – powerful-old, like the ancient rocks around her, or the huge cedars in the grounds of Holkham Hall. The first time she'd seen those trees, she had seemed to become a cedar with them, her top limbs touching sky, her deep roots clutching earth; endless noise and movement in her branches, the whine of wind, the flap and start of a bird. And it *had* been frightening, hadn't it, the pain she'd felt in her own hands and feet and skull when they'd felled trees or scythed back hedges: her raw wrists bleeding with the stumps, ears aching with the cries of murdered flowers. She could never tell her parents what she felt; would return to the house from her wild walks in the country as a different, tamer person – that timid tepid house where the only feelings permitted were her mother's disenchantment with the weather and the world, or her father's sullen grumblings at a change of syllabus. How strange that Robert understood – some of it, at least. She chewed her piece of grass, tried to sort her thoughts out.

'It wasn't quite like that, you know. Oh, I admit I had strong feelings, but I became a nun to *use* them, put them to some good. You see, all those convent rules are there for a reason, not to simply tie you down, but to make you free to . . . ' She stopped a moment, surprised by her own words. She was defending the whole system, as if she still believed in it. In one way, she still did, still missed it desperately, at least some aspects of it. 'Gosh, it's so hard to explain, but even the flagellation had a purpose, not just subduing the body for its own sake, but to allow the spirit to take over, so you could experience what the books called "spiritual adventures". That's what I really craved, I suppose – *spiritual* excitement.'

'But did you find it, Hilary?'

'In the early days I did, yes. I mean, the whole idea of being married to the God who made the world is absolutely breathtaking. If you really think about it, that's the greatest adventure possible to anyone, and any sacrifice is worth it, isn't it?' She nodded, as if to answer her own question, watched the sun add sparkle to her wine. 'But then the excitement seemed to fade, and after all those years of sort of . . . numbness, it's hard to quite remember what the early period felt like, or even believe it really happened. In fact, I'm beginning to realise that perhaps my entire life as a nun was something of a mirage – I mean even when I *had* a faith. The whole idea was to empty yourself for God, and I was pretty good at that, but I suspect I stayed empty, instead of going on to grow – you know, all outward rules and penances, but no inner development or spiritual maturity.'

'How could you grow, though, Hilary, when your whole character and temperament had to be denied, and you were cut off from so much – new ideas, different sorts of people, the entire male sex, for God's sake?'

'Some nuns do, you'd be surprised. Yes' – she laughed – 'Even deprived of men, they still manage to turn out wise and really holy.' She took a sip of wine, forgot to taste it, as she pondered. 'What's "holy", though? The trouble is all the words which meant something, like grace or sacrament or vocation, revelation, sanctity itself, seem to shrink to nothing without a God to give them point. I just can't get used to it.'

'Give yourself a chance. You've had your faith for nearly forty years; been without it just three days. These things take months to really filter down and change your basic concepts.'

'I'm so muddled though, I'm not sure what spiritual *means*, not even in a general sense. That's partly your fault, Robert. You're making me confused, teaching me to analyse too much.'

'I don't want to make you anything, except less violent with yourself. Promise me you'll never ever thrash yourself again?'

She banged her glass down, spilling half its contents. Why should he interfere, keep returning to that shameful stupid subject, extract promises about things he saw only from the outside?

'That's right, be cross with me! Go on, really lose your temper, tell me to mind my own bloody business and shut up.'

She sat in rigid silence, experiencing fear as much as anger. Only now had she noticed Robert's heavy belt – a brutal-looking leather belt, with a sharp-edged metal buckle. Violence was all around them – in nature, in herself. A lapwing flapped up suddenly, trying to frighten off a predator, startling both of them with its high-pitched squawking cries. She watched it dart against the crow, beak jabbing, wild wings threshing. The crow itself was strutting round in circles, then flailing up and back, a murderer-bird, thwarted in its urge to steal eggs, gobble young. She mopped the spill of wine, cuts burning and complaining as she leaned across the rug. They were worse because he'd mentioned them, stirred her up in general. He didn't understand that it was best to keep control – safer altogether, however high the cost. She grabbed a fistful of tall grasses, started shredding them to bits. 'I . . . I can't say things like that, Robert. It feels wrong to lose my temper, and also very frightening.'

'You were angry in your dream.'

'That's different.'

'Not really. It was still part of you, and perhaps a vital part, though I'm not really into the whole Freudian dream-analysis thing. Freud made it far too rigid. I think dreams are more like poems, which work with images and symbols, as a sort of way of using what we know to catch a glimpse of what we don't know. Hell! It's clouding over. See that belt of rain? It's heading south.'

Hilary looked up, surprised to see the difference in the sky. She hadn't even felt the drop in temperature, or noticed that the sun had disappeared.

Robert helped her to her feet. 'Quick! Let's get back before we're drenched.'

She started packing up the picnic hamper, pouring dregs of wine onto the grass. 'I ought to get back anyway – I mean to London, Cranleigh Gardens. Liz and co are arriving back tonight.'

'That doesn't mean that you must.'

'Yes, it does. Di needs me in the shop. And, anyway, the conference ends today, so they're expecting me.'

'I may not have a cooker, woman, but I do have a phone.'

'Oh, I couldn't phone them, Robert. Whatever would I say? You don't stay on at conferences.'

'You tell the truth.' Robert grabbed a last cheese biscuit before she stowed away the tin. 'You need a holiday. You're still absolutely knackered and barely recovered from all that dope and stuff the doc pumped into you. And you're also sore and bruised, and in no fit state to sew. Damn! Here's that dratted rain. We'll argue in the kitchen.'

She won the argument, felt surprised to do so, and almost disappointed. These strange few days with Robert had been a holiday already, and it was a wrench to leave the country and the tower, return to dingy London streets. She was also worried that Liz might see her marks, or ask too many questions.

'Look, don't bother with the car, Robert. I'll get the train – honestly, I'd rather. I bought a return ticket, so it's stupid to waste money.'

He laughed. 'You mean you don't want Liz to see you turning up with me? Okay, I understand. But don't deprive me of the pleasure of one last hour with you, or the chance to show you just how nippy my new car is. I'll drive you to the bottom of her road, and you can walk the whole way up it, puffing and panting, as if you've lugged your suitcase from the station. Will *that* do?'

She nodded sheepishly. They were sitting in the kitchen, where an ancient wood-stove, salvaged from a demolished Edwardian house, was drying out their clothes. The kitchen, frankly, was a mess, and not much more than a shell yet. Robert cleared a space to put his cup down. They'd made tea, to warm them up.

'I should have started on it first, I suppose, but I've still got to decide whether I'm staying here myself, or just doing up the place to sell. That'll determine the sort of kitchen I put in. Mrs Public wants microwaves and dishwashers, and double sinks with those waste disposal whatnots, whereas I'm content with a cold tap and a gas ring. Both of which I've got.'

Hilary sipped her tea, surprised to hear he might not stay, when he was obviously so taken with the place. He seemed always on the move, as if scared to settle, make anywhere his home. 'I suppose it's just too big for you,' she said.

'Miles too big. Though one or two brave souls from the commune did express some interest in moving in as well. And once they see my wonderful conversion, they'll be breaking down the doors to get a room.'

'I thought you said the commune didn't work.'

'It did in some ways. Though this wouldn't be a commune, just two or three of us. I don't think lighthouse keepers ever live alone. They have to share duties, in case one of them pegs out. Hey, is that the phone? Excuse me just a tick.'

She cleared up while he answered it, marvelling at the mixture of precious and expendable – gold-rimmed plates, hand-painted with petunias, stacked with plastic cups; calf-bound first editions half-hidden under motor magazines; a huge framed painting of a ship, propped against the wall, and standing in a tide of greasy rags. She started stuffing rubbish in the waste-bin, replacing precious books in boxes. He had tipped out the books that morning, to try to find the specific ones he wanted her to read, failed to put them back. Her hand struck something harder than a book – the corner of a metal photo frame. She drew it out, wiped a film of dust away. It was Robert – Robert black and white, and younger – lying face down on a bed, completely naked. Beside him lay a baby, also naked, their two sides joined, as if they had fused into one flesh, their skin the same light tone. She could tell it was his son, mainly from the eyes – expressive deep-set eyes, which, even in the infant, looked questing and intense. Yet the baby seemed so vulnerable, so tiny, as if its father's broad strong back might casually roll over and crush it underneath. Both faces were in profile, both fair heads gleaming in some hidden light-source; both bodies deeply shadowed.

Hilary kept staring at the photo with a sense of almost guilt, as if she had stumbled on a scene in Robert's private life and was peering through the keyhole back in time. She was also shocked to see him naked; that expanse of broad male body, which seemed more blatant even than Simon's, despite the fact he was lying on his front revealing nothing. Nothing? Those buttocks curving down to strong and muscly thighs, that coarse hair beneath his underarm, showing on one side? She had hardly looked at Simon, had kept her eyes averted, or closed them tight to try to ward him off. Yet this photo seemed to mesmerise her, so that she couldn't put it down; even touched Robert's shoulder with one nervous guilty finger, which she ran right down his back; then touched the child, the baby – stroked its fuzz of hair, traced the outline of its open mouth.

She remembered Robert lying on the rug with Luke, so at ease with him, relaxed. He'd obviously had practice, playing father to a son. She could see the magpie family he had drawn with Luke's crayons – the sleek and dazzling wife, the proud possessive male – *his* family, perhaps? She felt suddenly excluded, longed for her own family, or the nearest that she had to one, which meant Liz and Cranleigh Gardens. She'd been reluctant to return there; now she was impatient, anxious to be back in her small and sheltered room, with no males, save Luke next door. She rammed the photo back again, as she heard Robert's footsteps just outside, busied herself washing up the teapot.

'Leave that, Cinderella. We've just been invited to a ball – well, a bottle party, anyway. That was Hugh, a mate of mine, who's decided to break the tedium of Bank Holiday with a little serious drinking. Shall we go, join the merry throng, drive back first thing in the morning?'

Hilary didn't answer. How could he be so cheerful when he'd lost his son – that son who called someone else his father, who was maybe in his teens now, and had totally forgotten ever touching bones or sharing genes with Robert? Why were families so perilous, so fragile?

'What's the matter? You look quite shaken up.'

'N . . . Nothing.'

'You mustn't cry, my love. Hugh's not worth it. We don't have to go – of course not. I'd no idea it would upset you, or I wouldn't have mentioned it at all.'

She clung on to the teapot, a plain stout brown one, chipped. 'It's not that. It's . . . '

'I know. You're still feeling weak and weepy. That's only natural, but I wish you'd stay here for a few more days, instead of rushing back to London.'

She could see the photo in her mind, Robert's arm flung out, as if to protect his child from danger. She'd been murdering babies in her dreams, babies that she craved.

'Please don't cry. I feel it's my fault, somehow, but I'm not sure what I've done.'

She used the tea towel to mop her face, her eyes. 'You . . . You haven't done anything. You *wanted* me to cry – said I had to, earlier – to let my emotions out.'

He grinned. 'You're right, I did. Okay, let me tuck you into bed, so you can cry more comfortably.'

'No, I've got to go.'

'You haven't. There's no fairy godmother warning you it's midnight and your dress will change to rags. It's not quite four o'clock, in fact, and you still look beautiful.'

She ignored the compliment. 'Well, I want to go. I'd like to.'

'Can't wait to get away?'

'Robert, *no*, it's not that. In fact, I can't thank you enough – for everything. You've been so kind and patient.'

'Don't thank me, Hilary. It makes it sound so formal, and I'm very fond of you. You know that, don't you?'

Not too fond, she begged him, without answering aloud. It was too complicated, dangerous. Simon had said much the same, then turned fondness into lust. She wanted Robert as her brother, nothing else. So why did she feel jealous of his wife – the wife who'd borne his child, must have stretched beside him, naked, in the same way that he'd lain against his son? It was obsessing her, that photograph, so that, even now, she could see his naked body through his clothes; see those buttocks curving into thighs, the strong hair on his legs.

He took her hand a minute, trapped it in his own. 'Just stay until tomorrow, one more night.'

'No, really, I . . . '

'Come on. It's an order.'

'*No!*'

Her own fierceness startled her. She knew she'd hurt his feelings, hardly understood why she'd shouted at him like that, yanked her hand away. There was silence for a moment, a heavy wounded silence. Robert tried to mend it, make his voice sound casual, half-amused. 'Tell you what, we'll compromise. I'll drive you back immediately, but let's fix another date to see each other. How about tomorrow?'

'Oh, Robert, no, I can't. There'll be so much to do and Liz will think it very odd and . . . '

'Okay, next weekend.' He was hunting for his diary, found it on the floor. 'No, *I* can't manage that. The weekend after, then. Hell! I'm up in Sheffield. I know – St George's Day. That's perfect. The patron saints of soldiers and boy scouts, and I was both of those a hundred years ago.

285

And probably the patron saint of dragons, knowing how perverse the Church is. There, I've put it in my diary: "Rescue maiden."'

Except I'm not a maiden, Hilary thought bitterly, all her anger suddenly resurging, and now directed against Simon. She had chucked away her maidenhead on a man she didn't like and couldn't trust; had hoped to have his child – a child whose father would be God's representative, when there wasn't any God. She pressed her stomach, hard. Could she actually be pregnant? She'd read frantic letters in women's magazines from girls who claimed they hadn't gone that far, yet had still somehow conceived. She'd murder Simon, lynch him, march into his presbytery and . . .

Her hands were throttling Simon, aborting their gross child, pressing on her stomach, tearing at her grazes. She was wincing with the pain, frightened now by her turmoil of emotions, which seemed just as raw and shocking as the weals – vindictiveness and fury, aggression, even lust – emotions she had never owned, never dared to recognise. Yet Robert would accept them, probably call them natural, even urge her to express them, as healthy and more human. If she took that view herself, she could start her second-chance New Year as a new and different person – a wild explosive one.

She grinned at Robert suddenly, dared to touch his shoulder. 'Right, April 23. But don't be too surprised if you discover I'm the dragon, not the maiden.'

22

Hilary poured the top of the milk onto her cornflakes, added a sliced nectarine, swallowed the first spoonful very slowly, so she could relish all the different tastes and textures – crunchy flakes, cool and sharpish fruit, bland and creamy milk. She could still taste guilt, as usual, but it was far less all-pervading now. She was doing very well. Breakfast at eleven was almost decadent, yet here she was enjoying it. She had slept till almost ten, hadn't heard Liz get up, or Della leave for college. Those few days with Robert seemed to have taught her how to sleep, and also how to dream. She had moved from ships to horses; kept dreaming about horses with blue wings.

'Sure they're not dragons?' Robert had asked her on the phone.

'Oh, no. They're very cool, not breathing fire.'

'Well, you'd better have a dragon dream tonight. I'm planning a Mystery Day tomorrow, for St George's, but it will feature dragons definitely. You've got the day off, haven't you? I want as long with you as possible. I'll be there by noon, okay, and we'll stay out till the early hours.'

She felt excited and yet nervous. Although she hadn't seen him since the Easter Monday, he had phoned her every day, Liz growing more and more intrigued.

'What's up between you two? Bob keeps making out he's phoning *me*, to ask my advice about microwaves or fridges. Then, when we're through with the charade of comparing Zanussi with Iced Diamond, he adds – sort of casual and dead innocent – "Oh, by the way, if Hilary's there, I'll just have a brief word with her, okay?" And forty minutes later, he's still wooing you, care of British Telecom.'

Hilary put her spoon down, feeling real guilt now, and not about an out-of-season nectarine. She had found it quite impossible to confide in Liz, tell her about Simon and what had happened afterwards; had fobbed her off instead with some vague story about how Robert had dropped in at the conference and found her in her room, so they'd gone out for a drive together. All quite true, in fact, yet she knew she was deceiving Liz; felt worse when Liz regaled her with her own holiday romance. Liz had gone up to Scarborough, to stay with an old schoolfriend and her husband, who were hosting a silver wedding party, a grand one with a disco and champagne. She'd met Harry at the party, sixty, but well-heeled; a local councillor who owned a chain of estate agents and was a big noise in the town.

'I know sixty sounds quite ancient, Hil, and he's balding, I'm afraid, but still quite a lad, it seems. He outdanced all the young ones, then turned up in the morning at the crack of dawn – well, before ten, anyway – with this huge great bunch of roses. God! It was embarrassing. My friends weren't even up, so *I* went down, expecting just the postman or a canvasser or something, and looking quite unspeakable in my nightie and no make-up – came face to face with Harold, all smiles and aftershave, and with this bloody great bouquet done up in cellophane with yellow satin bows.'

Hilary smiled to herself. It was rather comic, really, both of them with suitors, both of them with flowers – Liz with roses, her with Easter lilies. And Harry, like Robert, had been phoning every day, though Liz was far less cagey about the content of the calls.

'He's really struck, he must be. That's the sixth time he's rung up. He says I've put the spark back in his life. Did I tell you he was widowed? Yes, seven years ago. He claims I'm the first thing that's happened in those whole seven years which has made him truly happy. Isn't that nice? I'm going up for the Bank Holiday again, staying at his house this time, instead of with the Jarrells. I must confess I'm feeling rather nervous. I mean, it's all happening a bit fast. I tried to play it cool that first weekend, hardly let him touch me – well, just a cuddle and a kiss or two, but you have to be so careful nowadays. Mind you, the Jarrells say he's safe enough – sort of pillar of the establishment, who's always dipping in his pocket for local charities, and never seen around with floozies, or any women much at all. That could be a bad sign, of course – may mean he's past it. Well, we'll have to see.'

Hilary had mumbled some reply. Talk of sex always made her nervous, even more so now. Anxious thoughts of Simon began to gripe and fret again, as she dragged the spoon around her cornflakes. Supposing she'd caught some vile infection, the sort of thing the papers kept discussing? And what had made her bleed like that? Was . . . ? She pushed both bowl and thoughts away, switched on the radio, tuned it to a Bach recital; refused to spoil her day with futile worries. Her marks had almost faded and she was determined that the whole memory of Simon should disappear as well, fade and pale to nothing.

She allowed the prancing harpsichord to change and lift her mood; tried to recall her small successes – as Robert said she must – not keep dwelling on her failures and her past. Di was really happy with her continued sewing skills, and she herself felt much less shy with customers – less shy altogether, could chat now fairly naturally, take part in conversations. She'd also learnt to set her hair without recourse to Della or a salon, and best of all, had missed two Sunday Masses without drowning in a tidal wave of guilt. It still felt very strange, though, to stay at home on Sunday, lie around in bed; to change the pattern of nearly forty years. Even as an infant, she had attended Sunday Mass, dribbling in her mother's arms, cooed at by the priest after the *Ite missa est*. It hurt – of course it did – to have Sundays hollow, vacant, but again she'd done her best to follow Robert's thinking, impregnate that hollowness with mystery, opportunity.

'And now Trevor Pinnock will continue his recital with Bach's harpsichord concerto in . . . '

The doorbell cut across the announcer's velvet voice. Robert! Fifty minutes early. Thank heavens she was ready, in the blue dress that he liked, new blue matching earrings, and hair freshly washed in camomile. She'd despised herself a little, taking so much trouble, as if she were a teenager preparing for her first important date. That was all too near the truth, though. She dived out to the hall, feeling still an adolescent; stomach seesawing with a mixture of elation and sheer nerves. She opened the door, half-expecting some surprise; dragons in stiff cellophane with yellow satin bows. Her smile faded as she saw not six-foot Robert standing on the doorstep, but a small and grubby child, face defiant, hands thrust in the pockets of torn and faded jeans.

'*Luke!* What are you doing? Why aren't you at school?'

'I hate school.'

As he spoke, she noticed that his two front teeth were missing. He looked strangely different with the gap, younger and more vulnerable, yet also sly, a Fagin.

'What happened to your teeth? Did you trip or something, or knock into a lamp-post?'

'No, they just felled out.'

She remembered now that children lost their milk teeth at round about his age. She still knew so little about children; was unsure even now what she ought to do with him – invite him in, or take him back to school.

'Come in,' she said, with a quick glance at her watch. She'd missed the boy these last few weeks. He'd gone back to his own home on the Monday before Easter, hadn't reappeared. There'd been a fight with Stephen, which had somehow escalated, involving both Luke's father and the school. Liz had shrugged the whole thing off, claimed children often quarrelled and they'd make it up eventually, and as for Craddock Senior, well, he'd obviously been plastered when he hollered down the phone, and was probably angry less with her or Luke, than with life in general or the VAT man in particular. Anyway, she said, it was probably no bad thing for Luke to spend more time at home, even with the problems there. So why had he turned up again, with the row still unresolved? Maybe fear of his own parents. From what she'd heard of boorish Mr Craddock, he wouldn't be too merciful to any truant son, nor, for that matter, to any stupid woman who aided and abetted him. Unless she could dream up some excuse for Luke.

'Are you feeling ill? I mean, you've not been sick, or hurt yourself, or . . . ?'

He shook his head.

'Well, I'm afraid you have to go to school, then.'

'No, I don't.'

'You do, Luke.'

'Don't.'

They were getting nowhere. She tried another tack. 'What's wrong with school?'

'Everything.'

'You used to like it, didn't you?'

He didn't answer, just kicked out at the skirting in the hall with one scuffed mini bovver boot. She winced for Liz's paint. 'Look, let's go into the kitchen and have a cup of tea.'

'I don't like tea.'

'Well, milk, then.'

'Milk's for babies.'

'How about a nectarine?'

'What's that?' He looked suspicious, was still punishing the paint-work. She'd never seen him quite so wilful.

'It's fruit. A sort of peach.'

'Let's see.'

She led him to the kitchen, picked out the ripest of the nectarines, the one she'd saved for Robert, held it out to him. He grabbed it rudely, squelched it in his hands, kept squeezing till he'd pulped it into mush, then chucked the soggy mess on to the floor.

'Luke, that's very naughty.'

He shrugged, wiped his juice-stained hands across his jersey.

'Pick it up, go on.'

He didn't move, just stood foursquare, defying her. And yet it was her he must have come to see, since no one else was ever in, at this time of the morning. She sat down at the table, pulled another chair up, patted it encouragingly. 'Come on, love. Sit down.' 'Love' was Liz's word, felt forced and false on *her* lips, especially as the boy refused to sit, just turned his back, kept whistling the same phrase.

290

'We're still friends, aren't we, Luke?'

'Nope.'

'So who did you come to see?'

Another shrug, a scowl.

'Have you been to school at all today?'

'No.'

She wondered where he *had* been, and whether either of his parents knew or cared that he was roaming round the streets. Surely they didn't let him out alone. 'How d'you get to school, Luke – usually, I mean?'

'My Dad takes me in the car.'

'So what happened this morning? Was he ill or something?'

'No, we went, but we was late, and I was scared to go in late again, so I waited till he'd driven off, then I walked back to the sweet shop.'

'And what have you been doing since?'

'Dunno.'

Walking, she thought, with a sudden surge of horror as she remembered just how busy the streets around his school were, and how bad he was at crossing roads. He tended just to blunder off the pavement, without a glance to either side. She sat at the table, drinking her cold coffee, wondering how Robert would react to the prospect of a threesome. No, she couldn't keep him here. His teachers would be worrying already and Joe Craddock would explode. 'Listen, Luke, let's go back to school together. We'll take a bus and sit right at the top, and on the way we'll play that game you like – you know, the one where you mustn't tread on any paving stones with cracks in, or the tigers eat you up.'

'Bears.'

She buttoned up her jacket. It was the first word he had spoken without that defiant angry hopelessness, so she must scoop him through the door before he changed his mood. She kept talking frantically to try to keep his interest – bears, tigers, magpies, dragons – while she grabbed her purse, did anxious calculations in her head. There was no chance whatsoever that she could be back by twelve o'clock, even if a bus came straight away. She could leave a note for Robert, tacked up on the door, but Liz hated them to do that, had already lectured Della on how dangerous it was, an open invitation to any passing yob or crook. There'd been two burglaries already in their street, one just a week ago. She glanced at Luke, saw he was about to speak, and, from the expression on his face, about to turn her plan down with an uncompromising no.

'Quick! The bears are out already. I can hear them roaring just behind us. We'd better run. Bet I can beat you to the bus stop and still not tread on any cracks.'

She lost her bet, which helped. Luke insisted she had bet him 50p, and softened quite considerably when she counted out the coins. She, too, felt more relaxed when a bus loomed up in minutes, with a Niki Lauda driver who seemed just as keen as she was to cut the journey time. If she were as lucky on the journey back, she'd be home by ten past twelve, and if Robert were delayed himself, he wouldn't even know she'd ventured out.

Luke was folding the tickets into tiny concertinas. 'Will you come right in with me, take me to my classroom?'

'Yes, all right.' She could hardly leave the poor kid at the gate again, when he'd been scared of being late and was now much later still. It would only take five minutes if she found his teacher quickly; invented some white lie, smoothed the whole thing over, then pelted back again. She felt strangely scared herself, though, as they walked in through the heavy metal gates. She had seen Luke's school several times, but only from the outside, had never heard that jungle noise yowling from the playground as children yelled and wrestled, charged like bulls with heads down, kicked dangerous balls around. They appeared to move in packs, like animals, surging one way, veering back; their bellow magnified by the cage of concrete buildings. How frightening to be unpopular, or shy; left out on your own while those cocky gangs swooped past you, cut you down.

She was suddenly as small as Luke, trembling in a corner, great louts twice her size advancing on her, threatening, trying to punch her face or trip her up. The girls seemed just as bad, many of them fighting, clawing at each others' clothes or hair, quarrelling over skipping-ropes or sweets. And how strange their outfits looked – girls in football jerseys worn with skin-tight leggings; girls in baggy sweatshirts; girls as young as nine or ten dressed in slinky skirts and jewellery. Her own rustic convent school seemed a million miles away, both in distance and in time: no frightening asphalt playground with lorries thundering past, but peaceful grounds with trees and fields beyond; tall white statues of a protective loving Mother, instead of hulking boys; no boys at all, just quiet well-mannered girls, playing hide-and-seek or hopscotch in their neat blue uniform.

Luke led her through a side-door and they entered to a whole bouquet of smells – sweaty feet, old gym shoes, hot pennies, urine, chalk. They trudged along a corridor, with graffiti on the walls and fluorescent lights glaring overhead, despite the sun outside. A bell clanged through the building and suddenly the playground roar was swooping after them – a whole tide of jostling children stampeding in from break – feet pounding, voices rising, as they surged along the passage.

'That's my teacher,' whispered Luke, pointing to a small dark girl in a crumpled denim skirt, her long brown hair escaping from its ponytail. 'Miss MacDonald.'

Hilary nodded, had met her once before, when she'd gone with Liz to pick the children up; thought then how young she looked. Yet this casual girl, barely in her twenties, had the power to terrify her, as she skulked with Luke against the wall, watching all his classmates marching in. She felt embarrassed by her own clothes, which were too dressy for the school, looked fussy, ostentatious, beside Miss MacDonald's denim. The teacher hadn't seen them, was busy sorting out a fight – two small boys wrestling on the floor. Hilary stepped forward, introduced herself again, begged a few brief words.

'I'm sorry. It's really not convenient. I'm about to start the lesson. Can't you wait till dinner time? Oh, I see. All right, then – just two minutes. But you'll have to come in here, otherwise they'll all start playing up.' She steered Hilary into the classroom, shut the door on Luke. 'No, not you, Luke Craddock. You can wait outside, and don't you move a muscle till I come and get you. Right?' She sauntered back to Hilary, voice lowered now, so the children wouldn't hear. 'Where's he been?'

Hilary heard herself prevaricating. Miss MacDonald's tone, though low, had been as uncompromisingly strict to her as it had been to the seven-year-old, and she wasn't finished yet.

'That child's been late every day this week and most of last week too, and, anyway, I thought it was agreed that he'd stay put in his own home, once he'd left the Kingsleys, at least for just this term. It's not good for him to keep moving from pillar to post, never knowing where he'll sleep at night. He needs security, for God's sake, if ever a kid did.'

'He . . . He's not living with us. And it's not his fault, honestly. It was his father who was late today and . . . '

'Nothing's ever Luke's fault – not the fact he forced a small boy's head right down into the toilet bowl, just a week ago – yes, even pulled the chain on him – and crashed another boy into the coat-pegs, really bruised his face.'

'*What?*' Hilary stared in horror, had always regarded Luke as the victim, not the vandal.

'Oh, yes. He's quite a bully. I assumed you must have known.' Miss MacDonald spun round on her heel, raised her voice to holler at her class. 'Be quiet, you lot, and get on with your work-books. I don't want all this racket. No, Chris, you can't have a drink of water. You should have thought of it at break.' She turned back to Hilary, one eye on the children still. 'Mrs Kingsley told me she'd filled you in on all the problems.'

'Well, I knew about his home, of course, and his father's spell in jail and . . . ' Hilary broke off. She couldn't quite believe that the small quiet Luke she knew – or thought she knew – could act the brute, smash faces. And why had Liz not told her the whole story? Did she know it all herself, or was she so absorbed at present in her do-gooder sexagenarian that she had no time to spare for a hoodlum seven-year-old?

'Look, forgive me. I'm sorry.' The teacher suddenly sank down on her desk, seemed to collapse into herself like a rag doll with no stuffing. 'It's hardly your fault, is it? In fact, it was kind of you to bring him in at all. I didn't mean to snap. Blame it on the flu – or perhaps it's just a cold. I feel lousy anyway, but there's no way I can be ill. I'm already doubling for a colleague who's off with tonsillitis, and everything that could go wrong has done so, plus a few thousand extra things.'

Hilary was still standing like a naughty child, started to apologise herself.

'No, it's my fault, really.' The teacher blew her nose, cautioned a small boy who was squabbling with his neighbour. 'It was most unfair to give you such an earful when I hardly even know you. Miss Reed, you said? Yes, I remember now – we've met before. Mrs Kingsley tells me you're very good with Luke. I shouldn't say this really, but I must admit he worries me, that kid. He's got a reading age of five, yet no one seems to bother, and he's obviously unhappy, as well as just plain cussed. I mean, I found him in the boiler room last week, shut up on his own and lying on the floor in all that grime. Things weren't so bad last term, in fact, but he's definitely been worse since he had that row with Stephen.'

'Yes, it shocked me too. They seemed so close and . . . '

'They *were* close. Stephen's very popular and that helped rub off on Luke. I'm afraid the other children taunt him quite a bit.' The teacher dropped her voice still further, to a hoarse and stagey whisper, her eagle-eye not shifting from her class. 'You see, somehow it got out that his Dad had been in clink, and of course kids are merciless when it comes to things like that. With a chum in tow, at least he had some measure of protection, but now Stephen's joined the opposition, so to speak. In fact, they were fighting like wild tigers only yesterday, and it was Luke of course who started it, gave far worse than he got.'

'But he's so much smaller, and so quiet and sort of . . . ' Hilary fumbled for the words. Those she might have used for Luke playing Ludo in his bedroom, or spooning in his Shreddies in the kitchen, seemed quite wrong in the context of his school. She kept seeing that wild playground in her mind; Luke no longer bullied, but lashing out himself with boot and fist. She switched back to the kitchen: Luke half-asleep at table, while Stephen rushed round like a steam train, knocking things off shelves. 'I mean, if you'd seen him at the Kingsleys', you'd have thought Stephen was the tearaway, not Luke.'

Miss MacDonald was working through a box of paper hankies, squidging them into soggy pastel balls. 'Some kids can surprise you – you know, sweet as pie at home, but little Hitlers in the classroom; others just the opposite. I'm afraid Luke is quite a trouble-maker here.' She checked her watch a moment, got up from her desk. 'Look, I'm sorry, but I'll just have to start this lesson, and I'd better go and fetch Luke in, or he'll be carving his initials in the floorboards or gouging lumps out of the walls.' Her laugh changed to a strangled choke of fury as she opened the door and revealed not Luke, but a stretch of empty corridor. 'You see? That's typical. Downright disobedience! If he hasn't run away again, he's probably hiding somewhere. We'll just have to smoke him out.'

A whole hour later, Hilary was sitting on a bus again, but not alone, and not the Cranleigh Gardens bus. Luke was still beside her, and they were heading for his home. In the course of her short talk with Miss MacDonald, Luke had slipped off to the kitchen, tried to steal some chips, sworn at all the dinner ladies, punched one in his way, and finally sicked up half his breakfast in the toilet. What had followed had been a nightmare – Hilary, suddenly responsible, *in loco parentis*, as she and Luke were summoned to the Head, who declared that Luke must go straight home and stay there. The Head had phoned his parents to ask if they could fetch him, but Mr Craddock was out all day, and Mrs Craddock stuck at home with a grandchild of four months and her own retarded daughter. Hilary, torn between worry over Robert, and horror at this new delinquent Luke, felt her duty was with Luke. She, too, had used the phone, rung both the shop and Cranleigh Gardens, to see if Liz could help. No answer from the latter, but Di informed her that Liz had left the shop and was probably buying half of Wimbledon before she drove back home. She had no alternative but to take Luke back herself. He had limped beside her, chastened, as they walked out along the corridors, the smell of vomit on his jeans now mingling with the odours of the dinner hour: curry, punished cabbage.

She had meant to spend her dinner hour with Robert, perhaps in some chic restaurant, where the only smells were sizzling steak or garlic butter; or maybe at a picnic, with a bottle of champagne tucked between them on the grass. She had been tempted to go first to Cranleigh Gardens, so she could warn Robert what had happened, ask him to hang on, but Luke had seemed too sick and miserable to make that tortuous detour, catch two separate buses. All she could do was deliver the wretched child, then rush straight back to Robert, hope to God he'd waited.

'Can't you walk a wee bit faster, Luke?' They had alighted from the bus now, but Luke was only dawdling, kicking out at empty cans, or just stopping for no reason, staring into space. The streets got narrower and dirtier, as they turned a corner, following the railway line, then crossed into an alley which opened into four high arches, their stained and sallow brick standing guard over a stretch of barren wasteground. It was Hilary who stopped now, stopped in shock. She was prepared, theoretically, for the scrapyard, the junked cars, but had never ever pictured it as large as this, as desolate. And could those piles of crippled metal ever have been cars – cars like Robert's, once cosseted and cherished? They were heaped one atop the other, as if of no more worth or interest than empty Pepsi cans, each one maimed in some way; some flattened, others twisted into grotesque distorted shapes. And around them spilled a tide of separate parts: engines ripped from bodies; orphaned wheels helpless on their backs; gouged-out headlamps staring like blind eyes. An abattoir for cars. And what of their poor drivers? Were they, too, lying shattered, either in hospital or grave, bones crushed, limbs dismembered?

She forced herself to walk between the dead and silent wrecks, stepping over abandoned tools, dodging a black pool of oil. A score of wrenched-off bumpers had been stacked against a row of sheds, which themselves spilled piles of junk – broken bits of motor-bike, old guttering, old pipes, collapsing cardboard boxes piled with cracked wing mirrors. A mangy dog slunk between two sheds, its hind legs caked with mud, a piece of string as collar. It nosed towards the shambles of a hen-run, cobbled out of posts and chicken wire, a gaping hole patched with rusting bed springs. She had hardly noticed the Craddocks' house itself, which seemed dwarfed by the lumber all around it. It was constructed, like the arches, of sooty yellow brick – two old workmen's cottages now knocked into one, its garden just a fringe of dandelions.

Hilary tried to change the expression on her face as she turned to speak to Luke, beg him to hurry, go and call his mother, but her voice was drowned by a sudden thundering roar. The whole place seemed to tremble as a goods-train rattled past, its noise and judder shaking through her body, whistling through her skull. Luke appeared not even to hear it, just slouched up to the house, pushed the front door open, disappeared. She followed nervously, stepped into a cluttered sitting room. A high old-fashioned pram took up all the space between a sagging three-piece suite, patterned with blue flowers, which had faded into indeterminate splodges. She peered in at the baby which was grizzling to itself – just a bald pink head beneath a pile of fancy coverlets. The satin-edged blue blanket and rose-sprigged eiderdown seemed too luxurious for this shabby room, where nothing else was new. The furniture was battered and mismatched, the 'fitted' carpet made from three quite separate offcuts, all green, but different shades.

Hilary stood by the window, feeling like a trespasser, wishing she could simply creep away. She could hear sounds upstairs, wails and shouts, then footsteps tramping down. A large and lumpy woman clumped in through the door, wearing red Scholls sandals and a grubby nightie, with two bows in her hair. Hilary came forward, tried to find her voice.

'Hallo,' she said, holding out her hand. 'I've brought Luke back. I'm afraid he's been quite sick and . . . ' Her words trailed off, hand dropped back to her side. It had not been shaken, just totally ignored. The woman was staring at her, staring like a cow stares, or a child; her face impassive, vacant; mouth hanging dumbly open, as if its hinge had broken. Hilary tried again. 'He may have a temperature. He seems a bit feverish to me. He was quite all right this morning, but . . . '

She cut the sentence short, suddenly realising her mistake. This wasn't Mrs Craddock, but her retarded daughter. She had heard about the daughter, knew how big she was, yet still she'd been expecting someone childlike, not this gross and bloated woman who looked as if she'd never been a child; seemed somehow old already; no colour in her pasty skin, no life in her small eyes. Those eyes were staring still, the silence growing more and more uncomfortable, as Hilary felt the smile freeze on her face. She must find Mrs Craddock, say goodbye and leave. Robert would be frantic, either with worry or with anger, or maybe both at once; pacing up and down the pavement outside an empty house, or sitting in his car fuming at her apparent lack of manners.

She started up the stairs, almost colliding with Luke, who chose that moment to come skidding down; followed more slowly by a thin and grey-faced woman in a baggy skirt and sweater, untidy hair straggling to her shoulders.

'Hallo, I'm Mrs Craddock – Rita. Come in and sit down, dear. You look smart! Going to a wedding? There's nothing smart round here, I'm afraid. You'll have to forgive the mess. The Hoover's just conked out, and if I wait for Joe to mend it, it'll be Christmas or New Year. I see you've met my Sylvie. Say "hallo", Sylvie, to the lady.'

Sylvie gave a grunt.

'Pull that chair up, dear. The sofa's got no springs. What did you say your name was? Hilary? I thought that was a man's name. Joe had an

Uncle Hilary, or was it a great-uncle? He's dead now, anyway. Want a cup of tea?'

'No, really, thanks. I must get back. I'm . . . '

'What, straight away? I was hoping you might stay a bit. It's nice to see a new face, isn't it? I don't get to see that many. And I'd like a little chat about the school, dear, before you just rush off. I mean, what the heck's he meant to have done *this* time? I don't believe half of it, do you? I never liked his teacher anyway. If you ask me, she's just a fancy stuck-up bitch. Where d'you get those earrings? Pretty, aren't they? Luke, go and put the kettle on and don't slop water on the floor.'

'No, I must go, Mrs Craddock, honestly. I haven't time for tea. I'm expecting someone and I'm very late already.' Hilary checked her watch, horrified. Robert would never wait that long, would assume she had forgotten or cried off. Unless Liz herself were back now and had found him on the doorstep. She ought to phone and check. 'In fact, if I could use your phone . . . '

'Help yourself. It's in the hall. Luke! Leave Sylvie's toys alone. You'll only make her cry.'

Hilary almost wept herself, with sheer relief, to hear Liz's friendly voice.

'Where *are* you, love? What's happened?'

She tried to cut the tortured explanations, ask the one important question – was Robert there?

'Here? Why should he be? I thought the whole point of today was that you were going out together.'

'How long have you been back, though?'

'Oh, an hour, at least, I'd say. No, longer. I was back at half past twelve. I remember that distinctly because I switched on the radio and "Brain of Britain" was just starting.'

'I must have missed you by two minutes, then.'

'What, you phoned before, you mean?'

'Yes. *And* the shop. Di said you were buying half of Wimbledon.'

'Bloody cheek! I bought a melon and a pair of tights which took approximately three minutes. But what's up, for heaven's sake? I still don't understand.'

As soon as Liz had grasped the problem, she was offering instant help. 'Don't worry, Hil, I'll come and fetch you right away. And I'll leave a note for Robert.'

'I shouldn't bother. He won't come now. Or he's already gone back home.' She felt absurdly disappointed. Each of Robert's phone calls in the last two weeks or so had increased her anticipation, her eagerness to see him – though she had done her best to control it. Robert wasn't Ivan, and she had no wish to get obsessed again, but all the same, it hurt that he should have apparently forgotten her.

'Don't be silly, love. He wouldn't have gone home after less than half an hour. Knowing Bob, he's far more likely to be late himself. I'll leave the key for him.'

'But what about the burglars?'

'Damn the burglars! You're more important. Look, give me twenty minutes. You caught me in the buff, and by the time I've dressed and . . . '

Hilary trailed back to the sitting room, feeling totally deflated. All that fretting over Robert and he hadn't even thought to phone to explain why he was late, or apologise for messing up her lunch. She was starving hungry now, could at least accept that cup of tea, hope there'd be a biscuit with it. She sank down in the chair again, explained to Mrs Craddock that Liz was coming to fetch her.

'Funny girl, that Liz. I can never make her out. Kind, though, isn't she? I can always phone her when I'm ill and she'll take the boy – no bother. I'm ill a lot, you know. Did she tell you? No? I get these dizzy turns. Everything goes black and . . . I like Luke going there. They got books at the Kingsleys and books is good for him. It's stupid, that damn school saying he should stay put in his own home. Any book that walked in here Joe would use for wedging a loose door, or propping up a table. Mind you, I'm not that hot at reading myself.' Mrs Craddock fumbled in her bag, brought out a small squashed pack of cigarettes. 'D'you smoke?' she asked, lighting up herself and settling back. She appeared to have forgotten all about the tea. 'What, not at all? You're lucky. I can't stop. I must get through forty a day now. Joe moans about the cost, but he smokes more than I do. Do call me Rita, by the way. Mrs Craddock's such a mouthful. Luke, stop it, will you! You'll only break that doll.'

Hilary glanced across at Luke who was taunting Sylvie, pulling at her doll – a pert and pretty creature whose rosebud mouth and doe-soft eyes only pointed up the contrast with her owner's ugly features. Luke himself looked ill, his face peaky, drained of colour. He ought to be in bed with a glucose drink, an aspirin. Perhaps she should offer to take him up herself, then once she and his mother were on their own downstairs, they could have that chat about his school which Rita had suggested. She could try to make her see how serious Luke's problems were, not just the inventions of some 'fancy stuck-up bitch'. She still felt shocked herself by the new and violent Luke, who had somehow taken over from the quiet shy boy she'd known – or thought she'd known.

She waited till a train had passed. Rita shouted over them, but Rita was in practice, and she herself still found it quite an effort to raise her voice at all. She opened her mouth as the last boom and rattle faded, but Sylvie got in first; let out a wail of fury as she pointed to her doll. Luke had snapped its head off, flung the pink corpse on the floor.

'Now look what you've done, Luke.' Rita sounded only mildly disapproving, as if she had long since tired of bawling out her children, and had no more strength or spirit to enforce real discipline. Though Luke seemed almost contrite now, and was trying to mend the doll, dry his sister's eyes, offer her his engine as a substitute. 'Blow your nose,' he ordered, dredging up a dirty scrap of Kleenex from the pocket of his jeans, then wiping her face deftly on his sleeve. He was obviously quite used to looking after her, yet it couldn't be that easy to have to share his home and mother with this retarded 'baby', have his rightful place as youngest child supplanted. The other baby was crying now, as well, woken by the noise; began to howl more and more hysterically, until Rita scooped him up, rocked him in her arms. 'Damn! He's poohed his nappy and I haven't got a clean one. Here, hold him, will you, dear, and I'll see what I can find.'

Hilary tensed in horror as the writhing choking creature suddenly plumped into her lap. In all her adult life she had never held a baby; had imagined them as passive pretty things, cooing in one's arms. This one seemed infuriated, was threshing with its arms and legs, as if to get away from her; its scarlet face contorted. She tried to copy Rita, rock the child, soothe it, make silly gaga noises, but the screams went on and on. She feared that she was holding it all wrong, or that her own tension had affected it; her own repugnance at its foul and fetid smell. Could a dirty nappy really smell that strong, and what if it were leaking? Its romper-suit felt soggy-damp already. Had it stained her best blue dress – Robert's dress?

Robert's baby. She could suddenly see that photograph – Robert with his child. That, too, had been a boy. She tried to imagine Robert with a squalling son, a smelly son, instead of that silent perfect specimen on celluloid. Had he been good with it, deft at changing nappies, handy with the bottles? She had no idea, only knew that she herself was quite inadequate, had no natural gift with babies. Yet this was what she'd longed for all those empty barren years – an infant in her arms.

Sylvie had come up to her, holding out her own truncated baby, talking to the headless china body, stroking the small feet. Hilary forced her features into the fiction of a smile. If this retarded woman had such deep maternal feelings, why did she herself feel only deep distaste? Sylvie touched her arm, let out a few noises which were completely unintelligible, yet sounded friendly in their tone, as if the girl were making some real effort to communicate. She knew she should reply, yet had no idea what to say, or even how to say it. Should she use baby-talk, or treat Sylvie as an adult?

'Yes, we're both mothers, aren't we, Sylvie? Is your baby good?'

More eager jabbering sounds, then Sylvie pulled her nightie up, displaying white and shapeless legs, kept pointing to her knee, repeating just one word, which sounded like 'Belay'; seemed frustrated when she wasn't understood. 'Belay,' she said again, began whimpering, screwing up her face.

'Nice knee,' said Hilary, desperately, praying that Sylvie wouldn't cry as well. 'Have you hurt it?' she enquired. 'I can't see anything.' She peered a little closer, though inwardly recoiling from the slack and bloated thighs, the white calves streaked with coarse dark hairs, the smell of unwashed flesh.

'Belay,' insisted Sylvie.

Hilary glanced towards the door, as if willing Rita to return – or even Luke, who might understand his sister, offer some translation. But he had rushed out with his mother, and she could only hear his footsteps overhead. The walls seemed thin, the ceiling insubstantial, the whole house far too frail, as if it had been weakened by a hundred years of trains, wearing down its structure and its will. A diesel train was passing now, which seemed even more intrusive as it shook the walls and furniture. She longed to get away, couldn't keep her thoughts from Robert, even with a baby wailing on her lap. Suppose he'd had an accident, was lying in the road, or . . . ?

'Sylvie, no! You mustn't eat your doll. That's very dangerous.' The girl had stuffed a china foot halfway down her throat. Hilary was terrified she'd choke, tried to ease it out, clutching at the baby with her one free hand. What on earth was Rita doing? Had she gone to buy some nappies, slipped out the back way without saying? She struggled with a rising tide of panic, as she imagined trying to cope all on her own. Yet Rita coped herself – all day and every day – had coped with seven children, seven writhing smelly infants, not to mention one who'd never outgrown babyhood. She wiped dribble off her dress, rearranged the infant on her lap. At least it had stopped crying, but still seemed fractious and uncomfortable, its tiny hands sawing at the air, its face puckered up and quivering, as if at any moment it might start again. This is what she'd risked with Simon – not a wooden Christ-child, who neither screamed nor soiled its nappies, but a complex human being who might be stubborn, sullen, violent; might even grow up handicapped, delinquent.

She banged back in her chair, jerking the baby almost callously, as if

301

trying to get at Simon, trying to shake his whole smug and rigid Church – that patriarchal Church which had refused Rita an abortion, when she knew the child she carried would be handicapped; refused her contraception all her married life. Luke had been unwanted, a mistake; conceived when his mother was in fact a grandmother, already tired of babies, and worn down by the problems of the other six. She must be only fifty, but looked distinctly older; her hair a brittle dingy-grey, her dull skin lined and faded; seemed a different generation from herself and Liz.

The phone shrilled from the hall. Hilary half-rose. Would she have to answer it, as well as hold the child, keep an eye on Sylvie? Relieved, she heard it stop, heard Rita's voice sounding frightened, yet annoyed. 'No, you mustn't, Joe, you *can't*!' she kept repeating, then the receiver was replaced and there was silence. Almost instantly it rang again. Was some row in progress, Joe furious he'd been cut off, or countered? No. Rita's voice was different now, less edgy altogether. The call was brief. Rita came back to the sitting room, still smoking.

'That was Liz. She says to tell you that your bloke's rung and you're not to worry – he's quite all right and on his way. And she's leaving now herself, she says. Okay?'

'Er . . . yes. Fine.'

'I didn't know you was worrying about a bloke. Though it don't surprise me. My mother used to say if there's a man, there's trouble, and I reckon she was right. Give me Kevin, will you? I've rinsed some nappies through. They're still sopping wet, but we'll fix him up in Sylvie's whatsits just for now. No, you come with me, dear. It's nice to have some company. Now the kids are grown up, they hardly ever visit, except to dump their own kids when they want to gad off somewhere. It's Joe's fault really. He's always shouting at 'em. I don't think he ever wanted kids at all.'

Rita led the way upstairs into her bedroom, a cramped and dirty room with little space for anything save the unmade double bed and a chest of drawers piled with clothes and clutter, including a tin of dog de-fleaing powder and a stale half-eaten doughnut. She laid the baby on the bed, removed its nappy, rolled it in a parcel, held it out to Hilary. 'Stick that in the bathroom, will you, dear? You'll see a bucket in the corner. Oh, and bring me in a towel. If there's none on the rail, you'll find one in the dirty laundry bin.'

When she returned, Rita was opening a packet of the largest thickest sanitary pads she'd ever seen.

'These are Sylvie's. They're the ones for nursing mothers who are losing really heavy. God! That poor child suffers every month. It's floods

302

she has, not periods. It's ridiculous for her to have the curse at all. I mean, she'd never going to have no baby, is she? I tried to get her sterilised, but they said it's not allowed.'

Who said? thought Hilary. The Church again, or doctors, lawyers? Yes, male ones, more than likely, who never had pregnancies themselves, never menstruated. She herself had had another period, which had just finished two days ago, the most welcome so-called 'curse' of her whole adult life to date, since it proved she wasn't pregnant. It had come on time, twenty-eight days exactly after that unexpected first one, as if her cycle had re-established itself, to accord with her re-entry to the world. She wasn't sure she welcomed that particular aspect of it; all its implications about fertility and womanhood. She watched Rita make a nappy from three pads and the towel, secure it with two pins. Why did she feel so bitter, so depressed? Liz and Robert were both now on their way. The rest of the day was hers to relish. Wasn't that the trouble, though? It seemed wrong now to enjoy herself, leave Rita here with three dependent children. Even at this moment, Sylvie might be trying to eat her doll again, choking on a foot, or fighting Luke.

'Is Sylvie all right downstairs on her own? I mean, should I go and check on her?'

'Oh, no, dear. She's no trouble, that one. She never seems to hurt herself, or even get bad colds and things, like all the others did. I suppose I shouldn't say this, but she's my favourite of them all. I know it's wrong for mothers to have favourites, but I really love that child. Well, I love them all, but Sylvie's special. People think she's stupid, but she's not, you know. I'm with her such a lot, you see, so of course I understand her, when other people don't. And I suppose we've grown very close after all these years. Joe got wild because I wouldn't ever leave her, or shove her in a home. We fought for years about it. He wanted her "put away". I hate that word, don't you? It makes her sound like a cup or plate or something, instead of a real person.' Rita took a quick drag on her cigarette, flicked ash on a carpet already grey with dirt. 'She really seemed to take to you. She always knows whether people like her and what they're thinking underneath. You're a nice quiet gentle type, you see, and she picked that up immediately.'

Hilary retrieved the Vaseline lid which had fallen on the floor, glad to hide her face. She had, in fact, felt quite a strong aversion to Sylvie's vacant stare and bloated limbs, the patchwork of old stains on her cheap and skimpy nightie. How *did* you love a child like that, look after it year in, year out; tie ribbons in its limp and greasy hair, even feel a pride in it? She watched Rita change the baby's clothes, button up its tiny knitted jacket. She appeared to know its language just as well as Sylvie's, replied

303

to its gurgles with a string of babbled words. Hilary felt a twinge of envy as Kevin smiled in answer. He hadn't smiled for her. The room was dirty, dust on all the surfaces, two waste-bins overflowing, but at least Rita Craddock knew what love meant; could call herself a normal woman, not a cold and heartless spinster who shrank from babies, from any human contact.

'It's sad for Sylvie, really. I mean, even her own flesh and blood seem to be ashamed of her. My oldest son don't come home at all now. He's made good, you see, married one of them bright types with GCEs and whatsits, and she don't like it here. I suppose you can't blame her, can you? They've got a patio at their place with those coloured stones, in squares, and a really fancy kitchen with everything electric and more switches than a power-station.'

Hilary said nothing. She had been offered just a glimpse of a small domestic tragedy, which had been playing out for over thirty years – an angry feckless husband who didn't want his kids; kids who'd managed to escape themselves, yet still felt bitter and ashamed. Liz had bailed out from bad marriages; Rita was still trapped, had neither house nor money of her own, was tied for life to Sylvie and to Joe. And what would happen when she died – to Luke as well as Sylvie? She was already in bad health, had constant spells of illness. Sylvie would land up in a home, no doubt, despite Rita's lifelong efforts to keep her out of one – but Luke . . . Where *was* the boy? She ought to say goodbye to him; could see Liz's car nosing slowly round the junk heaps, bumping on the rough uneven ground. She waved from the window, felt a little better as she saw Liz's cheerful grin.

'Know where Luke's gone, Rita?'

'He's in the airing cupboard. He often goes in there to have a sulk, or think, or something. It's like his – you know – burrow.'

'Can I say goodbye to him?'

'If you want.' Rita shrugged, pointed down the landing. 'It's the next door to the bathroom.'

Hilary tapped gently on the door. No answer, so she pulled it open. Luke was lying fast asleep on a pile of flannel sheets. She was amazed that he could sleep in that awkward cramped position, with his back hunched up and no room for his feet. He was breathing very heavily, as if sickening for a cold, nose running into open mouth, tear stains on his face. This was the vandal and the bully, the liar and the thief.

'Goodbye, Luke,' she said softly.

His eyes flickered in his sleep, as if aware that she had spoken. 'Good luck,' she added desperately, and walked downstairs to Liz, brushing dribble, ash and dog hairs off Robert's favourite dress.

23

'So what happened to Robert?' Hilary tried to sound casual as she fastened her seat belt, watched Liz negotiate the hazards in Joe's yard.

'Oh, half a dozen crises, by the sound of it. He went to some auction sale this morning; said something about how he was buying you a dragon, though I can't have heard that right. The line was dreadful, very faint and crackly. Then he had to go back home, to sort some problem out, and he was just about to leave when the phone rang – a client in Leicestershire he'd built a house for once, who was really in a state, complaining about . . . God! This is getting complicated, but then Bob's always complicated and often very late. Don't worry, love. He'll turn up for tea, at least.'

'But didn't he try to phone me or . . . '

'Yeah, 'course he did. Give the lad credit where it's due. He missed me by five minutes, just like you did, then he phoned again and the damn line was engaged. Then,' she shrugged and grinned. 'Third time lucky. Mind you, Hilary, you shouldn't have run away like that. If he *had* arrived on time, he'd have felt pretty miffed to find you gone.'

'Run away? I didn't.' Hilary jerked forward as Liz braked hard at traffic lights. 'I told you what happened with the school and everything. I couldn't just leave Luke in the lurch.'

'Actually, you could, love. And a lot of people would have done, in your shoes.'

'But that's cruel, Liz. He'd been sick and wasn't well and . . . '

'There's a perfectly adequate sickroom at the school. Or you could have brought him home to me.'

'You weren't in.'

'You knew I would be fairly soon. And at least you could have explained to Bob, not left him in a lather on the doorstep.'

'But he wasn't in a lather on the . . . '

'Look, forget it, love. I'm not trying to interfere. I'm just aware you're pretty bloody nervous of the guy, so maybe unconsciously you were giving him the slip.'

Hilary said nothing. Could that be true, in fact? She felt annoyed with Robert, certainly, though she couldn't quite say why; annoyed with all men – Joe, Simon, Luke, Luke's headmaster; even Stephen for quarrelling with Luke. But why should Liz take Robert's side, when he'd been delayed himself? She tried to change the subject, steer the conversation round to Sylvie.

'Yes, pathetic, isn't it?' Liz hooted at two cyclists who were weaving in and out. 'She and Rita even sleep together, in the so-called marital bed. From what I've heard, Joe doesn't get his oats now – in fact not since Luke was born. That birth almost killed her, and although she's over fifty she still hasn't had the "change", so she's absolutely terrified she'll be up the spout again. It must be more or less impossible at her age – but you just can't reason with her. She's paranoid about it, and who can blame her really? God! It's such a mess. I feel sorry for them all, in fact – even Joe – but Rita gets the worst of it, that's certain.'

Hilary sat silent. Never before had her vows seemed such a sham. Rita Craddock hadn't knelt before a priest vowing Holy Poverty. She merely lived it year by year – with debts and bills piling up around her, squalor on all sides. Poverty of hope and of surroundings; poverty of expectation. And what about the other vows? Obedience? Certainly. Obedience and subservience to Joe. Rita hadn't much alternative if he was tyrannical and violent. Enclosure? More or less. It couldn't be easy to get out if you were tied to a retarded child and used as a free crèche by all your grown-up children. Chastity? Oh, yes. Rita welcomed chastity, would envy nuns their vow of lifelong continence: a vow based on the premise that sex was valuable, something worth a sacrifice, worth renunciation. To Rita, it could well be an ordeal, another burden and demand, where she must obey her Lord and Master without question, and maybe without any shred of pleasure.

She said nothing more until they drew up at Cranleigh Gardens; felt strangely exhausted by her brief spell at the Craddocks', as if Rita's own fatigue and problems had descended on her shoulders. She followed Liz into the hall, took her jacket off.

'Oh, look!' said Liz. 'You've spoilt your dress. What's that? Shit or gravy? Probably both, knowing Maison Craddock. You'd better hurry up and change. Bob'll be here any minute, unless he stops off at another sale, or decides to make a detour up to Leicestershire.'

Hilary tried to smile, feeling dirty altogether, not just dribble, excrement, but a sense of grime engrained right in her pores.

'Wear your Laura Ashley. He'll really go for that. God! I'm dying for a cup of tea. No, I'll do it, love. You go up and change.'

Hilary walked slowly up the stairs. She had changed once already with an eagerness, excitement, which seemed pathetic, if not puerile, in her present state of mind. Where was Robert *now*, for heaven's sake? She had half-expected him to be waiting on the doorstep; had experienced a curious mixture of annoyance, disappointment and relief when she realised that he wasn't. They had been taught at Brignor that it was both disorderly and discourteous to be late, whatever one's excuses; a form of self-indulgence. What riled her especially was that *he* had made the plans, fixed the date and time, told her to be ready, made her take the day off, yet still he wasn't here. She dragged her dress off, removed her tights and petticoat as well. They weren't stained or grubby, but she somehow felt she wanted a total change of clothes, as if to start again, erase the past few hours. She was just unrolling a new pair of tights when Liz knocked with the tea.

'Just a minute.' Hilary snatched up her dressing gown, tried to scramble into it, but Liz was already through the door, had stopped with both cups poised. 'Good God! What have you done? Those marks. They look like bruises.'

Hilary darted to the wardrobe, concealed herself between its heavy doors, hiding both the marks and her embarrassment. The scars had faded, surely, were barely noticeable – at least far less so than they had been just a week ago, when she'd been extra specially careful that nobody should see her without tights on and long sleeves. She mumbled something half-inaudible, started searching for her dress in the crush and press of Di's clothes, which still cluttered up the rail. She was praying Liz would leave, but she plumped down on the chair instead, took a gulp of tea.

'Listen, love, I'm not trying to pry or anything, but Bob didn't do that, did he?'

'*Bob?*'

'Well, he's a funny guy, you know – a bit unpredictable. I mean, he's kind and generous to a fault and great fun and everything, but I've always thought there's something rather weird about him. And you've been so strange yourself, Hil, since you came back from that conference. You hardly said a word about the lectures or the programme, and even less about your time with Robert. And then you tried to kid me you only went out for a drive with him, when actually I know you stayed at his place, a night or two at least.'

Hilary let the wardrobe doors swing shut, anger fighting guilt. Had Robert betrayed her, confided everything to Liz when he had sworn to keep her confidence?

'It sounds as if I'm snooping, love, and honestly I'm not. It's just that Bob and I have got a friend in common – a guy called Hugh O'Connor. He phoned to ask me to a party on the Monday we got back, told me he'd invited Bob as well, and Bob had asked if he could bring this bird called Hilary who was staying the weekend.' Liz fiddled with her teaspoon, jabbed it in her palm. 'I've been quite worried, Hilary, if you really want to know. I mean, you've missed Sunday Mass twice running and you've never done that, ever, not before that conference. I assumed you must be what you call "in sin", and the sin was probably sexual, and I kept wondering what had happened, whether you were scared you might be pregnant, or if things had gone all wrong or . . . In fact, I blamed myself. I know it's stupid, Hilary, when we're not that far apart in age, but I felt I ought to have tried to help you more – you know, sort of like a daughter – fixed you up with an appointment at the Family Planning Clinic, or . . . '

Liz put her cup down, moved over to the bed, sprawled on the end of it, kicking off her shoes. 'Well, aren't you going to say something? I feel such a charlie jawing on like this, while you just stand there looking like the victim in a silent movie. Look, if Robert bloody Harrington laid a finger on you, I'll never let him in this house again.'

'He . . . He didn't.' Hilary went on hunting through the wardrobe, hardly seeing any clothes now, just a blur of dizzy colours, which seemed to strobe and flicker through her head. 'I just . . . bruised myself. It's nothing.'

'Nothing? But your whole body's marked and scarred. Oh, I know they're very faint now, but when I walked in through that door and you were standing in the light, I had this sudden ghastly memory of a friend of mine called Val, whose husband roughed her up. He actually used a strap on her, and the really awful thing was she encouraged him at first. I mean, they were into kinky sex and she liked to be tied up and even hurt, but then the whole relationship turned sour and the things they'd done for pleasure suddenly recoiled on her. Look, I'm sorry, love, you don't want to hear all this. It's just that since that time I've been much more aware of the peculiar things men do – well, some men, anyway.'

Hilary found a dress, the wrong one, pulled it on. It felt tight – tight and rather chilly, like her voice. 'No one hurt me, Liz. I hurt myself. And I don't wish to discuss it, if you don't mind.'

Liz swung up from the bed, rammed her shoes back on. 'Okay, please yourself. I thought I was your friend, but I'm obviously mistaken. In fact, I'm getting rather tired of what I see as just a one-way friendship. I tell you everything and you clam up completely. I fetch and carry, lend you clothes, cook you meals, and then you turn round and tell me to fuck off. Okay, I will fuck off, but don't expect me to come running next time you're in a jam.'

The door slammed shut behind her. Hilary stood paralysed, listening to her footsteps crashing down the stairs. Liz *was* her friend, her only real and close friend – her mother, aunt, sister, home and sanctuary. She could feel them all crumbling, the cold wind of the street blowing on her shoulders. It was Christmas Eve again and she was just emerging from the tube at Oxford Circus, totally alone, bewildered, guilty, terrified. No – that was stupid. She'd made enormous progress since December; found her feet, found a job. Yet even her job was tied to Liz; everything she had and did depended on the Kingsleys. One row with Liz and she'd be unemployed again, crawling round the Job Centres, inspecting shabby bedsits. But it wasn't only that, wasn't just a question of employment or security; she valued Liz's friendship, craved her affection and her interest.

She crept downstairs, pausing on each step, scared that Liz might shout again if she tried to make an overture. She remembered Mother Mistress saying that God had deliberately arranged that human friendship should be fickle, undependable and fragile, so that once His creatures had seen (and suffered) its obvious limitations, they'd fly back to Him alone, for an exclusive and reliable relationship. That was fine, if you *had* a God as Friend; lonely and unnerving if you hadn't.

She knocked timidly at Liz's door. No answer. She forced herself to enter, found Liz almost naked now herself, flinging off her clothes. '*Now* what d'you want? I'm going to have a bath.'

'I'm sorry, Liz, honestly. I must seem so ungrateful. I do realise all you do and I do appreciate it.' That bit she'd prepared; the rest was much more tricky. Easy to apologise; far harder to confide. Yet she remembered from confession it was never enough simply to say sorry. You had to change your ways, make a firm purpose of amendment. Which meant opening up to Liz, revealing all the details of her life, even the most private ones; explaining the marks, explaining Simon and her loss of faith, defending Robert from detraction. She tried to calm her breathing, make her voice sound casual and low-key. 'Mind if I come in?'

Liz didn't answer, simply gestured to a chair, pulled on an old housecoat. Hilary sat down, wished Liz would sit as well, instead of prowling round the room, fiddling with odd ornaments and knick-knacks.

'I don't mean to keep things from you, Liz. It's just my training. You've no idea how hard it is to break it.' No, that wouldn't do at all. You didn't make excuses in confession, or try to show yourself in a favourable light. You simply stated the facts fully and precisely, not leaving anything out, nor glossing over things which were embarrassing or shameful.

She was sweating when she'd finished, hands clammy, hairline damp – finished where she'd started – in Simon's bed. Now, at last, she allowed herself a laugh, a nervous shaky laugh. 'And I *was* scared I was pregnant, Liz. Though I'm not, thank God.'

309

'You just said you don't believe in Him.' Liz's laugh was equally uncertain. She was stretched out on the carpet now, head against the bed. 'Christ, love, you've been through it! I shouldn't leave you for a second, should I? You need a permanent chaperone. Look, I'm really sorry I blew my top upstairs. No wonder you've been secretive. I can understand it now.' She leant forward, rubbed her leg. 'I suppose the only good thing is that at least you've taken the plunge – sexually, I mean. Oh, I know it wasn't marvellous, but the first time's often quite a cockup, if you'll forgive the pun, and anyway, you had everything against you – wrong atmosphere, wrong guy – I mean, all those taboos about the priesthood and . . . '

Hilary pulled at a loose thread on her dress. Although she was embarrassed, it was a relief to share her fears with somebody experienced, unshockable. 'I've been quite worried, actually, not just about the pregnancy, but . . . ' She paused. 'Look, Liz, I know you're blaming everything on Simon, but I'm sure most of it was my fault. I mean, I didn't seem to . . . feel anything, or even like what we were doing or . . . '

'Give yourself a chance. You need more experience, that's all, and with normal healthy guys, not wimps in dog collars. It's funny, really, isn't it – Catholic priests seem to be insisting on their right to sex, just at a time when half us poor scared seculars are rushing into celibacy. I keep reading in the papers about Father This or That having it away, or marrying his housekeeper. I bet most of them are hopeless, though, after all those years of living like a eunuch. Try bouncy Bob next time.'

'But you just warned me off him, told me he was weird and unpredictable.'

'I owe him an apology – poor lad. In fact, I'm tremendously impressed with this new upstanding Robert Harrington. If it's true what you say and he didn't so much as touch you the entire weekend, I reckon he's a saint, not a pervert. He's wild about you, Hilary, and not just about your mind. He's a pretty randy bugger, if you'll forgive the phrase, so it must have taken considerable restraint on his part to keep his distance and his cool, especially if you were floating around in your nightclothes half the time, or sleepwalking more or less straight into his arms. God! You do have an exotic life. I feel quite envious sometimes.'

'Oh, Liz, how can you? You don't know how I envy *you*. I mean, all the things you do which I can't begin to tackle, like cooking complicated meals, and running this huge house, and driving a car, and understanding tax and VAT and things, and the fact you're – you know, normal – been married and had children, and know how to respond in bed, instead of . . . ' Hilary pummelled the chair arm, as if venting her frustration on it. 'D'you realise, Liz, I even envy Della. She's able to enjoy sex because she had a mother who regarded it as something good and pleasurable, not the disgusting sort of duty my own mother made it out to be, or the whole sin-thing of the convent.'

Liz sat frowning, one bare foot twitching on the carpet. Hilary watched her, worried. Liz was hardly ever silent. Had she offended her in some way, said something wrong or stupid? She could hear the bedside clock ticking almost feverishly, as if to fill the gap. Liz explored the pocket of her housecoat, found a crumpled piece of paper in it, screwed it up, smoothed it out again; spoke at last, though softly.

'It's funny really, Hilary, but the one thing you can't admit in my own particular circle, which is permissive and so-called liberal and sophisticated, is that you don't like sex. In fact, I doubt if you can even admit it to yourself. But now you've set me wondering. I mean, sex with Ken was okay, I suppose, though I was very young and green then, took it all for granted, didn't really question how I felt or what we did together. But once he'd upped and gone, I started plunging into bed with a whole stud-farm of odd men. I assumed I was frustrated, missing sex, craving it – but now I'm not so sure.'

Liz glanced across at Hilary, as if to check her face, get permission to continue. 'You see, divorce is such a put-down that you can easily go bed-hopping out of sort of fear, rather than plain lust – fear of being on your own, or feeling like a failure, or even to cock a snook at your ex-husband, show him other men do fancy you, even if he doesn't. I suppose *sometimes* I enjoyed it. I always thought I did. But I had to think that, didn't I, otherwise I'd lose that whole important self-esteem thing – you know, the sense of being normal and sexy and okay in the world's eyes. You just can't imagine how crucial it was made to seem – being good in bed, I mean – the sort of litmus test of human worth. If you weren't sexy, you were dead, or at least a failure and a write-off, who needed therapists and couldn't be accepted as a swinger or a super-woman. Superwomen were always multi-orgasmic – that went without saying – so women were totting up their orgasms like gold stars or Green Shield stamps, and cashing them in for goodies: gold bracelets or red roses or cruises to the sun.'

Liz was still torturing her piece of paper, had reduced it now to tatters. 'I'm afraid I wasn't a saint myself. I've traded sex for five-star dinners in my time, or paid back holidays or presents, but I wouldn't really call myself a gold-digger. It's much more complicated than that. You can agree to sex for such a mix of reasons, and sometimes I said yes because it just seemed easier, or I couldn't face my own cold and empty house, or I wanted to be wanted, or I was feeling specially plain that week and

311

needed reassurance that I could still turn someone on. And sometimes *I* was the one handing out the comfort. I remember once landing up in bed with a five-foot-nothing travel clerk with a stutter and damp hands, just because he seemed so shy and sad, and I knew he'd feel better for a cuddle and a kiss.' Liz smiled, as if remembering. 'I'm quite a good performer, if you know what I mean, so it's pretty easy just to fake the thing – a few gymnastics, or groans and moans of passion, and most men are preening at the way they've turned you on. The problem is with faking, though, you can confuse yourself as well, end up wondering just which you is you – the sexy one who's going through the motions, or the cynical detached one instructing from the sidelines.'

Liz eased up from the floor, stretched her legs, still frowning. 'D'you realise, love, I've never admitted this before, not to anyone? I hope I haven't shocked you. I think I've shocked myself. I mean, I *do* like sex, I know I do, and yet . . . ' She walked slowly to the dressing table, sat down on the stool in front of the large mirror, as if trying to see herself, perhaps a new self.

'I'm even confused now about Neville – you know, my second husband. I told you how cut up I was when that went wrong as well. And I especially missed the sex – at least I thought I did. Oh, he was a fantastic lover, no doubt about that, and everything was great at first. I felt desired and loved and settled, with my confidence restored, but after a few years, it . . . ' Liz reached out for her hairbrush, dragged it through her hair. 'Gosh! It's difficult to explain this, but sex was almost *too* good. It was always the same, you see – wonderful – but never any variation on that high-octane performance. I began to *want* it to be bad – or at least short and quick and basic – but Neville always went on hours, and I'd feel so tired, or pressured by all the chores I hadn't done, and in the end, I came to see it as just another chore itself. And yet I conveniently forgot all that, as soon as Neville left, saw myself as wronged and wildly sexy, and *him* as losing interest. In fact, it wasn't till just now, when you mentioned your own mother and used that word "duty", that something sort of clicked and . . . Good God! Is that the time?'

Liz swung round as the clock on the landing chimed the hour, checked it with her watch. 'Where's Bob, for heaven's sake? Is that his car?' She loped to the window, peered out down the street. 'No. False alarm. Even so, we ought to get our skates on. You can't go and meet him in that dress, Hil. It's really straining at the seams, and even his iron control will snap. You know, the more I think about it, the more I take my hat off to the guy. You say he didn't even kiss you?'

Hilary shook her head, still dazed and overwhelmed by Liz's outburst, hardly able to assess it, a hundred questions and reactions swarming in her mind.

'That's decent, isn't it? I mean, a lot of men would have insisted on their pound of flesh. It's the old payment thing again. He takes you in, looks after you, spoils you rotten, by the sounds of it, then claims his just reward – or rather doesn't. He must be pretty sensitive to have known how you were feeling, know you wouldn't want him, after what you'd been through. Most blokes are so big-headed, they'd have been offering themselves as instant sexual therapy, or couldn't wait to prove how much better they could do in bed than any puny priest. It'd be a sort of challenge to their pride, you see, and male pride is bloody strong. It sounds to me as if Robert really cares.'

Hilary tried to stop her voice from sounding bitter. 'So why is he so late?'

'Oh, that's nothing. You'll get used to it in time. You can't expect a guy to have no faults.' Liz turned back from the window, started collecting up her clothes. 'D'you know, I'm worried about Harry now. If we do land up in bed, I'll be all self-conscious, wondering if it's going to work and what I'm really feeling; and if we never make it, I'll assume I just don't turn him on, and get twitchy and neurotic. It's pathetic really, how much better he's made me feel already – I mean, just to have a guy in tow, paying court, and boosting me, as if I'm no good in my own eyes, only in a man's. Hey! Careful with that dress, love. You'll rip it in a minute. Here, let me help. Stick your arms up and I'll tug. God! It's tight. I don't know how the heck Di ever squeezed into it, except she was probably in her anorexic phase – you know, starving herself to please some man who only fancied Twiggys. Okay, relax, you're free.'

Hilary edged to the mirror, tried to see her back. 'Liz, do those . . . marks really show a lot?'

'No, honestly, they don't. In fact, I can hardly even see them now. It was just that particular light upstairs, coming from two windows, and with the sun streaming in as well.' She stood beside Hilary, staring in the mirror. 'It's funny how we're both marked by our men. Oh, I don't mean directly, but the sort of way the history of our love-lives is stamped on our bodies.' Liz untied her housecoat, looped it up. 'That's my Caesarian scar from Di, and that long sort of tramline on my thigh is a memento of my skiing trip with a ghastly chap called Tover, who dragged me from the nursery slopes to take part in a race. And see that lumpy patch of skin? Well, I fell off Neville's motorbike and though the cuts and bruises faded, it never quite went smooth again. And if you could see through to my mind, it must be scarred all over with guilts and fears and jealousies – all the things which bug you once you get involved

313

with men; all those ghastly dilemmas and decisions which almost kill you with the worry. Should I have slept with this guy, or given him the push? Should I have had that abortion or made the rotter marry me? Should I have married anyone?'

Hilary glanced at Liz's scars, embarrassed by their two half-naked bodies, almost touching in the glass. She herself was marked by her love affair with God: the faint line on her forehead which would probably never fade now, after all those years of wearing a tight coif; her feet permanently calloused by going without shoes – and if Liz counted all the inner marks, there was no part of her which wasn't stigmatised. Suddenly, she laughed.

'What's funny?'

'I don't know.' She went on laughing, clutching at her sides.

'Come on, love, do share the joke.'

She couldn't share it. There wasn't any joke. Yet she was doubled up with laughing, her muscles hurting with it, muscles out of practice, barely used before.

Liz began to laugh herself, watching her reflection in the mirror. 'Isn't laughing stupid? I mean, just look at our two faces.'

Hilary straightened up a moment, hooting still more wildly as she glimpsed her mirror-self. The laughter felt like pain, stabbing at her chest, hacking in her throat, stopping her from breathing. She fought and failed to gain control; her whole body racked, convulsed, tears streaming down her face now. Liz herself was choking as she laughed and coughed at once, making snorting noises which sounded like an animal – an animal in pain.

'God, Hilary, you're crazy! Do stop, for heaven's sake. I hurt all over and my mascara's streaking off. I'll end up like a panda. Anyway, it isn't even funny.'

'No, it . . . it's tragic.'

That set them off again, rolling round hysterically, Liz collapsing on the bed; Hilary still helpless, and hunched across a chair, trying to use a cushion as a gag. They were making so much noise, they hardly heard the door-bell, only froze when it pealed a second time.

'Bob!'

'Robert!'

'He can't see us like this. Quick! Tear upstairs, Hilary, and get some decent clothes on, and I'll go down and let him in.' Liz grabbed her housecoat, rushed out to the landing, scrubbing at her black-ringed eyes, smoothing down her hair.

Hilary didn't move. She was suddenly aware that this morning's wild excitement over Robert – heady Robert – had come flooding, rushing back; seemed to paralyse her outwardly, while it burned her up inside. Her own face was a mess, smudgy tear-marks scoring through the make-up she'd applied with so much care.

'Well,' she said to no one, with a last sudden violent laugh. 'He *said* I had to cry.'

Summer

24

Hilary could already smell the sea, its strong salt tang softened by the scent of flowers, a mixed bouquet of clover, daisies, meadowsweet; the sweet-sour reek of cow parsley foaming in the hedges. Gulls were screeching overhead; sanderlings wikwik-ing from the marshes. She closed her eyes a moment, stumbled on, aware of sharp stones jabbing through her sandals, clumps of coarse and tufted grass trying to trip her up; tensing as grass changed to sand and she felt her feet sucked into it, felt the fractious sea-wind on her face.

'What *are* you doing?' Robert asked, linking his arm in hers to stop her falling. 'You'll break your lovely neck.'

'I just can't bring myself to look,' she said. 'I mean, in case it's changed, or spoilt, or . . . ' How could he understand? He was just a tourist here, a visitor. For her, this slice of countryside was home and roots and childhood; almost half her lifetime marked and branded into it like growth rings on a tree. She had longed to see this coast again, wander on its beaches and pick her childhood up from them like shells, yet she was also apprehensive, the longing smirched with fear. Supposing they'd built beach huts, ugly cafés, kiosks; ruined her child's wilderness? Suppose the sea itself had changed?

She shook off Robert's arm, took a last step forward, dared to open her eyes. No beach huts, litter, whelk stalls, no caravans or shops, no human trace at all – just an immensity of ocean, a vast and empty sky. It was as if the world had suddenly expanded, its roof pushed up, to give more space and light; the horizon rolled back further, so that the endless booming ocean could fill the wide-screen landscape, overwhelm the eye. She longed to have a hundred eyes, like Argus, so she could watch every wave at once as it rolled slowly in, swelling, rising, breaking on itself, then frothing, sucking back in white-foam shards. Yes, the sea had changed. Whenever she'd recalled it, it had been winter in her mind, or at least a dull and grey day, with all the colours muted. Now green and golds and turquoise glittered in the sun; the sand itself seemed gilded and alive, rather than the flat and fallow dun-beige she'd remembered. It was not a coast noted for its sunshine; a coast for stoics, rather, with brisk winds always blowing from a stark North Sea, and no more land till Norway.

She had even heard Norfolk called an island, cut off from the main

319

north-south axis of the country, a remote and lonely backwater, closed
in on itself. But Robert had transformed it, thawed and tempered it,
altered its whole mood. Strange how he could change things – even
grimy London sparkling gold as they left Cranleigh Gardens in the early
hours and drove first to Leicester – a brilliant orange sun bursting
through blue mist to transfigure dingy streets, and matching the red-gold
of her excitement. It had been shining ever since, as streets gave way to
fields; the harsh but honeyed scent of hay replacing petrol fumes; every
tree and hedgerow lushly green.

Robert had reached his hand out, touched her fingers. 'I never
thought you'd come.'

Nor did I, she'd thought, but hadn't said. Why *had* she come, when
she was still wary of him, nervous; had spent two whole months avoiding
even one more weekend at his home, despite frequent invitations?
Because she craved to see her own home and he'd suggested it himself.

'I've got to drive to Leicester anyway. There are still problems on that
house I built and the client's in a tizzy – poor sod, I hardly blame him.
The builders have been useless, dragged their feet for weeks, then sent a
quite inadequate report. I promised him I'd go up there myself, try to
sort things out. Why don't you come with me? We could drive from
there to Norfolk – it's not that far – and once I've shown you my house,
you can show me yours, show me where you grew up as a child, take me
to your convent.'

'Oh, no!'

'Why not? I've heard so much about it, I feel I ought to see it, to prove
it does exist.'

'I couldn't. They might see me.'

'I thought you said the walls were ten foot high.'

'Yes, but . . . '

It had taken days and days to talk her round. So many fears had
crystallised; fear of Robert – being away with him, alone with him, away
with any man; fear of Reverend Mother, whose pale and bony hand might
reach out and claw her back if she dared approach that near; fear of her
parents rising up and chiding her as she crept back to their village, walked
across their graves; fear of re-finding Gloria – or worse, not finding her. She
even felt a certain aversion to Robert's client, a Mr Dermot Frazer. He was
the one who had delayed him on St George's Day. And what would he
think if his erstwhile architect turned up with a woman? Would she be Mrs
Robert Harrington, or merely some vague friend?

'Neither. You'll be my professional partner. I've just founded a new
firm – Harrington-Reed Associates, specialists in open-plan convents
and high-rise hermitages with all mod cons.'

Is that why she'd agreed? Because Robert made things fun, refused to fret or agonise, made her fears seem spoilsport or mean-minded? Or was it because she longed to see the sea again? She had been so close to it in Sussex, could have slipped out at the conference, taken a short bus ride to the coast, or driven from Robert's lighthouse in less than half an hour. Yet she hadn't even glimpsed it, might have been in Staffordshire or Shropshire for all the sense she'd had of being near the sea. The Sussex coast was different, anyway – white cliffs instead of flat and windy marshes; plush green downs in place of sea-stained saltings. She'd been a foreigner in Sussex; was a foreigner in London still, a country girl who felt increasingly the tug and pull of home. She had to see that North Norfolk coast again, see the dunes grey-shadowed by the clouds, the mud-flats loud with birds. June had produced a heat-wave which made London fretful, feverish: hard hot pavements which blistered feet as well as fraying tempers; claustrophobic buildings trapping fetid air. Even Cranleigh Gardens seemed stifling and on edge – Della sitting her exams, Di worried about bad business in the shop, Liz love-lorn, missing Harry.

She kicked her sandals off, ran down to the sea's edge, felt the icy water lap across her ankles, washing off the grit and fumes of London, all the Kingsleys' tensions, all her own fears and apprehension. She was here – she'd made it – despite all the voices which had said 'no', all those inner admonitions, chidings from her conscience, warnings about commitments; that crazy mix of terror and elation at the thought of closer ties. Even now, she felt the need to put more space between them; was glad that Robert had stayed up on the sand, trailing a swatch of bladderwrack behind him, like some slimy crested tail. They were sleeping on that sand tonight; side by side, with no dividing wall. Robert had offered her the best hotel in Norfolk, and she'd asked if they could camp. She had never camped, not even as a child. Her mother had forbidden it, as being messy, risky, and too much extra work. All her girlhood, she had longed to pitch a tent, cook beans in billycans, have canvas or the sky above, instead of a boring plaster ceiling.

Liz had seen it differently, been suspicious of her motives. 'I'm sure it's just another sneaky way of warding Robert off. I mean, zipped up to your ears in your own private sleeping bag, instead of lying in his arms in a nice big double bed.' Liz had said a lot of things: how she ought to see a doctor, get fixed up with a diaphragm or fitted with a coil; ought to have her hair re-bleached; ought to buy new and sexy clothes. She'd refused all the suggestions. She was a child returning to its home, needed only child's clothes – shorts and sandals, a summer skirt or two. And nothing would induce her to see another doctor; have rubber corks or metal plugs shoved right up inside her, a stranger's hands exploring her most private parts.

She kicked up sprays of water, curled her toes against the cool and clammy sand. She'd been sweltering on the journey, despite the open sunroof – a sticky, almost feverish heat, which seemed to be coming from inside, panting from their bodies – hers too close to Robert's in his scorching scarlet car.

She suddenly ran back to him, found him on his knees with a piece of broken razor-shell, inscribing their initials on the sand. She noticed how the R and H entwined, one growing from the other, embedded in the other. 'It's fantastic here,' he grinned. 'I never thought I'd see a beach so absolutely deserted – well, not in England anyway.'

'It's just knowing where to look,' she said. 'The sea is pretty dangerous at this particular point, so it's not much good for swimming. That keeps the crowds away. And that road we took is really just a track . . . '

'Don't remind me! I'll need four new tyres by the time this weekend's over. Or shall we stay here all our lives, sleeping on the sand, eating whelks and sea-birds – or at least sausages and mash? I'm starving now, aren't you? Shall we go and get our gear, pitch camp, cook those bangers?'

'We've only just had lunch.'

'Only just? That was hours ago. It's six o'clock, d'you realise?'

'It can't be! It's still so bright and sunny.'

'It's the longest day today, though; won't be dark till half past ten. And don't forget, once it's dark, we've got our little errand.'

She shivered in the sunshine. The sky was still unbroken blue, yet she could feel grey clouds closing round her head. She slowed her pace, feet dragging through the heavy clotted sand.

'Come on now. You promised, darling. You'll feel better once it's done.'

The 'darling' stopped her dead. He had never called her that before – nor had anyone. She could feel the word reverberating between them still, sending out small shock waves of mingled pride and fear. 'Darling' signalled affection and concern, but also implied an intimacy which she had neither earned nor sought. She felt a sudden rush of panic, an overwhelming urge to run away, pelt straight back to London – not just to avoid him, but to renege on that rash promise. What he called her 'little errand' was a huge and frightening undertaking, requiring courage and decisiveness she feared she hadn't got.

'Where you going, Hilary?'

'Just to get the camping things.'

322

He overtook her, helped unpack the car. They walked back to the beach together, lugging sleeping bags and groundsheets, food and water, pots and pans. She tried to kick her fear away, let the strong waves suck it back and down, in the same way that they pounced on bits of flotsam, spat them out as foam. It helped her to keep busy, so she worked as Robert's tenderfoot, surprised by all the equipment and utensils, all the complications. Camping wasn't simple, after all. Each small task took time, demanded skill: setting up the stove, getting it to light, despite the amused defiance of the wind, keeping sand out of the sausages, not spilling precious water, making cups stand steady, not losing spoons or salt. She was soon ravenous herself. Everything seemed sharpened by the fact they were outside – smells, taste, appetite itself. She finished off five sausages and half a can of beans, which she relished more than Mrs Frazer's salmon mousse and raspberry cream pavlova.

Robert scoured the plates with a piece of kitchen paper. 'Right, now pudding.'

'We didn't bring a pudding, only cheese and fruit.'

'Yes, we did. I put it in myself.' He scrabbled in the box, produced a small but heavy package, circular in shape, gift-wrapped in gold paper. 'Here you are – a present.'

'Another present?'

'Yes, a real collector's item.'

'But you already bought me the dragon and the . . . '

'Open it, go on.'

She tore the paper off, drew out a rusting tin, dented on one side, its label torn and stained. 'Whatever's this?'

'Condensed milk, vintage 1940. It's older than I am, came from my mother's larder, part of her stockpile for the war. She was turning out her cupboards once, when I was just a student of nineteen, told me to use it in my coffee. But I could never actually bring myself to open it, not in all those years. It seemed part of history, part of *her*. She's dead now, sadly, died the year my son was born.' He paused a moment, as if in silent mourning, trickling sand slowly through his fingers. 'You'd have liked my mother, Hilary. In fact, in some ways you're alike. She was petite and fair, with that surprising mix of serenity and passion which I love so much in you.'

There was a sudden nervous silence, as his sadness seemed to clash with her own embarrassed pleasure. He brushed sand off his trousers, reached out for the tin. 'Yes, I've had this more than twenty years. In fact, the longer I kept it, the more it became a sort of relic, if not to say a treasure. My Ma paid fivepence for it, yet a dealer offered £20, just two months ago.'

She glanced at it with new respect. 'We can't eat £20, Robert, and anyway I wouldn't dream of opening it. Relics have to be preserved.' She had a sudden grisly image of the precious Brignor relics: the bones of their Holy Foundress, brought from France; a fingernail torn from an obscure and early saint, which had been presented as a gift by an older richer Order. Both were enshrined in heavy gilded caskets, knobbed and bossed with jewels. It had been her job to dust the caskets, guard the bones.

Robert rummaged for the can-opener. 'No, they don't. All I've been doing is waiting for the right occasion and someone worthy of it. How lucky that I've found them both.' He touched her hand a moment, eyes still on the sand. 'It'll be our manna in the desert.'

She watched him struggling with the tin, trying to pierce the rigid metal. Its rust and stains seemed strangely out of place beside the brilliant orange brashness of the plastic cups and plates. 'But supposing it's gone bad?', she said, crumpling up the gift-wrap.

'It won't have.'

How could he be so confident? That milk was nearly half a century old, could surely never last that long without rotting, putrefying. She could hardly bear to watch as the sharp tooth of the can-opener bit into the rim. Would he open up a tin of writhing worms? If it *has* gone off, she told herself, then everything between us will go wrong, our relationship will sour, will never last. But if it's still unspoiled and fresh, then . . .

'Perfect!' Robert said, wrenching off the lid at last, and sniffing at the contents. 'A little stickier and darker than it was in 1940, but otherwise unscathed. Now the next big question is, do we spoon it or spread it?'

'Oh, spoon it,' she said fervently. It was far too rare and precious to be smeared on bread like common margarine.

He found the fold-up camping spoon, dipped it in the tin, held it to her lips. She was suddenly alarmingly aware of his solidity, his closeness, the faint and mingled smells of sausage, sun-cream, sweat, which seemed to breathe out from his pores. He had still not kissed her, never even tried, yet this act seemed more intimate than kissing. He was standing over her, blocking out the sun, the hard insistent spoon still nudging at her lips.

'Go on, darling, swallow.'

She swallowed, both the 'darling' and the milk, was startled by their sweetness – milk and honey. He went on feeding her with the same eager concentration with which he built his shelves or drove his car. Her teeth were twingeing on the almost sickly sweetness, but she somehow feared to say she'd had enough. He was allowing her to step into his past, drawing her into his family, his childhood, as she had included him in hers. She could feel time rushing back, could see his mother stocking up that larder, maybe wondering if she'd survive the blitz to produce a son at all.

Robert scooped a swag of milk from where it had dribbled down her chin, put his finger in her mouth for her to suck. She almost gagged on it, felt invaded and yet bonded, joined by just one finger in a strange and dangerous intimacy. His skin was slightly salty, undercut the sweetness of the milk. He shifted even closer, ran the same damp finger round the outline of her lips. She pulled away, uncertain how to handle all the confused and threatening feelings churning in her mind – her body, too, agitated, restless. She was *not* a child, however much she craved that state as being simple and uncomplicated, yet she was still unsure how to respond to him as a woman.

'My turn now,' he ordered, squatting on the sand and tipping back his head. She knelt in front of him, as if this were some strange sacrament, some secular Communion. Her hand seemed not quite steady, as it moved towards his mouth. He held it at the wrist, joining them once more, then licked the milk slowly off the spoon. She could see his teeth, his tongue, the whole soft pink private chasm of his mouth. How intimate mouths were, how almost dangerous.

'That taste really takes me back, you know.' Robert had his eyes closed, as if to relish the full flavour. 'We used to eat the stuff in sandwiches when I was eight or nine.'

'So you're a spreader, really?'

'I'm a spooner if you spoon.'

She flushed. 'I can make a sandwich, if you like. We've got a loaf of bread we haven't touched.' She scrambled to her feet, glad of an excuse to break the handcuff of his fingers round her wrist. 'Shall I cut it thick or thin?'

'Break it into bits and we'll give it to the gulls. I'm so full myself I couldn't eat another crumb.'

'But what about tomorrow?'

'I thought your Gospels told you not to take thought for the morrow.' He was already tearing chunks off, flinging them around him. The sky was wild and white with wheeling gulls – stabbing beaks, swooping wings, soaring jostling bodies. She hurled a piece herself, trying to reach the highest ones; remembered how she'd watched them as a child, longed to have their wings, so she could fly with them to heaven. She had always seen the sky, then, as a sort of lid to heaven, put on upside down, keeping in all the gold and glitter; only gleams of it escaping on bright days like today. Lonely, in the evenings, she had looked forward to the people she would meet up there – and talk to – not just all the saints, but people from her school-books who seemed interesting, exciting: people like Wat Tyler, Robin Hood.

They're rotting, she thought suddenly, not up there at all. The bread fell from her fingers as she gazed up at the sky. It was as if she had picked up the can-opener and peeled back the lid from heaven, found it empty, gaping; all its former inmates turning black and wormy in their coffin-tins; Robert's mother rotting, not pale and sweet and wholesome like her milk, but rancid flesh breaking down to bone – skull and bone and nothing.

'What's the matter?' Robert asked, as he pounded back to her. He had been running up and down the beach, throwing bread amidst a hail of birds.

'Nothing.' She watched a wave erase his jumbled footprints from the sand. 'Nothing,' she repeated; saw their Holy Foundress's bones, no longer honoured in their jewel-encrusted casket, but scattered to the winds.

Hilary stood within the shadow of the high stone wall, the letter in her hand. It felt huge and heavy, as if also made of stone. After months of indecision, she had written it in minutes, just a week ago, though only because Robert had insisted; more or less dictated those stiff and hurting phrases.

'I am writing to request formal dispensation from my vows. Though I entered in good faith, believing that this was my true vocation, I now feel that I should be living out a lie were I to continue in the religious life, especially as . . . '

The letter had to go to Rome, but must be sent via her convent and her Abbess. Robert had suggested that she deliver it in person on the first night of their trip, as a symbolic gesture, denoting her new freedom, proving the courage he admired. She wiped her free hand on her skirt, palm damp with perspiration. She felt no shred of courage, only abject fear, a sudden surge of loss and longing, as she stood outside the walls which had enclosed her all those years. They seemed taller even than she'd seen them in her mind, rising steep and dark to meet the darkness of the sky. She listened for some sound, but the whole night had been muzzled with a tight black gauze, stretched taut and straining over every field and copse, forbidding any leaf to stir, any bird to flap. The air was sultry warm still, scented velvet air, which made her feel she had travelled not just twenty miles, but to a foreign country. Brignor was a cold land, with sharp frosts and cutting winds. She had first entered it in winter, her parents' tense farewells a cloud of steamy breath as they turned away, growing smaller, fainter, as Mother Mistress surged and swelled to fill the hole they'd left – two parents in one tall and ice-cold nun. She had also left in winter, stumbling over bare and barren fields, a north-east wind scything through her play-clothes, her feet and fingers numb.

Yet now she felt sweaty hot, as if the whole three weeks of fierce June sun had been compressed and compacted in her body, then stoked and fuelled with fear. She'd been hot for days and days, hot with apprehension, hot with some strange restlessness she couldn't understand. She fumbled for her handkerchief, so she could wipe the perspiration from her forehead, then realised that she'd left it in the car. She had left Robert in the car, as well, knew she must complete this task alone; had even made him stop a good two hundred yards away, so that he hadn't glimpsed the convent yet at all. No one in her present life had seen it, not even a tiny snapshot, or a picture, despite the huge amount of space, of sheer emotion, it still took up in her mind. Yet she longed to have him there, his voice to break the silence, his bulk to dwarf the walls; have his strong hand seize the letter, march up to the gate and drop it through. Heroic, he had called her, and she, too, had seen herself as made of martyr's stuff, resisting tyrants, anti-Christs, for years. Yet, here she was, trembling before a harmless country mansion, which housed a dozen old and sleeping nuns.

Tomorrow was the great feast of St Alban, himself a martyr, Britain's first. In just an hour, the midnight bell would sound, the nuns get up for Night Office to celebrate that feast; and later, at tomorrow's Mass, the priest would vest in red – the red of martyrs' blood. She must leave all that behind, all that ritual and symbol, the whole circling year of feasts. Six weeks ago, her own feast had come and gone – the feast of St Hilary of Arles. To all at Cranleigh Gardens, it had been just another day, a boring busy Tuesday. She had tried to think that way herself, not look in vain for the posy of wild flowers which would have been tied to her mug in the Brignor refectory, the sheaf of holy pictures with promises of prayers, the smiles from every Sister as they wished her happy feastday. That evening, Robert had phoned. She'd told him, on an impulse, regretted it immediately, when he'd laughed and called her 'Sister Mary Arles'. The next day, he'd sent her flowers, a card tucked in amongst them, which said just 'Happy everyday'.

Suddenly, she marched up to the gate, not caring now if her feet disturbed the silence; thrust the letter through, heard it fall with a heavy empty sound, as she turned away, head down. She glanced back over her shoulder for a last view of the walls. She might never see this place again, was no longer part of it, no longer bound by the umbilical cord of her solemn holy vows. She kept stopping, stalling, looking back; almost collided with a tall shape in the gloom – Robert, come to fetch her. Neither said a word, just stood side by side, buttressed by the walls. She was glad he'd come, wanted him as witness to this place, witness to her past; willed him silently to understand, but not to speak. Anything he said might jar or wound. And she prayed he wouldn't touch her – not here, not now. It was enough that he was present; that naked as she was of robe or coif, he could clothe her in his strength and in his shadow. They stood as still as rooted trees, listening to the voices of the past. Could he hear the daily chanting of the Office, the grandeur of High Mass, the imperious bells pealing to direct her to the next task in her day, the next step in her life?

'Quick!' she whispered suddenly, seized his hand, almost dragged him after her as she blundered down the path, back towards the car. She slammed her door, sat feverish and impatient while he fiddled with the keys. 'Hurry, Robert, please!'

She had been trying to restrain him on the journey there, begging him to slow, not to let that needle keep creeping up and up. But now the car was hurtling down the lanes, as if all her own impatience was revving through its engine, spinning with its wheels. Already she felt different, her whole body lighter, freer, as if some crushing burden had been physically removed from it. The windows were wound down, her hair tangling in the wind, face slapped and pummelled by the rush of wild sea air. It was not quite midnight yet, not St Alban's day yet; still the feast of St Aloysius – the patron saint of youth. She was seventeen again, not a prim young virgin entering a convent, but a good-time girl out on her first date – unbridled, free as wind.

They were forced to slow as they bumped along the rough and stony track, which led to the beach they'd chosen as their camp site. The tide was far far out now, the beach huge, mysterious, beneath a thin-lipped crescent moon, a rash of stars. She checked her watch as she clambered from the car. Midnight. The nuns would be filing in to choir, eyes closed, hands joined, gait dignified and slow, as she herself streaked down the beach, eyes everywhere, drinking in the whole vast sea and sky. She increased her pace, arms and legs like pistons, barely needing any effort save the force of her elation. All the stored and frozen energy of her twenties and her thirties, when she had never run, never swung her arms, never used her body through the full range of its movement, had come flooding surging back. She craved some ritual to express her break with Brignor, flaunt her new-found freedom and relief. There were ceremonies for joining – simple vows and final vows – but none at all for leaving, breaking out.

She tugged off shoes and jacket, left them on the beach, raced towards the water, and into the first shallow froth of white. 'Be careful!' Robert yelled, his footsteps drumming after her, pounding on the sand. She took no notice, only plunged in deeper, bunching up her skirt, wincing as the icy water lapped and shocked her legs. Robert was much closer now, struggling through the breakers to try to catch her up, but hampered by the current and his clothes. Suddenly, she ducked down in the water, swam instead of floundering, felt herself lifted on the waves; rising with them, slewing down, spray breaking over her head. She could hardly hear Robert's voice for the noise of wind and water. He was swimming right beside her, his body tossed and buffeted.

'I thought you said this sea was dangerous.'

'It is!' she shouted back. 'Especially in our clothes.' She longed to be without them, to be naked like a fish. She had stripped off her long habit, stripped off Rule and vows, so why should she be hampered by that soggy spoilsport skirt, tangling round her limbs and trying to restrain her? She fumbled for the buttons, which went right down the front of it, tried to pull them free. A sudden violent breaker thwacked across her face, blinding her a moment, as she fought to get her breath, choking with the force of it, gagging on the salt. She closed her eyes, trod water, let two more waves surge past, then tugged the sodden skirt again, wrenching at the buttons. The third wave snatched it off for her, swept it back and down. She was free now, unencumbered; a sleek and streamlined dolphin, with no clothes, no nagging conscience, just a torso and good lungs.

'This is wonderful!' she shouted, as she cut across a swathe of glinting moonlight, plunged on into black. 'Let's swim all the way to Norway.'

They recovered, panting, on the beach, exhausted, muscles aching. 'God!' said Robert, rubbing his cold limbs. 'You're a fantastic swimmer, Hilary. You keep fazing me with all these hidden talents. What next?'

She flushed, tried to tug her tee shirt down, to hide her naked thighs. The saturated fabric was clinging to her breasts, outlining her nipples. The light from moon and stars was only very faint, but she was aware of Robert's eyes lingering on her body, returning to her breasts. His voice was low, and half-amused, as he laid a chilled and heavy hand across her naked leg. 'Why stop at just the skirt? You'd actually be warmer if you took your top off, too – *and* those stupid pants.'

She rolled away, hugged knees to chest, to hide both breasts and pants. So now he was demanding what Liz called 'payment', payment for his kindness, for the chauffeuring, the gifts. Why not? He deserved them, didn't he, and she herself had excited and aroused him by running wild, shedding all restraint. It now seemed unbelievable that she had flung away her skirt, with no thought at all for afterwards, or of how it might affect him; no thought of waste, or money.

'I'll . . . er . . . get changed in the car,' she said, jerking to her feet.

It seemed a long way back – darker, slower going, more broken shells and pebbles underfoot, things which jabbed and cut; a brisk sea breeze slapping her bare legs. So what happened to the good-time girl, she asked herself ironically, as she crouched shivering and awkward in the cramped front seat, trying to get dressed? She ignored her pyjamas, although it was now nearly one a.m.; struggled into a high-necked, long-sleeved tracksuit. She was still damp underneath it, but too frightened of her nakedness to take the time to dry herself. She wasn't sure where Robert was, or whether he were watching. She had passed him a towel, a torch, his own dry clothes, the knapsack and the groundsheets; suggested that he get dressed somewhere else.

She emerged still shivering from the car, her own feeble torch-beam almost snuffed out by the darkness which seemed to close around it. She was a nothing in this vastness, this blur of alien sea and sky, stretching to infinity – nothing but a grain of sand, a speck.

'Robert!' she called anxiously, but his name was blown away, shredded into spume. Supposing he had left her, stalked off in a huff, angered by her constant fears and scruples, her sudden shifts of mood, which encouraged then rejected him; swept her from elation to sullen prudishness. His own moods could change, as well. Liz had spoken of his temper, which could suddenly erupt, she'd warned, replace sunny calm with hurricane. She hadn't seen it yet, but now that she'd repulsed him, he might well be stung, resentful.

She stumbled down the path, across the dunes, suddenly saw a leap of flame, heard the crackle of dry wood. She ran towards the fire, found him crouching on the burnished sand beside it, breaking up distorted limbs of driftwood, both hands glowing golden as he fed the flames with sticks. Neither said a word. It was she who reached to kiss him – an adult kiss, mouth to dangerous mouth. She glimpsed his startled glance before shutting her own eyes, feeling the strange texture of his lips. His chin was rough and hurting, his tongue pushing at her mouth, as if to force it open. She kept it shut, afraid. The word 'kiss' sounded gentle and affectionate, but this kiss was urgent, fierce, as if she had struck a match and some new and frightening power she had never seen in Robert had leapt up like a flame. His whole body had joined in, was pressing, gripping hers, as if he wanted every curve and bone and plane to mould into his own. How long did kisses last?

As if in answer, he released her just a little, so he could see her face; touched her cheeks, her lashes, with one caressing finger. She let out a deep breath, half relief, half pleasure, but suddenly he clamped his lips against her open mouth, sought and found her tongue. She was taken by surprise; her own tongue powerless, captive, as his sucked and nuzzled hers. It seemed extraordinary, extraordinary, that someone else's tongue should be right inside her mouth – her private mouth, her small mouth, which somehow seemed more intimate than any other part of her. She could taste his supper, the lingering tang of sausages and grease, overlaid with wine. He must be tasting hers as well; their two salivas mingling, her own tongue moving now, as if he had forced it to respond.

She felt a hand slide slowly up her back, slip round to cup her breast. She tried to speak, to stop him, but she no longer owned her mouth or voice, no longer owned her body. He was unzipping her tracksuit, unbuttoning his own shirt. She hardly recognised him. He seemed larger than he'd ever been before; rearing tall and solid in the night, his features blurred and indistinct, as if he were no longer Robert Harrington, but Man in general, Man in abstract. She was frightened of him, frightened of his forcefulness; the way he seemed completely taken over, as if he had forgotten who she was, forgotten all her fears and inexperience; was simply claiming her as Woman – any woman. He had dragged her top off, was unhooking her bra, crushing his own bare and hairy chest against her naked breasts; and now his lower half, pressing thrusting closer, groin to groin. She could feel him far too big, bigger than Simon – far more headstrong and impetuous, as he seemed to rut against her, making noises like an animal. He tried to force her tracksuit bottoms down, but she grabbed his hand, pushed it off. She could see that label on the tin, Robert's precious relic tin – 'UNFIT FOR BABIES', printed in huge capitals on the torn and dirty wrapper. She *was* unfit for babies, could never be a mother, yet this act could make her one. In just a few brief minutes, her whole life could be changed and overturned.

He seemed not to hear her begging him to stop, not even to be aware that she was speaking. His own voice was the louder, as he kept stabbing out incoherent words, breathing very heavily. 'Christ!' 'Oh, yes, my darling.' He had dragged her trousers off now, was unzipping his own jeans. Suddenly, he clutched the zip, let out a strangled shout; seemed to hold himself, as if warding off a blow; then keeled over on his knees, head down, face hidden in his hands.

She crouched beside him, touched his shoulder nervously. He appeared to be in pain; must have pulled a muscle, strained his back; was still moaning very softly on his knees. 'Are you all right?' she whispered.

He looked up, gave a brief embarrassed laugh. 'Yes. Sorry. Rotten timing.' He reached out for his towel, mopped his thighs, his jeans. 'That hasn't happened since I was a wild lad of sixteen. I guess I'm out of practice. I really do apologise.'

What for, she wondered, picking up her clothes? Wasn't *she* the one who was meant to be apologising, for trying to stop him, fighting off his hands, worrying about things like contraception, when she should have been passionate, abandoned?

His voice was still unsteady as he buttoned back his shirt. 'Though you ought to take half the blame, at least, you know. You're the most exciting bloody woman – and completely unpredictable. I mean, to suddenly seduce me, when you'd just given me the brush-off . . . '

'Seduce you?'

'God! I feel a fool. *I*'m the virgin now, for heaven's sake.' He laughed again, more freely, went to fetch the groundsheet, fumbled in the knapsack, came up with a flask. 'How about a nightcap? I brought a drop of brandy, since you seemed to rather like it in that Easter tipsy trifle.'

She tensed, recalling Simon's brandy; her body feeling strange, unsettled, lips burning, almost sore. He touched his glass to hers, sat silent for a while, face half-dark, half-ruddy in the fire. She reached her hand out, but he didn't seem to see it. The hand felt lonely, stupid. Wasn't the sex act meant to join you, make you one heart through one flesh? She and Robert were in two entirely different places – he sitting on the sand, while she kept returning to the convent in her mind. The journey was a long one. Though Brignor was so close in miles, it seemed further in distance than it had ever been before. '*I am writing to request formal dispensation from* . . . ' She took a gulp of brandy, choked it down.

Robert flung his head back, so he could look up at the sky. 'The stars seem huge out here, far bigger than in London, and far more of them, somehow. D'you realise, there are five billion stars in the Milky Way alone, and five billion galaxies in the universe, and the population of the globe has just reached the five billion mark, and each of us five billion human beings has five billion neurons in our brain.' He swilled brandy round his mouth before swallowing it appreciatively. 'Five billion must be a sort of magic number. And if you work it out, it means there's one star apiece for every living person and one galaxy in the universe for each of us. Isn't that nice?' He eased his shoulders, rubbed his neck, before looking up again. 'We should have been designed with heads which tilt back comfortably, or with little levers on them, like those reclining airline seats. I could watch the stars for ever, couldn't you? There's a marvellous story about Anaxagoras – you know, the Greek philosopher chappie who inspired Socrates and Aristotle. Someone asked him once why a man should choose rather to be born than not, and do you know what he said?'

She shook her head, had never even heard of Anaxagoras, was astonished Robert seemed so changed – no longer rutting animal, but serene astronomer.

'Just this: "For the sake of viewing the heavens and the whole order of the universe." What an answer! Isn't it fantastic? And I think I'd go along with it. After all, we're made from stars ourselves. That's pretty damn fantastic in itself. In fact, someone else once said – I can't remember who now, but someone in our own time – that we're a star's way of knowing about stars.'

Hilary had focused on one faint and modest star. It seemed a mere pinprick in the darkness, yet she remembered reading somewhere that some giant stars were five hundred times larger than the sun. She tried – and failed – to imagine such a supergiant, to feel its light blinding her close up. All she felt was tiny, and alone. 'I feel just a speck,' she said. 'A nothing.'

'That's wrong, completely wrong. Just think what you are compared with an amoeba. You're a genius, a giant. And even in your own right, you're amazing – we all are. If only I could make you see it, Hilary.'

'I saw it when I had a faith. It was so much easier then, because we were created by an amazing God, and going back to Him – sort of handmade by a craftsman, and immortal.'

'We're still immortal.'

'No we're not. We just die and putrefy.'

'It depends which way you look at it. We all tend to focus on time passing, and of course the end of that is death. If we're stuck in time, we die. But once we get outside time, eternity is now.'

'How d'you mean, "outside time"?'

'Well, see it as a circle rather than a line. "In my end is my beginning" – all that sort of stuff. Past, present, future, all coterminous. It's quite difficult to grasp. You have to feel it, really, sort of in your gut – be aware the past is still around, continuing to affect us, and the future's here already, drawing us into itself; that all our different tenses are just a fiction, a convenience. Time *doesn't* pass, whatever we may say. Okay, you're not convinced. I can see that from your face. But look at it a different way. You can't deny we see light from the past. I mean, the sun's light, for example, is already eight minutes old when it reaches us, and light from Andromeda is a good two million years old, so their pasts are present for us.' He laughed. 'Just think – if Andromeda disappeared tonight, it would be two million years before we knew.' He folded two spare sweaters to make a cushion for her, arranged it on the groundsheet. 'But even on a simple level, there are other ways of achieving immortality – in the things we leave behind, for instance: children, works of art.'

'But I haven't any children and I've never been an artist. It's different for you, Robert. You've built houses, even churches; left your stamp on such a lot of things.'

'But so have you. What about those vestments that you made? They sound like works of art themselves. And you told me once you were looking after chasubles which dated from Victorian times, really precious things. Well, in another hundred years or so, someone may be cherishing *your* vestments, admiring all the skill which went to make them. And then there's prayer. You can't discount it as a force, even if you don't believe in God. Who can say for certain that your years and years of praying didn't touch and reach the people it was meant for, affect the world in some way? Prayer may be something we just don't understand yet – something like electricity, invisible but powerful. Do you know, when I was standing just outside your convent walls, I could actually feel a sort of . . . ' He frowned into his glass, shook his head impatiently. 'I just don't have the words. They all sound fey or batty, but those centuries of concentrated praying seem to have created a sort of force-field round the place.'

Hilary glanced up at his eager solemn face, so different from the face of half an hour ago, the grotesque grimacing face which had uttered those wild sounds. How strange he was, this man. Yet if what he said were true, then her convent years had not been wasted, fruitless. She had touched the world, as she had always aimed to do.

'And another thing, Hilary, you've affected *me* – yes, really left your imprint. I've never met another woman like you, and I've met a fair old number in my time. You're a marvellous sort of mixture – like a child, in some ways, and yet with such high ideals and iron self-will, and so serious about everything. I like that. Even if you ran away tomorrow – which I shan't allow, don't worry – I'd still feel your influence. You've made me change the way I see things.'

'*I* have?' Was he mocking? 'But you're the one who tells me everything. I know nothing on my own, Robert.'

'You know a lot of things.' He came to sit beside her. 'Including how to kiss. How about a goodnight kiss – just one?'

Her own mouth opened almost willingly this time, though the kiss was different – brandy-flavoured, gentler; less tongue, more nuzzling lips. She didn't need to pull away. He released her mouth himself, sat close and quiet, his arm around her shoulders. She could hear the jerky panting of the fire, the sudden hiss and spurt as flames surprised damp wood, the rhythmic roll and kickback of the waves. She followed Robert's gaze as he looked far out to sea, the furled power of the breakers swelling slowly, slowly, until they exploded on the sand.

'Do you realise, darling, it's not completely dark, not even now? There's a sort of gleam on the horizon.'

She looked where he was pointing, saw the sky not heavy curdled black, as it had seemed at Brignor just an hour ago, but pearled and fretted with the palest silver-grey. It must have been there all the time, yet she hadn't seen it, had called the darkness total. Robert shook his jacket out, draped it round their shoulders, joining them again.

'You know that time thing I was trying to explain just now, well it's rather like the movement of the sun. I mean, people long ago used to think the sun was dead, just because they couldn't see or feel it. The light and heat had gone; disappeared, apparently, for ever. We know it's there, of course; still hot, still bright, but simply in the other hemisphere. Well, you can also view the past like that. It's there, in some dimension, as much "now" as now itself is.' He reached out for his brandy, held it in the firelight, watched the flames flicker in the glass. 'In one sense, there can't be any "now", because even as we grasp it, it's changing, passing on, yet if you look at it another way, eternity is now, or now's eternity. Am I making any sense?'

She nodded, slowly. If the past were still alive, then her parents were still with her; Robert's mother still stocking up her larder; her old and saintly Abbess still praying on her knees – not in heaven, but in some infinite dimension. Heaven and hell had both vanished altogether: no need to dread the one, nor languish for the other. She could see them now for what they were – human and misleading ways of trying to understand Robert's subtler concept of an eternity beyond time. She kept her eyes focused on the faint gleam of silvery light, realised now it was vitally important, as a symbol of a new eternal life. Even her own small frail achievements were shining in a new dimension: she had sewn her vestments into history; helped to weave a force-field around Brignor; even stitched Robert to her, now their lives and mouths had joined.

The words of the psalm they had recited every night at Vespers suddenly welled up in her mind.

> Even the darkness is not dark for you
> and the night is as bright as the day,
> for darkness is as light with you.

She repeated them again, silently, wonderingly, as she watched the silver etch a little deeper in the black.

25

Hilary shut her ears and eyes against the brusque intrusive voice – a stranger's voice, a male voice. The bed was very hard, harder even than Brignor, but she didn't want to wake yet; felt lazy and contented, as if she had been told good news which she couldn't quite remember, but which had seeped right through her pores. She squinted through her eyelids, glimpsed a stretch of sand, a tartan-patterned sleeping bag, rumpled up and empty – suddenly remembered where she was. She rubbed her eyes, struggled out of sleep. Where and why had Robert gone, and whose was that rude other voice, which had now faded to a murmur? She turned in its direction, saw Robert and a policeman striding side by side across the sand. She sat up with a jerk. A policeman! What had happened in the night? Was Robert in some trouble? Were they planning to arrest him, wouldn't even allow him to get dressed? He was still in his pyjamas, and bare feet.

'Wait!' she shouted, as she wrestled with her sleeping bag, tried to force the stubborn zip. The policeman didn't hear, just picked up his push-bike, which he'd left lying on the dunes, mounted, pedalled off. Robert bounded back to her, wincing as he stumbled on a half-buried piece of rock.

'Hilary, my darling, you're now an official law-breaker, a felon and a trespasser. Which isn't bad for someone who's still technically a nun.'

'*Me?*' She hobbled up, still trapped in her blue sleeping bag. 'But why? Whatever's happened?'

'We're not allowed to camp, that's all. It's illegal on the beach – and also forbidden to light fires, or leave litter, or park cars. I didn't know, did you? He's moved us on, in any case, says he'll be back in half an hour, to check we're well and truly gone. I can't say I'm that sorry. I hardly slept a wink. I suggest we drive to the nearest grand hotel and order a decent four-course breakfast.' He yanked the zip to free her, bundled up the sleeping bag, turned back with a grin.'*Is* there a grand hotel in Norfolk?'

'I've no idea. I've never stayed in a hotel.'

'Never?'

'No.' She laughed. 'Nuns don't, you know.'

'Yes, but before that, as a child?'

She shook her head. 'My mother hated holidays.'

'*I* spent half my childhood in hotels. My mother didn't like it either, but she didn't have much choice.'

'You mean your father travelled for his job?'

Robert's face looked guarded, suddenly, as if a shutter had come down. 'Let's not talk about my father. I don't want to spoil this glorious morning. Look at the sun! And it's only half past six. That copper must have been a monk in another incarnation, if he's on his rounds so early.'

'Half past six was late for us. Positively indulgent.' She tried to keep her tone light, while reflecting on his words. Did Robert hate his father, fear him? The little idyll she had constructed in her mind of his mother stocking larders, his father building shelves, went crashing to the ground. She knew so little, actually, about his family, his background; still found it difficult to ask him personal questions, delve into his past – in that respect was still a nun.

Robert stopped her clearing up, removed the bedding from her arms, claimed them for himself. 'Talking of indulgence, don't I get a kiss this morning?'

His pyjamas seemed so flimsy thin, one silky layer between them. His chin had grown rougher in the night. He hadn't cleaned his teeth, and nor had she. All her old fastidious fears were surging back again. She was still a nun in far too many ways, despite that letter, which Reverend Mother Abbess might even now be reading. She shivered, pulled away. 'Look, we'd better get a move on. Half an hour's not long to get everything packed up.'

'Okay, you clear up here and I'll go and have a shave. I can see you don't like stubble.'

They were on the road by seven, washed and dressed, and in Robert's case, close-shaved. Hilary still marvelled at the way his sports car ate up distances which had seemed endless as a child; trudging in her wellingtons and red hand-knitted mittens against driving rain or wind. She never remembered warmth like this in Norfolk; the golden dazzling light which seemed to have been shaken out on all the fields and hedges, like glitter from a tube. And the colours she recalled were always greys, or dull and sober greens; not these startling vibrant yellows in mustard fields and gorse, these creamy clouds of elder flowers and meadow-sweet, that shout of scarlet poppies against a haze of golden-brown. The hedgerows seemed prolific – a tangled mass of jostling stalks and heads; ragwort dwarfing vetches, bindweed choking willowherb; every stem tussling for more space, every fat and glossy leaf thrusting to the light. And there had never been so many birds – not just sea-birds: curlews, plover, oystercatchers, but also larks and lapwings, stonechats, yellow-hammers; rainbowed pheasants strutting by the roadside, or skeetering to safety from the red jaws of the car. She watched a jackdaw preening on a signpost, spelt out the name beneath it. 'That's my village,' she said out loud, with a sudden lurch of longing, undercut by fear.

Robert swerved, swung the car off the main B road, and along the narrow lane. Trees grew high each side, so that they were in a private tunnel, the sun shut out except for glints and flickers, a sudden welcome coolness brushing her bare arms. They both fell silent, half-nervous, half-expectant, as the car emerged again into brilliant sunshine; a straggle of small houses, a church, a pub, a store – nothing changed, except the village seemed deserted, as if it had died and been forgotten; no gossips at the corner, no mourner in the tangled weed-choked churchyard.

Their footsteps echoed as they walked down past the church. The car looked wrong, parked blatantly outside it; too modern, too expensive, far too flashy bright. Even Robert seemed out of place in his stylish shirt, pale trousers; too healthy altogether for this ancient crumbling place; and certainly too big. The village was a toy, with a modest church, a midget pub, narrow small-boned houses squashed together. She was scared what he might think when he saw the house she'd lived in as a child – an unexceptional cottage with neither space nor charm, and built of dull red brick. The house he'd designed in Leicestershire had been grand-scale and distinguished, with a conservatory, a library, extensive formal gardens laid out with pomp and style. She stopped in front of the ragged patch of dandelions, somehow still expecting to see her father's tidy patchwork of paving stones interspersed with salvias, the blue edging of lobelia which led up to the door. 'FOR SALE', she saw, instead. The sign looked old and tired, as if it had advertised its wares too long, encountered little interest.

'There's no one here,' she said. What had she expected – her mother in the kitchen, her father marking school books?

'Good! That means we can go in and look round.' Robert was already through the gate, trying the front door. It was securely locked and bolted, the other doors and windows equally unyielding. Hilary trailed after him, as he rattled the back door; felt barred again, locked out of her past, as she had also been at Brignor. She peered in through the windows at the bare and grimy rooms, could feel her mother's outrage at the dirt, the desolation. She turned her back, walked slowly down the garden, remembering her father's Brussels sprouts, the way he lambasted slugs and caterpillars with the same weary sarcasm he employed for second-formers.

Her eyes were pricking, her chest felt tight, constricted. Suddenly, Robert was behind her, coaxed her round to face him, took her in his arms. She tensed at first, as if her parents were both watching from their poky bedroom window, shocked and disapproving. But this embrace was nothing like the wild kiss on the sands. His body wasn't bucking, stirring; nor his hurting urgent mouth prising hers apart. He simply held her, while tears slid down her face, ran into her mouth. She didn't wipe her eyes, just swallowed salt, remorse. She owed her parents tears.

They didn't stop again until they reached the obelisk. Hilary had almost forgotten that ugly and pretentious monument, pretending to be solid when it was only brick inside, thinly faced with stone; plaques on all four sides setting out the distances to neighbouring towns and hamlets.

'Oh, do let's stop a moment. My best friend Katy lived here and we spent hours just sitting by that thing, planning how we'd send down messages from heaven if one of us died first, and how we'd keep a throne warm for the other.' She smiled. 'What arrogance! It never crossed our minds we'd land up in the other place, or that God would object to our using all His busy angels to deliver paltry bits of information, like whether dogs had souls or if God allowed riding-schools in heaven.'

Robert laughed and slowed. 'It's an interesting piece of architecture, and very grand for such a tiny village. G.R., it says up top. Was that George III or George IV?'

She blushed at her own ignorance. 'I've no idea. I simply saw those as my own initials, which is partly why I liked the thing, I suppose. I told you I was arrogant.'

'Your initials? How? Liz said your name was Hilary, even before you were a nun.'

Hilary got out, smoothed her crumpled skirt. 'I was actually called Gloria, but I keep that very dark.'

'Why, for heaven's sake? It's a splendid name, full of fame and triumph.'

'That's the trouble. I just don't feel it's me.'

' 'Course it is. It also means glory in the sense of light. You know, like in the Christmas carol, "While glory shone around." That's exactly right for you, darling. I always think of you as bathed in light.'

'Oh, Robert, don't. You're mocking me.'

'I'm not. You're very fair and you've got this sort of inner light – bright both in and out. Anyway, I love the name. To tell the truth, I've never much liked Hilary. It seemed too plain and almost masculine. You're Gloria from now on. Glorious Gloria. I've just chiselled your initials into this rather marvellous obelisk for all the world to see.'

Hilary walked towards the plinth, resentment fighting pleasure. He hadn't asked if she objected to being suddenly renamed, made her

339

father's child again. 'I was named after Gloria Swanson, if you really want to know.'

'Even better. She was one of the most glamorous of females.'

'But I'm not glamorous.' She remembered the photo on her father's desk, the ineffable Ms Swanson in a silver frame, lips pursed and pouting, ostrich feathers in her hair. Katy's father had all his children's photos on his desk – Katy largest, in pigtails and a gymslip.

Robert traced her cheekbones. 'Yes, you are.'

'What, in this skimpy skirt and sandals?'

'Yes. In fact, we'll have to find a really swish hotel now. Glorias don't slum it.'

'Oh, Robert, *no*, we can't. It's far too grand.' Hilary gazed up at the panelled walls, the portraits; down again to the bowls of hothouse flowers. 'I haven't got the clothes or . . . '

'Don't worry. Ms Swanson's private valet just dropped by with a little blue silk number. He left it in the suite upstairs. You'd better come up now and see if you approve.'

She followed him upstairs, a wide and curving staircase with more flowers on the landing, chambermaids bobbing as they passed. They had stopped here just for breakfast, or so she'd thought as she'd sat in the palatial dining room, flushing as a waiter spread her napkin, another poured her coffee. After the most luxurious breakfast of her life, which started with fresh mangoes and ended with brioches, Robert had left her in the lounge with a pile of magazines, told her he was going to reconnoitre. An hour had passed before he reappeared, wearing a tie she hadn't seen before and an air of satisfaction.

'Yes, it *is* the best hotel. I've checked on a few more and they're nothing like as comfortable. I hope you like our room.'

They were standing now outside a panelled door, which occupied the prime place on the landing. Hilary touched her ring, felt the sharp arms of the crucifix hidden in her palm. He must have booked this room for Mr and Mrs Harrington, yet officially she was married still to God. He unlocked the door, which revealed another inner door, opened that as well. A huge four-poster dominated the room, its ruched and pleated curtains matching the frills on counterpane and pillows; the dark oak of the bedposts echoed in the antique chest of drawers, the tall broad-shouldered wardrobe, the highly polished table which held a bowl of fruit.

'Well, what d'you think?' he asked her, not waiting for her answer. 'Not just double doors, but two separate layers of curtains on the bed. See?' He pulled the white nets close, and then the heavy velvet. 'How's

340

that for privacy?' He crossed back to the wardrobe, took out a dress with a low plunge back, floating panels in the front, tiny shoestring straps. 'Ms Swanson's new creation. I only hope it fits. The shop said they'd take it back, but it's ten miles down the coast, at least, and there was nothing else as glamorous. Want to try it on?'

'Er . . . yes,' she said. 'I will in just a moment.'

'What's the matter? Did I get it wrong? I know blue's your favourite colour, but if you don't like it, we can . . . '

'No, it's beautiful.' Too beautiful, too chic; a creation for a film star or a model, not her style at all. She knew from working at Di's shop how much a dress like that would cost. She was in his debt again, his sexual debt. Could she ever pay him back, be worthy of the dress? She suddenly longed to be a child again, safe and small with Katy, sprawling by the obelisk in shorts and dusty feet; back in single figures when men were only Fathers, either parental or religious; or at least back on the beach in her shabby comfy tracksuit, her private sleeping bag. She had ached to camp for over thirty years, and it had lasted just one night. Though that was hardly Robert's fault. He must think her most ungrateful. After all, he was only helping out. She'd chucked one decent skirt away, thrown it to the waves; could hardly appear at dinner in this cheaper chain-store one, and a faded cotton tee shirt. It had been bad enough at breakfast. The woman at the table next to theirs had been designer-dressed, in linen, with pearls at wrist and throat.

'It's lovely, Robert. I don't know how to thank you.' She shook the dress out, draped it on a chair-back. 'I'll try it on later, once I've had a wash.'

'Yes, come and see the bathroom. Or should I say the art gallery?'

Even the bath was panelled in dark oak, the walls not tiled, but papered in a linen-weave maroon, the background for a dozen gilt-framed pictures, mostly coastal landscapes. A Victorian bowl and ewer of the sort they used at Brignor stood proudly on its floral china pedestal, serving here merely as an ornament. She glanced briefly in the mirror. Her face looked too informal for the room; seemed to need a frame as well, a famous artist's signature scrawled across her chin. She watched Robert's head approach hers in the glass, bend to kiss her neck. It was hard to concentrate. She had drunk four cups of coffee, needed now to void it; was feeling quite uncomfortable, in fact. Liz would say, 'Scat! I need a pee,' or even use the toilet in front of someone else. Unthinkable for her. Even things like cleaning teeth or washing seemed intimate and private, impossible to share. On the beach, she had walked miles to find a bush; cleaned her teeth in private by the car.

'I'll . . . just have a quick wash,' she said, willing Robert to leave. He did, but she could hear him still outside, singing, whistling, banging drawers. Which meant he could hear her. She had never emptied her bladder quite so gingerly before, drop by guilty drop; reaching out to run both taps as well, to try to mask the noise. She pulled the chain, frowning at its gurgles, then drifted to the window, gazed out at hedges cut like birds; roses trained to climb and curve in bowers. Liz would love this place. She, too, was staying in a grand hotel. It was Harry's birthday and they'd flown to Paris to celebrate in style. Harry had driven down to London, so she'd met the man, at last, just before he took Liz to the airport. She'd been surprised how old he seemed; embarrassed by the fact that she knew so much about him, all the private details of his sex life. Eager, Liz had said, with great interest in the subject, but the spirit far more willing than the flesh, alas. No, she wasn't complaining – he was gentle and considerate, and extremely generous both in and out of bed. What he lacked in passion, he made up in devotion.

She'd felt a twinge of jealousy when she'd seen them both in the Cranleigh Gardens kitchen, gulping a last quick cup of coffee, arms entwined, Harry in her chair. Liz and he seemed bonded now, and Liz talked of nothing else: Harry's house, Harry's business, Harry's hopes of being mayor. She and Liz were still good friends, of course, but they were no longer two girls on their own, and Liz was far less free – less free to spend weekends with her, or plan holidays together.

But why should she need Liz, when Robert was next door? And why was she not with him? Liz and Harry would probably be in bed together, laughing, chatting, cuddling, after croissants and black coffee, enjoying their hotel, revelling in the luxury. 'Go for it,' Liz had whispered, with a wink, when they'd kissed goodbye two days ago, yet here she was cowering in a bathroom, worrying about noises from the cistern. Liz had accepted flowers and gifts from Harry without agonising, totting up her debt; would have loved that blue creation, slavered at its price. 'You've got it all with Robert,' Liz had told her several times. 'He's even got *hair*, for heaven's sake. I've been trying to talk my poor bald lamb into a little Magic-Weave or stick-on, but he's resisted up to now.'

She splashed her face with water. Why was it so hot? They were no longer in the car, with the sun panting through the windows, burning on the glass, yet she still felt that sensation of being exposed to some relentless source of heat – itchy heat, restless heat, heat which seemed alive in its own right. She ran more water, lathered up the expensive floral soap, so she could enjoy its musky fragrance on her skin, dried her hands on the luxurious thick-pile towels, then squirted Liz's scent behind her ears. She must 'go for it', as Liz advised; be Robert's glorious Gloria. She would have all day to practise, to cool herself and calm herself, before she sauntered down to dinner in her Swanson gown, or tried out the four-poster. She could relax first in the shade, sit in that cool garden with its leafy walks, green lawns, maybe have a drink or two, and later a cold bath . . . By evening, she'd be perfect in the part, and by the end of the week, she could return to Liz triumphant, swap details, swap successes.

'Robert,' she said, as she stepped back to the bedroom. 'Have you seen their marvellous garden? Why don't . . . ?' She broke off in mid-sentence. Robert had vanished, only his possessions scattered all around, a whiff of men's cologne hanging in the air. She heard a muffled voice calling from the bed. 'It's incredible in here. Sort of back to the womb. Come and be my twin.'

An arm appeared between the heavy curtains, an arm naked to the shoulder. So he had taken off his shirt. What else, she wondered, with a surge of apprehension, as she unbuckled her child's sandals? He was going far too fast. It was only half past ten and they hadn't had their drink, or bath, or . . . 'Who cares about the time?' Liz said, grinning from the bed she shared with Harry, brushing flakes of croissant from his paunch. 'For God's sake, take your chances, love. Enjoy life for a change, instead of worry-gutting.'

Impulsively, she unzipped her summer skirt, let it fall around her to the floor, then climbed in pants and tee shirt through the curtains. He drew her down towards him, bare chest against the cotton of her tee shirt, corduroy legs capturing her naked ones. They were in their own small room, a dark and claustrophobic room, bounded by four walls of crushed red velvet; all the smells sharpened by the closeness of the space: the smell of frangipani soap still clinging to her hands; the tang of Robert's cologne; luncheon smells rising from the kitchen through the open bedroom window. It was hot again, stifling hot, as if all the heat she'd felt so far had climaxed at this point, culminated in the heat of Robert's body, the red furnace of the bed. She was aware of perspiration filming her whole body, prickling on her scalp; her heart itself pumping out more sticky dangerous heat.

He leaned up on one elbow, outlined all her features with a soft caressing finger. 'You've got a lovely mouth, d'you know that? See that little dip above your upper lip? That's a sign of passion.'

'You've got it too.' Her finger traced the same spot on his face.

'You see, we obviously belong together. I realised that from the first moment I set eyes on you. I've been pretty bloody patient, don't you think? Except for yesterday. I owe you an apology for that.' His hand was on her thigh, moving slowly up it, round towards her pants. '*No!*' He removed the hand himself, returned it to her face. 'This time it's real

343

slow motion. I promise not to rush things. We've got all day, all week. In fact, we can stay here all damn year, if you touch my chest like that again. Yes, my nipples like it, too. I'm not sure men's are meant to. Who cares? It's bloody marvellous. Yes, use your mouth. That's wonderful . . .

'It's fearfully hot in here. Are you sure you want that top on? Here, let me help. That's better. Now the bra. Damn! These hooks are tricky. Complicated things, bras. That's it, slip it off. Christ! They're beautiful. They drive me wild, d'you know that? I've only got to look at you and I'm . . .'

He reached up to turn the light on, a dim pink-tinged light, half-concealed in the hangings of the bed. 'Rose-coloured tits you've got now. I love those little dots all round the nipple, as if they're there to show it off. I've just got to touch them, darling. No, take your hands away. I can't see them if you do that. God! They feel so good. Your skin there's quite fantastic, all smooth and silky, with these tiny pale blue veins, which make it look translucent. Thin-skinned, that's what you are – thin-skinned in every way, not a great tough rhinoceros like I am.

'Shut up, Robert, you're talking far too much. It's just that I'm so nervous – yes, I am – nervous as all hell, worse than you. Crazy, isn't it? I just so want to please you, make it really good for you, as well. Look, let me kiss them, darling. That'll shut me up. Do you like them being kissed? Like this? Or just the nipples? Your skin tastes wonderful – sweaty, slightly sweet. I'm sweating like a pig myself, and your tummy's really damp. When I put my face against it, we're sort of stuck together, joined by our two sweats. I like that. It's exciting. It makes me feel you're hot for me and want me. You've got a marvellous navel, very deep and private, like an extra secret opening. I can hardly get my tongue in, just the tip. I'm not going too fast, am I? I am? I'm sorry, honestly. It's just so hard to . . . Okay, we'll stop. We'll cool it. Just a sec, my arm's bent back. That's better. Are *you* all right? You sure? We'll have a rest, just lie together, talk. It's so good to have you close.

'Look, I don't know how to put this quite, my darling, but the last thing I want is to be just some casual lecher who lures you into bed and . . . Of course I want you in my bed, but I want you in my life as well. Christ Almighty, Hilary, I've spent every night since April dreaming of this moment. I've missed you terribly, and my house has felt quite desolate and empty since that one weekend you spent there. I've been working like a black on it. The kitchen's finished now, and all the shelves are up, with my things arranged on them. If I sell the place, they'll all come down again, back in packing-cases. But if you came to live with me, it could be Gloria's Tower, a monument to both of us.

'What I'm really trying to say, darling, is you're special, very special. No – don't object, you are. I've had the wildest fantasies – except I don't think they were fantasies at all now. I've even thought we'd have a child together, then yesterday you said how much you envied Liz having two daughters of her own – I mean, just as if you'd read my mind, knew what I'd been thinking. Well, it's not too late, is it? We could have our own daughter. I'd love a little girl. What shall we call her? Gloriette? Gloriana? That was Queen Elizabeth's name. D'you think she ever slept here? With her Essex? Just think of the couples who've made love in this same bed, over all the centuries.

'Please talk, please say you're happy. I know I'm rambling on, but it's because I'm so unsure of you. I don't know what you're thinking, when you just lie there saying nothing. I haven't upset you, have I, suggesting that we live together? I know it's far too soon and you'll say we hardly know each other, but by the end of this weekend, I'll know every single inch of you. Well, I will if you allow me to remove those boring pants. Oh, *please*, my darling. I won't touch, I promise – just look, just worship you. God! It's beautiful. I've been wondering for ages if you'd be blonde down there as well. It's fairer than your scalp hair, and so neat, as if you trim it.

'Does that feel good? D'you like that? Or d'you prefer my fingers further in, like that? Just relax, my sweet, you're tensing up a lot. We *are* a pair, aren't we? I'm shaking like a leaf myself. You've made me feel sixteen again, as randy as all hell, but . . . God! I'm hot. Are you? I've just got to take these trousers off, or I'm going to melt away. Can you help me with the belt? That's it. Now tug them down. Christ! Your hands – yes, there, just there – yes, harder. That's wonderful, fantastic!

'Just a moment, we'd better use one of these damn . . . Don't shut your eyes. I like you looking at me – yes, all the time, even while I put it on. Don't look so worried, darling. I promise to be gentle, stop whenever you like. You just say, okay? Last night was *my* time, this is yours. I want to know exactly what you like. Oh, Gloria, my darling, just to feel you right against me. I never thought I'd . . . That's it – put your arms around me. Press really close – go on. I want to imagine we're one body, joined all the way from . . . No, wait. Lie still a moment. I'm sorry, darling, but I'm going to have to cool it, or I'm afraid I'll just explode again, like yesterday. I don't know what you do to me. I'm not usually like this. You make it so exciting, as if it's *my* first time, as well. Hey! – let's have a sort of fantasy, pretend we're celibates. I'm a monk and you're a nun and we met on a pilgrimage to Walsingham. It's only a few miles from here, in fact. Right – I'm very bashful, just a shy young virgin, not sure what to do with it. Can you help poor Brother Robert?

345

No, you can't. You're just as shy as I am, little Sister Mary Arles, even pretty scared. And we've both got these black habits on, yards and yards of them. I'm fumbling with your heavy skirts, fighting all those petticoats. You're trying to drag them down again, begging me to stop, but . . .

'No, forget about the habits – we're in our nightclothes now and I've just crept into your cell, and I'm lifting your white gown above your head. My hand's between your legs, sliding up towards your . . . Oh, come on, darling, let me. I must just touch you there again. You're wet, you know – you *are*. That means you really want it. *Say* you want it, darling. I love to hear you tell me. It really turns me on. Christ! You feel amazing – so hot and sort of . . . D'you like my fingers there? More fingers? My whole fist? Now let me just slide in. I can't hold on much longer. Your cunt! It's . . .

'No, wait – let's do it kneeling. Could you just turn over and sort of hump up on your knees? Oh, *please*. You must. We've got to kneel. We're monk and nun, you see. I'll go in really slowly. It won't hurt at all, I promise. That's it, that's quite fantastic. Now try and put your head down, so your body's sort of sloping, and I'll kneel over you. How does that feel, Sister? Can Brother Robert go in a bit further? He's not hurting, is he? Sure? Now, keep very very still, or Reverend Father Abbot may realise what we're doing and come storming up from chapel. No, you mustn't move like that, Sister. It's quite disgraceful for an untouched virgin. You'll have to do some penance. Christ! Do that again. Yes, grip like that, it's wonderful. Yes, I love it. I love you. Oh, Hilary, oh, Sister . . . !'

26

'Hey, Gloria, my sweet, don't you think we ought to celebrate tonight?'

'Celebrate? What for?' Hilary idled to the window, stared out across the downs. It was sad to see them parched and brown, the elms below the lighthouse already specked with rust, though it was officially high summer, when trees and fields were usually still lush, still flaunting in their prime.

Robert joined her at the window, stooped down to kiss her neck. 'You mean to say you've forgotten?' He shook his head, mock-angry. 'Try to work it out. What's the date today?'

The feast of Our Lady Queen of Heaven, she thought automatically. Our Lady's vestments at the Mass – the ones she'd sewn herself, in Mary's colours – white with a blue orphrey. She dragged her mind from Brignor, made it concentrate on Robert, on August in the world. 'Gosh! It's not your birthday, is it? I thought you said September.'

He laughed. 'No, not my birthday. Something we did together –very much together. I'll give you a clue. It's a two-months' anniversary.'

'Two months?'

'Mm.' He pulled her tee shirt up, slipped his hands beneath it, cupped them round her breasts. 'I can see I'm the real romantic, who remembers all the dates. Give up? Okay, I'll tell you.' He pressed his chest closer to her back, rubbed himself against her, like a cat. 'It's exactly two months to the day since our first night in bed together. I think that deserves a bit of a splash-out, don't you?'

'Yes,' she said, leaning back against him, eyes screwed up against the glare outside.

'You don't sound very keen, my love. What's the matter? Are you tired? I know I kept you up last night, but it was worth it, wasn't it?'

She nodded, caught her breath. Her nipples were still sore, and he was using both his thumbs to tease and fret them. She did feel tired, partly from the heat. It had been the driest, hottest summer for a decade; July a little cooler, but August aping June in its sweltering days and heavy sticky evenings, its mean and grudging rain, which had fallen only once in three long weeks. It seemed all wrong for England to see that thin and thirsty grass stretched taut across the dry bones of the hills; the pond reduced to a curve of hardening mud, the horizon lost in heat haze.

'So we'll have dinner out tonight, okay? Somewhere really grand.'

347

Robert smoothed her tee shirt down, gave a last tweak to the nipples through the fabric.

She dodged back to the fridge, to pour herself some orange juice, couldn't find the carton for the crush and scrum of packages jostling on the shelves – meat and fruit and salads they'd bought in last weekend, hardly touched at all. 'We've got so much food already, Robert. Isn't it a waste?'

'Gloria, my darling, am I ever going to change you?'

She didn't answer, just removed a pile of cheeses to try to find the juice. Robert said he loved her, then did his best to make her someone else – someone who loved going out, every night, and late; who kept chucking out expensive food; shrugged off waste and mess without a qualm. She glanced around the jumbled kitchen – lids off tea and coffee jars, books on greasy shelves. If she tried to make things orderly, he teased her, called her his boring little housewife. She was hardly that. The house was his – exclusively – his colour schemes, his furnishings, his choice of food and friends, his decision about mealtimes, even bedtime, his calendar, his clock. Yet why should she complain? He shared it with her, didn't he; invited her to come down each weekend, tried to make each special, did his best to please her? It was just that . . .

'*I*'d like to cook tonight,' she said, turfing out two mouldy heads of lettuce, then turning back to touch his arm, hot fingers on damp skin.

'You don't know how to cook.'

She flushed, withdrew her hand. 'I'm learning, aren't I?'

'Yes, but it's a chore.'

'No, it's not. I like it. I've never had much chance before. Liz always says she'll let me, then does it all herself.'

Robert yawned and stretched, revealing two wet patches spreading from his underarms. '*I*'d rather go out. There's this fantastic new restaurant just opened in East Grinstead.'

'Isn't East Grinstead rather far for just a dinner?'

He shrugged. 'Not really. We'll be there in twenty minutes, if we cut across country. Well – say half an hour.'

Fifty minutes, she corrected silently, as she rearranged the cheeses, softer ones on top. 'It's awfully hot for driving, though. It must be over eighty still and I've got this stupid headache.'

'It's far cooler in the car than stuck indoors, especially with the roof down.' He snapped a beer can open, foamed it over ice. 'They've got wild duck on tonight, braised in wine and juniper, and salmon in puff pastry, as a starter.'

'How d'you know?'

'I asked them. I phoned to book a table.'

She banged the fridge door shut. 'Why ask me what I want, then, if it's all arranged already?' She heard her voice sounding petulant, resentful, as she strode across the room, down the spiral staircase and out to Robert's patch of new-dug garden, now wilting in the heat. She needed to calm down, put some space between them. She was becoming sour and shrewish, getting far too blasé about her pampered life with Robert. Liz and Di would be grateful for those lavish dinners out, the constant generous presents – not carp because the gifts and meals were chosen not for her, but for some ideal abstract woman, or even for himself. She slumped down on a shelf of rock, stretched out her tanned legs. It was her fault more than Robert's: she couldn't love enough. The Abbess had remarked once that if you didn't love God, then you couldn't love man either – couldn't love His creatures or creation, couldn't love at all.

She looked up at the sky, a still and shimmering sky, inflamed with pink-tinged clouds. 'Teach me how to love,' she prayed, wondering if she'd ever stop these senseless prayers to No One. She had lost her God, and with Him, lost her capacity to love – if she'd ever had it. Even in the convent, where love of God and love of neighbour were stressed above all else, she had been more concerned with self, she realised now, with shame – saving her own soul, grooming herself to be a saint in heaven, an angel in the cloister, obsessively striving for her own cold and neat perfection. Had she ever really cared about another person, ever learned to give and share?

She bent to grub a weed out, hands hurting on the hard unyielding earth. She owed so much to Robert. He had taught her such a lot: how to sleep late; how to drive his car; how to choose flattering female clothes; how to play a score of games from golf to chess to tennis; how to view the world without blinkers or dark glasses; even how to live without a God. So why was she not satisfied; why resentful even now, as she glanced around his garden? *His* garden, yes – completely. She had suggested simple country flowers – lupins, foxgloves, hollyhocks – which wouldn't mind the dry and chalky soil, or need a lot of nannying. He had overruled her, insisted on exotic strains; showy flowers like tiger lilies, moody ones like edelweiss. His lilies were now dying, and even his azaleas looked limp and undersized.

She rubbed her forehead, tried to knead the pain away. Robert hated headaches, suspected she invented them. She couldn't really blame him. He was never ill himself, never even tired. He'd poured out care and sympathy when she'd truly been in pain, smarting from the cuts and weals she'd inflicted on herself. She couldn't expect that same intense devotion when there was nothing really wrong with her – nothing bar a throbbing head and a heavy cramping period, which had come on just that morning.

She eased up to her feet, climbed back to the kitchen. Robert was still sitting quaffing beer, eyes half-closed, blond hair dark with sweat. She wished he'd come to find her. It was always her who had to make the overtures. She jerked her head impatiently, flinching at the pain. Would she never learn to love him, think about his needs and pains, instead of just her own, put him first, for once? She crept up close behind him, arms around his shoulders, mouth against his hair.

'I love you,' she said softly.

He didn't seem to hear, just pulled her round to face him, hands reaching for her breasts again. 'So what are you going to cook?' he teased. 'For our celebration dinner? Shepherd's pie and junket, or bangers and baked beans?'

'No,' she said. 'We're going out. I've got this sudden weird craving for salmon in puff pastry and wild duck braised in juniper and wine.'

'So how was Sussex?' Della asked, bursting into Hilary's room in her new beautician's uniform.

'Er . . . fine.'

'Mum said you went to some new fantastic nosh-place and had morning-gathered frogs' legs, or whatever.'

'Yes, we did. Last night.'

'Lucky you! The food we get at Cedars is unspeakable.' Della frowned into the mirror, pulling at her skirt. 'You're back early, aren't you? Mum said I wouldn't see you, that Robert always whisked you back in the early hours of Monday morning, as if he couldn't bear to part with you.'

She flushed. 'Well, sometimes, yes.'

'Actually, you've saved my life. I'm meant to be off duty, but they're laying on this thrash tonight, and want me back at bloody six o'clock. I've got to help pour drinks and stuff and they insist I wear my uniform. Just look at it! I tried to take it in myself and messed the whole thing up. You couldn't be an angel and do something with it, could you, Hil? I'm desperate. I've got to catch the 4.14 from Paddington, which means leaving here just an hour from now.'

Hilary joined her at the mirror, inspected the botched seams. 'What's the problem with the fit? Is it just too big on top, or . . . ?'

'Well, it's very baggy there, but the waist looks really weird, as well. I've made it all uneven.'

'Yes, I see. Don't worry. We can sort that out quite easily. I'll just go and fetch the scissors and some pins.'

'Thanks, Hil. You're a saint. God! Was I relieved to see you. Mum's out, you see, and the thought of appearing at a party in this . . . They'd

350

go stark staring mad. They're paranoid about the way we look. I mean, we're meant to be professionals, trained and everything, and they're still treating us like schoolkids.'

Hilary started pinning, making darts around the bust, evening out the waist. 'I thought you liked the job.'

'It's okay, I suppose. I was thrilled at first, just because it's snazzy and a health farm sounded fun. But the hours are real slave labour. This is the first weekend I've had off in a month, and then they haul me back, expect me to act waitress, as well as mere beautician. Ouch! Those pins are vicious.'

'I'm sorry, Della, but if you could just stand really still. That's better.' Hilary took two paces back, to check the fit, secured a few last pins. 'Now, try to ease it off as gently as you can . . . Careful! Right, that's it. If you want to get dressed, I'll bring it down the minute that it's done. It won't take all that long.'

'No. I'll wait for it.' Della draped herself across a chair, feet up on the sides, thighs straining through her skintight lacy slip. 'It's too hot to get dressed, and apart from just my top things, I'm ready, more or less.' She watched Hilary unpick the seams, then examined her own nails, all scarlet and extremely long, bar just one casualty. She reached out for a nailfile, smoothed its jagged edge. 'D'you like that Robert character?' she asked.

Hilary looked up, startled. She was always thinking in terms of love, feeling all the burden of the word – its claims, its obligations, her own deficiencies. 'Like' was different, easier. 'Yes,' she said. 'I do.'

'*I* don't. He's a wanker. Still' – she shrugged – 'each to his own, as Mum is always saying.' She checked her watch. 'Where *is* Mum? I wish she'd get a move on. She's driving me to Paddington, but if she doesn't get back soon, I'll have to take the tube and lug my case. I only came back really to get a few last things, yet they seem to weigh a ton. God knows how I'll fit them in my room. You're jolly lucky, Hilary. Your room's twice the size of mine *and* gets all the sun. I've got one mingy little skylight facing north, and no room to swing a cat, and then they have the cheek to charge the earth for it, dock it from my wages. Mum's far too soft with you.'

Hilary was grateful for the whir of the machine, which prevented her from answering, covered her embarrassment. Della drew her chair up, peered down at the stitching, waited for a lull. 'You probably just don't realise how high most normal rents are. It'll be quite a shock, I bet, when you start looking for another place. You know Mum's moving, don't you?'

'*Moving?*'

'Yeah. Good old Uncle Harry! *He* suggested it – wants to share his home with her, drag her up to Scarborough to live. He says it's crazy for them to keep on two big houses and flog up and down each month, wasting precious time and petrol. I reckon all he's really after is a live-in cook and bottle-washer, but he'd never say that, would he? Anyway, Mum's hooked, agreed to go and everything. The only problem is she can't bring herself to turf you out, or even mention it. She's had a word with Ivan and he's already found another room in Richmond, but she's frightened you'll collapse, I think, if she so much as opens her mouth. I told her there were other pads in London and about half a million house-agents, all dying to let their flats, not to mention every local paper crammed with vacant bedsits, but . . . ' She made a face. 'To tell the truth, I'm jolly glad I'm out of it. I loathe that Harry character. I mean, the way he treats my mother like his lapdog, expecting her to move up North, away from all her friends. Why can't he come down here and live in London?'

Hilary tried to hide her shock, the sudden surge of panic which had clawed her chest and stomach, even lamed her voice. 'Well, h . . . he's tied down by his business, I assume. He couldn't leave it, could he, Della? It's very much a local thing. And isn't he important on the council, hoping to be Mayor or . . . ?'

'Oh, yeah, Mum loves all that. I suppose she sees herself as Lady Mayoress. What a hoot! By the way, perhaps I ought to tell you that Di's considering going up as well now. Mum tried to make me promise not to say a word, but you're bound to hear it anyway, from someone in the shop. They're really having problems. You must know that, at least.'

'Well, yes, I . . . '

'That bloody place – what's it called?'

'"Mam'zelle".'

'Yeah. Rotten pigs! I mean, setting up two doors away and snitching all her customers. That could mean instant death for Di, or at least a slow decline. Except Hero Harry comes up trumps again, says has she ever thought of moving North herself, that there's far less competition away from the South-East, and he could help her find really super premises, and if she's worried about the cost, well – nudge-nudge, wink-wink – he knows a good few people and could pull a good few strings. Talk about wooing the mother via the daughter, except it's usually vice versa. He's so old, poor Grandpa Harry, he should be moving to a rest-home, not trying to set up a harem with Mum and Di and . . . Do you know, he even tried to rope me in, as well, said he could help me land a job in one of Scarborough's top hotels. I'll get my own jobs, thanks.'

Hilary kept treadling the machine, guiding the white fabric with shaky sweating hands. If the Kingsleys moved up North, she would lose everything at once – her room, her job, her livelihood, her 'family'; would be alone again, and unemployed. She was appalled to think that nobody had told her, that Liz and Di had hushed the whole thing up, been discussing all their futures secretly and privately, without involving her. Was it true what Della said, though – that she was still too vulnerable and spineless to be included in such things, must always be babied, for fear she might collapse?

Della yawned and stretched, started jabbing with her nailfile at the chair. 'Hey, you won't tell Mum I told you, will you, Hilary?'

She shook her head, voice still understrength.

'Promise? Cross your heart? She'd do her nut if . . . '

'No, I won't, of course not.' She felt guilty promising, as if she were betraying Liz, keeping secrets from her, as Liz had done with her. She reversed the stitching on the machine, to finish off the seam, then stood up, shook the skirt out. 'I . . . I'll just give this a press, Della. I'll use the iron downstairs.' She had her own iron in her room, but she needed an excuse to be alone, to sort out the confusion churning in her mind. Why hadn't Liz included her, as well, suggested that she join them in the move, continue her work in Di's new Scarborough shop? Liz knew quite well that she didn't want to live with Robert, preferred her independence and her job, so that couldn't be the reason. Perhaps Harry disapproved of her, or Di had found another girl, more skilful, more congenial. Or maybe Liz herself had wearied of their friendship. Harry must have more or less proposed, yet she hadn't said a word about it, had left her out completely, left her in the dark.

She tripped on Stephen's engine, as she walked into the kitchen, paused to pick it up. The move would suit them all, even Steve. Di was worried about his school, and now she'd seen it for herself she couldn't really blame her. They'd probably find a better school in Scarborough, with smaller classes, fewer louts and bullies, even less pollution in the air. She and Luke would be left behind, to make out how they could.

She hadn't even seen Luke for a month, felt suddenly abandoned, totally alone. She was losing everybody – Ivan moving out to Richmond when she hadn't yet managed a *rapprochement*, still felt nervous and embarrassed in his presence; Luke stuck in his own home, the feud with Steve unhealed. Still no word from Eva, and no God to keep her safe. And now Liz, her closest friend, sneaking up to Scarborough in secret, concealing her big news, confiding in everyone but her. She couldn't even turn to Robert – they'd had their first real quarrel, just today, which was why she'd come back early, come back on the train.

She slammed the iron along the seams, furious with herself. She was useless at relationships. Liz saw her as a baby, Robert as a prude. She'd been spinsterish and squeamish to object to making love just because she had a heavy period; selfish to suggest a walk when she knew he liked to spend his Sundays drinking in the pub. She must phone him right away, try to make amends, return there next weekend and really make an effort, do the things he wanted, and do them with real love. Except that wouldn't solve the problem. She was still losing Liz, losing job and home. The lighthouse wasn't home, was too much Robert's project, and somehow too eccentric for a home. And how would she earn money, find herself another job in the middle of the downs?

Fear began to gripe again, knotting up her stomach, drumming in her head. She switched on the radio, searched through all the stations for a concert. That would calm her down, help distract her mind. Ah, Berlioz! The overture to *Beatrice and Benedict*, one of Robert's favourites – hers as well, since she'd discovered the opera just a month or so ago, instantly responding to its passion, its intensity. Only last night, Robert had been talking about a brilliant new recording of all the Berlioz overtures by a young Viennese conductor, still only in his twenties. She'd scour the shops for it, take it down on Friday as a present and a peace offering, a gift to match his own.

She rested the iron a moment, to relish the sudden rich crescendo, as clarinets and oboes joined the frenzied strings. She remembered him conducting it – chisel as a baton, leaping on a chair to control his wayward orchestra, arms flung up, hair wild – Berlioz himself.

'I do love you, crazy Robert,' she told him, told herself, as she continued with her pressing, iron dawdling now to match the slower tempo of the woodwind. Could there really be much wrong with their relationship, if they had Berlioz in common?

'Shall we play it just once more?'

'It's a bit late, darling – nearly two a.m.'

'Oh, come on, Sleeping Beauty, I'll let you off the rest, if we can just have *Le Corsaire* again. That last bit's so fantastic – the way he really drives the strings, as if he's got a whip behind them. D'you realise, he's only twenty-six?'

'Yes, you said.' Hilary stretched out on the rumpled bed, put the pillows back where they belonged. They had been out for dinner, then made love; a long and languid dinner, a fierce and almost frantic love. She'd tried her best to scorch her worries out of her, burn them down to ash in the heat and force of Robert's ramming body. It had worked, for half an hour.

354

'What's wrong, my sweet? You're not still fretting, are you? I'll kill that wretched Harry for upsetting you like this. Except if it wasn't him, it would be someone else – someone worse, most likely, who lived even further off, in the Hebrides, or something. I mean, it was bound to happen sometime, with Liz still so attractive – well, very warm and loving, if not a raving beauty, and anyway, that house is far too big for her. It must be quite a strain having to keep up all the payments and look after everyone.'

Hilary hardly heard him. She knew all the rational arguments. It was the irrational fears which hurt. She turned over, punched the pillow. 'Robert . . . ?'

'What?'

'Liz didn't tell you, did she? I mean, she seems to have confided in everyone but me. I'd hate to think you knew, as well, and didn't say a word.'

'No, honestly, I didn't know. I've hardly even seen Liz. I'm just not that surprised. Look, we'll discuss it in the morning, over coffee and fried eggs. My mind won't be so soggy then. Okay? Right now it's time for Berlioz.'

She leaned back, tried to concentrate, forget her need for sleep. It was not that easy anyway to sleep in Robert's bed. She'd never shared a bed till this last summer, found it wonderful in one way – the warmth, the closeness, the end to all her night fears – exhausting in another. Robert tossed and threshed a lot, got up in the wee small hours for drinks of water, visits to the bathroom, or to share some vivid dream or wild idea, or simply because his body demanded hers. Shameful to admit that she was sometimes quite relieved when she returned to Liz's house and enjoyed seven hours' unbroken sleep in her own tranquil single bed.

Robert stretched beside her, hand creeping up her nightdress. She wished he wouldn't fondle her to music. It seemed somehow disrespectful to that brilliant young conductor, to Berlioz himself.

'Happy, darling?'

'Mm.'

'We were great tonight, weren't we?'

She nodded, kissed his neck.

'You inspire me, drive me wild.' He laughed and grabbed her hand, bit the tip of every finger. 'You were pretty wild yourself, you know. Hey, where you off to?'

'Just to . . . you know.' 'Pee' was still a word she hadn't mastered. It seemed so vulgar, yet Robert hated all her coy alternatives. She slipped out to the bathroom, horns and trumpets following. Thank God they had no neighbours. Robert always played his music late and loud. The recording *was* fantastic – she was as thrilled with it as he was – but now she longed for silence, not that fierce exalting brass. She closed the door, shut them out, picked up a pile of bathtowels lying on the floor, started cleaning out the basin. Every time he shaved, Robert left his whiskers stubbling the white porcelain, plus a ring of dirty foam. Stupid to complain, or feel secretly resentful when he didn't clean the bath. They were such footling, petty things. Would Berlioz have worried about lids off Maxwell House jars or tidemarks round the bath? She grinned, left one damp and soggy towel still crumpled on the floor – deliberately, to prove she could – to break her links with fussy Sister Hilary, whom she was determined to kill off.

Hilary drained her orange juice, followed it with tea; seemed to share the thirst of the parched and languid landscape. She glanced up from the breakfast table. Everything looked dusty outside the lighthouse windows – dusty earth, dusty grass, even dusty air. The midges were already out, hanging in black clouds; other hidden insects throbbing out their ecstasy at another scorching day.

Robert buttered toast, dug his egg-smeared fork into the marmalade, eyes fixed on the jar. He'd said almost nothing since they'd first sat down to breakfast, seemed preoccupied and tense.

She filled his cup – and hers – passed him milk and sugar. 'Are you all right, darling?'

'Mm.'

'Not suffering any ill effects from those prawns you ate last night?'

'Oh, no, they were superb.' He rooted in the jar, speared two large snakes of peel, arranged them on his toast. 'I didn't sleep too well. I had this really way-out dream – all about Mohammed.'

'*Mohammed?*'

He nodded, pushed his plate away, suddenly snapped up from the table, started pacing up and down. 'He was on my mind last night.' His voice was nervous, almost brusque, as he spoke in jabs, addressing the slate floor. 'Mohammed was a great devotee of marriage, unlike Jesus Christ. He must have married nine or even ten times after his first beloved wife died, which makes him quite an authority on the subject.' He stopped, turned back to face her. 'And d'you know what he said about it?'

She shook her head, burnt her mouth on a gulp of scalding tea. His nervousness was catching. He was standing very close to her, eyes intense, both hands tightly clenched, as if he were trying to control some deep emotion.

'That marriage is half of religion and when husbands and wives hold

356

hands, their sins disappear through the touch of their fingers.' He paused, to clear his throat. 'You were talking about sin last night.'

'I *wasn't*, Robert.'

'Yes, you were – in your sleep.'

She blushed. Would she ever stifle Sister Mary Hilary, kill her off completely?

'You kept telling me you'd sinned, as if I was your priest and could absolve you.'

'Oh, Robert, no! How stupid.'

'Not stupid. Perhaps I can.' He uncurled his fingers, held all ten up and out to her, as if playing patacake. 'Will you be my wife?' he asked, his voice still gruff, uncertain.

She had never heard such silence. Every brash and boastful bird seemed to have stilled its morning prattle to listen to her answer. The kettle had switched off; both of them stopped breathing. She shifted on her chair, to prove she could still move, wasn't fully paralysed. A dozen different pictures were swarming in her mind – Captain Robert Harrington rescuing her from drowning, his Easter Sunday lilies smiling on her altar; the sweltering four-poster with its stifling blood-red curtains; his red-flame voice as he lambasted her last Sunday. The pictures gave no answer, were shouting at each other, quarrelling, conflicting, like the voices in her head. Yet Robert's hands were still held up; must be really aching.

She tried to form a word, except she didn't know which word. There were only two available, and both seemed quite impossible. The hands themselves were mesmerising, strong tanned hands, clever hands – imploring her, beseeching.

Slowly, very slowly, she lifted up her own hands, so that palm grazed palm, fingertip met fingertip. Then, suddenly, his fingers slipped down between her own, gripped, and slowly closed. She shut her eyes, felt her sins evaporate, as Mohammed's words had promised; her guilts and fears drift away like smoke – all her petty grievances submerge beneath a soaring wave of sudden total joy.

27

Gloria could feel every eye upon her, admiring the full skirt and sweeping train of her wild silk wedding dress. A borrowed dress, like her borrowed seed-pearl necklace, her borrowed high-heeled shoes, her borrowed brace of bridesmaids, her borrowed father. Her 'father's' arm felt stiff and almost cold. She herself was burning with excitement and sheer nerves; melting in the lights, melting in the heat of the candles in the church. She only hoped her hair would keep its curl. She had suffered agonies last night trying to sleep in rollers, trying to sleep at all. She had never worn it quite so long; had grown it specially for today, could feel it now, heavy on her shoulders. She shouldn't be thinking of trivial things like hairstyles, but reflecting on the service, on her future.

It was hard to concentrate on anything save each wobbling step along the treacherous shiny parquet. The shoes were quite absurdly high, made walking near impossible, and though she'd practised for at least half an hour last night, it was much harder with an audience, a train. The veil, too, felt very strange, floating out behind her, gauzy round her face, anchored by a wreath of heavy flowers. More flowers on the altar, their heady fragrance mingling with the odour of hot wax; the solemn scent of incense choking in her throat. Sun flooded through the windows, made a shifting pattern on the floor. She walked across the golden latticework, watched the sunlight explode against brass vases, rainbow whitewashed walls. The weather was still sultry; a ripe and lush September gilding the brown dregs of shrivelled August.

She almost missed her footing, was steadied by the burly man who was acting father, giving her away. She wished she knew him better, longed for her own father to be there instead, on this key day in her life. And if only the six bridesmaids were her nieces or her cousins, not someone else's relations – the whole troupe of them in pale pink tulle and matching floral wreaths. Six was far too many and tulle absurdly fancy. She would have preferred a simpler ceremony, with fewer frills, less pomp, but she'd been completely overruled. Everyone had told her that this was her big day, the most crucial in her life so far, so she had to make the most of it.

She smiled at the smallest of the bridesmaids, entrusted her bouquet to the taller gap-toothed one. All their names were muddled, all the smiling faces swimming in a haze of jumbled colours. Her own smile seemed far too broad, pulling at her ears, eating up her face; sweat sliding down her body beneath the silky dress, as she walked along the passage towards the heavy enclosure door. Her 'father' had to leave her there, let go her arm, withdraw. She felt orphaned, suddenly, as he unlatched his arm from hers; as flimsy as a scrap of tissue paper, which might simply blow away. Her other Father seemed to tower above her, as she knelt before him on the polished wood; he, too, dressed in white, elaborate white brocade; strange contrast with his battered broad black shoes.

'Bless, Reverend Father, my entrance into this holy house.'

Drops of holy water splattered on her face, a welcome shock of cold against her flaming cheeks. The Latin blessing sounded as if it came from miles away, the well-known words barely making sense to her. She struggled to her feet again, hampered by both train and veil, tried to find her mother's face in the crowd of friends jostling round the door. Could they be her friends? They seemed so unfamiliar, people from another life; their faces looming, blurring; their garish fussy outfits smudging like wet paint. She turned her back, then slowly, tremblingly, stepped across the threshold; the enclosure door swinging shut behind her, a weighty wooden barrier which would cut her off for ever from the swarming world outside. For a second, she was dazzled, blinking in the blaze of fifty flickering candles; light glinting on steel spectacles, reflected back from shining silver crosses; white teeth bared in smiles, black robes closing in. High and joyous voices were shrilling out a welcome.

> I rejoiced when I heard them say
> Let us go into God's house.

Dry lips pecked her cheek, toothpaste breath wafted in her face, as each nun bent to kiss her – no real contact, just stiff coifs poking in her eyes, the brush of musty habits against her own silk dress. Then she took her place in the file of chanting nuns, white against their black; each holding up a candle, as they processed through the enclosure, past the vestment room, the chapter room, the refectory, the kitchen. She glanced in at the kitchen door, hoped to glimpse the wedding cake. Sister Cook had baked it – a grand two-tier affair, with icing sugar doves for peace, icing sugar lilies for purity, virginity. Two separate tiers, two separate teas. The nuns would have theirs in the dim and panelled refectory, shielded from the sun; the family and visitors in the newly painted extern parlour which had bigger windows, slightly softer chairs. Her mother would abhor that, still didn't understand why they couldn't eat together, might even weep into her cake, as she had been weeping in the chapel, weeping through the service; her sobs a racking descant to the singing. Mr Reed was absent, had brought his wife and daughter to the convent gates, but refused to come inside, refused to give his child away; couldn't face the sight of the rich and glittering bride being stripped and plucked and shorn; reappearing as a beggar in black robe and bare feet.

'It's a day of *joy*,' she whispered to him silently. 'Not mourning, not hostility.' Doves for peace. If only he would make his peace with her, turn up even now, in time for the second and most crucial part of the ceremony, or at least in time for tea. She reached forward to cut him the first and largest slice of cake, a slice with two white doves on. The doves were works of art, with silver beaks and eyes, even the details of their plumage tooled into the icing. She felt her hand slam against a pane of glass, reeled back in pain and shock. She was standing in the High Street, outside Liz's favourite bakers, the window full of buns and bread, a two-tier wedding cake resplendent on a silver stand. The same icing sugar lilies, the same icing sugar doves, the same four white fluted pillars holding up the top tier. Just one small difference: this cake had a couple on, an icing sugar bride with an icing sugar bridegroom.

Her own Bridegroom had been invisible; ineffable, but invisible. The eye of faith could see Him, standing there beside her satin-covered prie-dieu, stretching out His nail-pierced hands, as she made her vows to Him. But the eye of faith was blinded now. Her Groom had died two thousand years ago, died again this April, at the conference. She had been a widow on her wedding day, lacking both her husband and her father.

Suddenly, she pushed the door, strode up to the counter. 'Do you sell those icing sugar figures – you know, like the ones on that big cake in the window, the little bride and groom?'

'I'm sorry, Madam, but they're not sold separately – only with the cake itself, and that cake's cardboard, actually. But if you're planning a wedding, we can make you an identical cake, or any design you choose.'

She shook her head, kept hearing that word 'cardboard'. A cardboard wedding, cardboard faith.

'Or if you'd like to try the mixture first, we've got these miniature cakes. They're really just for fun – only four inches across, but they're very good, very rich. We don't do a wedding one, but we've got happy birthday, happy anniversary . . . '

She walked out of the shop, her miniature anniversary cake ribboned in its box. Her steps faltered as she ran into the rude slap of the sun again: busy traffic, bustling shoppers, trembling in its glare – the same hot relentless weather as twenty-one years ago, and exactly the same date. September 8, the birthday of the Blessed Virgin Mary and the solemn anniversary of her Clothing.

'What's a Clothing?' Liz had asked her, just a week or so ago, and she'd felt the same surprise that Liz didn't know the word, as Liz must have felt herself when trying to explain the meaning of words like gig or Watergate. Despite her explanation, Liz seemed unimpressed; didn't seem to understand the bridal symbolism – how you had to look your best, like any worldly bride, wear finery and jewels to be worthy of your Bridegroom; how she'd grown her hair specially for her Lover, so there'd be more of it to sacrifice.

'It sounds quite macabre to me, and anyway, the whole affair must have cost a bomb. Who paid for all that junketing and where did you get the dress?'

'Oh, the convent always had a few. Some real brides donated them. I suppose they liked to feel their wedding dress would be worn again by a bride of Christ, rather than moulder in a cupboard gathering moth. Or some girls' mothers made them.' Her elaborate borrowed gown had belonged to a Sister Mary Julia, whose mother had sewn it as an act of love, all fifty yards of it, including train and veil; a last tribute to a treasured honoured daughter. It was, indeed, last tribute, as Sister Mary Julia had died within six months of her Clothing; obviously beloved of God, so Mother Mistress said, since He had claimed her back so soon. The seed-pearls and the bridesmaids' dresses were also Sister Julia's. She had felt a little uneasy with a corpse's necklace round her throat, a corpse's glamour disinterred to grace a second ceremony; had longed, in fact, to have her own much simpler dress, home-sewn with love and pride.

She had tried to reassure Liz, who'd still seemed disapproving. 'It's completely different these days. They've done away with all the bridal trappings and replaced them with a very simple ceremony, with no special dress or cake or anything. In fact, my Clothing was the last one in our convent.' Which made it very special, she'd thought, but hadn't said. The older nuns looked back to it, remembered it with awe and deep emotion, still got out the photographs to marvel at her dress. The dress itself had been made into a chasuble and was worn by the chaplain at Easter, Christmas, all important feasts. Was that why she had left on Christmas Eve – because she couldn't face the sight of Father Martin vested once again in that wedding-shroud which coffined all her girlish hopes, aroused such deep emotions?

'Thank God for that!' Liz picked up her knife. She had been preparing vegetables, continued chopping carrots with an indignant jabbing relish. 'I think it's plain sadistic, dressing nuns as brides.'

'It had its funny side,' she'd said, trying to take a lighter tone, damp down Liz's anger. 'I mean, you should have seen my shoes! They were dug out from the play-clothes trunk and dated from the early 1930s –white satin things with ankle straps and diamanté buckles, and so high I couldn't walk. Mother Mistress made me practise parading up and down the refectory. I must have looked a sight. I had to wear the shoes above my thick black woolly stockings and with my postulant's black dress. And then she pinned these two huge white bathtowels on my neck, so I'd get used to walking with a train.'

'You're joking!'

'I'm not. In fact, I was terrified I'd laugh. She took it very seriously and we practised in dead silence. It was awful being the one and only postulant. If there'd been a couple more, at least we might have shared a private giggle. But vocations were already falling off. Everything sort of blew up in the sixties. Nuns started leaving, especially in America. The year I entered – 1966 – they were walking out in thousands in the States, even those who'd been in half a lifetime. I heard that as a novice and was deeply shocked.'

'And then you left yourself. How ironical, my love.'

Yes, how ironical, she thought, as she forced herself to walk down to the jeweller's, three doors from 'Mr Bun'. She had come out to the High Street not to buy a cake, but to get her ring sawn off. She'd been trailing up and down for half an hour, not daring to go in. She had phoned several different jewellers to ask if they could do it; only Ratners had the special instrument. 'It's called a ring-saw,' the friendly man had said. 'But it's really only like a pair of scissors with a little wheel on top.'

She bowed her head, glimpsed the shining pointed scissors in Reverend Mother's hands, felt the sudden shock of steel against her skull, heard the scrunch of butchered hair. Fair curls falling, foaming, into the little wicker basket held out by Mother Mistress. The basket filling, overflowing, as the nuns sang the *Magnificat*; her mother's anguished wails cutting through the hymn of thanks and praise. She stared into the steel-framed jeweller's window, saw not rings and bracelets, but her ragged convict's head, the hair hacked off anyhow, standing up in ugly stupid tufts. For a second, she felt outrage, disbelief; the same shocked incredulity as she had experienced at the ceremony itself. She had gone to all that trouble setting it in rollers in her cell, and without a mirror, which made it much more difficult. She had been a woman then, a woman with her accoutrements of hairnets, setting lotions; a pretty girl with thick blonde hair swinging round her shoulders. Now she had been neutered at a stroke. She checked herself in horror, guilty at such thoughts. She was a bride still, not a convict, a virgin dying to the world, who must make this gift with joy, a gift demanded by her Bridegroom who demanded everything, including her whole womanhood.

She had tried to pray, beg pardon for her vanity, rebellion, as they led her to the robing-room just outside the chapel. She had stood motionless and contrite as Mother Mistress's bony hands started tugging at her clothes; other hands reaching out to undo fiddly buttons, unpin her heavy wreath. A rustle of white silk, and she was blinded for a moment as the wedding dress was whisked above her head, replaced by heavy serge. She was no longer tall and wobbling on high heels, but small and safe and humble in bare feet. Drawstrings pulled tight, tight, around her head, to restrain her vain and worldly thoughts, keep her mind fixed on God alone. There seemed so many layers; layers of fabric muffling sounds, denying all her curves; layers of padding between her and other people, so they would never come too close. She was moving in a daze, blinking once again in the bright lights of the chapel; kneeling at the grille to receive the white veil of the novice, the girdle, cross and rosary, the Rule and breviary, but not the ring, not yet. That came four years later, when she made her final vows; slipped on her finger by her Bridegroom's representative, never to come off.

'Never?' she whispered, as she pushed the plate glass door, walked into the shop. A young but shabby couple were choosing matching wedding rings, their two heads touching as they leant across the counter. She approached the other counter, spoke as low as possible.

'Yes, no problem, Madam. You're the one who phoned, aren't you? I was expecting you today. Just relax. It'll only take a moment.'

She couldn't watch as the vicious metal wheel cut into the silver with its sacrilegious teeth. 'This won't hurt,' the man said, reaching for the pliers. She heard only the priest's voice, deeper and more solemn. 'Receive this ring, for you are betrothed to the eternal King. Keep faith with your Bridegroom so that you may come to the wedding feast of eternal joy and . . . '

'Madam, madam!' She felt someone tap her face, strong fingers grip her arm. 'Are you all right? You're not going to faint on me, I hope. It's all finished now, all over.'

She opened her eyes, stared down at her marked but naked finger; the desecrated ring hacked apart, so that it no longer formed a circle, symbol of eternity, of union.

'You had me frightened for a moment. You went so pale, I thought you'd just keel over. I didn't hurt you, did I?'

'No,' she lied; wished she could remove the hurt as simply as the two small scraps of silver, which she wrapped in a Kleenex, transferred to her purse. The cross itself was whole still, but the 'J' had been severed from the 'oy', her always elusive happiness now reduced to gibberish.

'What a darling little cake, Hil. Where ever did you get it?'

'"Mr Bun".'

'I've never seen them there.' Liz smoothed out the ribbon from the box, tied it in a bow in Hilary's hair. 'You are a funny girl, you know. I'd have thought the last thing you wanted was to celebrate that gruesome anniversary.'

'It's not for that. It's . . . another celebration. One they didn't have a cake for.' Hilary rummaged in the cupboard, made a pretence of looking for a cake-stand, so she could hide her burning face, prepare that one brief line, which still seemed so difficult to phrase. She'd been rehearsing it for days now, trying to break her news to Liz, yet somehow always hesitant, embarrassed. She'd kept hoping Liz would get in first, divulge her own proposal, discuss the move to Scarborough, the plan to live with Harry; couldn't mention it herself without betraying Della. She had resented Liz's silence, seen it as a barrier between them, the first failure of their friendship. Whatever Liz's motives, her secrecy still hurt.

She was also worried that Liz might think she'd agreed to marry Robert only because she'd lost her home and job and had nowhere else to go. That wasn't true, in fact. Even in ten days, she had learned to love him more, come to see that his dominance, untidiness, had their positive and good sides. The untidiness meant he was relaxed, not fussy and uptight as she still was, alas. And his dominance made him confident, decisive; helped overcome her own constant dithering. It was Robert who had urged her to have her ring sawn off, so she'd be free to wear his own ring, break with her nun's past. Life at Brignor had been totally unreal. Stupid, even selfish, to try to recreate it in the outside world, its rigid punctuality, its pettifogging rules. With Robert's help, she could throw off those restrictions, learn to live more fully and more freely.

She turned back to Liz, still without the cake plate, took a deep breath in. 'Robert asked me to marry him,' she said. 'We . . . We're officially engaged.'

'*What?*' Liz leapt up to her feet, her whole face and stance and body expressing amazement and delight. 'You said "yes", I hope, my love.'

She nodded.

'Hilary, that's wonderful, fantastic. Hell! I wish we had champagne. Shall we drink a toast in sherry?'

Hilary groped towards a chair, feeling shaky suddenly. 'I'd rather have a nice hot cup of tea.'

Liz laughed and filled the kettle. 'You're still the nun, aren't you?'

'No,' she said more sharply than she'd meant. 'I'm not.'

'Christ! I'm so excited for you. When's the wedding going to be?'

'I don't know. Robert said this month, but . . . '

'This month? That's far too soon! What about your dress and . . . ?'

'I want to keep it very simple, Liz, no fuss and frills at all.'

'But you'll have to have a party – just a little one, and a cake, of course, and . . . Look, I'll arrange it, love. You needn't worry about a thing. If the weather holds, we could have it in the garden, maybe even hire a small marquee. Gosh! Wait till I tell Della. I'm allowed to tell, am I? It's not meant to be a secret?'

'No.'

'Well, let's cut this dinky cake and drink our Château-bottled Typhoo. Here's to you and Bob. Long life and happiness.'

Hilary cut the cake in two – half for each of them – felt fiercely disappointed to discover it was stale, the mixture dry, the icing hard and yellowing. Had it been there months – the baker's customers more concerned with fighting for divorces than counting anniversaries? Liz hardly seemed to notice, ate her piece with relish, using the cardboard box as plate. Her relief was almost palpable, spreading through the kitchen like the glow from a log fire. She hadn't said, 'Thank God you're off my hands, love,' but surely she was thinking it, and must certainly be wondering how to break her own news, since there was no excuse to hide it any longer. Hilary felt embarrassed for her, in the sudden pause which followed, realised she was searching for the words, as she had done herself. She longed to say, 'I *know*, Liz. You don't have to spell it out,' instead of feigning ignorance, as Liz suddenly leaned forward and started pouring out her story, though a rather different version from Della's, just two weeks ago.

'Congratulations, Liz!' she said, at last, having forced her face into various expressions of surprise, delight and sympathy, yet despising her deception while she did so. 'It sounds a marvellous plan. I mean, I presume you're keen to go, are you, and don't mind leaving London?'

'Well, it's a big upheaval, obviously, and I'll miss this house, in some ways, and things like shops and theatres, and all my friends, of course. But my immediate gut reaction was to get the hell up there, as fast as I could make it. The only thing which stopped me was *you*, my love. I've been half-paralysed not knowing how to tell you, and feeling such a heel at the thought of leaving you alone down here in London, without a room or job.' She licked her finger, scooped some cake crumbs up with it, retrieved a last raisin from her lap. 'Then Di got all upset, accused me of caring more for your concerns than hers. She's so worried about the shop, you see, not just that damned "Mam'zelle", but the fact they've

365

put the rates up for the second year running. Wimbledon's impossible – expensive, snobby, fickle. She can start again in Scarborough. It's a much more friendly place, and with Harry there to smooth the way . . . God! I'm so excited. I feel a new-born woman, now I can enjoy it, and make proper plans and everything, instead of fretting all the time about how it would affect you. It'll be a new start for us all – you and Robert, me and Harry. You must both come up and visit, come to one of Harry's ''dos''. Bob would love that, swanking in his tails and . . . '

Hilary put her piece of cake down, feeling still a little hurt that Liz should be so patently relieved; express no regret at all at their imminent separation, the two hundred and fifty miles which would divide them from now on. She understood the attractions from Liz's point of view – a smaller and more modern house, some help with all the bills, a man to share her life again – but all the same, she'd like to feel she mattered more to the first friend she'd ever had.

She touched her ringless finger, its narrow band of pale white skin a strange contrast to the deep tan of the rest. That finger was still branded, felt not light, but heavy, without its silver shackle, as if it weighed her down. The whole of Wandsworth seemed to have been staring at her hand as she walked back from the jeweller's; the hand itself swelling and distending with every step she took. Yet Liz hadn't appeared to notice it at all.

She kept rubbing at the mark, as if to add some colour to it, make it less conspicuous; wished she had Robert's ring already, to conceal that shaming symbol of the failure of her first life. She longed to start her second life – to experience success, and even joy – not joy in cold dead silver, but in a warm and living bond. Had he bought the ring, she wondered, and what would it be like? Unusual and expensive, almost certainly, since he was a generous and unusual man himself – two other things she loved him for, in fact.

Liz reached out for the sugar, seemed to read her thoughts. 'I must tell Harry your big news. It may spark the darling boy to propose himself.'

She looked up in surprise. 'I thought he had proposed.'

'Well, not officially. He's a real romantic underneath, but when it comes to things like property or houses, the businessman takes over, I'm afraid. And of course we've had so many problems as a family – Di's shop and my insurance and the mortgage on this place.' Liz stirred her tepid tea, now stewed, with scum on top. 'The poor lamb's been a brick, sorting out anything and everything. But give him time and he'll probably pop the question in his usual ardent style. In fact, he'll have to, won't he? I mean, as a councillor and a pillar of the community, he's in the public eye a lot, and I can see that public eye narrowing in horror if

366

he sets up home with a woman not his wife. I'm sure he'll have to regularise our union, to use a phrase his prissy fellow councillors are probably tossing round themselves. Mind you, I'm not so sure I want to change my name again. You'll be doing the same, of course. Mrs Hilary Harrington.' She frowned. 'Two H's. Bit of a mouthful, isn't it?'

'I wouldn't let it worry you. Robert calls me Gloria all the time now. I told you, didn't I? I wasn't keen at first, but I do think Gloria Harrington sounds better.'

Liz nodded. 'Yes, you're right. It must be rather muddling, though, to change both names at once.'

'I'm muddled up to here.' Hilary grinned, gestured to her forehead. 'There's so much to get used to.'

'You'll manage. Robert's worked wonders already. You're so much more relaxed now, different altogether.' Liz gave a sly collusive wink. 'Amazing what a bit of sex does, isn't it?'

Hilary tensed, got up to wash the teapot. There were certain subjects she had no wish to discuss; subjects best avoided even in her inmost private thoughts. Okay, so there were problems, but time would sort them out.

Liz joined her at the sink, reached out a friendly hand. 'Look, forgive me prying, love, but once you're married, are you going to . . . you know, think about a little Harrington Junior? I mean, is that the whole idea – marriage and a baby?'

Hilary swirled tea leaves down the sink. She could smell the dirty nappy which Rita Craddock had pushed into her hands, all those months ago, could still recall its repellent heavy sogginess. She had seen the baby since, on a visit to the Craddocks, way back in July, listened to it wailing the whole time she was there. 'Teething,' Rita said, as she got up for the umpteenth time to soothe it. Babies were so basic, so demanding. Could she really cope with dribble, vomit, faeces; be invariably supportive through teething, broken nights? If she had a baby in a year or two, she would be nearly the age that Rita was herself when she'd given birth to Luke – too old and tired for babies, and without Rita's simple capacity for love.

Liz was still waiting for her answer. 'Well, Robert's keen,' she forced herself to say, as she cleared the last clogged tea leaves from the plughole. Even with the condoms – which she loathed – she always felt frightened of conceiving, totally unsafe. The very possibility of creating a new life seemed overwhelming, arrogant. It was awesome enough to be co-creator with God, but to cobble up a baby with a mere mortal man who had his mind on other things was surely irresponsible.

Liz shook out a tea-towel, dried the heavy pot. 'You and Bob are bound to have a super kid – all blond and beautiful. His first son's quite a stunner, or he was when I last saw him, which was years and years ago. He can hardly be a child now, I suppose.'

Hilary rubbed tea-stains off a cup. Robert never appeared to phone his son, or write; had no recent photos of him, rarely mentioned him at all. He might be just as casual with a second child; crave it now, ignore it later on. If they had a child together, could either of them love and give enough? They were both divorced now – she from God, he from his first wife – and divorcés could be selfish and unstable.

'I'd be thrilled to bits to be Grandma Liz again. Or maybe I'll be unofficial godmother. A bit long-distance, though – that's the only problem. Can't you talk Robert into buying a new lighthouse on the north-east coast, or a Martello tower at Scarborough?'

'He may well do just that. He's involved with this new Trust, which saves threatened historic buildings. He got such a kick from doing up the Sussex place, he's keen to do some more. And he says it's a pretty painless way of making money.' Not completely painless, she reflected silently, as she rinsed the last odd teaspoon – at least not for her. She'd prefer to be more settled, to live in a conventional house, rather than a folly. Strange how other people were always sure you wanted things they wanted for themselves – lighthouses or five-star grand hotels, sexual games and fantasies, champagne, even babies. Or was she just a coward, scared of giving birth? She glanced across at Liz, could still recall that Caesarian scar, running down her stomach from her navel to her groin. Thirteen stitches, Liz had said. She shivered, changed the subject.

'When will you be moving, Liz?'

'I've no idea. I'll have to sell this house first – though that shouldn't be too difficult. I've already seen a couple of estate agents – one just down the road – and they both assured me that a family home in quite good nick in this particular part of Wandsworth won't be on my hands long. And Harry said the same.'

Hilary wrung out the dishcloth, started swabbing down the table. Again, she felt betrayed, as she realised Liz had been planning her new future, despite the paralysis of guilt she'd claimed; creeping off to house-agents, having secret talks with Harry, Ivan, Di – involving everyone but her. She flexed her ringless finger, still irrationally upset that Liz had failed to mention it. Thank God for Robert. He had saved her, in a way, saved her from herself, saved her from a bedsit in a strange and hostile house, spared her from returning to the Job Centre. How could she criticise him, when she owed him such a lot; when he'd offered her the chance to be a normal married woman, not a freak or outcast? His local pub in Sussex was called the Hope and Anchor. Wasn't that symbolical? He would be her security, her future; anchor her to this world, show her all its wonders, so she'd stop continually pining for another non-existent world, or a different sort of Saviour.

'Liz,' she said suddenly, abandoning the dishcloth and reaching for her bag. 'You know you said you wished we had champagne. Well, let's go out and buy some, the best bottle in the shop.'

28

'Drink up your champagne. It's only five minutes to closing time and it seems a shame to waste best bubbly.'

Hilary took her glass from Robert, drained it in one draught. She'd had too much already, felt strangely light and weightless, cut off from her body. Robert helped her up, said goodbye to Tony at the bar, strode out of the Hope and Anchor, sniffing the night air. 'Stale beer and honeysuckle. What a mixture! D'you want to drive, darling, or shall I?'

'You, please. I'm sure I'm past the limit, and anyway, I almost killed you last time.'

'No, you didn't. You're doing very well. I knew you'd be a natural all along. Otherwise I'd never have let you touch my precious car.'

'I'm honoured.' She glanced across at his low-slung scarlet sports car. It still felt very strange for her to drive it. It was so much Robert's toy – his aggressive shade of red, his powerful fine-tuned engine, his streamlined racy style. Yet she'd spent countless hours enthroned in that cramped driver's seat. Robert came to fetch her every Friday evening, and she drove him back to Sussex; then practised her night driving on the return run, late on Sunday. She got tired of travelling sometimes, but had no wish to lose her job before she had to, or before Di sold the shop, and it was still three weeks to the wedding. They had settled on the first week of October, to give Liz time to prepare her little party before she moved herself, moved up North with Harry, later in the autumn.

Robert helped her in, slammed his own door, then leaned across to kiss her. Her mouth felt slightly swollen. They'd made love all afternoon. He'd seemed voracious, almost violent, as if he couldn't get enough of her; had used his teeth, as well as just his tongue.

At last, he took the wheel, one hand on her thigh still, as he drove along the dark and narrow lane, humming his own slightly off-key rendering of the triumphal march from *Aida*.

'Where we going?' she asked, as he swung off to the left, instead of following their usual straight road home.

'Wait and see!'

The road began to climb, zigzagging through downland, a three-quarters moon bulging in the sky, showing up blurred trees and murky hedges. The swerving headlamps flushed out startled rabbits; a bird flapped up, a rush of wings, a cry. The countryside looked better in the darkness. The long relentless heatwave had sucked out all its green, parched and shrivelled it. It was only mid-September, but many leaves were already brittle brown; bracken fronds yellowing and tired; all nature limp and listless. Now it seemed revived. A lively south-west wind had started up that afternoon, heralding a change. Hilary could feel it gusty on her face as she wound the window down. It seemed to match Robert's own excitement. There was a tension in the car, like a live electric current charging her, as well, sending the speedometer slowly up and up. She never dared to drive so fast herself; was often scared when he did, but tonight she didn't care. Speed, champagne and shadows were flickering in her head, strobing her whole body, dissolving any fear. She shut her eyes. The motion felt like flying. She was soaring through the aether, an astronaut cut off from her spaceship, spinning into darkness, rotating with the earth.

'Hey, wake up, darling. This is where we stop.'

'I'm not asleep. I'm flying.'

'Good. You'll need to fly. It's the highest point in the entire South Downs. The officials got it wrong. They say it's Butser Hill, which must be forty miles away, across there to the west. They've set up a marker, with public loos and a kiosk selling ice lollies, turned it into a dreary tourist-spot. But this is my own private hill, and I'm pretty sure it's higher. Okay, I haven't actually measured it or done an ordnance survey. I just feel it in my gut. If you stand up on that knoll, your head knocks against the sky.' He gestured through the window at a dark and lowering shape. 'I wanted to bring you as close to heaven as I could. If we get out here and just walk up to the top . . .'

She could hardly stand against the wind, which seemed to be blowing straight from the Atlantic, spray and salt and all; no trees to break its force, no buildings to deflect it. The hill was like the highest deck of a huge ocean-going liner, totally exposed. She could see the lights of other ships pinpricking the horizon twenty miles away; coastal roads like narrow golden streamers flung down from the deck and shining far below. At their height, all was shadowed; swollen clouds caging in the moon and stars, then releasing them again – moody gaolers, now angry, now relenting.

'What a sky!' said Robert, clutching back his hair from the fierce grip of the wind.

'Yes, it's so dramatic, isn't it? The clouds look almost alive.'

'What d'you mean, "almost"? Of course they're alive. Everything's alive. We're part of it, all one.'

They didn't speak again till they reached the summit of the hill, needed all their energy to climb, all their concentration to see where

371

they were going. The moon's light was only grudging, the grass tussocky and rough. Hilary stopped a moment, gazed around at the sombre sweep of hill, aware of ghosts and presences. Neolithic man had farmed this land, mined its hills for flint. Bronze Age burial mounds still humped up from the ground, overgrown with brambles. Iron Age hill-forts had been set up on its heights, the dry chalk ridges offering sanctuary from the dense and humid forests which once threatened from below. If Robert were right and the past were still alive, then early man walked with them here; Roman traders were marching from the coast, unruly Saxons looting Roman settlements; the first Christians building churches in the foothills. Or was she being fanciful, merely reacting to an excess of champagne?

Robert had come back for her, took her arm, helped her up the hill. Despite the wind, she could feel his body burning hot, as it pressed against her own. He seemed still fuelled by that impetuousness she had experienced in the car; his strides too long for her, his fingers almost hurting on her arm. They were nearly at the top now. Robert surged ahead, scrambled up to the summit, stood motionless a moment on the topmost spur, arms outstretched, as if he were a statue of some ancient stone-carved priest. She felt out of breath, light-headed, as she stumbled up the last few yards to join him. He took her in his arms, no longer priest or stone, but man and flesh – though his kiss was brief, this time, an impatient kiss, followed by a sudden nervous laugh.

'I'm king of the castle. Will you be my queen?'

She choked back her own laugh as she realised he was serious, that this was not a game, but a second proposal – one sanctioned by a ring. The clouds had swept apart again, allowed the moon to shine, its light glinting on the trophy he was holding out to her. Pearls. A swollen central pearl, framed by smaller seed-pearls in an elaborate wide gold setting. They had been discussing stones together, what they symbolised – diamonds for light, rubies for royalty. She hadn't wanted either, felt both were far too grand for her. Pearls stood for innocence, purity, virginity. She closed her eyes a second, saw not Robert's hand, but Reverend Mother Abbess's closing over hers as she spoke her solemn vows.

'I resolve with the help of God's grace to undertake a life of perfect and perpetual chastity . . . ' She could feel her body hooked and trapped as Robert's thrust above it. He was stuck to her with sweat, his rubber-covered penis pumping like a piston engine. She had to try to like it, had to make him happy, move as he was moving, up and back, up and back. Perspiration was sliding down her breasts, the heat of the four-poster intensified by the weight of Robert's body crushing into hers. She rocked and tipped her pelvis, memories of Ivan increasing her confusion. She forced herself to concentrate. Her body was responding now, doing what it should, picking up the rhythm from Robert's own wild thrusts. Only her mind refused to go along with it, distracted by the flood of words; Robert's voice ramming her and ramming her, like a second violent organ. The act of sex was sacred –*with my body I thee worship* – should be silent, surely; dignified and silent. She tensed against him as he tried to play the game again, that game he liked so much, but which angered her, embarrassed her, made her almost hate him.

'Is it good for you, Sister? Brother Robert's not hurting, is he, naughty Sister Arles? You shouldn't move like that. It's disgraceful for a virgin. Reverend Father Abbot punished you last time. He whipped you, didn't he? Took off your habit and spanked your bare white bottom. And this time he'll . . . '

She was now so tense, so furious, surely he must realise what she felt. Her whole body closed against him, though it kept moving, moving, as she tipped and rocked, tipped and rocked, obeying Ivan's orders. Liz had paid for all those lessons, so she had to get some good from them, do as she was told.

'Oh, wonderful, my darling! It's quite fantastic when you push like that against me. Oh, I love you, Gloria. Oh, it's absolutely . . . '

She was being good, pleasing him, pleasing all of them, suppressing her own distaste and prudish fears; doing what the sex books said, what Ivan said, what Liz said. All the voices telling her: 'Go for it,' 'Let go,' 'Relax,' 'Have a climax,' 'Have a baby,' 'Indulge your man and fantasise,' 'Eat these oysters,' 'Wear this dress,' 'Marry me,' 'Wear my ring.'

'No,' she said suddenly. 'I won't.'

He couldn't hear. She was speaking dumbly, as she had spoken in his bed, this afternoon; spoken to the pillows, to the sperm-stained sheets which he'd refused to let her change; crying out without a sound: 'Not so roughly, Robert. You're hurting. I don't like it. And please don't use those words. They upset me. They're so crude. I love you, darling, honestly. Just hold me, will you, hold me in your arms. That's wonderful, so peaceful. I love it when you kiss me really gently . . . No, Robert, *please* – not that game again. I loathe that game. Can't you understand?'

She opened her eyes, saw the ring moving towards her finger, an expensive antique ring, pearls shining in the stippled silver light. Pearls for fertility, fecundity, rebirth. Lightning piercing through the oyster shell and seeding a white gem. Robert's sperm seeding a fair child. White for immortality. A union for ever, till death do us part. Robert's for ever, his worldly goods, his body; for richer for poorer, for better, for ever. His voice dinning on for ever, his penis thrusting, ramming in for ever; she his nun for ever, part of his collection, a strange unusual object for his shelves; an object still too artless, which must be planed and sanded, polished, buffed, till it was worthy of him, glamorous, matched his expectations and his style.

She felt the ring graze against her fingertip. He was about to slip it down, bind them both inexorably. *With this ring I thee wed . . .* Her finger had been free for just five days. She didn't want it shackled once again, fettered with an eighteen carat manacle. Yet she couldn't move her hand. It felt rigid, paralysed, stretched out towards his own hand.

'Gloria, my darling, will you marry me?'

'No,' she said. 'I can't.'

This time, she heard the sound. The three brief syllables seemed to boom and rumble in her head, re-echo through the entire South Downs. She was breaking a contract; had said 'yes' before, two weeks ago; was engaged already, bound to him already. She took a step away, broke the contact of their fingers.

'Gloria?' His own voice was stunned and shaken, the ring still held out to her, symbol of their union. Pearls for wisdom, for enlightenment.

'I'm not Gloria,' she said, her voice lower, but more confident. 'And neither am I naughty Sister Arles.'

'What in God's name are you talking about? Of course you're Gloria and of course you can't say no. It's all arranged. We're getting married in exactly twenty days. You know we've booked the registry office, and invited all our . . . '

'No,' she said, third time. He had proposed three times, so she must match him each for each. She shook her head, squeezed his hand a second, fighting back tears of loss, regret, then turned her back, stumbled down the hill.

Fall

29

'And this is the utility room. It's quite handy, really, for the washing machine and tumble drier. And there's another toilet just through here. Yes, that leads into the garden. Careful! The steps are rather dark.' Hilary shivered in the draught from the back door. Autumn had been mild so far, but now they were a week into November, and the nights were turning cold.

'We must come back in the light, Tom, see the garden properly.'

'Yes, of course. Come any day you like. I'm always here. Just phone, or get the agent to arrange it.'

Hilary smiled, showed the couple out, then sank down in a chair and put her feet up. There'd been twelve prospective buyers this weekend, and that last unwelcome pair had turned up at half past ten, breezed in off the street as they were passing the 'For Sale' boards. It wasn't just her feet which ached – her face ached, too; ached from smiling, ached from talking, pointing out amenities, playing down the problems. Just a week ago, a new board – 'Under Offer' – had replaced the three 'For Sale' boards, but the buyer had withdrawn when his surveyor found dry rot. Liz had been appalled, had assumed her house was in very good condition, expected a quick sale, a hefty profit. It was she who'd had to soothe her, long-distance, on the phone; she who'd seen the agents once again, negotiated a lower price, approved the new euphemistic wording on the handouts.

'Exceptionally well-appointed character residence in sought-after position. Immaculate decorative condition, excellently presented throughout, though in need of minor repairs.'

She phoned Liz every day, sometimes twice a day, to report on any developments, advise on any problems.

'You're a wonder, Hil, honestly. I don't know what we'd do without you.'

She had glowed at Liz's praises, secretly agreed with her that she had made some genuine progress in the last two months; was far less frightened of meeting total strangers, less hesitant and ignorant in discussing business matters. She had learnt a lot about property and prices – not to mention human nature – had steeled herself to live alone in a large and lonely house. Even Di had gone now, sold the dress-shop to her rivals in one of the quickest deals on record, was already setting up a new boutique in Scarborough. She herself had been invited up to join them, as soon as Liz's house was sold: help with Stephen, help Di in the shop, find a room nearby. She had turned the offer down, even when Liz pleaded. She suspected Liz was acting out of pity, and she had no desire to accept favours based on pity, not from anyone. It was time to strike out on her own, without help from Auntie Liz or jobs from Auntie Di.

She had found herself a job, in fact – and quite a decent job, one with board and lodging; had bypassed the Job Centre, found it on her own. Everyone had told her that would be impossible; bored and snooty girls at employment agencies shaking their heads, always saying 'no', rubbing in her lack of qualifications, reiterating the scarcity of residential posts, especially when she'd had no real experience. Then, one morning, when she'd been looking through Appointments Vacant, finding nothing, trying to quash her growing sense of panic, her eye had strayed to the Educational column. An American college for international students was advertising courses – everything from Fine Art to Computer Studies: mature students especially welcome, and those from overseas. The college was in Oxfordshire, described itself as friendly, small, and set in glorious countryside. How nice, she'd thought, to have the time and money to do a course in literature or art, get out of grimy London, meet people from a host of different cultures, live amongst trees and fields again. On impulse, she had phoned them, not as a prospective student, but to ask them if there were any chance of working there, as receptionist or housekeeper, even a gardener or a kitchen hand. An American had answered. No, he'd said, no way – though he said it not unkindly, seemed surprised she'd phoned at all. Why was she so desperate, why so keen on Roosevelt College?

In the end, she told him far more than she meant to, including the fact she'd been a cloistered nun for twenty years. He began to ask her questions, obviously intrigued. The questions were embarrassing, began to get too intimate. She returned the conversation strictly to employment. Could he possibly advise her where else she might apply to get a job? He'd laughed, seemed more relaxed and even jokey. Yes, maybe he just could. It wasn't every morning he got ex-nuns calling up, especially not the sort who wore medieval robes and shut themselves away for half a lifetime. And he'd always heard that nuns were real good workers, never slacked or went off sick. They owned a sister college, a larger one in Hertfordshire, and if he had a word with Andy, there was just a chance he'd find her something, though it might be pretty lowly. 'That's all right,' she'd murmured, with the first stirrings of excitement and relief. 'I'll take anything at all.'

The position Andy offered was less humble than she'd feared, even had a title – assistant domestic bursar – though the title sounded grander than the job. All she really had to do was help out in the kitchen, do the washing up and cleaning, then once she'd mastered that, graduate to waitress work. In return, she'd receive room and board and a low but adequate wage. Andy also promised that if she proved reliable, she might increase her pay and status by taking on the extra job as warden to the girls; on call at nights to deal with any problems which arose among the female students. She was to start in early January, when their new college term began and one of their key kitchen staff was leaving to get married. The timing, too, was perfect, gave her two whole months to sell the house, wind up Liz's affairs; and if the sale went through much sooner, well – she could always spend a few odd weeks in Scarborough. At least she'd be a guest there, a temporary visitor, not a permanent drag.

She eased up from her chair, moved into the kitchen to make herself a drink. She'd indulge herself this evening, had worked hard all day, tidying and cleaning, showing people round. She sat at the table sipping her hot chocolate, made with full-cream milk and frothy on the top; smiled as she remembered the bitter Brignor cocoa, always made with water, always sugarless. 'Congratulations, Hilary,' she murmured to herself, as she spooned half-melted sugar from the almost empty cup. 'You've got your job. You're coping.'

She washed the saucepan, put everything away, wiped down all the surfaces, removed the soggy tea towels. Liz would hardly recognise her house – no coats flung on the banisters or books left in the lavatory, no cluttered shelves or messy bulging cupboards. The huge fridge held just two small eggs, a paltry cube of cheese. All the rooms seemed larger with their furniture removed. Liz had moved out half her things, sold the rest, or passed them on to friends. Her plants had gone, her ornaments; all the family flotsam which had surged or drifted in through thirteen years. The piano was still there, though that, too, was up for sale, and at least a dozen different people had already called to try it. She found it almost painful to hear their rough and ready music, or – worse – their skilful playing. She herself had still not played a note. Just to touch the keys might undam a whole wild flood of raw emotion, prove too overwhelming. Music was something she had renounced completely, save as a rapt but passive listener. Liz had left her half her records and an ancient stereo, insisted that she keep them, since Harry had progressed to compact discs and owned a far superior system. Dear Harry had his uses, she thought, grinning to herself.

She closed the door, locked up back and front, began to feel her usual twinge of nervousness as the clock hands on the landing moved to

379

midnight. The nights were always difficult. She was still not used to sleeping in Liz's bedroom, which seemed too big for her, too fancy altogether, despite the fact it had been denuded of its luxuries, stripped of Liz's frills. Liz had insisted that she move down from the top floor. 'It's not safe, love, with you stuck away up there. If there was an intruder, you wouldn't hear a dicky bird. Anyway, my room's much nicer, much more comfortable. And you'll have a bedside phone.'

The phone was ringing now. 'Damn!' she muttered, as she reached to pick it up. Surely not house-hunters in the middle of the night – though a month of trying to sell the place had prepared her for anything. One cheery family had taken over the kitchen, casually demolished her modest lunch-for-one, and a man had come just yesterday with two delinquent dogs in tow. One had fouled the garden, the other tried to maul her.

The phone lead was twisted, the line fuzzy and unclear. 'I'm sorry, I can't hear you. Who? Oh, hallo, this is Hilary, the girl who . . . No, Liz isn't here. She's moved away. I thought you'd know, actually. She's gone up North to Scarborough.' Hilary sat down on the bed, thrown by the tremor in Mr Craddock's voice. She'd met Luke's father only twice, and only very briefly, and both times he'd been angry, bellowing like a bull. Now he sounded subdued and almost panicky.

'What's happened? What's the matter? Can't I help instead? I'm looking after things for Liz and she told me to . . . Rita? Oh, how awful. Is she bad? Oh, I see, they've taken her in. Yes, of course I will. I'll come first thing. He'd better stay here, hadn't he? I mean, if you're going away and there's no one else to . . . '

She heard her voice sounding calm and confident, though it was contradicted by the churning agitation in her mind. Was she crazy to have invited Luke to stay? She hadn't had much choice. Rita Craddock was bleeding like a skewered pig, as her husband put it baldly; had thought at first it was a really heavy period, until it turned into a haemorrhage. She'd been rushed into hospital earlier that evening, and was now under observation. Joe's middle son had offered to take Sylvie, and had just driven back to Harlow with the bewildered girl whimpering and dribbling in the back. Luke was more a problem. He'd missed so much school already that Joe was reluctant he should move away from Wandsworth. He had banked on Liz helping out, as she had before, several times, when Rita had suffered less dramatic ailments.

Hilary stood up, started pacing to and fro like a caged and anxious animal, tethered by the phone-lead. If only Liz were here to take control. She was surprised Joe didn't know that she and Di had moved. Wouldn't Stephen have told Luke, or Luke himself reported to his parents that Steve was changing schools? No. The boys were still at loggerheads, had kept up their long feud. And as for Liz herself, the last two months had been so full, so hectic and disruptive, she had hardly seen any of her friends, let alone the Craddocks. She, too, had quite ignored them – apart from that one visit, way back in July, when the baby had been teething. Luke had obviously resented all the attention being lavished on the screaming feverish infant, and had behaved extremely badly, breaking things and kicking at the pram. 'I'm teething too,' he'd whined, pointing to the gap in his front teeth. 'And I don't scream and shit my cot.' She had found herself recoiling from both boy and baby, had not returned again. And since mid-September, her own problems seemed too pressing to take on someone else's. Now she had to help. Joe was off to Birmingham first thing in the morning and the boy would be alone.

She made the last arrangements, sat staring at the carpet, the dead receiver still cradled in her hands. Could she act as mother? Luke might well be very difficult with his own mother ill in hospital, his whole home life disrupted. She'd have to cook and wash for him, take him to and fro from school, amuse him after school, keep him clean and tidy. So what? Most women did that all the time, for several different children, and often with a full-time job as well. She replaced the phone, stood frowning and preoccupied, her mind on meals and shopping lists, homework, sheets and blankets. She'd better get up early – air the bedding, prepare his room, try to find some toys for him.

She went to draw the curtains, shivering in the large unheated room, pausing at the window, to peer up and down the street. It seemed totally deserted, curtains drawn, bedroom lights extinguished, only she awake. Perhaps she was alone not just in the house, but in the whole of Cranleigh Gardens; all the other occupants packed up and moved away, their houses stripped and plucked, their silent gardens jungled. She let the curtain fall, undressed quickly, pulled the bedclothes right up to her chin. She was still not used to Liz's double bed – to have all that space for one unimportant person, all that luxury: the goose-down duvet which Liz had left behind for her, the pile of feather pillows.

Sleep refused to come. She kept worrying over Luke. Suppose he played up, ran away from school? If he were difficult and sulky in his own home, he might be quite impossible in hers. She groped for the light switch, sat up against the pillows. She should have just said no, made some quick excuse, said the house was half-dismantled, so nobody could stay. The Craddocks had a brood of older children. Couldn't one of them help out, or one of Rita's family? She had enough to do already, keeping three floors clean, coping with the garden, the constant stream of house-hunters, without a sullen and rebellious child disrupting her whole . . .

'Completely bloody selfish, that's what you are, Hilary. You may have been a nun for all those years, but you don't really give a damn about anyone but yourself.'

She flinched, dodged back, as if recoiling from a blow. Robert's voice, angry and accusing. She had tried to blot it out for eight whole weeks, forget that frightening outburst on the downs, but now the ugly phrases were roaring in her ears. She *was* completely selfish, lying in a feather-bed feeling sorry for herself, when Rita Craddock was bleeding in hospital, Luke motherless and miserable. She had realised, long ago, how serious Luke's problems were, how much he needed help; the whole wretched Craddock household crying out for friendship and support. And what had she done? Turned her back on them, indulged in her own selfish petty pleasures, and when those pleasures ceased abruptly in September, she had retreated into herself, made Liz's house a private sanctuary, a convalescent home with her as the sole patient. She had put her need for safety and survival before everyone and everything; creating order, organising, tidying, so she wouldn't sink or crack. If other people cracked, too bad. She couldn't take their problems, their messy feckless lives.

Selfish? Yes, completely. She had never loved anyone, never lived close enough to another human being to nurture and support them through sickness, crisis, breakdown, or even through the endless petty daily aggravations, as most normal women did. It had been much the same with Robert. She couldn't love him because he threatened her whole neat and tidy life, her safe and sterile order; had rejected sex because she wanted it a sacrament, a spiritual communion without noise or sweat or bodies, without any violent passion, any real abandon. She grabbed a pillow, hugged it, tried to turn it into Robert, warm and solid Robert saying she was beautiful, stroking her bare breasts. It wouldn't work. She could only hear his fury.

'You've made me look a total fool. I spent bloody hours searching for that ring, scoured every shop and sale room. You've just used me, haven't you, led me on, let me think you cared, when you didn't give a shit? Let's face it, woman, it's been all take and no give from the moment we first met. I tried to make excuses for you, give you time to change, but you'll never change – you're just plain bloody selfish.'

She hurled the pillow out of bed, leapt out the other side, stood trembling by the wall. Who was Robert Harrington to use the word 'selfish'? He had encouraged her to be herself, then tried to change that self, mould it to his whims, replace the rules and duties of the convent with another set of disciplines: the duty to be sexy, the duty to look good, to grace his lighthouse, charm his friends. He had dismissed her own perfectionism, as well as his ex-wife's, yet was selfishly perfectionist in the pursuit of his own ends – his work, his home, his projects. He had urged her to fulfil her needs, then ignored them all himself: her need for space and privacy, her need to choose occasionally, choose meals or books or clothes, or even a whole lifestyle. He was determined to possess her, possess her mind and body, control her tastes, her mood. Wasn't that selfish, even ruthless? And he'd been rough in bed, insensitive, hurt her and embarrassed her, and not even had the insight to realise she abhorred it. He was generous, yes; adoring, yes; but also brash and violent. He'd attacked her on the downs – actually pummelled her and slapped her, because she'd hurt his pride. She could feel his hands stinging on her face, hear his angry ranting voice scorching the whole county.

'I've met girls like you before – pretending butter wouldn't melt in their mouths, but really hard as nails. Well, don't think I'm taken in. I'm not. I'm . . .'

She had heard about his temper, never quite believed it till she experienced it that night; found it so unnerving, she'd done everything she could to erase it from her mind, pretend it never happened, pretend Robert was unreal. He was probably doing much the same himself, since she'd heard nothing further from him – not a letter, not a phone call, not a single word of sorrow or regret.

Impulsively, she reached out for the phone, dialled his Sussex number. He wouldn't be asleep, rarely went to bed before the early hours. Despite the cold, her hands were clammy wet, her heart pounding through her flimsy nylon nightie. Her whole stomach seemed to heave as she listened to his number ringing out. She had no idea what she planned to say. 'You brute, you bully, hitting me like that. I never want to see you in my life again.' 'I love you, Robert – truly – please come back.' 'I'll never forgive you, never in my life.' 'I'm sorry, it was my fault. I was just too prim and scared. Let's try again. Let's . . .'

She was speaking to herself, speaking to a piece of deaf white plastic, voice desperate now, imploring. 'Please answer, please say anything. Please wake up and hear the phone.' The ringing tone sounded tired and jaded. She hung on one more minute, let it drag to two, to three; still sat there, hoping, pleading, clutching the receiver as if it were his arm. Perhaps he'd moved away, sold his tower – 'Gloria's Tower' – bought a new folly which wouldn't bear her taint, a water-mill or castle named for someone else.

She groped for her slippers, stumbled down the stairs into the sitting room. She had to have a drink, something to anaesthetise the seething mass of memories, remorse. The room looked bare and barren, with all Liz's softening touches swept away. She had turned the place not into a sanctuary, but into a remand home, where everything was disciplined and stark; had become a nun again, a strict old-fashioned nun.

She poured herself a glass of Southern Comfort, another gift from Robert, sat staring at the blank uncurtained windows, trying not to think; suddenly giggled to herself as she began to gulp it down. Strict old-fashioned nuns didn't sprawl in low-cut lacy nightgowns, knocking back strong liquor. Robert had affected her far more than she realised, given her a taste for alcohol, made her more extravagant, more worldly altogether. He'd also changed her views and her philosophy, taught her 'God is Truth', instead of 'Truth is God'. She could salvage most of that, value what he'd given her, preserve the best of it, while throwing out the rest; rejecting his demands, his domination. She had chosen not to marry him for sound and rational reasons; had actually made a decision on her own, broken with her former convent habit of always seeking guidance and advice. That was some achievement. She'd also decided not to go to Scarborough – another key decision – had resisted Liz's fussing, Di's urgent overtures as she realised alteration-hands were as rare up North as they'd been in Wimbledon. Liz was still keeping her, paying for her services as secretary and agent, but that would end in just a month or so. And once she moved into the college, she would be entirely self-sufficient.

'About time too,' she murmured, as she fiddled with the bottle-cap, curled up in her chair. She had seen Robert as a teacher, Ivan as a priest, used Liz as aunt and nanny; was still searching for her real aunt, had even sent a letter to Eva's old address in Gloucestershire, in case she'd moved back there. She'd have to change her outlook, learn to stand alone now, without priests or teachers, mother-figures, elusive Evas, sanctuaries; even do some mothering herself, offer Luke a home. She lurched to her feet, dragged herself upstairs again, bottle in her hands. She'd use it as a nightcap. Joe Craddock was expecting her first thing in the morning, so she ought to get some sleep, conserve her energies. She might need them in the next few days – or weeks.

The bed seemed even vaster, her mind more helter-skelter, as it plunged from Robert down in Sussex to the Kingsleys up in Scarborough; from Sylvie in Harlow to Rita in her ward; from Luke's concrete-jungle playground to her job at Claremont College. She hadn't drunk enough, was still restless and keyed up. She uncapped the bottle, filled her glass again; realised she was missing Robert, actually missing that male body she had criticised, rejected. She had allowed her thoughts to dwell on him, broken through the barrier she had set up round his name, recalled him from limbo, from the dead. She pulled her nightie up, let her hand stray across her thigh. She had never touched herself, even though he'd begged her several times; said it turned him on, said she ought to masturbate as part of being adult, being fully sexual. The hand groped lower, moved between her legs, began to stroke guiltily and nervously. She closed her eyes, tried to rock her pelvis the way that Ivan taught. It didn't seem to work. She kept remembering sex with Robert, the way her rocking thrusting body wouldn't link up with her mind, wouldn't register as pleasure, refused to burst into excitement, was simply movement, simply automatic.

'Pretend,' she urged herself. 'Fake it just to start with.' Liz had told her that scores of women faked their sexual pleasure, at least in the beginning; went to bed more to please their men, or make themselves feel normal, loved, secure. She'd done the same herself, might have become a truly sensual women, if she'd only persevered, allowed herself more time and more experience. She thrust her legs apart, even dared insert a finger, tried to think of nothing but herself – her pleasure, her enjoyment, the passion which would follow once she'd shammed a bit. 'All you need is practice,' Liz had said so often. 'Sex is just a skill you have to learn, like any other skill.'

She licked the finger, tried to push it deeper, explore herself, get to know her body. She'd read the sex books, knew what was expected. It was important to relax, they urged, maybe even fantasise. She tried to think of Robert, a different Robert, gentler, less explosive; a man who didn't sweat or swear, didn't boast about the prowess of what he called Big Bob, didn't have genitals at all; a man who had no body-hair, only long blond ringlets falling to his shoulders. She sat up with a jerk, snatched her hand away. She'd turned Robert into Jesus, and still it hadn't worked. She was still dry, still tense and squeamish. She tugged her nightie down, wiped her finger on the sheet. They didn't write sex manuals for women like herself, eccentric semi-nuns who weren't sexually frustrated, as single manless females were expected invariably to be, but spiritually frustrated. The craving was still there, the craving for a God, a faith, a meaning to her life. She smoothed her tousled hair, let out a sudden laugh. She was spiritually randy, to use Della's word, and Robert's. It *was* a randiness – a constant urge and restlessness, an aching rutting search. Did no one else experience it? There were so many other urgent hungers in the world, for food, success, achievement; hungers on the television – complexions craving moisturiser, digestions lacking fibre. Could she really be so unique in panting after angels, searching in the supermarket for spiritual adventures in convenient packet form, bottlesful of grace?

She reached out for her glass. The only bottle in her grasp was Robert's Southern Comfort. She had bid goodbye to grace, would have to settle for good old-fashioned liquor. She'd drunk only one small glass, so far; not enough to anaesthetise so many different worries. She tucked the duvet round her shoulders, lolled back on the pillows, kept sipping steadily; pausing for a moment to swill the amber liquid round her mouth, relishing its warmth, its kick, as it tingled down her throat. If she couldn't find her God, at least she'd find whisky-flavoured oblivion.

The alarm clock and the doorbell shrilled at the same time. Hilary struggled out of bed, a foul taste in her mouth, a cruel relentless hammer banging in her head. She had been dreaming about wounds; her whole body a deep wound, a red and pulsing opening. Still dazed, she took the parcel from the postman, a pile of bumph, two letters – one addressed to her, with a smudgy Norfolk postmark. Her entire attention focused on that postmark, on the neat and spidery writing, Reverend Mother's writing, which acted like a dose of Angostura bitters; cut right through her hangover, jolted her to wakefulness, even to alarm. She plunged into the kitchen, collapsed on a chair, heart pounding now, as well as just her head. The envelope was bigger than the usual small pale blue ones the Abbess always used, looked quite fat and bulky, as if it held more than just a letter. She tore it open, found the letter, and another envelope – an important-looking white one with an Italian stamp. She closed her eyes a second, as if to blank it out. That second stiff white letter was from Rome, from the Sacred Congregation for Religious, their name spelled out in Latin on the envelope; *Città del Vaticano* screaming from the postmark. It could only be one thing: the formal dispensation from her vows.

She picked it up, put it down again, longed for Liz, for Robert – somebody to help her slit the envelope, face those chilling phrases. Already she could feel a wave of loss, regret, a sensation of near panic. Right up to this moment, she had been officially a nun – even with a hangover, even making love to Robert, or driving his red sports car – could still return in theory, take up the life again, re-enter the safe Brignor womb. Now the cord was cut and she was thrust gasping, blinking, into the harsh glare of the world, with no way back, no bolthole or emergency escape. A dispensation was final, absolutely final. If her faith returned, or even her vocation, she would be cut off from the convent, permanently, completely; all legal and religious ties severed by that document for ever. She fiddled with the other mail, tried to read a catalogue from Comfy-Fit Footwear, concentrate on arch supports and slingbacks, but her mind refused to shift from the white official envelope which contained her fate, her future. She reached out for the sheet of pale blue paper, Reverend Mother's letter. If she couldn't face the document itself, at least she could read that, take one thing at a time, ease and spread the shock. She unfolded it, hands clammy, glimpsed just the first two lines.

'Dear Sister Mary Hilary,

I regret to inform you that . . . '

She dropped the letter instantly, as if it were scorching hot and had already burnt her hand; pushed it to the far end of the table, trying to ignore the sudden queasy churning in her stomach, far worse than any hangover. It was not her dispensation. She was still Sister Mary Hilary, and Reverend Mother Abbess was writing to inform her that the Sacred Congregation had refused her application, refused to release her from her solemn vows. They had that right and power, though they used it very rarely, and only in cases where the reasons given for requesting dispensation were judged frivolous, unworthy, or when the applicant's Superior had serious reservations of her own. She had heard of just one case before – a Trappistine who had applied for dispensation in 1959, and had died of cancer twenty-two years later, still under vows and buried in her habit.

'No,' she mouthed in horror. 'You can't refuse. You can't!' It was only at this moment that she knew suddenly, indubitably, that she could never be a nun again, that the life was wrong for her, had been always wrong, even from the start. She'd been ambivalent about seeking dispensation, but now she craved it; realised that it spelled relief and freedom, not remorse and shame. It was total folly to imagine that her old faith would return. Robert had shown her a much wider and more complex world, displaced her simple vision of God and Satan, heaven and hell, her one narrow rigid Truth. She had rejected Robert's ring, but she could still respect his views. It didn't even matter that they had gone their separate ways. There were other options to being Robert's wife, different sorts of future. She required her formal freedom so she could search those options out, learn to find and be herself. 'I won't go back,' she whispered. 'It would be absolutely crazy. I know that now. I'm certain.'

She must ignore the letter, flout it, tear it into pieces, go her own way anyway, regardless of the Sacred Congregation. If she had no faith, then they were just a group of bureaucrats; Reverend Mother Abbess not reverend at all, but a rigid martinet, clinging to old outmoded standards. Except it didn't feel like that. Reverend Mother's sanction, the Congregation's permission and release, seemed desperately important. Without them, she was tied – legally, symbolically – would always be a misfit in the secular world; someone who was barred from it officially, belonged back in her cloister. She picked up the envelope blazoned with the Congregation's crest. She'd better read their letter, face their petty cavilling about frivolity, light-mindedness, their relentless admonition that she go back to her convent.

Still she hesitated, scared of her own anger, of all the difficult decisions she would be forced to make once she'd read their case. Did she appeal against their verdict, or ignore it totally? Should she return to see the Abbess, or cut all links with Brignor? Might it not be easier just to burn the letter, pretend she'd never seen it? She sat staring at the Italian stamp, which showed a crenellated building, with solid four-square walls, lowering battlements. She envied it its strength, while blenching at the words which ran beneath it: *Poste Vaticane*. Could she really burn a letter which had come from Rome, the Pope's own Holy City? Mixed in with her anger was a whole morass of fear, an instinct to surrender – a remnant from the past, when the Pope had towered above her life for nearly forty years, insisting on obedience and submission. The hall clock struck the hour. She dropped the letter on the table, dragged herself upstairs. She'd been lost in her own problems, while ignoring Luke's completely, forgetting he was waiting. Selfishness again. She washed and dressed in under fifteen minutes, returned to the kitchen, gathered up the mail, to sort out on the bus, grabbed a few stale biscuits from the tin, in case Luke, like her, had found neither time nor appetite for breakfast, then stepped through the front door.

It was still half-dark outside, a glaze of silver covering the grass, etched across the privet hedge: the first frost of the season. She shut the gate, turned the corner and walked down Atwood Avenue into Marefield Crescent, a tree-lined street, unlike Cranleigh Gardens – stopped in sudden shock. The trees had lost more than half their leaves, which were lying on the pavement ankle-deep; the trees themselves skinny and denuded. Yesterday, the weather had been mild: blue sky, weak shafts of sunlight, a golden glow at dusk. Yesterday, the plane trees still had leaves, brown and sapless leaves maybe, but still bulking out the branches. She knew it happened sometimes – an almost instant leaf-fall, when a sharp and unexpected frost followed on a mild spell, but it still seemed quite traumatic, as if the trees had been bereaved, suffered a sudden jolting shock. Winter had arrived – arrived this morning with the post – come in cold and grey.

Impulsively, she rummaged in her handbag, took out both the letters, stiff white and flimsy blue. She had to face her own shock, not run away from it, or try to fool herself that things were bright and sunny. She was no longer angry, merely numb, resigned; no longer even scared. If she had to appeal, so be it. She could get advice from someone, maybe consult a lawyer or a priest. She checked her watch. She wasn't late; had washed and dressed so quickly she'd left earlier than she'd planned, could easily read two letters and still be at the Craddocks' at the time she had arranged. She shivered suddenly, moved closer to a plane tree, as if seeking shelter from its dark and solid bulk before unfolding the blue paper – Reverend Mother's letter.

'Dear Sister Mary Hilary,

I regret to inform you that the Order will not be able to grant you any financial assistance for your return to the secular state, since the circumstances of your leaving were . . . '

Incredulous, she checked the words again. 'Your return to the secular state.' That must mean . . . She clutched at the tree trunk, steadied herself a moment before ripping open the stiff white envelope. Two dozen lines of typing on heavy bonded paper, with an insignia above, a long impressive signature below. She tried to read, realised with a shock that the typing was in Latin, and her own knowledge of the language appeared to have completely disappeared. She was gazing at a tide of foreign words – no sense to them, no meaning – just empty mocking hieroglyphs. She shook the paper angrily. Crazy to communicate in a dead and arcane language, which most normal people couldn't understand. She had loved the Latin once, revered it as precise and universal, but now it seemed a symbol of all that was wrong about the Church – its archaism, its rigid hidebound pedantry.

She took a deep breath in, tried to exhale her anger; tried to make some sense of the still baffling alien words. This must just be tension, or temporary amnesia. The Latin would come back, if she calmed down, took her time. She forced herself to concentrate, picked out her own name: *Soror Maria Hilarius*. No, that wasn't her. Why should she be Latinised and fossilised; men keep forcing names on her – *Hilarius* and Gloria – names she didn't want? She struggled with the next line, face screwed up in effort until she spotted a key word – the one word she was looking for: '*dispensationem*'. She repeated it aloud as her eye went racing on, the lines now making sense, instantly, dramatically, as if the word had brought her skills back, restored her to her powers. She could translate now quite effortlessly, the once obdurate Latin slipping, smiling, into English.

'Having given due consideration to the aforesaid documents forwarded to us at . . . ' She skipped a line, plunged on – on towards that magic word, '*dispensationem*', repeated further down the page and yoked this time to her name. She translated once again without the slightest hesitation. 'This Sacred Congregation is willing to grant to Sister Mary Hilary dispensation from her solemn vows.'

She was still clinging to the tree trunk with one hand, her palm hurting on its rough uneven bark. She rubbed it on her skirt, let the letter drop back in her bag, as she tried to take it in, tried to still the wild emotions welling up inside her – a heady mix of triumph, shock, relief. 'I'm free,' she mouthed. 'I'm free!' A bird flapped up, a lean black cat jumped a fence, streaked across a lawn. Free like them, with no cages and no walls. Free to be a normal human being, free to find a role – not as *femme fatale* or collector's acquisition, but a role she'd choose herself. She could be scruffy if she wanted, celibate if she wanted; a tomboy or a tearaway or a pillar of society. It was up to her alone now. She no longer had a Superior, no longer had a fiancé; had cut all ties, finished with all gurus. She'd make her own rules, if she needed rules at all. So the Order couldn't grant her financial help? No problem. She hadn't expected any help; didn't need it anyway. She had a job, a future, could be truly self-supporting for the first time in her life. Her headache had quite gone, even the foul taste in her mouth replaced now by the honied tang of freedom.

She glanced down at the pavement. Every autumn as a nun, she had fought a childish urge to shuffle through the fallen leaves, as she'd done as a young girl, hear them scrunch and crackle underfoot. Instead, she'd had to sweep them into neat and tidy piles, work in silence, with her mind on God alone. She broke into a run, kicking up a storm of leaves, brittle crackly leaves, like the stiff and crackly paper which had granted her release. She zigzagged up and down, jumping wind-blown drifts, paddling though the tide of brown and yellow. She'd bring Luke here this afternoon, so they could play leapfrog with the leaves together, then pick out a few perfect ones, brilliant coloured specimens, she would press and keep for ever. She needed a memorial, something to preserve this day, save it from oblivion.

She stopped a moment, looked up at the sky. It was light now, fully light, the first weak sunlight breaking through; the first frost of the season melting, vanishing. With any luck, it might be quite a good day, even bright and sunny. She'd been wrong about the season. It wasn't winter yet.

Winter

30

Hilary secured a tinsel halo around an angel's white-blond hair. All the angels were fair, and all were girls; Gabriel with waist-length platinum curls. Technically, angels should be males, but Wandsworth Junior School seemed blithely unaware of that. They had done better with the Magi – all Three Kings swarthy dark: a gangling child from Zambia and two smaller Pakistanis. She darted across to Melchior, adjusted his gold-trimmed velvet cloak. She had made the cloak herself from a pair of old school curtains; made a good half of the costumes. Luke's teacher, Jean MacDonald, had roped her in to help, as Jean was joint producer of the school nativity play. Today was the first official dress rehearsal and Hilary felt honoured to be there at all, one of just three mothers painting cardboard camels or gluing angels' wings, amidst the excited tide of children, the crowd of anxious teachers. She felt something of a fraud, since she wasn't even a mother, only Rita Craddock's stand-in, who happened to be skilled at making clothes.

Rita was still ill, had recovered only poorly from a hysterectomy; been home just one weekend before landing back in hospital again. Luke had reacted very badly, become even more withdrawn; missed his mother, missed his home surroundings. She scanned the room for him, saw him skulking in a corner, jabbing at the wall with his foil-and-cardboard spear. She wished he had a better part, wished he could play Joseph, or even Pontius Pilate. It might have helped him, made him feel important. He had no words to speak at all, had been cast as a centurion with three other playground toughies, all dressed in short black tunics, worn with crested silver helmets and shiny wellingtons.

She felt hot just looking at the boots. Despite the chill outside, the school hall was airless, stifling, as if the crudely crayoned backdrops of Judaea and Galilee had brought their own heat with them; a relentless desert heat. The smells were different, though – not sweaty mules or camel dung, but newly painted radiators, children's feet, pear drops, glue and greasepaint. The hall was really crowded, children laughing, shouting, pounding up and down, while they waited for the rehearsal proper to start. Many were transformed. The Bangladeshi Mary who was something of a tomboy and always had grazed knees, was now dignified and gracious in her long blue robe and veil. The Three Kings seemed bemused by their own grandeur, jangling in their mothers'

393

beads and baubles, bearing gifts of decorated tea caddies.

'Those cloaks are really smashing.' Gill Lawley, Herod's mother, was also looking at the Kings, admiring their three outfits, as she slumped down next to Hilary. 'I've never seen such workmanship. You must be a professional.'

Hilary shrugged. 'Not really.'

'Come on, don't be modest. I was so impressed with Nicky's purple robe, I almost borrowed it myself for my husband's office party. I mean, all that marvellous braiding, and the way the inside's just as perfect as the outside. Most of these school costumes are just thrown together, but yours are works of art.'

Hilary flushed. Robert's phrase – the one he'd used in Norfolk, about her Brignor vestments – though it gave her still more pleasure to hear it on Gill's lips. Gill was something of an artist herself, professionally trained in stage make-up; had been dragooned today into painting fifty small scrubbed faces; was now recovering, exhausted, rubbing blusher off her fingers.

'In fact, I was wondering if you do dressmaking at all – I mean for private clients? I've got an elder daughter who's scoured the whole of London for an unusual wedding dress and still can't find exactly what she wants. I told her she ought to have it made, but she said dressmakers were as rare as decent dresses. It just struck me that perhaps you could help us out.'

Hilary shook her head, about to say an apprehensive no, then changed it to a question: what date was the wedding and what style of dress did the daughter have in mind? It might be rather fun to make a wedding dress, and certainly a way of earning money. Liz's payments were becoming more erratic and Joe paid her very little for Luke's keep, though the boy had stayed a month now. Sometimes Joe descended with exotic gifts – toys for his son, flowers or scent for her, but you couldn't eat chrysanthemums or Chanel No 5.

She and Gill started discussing styles and fabrics, chairs drawn close together, so they wouldn't have to yell. The noise was getting louder: someone thumping the out-of-tune piano, a teacher taping carols from an old LP, and two angels swapping angry shouted insults. Jean MacDonald had announced what she called a toilet-break, before running through scene one, and a crowd of children were scrambling to their feet, rushing to the door. Gill dodged a punk-haired shepherd, who crashed past her with a woolly lamb in tow.

'Why not come to tea, Hilary, one afternoon this week, bring Luke after school. I live just round the corner. You can meet my daughter then, and fix a price and everything.'

They exchanged addresses, Hilary excited by her new role, new commission. Luke's reputation as a bully and a troublemaker had rebounded back on her, so she'd made no friends, so far, amongst the other parents, despite her shy attempts to barter names and smiles. They had all seemed rather wary, kept their distance, wouldn't lift their guard. It was a welcome change to be accepted by this woman, with her vivacious lively face, her striking arty clothes; invited out to tea like the normal friendly mother of a normal friendly child. Her labour on the costumes had been certainly worthwhile, had involved her with the school, made her part of a community, a work force. It was ironical, in fact, that her month with Luke had done more for her personally than it had done for the boy: given her a new routine, improved her social skills, even taught her how to cook – the basics, anyway. But Luke himself remained sullen and depressed.

Perhaps she ought to speak to Gill about him, bring the matter up when she went to tea with her, ask for her advice. Gill had two daughters and three sons, might well be able to help. She was going to need some help from someone, if Luke stayed any longer. She had expected to look after him for just a week or two; had suggested tentatively, after the first fortnight, that Joe might take some time off, so that his son could go back home – not just for her own sake, but for the wretched child's, as well. He was obviously unhappy in his new surroundings, missing Liz as well as Rita, uneasy in the half-denuded house. She had found him several times just lying on the floor, eyes closed, though not asleep; doing nothing, saying nothing, as if he were trying to stop the world, or block it out. He'd lie on tiles, or lino – anywhere, despite the cold, discomfort. Or he'd shut himself in cupboards, climb in under brooms or cardboard boxes, refuse to be coaxed out.

She'd tried to make Joe realise he needed more security, but Joe seemed almost frightened of his son; the big bully father reduced to funk and bluster, now Rita was away. He couldn't cook, couldn't run a house; was rarely home, in any case; always scavenging for scrap, touring dumps and car parks in his tow-truck, making shady deals in shabby pubs, checking other scrapyards, nipping in and out of bookmakers to put money on a horse, or taking time off, not for Luke, but to drive out to a race meeting, watch the horse he'd backed. If Rita Craddock kept on running temperatures, kept on losing weight, it would be Christmas Day before Luke was off her hands. Except they'd both be nomads then, both out in the street, since Liz's house was sold, the completion date fixed for mid-December.

'Right, time to start, everyone. Gabriel and Mary up on stage. Pontius Pilate, will you please not pick your nose. You're an important Roman

Governor, in case you'd forgotten. And if I have to tell you one more time about that spear, Luke Craddock, you'll feel it on the seat of your pants. Okay, kids, let's go . . . '

'You were marvellous, Luke.'

'I wasn't.'

'Yes, you were. You looked just like a real soldier.'

'It's stupid dressing up.'

'No, it's not. It's fun.'

'Bet you've never done it.'

'Yes, I have, lots of times. I was the Virgin Mary once and Joseph twice.'

'Girls can't be Joseph.'

'Yes, they can. I was even a King once, with shoe-black on my face.'

Luke looked disbelieving. She herself now felt it quite extraordinary that a bunch of aged nuns should have acted out their pathetic little playlets, taken them so seriously, crowing like small children over cardboard crowns, or turbans made from tea towels. Their cast had been so limited – no males, no Pakistanis, no playground bullies to take the baddie roles. Yet hadn't it been fun? She recalled her own star role as Pontius Pilate, fifteen years ago; the sense of almost sinful glee that she was allowed to stride around and play a man, even play a bad man; allowed to raise her voice for once, shout orders, snap her fingers, if only for ten minutes out of the five hundred thousand silent minutes which formed the normal convent year.

She fumbled for her keys as she and Luke turned the corner into Cranleigh Gardens, stopped outside the 'SOLD' sign.

'D'you like them people, Hilary?'

'*Those* people.'

He looked at her, confused. 'What people?'

She opened the gate, clicked it back in place. It was a losing battle to try to teach him grammar. 'Well, which people did you mean?'

'The ones what bought the house.'

'Yes, they're very nice.'

'*I* don't like them.'

'Why?'

'They're werewolves.'

'Oh, are they?'

'Yeah.' He kicked out at the dead hydrangea bush. 'Can we go and see my Mum?'

'Not today. She has to be kept quiet.'

'I won't talk. Honest.'

396

'I know you won't, darling, but . . . '

'I won't say a single word. Cross my heart and hope to die.'

'We'll try to go tomorrow, or the next day. That'll give you time to make her a nice card. I've got some real gold paper, that lovely shiny sort.'

'I don't want to make no cards.'

'Oh, come on, Luke. I'll help you.'

'No.'

'Why not?'

'I want to watch *Dracula*.'

'It doesn't start till nine. You'll have heaps of time before that.' She had tried to wean him off the television – all those horror films and cop shows he claimed to watch with Rita, despite the fact they were often very late; had given up the struggle now, and simply sat beside him, flinching at the gunfights, recoiling from the gore.

He switched on *Battlestar Galactica* as soon as they got in, crouched down on the carpet, still in scarf and anorak, eyes glued to the set. She switched it off again, poured him a glass of Seven-Up, as minor compensation. 'Remember what we agreed, Luke – reading first.'

'Reading's crap.'

'No, it's not.' She went to fetch his dragon book, one she'd bought herself, to provide some welcome contrast to the dreary reading-schemes they insisted on at school, with their safe and small vocabulary, their lists of repeated words. The dragons were exotic, very much in Robert's style, with threshing tails and plumes of fiery breath. 'Look, this one's called Demetrius, and that's his wife, Drusilla. Can you read me just the first page? I know the names are hard, but try these few lines here.'

Luke peered down at the print, stuttered out a word or two, then tried to close the book against her hands. 'Let's find another book.'

'What's wrong with this one?'

'Everything.'

'You liked it in the shop.' She should have saved her money, bought him shoes instead. She glanced down at his scuffed and battered trainers, the patches on his jeans. He had arrived with one small duffle-bag, stuffed with torn and dirty clothes; his usual long and floppy hair shorn to prison-length. She suspected Joe himself had acted barber, since, even now, it was sticking up in tufts. It angered her to see it hacked about like that. If Luke had been born a Lawley, not a Craddock, someone might have found the time to replace his worn-out clothes; made him feel he mattered; made him an appointment with a decent children's hairdresser.

She moved his glass to the safety of the coffee table. 'Well, if you don't like dragons, how about a magpie story?'

He didn't answer, just stared at the blank screen, as if the intensity of his gaze might somehow have the power to switch it on again.

'A crow ate all them chicks,' he said, at last, talking to the set.

'Which chicks?'

'The ones you said flew off to the seaside.'

She flushed. 'Who told you that?'

'Tim Wentworth. He lives just down the road, right beside that big tall tree the magpies built their nest in. His Dad saw these crows attack it. They had this awful fight, he said, and the mother magpie screamed like she was dying. Then the biggest crow gobbled all the babies up, except just one he dropped. Tim found it on the pavement. It was bald, he said, and dead.'

Hilary said nothing. She had known about the carnage. It had happened back in May, and it was now the first week in December. Had Luke only just found out, or had he been brooding on the tragedy all those seven months? The magpies had backfired on her in other ways. She'd got a book out of the library, just a week ago, to garner more details for her stories; discovered that according to the folklore, they were birds of evil omen, which heralded disaster, even death. The ancient legends claimed that they'd refused to wear full mourning at the time of the Crucifixion; were even called the Devil's Birds in Scotland, believed to conceal a drop of Satan's blood beneath their coiled black tongues.

She glanced out of the window. She hadn't drawn the curtains yet, and the dark night seemed to press against the pane. The whole room looked bare and desolate, with only the piano left, a makeshift coffee table and two hard wooden chairs. Once a house was sold, it seemed to lose not only all its comforts, its furnishings and fittings, but also lose its soul. No wonder Luke was nervous, kept asking to go home.

She pulled the heavy curtains, went to squat beside him. Her own fictitious magpie stories were still entirely innocent. She refused to change her kindly Mrs Swagger-Tail, her blameless Droopy-Wing; or let Luke know that magpies were a type of crow themselves, which gobbled eggs and fledglings with that same aggressive relish. She unzipped his anorak, tried to peel it off. 'Mrs Swagger had her chicks, though – a good half dozen, wasn't it? Shall we have that story while I'm putting you to bed?'

'What d'you mean, "bed"?' He pushed her hands away, refused to shed his coat. 'You said I could watch *Dracula*, and it starts in fifteen minutes.'

They were halfway through it when the doorbell rang. Hilary was glad of an excuse to miss the next slow and gloating blood-sucking; less pleased when she saw Ivan on the doorstep. She had never quite recovered from her initial shock on discovering that she'd allowed herself to become romantically involved with what Della called a poof. Since then, she'd learnt more tolerance, become fond of Ivan in a different sort of way, admired him for his kindness, his sensitivity, yet she still felt a shade uneasy with him, especially on her own. He had somehow become entangled in her sex life. Every time she'd been to bed with Robert, Ivan had been there, as well, as she tried to tip and rock her pelvis, remember what he'd said about relaxing, opening up. And occasionally she'd wondered – secretly, shame-facedly – that if it had been Ivan in her bed, instead of preening Robert, would she have responded any better; felt more sense of being in her body, owning it, enjoying it, able to experience ecstasy, release?

The thought had quite confused her, made her realise that her feelings for Ivan still went far too deep, despite the fact they were completely inappropriate, could never be reciprocated. Once she'd ended things with Robert, she'd also found herself avoiding Ivan, trying to keep their conversations as brief and bland as possible; had been frankly quite relieved when he'd moved out two weeks later, on the last day of September, found himself another room in Richmond. She hadn't seen him since.

'Come in,' she said, trying to force a casual smile. 'Have a cup of tea. I'm afraid I haven't got your herb tea, but . . . '

'No, I mustn't stay. I'm on my way to Croydon. I've just brought you round a present.'

'A present?' He was holding nothing but a bunch of keys, and what had she done, anyway, to deserve a gift from Ivan?

'It's out there in the van. I'll need a hand to bring it in.'

'What is it then – a grand piano?'

He grinned. 'You're getting warm.'

She followed him out into the road, gasped to see the rocking horse stabled in a battered van, its red nostrils flaring still, its majestic tail lustrous-long and black.

'I've no room for it in Richmond. My pad's so small, there's hardly room for *me*. I thought you'd like it, you and Luke. Liz told me about Luke – all the problems with his mother. I'd like to help, but . . . ' He shrugged, embarrassed. 'I couldn't think of anything but this.'

'Oh, Ivan, no, it's far too precious. I couldn't take it, honestly.'

'Well, I'm afraid you're going to have to. I've already filled the space it took, bought a new stereo which will give me far more pleasure than poor old Dobbin here.'

'You can't call him Dobbin, not a thoroughbred like that.'

'You see, you do deserve him. Give him a grand name and stable him in Liz's sitting room. He needs a bit of space.'

'But I'm moving out as well, Ivan.' She gestured to the 'SOLD' board. 'I'll be gone in just ten days.'

'Don't worry. Luke can have him then. He's more a child's thing anyway. Just be careful Craddock Senior doesn't break him up for scrap. Right, if you can steer the front part, I'll try to take the main weight. Up she goes!'

Dobbin had changed his sex in seconds – which reminded her of something. Once the horse had been installed inside and Luke was in the saddle, she asked Ivan if he'd wait for just a moment, disappeared upstairs, returning with a puppet in her hands, a pretty boy in trousers, with a cloud of girlish curls.

'Your turn now – a present in return. I bought it months and months ago and forgot to give it to you.' Not quite the truth, but near enough. She handed over the smirking doll, which had been stuffed into her sock drawer since his birthday in late March. What progress she had made since then – no longer a limp doll herself, a strange androgynous creature who feared to be a female, yet was frightened of all males; a dangling marionette who couldn't take a step without a puppeteer to pull her strings. Now she felt human and very near autonomous; if not quite fully adult, at least well on the way.

Ivan was still lingering in the hall. 'Look, if you ever need a hand, Hilary, or the loan of anything, or a lift in this old banger, which I've loaned myself from one of my old chums, or even just a chat, if you feel you're going spare, please do ask me, won't you? That's what friends are for.'

She mumbled something trite, wished she could express the surge of genuine pleasure his words had roused in her. He *was* a friend, a true one, and friends were very precious. She had become far too isolated, would have to start to change. Today was quite a landmark: a *rapprochement* with Ivan, an overture from Gill. Crazy to be ill at ease with Ivan because of something that had happened – or rather hadn't happened – eight whole months ago, and which she'd blown up since to a confused and senseless tangle. The whole affair was totally one-sided, Ivan himself completely unaware of it. He was offering simple friendship, which he'd offered from the start – nothing more, nothing dangerous. She dared to touch his arm, steer him from the door. 'Ivan, please do stay, just for one quick drink. Forget the tea – let's have a glass of wine. Liz left me all her booze, and I need an excuse to drink it up.'

'Okay, just five minutes.' He turned back to the sitting room, repocketing his car keys. She went to fetch the wine, returned with two full glasses and a thimbleful for Luke. She had cause to drink to Ivan. It was he who'd first relaxed her, returned her body to her, given her her bones; sown the first frail seeds of her present confidence, however gauche and groping it might have been at first. 'Cheers!' she said, as she arranged the two small chairs in a corner on their own, so they could talk above the chilling strains of *Dracula*, the creaking of the horse. Luke was watching his programme from the saddle, plunging wildly to and fro, feet rammed in the stirrups, reins bunched up in one hand. 'Careful, Luke!' she warned him. 'It's not a Ferrari.'

Ivan grinned, touched his glass to hers. 'Good luck in your new job. Liz told me all about it on the phone. She also said you've been a saint, helping out with Luke, and stuck with all the problems here, while she's free as air in Scarborough, wowing local councillors and enjoying the sea breezes.'

Hilary looked down. 'Oh, it's nothing. I enjoy it.'

'It isn't nothing, Hilary. It's really pretty decent of you. I feel bad myself. I haven't done a thing.'

'You brought the horse. He loves it.'

They both glanced across at Luke, who was now talking to his steed out loud, explaining some new twist in the film. 'His father buys him all these awful war-toys – Thundertanks and Doom Rollers, and robot anti-terror squads.'

Ivan shrugged. 'I had all those myself – or the equivalent, in my day, and they didn't do much harm. I'm still a pacifist.'

'I'm not sure Luke is, though.' Hilary laughed, leaned back against her chair. It no longer seemed so uncomfortable and hard, nor the room so bleak and empty. They had furnished it themselves, with their presence, conversation; become a little family – man, woman, child – the child even quite content now, as he dismounted from the saddle, fed his horse a toffee.

'Hey, Luke,' said Ivan, swivelling round to face him. 'What you going to call your bucking bronco?'

'Demetrius.'

She smiled. The dragon's name. She was surprised he could remember it, let alone pronounce it. Perhaps, after all, that book had done some good.

Ivan drained his glass, rezipped the knitted jerkin which served him as a coat. 'I'm sorry, but I'll have to make a move now, or I'll never get to Croydon.'

'Okay,' she said, getting up herself. 'But don't lose touch, will you, Ivan? Come and visit me in Hertfordshire. I'll remember to stock up with your favourite fennel tea.' She heard herself sounding like a normal friendly woman, no longer shy, embarrassed; realised she'd come light-years since the spring.

'Right, I will.' Ivan said goodbye to Luke, slapped Demetrius on the flank. 'And if you need anything before that, including a free lesson, don't hesitate to ring.' He paused a moment in the hall, fiddling with his car keys. 'I don't know how to put this quite, but I won't forget you, Hilary. I mean, even if you flitted off to China, instead of just to Letchworth, I'd still . . . ' He broke off, frowning, as if impatient with the language, or his own unaccustomed awkwardness. 'I meet a lot of different people in my work, often get to know them from the inside out, if you follow what I mean, and your "inside" is . . . Hell! I can't find any words tonight. I must be tired or something. What I'm trying to say, Hilary, is you've got a special kind of strength – what my army Dad called "spunk", or perhaps I should call "backbone", to fit my own profession. You may not be aware of it yourself yet, but it's there all right, believe me.' He stepped over Luke's discarded shoes, moved towards the door. 'Look after it. It's rare.'

She kept her gaze on the pockets of his jerkin, so he couldn't see the expression on her face, its mix of sheer pleasure and surprise. Robert had said something much the same, but it startled her still more to hear such words from Ivan, who wasn't out to flatter her, or woo her. She had regarded herself since the age of seventeen as the frailest of all sinners, and since her early thirties as a total abject failure, yet two very different men had called her special, praised her courage. Perhaps her past, however gruelling, had taught her perseverance, tempered her like steel.

Ivan opened the front door, gripped her hand a moment, as he turned to say goodbye. Impulsively, she took a step towards him, reached up to kiss his cheek.

'Thank you,' she said simply. 'And I mean for everything.'

'Bedtime, Luke. Come on.'

He shook his head, climbed back in the saddle, wrong way round this time, face towards the tail. 'I want to see the Western.'

'You can't. It doesn't end till midnight.'

'So?'

'Don't be rude, Luke. I'll count to ten, slowly, and if you don't get off that horse by the time I've . . . ' The phone cut across her threat. She went to pick it up, annoyed to hear Joe Craddock's beer-slurred voice. He always rang so late, disrupted Luke still more, sometimes gave her orders, seemed to forget she wasn't Rita, or his young delinquent daughter.

402

'Joe, it's very late. I'm just getting Luke to bed. Perhaps it might be better if . . . What? Oh, wonderful! That's really marvellous news. Yes, of course you can speak to him. He'll be thrilled to bits.'

Luke said very little, but she watched his face, saw it lift and brighten, as he hopped from foot to foot with the phone still in his hands. His mother was much better, had responded to the drugs, at last, would be home in just three days. Hilary collected up his toffee papers which were scattered on the floor, along with two burst crisp bags, ashamed to feel such sweet relief herself. It hadn't been that easy to take the role of mother, with no rehearsals and no script, and she'd been especially nervous recently, with the completion date so imminent, the end of term so near. Whatever Rita's state of health, she had no desire to drag a self-willed seven-year-old up to Scarborough with her.

He was gambolling round the room now, mock-wrestling with imaginary opponents, his whole mood and mien transformed. The receiver was still off.

'Luke, did you say goodbye?'

'Yeah. Dad wants to speak to *you*, though.'

'Well, thanks for telling me.' She rushed back to the phone. Joe sounded half-embarrassed now, a new emotion for him. 'We was wondering, me and Rita, if you'd like to come for Christmas. It would be our way of saying – you know . . . ' The words faltered and broke off, as if Joe couldn't bring himself to say thank you directly, shied away from any fancy sentiments. 'You won't have to lift a finger. My daughter's coming over and she'll be doing all the dinner. We always eat well, Christmas, have a goose and that.'

'Thank you, Joe,' she said herself. 'That's very sweet of you, but I've already made my plans. I'm going up to Liz's, spending Christmas there.' Her words triggered off a twinge of real excitement. She was longing to see Liz again, stay in a house which had cushions, plants and ornaments, in place of packing-cases; revive their friendship, catch up with her news; yet know she'd be returning to a complete new start, new job. The old bad year was over, Rita's illness over, and she was almost free, at last. Free, but very busy. She had a house to strip in ten days' time, all her Christmas shopping still to do, a wedding dress to make, and three more shepherds' costumes to complete. She switched the lights and fire off, straightened up the hearth rug. 'Come on, Luke. Upstairs! If you don't need sleep, I do.'

He didn't move. He'd stopped his frisking now, was squatting by the rocking horse, fiddling with its tail. 'D'you think my Mum would come – I mean, now she's better?'

'Come where?'

403

'To the play.'

'Let's invite them all – your Mum, your Dad, your brothers . . . '

'Don't be stupid. *They* won't come.'

'Not your Dad?'

'Nope.'

'He might if *I* ask.'

'No, he won't.'

'Want to bet?'

'Okay. How much?'

'50p. No, make it a whole pound.' She unplugged the television, shooed Luke through the door. Joe Craddock was already in her debt. He had offered her repayment in the form of Christmas dinner – a goose, a slap-up meal. That she didn't want, preferred Liz and Harry's turkey. But she could be tough for once and take a stand; insist he paid her back in the currency she chose.

31

'Merry Christmas.'

'Merry Christmas.'

'Come on in, dear. You look loaded down. What *have* you brought – the contents of your house? This is Ron, my second eldest son. Terry's two years younger, though you wouldn't think so, would you, the way he's losing half his hair? That joker in the paper hat is Gareth. He's married to my daughter, Maureen. And that body on the sofa is . . .'

Hilary stepped into a fug of smoke, her cheeks burning from the cold outside, burning from embarrassment as four strangers turned to stare. Was she just imagining it, or did she sense a slight hostility, a shade of suspicion in the air, or even mockery? She felt very much the alien, the prissy goody-goody with the stuck-up voice, the over-fussy clothes; the weirdo who had been a nun, lived all on her own, and was now intruding into a strictly family Christmas. She put her parcels down, began to fret about those too. Money was still short, so she'd made most of them herself, but perhaps it was absurd to bring chi-chi patchwork cushions and a hand-embroidered tablecloth to such a shabby house. The room was still more cluttered than before, crates of drink piled behind the sofa, Ivan's piebald rocking horse blockading the whole sideboard.

Ron and Terry shook her hand – both thickset swarthy men, smoking fat Havanas. The reek of their cigar smoke curdled with the queasy smell of goose fat, which filled the small squashed room. Multicoloured paper chains were looped across the ceiling, Christmas cards curling on the mantelpiece above a fierce coal fire. Gareth sidled up, a smaller shyer man, with a scraggy beard, damp hands; his purple paper crown clashing with his wiry ginger hair.

'What's the box?' he asked.

'Oh, that's for Luke.' She tried to shrug it off, wished it wasn't quite so big and bright. Her Magic Lucky Dip Box, which had seemed such fun a week ago, was probably a bad mistake as well. Luke liked action toys, and preferably violent ones, not babyish bits and pieces. She had almost killed herself trying to bring it on her bike, with all the other parcels. The bike was very ancient, a gift from Joe, who had rescued it from a scrapheap, done a few repairs, fitted it with panniers and basket, then called it her Rolls Royce.

'Where *is* Luke, by the way?' she asked, unbuttoning her coat. The heat was overpowering.

'In his room. He's sulking.' Rita took the coat, parked it on a chair.

'Could I pop and see him?' 'Sulking' could mean anything – despairing, crying, breaking up the place. She wished he'd come to greet her, at least said a brief hallo. She was only there for his sake; had come because he'd asked her, a week or so ago. He'd actually ventured out alone and found a call box, so he could talk to her in private; had struggled with the coins and the instructions, got through at last, after several failed attempts; said not 'Hallo', or 'Is that Hilary?', just 'My face is hurting.'

She'd been shocked to hear that forlorn and listless voice, dismayed to know he was still in pain. She'd heard about his face already; had thought of little else since his father had described it, just three days before – the closed and blackened eye, the purple bruising, swollen puffy lids. Joe had claimed quite casually that Luke had inflicted all that damage on himself, bashed his own face in, just to get attention. At first, she'd not believed him, suspected Joe was lying to protect himself. *He* had hit his son, most likely, and was scared of censure, frightened of reprisals and reproach. But Gill Lawley phoned herself, just minutes after Joe's call, confirmed the tale was true. Her own son, Nicholas, had returned from school with some garbled story about what he called 'that Craddock nut' banging his face against a wooden desk. Apparently, Luke had left the playground in the lunch hour, thinking nobody would miss him, skulked back to his classroom, where he assumed he'd be alone. But his teacher had returned as well – returned too late – found the child already bruised and sobbing.

It had happened on the final day of term, the day after the nativity play, which neither Joe nor Rita had attended, despite their promises. Rita was genuinely unwell; Joe simply got cold feet, had no desire to meet hostile stuck-up teachers, who might take this chance to grab him, berate him for his son's deficiencies. She had gone herself, of course, but she'd been kept so busy making last adjustments to the costumes, helping Gill with make-up, she hadn't even realised that the Craddocks were not there, or not until the play was almost over. Naively, she'd believed they'd come. Hadn't they given her their word?

Now, glancing round the messy room, she felt a surge of guilt. Wasn't it partly her own fault for trying to interfere, trying to work miracles and make Joe the sort of loving caring father who featured in Luke's reading-schemes? No wonder Luke loathed reading, when his books chronicled those happy cosy families with two cute children only, not a brood of seven; a young and healthy mother instead of an invalid of fifty;

a neat and shining house with roses round the door, home-baked cakes cooling in the kitchen. She should have come round sooner, offered Luke some help, tried to win his confidence, or at least showed him someone cared. But when she'd phoned the Craddocks, to suggest it, they'd been wary and offhand, still shaken from the social worker's visit, unwilling to discuss things with anybody else. Perhaps they'd been just tired, or frightened she would blame them for this further bout of trouble, or maybe they regarded her as another sort of social worker – middle-class, childless, interfering.

She had also tried phoning Luke's class teacher, tracked down her home number after a dozen false attempts, but the man who answered said Jean MacDonald had already left for Scotland, to spend Christmas with her parents. She'd stood motionless, still holding the receiver, seeing nothing save the grisly scene she'd run twenty times already in her head: Luke banging his own face mechanically, cold-bloodedly, as if he were punishing some crude inanimate object, not his own live and feeling flesh.

How was he now, she wondered – still bewildered and resentful, still crying out for help? He wouldn't get much help in this anarchic household, where they'd dismissed his pain as 'sulking', left him on his own on Christmas Day. Rita seemed reluctant that she should go up to his room; sounded more annoyed with him than anxious. 'Oh, leave the wretched boy,' she'd said already. 'He'll come down when it suits him.'

She tried once more, edged towards the stairs. 'But can't I just . . . ?'

'No. He's in a mood – forget him. Stop fussing and sit down. I'm gasping for a drink, aren't you? Park your bones, and I'll go and get our tipple.'

Hilary submitted, did as she was told – sat, or rather tried to sit – since all the chairs were littered with presents, toys, torn and crumpled gift-wrap, discarded coats and mufflers. She removed a leather jacket, draped it on a chair-back, squeezed herself between a box of crackers and a large black cat with scurfy-looking fur. Floor space, too, was rationed. Kevin's pram was parked beside a giant-sized Christmas tree, which seemed too grand for its surroundings and was already shedding needles, as if the noise and heat had overpowered it before Christmas Day was even halfway through. A dark man in an anorak was stretched out on the sofa, fast asleep, despite Les Dawson's Christmas Party, which was in full swing on the television, his manic guests hurling streamers, gulping down champagne. Sudden wild unnerving bursts of laughter shook the room each time Les cracked a joke. The sound was turned up loud, though no one else seemed aware of it at all; not even Sylvie, who was crouched right beside the screen, playing with a plastic

407

Mickey Mouse. She was decked for Christmas, like the tree; a red bow in her hair, a silver bauble pinned on to her nightie, strands of tinsel tangled round her neck.

There was no sign of Craddock Senior, though both his elder sons looked like slightly slimmer copies of him; the same broad shoulders and sturdy compact bodies, dark eyebrows, stubborn jaws. Both had totally ignored her, after the first brief introductions. They were still standing by the door, engrossed in private conversation, perhaps an argument, judging by their raised and heated voices. She had also met Joe's aunt, who was sitting in a corner and kept nodding at her, smiling, though she hadn't said a word; an anxious-looking woman, whose timid smiles failed to reach her eyes. The eyes were caged in spectacles, her freshly permed grey curls fettered by a spangled nylon hairnet. Hilary fought an aching longing to see her own Aunt Eva, share her Christmas with her, claim just one relation who was hers by blood and right. There had still been no response from her, no answer to her letters, no scrap of news or hope. She had done her best to remove her from her mind; somehow knew her aunt was dead, as her parents were both dead, her Father-God stone-dead. She had no wish to dwell on funerals, weep and rage for what she couldn't change.

She was relieved to see Rita returning from the kitchen with a glass of sherry in each hand, filled so full it was spilling on the carpet. The men were drinking Guinness, Auntie Dot nursing a large tumbler of something red and fizzy. Rita turfed the cat off, sank down on the chair arm. She looked shockingly unwell, as if she had aged a decade in two months; her skin ashen grey and lifeless, her eyes red-rimmed from crying. Hilary had heard about her crying spells, which she suspected must be due to some hormonal change, triggered by the recent hysterectomy. Joe's own diagnosis was less civil altogether. He was losing patience with his wife, fed up with 'women's troubles'; had told Hilary on the phone that if *he*'d made bloody women, he'd have made them without wombs.

'Where's Joe?' she asked.

'He's working.'

'What, on Christmas Day?'

'Makes no difference to him. If he wants to drive out somewhere, booze with all his pals, and call it work, that's his business, isn't it? I don't ask no questions. He'll be back for dinner, anyway. Joe don't miss his meals.' She reached out for her cigarettes, fumbled for a match. 'You don't smoke, do you, dear? The doctors tried to make me stop, but I'm smoking worse than ever. I'll stop tomorrow. I said that yesterday.' She laughed, an unconvincing laugh, got up again to try to find an ashtray.

'Can I help with something, Rita?'

'It's mostly done, but come and meet my daughter. She's been stuck out in the kitchen since eight o'clock this morning. I've never been so idle in my life. I don't like being idle, tell the truth. It only makes me restless. Mind that train-set, dear. I told Luke to pick it up, but it's like talking to a brick wall.'

Hilary eased up from her chair, tempted to cut upstairs to Luke, instead of following Rita. Her mind kept circling back to him: was he crying, still in pain? Had anyone given him breakfast, wished him 'Happy Christmas'? She tried to hide her shock at the filthy cluttered kitchen, as she was introduced to Maureen, a flamboyant fat-faced girl, whose brilliant scarlet lipstick and tinted auburn hair made Rita look still paler and more gaunt.

'Pleased to meet you, Hilary. You're the nun, aren't you? I've heard a lot about you. Amber, put that bowl down. No, you can't have a sweetie – they're for later. You've met my Kevin, haven't you? This is Amber, his big sister. She'll be four in February.'

Hilary forced a smile, to counteract the hostile stare in the huge blue eyes now fixed on her. Amber was dressed exactly like her mother, in a miniature version of her frilled and checked shirtwaister; even had her ears pierced, to match Maureen's own gold hoops, and her tiny nails varnished in the same pearly shade of pink. Both wore fine gold bracelets, gold lockets round their necks. Could they really belong to that shabby shambling Gareth, with his crumpled slacks, his patchy scruff of beard? No one else had bothered to dress up: Rita in a baggy skirt and sweater, Aunt Dot in limp beige Crimplene, and both Ron and Terry in their jeans.

She herself felt ill at ease in the smart cream suit she had chosen specifically for Christmas at the Kingsleys, hoping Di would admire her slowly growing dress sense, and not realise it was second-hand, from a highly useful shop she'd found, called 'Second Time Around'. The state of Rita's kitchen warranted a boiler-suit or a set of industrial overalls, not a pale two-piece which had to be dry-cleaned. The walls were streaked with condensation, the cooker clogged with grease, every surface piled with dirty pots and pans. The sink was leaking into a stained old plastic bucket wedged beneath it; a second cat was sitting on the table, its tail flicking over a bowl of cranberry sauce. The lino on the floor was torn in several places, its pattern faded to a dingy greyish blur. The tiny window looked out on the backyard, a wasteland of defunct machines, broken rusting tools.

Maureen seemed flustered, not quite in control. The sprouts were boiling over and an acrid smell of burning began seeping from the oven.

She darted over, rescued the potatoes, already semi-black. Hilary glimpsed the goose, a huge hump-backed bird which seemed to jam the oven, its fatty smell now almost overpowering.

'Look, please do let me help.'

'No, honest. It only makes me worse to have people flapping round me. Okay, I'm not the world's best cook, but I said I'd do the dinner and I will. I've told Mum a dozen times to go and put her feet up. What's the point of us all trooping over, if she still wears her fingers to a frazzle?'

Rita didn't seem to hear. She was fussing with the sprouts, mopping up the hob. 'You need the oven lower, dear. I told you that before.'

'Look, scat, Mum, or shut up. If I turn it any lower, we'll never eat at all. That goose is semi-raw still. God knows where Dad got it. It's as tough as old boots.'

'He shot it in the Royal Mid-Surrey Golf Club, way back in the summer. It's been sitting in the freezer ever since. That always makes things tougher, and it's a wild goose anyway.'

'Shot it?' Hilary looked aghast.

'With a crossbow, so it wouldn't make no noise. He and some old pal went out at five o'clock, when it was still just getting light, bagged a Canada goose and a couple of pheasants each. We've eaten both our pheasants, had them for Joe's birthday. That golf club's like a nature park, he says – every bird you ever saw, and some you wouldn't recognise outside a fairy tale, and all so tame they almost say "good morning", shake you by the claw. They was out again by half past five that morning, and no one any the wiser. He nicked the Christmas tree as well, dug it up from Oxshott Woods last week. No point wasting money.'

Hilary's mind was on the goose still, anger fighting shock. Canada geese were a protected species; handsome ornamental birds, born for flight and freedom, not for Christmas tables.

'Joe's an ace shot, I'll give him that. Take a look in here, dear. Even when we've no cash for the necessaries, at least he keeps my freezer stocked.' Rita opened the door of a battered rusting freezer, pointed out half a dozen wood pigeon, two mallard from the river, skinned and jointed rabbits in bloody plastic parcels, even a whole hare. 'He got the freezer free, as well. Fell off the back of a lorry, didn't it? Funny how much stuff falls off them lorries. I reckon we've furnished our whole house with what my old man calls "liberated goods".' She slammed the door, opened up the fridge instead. 'Have you made the bread sauce, Maureen? I'll do it, if you like.'

'Hop it, Mum, I've told you. I'll do everything in time. Just get out of my hair.'

Hilary stood staring at the open fridge, could hardly believe its squalid jumbled state; food crammed in anyhow, pots and jars without their lids, mouldering hunks of cheese; remains of meals which looked as if they dated from a month or more ago; nothing covered, nothing wrapped. Never before had she ventured into Rita's kitchen. Both times she had visited, they had stayed in the main room, and though Rita offered tea and snacks, they had never quite materialised. Thank God for that, she thought now, her mind on germs, bacteria. But she could hardly avoid eating Christmas dinner. She paused outside the sitting room, had no desire to go back there, face the smoke, the noise; could already hear a burst of wild applause exploding from the television, the pounding of a rock band. She must see Luke, whatever Rita said, must check on how he was. That was what she'd come for.

'Look, I'd like to say hallo to Luke. I won't be long, I promise.'

'Okay, please yourself. Maybe you can make him see some sense. He won't listen to a word I say, won't even get his clothes on.'

She found Luke in his vest and pants, stretched out on the floor, wrecking his toy cars. Several lay immobile on their sides; two more collided with a defiant-sounding crash as she closed the door, joined him on the lino.

'Pile-up on the motorway? Too much drunken driving over Christmas?'

He didn't answer. It was hard for her to speak herself, keep her tone jokey and offhand, while she had to sit there looking at his face. She was prepared for it in theory, but the reality was worse. The bruising covered more than half his face, mottled dirty purple on his cheeks, fading on the neck to a dingy greyish yellow, the blackened eye still bloodshot and inflamed. Thank God she'd come, she thought at once – put him first, done what he had asked, despite her strong aversion to spending Christmas with the Craddocks. She'd been tempted to refuse, at first, when he'd phoned her from the call box; use Liz as her excuse, explain that Liz and Harry had invited her themselves, made all the arrangements. He'd hardly seemed to listen, just rammed in his last coin. 'Please come,' he'd said. 'I want you to.'

Still, she'd hesitated, aware they could be cut off any moment. How could she agree? The Craddocks might not welcome her – not now – and she'd be letting Liz and Harry down, upsetting all their plans. Yet Luke himself had been let down, had no one to say yes to him.

'All right,' she'd said, suddenly, speaking in a rush, before the avaricious phone could axe her voice. 'I'll *be* there, Luke, I promise.'

Easy to decide that; far more delicate and difficult to explain her change of plan to Liz, who'd rung herself, later on that evening, to elaborate the programme for their own jolly Northern Christmas. She'd

411

found herself prevaricating, realised she felt guilty, like the Craddocks, fearing Liz might blame her for the whole affair, call her arrogant and foolish for trying to pressure Joe into attending a school function, without foreseeing what might happen as a backlash. In the end, she hadn't mentioned Luke or Joe at all. There were several other reasons – sound and pressing reasons – for deciding she had to stay at home. The completion date had been postponed, to start with, and she was genuinely nervous about leaving the house empty, especially over Christmas when break-ins were more likely. Liz had almost exploded down the phone.

'Are you out of your tiny little mind? That blessed house is almost off our hands. Let the Philpots worry – it's theirs now, legally. Okay, they're having trouble finding money, but you say they're still dead keen. So why ruin your whole Christmas nannying a pile of bricks and mortar which belongs to someone else, when you could be up with us in Scarborough, having a real ball?'

She'd changed tack quickly, tried to explain instead about the wedding dress, how it wasn't finished yet, how she'd agreed to make the bridesmaids' dresses, too; and how Gill Lawley's headstrong daughter wasn't the easiest of clients, kept changing her mind about length and style and fit.

'She sounds a right spoilt bitch to me. But never mind, bring the damn stuff with you. It'll be quite like old times to have you sitting sewing seams.'

'Liz, I *can't*! There's yards and yards and yards of it. The wedding dress alone is like a crinoline.'

'Okay, I'll come and fetch you in the car – *and* the bloody sewing. Or Harry's car. That'll hold a dozen crinolines.'

In the end, she'd told Liz – had to, more or less. Liz was getting ratty, piling up reproachful details of the outings she'd arranged, the Mozart concert she'd booked at great expense, the gifts she'd bought which were far too big to send.

Their last long-distance phone call was late on Christmas Eve. 'Are you sure you're not still cross, Liz?'

'Yes. I mean, no, I'm not – of course not. It's just a rotten shame, that's all, a ghastly bloody mess.'

'But you do agree I made the right decision?'

'Yes, I s'pose so.'

She had debated it herself through a mainly sleepless night last night, wondered if she'd blown the whole thing up, casting herself as the self-sacrificing figure, or the wretched humbled sinner seeking a new penance. Now, she was quite certain she'd been right to come, faced with Luke's grim and swollen face. If a child could do that damage to himself, accept that pain and bruising as the price of being noticed, then it was vitally important he got that notice; that someone said 'Yes, I'm here. I see you.' She was also uncomfortably aware of the parallel between them. Both of them had turned on their own bodies – she even more extremely by drawing blood with a vicious leather belt.

She sat back on her heels, picked up a toy Ford, which at least gave her an excuse to stop looking at his bruises. 'Did you get these cars for Christmas, Luke? A lot of them look new.'

'Yeah.'

'What else did you get?'

'Stuff.'

'Nice stuff?'

He didn't answer.

'I've got a box for you downstairs.' She noticed just a flicker of new interest, as he sat fiddling with a wheel-less pick-up truck.

'What d'you mean, a box?'

'A Magic Lucky Dip Box. Why not come and see?'

He dropped the truck, slumped against the wall. 'Too fagged.'

'Couldn't you sleep last night?'

He shook his head.

'Nor could I. We should have been together, had a snakes and ladders marathon.'

'What's a marathon?'

'A sort of race – a long one.'

'I don't like snakes and ladders.'

'You used to.'

'No, I didn't. I just played it to please you.'

'Well, I owe you a favour then, don't I – something in return? What's it going to be?'

He scowled. 'Stop taking the mick.'

'I'm not. You *can* have a favour, Luke – just one – a special Christmas one.'

'You mean anything I like?'

Now it was her turn not to answer. She was acting irresponsibly again. She shouldn't promise anything, when she might have to let him down. He hunched his legs up, stared at her defiantly. 'Okay, then, don't let them send me to that school.'

'Which school?'

'The one for bad boys.'

'What d'you mean, Luke?'

'I heard them talking.'

413

'Who?'

'That woman and my Dad.'

'You mean the social worker?'

'Yup.'

'She said I've got to go back to my own school after Christmas, but then they're going to send me somewhere else.'

He must mean a remedial school, the sort of place they dumped the kids they'd once called 'maladjusted', or 'educationally sub-normal'. No doubt they'd changed the terms now, prettied them with euphemisms, but the reality was probably much the same – dropouts and delinquents all herded up together, labelled as failures early in their lives, removed from the mainstream. That was wrong for Luke – she knew it, knew he was intelligent, didn't want him branded as a thickie or a yobbo, shunted to some siding where he could stay his whole school life, with no chance of catching up, no chance of being normal. And even when he left school, the stigma would remain; employers losing interest once they checked his records, realised he'd been 'dustbinned' since the tender age of seven.

Why had Joe said nothing, hushed the whole thing up? Because he suspected she'd object? How could she? If Luke's Head had decided he was unsuited to the school, needed special educational provision, she was powerless to oppose him. For all she knew, the process could already have been started: educational psychologists alerted, the social worker preparing her report. She glanced across at Luke, longed to wrest him away from all those so-called experts who would turn him into a 'case', probably put him on some huge computer, make him just a number and a file.

'Hilary! Where are you? We're going to open presents now. Come down here and join us, and bring Luke with you, please.'

Maureen calling from the hall. Hilary got up, reached out a hand to Luke, to pull him to his feet. He ignored the hand, slumped lower.

'I don't want no more presents.'

'Not even mine? I bought you twenty different ones.'

'Twenty?'

'Well, just tiny silly things. Why not come and see?' She retrieved his jeans and sweatshirt from the pile of clothes discarded on the floor, helped him on with them, tried to hide her shyness as they walked into the sitting room together. It seemed even more noisy and crowded than before; Kevin wailing in his pram, Amber teaching Sylvie carols, and the television party in its final frenzied throes. At least there were no trains today, though the roars of canned laughter and storms of canned applause still seemed to shake the room. The dark man on the sofa had

414

disappeared, perhaps woken up, at last, by the gang of party guests on screen, who had wrapped themselves in paper chains and were chasing round the studio; clutching glasses, knocking over chairs.

'Lovely cushions, dear,' said Rita, who was already opening presents. 'The cloth's too good to use, though. Joe's such a pig at meals, we never have no cloth. Here, park your bones and open these few things. The ones in the red paper are all from me and Joe. The shiny one's from Maureen and that little box is . . . '

She was astonished by the pile of presents, all brightly wrapped, with gift tags. 'Love from Auntie Dot', 'Cheers from Terry', 'Merry Xmas, Joe and Rita'. She had called herself an interloper, intruding on this family, but now they'd made her part of it, included her as well. Never in her life had she received so many gifts. As a child, relations had been rationed – not to mention money. One present from her parents, one from Auntie Eva, a few small things from Katy; a box of hankies from the couple in the shop, perhaps toffees from a neighbour – that was it. She tore the wrappings off a pair of weighty bookends, a ceramic boy and girl in tartan trews, with matching pouts and hats.

'We know you're into books, dear. Pretty, aren't they? We could have got elephants, or owls, but I thought those were more unusual. Hey, you'll never guess what that is. A nail dryer! Yes, so your varnish doesn't smudge. Clever, isn't it? You just stick your nails in here and . . . Ow! It's blowing cold. Now open up that big one. D'you like it, dear? It's a Piccadilly Raindrops Lamp. When you switch it on, it looks as if it's raining, but the lady in that bandstand thing stays sheltered all the time. Saucy, isn't she, with just that wisp of clothing?' Rita laughed. 'She can't feel the cold like I do. I get arthritis the minute that it's damp. No, you can't see it raining, Luke. It needs a plug on first. Anyway, you saw it in the shop.' She pushed his hand away, turned back to Hilary. 'They had one on display, dear, and we thought of you immediately. The rain looks sort of golden and them lilies at the bottom light up pink and mauve. We reckoned it would be nice for your new place.'

'Yes, thank you. It's . . . ' Her voice all but tailed away. She was disappointing Rita, as Rita had disappointed her. 'Lovely cushions, dear' wasn't quite enough for the hours of love and labour which had gone into the patchwork, and the hand-embroidered tablecloth would probably end up in a drawer. Her Raindrops Lamp would be more difficult to hide. It was nearly two foot high, with a plastic goddess smirking in a shiny golden temple, her feet growing out of a bed of garish flowers. She felt a sudden pang for the tiny humble things they'd be opening now at Brignor – a box of pins, a biro, a skein of darning wool. They had seemed such treasures at the time, engendered such excitement. She glanced around the room: Ron and Terry shrugging off gold cuff-links and silver Parker pens; Amber complaining about her pastel fake fur coat. Where had all the money come from for these expensive lavish gifts – or were they 'liberated goods' again?

She felt even more embarrassed now by Luke's Magic Lucky Dip Box, the trifles it contained. She had never intended him to open it in public, have all those mocking eyes turned towards the Woolworth's jotters, supermarket sweets, home-made bits and pieces she had assembled in a Sainsbury's cardboard box. It had cost her only time – the time and thought and trouble it had taken to make each parcel special, to paint the box itself in brilliant reds and blues, stencil out his name along the top. Luke had hardly noticed it, barely glanced at all the wrappings, just ripped off the snakes-and-ladders paper she'd drawn herself, coloured in so carefully, using his own crayons; or crumpled up the carton she'd turned into a hedgehog, with matches as spines and round brown button eyes. She'd wrapped one tiny present in twelve separate sheets of paper, like the game of pass-the-parcel – thought it would amuse him – but he only seemed impatient with it, ripping off the dozen fiddly wrappings, until he finally found a plastic pencil-sharpener, tossed it to one side. At least she'd diverted Sylvie, who was collecting all the papers up, exploring empty cartons, chewing a rosette. Rita removed it from her mouth, swapped it for a Mars bar.

'You're hungry, lovey, aren't you? We should have sat down hours ago, if only that damn bird was ready.'

'It *is* ready, Mum, I've told you.' Maureen shook out Amber's coat, smoothed down the pink fur. 'And the sprouts are cooked to pulp. It's Dad we're waiting for. Which means we won't get any dinner till the pubs are shut. We'd better follow his example and knock back a few ourselves. If we all get tiddly, at least we won't notice if the meal's spoilt. No, Amber, I haven't any Mars bars, and you're not allowed them anyway. Sylvie's different – she's grown up. I know you're starving hungry. We all are. No you can't have sherry, neither. I don't want you ending up like Grandad. Oh, look! *Diamonds* is just starting. I've just got to see it. D'you know thirty million people watched it on Christmas Day last year? I read that in the *Sun*. D'you watch it, Hilary?'

'Well, no, I . . . '

'See that woman in the lurex gown? That's Amanda Carson. She's the star, the bitch, the one with all the diamonds. And that guy just bending over her is her ex-husband, Dale – except they're going to get remarried. That sulky-looking blonde bit is Dale's second eldest daughter and she hates Amanda's guts. She's so thin, she makes me sick. I like her dress, though, don't you, and the way she . . . ?'

'Shut your trap, Maureen. We've just missed the whole beginning, with you yapping on like that.'

'Okay, keep your hair on. I've got to explain to Hilary or she'll get completely lost. Hey, look at that mink wrap! Amanda must have got it from Guy Lowndes. He's another baddie, Hilary, but he always . . . '

'He's not a baddie, stupid. He's the hero of the thing.'

'And what about his wife, the way he just abandoned her?'

'She asked for it, going off with . . . '

'Oh, shut up, all of you! Hilary's not blind or deaf. She can follow it herself, or have a snooze.'

Hilary longed to have a snooze. She was already weary from her night awake, drugged by too much sherry, yet she dared not close her eyes. It would seem an insult to the family on screen, a two-dimensional family, who were obviously more solid and important than any real or living one; engendered strong emotions. She had just sorted out the Craddocks, their relationships and names; now she struggled with the Carsons – who belonged to whom, who was sister, son, ex-wife, or merely lackey. She watched them exchanging gifts and greetings, just as they had done themselves, though sentiments and presents were both more elevated. These were exceptional people, as far above the norm as the Saints had been to her, once; set up as idols, models; the non-Christian's Holy Family. Amanda Carson was Our Lady of the Sitting Room, whose mystique and miracles excited awe and veneration; thirty million worshippers watching at her shrine. She tried to imagine all those separate congregations, up and down the land, revering the same saints, attending the same service, like a new united Religion of the Box; or like the ancient monasteries had been – every Order in the world chanting the same Office at exactly the same time.

The thirty million contracted to eleven – eleven aged nuns singing in the Brignor chapel – and she not there to swell the sound. A year ago today had been her first full day in the world, so today was an anniversary, as well as Christmas Day – even her birthday, in a sense. She was one year old in secular terms. Maybe that explained why she felt so small and vulnerable, why her thoughts kept sneaking back to Brignor, missing its traditions. She'd feel better once the Christmas con was over. It *was* a con, without Christ in it, or God. She had longed to go to Midnight Mass, even as a non-believer; hungered for some ritual, if only a pagan one, so long as it were sacred. The television rituals couldn't compensate: too much bread and circuses, too little soul and spirit. They were advertising space-guns now, farting Santa Clauses; interrupting *Diamonds* with commercials. She waited till the Carsons leapfrogged back, then sank back on the sofa, sipped her refilled sherry, watched debonair Dale Carson drinking his. At least everyone was quiet now, every eye riveted to the screen, even Amber's, Sylvie's. This was their own family – surrogates, ideals; a circle they were intimately involved with, who kindled the emotions maybe dormant in real life – desire, excitement, wonder; a focus of high passion, gods to fill the void.

She felt her own mouth water as Amanda Carson carried in the turkey, entrusted it to Dale to carve. Jewelled hands around the table reached out for vegetables: roast potatoes, uncharred and golden-brown, tiny *petits pois*. She heard her stomach rumble, quickly masked it with a cough.

'Enjoying it?' asked Maureen.

'Oh, yes,' she said, swallowing and smiling. Delicious tender turkey breast was melting in her mouth, crisp and perfect sprouts dispelling the sweet sickliness of Tesco's British sherry.

'More sprouts for you, Hilary?'

'No, that's plenty, thank you.'

'Swedes?'

'I've got some, thanks.'

'Joe grew those himself. He's got a little patch of garden next to his menagerie. The rabbits got out once and ate everything in sight, including all the swede tops.'

Joe gave a boozy guffaw. 'Greedy buggers! I got my own back pretty quick – killed the biggest blighters and put them in a pie. Terry called it swede and bunny pie.'

Hilary put her fork down. It was bad enough trying to eat the goose. She kept remembering the Sunday when she and Luke had gone down to the river, fed a pair of Canada geese with scraps of bread and cake crumbs. They'd been so tame and trusting, they'd eaten from her hand. Now their flesh was skewered on her fork, its gamey taste rancid in her mouth. The whole meal seemed tainted, germy. Both Amber and Sylvie had prodded half the dishes with sucked or dirty fingers, before anyone was served. The dishes had no lids, were just cracked white pudding basins, one leaking greenish fluid on the table. Then Rita had dropped the carrots, scooped them from the carpet, fluff and all. She seemed unsteady on her feet, had spilt gravy down her skirt, upset several glasses. There had been a row when Joe returned, and she'd dis-appeared upstairs, come down pale and shaky, as if she'd been mixing drink with tranquillisers. Joe had refused to wash his hands, or change; was sprawling at the table in an old blue donkey jacket, with a grubby yellow tee shirt underneath. His hands were filthy, oil and grime engrained into the skin, nails black and bitten off.

'They'll get a wash later, when I do the dishes. No point wasting water.' He grinned and turned to Hilary. 'I always do the Christmas washing up. It's my gift to Rita. She won't get nothing else.'

'Some gift! He always breaks the glasses, or bungs 'em in the sink with the greasy baking tins.'

'You're an ungrateful bloody cow, Rita. Some wives would give their . . .'

'Shut up, Dad. We've got company, remember.'

Hilary tried to hide her embarrassment in her beaker of champagne. The champagne was pink, expensive; the beaker stained brown melamine. It was a household of extremes: expensive toys and presents, yet no proper dining table – just a table-tennis top set across two trestles; no cloth to hide the bare and cracked green wood. She understood about the cloth once she saw Sylvie try to eat. The girl paddled her hands in gravy and bread sauce, then wiped them on anything or anyone who happened to be near. She dropped food all around her, mauled it, played with it; uttered piercing wails or piggish grunts to indicate she wanted second helpings. She seemed never sated, never full. Before lunch had even started, she had eaten two whole Mars bars, half a packet of ginger nuts, and various greasy titbits Rita fed her from the kitchen, to prevent her devouring newspaper or toys.

Hilary wished she could offload her own still bulging plate, employ Sylvie's mouth to clear it. The swedes were the main problem. Swedes spelled penance for her, and despite her years of practice, when she'd always asked for double – done her best to relish them, to release holy souls in Purgatory or ease Reverend Mother's rheumatism – that all seemed arrant nonsense now. The Abbess needed cortisone, not swedes. She pushed them round her plate, made patterns with them, hid a woody lump beneath a piece of goose skin. Luke was also messing with his food, had hardly eaten anything. He was sitting next to Amber, whom he obviously despised. The contrast was quite painful. Amber was a pink and perky child, who enjoyed chatting with the grown-ups, flirting with her father, and had even managed to finish up her goose, whereas Luke looked tired and sullen, ignored everyone around him, and was using his knife to cut the table, rather than his food. Hilary wished they'd put her next to him, instead of next to Joe, with a rowdy beery Terry on her left. Both men were gnawing bones, talking with their mouths full, so that tiny particles of mingled food and spittle sprayed onto her face.

'Pass the stuffing, Terry. More for you, Dot?'

'No, thanks, Maureen, love. I can't eat much these days. The last op I had they took away so much, I reckon I've only got a shred of stomach

419

left.' Long speech for Auntie Dot, who had hardly said a word so far, seemed cowed by Joe, awed by his two sons, kept flashing on her nervous smile, as if she hoped it might protect her, or at least be accepted in lieu of conversation. Hilary herself found it hard to talk. Every subject which came naturally to mind seemed either out of place, dangerous, or tactless: Luke's schooling, Luke's bruised face, her stupid disappointment that he hadn't bought her anything for Christmas; Brignor, and its Office, the fact she missed it still. She was missing Liz, as well, her mind continually sneaking back to Norfolk, then on to Scarborough, so that she was living through three Christmases at once – the convent one, the Kingsleys' and the Craddocks'.

'Hilary's a nun,' Amber suddenly announced, in a tone of obvious relish. Everybody laughed, even Hilary herself. Much of Amber's chatter she couldn't understand. The child was obviously intelligent, even quite precocious, but she used her own child's language, with private or invented words; spoke so indistinctly Hilary felt embarrassed when she couldn't grasp her questions, or failed to laugh at jokes which the others found so cute. Ron and Terry talked mainly to each other, discussing subjects she knew nothing of at all – greyhound racing, souped-up Kawasakis, Chelsea's shaky prospects in next week's FA Cup. Joe seemed only keen to pick a fight, kept contradicting everyone, complaining about the food, the heat, the government, the snooping bloody VAT man whom he threatened to castrate, and the way they ran the tote at Kempton Park. He reached out for the potato dish, not to take some more, but to put his own five back, despite the fact they were soggy-wet with gravy, and already hacked about.

'It's time you learnt to cook, Maureen. These spuds are so damned hard, I almost broke my teeth on 'em. No wonder Gareth looks like he's always got the trots and Amber's cadging chocolate half the time.'

'Lay off, Dad, can't you? I've spent half my bloody Christmas slaving in the kitchen, and that's all the thanks I get. And if you're going to start slagging off my family, we'll stay at home next time.'

Joe ignored her, heaped his plate with swedes, bloodied them with ketchup, then waved fork and swede at Hilary. 'My fucking stupid daughter didn't want to cook these; said they weren't the thing for Christmas. "Weren't the thing".' He imitated Maureen's high-pitched voice. 'Christ knows where she gets all her stuck-up fancy notions – not from me or Rita, that's for sure. I spend all year trying to grow the buggers in soil that's more like gravel, and they're not good enough for . . . '

'Watch your language, Dad. We're used to it, but . . . '

420

'I won't watch fucking nothing. You've all been picking on me since I walked into this house. If you don't like it here, get out.'

'Cool it, Dad.' Ron now intervened, ripped the tags off half-a-dozen cans, poured his father a glass of light and bitter, as if that might calm him down, refilled his own pint tankard. Joe had already damned the pink champagne as 'woman's bloody piss'.

Hilary sipped her woman's piss, laid her knife and fork together, to indicate she'd finished, leant back in her chair with a ripple of rebellion. She wouldn't finish up her swedes, wouldn't eat her goose. She wasn't a nun, wasn't seeking penance, and if Joe could be so rude, she'd be impolite herself, risk offending him by leaving food he'd shot or grown. This was Christmas Day, so she'd indulge herself for once, fill up on dessert, which wasn't spoilt, since Rita had looked after it herself, saved the Christmas pudding from death by drowning, the mince pies from cremation.

She looked up at the small and grimy window pane. It was already almost dark. They had missed the Queen's speech, which had just been starting as they all trooped in to dinner, though she'd heard Gareth say he'd record it on the video for Maureen. Christmas Day was already half over. She felt a sudden droop of failure. What difference had it made to Luke to have her there, share his Christmas with her? She'd had so little chance to talk to him, make things better, present him with some chink of hope. And even when she'd tried, offered to play Snap with him while they were still waiting for their lunch, he'd merely shrugged, slunk back to his room. He seemed uneasy and on edge, pulled between his family and her, as if even he could see the gulf between them, felt he belonged to both and neither. How could she help him, anyway, when his problems were so grave, when so many other people would soon be clamped onto his life – well-meaning dangerous people like so-called welfare officers?

She must make one last big effort after lunch, maybe take him for a walk, dark or no – try to get him on his own and draw him out, ask him what he wanted, find out what he feared. At least she could promise to keep in touch with him, write to him from Hertfordshire, perhaps invite him up to visit in the holidays, if the college and the Craddocks both allowed it. Then, once she'd reassured him, let him know she wouldn't simply vanish, she could say goodbye all round, make her getaway, slip back to Cranleigh Gardens after tea, spend Boxing Day mercifully alone. She had just ten days to finish off the bridesmaids' dresses, complete her last few jobs, before she packed up her belongings and decamped to Claremont College. Despite her worry over Luke, she was really looking forward to it. December was a feverish month, with all the fuss and fret of Christmastide, its painful lacks and memories, but cold and steady January would blast her back to health. She'd been to see the College, taken to it instantly, liked its friendly atmosphere and spacious well-kept grounds. She'd even seen her room – small, but bright and cheerful, with a marvellous view, looking out across a beech wood. She knew she'd settle down there, begin to put down roots, be able to start again as a new and different person – not ex-nun or Liz's protégée, but as assistant domestic bursar, future warden to the girls.

The room was growing dimmer, the one weak unshaded light bulb no match for the wintry dark outside. The table was now littered with nutshells, chocolate wrappings, dismembered Christmas crackers and a pool of spilt custard congealing round Sylvie's empty place. Sylvie herself was sprawled out on the floor, still engaged in eating. She had returned to savouries again and was picking at a goose bone, her nightie hitched up high above her knees, displaying gross white thighs and a drooping bulge of sanitary towel, which looked more like a nappy. Amber was asleep, had nodded off after the dessert, and was now stretched out on her mother's lap, blue eyes closed, chic dress splashed with gravy.

Hilary shifted in her seat, longed to leave the table, as Luke already had. The room was getting chilly, cold draughts sneaking in through the small ill-fitting windows. It was a mean low-ceilinged room, which held nothing but the table and eleven makeshift chairs; had once been just a lean-to, only annexed to the house when the Craddocks had their fifth child and could no longer fit the kitchen. She was feeling claustrophobic, closed in by the circle of slumped and sated bodies, and weighted down inside with heavy Christmas pudding, over-sweet mince pies. The trinket in her cracker had been a tiny plastic gun, which seemed somehow menacing, even when Luke swapped it for his thimble. They all wore paper hats now. Gareth sported two, one above the other. Sylvie's was too small, had started disappearing down her throat.

'Coffee!' Joe demanded.

'You don't want no coffee, Dad. The doc told you to keep off it. Anyway, I want to put my feet up. We'll have tea in half an hour. You can bloody wait for that.'

'*I'll* make it.' Rita got up, starting stacking plates. 'I ought to clear up, anyway.'

'No, don't, Mum. You're meant to take it easy. If Dad wants coffee, can't he put the kettle on himself? Or is he paralysed or something?'

'Don't you take that tone to *me*, girl. You don't know what work is. What is it they call you at your job – a receptionist? That's just a fancy

422

term for sitting on your arse all day and getting someone else to mind your kids. You've always been the same – bone idle.'

'For fuck's sake, Dad, I've just cooked Christmas dinner for eleven.'

'Ruined it, you mean. If your mother wasn't always running to the doctor and living on them pills, we might have had a decent meal for once.'

'Oh, you're starting on *her*, are you? I'd have thought she'd had enough from you already. She almost died in hospital, and all you cared about was who'd wash your shitty pants or cook your rotten dinners.'

'And what fucking help was you, I'd like to know? You didn't lift a finger, didn't even visit. You're all the same, you lot, only come here when you want something, or when I've got a few bob spare. I've worked my arse off feeding seven kids, yet when Rita falls apart, I have to send the youngest to a stranger, because his own flesh and blood just don't want to know.'

'So Hilary's a stranger, is she? That's nice for her, I must say. She must feel really great, sitting there beside you, while you use that filthy language, then insult her.'

'And what about your own language? Not that marvellous, is it? Oh, you try to play Miss Prim and Proper, but it don't cut no ice with me.'

'Look, shut up all of you!' The mild and shambling Gareth suddenly exploded, sprung up from his chair. 'I'll make the coffee myself. Maureen, go and watch the Queen. The video's all set up. If your father can't be civil to you, then keep away from him.'

'She's not watching no video. *Lucky Break* is starting in five minutes and I'm not missing that for anyone.'

'The speech only lasts five minutes, Dad. You won't miss nothing. Anyway, we could have watched it hours ago, if you hadn't hung around the boozer and made us all so late.'

Joe lunged forward for his glass, drained it in one defiant gulp. 'I don't know why I stay here. You're always on my back, always yak-yak-yakking. I sometimes think I'd have been better on my own, without no wife and kids at all.' He wiped beer foam off his mouth, pushed his glass away. 'Rita never should have had no kids. She's not built for it, not got the right equipment. It went wrong from number one, when she produced that . . . that . . . ' He seemed lost for the right word, finally swung round on his chair and jerked his thumb at Sylvie, who was sitting vacant-eyed now, grease and dribble curdling on her chin. 'Kids like her should be done away with – yeah, right from birth, before they break no hearts. It's kinder in the end. Once *that* was born, we didn't stand a chance. Oh, for Christ's sake, Rita, don't turn on the bloody water-works. I've got to talk straight sometimes.' He heaved up from the table,

423

flinging back his chair and waking Amber, who broke into a wail. 'Yeah, go on, bawl, the lot of you. I'm going to watch the box.'

'Oh no, you're not, Dad! I'm watching the Queen's speech first. I don't care what you say.'

'You'll quiet your bloody brat first – *both* your bloody brats. Now the little un's started.'

'Only 'cause you shouted. Look at you, you bully, you've made everybody cry. It's a wonder Hilary's not howling her eyes out, too. Come on, Hil, d'you want to watch the Queen?'

'No. She's watching *Lucky Break* – same as me. She's my guest, isn't she? I asked her here.'

'Some guest! You're treating her like shit. She's not used to this, you realise. She's probably never heard such language in her life.'

Joe ignored his daughter, made an elaborate show of offering Hilary his arm, easing back her chair for her. 'You come with me, sweetheart. And how about a little drop of whisky? It's good for indigestion and I reckon we'll all finish up with that, after Maureen's shitty cooking.'

Hilary was steered into the sitting room, seated on the sofa, a drink placed in her hands. She could hardly think for all the noise, commotion. Both the children were howling still, Amber near-hysterical as she tried to fight her mother, lashed out with feet and fists. The row had upset Sylvie, too, and her frightened wails were resounding from the dining room, countered by Terry's angry shouts. And now the Queen's voice was added to the uproar, as Maureen struggled with the video, managed to switch it on, despite one child screaming in her arms, one kicking at her skirts.

'The Christmas message is a very lovely one: peace on earth to men of good will. At this universal festival, we should aim to see the world as one, united by our common bond of humanity, our desire for peace, our fervent hope for that good will mentioned in the . . . '

'Shit! He's soiled his nappy.' Maureen sniffed her son's lower half, wrinkled up her nose. 'That's all I need! Amber, if you don't stop that noise this minute, I'm putting you to bed and you'll stay there till we leave. Okay, that's it – you've had it. Come on, both of you.' She swept them out, Kevin bundled under her arm, while she steered Amber by the ear; paused a moment at the door, to yell some last invective at her father.

'Good riddance!' Joe grinned, got up, started fiddling with the controls. 'Now we can watch *Lucky Break* in peace.'

'I'd like to watch the Queen first, if you don't mind.' Hilary's voice was quiet, quiet but steely.

Joe stared at her in shock, mouth open, legs unsteady. 'You what?'

'I said I'd like to watch the Queen's speech. I've never seen it, ever.'

'But *Lucky Break* must have almost started. I can't miss that. I watch it every week.'

'It goes on for fifty minutes, Joe. You'll only miss the first bit.'

Joe took a step towards her, part threatening, part incredulous, stood uncertain by the sofa, sweat beading on his forehead. The room was stifling hot, in contrast to the draughty dining room. The fire seemed far too fierce; cruel flames twisting round the logs, which appeared to be in pain as they hissed and spurted, gave sudden twitching spasms before charring into ash.

Joe grabbed the sofa arm, to steady himself, crouched right over Hilary, so that his whisky breath was blasting in her face. 'You're as bad as bloody Maureen. I might have guessed. All you fucking females are the same.'

She tried to edge away. 'Would you kindly watch your language, Joe. Maureen's right. I do find it rather shocking.'

'Oh, you find it rather shocking, do you?' He lurched back, almost fell. 'I suppose ordinary working people aren't good enough for you. I'll have you know it's blokes like me what keeps the likes of you, shut up in those nunneries, never doing nothing, or sponging off the state.'

'Look, please, Joe, I'm trying to listen to the Queen.'

'What does *she* know, neither? She never had to earn no living, or scrimp and save to bring up seven kids. It was all nannies, weren't it, and dirty great palaces, and handouts from the state.' He was silent suddenly, staring at the Queen's pale face, an old face like his own, which looked strained and almost weary, despite her duty smile.

'At this season of Christmas, when we share our love and happiness with family and friends, we must also recall all those who live without love, or who are on their own, or battling with poverty or sickness . . .'

'Where's Rita?' Joe demanded. 'Where's my coffee? If a man can't get a cup of coffee in his own house on Christmas Day . . . I bet Prince fucking Philip isn't told to wait till teatime. Ah, here it is, and about bloody time.'

The door burst open – not Rita with the coffee, but Luke with his new vampire book. 'Will you read this to me, Hilary?'

'No, she fucking won't, lad. She's watching the Queen's speech and no one's allowed to say a bloody word. We've got two royal highnesses in here – Her Majesty the Queen and Princess bloody Hilary.'

'Joe, *please*. Don't use those words in front of Luke.'

'He's heard 'em all before. And don't you tell me how to treat my lad. You've never had no kids yourself, so you don't know nothing anyway.'

'Yes, I do.' Hilary suddenly sprang up, banged her whisky glass down, strode across to Joe. She saw Luke dart out as swiftly as he'd entered, heard his footsteps thudding up the stairs. Her own heart was thumping in her chest, but she hardly even noticed it, was too startled by her voice – a new aggressive voice now booming through the room.

'I know that kids are meant to have some love, and live in peace and quiet without all these rows and upsets. And I know it's wrong for them to hear that no one wanted them, that their fathers considered drowning them at birth, or . . . '

'Look here, my girl. I said that about Sylvie, not the boy, and, anyway, I . . . '

'It doesn't matter.' She interrupted Joe as he had done with her, though for her it took some courage, was a completely new experience. Ivan had talked about her strength, used words like 'spunk' and 'backbone' – high time she proved him right then, used that strength and courage, for a change. 'If Luke ever heard you say it, even about Sylvie, he might well think you felt the same in his case, wished he'd not been born or . . . Maybe you do think that, but it's too late now, isn't it? He *is* born. He's here, alive. He needs a chance at least.'

There was a sudden threatening silence, save for the gasping of the fire, the Queen's gentle measured phrases about the Commonwealth, our Christian heritage. Hilary hardly heard the words, was fighting fear and guilt now, as she still stood her ground to Joe. Had she gone too far, sounded too belligerent? An image suddenly flashed into her mind: a Canada goose with Luke's own wary eyes, feeding from Joe's hand. Phhtt! She heard the arrow strike, pierce the creature's breast; watched it struggle, collapse into itself, in a writhe of bloody feathers. If she submitted now, who else would dare defend those smaller weaker creatures, which men like Joe shot down? His two elder sons had roared off on their motorbikes, their first instinct to escape; Rita was still sobbing in the kitchen, Auntie Dot paralysed with fear.

She refused to join those cowed and weeping women, who would go on suffering passively, never answer back or take a stand. She'd been the same herself – all her life, in fact – had let her father bully her, then allowed a whole succession of powerful tyrant men to tell her what to do – bishops, priests, the Pope, the Brignor chaplain: tyrant women, too – her Abbess, Mother Vicaress, cold-eyed Mother Mistress. She hadn't even dared reply to Robert Harrington, had let him slap her, shout at her, call her selfish and unprincipled. She *did* have principles and she'd damn well make them clear.

'Luke's got to have some help, Joe, and he's got to have it soon.'

'He's having help, for Christ's sake – far too bloody much of it. I've

426

already got the Social on my back, and now they say they're sending round some fancy bloke connected with his school.'

'Yes, what about his school? He told me they were going to send him somewhere else. Where, I'd like to know? To some school for hardened cases, which will only make him worse?'

'It's nothing to do with me. It's that fucking Head at Wandsworth. He says he won't put up with Luke no more, says he needs . . .'

'But it *is* to do with you, Joe. You're his father and you can push for what seems right for him, not allow them just to shunt him to some . . .'

'He's not going bloody nowhere – not for months. It takes an age, the Head said. He has to be assessed first, and every fucking busybody from our doctor to his teacher has to poke their nose in first, or come snooping round to spy on me and Rita, write their damn reports about what a pigsty it is here.'

'But can't you stop them, Joe, send him to another school before the assessment even starts – just an ordinary school, but a homely simple kindly sort of one, with a Head who has ideals, believes that boys like Luke need love and understanding, not constant threats and punishments. Luke's own Head seems so callous, as if he's really got it in for Luke, and has now simply washed his hands of him.' She moved over to the window, stared out at the scrapyard, at the piles of junk and wreckage. 'It's wrong for children to be beaten down – wrong for anyone – to be made to feel they're wicked all the time, or worthless human beings, damned to an existence where there isn't any happiness or simple human love, only sin and penance. I know that, Joe, believe me. I know what harm it does, how soon it saps your confidence, removes all your joy in living, all your self-respect.'

Joe strode towards the television, turned the volume up, so the Queen's high-pitched voice was shrilling through the room, drowning Hilary's own voice.

'I just don't understand you women. You made all that song and dance about this fucking bloody speech, and you haven't heard a word of it. Why don't you listen, girl, instead of yakking on yourself? I've had enough of bloody yap today, from you and all the rest.'

Hilary winced against the noise, which was jarring in her ears, stunning the whole room. She darted forward, turned the volume down again, stood trembling by the set as the Queen's face loomed into close-up, the age lines in her forehead cutting deeper now, the lipsticked smile less steady.

'To all of you, of every faith and race, I send you warmest wishes for a time of peace and joy during this most important festival of Christmas, in which we celebrate the birth of a small child. To you, and all your

427

children, to all the children in the world, especially those unprivileged, I should like to say . . . '

'Christ! She do go on – like every bloody woman. Can't she wind it up, for fuck's sake? Ah, she must have heard me – that's the sign-off. "A very merry Christmas to you all."' Joe repeated the greeting in his own mocking version of the Queen's high breathy voice, then put two fingers up to her. 'Ta, Ma'am, very much, and the same to you and yours. Now maybe I can switch on *Lucky Break*, or d'you want to hear the fucking national anthem?'

'No, I don't, Joe, thank you, but I don't want you to swear. Almost every word you've used since I mentioned it before has been a . . . '

'Christ all fucking mighty, woman, I didn't invite you here to tell me what to do. I've had just about enough from you, poking your nose in where it don't belong, like all them other buggers who keep bloody interfering. If I want to teach my son every swear-word in the book, or even stick the lad in bloody borstal, that's my affair, thank you very much. Mind your own bloody business, will you, and if you don't like my language, or the way I run my life, well you know where the fucking door is.'

'Yes, I do.' Hilary swept towards it, cymbals clashing, trumpets blaring, as the national anthem surged across the room, its last triumphant phrase braying out, full-volume, as she tugged the door, slammed it, hard, behind her.

32

Hilary strode round and round Liz's half-denuded sitting room, still out of breath, still sweating from her frantic breakneck bike ride. The room was cold, the heating all turned off, yet she was burning with a mixture of anger, guilt and shock – anger with Joe Craddock, anger with herself. What in God's name had she done, screaming like a harpy, deluding herself she was standing up for Luke, when she'd only made things worse for him? She'd left Joe so virulent, he'd probably turn his rancour on the boy, victimise his family. Easy for her to hurtle off, escape like Ron and Terry. Luke had no such option, had to stick it out. How naive she'd been, and stupid, to imagine simple love could heal his wounds; to have taken that heroic stand on behalf of bullied children, bludgeoned geese; seen herself as champion of the oppressed, challenging Goliath. That was pride and foolishness, not love.

Yet the anger was still there – resentment that Joe Craddock should be allowed to tyrannise; rage with Luke's headmaster; frustration with the boy himself that he wouldn't even try to be less truculent. Almost without thinking, she sat down on the piano stool, banged back the lid of Liz's ancient Broadwood. The husk of a dead fly was lying upside-down on middle C. She slapped it off, brought down a wild right hand, began to hit the keys at random, wincing at the maddened tide of sound; both hands thumping down now, feet vicious on the pedals. She was killing Goliath not with stones, or arrows, but with sheer booming hurting sound; hitting out at priests and Popes, attacking Joe and Robert, attacking her Superiors. She was startled by the noise, the volume of it, resonance; the way it seemed to fill and cower the room. That piano had more power and tone than she'd ever realised.

She was even more astonished to realise she was playing – that what had started as brute fury now had sense and shape. Several chords had somehow come together to form a phrase she recognised, a phrase which spawned another, and another; had begun to flow, develop, grow into a tune. How extraordinary, incredible, that her hands still knew the notes, knew where to go and what to do, despite a practice-gap of over twenty years. They were stiff, admittedly, clumsy and unsupple, the nails too long, one finger sore from sewing, yet still retained their basic skills. She was no longer merely crashing chords, but actually making music – rough and simple music, yes – but with melody and structure, a

429

growing sense of rhythm. It was like a minor miracle, something resurrected from the dead.

She dared not stop, in case the magic vanished; continued playing fragments, weaving them together; suddenly changing to a piece she'd once practised quite obsessionally – the Beethoven Sonata she'd prepared for her Grade 8 exam, as long ago as 1966. She'd never taken the exam, had entered Brignor that same year, renouncing music as a dangerous source of pride, along with all the other skills which might tie her to the world. She was amazed she could still play the piece – or at least play parts of it – though she was making such a hash of it, the examiner would have shuddered, ordered her to stop. She was fluffing notes, forgetting notes, breaking off completely several times, yet hearing the whole movement perfect in her head, as if she'd recorded it on tape. She stumbled on an ascending run of semiquavers, groped for the arpeggios which followed; realised with a sense of shock that she had never really given up her music. Those phrases had been sounding for more than twenty years; muted, maybe, officially denied, but still always faintly playing in the recesses of her mind, despite her nun's resolve to strip that mind of everything but God. Another sham, but one she now rejoiced in, since it had preserved her music, kept it still alive, like a valuable possession she had buried in the sand to conceal it from its predators, and was now digging up with excitement and relief.

She went on playing, her already tired left hand repeating and repeating that mournful pleading figure in C minor, which sounded bitter, elegiac. As a girl of seventeen, she had never been aware of that edge of mounting anger beneath the desolation, the subtle change from endurance to revolt; the sudden switch of mood again, as a mocking second subject undercut the grief. There were whole new depths to this sonata, depths which as a schoolgirl she'd had no power to express, or even understand. Oh, she had assumed she was mature then, had prided herself on her artistic sensibility, even in her teens, but her emotions were too narrow, her whole life and mind too narrow. Only now, could she understand the vast new range of feeling which her one year in the world had opened up, and which made this music new and almost dangerous.

Yet she was still betraying it by her infuriating clumsiness, her lack of all agility, her constant shaming lapses when she forgot whole passages; heard them in her mind still, but hadn't the ability to convey them to her hands. She longed to play the piece with all the deft technique she'd had at seventeen, but added to the intensity of feeling she'd developed only recently; to make it soar and sing, bring out all its meaning and its power.

430

Abruptly, she broke off, sat staring at the keys. She *could* do that, in fact. It needn't stay an idle wish, some unrealistic fantasy like living in a lighthouse and becoming Gloria Harrington. Robert himself had told her she was passionate, had talents she must use. *This* was her main talent, a gift which hadn't died, only been neglected. She could restore it if she wanted, nurse it back to health, start playing every day again. There were three pianos at the college, two uprights and a grand. She'd noticed them particularly, flung them envious glances as Andy showed her round. They'd probably let her use one, at least the oldest battered one, and if she really scrimped and saved, she could use every spare penny for piano lessons, find a teacher who didn't charge too much, someone who might realise just how keen she was, how desperate to play.

She jerked up to her feet, a dozen different pieces clashing in her head as she began fidgeting round the room; her fingers flexing as they remembered leaps and stretches, her mind churning with new schemes. She must re-plan her college term, to fit in daily practice; forget the footling hobbies she'd been planning for her leisure time. Tennis, sketching, swimming, were of no importance now. She could even start preparing for her Grade 8 examination, take it after all – a mere twenty-two years later – just to prove she could, provide her with a goal.

She crossed the room again, unable to keep still; ran a restless thumb along the hard grooved ridges of the music-rest; traced the spray of ivy carved into the wood. She felt a real affection for this battle-scarred piano; its worn and yellowed keys the colour of old teeth, its left flank streaked and faded by the sun, the bite-sized piece missing from the top. It had given her her freedom and her future, restored her to her powers.

She opened the hinged lid of the padded music-stool, started sorting through the music stored inside; discovered favourite pieces, longed to play them all; longed to be a girl again, with her whole adult life in front of her, so she could devote it now to music, not to God. She couldn't find the Beethoven, but why not start with Haydn, try to choose something quiet and calming? There was a book of Haydn sonatas crumpled at the bottom, its stained and curling pages filmed with dust. She wiped it with her sleeve, admired its handsome cover, which was decorated with a scroll of leaves and flowers, the composer's name picked out in Gothic script, 'Franz Joseph Haydn, 1732–1809.'

The book slipped from her hands. Joseph Haydn. Joseph Craddock. She had forgotten Joe entirely, forgotten all her guilt and fury, even forgotten date and season. Yet just a mile or two away, the Craddocks were continuing their relentless Christmas Day, the one she'd hoped to leaven with her presence. Leaven! She eased up from the floor, fretted

431

to the window with a shudder of embarrassment; peered out at the dark and shadowed garden. She could see not grass and shrubs, but Luke's bruised and swollen face; see him in his bedroom, slumped down on the floor again, or maybe in the middle of a full-scale family row: Rita sobbing still, upset about her vanished guest; Maureen's children squalling; Joe himself bellowing and cursing. She ought to phone immediately, apologise to Rita, ask to speak to Luke, at least try to reassure him, explain that . . .

What could she explain? And supposing Joe picked up the phone, a still more drunk and bitter Joe, who might shriek at her again, use every ugly swear-word in his repertory? How would that help Luke? She couldn't help him, could she – not in any way – despite her good intentions, her irrational assumption that she knew better than the experts, and could save a child whom they would only harm? She blushed at her own arrogance. She was completely inexperienced, not to mention ignorant, knew nothing of remedial schools, had simply jumped to rash conclusions, condemned them all as useless, with no evidence at all. She must leave Luke to the social workers, the educational officers – trained professional people who were used to handling cases as complex as his own. She could actually do him damage by her amateurish meddling, simplistic good intentions. Luke wasn't just a separate individual, but part of a whole family, part of its very hopelessness, its problems, and it was sheer delusion to imagine she could solve those on her own. Liz herself had tried and failed, yet Liz had so much more to offer: a proper home and family, a grandson the same age, all her long experience as a mother and a home-maker.

She sagged down on the window-seat, shivering now in the cold and draughty room. Liz had acted out of simple kindness, but her own motives were more suspect. Was she trying to seek penance still, search out worthy causes? She had suspected that last night, in fact, dismissed it far too glibly; realised only now that her training as a nun was still nowhere near totally destroyed. She would have to hack more fiercely at those remaining Brignor roots, yank them out completely; change the medieval concept of living for one's Creator to the modern one of living for oneself. She was still denying self – had spent eleven months in a house with a piano and never touched it once before today. There was irony in that. The piano was now sold, would be moved to its new owner the day after tomorrow, so she had found it only to lose it. She blessed the fact that she was moving, too, to somewhere she could play, make up for those lost and wasted months. It was sin, in Robert's book, to let her talents shrivel, ignore her gifts, deny her strongest feelings. She must follow his advice, give expression to those feelings, display her obvious passion – not in bed, in music.

She drifted to the mantelpiece, picked up his small bronze dragon, smiled to see its furious expression, a metal tongue of angry flame exploding from its mouth, bulbous eyes distended. She held it on her palm, stroked its sharp ridged scales. Why still chafe at Robert, when he'd given her so much, and would actually help her music by the fact he had encouraged her to dig up buried feelings, unwrap her shrouded self? Even the pain and violence of their parting had taught her something more about humanity, helped her gain maturity, rely more on herself. She realised now that suffering could have point – not as penance, or for God, but because it gave you wider sympathies, deeper understanding, and she could use those in her music.

She returned to the piano, discarded the Haydn for no other reason than the poor man's Christian name – picked out a Mozart Sonata which she set up on the music-rest instead. Wolfgang Amadeus. Amadeus meant 'love God'. She *would* love god – the god in her, her talent, all Robert's subtle complex gods which included art and music. She adjusted her position on the stool, tried out the opening bars, surprised again to find her hands obeyed her; elated by the vigour of the piece, its zest and sheer resilience – qualities she'd forgotten still existed. She had returned her silver ring to Mother Abbess, two severed scraps of lost and broken joy, yet here was joy intact.

Christmas faded, the Craddocks faded. It was no longer bitter winter in a faceless London street in the dreary 1980s, but summer in Vienna two centuries earlier, Wolfgang Amadeus scribbling down these bars. Nothing was important save that she played them as he wished; nothing even existed save her fingers on the keys, that crescendo in the next line, followed by a sudden pianissimo, that marking at the top: '*Allegro con spirito*'. She'd caught the mood – the liveliness, the spirit – but the technique was still eluding her. She bungled a transition, botched a change of key, almost exploded with frustration as she heard the music limping, refusing to match the perfection of the score. It needed work – endless work – discipline and patience, total dedication. Those qualities she had; had learned them as a nun, practised them for decades as virtues in themselves; could put them to some use, at last, justify those years of arid training. Nothing would stop her now she'd returned to the piano, neither lack of time or money, nor any guilts and scruples.

She turned back to the beginning of the Mozart, to the lively scampering figure which had slowed her down, spoilt the flow and sparkle of the piece. She cursed as she went wrong again, fingers stumbling, left hand still too feeble, even the pedalling unsubtle, overdone. She must find a proper teacher, however much it cost, start her practice the very day she arrived at Claremont College; keep

433

playing, persevering, so that by Christmas Day next year she could sweep through this sonata as if those two dumb and silent decades had simply never been.

33

Hilary snipped her thread, took a final appraising glance at Emma Lawley's wedding dress, before she returned it to its special padded hanger. She had to admit it did look rather special, modelled on an Elizabethan court gown, with elaborate sleeves, yards and yards of frothy swirling skirt. She stretched her cramped fingers, tried to ease the tension in her neck. Her whole body seemed to ache from the strain of so much close and finicky sewing. Over these last weeks, she had worked with something very close to passion, becoming more and more involved as the gown grew from paper concept into organza actuality. She had come to regard it as her own dream dress – Gloria's dress – the one she'd never had, either for her Clothing or her almost-marriage. The bridesmaids' dresses, too, had become part of the whole fantasy, as she'd helped Emma choose a more tasteful style and colour than her own borrowed frilled pink tulle of twenty years ago. It would be quite a wrench to hand the dresses over. She knew she'd be renouncing her last romantic dreams, her last vain hope of leaning on some stronger wiser figure, or following a Master, be he God or man.

Yet she wasn't miserable, had felt instead a sense of real achievement, especially last night, when she had sat up late, like half the world, to see the New Year in. She had heard laughter from next door, garbled shouts and greetings from the drunken guests who'd left at 2 a.m.; had felt no twinge of envy as she watched a second party spill over into the street from the big house opposite. She was doing what she wanted – practising the piano, finishing the dresses – almost relieved to be alone, so she could achieve so much: four hand-sewn hems, fifty fiddly buttonholes and a definite improvement in the Mozart. Anyway, at least she'd had the television to enliven things at midnight, wish her happy New Year. She'd poured herself a glass of sparkling wine, drunk to that New Year with real hope and conviction; drunk a second toast to Liz and all her circle, and a final one to Mr Humphrey Sheed.

Mr Sheed was the new owner of the piano, a sprightly septuagenarian, whom she'd managed to charm into allowing her to keep it for an extra week. She had somehow felt a quite irrational terror that if she didn't play again until she moved to Claremont College, her resurrected gift might simply vanish. She had told Mr Sheed a slightly different story, but at least he had accepted it, rebooked the removal van for tomorrow afternoon. The day after was completion day; her own carrier arriving to transport her bike and luggage up to Hertfordshire; all the precious things which Liz had given her, to transform her humble room – the stereo, the radio, the two framed watercolours, the old but eager sewing machine, plus the kitchen bits and pieces which she didn't actually need, but which no one else had use for.

Her excitement was building like Emma Lawley's wedding nerves. She had made the last arrangements with Andy at the College, even got permission to use the college piano – not the battered one, the grand – so long as she practised when no one else required it, and not after ten at night. The piano lessons were still a source of worry. How could she afford them on her meagre wage? Yet she'd been considering having driving lessons, to carry on where Robert had left off, and they'd be more expensive still. She'd take her test eventually – that, too, was an ambition – but music took priority, both in money and in time.

She tidied up her sewing things, sat at the piano, began a flurry of arpeggios and scales, only stopping when the phone rang. It was probably Gill or Emma, impatient to collect the finished dresses. She picked up the receiver, tensed at the male voice – not a cultured Lawley voice, but a rough untutored bark.

'You left your coat behind.'

'I know.' Her own voice became immediately defensive, hand gripping the receiver as if throttling Joe's thick neck.

'And all your Christmas presents.'

'Mm.'

'Don't you want 'em, then?'

'Well, I . . . '

'I could bring 'em over in my van – like now.'

'*No.*' The word came out like a shout, as she tried to think up some excuse, protect herself from a further dose of Joe.

'It won't be any trouble. I've got to fetch a set of wheels, so I'll be passing your street anyway.'

'No, really, I . . . I'm going out. In fact, I'm late already. I ought to leave this minute, or I'll miss my train.'

'Don't go. Please. Don't ring off.'

She was astonished by the tremor in his voice, a new note of desperate pleading. Joe must be simply acting, putting on a show. 'I've got to, Joe, I'm sorry. There's this friend of mine who's . . . '

'Rita's left.'

'*What?*'

'Rita. She's walked out. Last night. Took Sylvie and the cats.'

'Walked out?'

436

'Well, drove – went roaring off with Maureen in the car. They came down again last night, my daughter and her bloody brats, came to see the New Year in. Except we never saw it, did we? They was gone again by half past ten. Yeah, another fucking row, with everybody screaming and Rita quite hysterical. She's mental, my old woman. Maureen says she's ill, but it's worse than that – she's losing her marbles. I blame that hospital. She's never been the same since they took her womb away. I reckon they took a good bit more than that . . . '

'Where's Luke, Joe?'

'He's here, with me. Maureen wouldn't take him. She said Sylvie was enough. Well, I hope our fucking halfwit really gives her hell. That's what she deserves, for winding Rita up, telling her to stick up for her rights and not take shit from me. She . . . She . . . ' The last words faltered to a halt, as if Joe were running out of steam and even fury. She heard his laboured breathing fill the gap, heard the silent fear behind the swearwords and the rage.

'She'll be back, Joe, in a day or two. She won't leave Luke, I know.'

'She's bloody left him, ain't she? *And* me. She told me she weren't never coming back, yelled it in my face, really lost her rag and . . . '

'Well, she was probably just upset. People often say things when they're angry, and don't mean half of them. Once she's cooled down and had a day or two to rest, she'll be on the phone to say she's coming home.'

'Not with Maureen there, she won't. Maureen's had it in for me for years. She's won now, ain't she – split me up from Rita, got her own back.'

Hilary struggled with a ferment of emotions – selfish irritation that Joe had burst into her life again, worry over Rita, mounting fears for Luke, and a strong desire simply to put the phone down. She fought the last, tried instead to make her voice sound reasonable. 'It's not a question of winning, Joe. Rita really isn't well. She's never had a chance to get her strength back. She'll be better for a break, a bit of convalescence, if you like, with someone else to cook and shop, and help her out with Sylvie. She'll probably be a completely different person once she . . . '

'And what about *my* cooking? Who's going to help *me* out, I'd like to know? Or the lad?'

Hilary drew her breath in. She already knew the next line, and already knew her answer. This time, she didn't need excuses, fabrications. 'Well, *I* can't have him, Joe. It's out of the question. I'm moving in two days and the Philpot tribe take over. I'm already half packed up. All the beds have gone, and there's no proper furniture. I'm sleeping in a sleeping bag and living out of a suitcase.'

'If you need a place, you could always move in here. I mean, it would help us both out, wouldn't it? We've got half a dozen beds and so much bloody furniture we're always tripping over it.'

She shuddered at the thought of living in a breaker's yard, alone with Joe and Luke. The idea was quite grotesque. 'I've *got* a place, I told you, Joe – weeks ago, in fact – a residential job with room and board.'

'Well, this could be another job, a better one. I'll make it worth your while this time. Just tell me what they're paying you, and I'll up it by a tenner, and the whole lot cash in hand. I had a big win on the horses, so I'm not short of a bob or two.'

'Joe, I'm sorry, it's impossible. This job is really important. It means a lot to me.'

'And I suppose my poor lad's not important?'

'Yes, of course he is. But you said yourself I wasn't any good with children, that I'd never had any of my own and . . . ' She realised with a twinge of guilt that she was actually taking pleasure in throwing back his words at him, evening up the score from Christmas Day. Yet if he could blackmail her, call Luke his 'poor lad', to appeal to her compassion, when he'd been a 'bloody bastard' just last week, then he deserved what he was getting. She *was* worried over Luke; horrified, in fact, that now even Rita had walked out on him, but she must harden her own heart, refuse to get involved. She couldn't help – she knew that now – had been making a real effort to cut off from the Craddocks since the hideous debacle of Christmas Day.

She was aware of Joe's embarrassment as he mumbled an apology. He was obviously unused to saying sorry, only doing it now so he could try to change her mind.

'I said a lot of stupid things on Christmas Day. Blame it on the drink, dear. Or blame my bloody daughter. She got me all wound up, and it's like you said yourself about people getting angry. They say things they don't mean.'

'I think you did mean some of them. And it's true I've no experience of children. Your poor lad, as you call him, would be far better off in a proper family, with other children, and a normal kindly mother who knows what she's about.'

'There ain't no fucking family like that. If my own kids won't help me out, then how the bloody hell d'you think . . . ?'

'Joe, if you keep on swearing, I'm going to put the phone down.'

'Okay, okay, I'm sorry. It's only bloody habit. My own Dad used them words and his Dad before him. I don't know any other words, that's all. But look, I've got a new idea. There's this pal of mine – Charlie – rents this shop in Tooting where they sell batteries and car parts. He owes me a favour, several favours, actually. If it wasn't for his old pal Joe, he'd be doing a stretch in the Scrubs. But never you mind that – what's important is he's got this empty flat above the shop. If you take Luke, help me out till Rita's had her little rest – it's yours. Yes – no rent, no charge, no questions asked. You can take Luke there to start with, and when the laddie's back with us, you just stay on, however long you want. And don't worry about furniture. I'll take care of that. If you're short of beds, no problem. I can . . . '

'I'm *not*, Joe. You don't listen. I've already got everything I want – a bed, a room, a job, a . . . '

'Look, a flat like that's worth hundreds. Tell you what, I'll throw in a colour telly, one of them big fancy ones with remote control and . . . '

'Joe!' She raised her voice, made it almost threatening. 'The answer's no. D'you understand? And I've simply got to go now. I was late before you rang.'

'Wait, please wait! Forget about the flat. I'll sort out something else. Forget I even asked you to help out with the lad. It ain't fair – I realise that. But just do one small thing for him. Find him a new school.'

'Joe, I can't. I . . . '

'But you said yourself how he must go somewhere different. I mean, you made a fucking speech about it, didn't you, as if you was up there on your soap-box – how he needed a new Head who'd give kids like him a chance, even give him love, you said, love and understanding.'

Hilary swore beneath her breath. Now Joe was doing what she had done herself, throwing back her words at her, words which made her cringe now.

'You see, I don't want them people coming here – them snoopers from the Education whatsit – when Rita's not at home. It don't look good, do it? But if we moved him to another school, we could stop the whole damn – what's the word?'

'Assessment.'

'Yeah, assessment. That word sounds like trouble – you told me so yourself – and I don't want no more trouble. I've had enough, and so's the boy.'

'But term starts in a few days, Joe. How on earth can . . . ?'

'All the better! I'll go and see his old Head the first day of fucking term, tell him we don't need his school no more. And if you sort him out a new one, I'll fix him up a place to live, okay?'

'But can't he stay at home, Joe? I mean, you're there at the weekends, aren't you, and almost every evening?'

'No, I'm fucking not. I'm sorry, I don't mean to swear, but there's no way I can have that boy at home – not without his mother there. Don't

439

worry – I'll ask Les again. He's my eldest son, married to a prize cow who thinks she's far too good for us, but even cows can change their minds, if you make it worth their while. They live quite close, so the lad could pop back here from time to time. That way, I'll see him, won't I, and . . . ?'

It was several minutes more before Hilary managed to ring off; stood trembling by the window, her whole day and mood destroyed. What a way to start a brave New Year, struggling with this weight of guilt and anger. Joe had bawled her out on Christmas Day and was now grovelling back to ask her help. Yet how could she not give it, when Luke's future was at stake? She must at least try to find a school for him, if only for partly selfish reasons. If she left him in the hands of some kind but firm headmaster, or perhaps a motherly headmistress who understood his problems, then she could depart for Claremont College with a distinctly lighter conscience.

Impulsively, she rushed upstairs to fetch her bag and jacket, wheeled her ancient bike out through the gate, cycled full-pelt to the Lawleys, found Gill in an old dressing gown, recovering from a hangover.

'What's the matter, Hilary? What's happened? You look as if . . . It's not the dresses, is it? Christ Almighty! Nothing's happened to Emma's precious dress?'

'No, it's fine – they're all fine – finished just this morning.' She sank down on a chair, mopped her eyes which were watering from the wind. 'I do feel pretty low, though. I've just had Luke's father on the phone – more trouble, I'm afraid. Look, I'm not intruding, am I? I mean, if you'd rather rest or . . . '

'No. I'm glad to see you. All the kids are out and Ben's clearing up the debris in the garden. Hold on just a sec – let me get an Alka-Seltzer. My head's splitting from last night. It must be lunchtime, isn't it? I've lost all track of meals, but if you're hungry, there's some soup.'

They discussed Luke's future education over home-made mushroom soup and Alka-Seltzer. Hilary had already mentioned the assessment, when she'd phoned Gill several days ago, asked her opinion on remedial schools, admitted her own prejudice.

'Perhaps I'm wrong, Gill. I've no facts at all to go on. I'm just following a hunch.'

'No. My hunch is much the same. I mean, those special schools are often pretty good, with smaller classes and loads of individual help and visiting psychiatrists and things, but the trouble is they're "special" in the wrong way. The kids who go there must feel singled out, made to feel they're different, all black sheep, cut off from the norm. And anyway, assessments take for ever. I knew of one case, not unlike Luke's, in fact, where it dragged on for a year, and all that time the kid was getting worse.'

Gill drained her fizzing Seltzer, slumped back in her chair. 'The problem is where d'you send the lad? I mean, his present school's no good for him, even if the Head were on his side. That man's a real traditionalist, who puts the three Rs first, believes kids are there to learn, so he cracks down pretty fiercely on anything or anyone who interferes with that. It's fine for Nick – he's bright, and really thrives there, but different schools suit different sorts of children.'

'That's what I said to Joe. I mean, I thought a more progressive school might . . . '

'That could be just as bad. The more anarchy a kid has in his home, the more structure and security he needs at school. Those progressive schools sometimes go too far, throw out timetables and rules and any sense of discipline. I'm sure that's wrong for Luke. If I were you, Hilary, I'd go for a small church school. They're often very good, get the balance right between strictness and permissiveness. There's one just down the road – St Matthew's and St Mark's.'

Hilary tensed at the familiar names, felt an immediate opposition to the school. 'Is . . . Is it Catholic?' she inquired.

'No, C of E.'

'But Luke's not C of E.'

'Doesn't matter. They take all kinds and creeds. Were you looking for a Catholic school particularly?'

'No.' Hilary removed a shred of mushroom from her tooth. 'Definitely not. Luke's officially a Catholic, but . . . '

'Mind you, there *is* the convent in Upper Westmead Gardens. That's meant to be extremely good, as well, and the only convent state school in the area. They take boys as well as girls, right up to eleven.'

Hilary wiped her mouth, pushed her soup away. 'I'm . . . er . . . not too keen on convents.'

'Well, they've got a lot of lay staff. They had to take them on, because they couldn't get the nuns. I suppose girls these days are itching to be astronauts or nuclear physicists, rather than give themselves to God.'

Hilary forced a laugh, tried to change the subject. Gill Lawley knew nothing of her past. 'I'd prefer a non-denominational school, if possible. What about that one in Lambourne Crescent?'

'Not your catchment area. That's another problem, Hilary. You're restricted to the schools within easy walking distance – which usually means a choice of only two or three. And if they're all full up already, or object to a kid who's labelled difficult . . . Good God! Is that the time?' Gill leapt up from her chair as the hall clock interrupted her, struck two

441

across her words. 'I promised Fran I'd collect the boys on the dot of two o'clock, and it's ten minutes' drive at least. Look, make some tea or something and we'll continue the discussion when I'm back. There's nothing you can do in any case, until term starts on the 7th. All the schools will be dead as dodos now; no one there but caretakers. Why not have a little zizz, or read my new *Vogue*, or if you fancy a wee tipple, there's sherry in the sideboard. Help yourself to anything you want – including the phone, if you need to check on Luke. *Au revoir*.'

Hilary stood motionless, as Gill scorched out of the house. She had totally forgotten such basic things as holidays, overlooked the obvious fact that all schools would be closed. What an utter fool she was, and with no excuse at all, since her own Claremont College was similarly shut. How could she find Luke a place, when she was leaving on the 3rd, starting work the day the schools reopened? She would have to take the day off, come down on the 7th and try to solve the problem there and then, before racing back to Hertfordshire again. But it would create an extremely bad impression to be absent on her own first day of term, make her seem half-hearted, irresponsible.

She fidgeted around the room, unable to relax, drifted out into the hall, started fiddling with the ornaments arranged on the hall table. She must do something now, while she was free and had the time. Might not *some* schools still be open – one or two exceptions, where a keen or busy Head was working in the holidays, catching up with paperwork? She seized the Yellow Pages from the shelf below the phone, rifled through the entries until she came to 'S'. All the schools seemed jumbled up together – primary and secondary, boarding, comprehensive; even Schools of Slavonic studies, Schools of Meditation. She sleuthed out all the primary schools with addresses in the area. There seemed to be a lot, not the paltry two or three which Gill had mentioned. Perhaps some of them were private, though, or out of the state system, or restricted to certain sorts of children. She knew nothing about schools – which ones were suitable, or how free you were to pick and choose at all; cursed her ignorance as she reached out for the phone. Gill said that she could use it, to check on Luke, rather than on schools, but she could always pay her back for any calls.

She dialled the Robert Browning School, merely because she liked the name, judged a poet safer than a saint. No reply. She tried the next – Grove End School – no answer. She rang another five schools, almost out of obstinacy, or a quite irrational hope, got nothing but the ringing tone. The eighth one took her by surprise. Someone answered instantly, but he turned out to be the caretaker, and a bad-tempered one at that. So Gill was right – as usual. She rammed the Yellow Pages back, trailed

442

into the sitting room, tried to concentrate on *Vogue*'s spring fashion forecast, but her mind refused to shift from Luke. She jumped up again, grabbed her bag and jacket. She couldn't wait for Gill, felt far too tense and edgy to sit around for hours. Gill was often late, lost all track of time, was probably telling Fran the whole grisly Craddock saga. She scribbled a note about an important chore she'd totally forgotten, reflecting with a grimace that her lying skills were improving every day; then waved goodbye to Ben, and cycled off.

She pedalled down Gill's tree-lined street, turned into the next road, braked suddenly as she realised she was passing a small school, the school which Gill had mentioned. She stood reading the large sign. 'St Matthew's and St Mark's Church of England Junior School. Headmistress: Miss B. Craig. B.Ed.' The school looked shut, deserted, with its crate of empty milk bottles, its smeared uncurtained windows, but perhaps by some miracle Miss B. Craig was there. She could have just popped in, to check a record, inspect the building, make sure there'd been no vandals over Christmas.

She locked her bike, ignored the notice 'No Entrance. Private Property', slipped in through the gate; glanced around at the straggle of low buildings, their flat roofs stained, discoloured, a row of battered dustbins blocking half the asphalt playground. She tried all the doors, back and front, but every one was locked; peered in through the windows, spied empty classrooms, a draughty-looking hall. She was suddenly reminded of a photograph she'd seen in the *Observer*, of a village school in Italy which had been abandoned after a local flood disaster – the desks still there, the coat pegs, even the children's drawings on the wall, but no actual spark of life.

'Miss Craig?' she said out loud, as if the name alone might summon the headmistress, bring the children back. A lorry thundered past, the first drops of heavy rain began to spatter on her face. She trailed back to her bike, cycled slowly, head down against the rain, turned right, instead of left, at the second set of traffic lights, found herself approaching Upper Westmead Gardens – the convent Gill had mentioned. She was headed there for a purely selfish reason: convents didn't close. Nuns had no other home, didn't leave for holidays, so a convent school could actually solve her problem. Yet it might make Luke's much worse, load him with new guilts, weigh him down with penances, so that he became sin-obsessed and narrowed, began to draw harrowing Crucifixions instead of cars and planes; suffer just as she had from the dark side of religion.

She dithered, wobbled, almost hit a passing car, mouthed 'Sorry!', cycled on. There was no real comparison between medieval Brignor and a modern school. She'd been a cloistered nun in one of the strictest Orders left anywhere in Europe, shut up within four walls, going barefoot, fasting on dry bread. Luke would be a dayboy at a small mixed school, which Gill herself had praised, with free access in and out, lay staff as well as nuns; a school open to inspection to prevent excess or abuse. And yet hadn't Simon Tovey said how bad some Catholic schools still were, how the stress was on God's anger, rather than His love? Could she really risk Luke's happiness, add Hell and Satan to the long list of his fears? She knew the answer; knew she must turn back, phone Andy at the College, try to make him understand why she'd have to have a day off, have to miss the . . .

'Our Lady, Queen of Peace.' The sign was blue, Our Lady's colour, and set outside the garden of a large Victorian house, with a mass of Virginia creeper almost concealing the red brick, and a monkey puzzle tree guarding the front gate. Hilary stood peering through the fence, ignoring the rain, the fact her clothes were soaked, battling with a surge of strange emotion. Even now, convents still attracted her – attracted and repelled – the order and the harmony, the strictness and the rules, the knowledge that inside those walls, women like herself were living out a faith and an ideal. Would that really be so bad for Luke, to have some glimpse of the spiritual, some knowledge of the Christian heritage?

Queen of Peace. Luke needed peace, was crying out for harmony and order. In a convent, he would be regarded as a soul, not just a naughty boy, a soul made in God's own image and therefore valuable. That alone could help him, to be given worth, importance. The nuns would take real pains with him, see that as their job – to mould and nurture every soul for God. But wasn't that the problem, the one she kept returning to? The 'nurturing' would mean indoctrination; so-called truths and dogmas which were really fairy tales, dinned into his head. 'Give me a child before he is seven . . . '

Yet Luke was nearly eight, had passed the dangerous age. If she countered Catholic doctrines with her own wider, less restrictive views, views culled from Robert and a host of different books, might Luke not get the best of all worlds? Some training in religion could actually be a help to him. He might enjoy the ritual, respond to concepts such as mercy, meekness, goodness, when all he'd seen so far was vice and vengeance. And the other children were bound to be less rough than the toughies in his present school. Whatever else was wrong with convents, they did insist on manners. She remembered from her own school how they'd been taught to treat their classmates with courtesy and kindness, not to snatch off hats, or shout, or tease or point or snigger, or leave

444

other children out. Luke had told her once how he dreaded the school breaks, how no one talked to him, except maybe to yell taunts.

She propped her bike up, trudged in through the gate, rang the bell. No one came, no one seemed to hear it. Supposing she were wrong and this school was just as empty as the rest? Nuns did go away – modern nuns, teaching Orders – if only to a sister convent, or to visit parents, siblings. She rang again, heard the bell echo down the hall; felt a sudden rush of panic, as if this were Brignor and she were begging readmittance. Any moment, her Abbess might appear, refuse to let her in, force her to her knees on the cold and rain-splashed doorstep, to beg pardon for her apostasy in leaving. She turned swiftly on her heel, about to sprint back to her bike, when the door suddenly creaked open and an old and wizened nun, dressed in a floor-length full black habit, caught her by the sleeve.

'I'm sorry, dear. Have you been waiting long? I think I must have nodded off. Good gracious! You're wet through. Come in and dry your clothes. You're from St Andrew's, aren't you?'

'Er – no, I . . .'

'I thought I'd seen your face before, but I get so muddled nowadays. D'you know, I'm eighty-five next birthday and Father says I don't look sixty-five.'

Hilary smiled. A vain nun, obviously, and one still hanging on the words of priests. Wasn't that a warning? She ought to leave immediately, before she got enmeshed in tyrant Fathers, Reverend Mothers.

'Is . . . er . . . Reverend Mother in?' she asked, still standing on the doorstep, as if to be sure of her escape.

'You mean, Sister Anne, the Head?'

'Well, yes, I . . .'

'She's in chapel at the moment, but if you wait in the parlour, I'll tell her that you're here.' She ushered Hilary in to a light and cheerful room, with a high ceiling, generous windows, a bowl of gold chrysanthemums arranged on a low table.

'What's your name?'

'Miss Reed.'

'I may forget it. I'll switch the fire on, shall I, and you can dry off in the warm? No, have this comfy chair, dear. You look tired.'

A kind nun, not just vain. The headmistress might be fiercer, even frosty. Hilary shifted on her chair, her apprehension growing, now she was actually inside and had seen that long black habit. It was surely a bad sign that the Order hadn't modernised, signified rigidity, hostility to change. Though the room itself was modern – in its furnishings at least – vivid colours, comfortable armchairs, even an abstract painting on the wall; so unlike the Brignor parlour, with its framed and frowning Popes, its hard-backed chairs, its gloomy greys and browns. And yet all the nun-like touches were still there: the hand-embroidered cushions, thick with peonies, the highly polished floor, the smell of wax and flowers. Luke's house smelt of cats, and no one polished anything, or had time to grow and gather flowers, let alone embroider them on cushions. Wouldn't it be good for him to live amongst such things, to meet gracious soft-voiced women who didn't swear or scream, and who believed in keeping their surroundings always neat and shining?

No. Those were only details. He would be actually surrounded by frightening figures in long black robes, who wouldn't even seem like women; might reappear as demons in his dreams. The habit had decided her. Any Order which still wore a full-length habit, unmodified in any way, with not the slightest concession to the modern age, was clearly wrong for Luke. No point wasting time here, except it was too late now to leave. Sister Anne would be on her way, gliding from the chapel to this parlour. She tried to picture her, could only see the scathing Brignor Abbess, annoyed at being disturbed at her devotions; mouth set, eyes cold and narrowed.

She jumped as the door swung open, and a dumpy, rather shabby-looking woman, with a thickening waist and thinning hair walked in with an apologetic air, a dirty-white Sealyham ambling at her heels. Her calf-length navy skirt was creased, her home-knitted chunky cardigan a different shade of blue. This must be the secretary.

'Miss Reeves?' She held her hand out, a stubby ringless hand.

'Miss *Reed*.' Hilary shook the hand, was surprised at its firm grasp, which seemed to contradict the sagging skin, the wrinkles round her eyes.

'I'm so sorry. Sister Mary Philip is a little hard of hearing. I'm Sister Anne. I believe you wanted to speak to me.'

Hilary tried to hide her shock. Where was the black-robed martinet she'd been picturing in her head, the pale pinched face encased in starch, the cruel eyes blinkered by a coif? Sister Anne had kindly eyes, a high-coloured complexion, roughened by the sun and wind, as if she'd once been a farmer or a gardener. She had little actual beauty, except in her expression. Her face was round and fleshy, as if it had lost its supporting bones, and the faint trace of a moustache streaked her upper lip. Her hair was straggly grey, barely hidden by a headdress, which was little more than a flimsy sort of scarf, and was slipping anyway. So the Order *had* modernised, and not just in minor details. Sister Anne looked almost like a secular, apart from the unobtrusive cross around her neck, and that, too, could have passed for a piece of modern jewellery. Sister

Philip had misled her – though she remembered now that the old nuns in an Order often retained their former dress; feared the newer modern habits would reveal their veiny legs and balding heads.

'I hope you don't mind dogs, Miss Reed?'

'Oh, no. I like them.'

Sister Anne scratched the stained white ears, one ragged and half-bitten off. 'This is William. He's quite a hardened sinner, I'm afraid, but he wandered in one day without a collar and very near collapse, and he's been here ever since. Do sit down, my dear, and tell me how I can help.'

Hilary sank back in her chair, hope and conflict still fighting in her head. She had warmed to Sister Anne from the moment she stepped in; liked her plain but honest face, her lack of all pretension, so that she could have been the caretaker, rather than the Head; but she was still a nun, modernised or no, still tied to one narrow faith, one rigid view of life. She opened her mouth, shut it, smoothed her damp creased skirt, kept wondering how to start, or even where. Could you really grasp Luke's problems without knowing about Sylvie, or even about Joe's own spell in jail? Yet she felt some strange sense of loyalty to Joe, feared to blacken him too badly.

William suddenly shifted on the floor, got up and shook himself, as if impatient of her dithering, and about to leave the room. She leaned forward, grabbed his collar, used him as her anchor as she began blurting out her story, saying far more than she'd meant; only stopping in confusion when she heard the pleading in her voice, the sheer note of desperation. She was begging Sister Anne to take Luke on, before she'd even viewed the school, or asked important questions about rules and punishments, religious education, attitudes in general.

'I'm afraid it's quite impossible, Miss Reed. We're full up for this year, already got a waiting list, in fact. Look, come into my study and I'll check the records, see if there's a space for next September.'

She followed Sister Anne along the passage, sick with disappointment. Next September was far too late. Luke would be in a remedial school by then, or being passed from psychiatrists to social workers to educational welfare. She had an overwhelming feeling that he'd be better off right here, with Sister Anne, her Sealyham, the hutches full of rabbits which she'd just seen in the garden, the slide, the coloured wigwams, the climbing frames and sandpit. This school seemed basically a home, not just in its building, its lack of concrete, asphalt, but in its scale, its general atmosphere: the cheerful classrooms they were passing now, all with plants and pictures, brightly coloured desks and chairs, each child's self-portrait tacked up on the wall, with a crayoned name

447

beneath. More pictures in Sister Anne's small study, children's art next to Botticelli – a large framed reproduction of the Annunciation.

'Sit down. No, not you, William. That's Miss Reed's foot you're lying on.'

She tried to smile, though it would have been easier to cry – weep with sheer frustration. She somehow knew, just looking at this study, that Sister Anne could help Luke, if she could only find a place for him. Everything about the room revealed an interest in her children: their crooked paper sculptures displayed on two wide shelves, their home-made Christmas cards tacked all round the walls, the photos of old pupils on her notice board. Luke's present Head had nothing in his study save books and papers, metal files, and a few confiscated objects such as roller skates and chewing gum, returned only in exchange for stringent punishments.

'Look, Sister, *please*, even if you're full, couldn't you make an exception in Luke's case?'

'No, I'm afraid I can't, Miss Reed. You see, so many parents ask us that, I feel it wouldn't be quite fair. And, anyway, I have to consider all the other children. Poor Luke sounds quite a handful, and one disruptive child can upset a whole class.'

'Yes, but if no one helps him out, he'll be more disruptive still. He's never had a chance, Sister. Everything's against him – his home, his parents, his position in the family as last unwanted child, his . . . '

Sister Anne reached her hand across the desk. 'Let's go to the chapel, shall we, and pray about his case? The good God may suggest . . . '

Hilary ignored the hand, leapt up to her feet. 'There *isn't* a good God. How could there be, if He allows poor defenceless children to suffer for no reason, to lose their mothers, bash and bruise their faces, have no one in the world to care or . . . ?'

'He's got *you*, Miss Reed. It sounds to me as if you care a lot.'

'No, I don't, I don't! I'm only thinking of myself.' She broke off, confused and angry, her head throbbing with the effort of trying to keep control. 'I'm sorry, Sister, I didn't mean to shout, but I'm so worried and mixed up. I feel I ought to help the boy, yet in another way I can't bear the thought of "duty" any more. You see, everyone expects me to be the perfect nun, do good all the time, even though I've left and . . . I mean, Luke's own father accused me just today of being selfish and a hypocrite.'

'I'm sorry, I'm a little lost. What d'you mean, my dear, "the perfect nun"?'

'I *was* a nun, Sister – yes, for twenty-two years – a Sister of Notre Dame de Bourges. I wasn't going to tell you. I've swamped you with

Luke's problems, without adding mine on top. But I left a year ago, then lost my faith, as well.' She stopped, aware that she was tensing, hands clenched, shoulders rigid, as if prepared for Reverend Mother's shocked reproaches. Sister Anne only looked concerned.

'That must have been a terrible upheaval. I do understand, believe me. One of our own community left two years ago, and she's still not really settled, even now. Would it help to talk about it?'

Hilary shook her head. She was here to discuss Luke's future, not her past. She had solved her own problems, carved out a new life – if only Luke and his brute father would leave her free to live it. Yet Sister Anne was already gently probing, asking kindly questions about her Order, her vocation. She answered tersely, her mind still fixed on Luke. The boy was at a crossroads, as she herself had been – not at seven, but at the age of seventeen. If someone had miraculously appeared then, weaned her from the convent, changed the whole direction of her life, she would have been spared those years of misery, that sense of being cut off, shut away, turned into a 'case' – a different sort of case from Luke's, but still branded and 'abnormal'. Luke could still be saved, if only this headmistress would change her mind, move from Brignor back to Wandsworth.

'It's interesting that you opted for the contemplative life, rather than a teaching order. Did you feel that . . . ?'

Hilary shook her head impatiently, hair clammy on her neck. 'I'm sorry, Sister, but I just can't see how this is helping Luke. You haven't got a place for him – okay – I'd better tell his father, and maybe *Joe* can pull some strings, get him into Borstal.'

Sister Anne stood up, moved around the desk to her. 'I do realise how upset you are, but as you've seen, I've checked through all the class-lists, and they're all jam-packed already. But look, there is the possibility that a few children may drop out. I won't know that till term's started, but why not get in touch again, about a week or so from now, and I'll see how things look then?'

'A week or so's too late. He'll be lost by then.' As *I* was lost, she added to herself, as she snapped up to her feet, grabbed her jacket, strode towards the door. It was all talk with this nun – pious platitudes, even tolerant acceptance of her own sarcastic outbursts, but nothing of the slightest help to Luke.

Sister Anne pushed back a wisp of hair, touched her silver cross. 'I'm sure God won't allow . . . '

Hilary swung back again. 'I don't *believe* in God,' she shouted. 'I've told you that already. And I'm not sure now if I even believe in goodness – anybody's goodness. It seems to me there's nothing in the world except

449

misery and suffering and endless hopeless problems, so that just as you dare hope you've found a sort of life, and can leave the past behind and start again, the bloody rotten phone rings and you're saddled with a problem child whom no one else will help you with, because everybody's too full, or scared, or busy, or frightened he'll disrupt their precious . . . ' She lunged towards a statue of Our Lady, simpering in a niche with a gold crown on her head, blue roses on her feet. 'Queen of Peace. Yes, wonderful, except Luke won't get that peace – won't know what the word means, and if he grows up to be a criminal or a thug, then it'll be partly *your* fault, Sister Anne. Goodbye.'

She marched back along the passage, eyes blinded with hot tears of rage and shame, so that she didn't see the small dog racing after her, darting between her legs to overtake. She tripped and fell on him, sprawled full-length on the floor. He wriggled out, yelping, sat cowering by the skirting, while she herself lay stunned, remembering only that she'd said 'bloody' to a nun, and that nun was kneeling on the floor beside her, passing her a handkerchief, even dabbing at her eyes, as if she were a child.

'I'm so sorry about that wretched dog. Have you hurt yourself?'

'I . . . I'm not too sure.'

'Let's help you up and see.'

Hilary took the hand offered her, struggled to her feet, checked her knees, which were only bruised, rubbed her smarting palms; flushing scarlet with embarrassment as she recalled her words, her fierce vindictive tone. She mumbled an apology, tried to creep away, edge along the passage to the door.

Sister Anne followed, headdress knocked askew. 'It's me who should say sorry. William could have killed you, dashing out like that. Come back to my office and sit down. You ought to rest a minute, after a nasty fall like that.'

'No, really, Sister, I . . . I must get back.' She took another step towards the porch. Essential to escape before she disgraced herself still further. She should never have set foot inside a convent. The memories were too acute, too painful.

The nun retrieved her handkerchief, freckled now with blood. 'Look, both your hands are bleeding. I can't let you go without a cup of tea, and something for those grazes. I'll ring through to Sister Catherine. She can probably find some witch hazel, as well as make the tea.'

Hilary followed her reluctantly, subsided on the same small chair, which felt chilly now and damp. Her inbuilt habit of obeying her superiors was still too powerful to ignore. Yet she resented that submission, felt awkward, hypocritical, as she sat exchanging pleasantries – the weather, Christmas, the wicked ways of Sealyhams; forcing down the convent tea, which was too sickly sweet and milky for her taste. She longed to slip away, begrudged the waste of time, the trivial conversation which they were using as a poultice to try to heal the breach, remove the sting and venom from her recent bitter tirade.

Yet, even now, her voice still sounded petulant – an abrupt unfriendly voice, with an undertone of anger which seemed completely inappropriate to the safely anodyne subjects they were tossing to and fro. She was frightened of that anger, terrified she'd shout again, rail at Sister Anne as if she were the Abbess and she'd at last decided to end her cowed obedience and express her screaming grievances, muzzled all those years. That was totally unfair. Sister Anne was nothing like the Abbess, had been exceptionally long-suffering, and even now was supplying her with details of an organisation set up specially for ex-nuns, which provided information and support.

'I'm *not* an ex-nun,' she muttered half-inaudibly, aware how rude it sounded, yet bridling at that 'ex', its implication that she had only a past – not a present or a future – a troubled past, which cried out for support.

Sister Anne said nothing, started sorting through the papers on her desk, abandoning all attempts at further conversation. Hilary watched, abashed. She had obviously upset the nun by her ungracious manner, her impatient brusque replies, that final clinching rudeness. Her face looked closed and pained now, one hand twitching slightly, as if she, too, were annoyed, but trying to control it. She was probably reflecting that if Luke were half as difficult as his so-called champion, then she'd been wise to turn him down. She had also closed her eyes, which only served to emphasise the sudden chilly distance which seemed to have sprung between them. Or was she simply praying – perhaps for patience, or endurance?

Hilary cleared her throat, fiddled with her teaspoon. She could hear her watch gasping through the silence, its tiny strangled tick an expression of her own unease. Her hands and knees were throbbing still, the accusing smell of witch hazel lingering in the air, like another veiled reproach. She tried to fix her gaze on the Botticelli painting which faced her on the wall, stitch her eyes and mind to it, to calm her agitation, distract her from the curdled mix of shame and sheer frustration still churning in her mind. She'd seen the work before, in one of Robert's glossy books on Italian Renaissance art; had noticed it particularly, since the Virgin wasn't passive and obedient, as in most Annunciations, kneeling humbly, with her hands crossed on her breast, but was reeling back in shock and almost horror, arms stretched out in front of her, as if to ward the Angel off.

'Miss Reed?'

She started, jolted back from Nazareth to Upper Westmead Gardens. She'd been semi-mesmerised by the brilliant blues and scarlets of the picture; by the Angel's rippling hair and billowing robe; the stiff and waxy lily, whose glinting green and gold was echoed in the Angel's feathered wings. She shifted her gaze from Mary's pale and fine-boned face to Sister Anne's rounded ruddy one. The nun was looking up, her expression grave and frowning still, hands tightly clasped together on the desk. Hilary lowered her own eyes. She knew now what was coming – the pained recriminations, the soft but stern reproof, the quiet insinuation that she was hardly a fit person to be pleading for a problem child.

'I've been thinking about what you said . . . ' Sister Anne paused, as if embarrassed, gave a vague pat to her still dishevelled headdress. 'How you don't believe in goodness. That worries me, a lot, and I fear it's partly my fault – perhaps the fault of all of us who are too concerned with keeping our lives simple and uncomplicated, leaving someone else to mop up the disasters, deal with all the crises. You're right in what you said, you know. I do have a responsibility, towards you, as well as Luke.' She picked up her pen again, ran it like a pointer up and down her class lists. 'We *are* full this term, bursting at the seams, in fact, and Luke may well be difficult, but as you pointed out yourself, he's got as much claim on my conscience as on yours. What I'm trying to say, Miss Reed, is I feel I turned him down too hastily and perhaps we ought to offer him a chance.'

Hilary leaned forward. Had she really heard those words, and not the more reproachful ones she had scripted in her mind? The rain was flailing down outside, its dull insistent drone confusing and distracting her. She gripped the teaspoon tighter, felt it hard and hurting in her palm.

'From what you've said already, he may, of course, need remedial education at a special school. I can't judge that until I get to know him. So what I'm suggesting is that I give him a term's trial, and assess him myself – you know, unofficially, keep an eye on him, liaise with his teachers.'

'In September, you mean?' Hilary forced the words out, not daring yet to hope. September was too late. Had Sister Anne not grasped that?

'No, in January – in five days' time. Our term starts on the 6th.'

She sank back in her chair, still half-incredulous, still fighting shame and guilt. She had criticised this nun, deplored her so-called platitudes, yet she'd had the courage, the humility, to change her mind, offer Luke a place. The 6th was perfect, absolutely perfect, the day before her own college term began. She'd already be in Hertfordshire, but was bound to get permission to return for just one night, so she could bring Luke here herself, imbue him with some courage, at least on his first morning.

Sister Anne capped her pen, glanced across at William, who was asleep now on the rug. 'It's just a trial, you understand? If he settles down, that's fine. I'll be very happy to keep him till he's eleven, but if it does turn out he's in genuine need of special education, then I'm afraid he'll have to leave – for his sake, as well as ours. You do see that, don't you, dear?'

She nodded, light-headed with relief; could hardly think beyond one blessed term. 'Yes, of course I do. That's fine. It's just this one first chance he needs, so *he* can believe in goodness, if you like.'

'Well, we'll do everything we can – that I guarantee. I'll give him a hand with his reading, squeeze it in after lunch each day. I often take the slower children for individual sessions, and it's amazing how they improve, once they get some extra help. We also have a system where each new child is looked after by another child of roughly the same age, who shows him the ropes, sits next to him in class, helps him feel at home. But we're going a bit fast. I shall have to meet Luke first, of course, and interview his parents – or at least the father, if you say the mother's left. Will Mr Craddock come, d'you think?'

'Yes,' she said, vehemently. 'He will.' If I have to drag him by the hair, she added silently. 'Though it might be better if he came with me – perhaps later on today, or in the morning, or whenever suits you best. He's a little . . . ' She paused a moment, considered various adjectives: violent, angry, moody, unpredictable; realised to her shame that they all applied equally well to her. It was high time she got away, if she were modelling her behaviour on Joe Craddock's. One 'bloody' was enough, two outbursts in a week a shade excessive, especially following a lifetime of submission. At least Robert would be pleased with her, and proud.

'And I'll need all his particulars. I'll take those now, shall I, since we're rather short of time before term starts? I'll have to phone his present Head, before I do anything official – I'm sure you realise that – but I know Mr Stanthorpe very well, in fact, so I don't see any problem there.'

Hilary offered up a silent prayer of thanks. So she wouldn't have to face the man herself, endure another hostile confrontation, or take the risk that Joe might come to blows with him. She started spelling out Luke's name, address and birthday, feeling a huge weight leave her shoulders, as if she were handing over not just facts and figures, but the boy himself, with all his problems, his whole sad and chequered history; transferring the burden to Sister Anne instead.

'Right, that's it for the moment, until I meet Luke himself. How about ten o'clock tomorrow? Would that suit Mr Craddock? You can always phone me if it's inconvenient. And now, let me show you round. Come and see our chapel. I know you said you don't believe in God, but it's a lovely peaceful place, and we all need peace these days.' She held the door for Hilary, gestured down the passage. 'Perhaps peace *is* God.'

Hilary turned to stare. Robert could have said that – almost had. She was also astonished by the casual way the nun had referred to her loss of faith, appearing to accept it without expressing any outrage, or trying to reconvert her. She knelt beside her in the modern elmwood pew, feeling something of a hypocrite as she bowed her head, joined her hands, purely out of habit. Sister Anne knelt motionless, her pale eyes never wavering from the red glow of the sanctuary lamp, as if it were a magnet drawing her attention, her total concentration. Hilary raised her own eyes, fixed them on the altar; recalling Robert's words about the power of prayer – even without a God to sanction it – how it could touch and reach the people it was meant for.

'Help Luke,' she murmured silently, invoking any Force or even Deity which lay beyond her narrow understanding; trying to rally her own powers, draw strength from Sister Anne's. She felt sure the nun was praying for her personally; was aware of some strange lightening in the atmosphere, some lightening of her self, as if she was sloughing off dead skins, pushing back the dragging weight of winter. She closed her eyes a moment, saw herself standing on a lonely Norfolk beach, a summer sea slowly threshing in; one huge wave swelling, swelling, until it broke across her shoulders in a slap and fling of spray. All her agitation seemed to swirl and stream away, blowing off like spume; a clean south wind purging her and wringing; replacing fear, exhaustion, with boundless space and peace.

She glanced up at the sky. It *was* a sky – the chapel ceiling painted with white clouds, God's finger pointing down in a blaze of golden glory. Even on this rain-washed afternoon, with dusk already fingering the windows, the room seemed full of light – silver angels blazoning the walls, more gold in the chrysanthemums ripening in bronze vases, the haloes of the statues she remembered from her childhood – patient Joseph, rapt Teresa, kind maternal Mary. How would it strike Luke – as strange, outlandish, soppy, or like something from a fairy tale, which did have its own truth, its own majesty and wonder?

Sister Anne turned back to touch her arm. 'We mustn't pray too long. I expect your knees are hurting. How about a quick look at the garden, before it's too dark to see out there? The rain's just beginning to ease now, so I can show you our menagerie. You won't believe this, but our

454

four white rabbits are called after the four Evangelists, and the biggest
and the baddest is – well, guess – yes, Luke.'

34

'*Magnificat anima mea Dominum, et exsultavit spiritus meus* . . . ' Hilary swerved, narrowly missed a passing car, cycled on unscathed, repeating that soaring '*exsultavit*'. They had always sung the *Magnificat* at Brignor, on feastdays, Golden Jubilees, or whenever they wished to thank and praise their God – though not, of course, on bicycles, or in the pouring rain. She was still a nun, at heart; would always be, in one sense, but did it really matter when there were nuns as wise as Sister Anne, as kind as Sister Catherine, as humorous as Sister Magdalena, who would be teaching Luke art, and whom she'd met just now over a second tray of tea? His class teacher would be not a nun, but a Mrs Margaret Rowlandson, who'd had thirty years' experience in the classroom and four children of her own. Everything was working out far better than she'd dared to hope. She even had a blazer in her saddlebag, a boy's striped blazer, just Luke's size, which had been left behind a year ago, unmarked and never claimed.

'You take it,' Sister Anne had urged. 'That's all he'll really need, apart from grey shorts and a tie, and a clean white shirt or two, which most boys have already.'

She'd had to hide a grin. Luke in uniform! The thought was quite diverting, when she'd never seen him in anything but jeans. She was sure he didn't own a tie – any more than Joe did – let alone grey shorts. Would it involve another battle to get him dressed correctly, and could Rita cope with ironing shirts, when she returned from Maureen's, maybe already more rebellious after her daughter's rabble-rousing? She was sure she *would* return. A few days cooped up with Maureen in a tiny terraced house with Sylvie and two babies was bound to bring her back, if only for some peace and space. And however much she complained about her husband, Joe was still the pivot of her life. Seven children and more than thirty years of marriage had welded them together in some creaking cast-iron partnership, which she couldn't imagine either of them breaking. Rita had acted out of character by deserting Joe at all; must be still affected by her hormones, the whole trauma and disruption of her hysterectomy. And the season didn't help. New Year's Eve and Christmas were always fraught explosive times, when domestic quarrels rocketed.

Today was January 1 – time to start again, heal the wounds. She only prayed the healing would be swift; that Rita would come grumbling home in just a day or two, so she could call on her herself, explain the situation, spell out the advantages of Our Lady Queen of Peace. But first she must report to Joe, and with any luck, he'd ring Rita straight away, use the news as bait to lure her back. She picked up the phone the minute she walked in, not even taking off her dripping jacket.

'Joe? I've done it! I've found a school and got him in – well, almost. They want to see him first, and you, of course, but I'm pretty sure they'll take him. The head promised, more or less. She's a nun – Sister Anne. It's a convent, you see, but a really nice and modern one, with . . . What? I can't hear you, Joe. You're mumbling. What d'you mean, "take him into care"? They can't do that. They *can't*, Joe! Does Rita know? I don't believe you. She wouldn't let . . . '

Joe's indistinct mutter suddenly changed into a bellow. Hilary sank down in a chair, listening to the tirade: complaints, expletives, threats. She longed to block her ears, couldn't bear to know that absolutely nobody would agree to take Luke on – none of Joe's large family, none of their acquaintances. Les had merely snubbed Joe, and when he'd begged his daughter to send Rita back at once, or look after Luke herself, all he'd got was 'a bloody fucking earful'. Rita, it appeared, was haemorrhaging again, and in no state to go back anywhere, except to hospital. Maureen, already barely coping with Amber, Kevin, Sylvie and now an invalid, had refused point-blank to add Luke to her household. She lived miles away, in any case, so he'd have to miss his schooling, and she couldn't stand the thought of 'that bolshie kid' at home all day, tormenting all the others, upsetting her routine.

Joe disposed of Maureen in a final burst of scorn, then turned on Hilary. 'It don't matter whether you've found him fucking Paradise, there's no way he can go there. They'll arrange his education when they take him into care. Look, it's no big deal – I don't know why you're carrying on like that. I was in care myself when I was only half his age, and it's never done *me* no harm. My Mum pissed off, didn't she, and I never saw her in my life again. I was in seven different children's homes, and that was bloody years ago, when it was canes and belts and leather straps, not all this piss-balling about with psychologists and suchlike. I've spoken to the Social and they're coming round tomorrow. Stop squawking, can't you, woman? It was your fault I had to phone 'em in the first place. If you'd taken Luke yourself, snapped up that nice little flat above the shop . . . '

Hilary slammed the phone down. That was blackmail, and a pack of lies as well. Nice little flat! A dirty grotty noisy slum in the worst part of Tooting, with a jailbird living underneath, when she was about to move to a large and gracious college with rolling grounds and country air. And he wouldn't stop her moving – oh, no! She could see through all his wiles, his base attempts to make her feel guilty and responsible. She'd done her best, for God's sake, spent her whole damned day on Luke, and not got a word of thanks. Joe was quite impossible – the rudest, crudest, most ungrateful bloody man she'd ever met. Yes, she *would* swear. Everything was ruined. She couldn't think, couldn't settle, couldn't even go upstairs and change her clothes. She was too wound up, too angry, pacing round in circles, shivering from cold and wet and rage. Impossible for her to take the role of mother, when she didn't love the wretched child, didn't even like him much.

She slouched to the window, stood leaning on the sill. It was shocking to admit that, even to herself, and she'd been trying to dodge the truth of it for weeks; trying not to face her own changed and shameful feelings. She felt sorry for him, yes, felt guilt, compassion, pity, but the genuine bond between them, which had sprung up in the early days when he'd been staying here with Liz, had somehow snapped and spoiled. He'd been just a guest at Liz's, had seemed a quiet and harmless lad, who shared her own insomnia and loneliness, and whom one could safely comfort and befriend. But since he'd come to live with her, as her own sole charge and obligation, things had been more difficult, sometimes near impossible.

She had never confided that to anyone, save a few vague hints to Gill; was ashamed of seeming selfish, unmaternal. Though Luke was hardly the easiest of children – was fussy with his food, refused to flush the toilet, and would only wash or take a bath after endless chivvying. Even his appearance had seemed to subtly change, those weeks he stayed with her: his fair hair turning darker, his face thinner, almost sly, his new front teeth coming down just slightly crooked, as if to match his uneven jagged haircut. It was wicked not to love a child because he was no longer blond and pretty, but how could she dissemble love, if it simply wasn't there? Up to Christmas Day, it had, in fact, been possible. She'd still felt a deep concern, which was very close to love, but Joe himself had helped destroy it, by pushing her too far.

Okay, so she was selfish, but wasn't everybody selfish – Joe himself, Rita, Maureen, Les? If Luke's own flesh and blood refused to help him, why should she step in? She had made her decision to develop her own gifts, live life for herself, and if she changed her mind and involved herself with Luke, she would lose everything in one disastrous stroke – her job, her room, her future and her music.

She moved to the piano stool, head bowed above the keys. Her music meant so much now. She had already got the syllabus for her Grade 8 examination, discovered with surprised delight that they'd set the very same Beethoven sonata as in 1966. It seemed more than just coincidence – almost like a sign that she was meant to play, take up again where she had broken off before. She'd been practising it daily, and even in a week had made some definite progress, especially with the slow movement, which had always been her favourite. She could struggle through that movement now, if not with inspiration, at least with no wrong notes, and though it needed months of work to reach the tough new standards the examiners demanded, she was still elated to be playing it at all. The score lay open on the music-rest. She'd been intending to tackle it this morning, after her usual hour of exercises for loosening up the fingers. Those too were paying off. She could stretch an octave with far less ache and stiffness, play her scales more evenly, make her chords sound crisper and more balanced.

She removed her jacket, rubbed her hands, to warm them, then began the solemn lingering chords which opened the slow movement. The music sounded muted and severe, the phrase-ends drooping, as if exhausted or discouraged; the whole mood tired, forlorn. A throbbing left-hand tremolo kept breaking up the melody; the strong chords petering out, as if they'd lost hope, lost direction, even a heavy brooding pause. She seemed to hear Luke's sadness in the mournful modulation which followed that taut silence; his small but grim despair in the listless limping rhythm. She broke off in mid-bar. If she refused to lose her music, then Luke would lose far more – his convent school, his one last chance, his home and both his parents; would be taken into care, treated like an orphan or delinquent. He had missed his home and family when he was staying with her here, and that was just a few short weeks. How would he react if he were permanently removed from them, shut up in some dreary faceless home, with no one special person to act as mother, anchor? He'd end up like his father – aggressive, bitter, loveless, cursing the whole world. Could she really blame Joe Craddock when he'd suffered seven children's homes himself, lost his mother at the age of three or four? That cycle could continue endlessly – Luke's own children equally disruptive and deprived – if someone didn't stop it, stop it now.

But who? She had yelled at Sister Anne that if she didn't take Luke on, it would be partly her own fault if he grew up to be a criminal or a thug. The same applied to her – and far more so. She had voiced her indignation that he'd never had a chance, no one in the world to care or help. And here she was, breezing off to fulfil her own ambitions, leaving him to a life of institutions.

No, that was too extreme. She had no real proof Luke was going into care – only Joe's own word for it, and Joe could well be bluffing, so as to

459

make her change her mind. And, even if it were true, surely these things took longer to arrange? Wouldn't they require a court order first, or at least a lot of paperwork? By the time they'd worked through all the small print, Rita might be back. In fact, that itself would surely bring her back. Whatever Joe alleged, she refused to believe that decent loving Rita, even with her failings, her recent moods and outbursts, would simply stand by passively while they took her son away. It was absolutely crazy for her to risk her own whole future, resign her job, for the sake of just a week or two. She must bring Rita back herself – and much sooner than a week or two – entreat her back to Wandsworth tomorrow, or the next day; save Luke from his court order, herself from the scrapheap. Impulsively, she seized the phone, dialled Maureen's Swindon number. She'd insist that Rita listen, refuse to put the phone down until she'd extracted a firm promise from her, even if she had to plead all night.

'No, I'm sorry, you can't speak to Mum. She isn't here. No, you can't phone her there, neither. The nurses won't allow it. She's sedated for the night. The op's tomorrow morning – nine o'clock – and I'm bloody worried, if you really want to know. The doctor said she's been doing far too much, and . . . Yeah, I know all about my rotten little brother. Dad's phoned already – seven times, in fact. Sorry, I can't help.'

Hilary replaced the dead receiver, slumped down by the window. She was feeling tired and almost feverish, perhaps sickening for a cold. Not surprising, really, when she'd sat around in sodden clothes all day. She shut her eyes a moment, could see herself back with Sister Anne, her hair dripping down her neck, her wet skirt clinging damply to her thighs. She tensed, dodged back; sweat, not rain, now clammy on her forehead. Botticelli's Mary seemed to loom above her, in that tormented swooning pose she had noticed in the painting; the figure's red-robed arms stretched up and out, as if trying to block the news off, refuse her sudden motherhood, dismiss the radiant Angel at her feet.

She did her best to struggle up, dislodge that violent picture from her mind, but her legs seemed weak and papery, the figure still more real – Mary's eyes half-closed, her features deathly pale; even the folds of her blue mantle looking frenzied, disarrayed. She jerked her head irritably, as if impatient to dispel the words now throbbing through it – words she knew so well: St Luke, 1: 29 – all the different translations, old and new: 'Mary was deeply troubled at his saying', 'Mary was much perplexed', 'Her heart was disturbed within her.'

She could feel that fear herself, that perplexity, disturbance, feel it in her sweaty hands, her queasy churning stomach. She had always thought of Mary as a quiet and gentle woman, passively consenting to God's will; had never grasped her sense of almost panic, the agonising conflict in her

460

mind. Mary wasn't married, had not expected motherhood, maybe even dreaded it – not just the gossip, the whispered innuendos, but the shock, the work, the suffering, the total loss of freedom. She had been reading at her lectern when Gabriel burst in, an elaborate wooden lectern which looked just like a music stand. She had noticed that particularly as she gazed up at the painting in the office, her mind on music even then; Mozart, Grieg, Rachmaninov, muddled with her fury, her hopes and fears for Luke.

She forced her eyes to open, staggered to her feet. She ought to do her practice – sick or no – mustn't miss a day, or fall behind. She groped towards the piano, which looked only a dark blur; stopped halfway, disorientated. The ground seemed not quite steady and she could hear the noise of wind. Had the weather changed from rain to storm and squall? No. The wind was in the room. She could feel it on her face, see it blowing back her mantle. She must be feverish, delirious – not just sickening for a cold, but for something much more serious. She limped back to the wall, eyes blinded by the light; an intense and dazzling light, which appeared to have no source.

She tried to reach her arms out, to ward the Angel off; felt the red sleeves tight, confining, the gauzy veil slipping from her head. Her long brown hair was heavy on her back; all her clothes too heavy; the sweltering velvet mantle tangling round her feet, the rough fabric of her underskirt prickly-hot and chafing. She could hear the rain still drumming down outside, echoed in her nervous thudding heartbeat. The Angel's outstretched fingers were only inches from her own now; the scent of the white lily choking in her nostrils, cloying, queasy-sweet.

'No!' she cried; heard different words, spoken in her own soft voice, spoken obediently and humbly, as she bowed down by the music stand, hands folded on her breast.

'Be it done unto me according to Thy word.'

Epiphany

35

Hilary slipped out of bed to fetch another jersey, shivering as the cold night air lunged between her legs. Perhaps she ought to sleep in thick wool trousers – add a winter coat as well, a scarf and fur-lined gloves. She had already pulled a sweater over her flimsy nylon nightie, doubled all the thin and scratchy blankets. The room was dank, as well as cold, one wall darkened by a damp and mouldy stain. Joe had brought her oil heaters, but she didn't like to leave them on all night, and, anyway, they stank – their sickly nauseous odour still clinging to the room. She trailed to the window, lifted the curtain, which was really an old car-rug rigged up on two nails; peered out at the mean and narrow street. A drunken lamppost reeled towards its neighbour, the abandoned Ford beneath it slewed half across the kerb. Most of the other windows were boarded up or smashed; shop signs missing letters, so they lisped a strange starved language of their own.

She turned her back, checked her watch, still the Mickey Mouse one she had never yet replaced. Four a.m. The last hour had really dragged, despite her tot of whisky. She'd better watch her drinking. Joe kept bringing liquor, perhaps in lieu of decent furniture, or out of simple guilt. What furniture she had was an uneasy mix of Craddock, Liz and junk shop.

She gazed around the room, half-shadowed now in the grudging light of the bedside lamp, itself a Craddock offering, and still lacking any shade. The Piccadilly Raindrops lamp took pride of place in the centre of the room, on a low and battered coffee table, which was all they had to eat off at the moment. The kitchen was too small for any table, Luke had bagged the only decent bedroom, so this one main room combined several different functions – dining room, sitting room, Luke's playroom (toys still littered on the floor, rocking horse stabled in one corner), and was transformed into her sleeping quarters after ten o'clock at night. The second tiny bedroom was crammed with rolls of lino, offcuts of old carpet, a huge dismembered wardrobe, and boxes full of cracked pink bathroom tiles. She hadn't found the strength to clear it out yet, preferred sleeping on the sofa bed. That black and bulky monster was the best of Joe's bequests, so far – not new, of course, but versatile, though she still found it rather tricky to set up and fold away, had to fight its heavy legs and faulty hinges; also fight her longing for a permanent bed, ready-made and waiting, which she could collapse exhausted into, after a long day like today.

Except today was now tomorrow, first day of term for Luke, and one of the chief reasons why she was lying wide awake at four o'clock. Pre-school nerves – hers, not Luke's. Luke seemed merely numb, too miserable for nerves. He had also caught her cold. She had dosed him late last night with aspirin, malt, hot lemon, and a dash of Johnnie Walker, which at least had made him sleep. She'd crept into his bedroom every hour or so, to make sure he was all right. He'd seemed restless, apprehensive, even in his sleep; muttering garbled words, hands twitching on the duvet. She had left him half her giant-sized box of Kleenex, the other half mere damp and crumpled balls now. She'd been using them all night, mopping, blowing, sneezing. Luke's cold was far less heavy than her own, and though it was unsociable and selfish to take even a snuffly child to school, she knew it was imperative that he was there on the first day. Hard enough for him to start in January, rather than September, without turning up three or four days late.

She'd been sly – or was it sensible? – bought him cold-suppressants from the chemists, to feed him with his breakfast. He must start school like the others, a normal law-abiding boy, neither late, nor ill, nor special; and he must also be in uniform – another source of worry. He had refused to wear his blazer, loathed it on first sight. She'd done everything she could to coax him round, put Mars bars in the pockets, bought him a school case with new and shiny pencils, even planned an offbeat breakfast of both his favourite foods: Heinz spaghetti hoops and pink ice cream.

She trailed out to the kitchen to check everything again: bowls and saucepan ready, school case stuffed behind a cushion in the highest of the cupboards. She was keeping it well hidden, to produce as a surprise, hoped it would distract him while she somehow slipped his blazer on; told him only if he kept it on, could he keep or eat the Mars bars.

She filled the kettle, lit the gas. She knew she'd never sleep now, so she'd treat herself to breakfast – a simple pre-dawn breakfast before her second one with Luke. She needed to keep busy, to calm the skein of worries in her mind, all tangled round that wretched stripy blazer. Would the convent do him any good, or had she only sent him there to suit herself, secure her precious freedom? Now she'd lost that freedom anyway, she kept questioning her motives, wondering whether uniform and chapels were really right for him; whether nuns with names like Sister Magdalena could gain his trust or only make him jeer. Would he even last there, or would Sister Anne decide he wasn't suitable and must be moved to a remedial school, so they'd be back to where they'd started, after just one short trial term?

She watched the slow and lazy gas flicker in a draught. There was no permanence in anything, at present. When she folded down her sofa bed each morning, she was surprised the house itself still stood, hadn't collapsed exhausted in the night. This row of shops was structurally unsound and officially condemned, several of them vandalised, only Charlie's functioning, and even that to close by next October. Rita's health was similarly precarious. She was still in hospital, and no one knew how long she might be there. Although weak, depressed and listless, she might suddenly make progress, or be sent home anyway because they were desperate for her bed – go home not to Maureen, but to Wandsworth; resume her former role as wife and mother. Which meant she'd lose her own role, as she'd already lost her job at Claremont College. Andy had been fiercely coldly angry. She had hardly recognised the urbane and friendly fellow who had shown her around two months ago, as he lashed her with his tongue, called her selfish, irresponsible and totally ungrateful. Liz had called her wonderful – and crazy.

She made the tea, poured herself a bowl of Luke's Oat Krunchies, removed the plastic Rambo from her bowl. There was also a coupon on the packet for a free real linen tea towel. Two pre-birthday gifts. It was her fortieth birthday in just four days' time – that at least was certain – the official start of official middle age. In the convent, age had been irrelevant, except that the older you grew, the closer you approached to the afterlife – and God. Old nuns were respected, often held high office. If she'd stayed herself, kept her faith and fortitude, she might well have become assistant to the Abbess. She was nothing in the world – a spinster, out of work – and with each successive birthday, she'd lose a little more, grow plainer, tireder, creakier; depreciate in value like a car. Perhaps better not to recognise her birthday, just totally ignore it, tell nobody at all.

She carried bowl and cup into the sitting room, switched on the television, the most luxurious object in the flat. Joe had somehow found her a twenty-six-inch colour set, with remote control and a video recorder. The videos themselves he'd bought cheap as a job lot, an extraordinary assortment of sex and violence, blood and thunder, and a few old classic movies of the sentimental kind. Luke had refused to watch *Lassie*, preferring *Son of Werewolf*, so she put it on herself now, lolled back on the sofa. What luxury! Breakfast in bed, in-room movies, bathroom *en suite* (well, a shower which leaked and a toilet minus seat), and full bar service day and night.

She removed her whisky from the bedside table (an upturned wooden crate), to make room for the tea, drained the last half-inch of liquor in the glass. It was an expensive malt, which had aged so long, Joe claimed it was getting on for near as old as he was and had cost an arm and a leg. Poor Joe. He was trying quite pathetically hard to keep her happy, keep her there, control at least one section of his life. He seemed stunned by Rita's second operation, totally confused at living in his house alone, with no noise but the passing trains, after more than thirty years of wife and kids, racket and commotion. He kept dropping in to bring her things, or was it more for company, or even reassurance? Her former anger with him had totally subsided. In some strange way, he had become her own father – complaining, grumbling, never really happy, uneasy in a world he no longer seemed to fit. She had longed to have her father back, so she could say those things she'd never dared express, explain her guilt and sorrow at being absent from his funeral, somehow forge a bond with him. Her shy and stilted relationship with Joe could hardly compensate, yet, nonetheless, even in these few short days, it had helped her come to terms with her own parents; their inadequacies, their failure, the fact they, too, had been fashioned by bad parents in their turn, which somehow lessened her resentment, made it easier not to blame.

She spooned in Krunchies, washed them down with tea, lined up her Kleenex to cope with the next sneeze, or perhaps a tragic end to *Lassie*. She hoped it was a long film, to fill the gap till Breakfast Two, distract her from her worries. She drained her cup, settled back, kept her mind firmly on MGM's Welsh collie, to prevent it darting up to Claremont, or, worse still, running through her pieces for Grade 8.

Three hours later, she was woken by the postman, groped up in confusion, still half-drugged with sleep. A pool of sodden Krunchies was congealing on the carpet, and the television talking to itself – no longer *Lassie*, but a hearty-sounding weatherman predicting gale-force winds, persistent rain. She took the narrow stairs as quickly as she could, throwing on a coat above the nightie and the sweaters.

'Mornin'!'

'Good morning.'

'Rain again.'

'Yes.'

'Well, I suppose we're lucky it ain't snow.'

'Mm.'

'The parcel's for old Charlie, but I thought I ought to ring. Anything you leave outside gets nicked.'

'Yes, thank you. That was kind.'

'And a letter for you. Postmark says Madras.'

'Madras?' She took it from him, tried to close the door. The rain was blowing in.

'Yeah. Been in those parts, have you?'

'No, I . . . ' Her voice trailed off as she suddenly saw the writing on the envelope – three sets of writing, actually, and two of them she knew. She dashed upstairs, dread and wonder clashing in her mind. The first writing was Aunt Eva's, dead and lost Aunt Eva, whom she'd hunted down for months – chased, pursued, and chivvied – then finally abandoned, deliberately uprooted from her mind, so she wouldn't waste more time on fruitless visits, unanswered futile letters; wouldn't have to mourn. Yet here was Eva addressing her from India, and addressing her as Sister Mary Hilary at the Convent of Notre Dame de Bourges, as she had done every Christmas since 1966 – every year except the last. She'd know that writing anywhere: a large lopsided scrawl with generous leaping upstrokes, i's dotted only randomly, j's with fancy loops. Reverend Mother's writing was far more neat and cramped, still produced a ripple of unease. The Abbess had forwarded the letter to Cranleigh Gardens, where it had been sent on in its turn by Mrs Philpot; caught up with her, at last, at her new Tooting Bec address. It now looked tired and tattered, despite its bulky size – scarred with postmarks, smudged with rain, even a grubby thumbprint on the back.

She ripped it open, a hundred questions racing through her mind. Had Eva emigrated, or was she just on holiday? And why India, for heaven's sake, when she'd always been on walking tours to quiet and temperate places like the Dales? How could she afford long-distance air fares on her meagre nurse's pension? Why had she not written a whole year ago? Had she been in Madras all that time, or fallen ill, or . . . ?

She sank down on a chair as she tried to take the letter in, still hardly daring to believe that it was, in fact, from Eva; that her Aunt was still alive, not coffined or cremated.

'Yes, shoot me, darling! I deserve it. I've always been a lousy correspondent – well, you know that, don't you, pet – just my one scrawled letter every Christmas, and even that went by the board last year. I know I promised you I'd write, on that tiny mingy card I sent, and you must have been wondering all this time how my round-the-world cruise went off, or where the heck I'd landed up, or even imagined I had drowned or something, or run off with the Captain. No such luck!'

Hilary laughed aloud, not so much at the thought of spinster Eva eloping with a Captain, but in sheer stupefied relief that her Aunt had turned up from the dead, was writing in her usual lively style. Drowning hadn't crossed her mind, but several other forms of death had seemed all too sadly likely – cancer, or a stroke, a smash-up in a car, even a fatal mugging in the dark streets of North London. Yet she was still completely mystified. How could modest Eva afford round-the-world cruises when she'd never saved enough to fly to Benidorm? And what 'tiny mingy card' was she referring to? She'd received no card at all, no single word from Eva since Christmas two whole years ago.

'I don't think I even told you how Edward and myself happened to be cruising the high seas at all . . . '

Edward? had her Aunt got married, or, even more unlikely, found a sugar daddy? She fought an irrational surge of jealousy, raced on through the letter, discovered Mr Edward Unsworth Taylor was a man of nearly eighty, who already had a heart condition, but was determined to see the world before he met its Maker, as Eva quaintly put it. He had advertised in London for a private nurse who would also act as chaperone, companion, on a ninety-day world cruise. Eva, hating both retirement and her move from friendly Gloucestershire to a vast impersonal city, had answered the advertisement, been finally selected in preference to a host of younger girls. They had set off on the P&O, called at Gibraltar, Malta, Port Said and Suez; then on to Madras, via Mahé and Colombo, with at least one day ashore at every port and still twenty-odd more ports to go.

'Alas, my love, we never got to see them, never made it past Madras. Edward collapsed right in the middle of a bustling Madrasi market, which sold everything from curry to dead bats – collapsed not just with heatstroke, but with a full-blown heart attack. Our three-month cruise was cut to just three weeks.'

Eva's writing, always hard to read, had now become illegible, as if it were suffering from the shock of Edward's coronary. Hilary jumped two crippled lines, picked the story up again, with Edward in St Thomas's, an expensive private nursing home, where he survived nearly a whole month, Eva at his side. When he finally expired, she was genuinely upset, had come to like the spirited old gentleman, with his eccentric ways, his little fads and fancies. She was equally sad at the thought of leaving India, which she had also grown to love; the nurses at the hospital who had accepted her as one of them, permitted her to nurse her charge, administer his drugs.

'Why not stay on here and get a job?' one of them had asked her, almost casually.

'Why not indeed!' Eva wrote, the ink smudging on the letter here, as if her hand were sweating in the heat. At least half a dozen reasons why she couldn't think of staying. She was past retirement age, had never lived abroad in all her life, and had a house in London which was standing empty, only checked on once a week by a rather vague acquaintance who lived in the next street. There were also endless rules and regulations about getting jobs in India, problems over visas, red tape by the mile. Yet the wild idea was somehow most appealing, and once it had rooted in her mind, she couldn't seem to dig it out again.

'It's not actually impossible, I allowed myself to think.' (More smudges and the writing getting wilder.) 'I'd nothing to return for, after all – no single living relative save you, my darling girl, and you were cut off anyway by those high walls and your vows. I'd no job and no real home, except a tiny terraced house in the most unfriendly street in London. I don't like London, Gloria, and I'd never found my feet there. India's a crazy place – chaotic, overcrowded and too damned hot for a paleface like Yours Truly, but the Indians are darlings (most of them!) and so wonderfully attentive. I mean, I find I'm now respected – revered out here as old and wise, rather than slung out on the rubbish heap, as I would be back in England. And anyway, I rather liked the feeling of landing up five thousand miles from home, with a circle of real friends already, and not actually starving, because my dear old generous Edward left me a few bob and . . . '

Hilary paused a moment, felt out of breath from the tidal wave of Eva's words. Eleven sides she'd read so far, with at least another dozen still to go. She dithered, checked her watch. The postman had come early, but even so, she was pressed for time, had a child to get to school, maybe a battle to be fought over a blue and gold striped blazer. She ought to wake Luke up, give him time to eat his breakfast with no sense of rush or hassle, take things really calmly. Yet she burned to know what happened next in Eva's Indian saga, and once he was awake she'd have no chance of finding out. He'd probably be rebellious; would need her full attention, all her 'mother's' skills. She stuffed the pages back into their envelope. Best continue with it later, once she'd delivered him to school. Easier then to concentrate. She could spin the letter out, relish every word, free from all distractions.

She moved into the kitchen, lit the rusty oil stove, put the kettle on the gas, so she could wake Luke with a cup of tea; picked him out the Batman mug, the last two custard creams. She started pouring juice into the milk jug, cursed, and tipped it back. Her mind was miles away – cruising from Gibraltar to Madras. Would Luke really need so long to eat his breakfast? Too much time to hang around could be just as bad as rushing him; might only build his nerves. She was wasting time right now. No point watching kettles, especially sluggish ones.

She dived back to the sitting room, snatched the letter up again, skipped the next few pages – endless snags and setbacks in Eva's bid to get a visa, land herself a job. By page fifteen, she'd wangled both – a visa for a year, and a nursing job not at chic St Thomas's, but at a smaller shabby mission hospital run by nuns. Nuns! She gasped, couldn't quite imagine Eva's strident tones and scarlet-painted fingernails ringing out against the soft-voiced pallor of the Mission Sisters. Yet she appeared to have enjoyed her work enormously; admired the nuns: their gentleness and patience; the endless hours they toiled – she, too! – with no real rest or recreation. She'd been meaning to write for months, she said, kept starting letters, but never finishing them, on account of the pressure of the job, the constant stream of patients, the fact that overtime was just a normal unpaid part of every day.

She also apologised – again – for sending just a card last Christmas, and that three weeks too early. She and Mr Taylor had departed on the first day of December, so she'd posted all her Christmas cards that morning, adding a brief and scribbled promise to her niece's that she'd write again more fully on the ship – a promise she had broken. Even on a so-called leisure cruise, every day seemed hectic, from early morning tea to late night cocktails. Then, once Edward had his heart attack, she was swamped with correspondence to his family, arrangements for transporting back his ashes, queries over the changes in his will. There followed her long battle for a visa and a job, and when she'd won both those, she'd been forced to sell her London house. She was running short of money, had no other source of capital. Her legacy was almost gone, and the nuns were offering little above basic room and board. She was also very anxious about leaving the house empty for a year, at risk from vandals, squatters, even fire. More prudent to dispose of it, release some ready cash, remove one source of worry from her mind. She'd had to arrange the sale long-distance, re-contact the solicitor she'd used to buy the house.

Hilary glanced up at the window, the dark still pressing close; one tattered rag of light from the crippled lamppost opposite, patching the old curtain. She recalled her lonely visits to Hurst Road, N14; those hoping hopeless odysseys to a deaf and empty house. While she'd trailed along that dark north London cul-de-sac, fearing Eva cold and dead, her aunt had been a world away, working like a beaver, or romping in the sun. Typical of Eva to buy a house, then sell it; survive all that aggravation, and still keep bouncing back. She grinned at the drawing scribbled on page twenty – a rickety 'For Sale' board, tied to a huge boulder, with a screaming, squint-eyed woman half-crushed beneath the rock, but doing her wild best to push it off.

'You'll probably think I was out of my small mind, getting involved in all that hassle, with letters firing back and forth, and a whole tangle of new problems, but that house was like a millstone round my neck, seemed to tie me to a life I didn't want. Anyway, I'm sure you'll understand, my love, why your own letter got put off, especially once I'd actually started work. And now blow me down if it isn't almost Christmas once again, and in just a month or two, my wretched precious visa will expire, so I'll have to come back home, like it or no.' Several lines were crossed out here, a brownish stain splashed across the writing. Had Eva stopped for tea, spilt it on her letter?

Tea! Hilary sprang up. She could hear the kettle whistling from the kitchen, calling her, reproaching. She rushed to turn it off, ignored the pool of boiling water which had spewed across the hob; cursed the officious kitchen clock striking the half-hour. Luke really should be up by now. Disastrous to be late this first and vital morning. She turned the clockface round, spooned out the spaghetti hoops, put them on to warm. The boy could dress in minutes, when she made it worth his while, and if she invented some new eating game, she could speed breakfast up, as well. She just had to read those few remaining pages, find out if her crazy aunt were truly coming home. She skipped the messy brown patch, continued at the bottom of the page.

'You won't believe this, darling, but P&O have agreed to fly me back – yes, after all this time. Mind you, I'm not that keen to come back, and I don't intend to stay, but I must sort out my things, and tick off that solicitor. I'm pretty sure he diddled me, and his bills were astronomical. (Can't spell that!) Then I'm off again – I don't know where exactly, but now I've seen half the world, I'm determined to see the other half. I've heard they're short of nurses in the States and are even recruiting oldies like myself. Or I may find another Edward, land up in Timbuktu next time. Who knows? I've got my health and strength, thank God, and the last thing I intend is to sit around on my backside, turning into a professional old age pensioner. But before I set off anywhere, I promise you one thing, my love – I'm going to come and visit you – yes, brave those nuns at last. You know how scared I've always been of setting foot within a mile of Brignor, and your Mother made it worse by harping on about the grilles and things, and how she couldn't say a word without some black-robed figure listening in, and your Father half-suspected there were even hidden microphones . . . Well, I'm far more used to nuns now. In fact, I was almost shocked, at first, by how free and easy those Mission Sisters were – I mean, the way they rode bicycles and didn't turn a hair at the sight of naked men . . . '

Hilary grinned in disbelief, zipped through the last few pages to the end, then made straight for Luke's bedroom, forgetting tea and biscuits, only pausing at the door. She longed to share her news with him, share it with the world, but would he really care a fig about some fuddy-duddy aunt he'd never even heard of? Unless she made it sound exciting, used it as a lure to get him up. She pushed the door, sat down on his bed.

'Wakey-wakey, Luke, my love.' That was Eva's voice, lively, loving, cheerful. The letter was awash with 'loves' and 'darlings', had made her feel cosseted and cherished. She hugged it to her in the half-light of the room. Eva – coming home; her next of kin face to face with her, without even grilles or chaperones. 'Luke, are you awake?'

He didn't answer, just squinted up at her, still groggy from his Scotch-and-aspirin cocktail.

'Luke, we've got a new relation.'

'What you on about?'

'Aunt Eva. She's coming to see us. She'll be your Aunt, as well as mine. She'll have lots and lots of stories. She's been in India a year. There are elephants in India and great fierce tigers, and alligators which bite your head off and . . . '

'Shove off, can't you, Hilary, it's the middle of the night.'

'No, it's not. It's late. I've given you twenty minutes extra.'

'I don't want to go to school. My nose is sore.'

'We'll put some Vaseline on. And don't forget we've got ice cream for breakfast. Guess what Auntie Eva eats for breakfast?'

He shrugged, turned the other way.

'Mangoes and papayas and chocolate-covered ants.'

'*Ants?*'

'Yes, two dozen every morning, twelve milk and twelve plain.'

He sat up very slowly, wiped his runny nose on his pyjama sleeve. 'How do they put the chocolate on – when the ants are still alive?'

'Yes, I think so. You have to gulp them down very very quickly, or they fly out of your mouth.'

'Ugh! I'd hate to go to India.'

'No, you wouldn't. You could ride on an elephant, right high up, on a sort of wooden throne, and the elephants have gorgeous coloured rugs on, and medals round their necks and . . . Want to see a picture?' He was watching her intently now, as she fumbled for the photograph. 'There! That's our Auntie Eva, holding her umbrella up, for shade. It's very hot on elephants, because you're closer to the sun. And see that little boy sitting on its head? He's the driver and he's not much older than you are.'

Luke grabbed the photograph, studied it close up. 'When's she coming?'

'Oh, it'll be quite a little while yet. We'll have to get the place nice first, so we can invite her here to stay. Would you like her to come and stay, Luke?'

'Don't mind.'

'Right, up you get. 50p for the one who gets dressed first.'

'That's not fair. You're dressed already.'

'No, I'm not. I've got my nightie underneath this coat. In fact, you're bound to win, because I've got layers and layers of clothes to take off first. Okay, starting now!' She dashed back to the sitting room, trying to generate excitement. It wasn't hard. Her whole body seemed lighter and less weary. Even her cold was less oppressive, as if Eva's thirty pages had acted like an instant cure. Her mind kept darting back and forth, reflecting on the letter, filling in the gaps, solving any puzzles like last year's Christmas card. No real mystery there. It would have arrived in the first week of December – already Advent, when no letters were allowed; would have been kept by Reverend Mother for Christmas afternoon. Except Sister Mary Hilary had disappeared by then, run away on impulse with no forwarding address. And why should Reverend Mother forward letters anyway, when the nun in question belonged back in the convent, had taken formal solemn vows never to leave it in her life?

She must dash off a reply, maybe even send a telegram, tell her Aunt not to visit Brignor, but to come and stay in Tooting – and to come immediately, before she'd moved herself, lost the only fragile home they had between the two of them. Eva would be absolutely stunned to find her niece not a virgin Sister, but the 'mother' of a seven-year-old, and no longer living in an eighteenth-century mansion, but in a condemned flat above a shop. She laughed out loud, sharing Eva's shock and sheer astoundment. She'd have to work really fast, clear that second bedroom, get it painted, furnished – maybe refurbish the whole flat. And Joe would have to help. She'd take a tougher line with him, insist she got her wages the day that they were due, instead of always late, so she could buy material for curtains, make a bedspread for Aunt Eva, cushions for this sitting room, perhaps a . . .

A silent mocking voice cut through her plans. 'Look, your precious Aunt will probably only stay for just a month or less – if she comes at all. Nothing's certain, is it? She said herself she's only passing through, before she flies off somewhere else, hates the thought of London, is agog to see the world. Why go to all that trouble for . . . ?'

For who? Hilary flung back the car-rug curtain, glanced around the room. Why not for herself? She'd made no plans at all to improve this tatty flat. It had seemed hardly worth the effort, when both her tenure and her role were equally provisional. Yet she had one whole term, at least. Even if Rita were discharged from hospital, she was unlikely to be strong enough to take on Luke immediately, was bound to convalesce first. And, anyway, she didn't have to move. Joe had promised she could remain here in the flat, even after Luke was off her hands – which gave her till October; maybe longer, if Charlie wangled extra time, or the developers delayed in pulling down the place. It was nine months till October, plenty long enough to transform it into something of her own, stamp it with her taste, not Joe's or Liz's. She'd never had a home before, never had the chance to do things as she wanted, choose a colour scheme, hunt down odds and ends in second-hand shops, things she'd picked out for herself, instead of making do with other people's cast-offs.

It might actually be fun – a challenge, an achievement, and who cared if it were temporary? Everything was temporary, in one sense, especially Eva's own jobs. Yet that didn't seem to stop her aunt from trying to grab at life, relish her small crumbs of it. And Charlie wasn't moping in his shop downstairs; still kept it open, kept it fully stocked, still hoped for a reprieve. Both he and Eva were already in their sixties, had far less time than she did – time to simply live. Her aunt had less in every way: no home, no wage, no job, no friends in London, no supportive Sister Anne; was returning home to complete uncertainty. At least she'd find a roof, a *pied-à-terre*, a resurrected niece to meet her at the airport.

She rifled through the photographs again – Eva grinning with the nuns, her brilliant crimson sundress hogging all the limelight; Eva with a bald and bearded Indian, who looked less than half her size; Eva in her swimsuit, challenging the waves. Her aunt was officially a spinster, officially retired, alone in the world – as she was – yet she had refused to wilt or wither, wallow in self-pity, view her birthdays as simply signposts to the grave. Instead, she made things happen, lived life for herself, made that self important – and enough in its own right. She could do the same; create a home right here, even plant a garden, transform the cluttered junkyard into a splash of scent and colour. She needed colour everywhere, inside as well as out; could paint these dreary khaki walls a deep dramatic shade; buy a few bright posters –perhaps a Botticelli, like the one in Sister Anne's room.

She closed her eyes, suddenly uneasy, could see not grinning Eva, but the pale and shocked Madonna; recalled that strange and blinding light, the fierce wind on her face. She had never understood that extraordinary experience. When she'd been to see Sister Anne next morning, the nun divulged that she and all the Sisters had spent that night awake, praying for herself and Luke, imploring God to make it clear what He wanted for the boy. Had that been His answer – the rushing wind, the light – or were they just the side effects of the feverish cold which started that same evening, or simply the result of too much stress? She would probably never know, would have to accept the whole improbable phenomenon as one of Robert's mysteries. And one which smacked of blasphemy. Why should she be granted an annunciation, when she was no longer even a virgin, let alone a Blessed one, and she and Luke (and Joseph) comprised no Holy Family?

'I won, I won! You haven't even started.' Luke burst in, shirt unbuttoned, shorts unzipped, one sock on, one off. 'Where's my 50p? I need it now, this minute. I want to go and buy a glider. There's this really cheapo one I saw in . . . '

'Breakfast first, then gliders. We'll get it on the way to school, but only if you hurry.'

'You're not hurrying.'

'No, I'm not, you're right. Go and start your ice cream and I'll be washed and dressed by then. Did *you* wash, by the way?'

'Yeah.'

They both grinned at the lie. 'Well, I'll let you off today, but only because it's my fault that we're late – or Auntie Eva's fault.' Hilary was tugging off her sweaters as she talked, rifling through her suitcase for clean clothes. 'D'you know, I think we ought to celebrate this Saturday, have a treat or something, first because my Aunt's not dead, and . . . '

'Dead?'

'Yes – I thought she was – and second, it's my birthday.'

'You're fibbing.'

'No, I'm not.'

'Why didn't you say before, then?'

'It felt too old, I suppose. I'll be forty in four days.'

'My Mum's nearly fifty-one.'

'Well, forty's still important. It's rather like you reaching double figures. What would you like to do?'

'Nothing.'

'Oh, come on, Luke, we must do something.'

'Okay, chocolate-covered ants for breakfast.'

'You can't get those in Tooting.'

'A ride on an elephant with me sitting on its head.'

'I'm not sure we'll get that either, unless we . . . Oh, yes, we can! We'll go to London Zoo – ride on an elephant and see all Eva's animals. Would that be fun?'

'Dunno.'

'It's meant to be a marvellous zoo. I've never been. Have you?'

'Nope.'

'Well, let's try it, shall we – go early, spend all day there? We could even have a camel-ride, as well as just the elephant. Now, shoo, Luke! I'll see you in the kitchen in two ticks.'

'Hilary . . . ?'

'Mm.'

'Can I ask you something?'

'Well, gee up with it. Or we'll be eating our spaghetti on the bus.'

He didn't answer for a moment, seemed embarrassed, almost diffident, scuffing one socked foot against the lino.

'You know that letter thing they gave you?'

'Who gave me?'

'That lady. Sister – you know . . . '

'Sister Anne?'

'Yup.'

'What about it?'

'Well, it had my name on, didn't it?'

'Did it?'

'Yeah.' He paused. 'Luke Craddock.' He stood, restless, scowling, pulling at a button on his shirt. 'Craddock's not your surname.'

'No.'

'Well, I don't want them to know.'

'What d'you mean? Know what?'

'That my Mum walked out. They'll only laugh, or . . . '

'They won't, Luke, not at this school. Anyway, your Mother's ill. All you have to say is she's had an operation and is still in hospital.'

'They won't believe me. We said that about my Dad when he'd really gone to prison, and Gary Eaves found out and bent my arm up right behind my back, held it there five minutes. Will you say you're Mrs Craddock, so your name's the same as mine? Just at school. Not here.'

'But what about the nuns? They know I'm . . . '

'I don't mind *them*. It's the others in my class.'

'But how can . . . ?'

'Please. I'll give you back the 50p.'

'I don't want that.'

'But *will* you?'

'All right, I suppose so, if it really . . . '

'Say you promise.'

'Okay, I promise, Luke.'

He dashed out, slammed the door, as if frightened she might change her mind. She checked her watch, hadn't time to wash. She was picking up Luke's bad habits now, as well as Craddock Senior's. She doused herself with talc, instead, then tossed aside the neat grey skirt she'd selected from her case; the sober navy sweater she'd chosen for its convent-plain restraint. She replaced it with a frilled red blouse – Eva's singing red – a swirly patterned skirt. She must celebrate this morning, not wait until the 10th, celebrate her two new close relations – Aunt Eva and a son.

36

'Can I have the piece with the "B" on?'

'Okay. Why the "B"?'

'B for big.'

'All right, but don't make crumbs. This sofa bed's uncomfortable enough, without sharing it with bits of soggy cake. You've already dropped jelly in my slippers.'

Luke giggled, gulped his drink. 'Aren't you having any?'

'It's a bit early for sponge cake, Luke.'

'No, it's not. It's nearly half past eight. That's late for us.'

Hilary cut herself a finger, lay back against the pillows, chewing very slowly, so she could judge the taste and texture of the sponge. She had made the cake herself, even used an icing set to write a wobbly 'Happy Birthday' in pink on white. She thought back to a year ago – that swede and carrot hotchpotch she had made for poor Miss Pullen, then devoured as penance cake. She'd come quite a way since then, and not just in her cooking skills. She'd left behind that panicky insomniac – crop-haired, dressed in cast-offs – still pining for its convent, its safety net of rules; somehow found an identity, a self; even strengthened it these last few days, in response to Eva's letter. Eva would approve of this offbeat birthday breakfast – red jelly and iced cake, washed down with Seven-Up. In the week they'd been at Tooting, they hadn't yet had one conventional meal. She let Luke choose the menus. Not only was it easier, since he asked for things like Chow Mein from the takeaway, or peanut butter sandwiches, but it also meant he ate more. All meals were casual picnics, usually eaten on the sofa bed with the television blaring. This morning it was Boss Cat and the Smurfs.

Luke broke his 'B' off, wrapped it in a Kleenex, then stuffed his mouth with icing, talking as he chewed. 'Now your cards. You've got – let's count – one, two, three, four, five. Can I open them?'

'Yes, do. My fingers are all sticky. What's that really fat one?'

Luke tore it open, found a card, a bulky letter and a smaller envelope. '"Love from Liz", the card says. Don't read the letter. It looks boring.' He snatched it from her grasp, handed her the second card, instead.

'Don't be such a Boss Cat!' Hilary grabbed the letter back, flicked through it very swiftly, fighting an immediate surge of guilt, as Liz detailed all the presents she and Harry had for her – Christmas gifts still

480

waiting for her visit, and now birthday presents, too – clothes from Di's new shop, books and records, classy bits and pieces to mitigate the squalor of her flat. Her first instinct was to refuse, write straight back to Liz and say she couldn't take so much, until she realised from the letter that Liz, too, felt plagued with guilt; that the presents were a way to quiet her conscience, minimise the growing gulf between them. In Liz's view, she herself had everything – money, status, a gracious house, elegantly furnished, and now, at last, a definite (and romantic) wedding date – February 14th, St Valentine's – whereas 'you, my love, have landed up with zilch'.

Hilary refolded the letter, returned it to its envelope. No self-pity. Anyway, a lot of things which Liz had, she didn't envy in the least. She had never wanted marriage – save to God – nor an expensive gracious home; preferred Eva as her model, Eva who had lived alone on boiled eggs and custard creams, rarely cooked at all, except for sudden generous dinners for her friends; chose to spend her money on books and outings, or saving whales and seals, rather than *Homes and Gardens* clutter. She glanced at her new ring – no crucifix, no pearls – just a cheap and gimcrack thing she'd discovered in the toy shop while Luke was picking out his glider. A toy ring, to help her play the game of being Mrs Craddock, and which could be discarded with the name.

She slit the smaller envelope, found a home-made card from Stephen, admired the bright collage of ships and cars.

'Get a move on, Gee! You've still got four more left.'

She grinned at her old nickname; had told Luke just two days ago that she'd been 'Gee' at school, from the age of seven to the age of seventeen. He seemed to like the name, had used it ever since. It made her feel a child again, with Luke as her kid brother. She could love him as a brother. That brand of love was easier.

He was jumping on the bed now, endangering its springs, jabbing the last cards against her stomach. 'One's from Di and one's from Dad. You're lucky! He never sent my Mum no card. And who's this third one from? I can't read a word of it.'

Nor could she. The writing was a scrawl, and completely unfamiliar. She held it to the light. 'Oh, it's Charlie! Charlie Cook downstairs. He says "Forty's nothing, wait until you're sixty!" How on earth did *he* know?'

'I told him.'

'Luke, you rotter! Right, let me see your Dad's now.' She took the padded satin card, which showed three kittens in a basket, pink bows around their necks; a sentimental verse inside, wishing her sunny days and silver linings to any tiny cloud. Joe himself had written just three words – 'Thank you' and his name. She stared down at his writing, which didn't seem to fit him, a timid spindly hand, which looked diffident, uncertain. The brief message meant a lot, though. It was the first time he had thanked her, either in writing or in person. She glanced back at Charlie's card, pleased he, too, had bothered. Even the postman had wished her happy birthday, stopped to chat a while. She was slowly making friends. Some of Charlie's 'regulars' had got to know her name, and the woman in the paper shop often had a friendly moan about the weather or the Unions. She liked the feeling that they were relating to her as her, and not merely as an appendage of the Kingsleys, as had always been the case at Cranleigh Gardens.

Yet she still had Liz's family, as well. They had all remembered, even Della. Luke was just squinting at her card, which he described as 'squashed red flowers'. She scanned the reproduction of Monet's Poppy Field, Della's sweeping signature inside. This must be a duty card, sent only on Liz's orders. All the same, it touched her – as did the offer of free highlights any time she found herself in Berkshire. Impulsively, she slipped down from the bed.

'I need the bathroom, Luke. Won't be a sec.' She did need it, urgently, had drunk two cups of tea before the Seven-Up. It was also the only room which had a mirror. She'd been ignoring mirrors recently, fighting off her fear of being forty since dawn that morning when she'd woken to pitch darkness, aware that half her life was over, maybe more. Her father had died when he was only in his fifties. If she took after him in that respect, she was old, not middle-aged. She peered closely in the cracked and dingy glass; knew already she'd find her first grey hairs, had been trying to ignore them now for weeks. She counted them – just seven – and they didn't really show. Her hair was still the wheaty colour it had been in her girlhood. Della's highlights had grown out now completely; no traces left of the chic and clever cut. It was child's hair – thick and straight, but somehow she preferred it. She'd leave the grey hairs grey, leave the rest unstyled, not continue with the blonding or take up Della's offer.

She unlocked the door, about to leave the room, then suddenly dived back, turned the key again. She had to see the rest of her, somehow feared that she had aged, subtly but irrevocably, breasts sagging, waistline spreading, as if to mark the start of official middle age. She unzipped her dressing-gown, tugged her nightie off, shivering in the dank unheated room. She looked much the same as always – perhaps a little thinner – a bruise on her left leg where Luke had rammed it with his Thundertank. She touched one breast, felt it firm and girlish still. Robert would approve – her waist still well-defined, what he called her 'thatch' still blonde and crisp. She stroked her hand across it, remembering his hand, the pressure of his fingers, his high-flown compliments. It was the clothes which spoilt the image: a boring long-sleeved nightgown, and a new bargain-basement dressing-gown, bought for warmth, not glamour. Yet why should she be glamorous, dress for vanished Robert, or the editor of *Vogue*, rather than to suit herself or the cold climate of the flat? She and Liz had parted, not just geographically, but in more fundamental ways. Liz was seeking wealth and gloss, still trying to outwit nature, force her face and hair and figure to fit a glamorous mould, whereas she herself had renounced such futile struggles.

She leaned forward, touched her mirror-face, realised with a sense of shock that the high glass wall she had always felt surrounding her, had totally dissolved. It hadn't needed shattering, with all the pain and danger of cut and bleeding hands; had simply melted, vanished. She was no longer cordoned off from other people, shut out from the world.

'You was long enough,' said Luke, as she returned to the sitting room, buttoning up her dressing gown. He was squatting on the carpet, prising lumps of icing off the now half-balding cake. She was tempted suddenly to hug him, just to prove she could, show the world the barriers were down. Yet she knew he'd pull away – squirming, scowling, embarrassed by the contact. Best to leave it for a while – next week, next month, next term.

'Hey, no more of that icing, Luke. It'll only make you sick.'

'I'm never sick.'

'What about last Monday?'

'That was eggs, not icing. I don't like eggs. They're chicks.' He dashed off to the bathroom, clutching at his jeans. He always left his visits far too late, sometimes right till danger point. Monday had been bad – vomit, then a puddle.

She removed the cake, collected up the dirty plates, the torn and scattered envelopes. Two cards missing: one from Robert, one from Luke himself. If Joe had never sent a card in thirty years of marriage, was it any wonder his son had failed to bother? She'd have to train him differently, as Di had done with Stephen. And as for Robert, she had his gifts already, and more important, still had his views and insights; views she must impart to Luke, to supplement the teaching of the nuns. If she were acting mother, then Robert must be father, in the sense of influence, must point Luke to a wider world which would undercut the narrowness of one coercive faith.

She moved to the window, peered out at the sky. It seemed to threaten snow, pressing grey and leaden on the stained and steep-pitched roofs. She shivered, flexed her fingers. She had lit both the ancient oil stoves, yet the cold still seeped through cracks, thrust against the glass. She rubbed the steamed-up pane, looked beyond the roofs, to where the grey was slowly lightening into white; a white so intense, so potent, it seemed to eat into the obstacles which tried to interrupt it – telegraph posts or aerials or ugly factory chimneys, dissolving in its bleak but brilliant light. She gazed higher still, up to Robert's region, where the eye could pierce through barriers of sky and space and time, to a vastness and intensity she still could hardly fathom. Would she ever really grasp it or – still more difficult – impart some vaguest sense of it to Luke? She felt a sense of duty to the boy, to give him at least the barest intimation of Robert's complex world, and to present it as a wonder, not a threat. She could hear him tramping back now, hear his tuneless whistle, the muttered 'Shit!' as he tripped on a torn patch in the lino.

'Did you flush the loo, Luke?'

'No.'

'Well, go and do it.'

'No.'

'We can't go to the zoo, then. What a shame. It opens in three-quarters of an hour, and I thought it would be rather nice if we were the first ones through the turnstile.'

Luke threw the last piece of birthday cake to a mangy-looking ostrich which appeared to be losing half its feathers. The bird bent and looped its long elastic neck, to investigate the offering, disdained it, minced away.

'Fuck!' said Luke, full volume.

Hilary dragged him from the ostrich cage, helped him zip his anorak, put the hood up for him. It had just begun to snow, light uncertain flurries which blew into their faces, made it hard to see. Many of the animals were confined to their enclosures; the zoo relatively deserted, trees leafless, flowerbeds bare, shivering birds huddled in their feathers. The lion-moat had frozen over, the lions shut up inside. She and Luke had seen them through the glass – the male snappish and bad-tempered, his harem half-asleep – not prowling wild, majestic, through their paddocks. The giraffes seemed sad and rigid, as if they had stiffened in the cold, no movement in their painted necks and legs. Luke was disappointed, especially by the total lack of rides. She should have phoned the zoo first, before making random promises. Camel rides and pony rides stopped in late October, and elephant rides simply didn't happen, had been discontinued thirty years ago. Elephants were dangerous, could bolt with their riders, dislodge them, throw them off.

'Why don't they bolt in India?' Luke enquired, disgruntled.

A keeper overheard him. 'They do,' he grinned. 'There've been some nasty deaths out there, and one man I know lost both his legs.'

Hilary backed away, as if suddenly aware of all those warning notices: 'These animals are dangerous'; 'Do not cross the safety barrier'; that vivid coloured symbol of a bleeding bitten hand. Wild beasts all around them, wild nature pressing in. Only narrow bars and insubstantial cages between their naked human skin and those manes and fangs and claws. White teeth bared, black tongues coiled, huge mouths gaping open; powerful jaws which could smash and crush an antelope; killer paws which could stun and trap and tear. She could smell the reek of urine from a score of dens and lairs, the odour of soiled straw; hear the angry cries of birds of prey, their cruel hooked beaks ripping through warm flesh. She turned to Luke, as if for reassurance, took his hand in hers. He pulled away, wiped the hand, as if somehow she had soiled it, started striding on ahead.

'What's that?' he asked, turning back a moment, and pointing to a cage with just three sides.

'That's for us,' she answered, as she read the sign: 'London Zoo Presents The Most Destructive Animal In The World.'

'What d'you mean?'

'A cage for man. You can stand in there, with your feet in those two hollowed-out man's footprints. Then you're an animal yourself – the only one which kills its own species and destroys its own environment and . . . ' She broke off. Luke had already dashed inside and was grunting and grimacing through the wire; had hardly heard her pious little homily. Well, at least it had distracted him, and perhaps a pizza in the café would do much the same, besides providing shelter from the snow.

The pizzas were expensive, the coffee watery. They sat at a small table littered, like the cages, with discarded crusts, orange peel, the greasy uncleared debris from other people's meals. Luke spat out an olive stone.

'I want my Mum,' he said.

'She'll be back.'

'When?'

'Quite soon.'

'You're just saying that, aren't you?'

'No, I'm not.' Hilary laid her plastic fork down, leaned closer to the boy. 'Look, my Auntie Eva went away, disappeared completely, didn't write or anything. I had to wait a year, or more, but she still came back, didn't she? Your Mum will, too – you see. She's not even far away. Shall we buy her something, send it to her in hospital – something from the zoo shop – a biro with a lion on, or . . . ?'

'No.' He gouged a hole in his pizza base, jabbed his finger through it.

'Why not?'

'She don't write.'

Hilary added whitener to her coffee, watched it clog and curdle. Eva hadn't written, either – not a second time – in reply to her own telegram which she'd sent four days ago. Four days wasn't long, but even so . . . She'd expected some reaction by return, an amazed excited telegram, expressing Eva's sheer delight that they could embrace as aunt and niece, meet freely without walls or grilles, stay together, live together, if only for a month. But perhaps her aunt was shocked, or simply preferred things not to change; was so accustomed to a captive niece, safe behind her bars, that the thought of her set free was somehow threatening or distasteful.

'I'm cold,' said Luke, abandoning both seat and plate, and ripping up his paper serviette. 'Can we go home now?'

At least he called it home. She didn't – yet – nor wish to spend her birthday afternoon in that cold but claustrophobic flat, with the winter darkness closing in, the growing silence as Charlie shut his shop.

'Let's stay a wee bit longer. The chimps are being fed in just five minutes, and we don't want to miss that. Anyway, the snow's stopped.' She tied her woolly muffler round his neck, lent him her old gloves. He had refused to wear his own, refused to change from his thin and holey gym shoes.

They followed the sign for apes and chimpanzees, careful not to slip on the wet and treacherous paths. A party of Cub Scouts in their green and grey uniform were gathered round the chimps' cage, waiting for the keeper. He strode in with a bucket, started scattering the food. All the chimps seemed suddenly to come alive, rushing, grabbing, pouncing; snaffling up celery and apples, fighting each other for sunflower seeds, banana; flinging husks and debris to the ground. The one large male was particularly aggressive, snatching food from females, swinging from the bars to attack the smaller chimps, threaten them with howls or ugly leers. A female with saggy drooping breastlets sat picking at her fruit, her huge pink naked bottom swollen like some grotesque diseased attachment. Several of the Cubs were already pointing at it, shrieking with embarrassment, distaste. Hilary read the notice tacked up on the cage, which explained the swellings as cyclical and sexual, appearing when the females were on heat, and acting as a signal to the males. She prayed Luke wouldn't ask her what it meant, question words like 'oestrus', in a piercing public voice. Fortunately, he was round the other side, mercifully intent on a baby chimpanzee who was poking at a waterspout, trying to get a drink.

Suddenly, the male reared up, and she saw its thin pink penis, pointed at the end and now erect. It lunged towards the female, who struggled to escape, her shrill cries growing louder, her gait awkward, panicky. The male was bearing down on her, felled her to the ground, climbed on top, clung on. Hilary watched, appalled. The female seemed so passive, the piece of apple still clutched in one limp hand, her body pinioned by the male's full weight, as it jerked and thrust, shot its semen into her, then suddenly withdrew, in the same abrupt and casual way as it had entered.

'See that?' said Luke, who'd come racing back, wide-eyed.

She nodded, tried to coax him from the cage towards the Reptile House. He shook free, pushed her arm away, pressed closer to the bars.

'They was fucking, wasn't they?'

'Yes,' she murmured, hoping her own whisper might temper his wild voice. It hardly mattered, really. Nobody else could hear him, with that pack of raucous Cub Scouts catcalling and sniggering, trying to urge the male to repeat its brief performance, so they could point and jeer again.

The female chimp stuffed her mouth with peanuts, started spitting out the shells angrily, vindictively, as if furious at her rape. The male sat sullen on its own, scratching at its fur, its penis still erect, its small eyes hostile, narrowed.

'Look, Luke,' she said, still trying to distract him. 'The chimps have all got names. They're written up over there, with pictures of each one. Shall we see if there's a Luke?'

'There won't be.'

He was right. Bobby, Johnny, Barbie, Jane and Fanny, even Amanda and Rosanne. Human names. She stared up at the chart which showed man grouped with the apes, listed all their similarities – their frontal vision, grasping hands, their closely related anatomy and structure, even their similar blood groups, biochemistry. What had Robert said – way back in April when he'd first brought her to his lighthouse – that there was only a one per cent difference between man and chimpanzee? At the time, she had hardly deemed it credible, suspected that he'd got the figure wrong. One per cent seemed ridiculously little, impossible, in fact. Yet they'd discussed it at a later date, and Robert had explained the new and clinching evidence which showed man was closer to the chimp than a donkey to a horse; that chimps, gorillas, humans, were virtually identical, at least as far as genetics were concerned. She'd continued to resist the notion; somehow found it most distasteful to imagine Mother Mistress or Reverend Mother Abbess composed of the same chemical components as a gross and hairy ape. Yet now she could actually see it for herself, pictured on that chart – naked man crouching beside a row of fellow apes, all with roughly the same head-shape, the same muscles, joints and organs, even the same expression on their faces, one of cunning, guile.

Luke was tugging at her arm. 'Come back to the cage. The chimps are fun.'

'But we haven't seen the reptiles.' Reptiles were much safer, far removed from man – cold-blooded, with small brains.

'No. I like the chimps best. Oh, look! They're fighting now.'

The male was in pursuit again, howling with frustration as a younger slimmer female managed to elude him. She was screeching too – high-pitched yowls of rage, as she swung high up on the bars, then turned her back and urinated, directing the fierce jet at her pursuer. Luke crowed with vulgar laughter, the Cub Scouts joining in, mimicking the male's outraged expression. Hilary glanced from boys to chimps: the same open mouths, bared teeth, the same crude and braying noises, piggy eyes screwed up; the same grabbing snatching hands. The bars were down, the cage dissolved; boys and man and monkeys all muddled up together, all chewing, spitting, defecating; hurling nutshells, picking noses, scratching heads and rumps.

Luke was in the centre of the scrum, stuffing his mouth with rotting fruit and vegetables, hitting out at smaller boys as they tried to grab his share; Joe, yowling with frustration at his women, threatening them with leers; Robert, too, and Simon, pink penises erect; she herself swollen and on heat, submitting as they covered her and thrust. She could feel their hairy bodies rutting into hers, their rough coarse pelts hurting on her breasts; the constant stabbing pain as they rammed again, again; the heat, the sweat, the smell of dirty fur. Her head was like a cage itself, fetid with their droppings, jarring with their noise – snortings, gruntings, sudden yelps of triumph as they spurted into her, as suddenly withdrew.

She limped away, found an empty corner, slumped against the wall. She had to be alone, remove herself from that barbarous savage pack. She opened her eyes, saw all the colours blurring, solid shapes melting and distorting; heard discordant shouts and laughter, jumbled up and booming through her skull. She *was* alone – totally, completely – alone in this new terror, this sudden choking panic. She wouldn't make it, couldn't cope. She had tried to believe that she was sufficient in herself, a fighter like Aunt Eva, who no longer needed gods or nannies, glass cocoons, high protective walls. Now she realised she was nothing, too feeble and defenceless to save herself, let alone a child. She was just an animal, a mix of random chemicals no different from a monkey's. She stared up at the chart again, man beside the apes, five squatting snarling figures on a level – man crude, uncouth, unfinished.

'No,' said Robert. 'You haven't understood.'

She started, glanced around. No one there; only the dark shapes on the chart, which she watched through half-closed eyelids, still uncertain where she was, or what was happening. One figure seemed to move, appeared to struggle to its feet; naked man standing slowly upright, towering now above the four crouched apes. She moved swiftly back, as he took a step towards her, a grotesque and lumbering man, reaching out for berries, digging for small grubs. Already, he had moved past her, was fashioning an axe-head from an unshaped lump of stone, building a rough shelter, striking flints together and sparking off a fire – man's first and potent fire. The flames flickered in her face as he roasted deer and buffalo, kept wild beasts at bay; then joined his fellow hunters, trekking the broad plains to pursue and trap his prey; no longer naked, but dressed in skins and furs. His face was slowly changing, finer-honed, less savage, as he settled down to farming, cleared forests, grew new crops, domesticated animals, carved out settlements; his dress less wild and shaggy, his brain and tools more subtle. She watched him as he learned to write, drew up laws and codes, founded cities, raised temples to his gods; marvelled as he mastered mathematics, tested scientific theories, reasoned and debated, reflected on himself.

She rubbed her eyes, disorientated; glanced down at her hand, surprised to see it bleeding where she'd scraped it on the fence. She'd felt no pain at all, only a strange elation at the sense she had of the whole pattern of existence, with herself as an essential part of it; part of her own awesome human species. She needed Robert to put it into words for her – that startling concept of her own infinitesimal speck of life, touching on the infinite – a life which reached right back to slime, and on to sages, seers.

She swung round, still half-dazed. A raucous tinny pop tune was jangling out behind her; a lanky boy with acne nursing his transistor, though radios were forbidden in the zoo. That insistent thump-thump-thump had broken up her vision, dispersed those mysterious figures in her head. Now, all she was aware of was the whine of a guitar; the banal and jaunty twang of an electric piano. She swore beneath her breath, about to stalk away; stopped, transfixed by one repeated phrase. She knew that phrase – the ascending run of semiquavers from her Beethoven sonata. Had the pop composer stolen it, or was it sheer coincidence? The phrase rang out again, seemed to throb through her whole body, repeating and repeating, as if she herself were a soundbox or a keyboard. The boy had mooched away now, turned the volume down, but she was still hearing that same phrase, amplified, insistent, and then the flurry of arpeggios which followed in the score, the spirited crescendo which brought the movement to a close.

There was no close. The second movement was now clamouring in her head; the sustained dark chords which opened it; the forlorn and brooding theme with its restless left-hand tremolo fretting beneath the triplets in the right; and then the slow and groping change as the melody enlarged – gradually, uncertainly – the sombre mood shattered by abrupt explosive chords. She felt her own mood change with the arresting modulation which ushered in the serene and song-like passage in the major. That chain of rising fourths seemed to promise hope and certainty; those bold assertive chords to challenge and sustain her. The words of Isaiah suddenly jolted through her mind: 'The land that was desolate and impassable shall be glad.' She could feel that gladness suffusing the whole movement – a dazzling spill of quavers shimmering in the treble; lifting her spirits with its buoyancy, its verve. 'The wilderness shall flourish like the lily.'

The melody was now in the left hand, the right hand playing a steady ostinato, its compelling rhythm ripped apart by those sudden offbeat accents, which had always thrilled her and defeated her. She tensed instinctively, at the tricky treacherous passage which followed in the minor, with its unexpected cadences, its sudden change of key. It needed practice, hours and hours of practice, as man himself had needed years and years before he evolved a hand and brain. She would have to work on it, daily and meticulously, until the whole piece flowed, refined; developed power and meaning; became a vital part of her, as she herself was grafted into it, rooted in the score.

She unzipped her heavy coat, flung it open, ran a sweaty finger round the collar of her shirt. She was burning hot, despite the freezing air, yet everything was clear. She had to play – she knew that now – had to use her one great gift which saved her from the apes; had to battle, struggle, for her own small evolution, use claw and wile and guile to get her own piano, deny the voices shouting out 'Impossible!' Joe could help, had started clearing houses as well as selling scrap, might well hunt down an instrument which at least would get her started. She must simply quash her pride, overcome her scruples, beg for what she wanted, make it paramount. She had never really given up her music, not even in the convent, not through more than twenty years. And she refused to renounce it now. Music *was* that one per cent, or at least a vital part of it; that unique and crucial element which had made man what he was: a thinking reasoning animal who had moved beyond the apes, infinitely beyond them as he wrote and built and calculated, painted and composed. Robert was right – she hadn't understood. That one per cent was huge; accounted for the whole of consciousness and culture, for philosophy and science, literature and language, art and music. Music.

She stretched out both her hands – amazing agile hands, which had evolved through those millennia of grasping, shaping, whittling; refined themselves through every skill and subtlety, until they could write and sew and play – though not with that precision yet, that heady combination of passion and control she was hearing in the music, as the final movement swept into her head. She could never match that perfect tone, the audacious power of those relentless rushing triplets, but at least she must attempt it, wring out any shred of skill she had. When she'd entered Brignor as a novice, every nun had repeated to her in turn, 'May the Lord grant you peace and perseverance.' She had found neither in the convent, had lost the Lord Himself; yet now she felt a spacious peace, a wild determination. This time, she'd persevere.

Of course there were problems, absolutely basic ones: no space for a piano, no cash for one, no chance of getting lessons, no money spare for buying music. But there would also be solutions, as there had always been solutions – had to be, for man to survive at all. She was suddenly aware again of that strength which Ivan had mentioned, that sense of possibility – and not only in the music – the strength to stand alone, or maybe not alone, the strength to grow and give. The exultant dancing rhythm of the coda seemed to blazon out her confidence; the insistent rising bass asserting, reasserting, her resilience, conviction; the sudden threatening chords dissipated instantly in a glittering run of semiquavers; all doubt and fear resolved. She was going to play – and soon – next month, next week, tomorrow; not just in the future. There wasn't any future, only Robert's eternal 'now', with those triumphant closing cadences soaring out across the zoo, seeming never quite to reach their final bars; the notes building, building on themselves, as if the sound were solid, like a monument.

She plunged back to the chimps' cage. Three billion years or more had passed, as man struggled from the slime, but Luke hadn't seemed to notice she had gone. He was still laughing at the chimps, his pale skin chapped with cold, her gloves stuffed in his pocket, scarlet muffler trailing.

'They had a drink,' he shouted. 'The keeper gave them fruit squash from a bottle. Can *we* have orange squash?'

'You've just had some in the café.'

'I want another one.'

She began to tell him 'no'; they were short of money, the café was too far, it had just begun to snow again and they ought to . . . She broke off in mid-sentence. 'All right,' she said. 'Why not?'

491

She retied his muffler, took his hand. He didn't pull away this time, not even when she broke into a run. His chilled and grubby hand began to thaw into her own, as they galloped on together, dodging puddles, tripping, noses running in the cold.

'Can we have ice cream as well?' he yelled. 'It *is* your birthday, Gee.'

He was pushing his luck, to use his father's phrase, demanding what he wanted, challenging her to provide a few indulgences. She'd better do the same, push her luck, believe in it; start scrounging cap in hand, insisting life gave her what she needed. It *was* her birthday – yes – time to start again; put pleasure and achievement before penance, abnegation; time to put her new self to the test.

'Okay,' she shouted back, above the echo of their footsteps, the rush and blur of snow. 'Let's be devils, for a change.'